SUMMA THEOLOGICA

Copyright © 2007 BiblioBazaar
All rights reserved
ISBN: 978-1-4264-9429-1

SAINT THOMAS AQUINAS

SUMMA THEOLOGICA

PART II-II
("Secunda Secundae")

VOLUME I

TRANSLATED BY
Fathers of the English Dominican Province

BIBLIOBAZAAR

SUMMA THEOLOGICA

DEDICATION

To the Blessed Virgin Mary Immaculate
Seat of Wisdom.

CONTENTS

TREATISE ON THE THEOLOGICAL VIRTUES (QQ. 1-46)

1. OF FAITH 13
2. OF THE ACT OF FAITH 36
3. OF THE OUTWARD ACT OF FAITH 56
4. OF THE VIRTUE ITSELF OF FAITH 59
5. OF THOSE WHO HAVE FAITH 75
6. OF THE CAUSE OF FAITH 83
7. OF THE EFFECTS OF FAITH 87
8. OF THE GIFT OF UNDERSTANDING 90
9. OF THE GIFT OF KNOWLEDGE 104
10. OF UNBELIEF IN GENERAL 111
11. OF HERESY 135
12. OF APOSTASY 144
13. OF THE SIN OF BLASPHEMY, IN GENERAL 148
14. OF BLASPHEMY AGAINST THE HOLY GHOST 154
15. OF THE VICES OPPOSED TO KNOWLEDGE AND UNDERSTANDING 164
16. OF THE PRECEPTS OF FAITH, KNOWLEDGE AND UNDERSTANDING 169
17. OF HOPE, CONSIDERED IN ITSELF 174
18. OF THE SUBJECT OF HOPE 185
19. OF THE GIFT OF FEAR 191
20. OF DESPAIR 212
21. OF PRESUMPTION 219

22.	OF THE PRECEPTS RELATING TO HOPE AND FEAR	225
23.	OF CHARITY, CONSIDERED IN ITSELF	229
24.	OF THE SUBJECT OF CHARITY	243
25.	OF THE OBJECT OF CHARITY	267
26.	OF THE ORDER OF CHARITY	286
27.	OF THE PRINCIPAL ACT OF CHARITY, WHICH IS TO LOVE	310
28.	OF JOY	323
29.	OF PEACE	329
30.	OF MERCY	336
31.	OF BENEFICENCE	343
32.	OF ALMSDEEDS	350
33.	OF FRATERNAL CORRECTION	371
34.	OF HATRED	389
35.	OF SLOTH	398
36.	OF ENVY	406
37.	OF DISCORD, WHICH IS CONTRARY TO PEACE	414
38.	OF CONTENTION	418
39.	OF SCHISM	421
40.	OF WAR	430
41.	OF STRIFE	438
42.	OF SEDITION	442
43.	OF SCANDAL	445
44.	OF THE PRECEPTS OF CHARITY	462
45.	OF THE GIFT OF WISDOM	474
46.	OF FOLLY WHICH IS OPPOSED TO WISDOM	485

TREATISE ON THE CARDINAL VIRTUES
(QQ. 47-170).

47.	OF PRUDENCE, CONSIDERED IN ITSELF	489
48.	OF THE PARTS OF PRUDENCE	513
49.	OF EACH QUASI-INTEGRAL PART OF PRUDENCE	517
50.	OF THE SUBJECTIVE PARTS OF PRUDENCE	528

51.	OF THE VIRTUES WHICH ARE CONNECTED WITH PRUDENCE	534
52.	OF THE GIFT OF COUNSEL	541
53.	OF IMPRUDENCE	548
54.	OF NEGLIGENCE	557
55.	OF VICES OPPOSED TO PRUDENCE BY WAY OF RESEMBLANCE	562
56.	OF THE PRECEPTS RELATING TO PRUDENCE	574
57.	OF RIGHT	577
58.	OF JUSTICE	584
59.	OF INJUSTICE	604

TREATISE ON THE THEOLOGICAL VIRTUES (QQ. 1-46).

1. OF FAITH (In Ten Articles)

Having to treat now of the theological virtues, we shall begin with Faith, secondly we shall speak of Hope, and thirdly, of Charity.

The treatise on Faith will be fourfold: (1) Of faith itself; (2) Of the corresponding gifts, knowledge and understanding; (3) Of the opposite vices; (4) Of the precepts pertaining to this virtue.

About faith itself we shall consider: (1) its object; (2) its act; (3) the habit of faith.

Under the first head there are ten points of inquiry:

(1) Whether the object of faith is the First Truth?
(2) Whether the object of faith is something complex or incomplex, i.e. whether it is a thing or a proposition?
(3) Whether anything false can come under faith?
(4) Whether the object of faith can be anything seen?
(5) Whether it can be anything known?
(6) Whether the things to be believed should be divided into a certain number of articles?
(7) Whether the same articles are of faith for all times?
(8) Of the number of articles;
(9) Of the manner of embodying the articles in a symbol;
(10) Who has the right to propose a symbol of faith?.

* * * * *

FIRST ARTICLE [II-II, Q. 1, Art. 1]

Whether the Object of Faith Is the First Truth?

Objection 1: It would seem that the object of faith is not the First Truth. For it seems that the object of faith is that which is proposed to us to be believed. Now not only things pertaining to the Godhead, i.e. the First Truth, are proposed to us to be believed, but also things concerning Christ's human nature, and the sacraments of the Church, and the condition of creatures. Therefore the object of faith is not only the First Truth.

Obj. 2: Further, faith and unbelief have the same object since they are opposed to one another. Now unbelief can be about all things contained in Holy Writ, for whichever one of them a man denies, he is considered an unbeliever. Therefore faith also is about all things contained in Holy Writ. But there are many things therein, concerning man and other creatures. Therefore the object of faith is not only the First Truth, but also created truth.

Obj. 3: Further, faith is condivided with charity, as stated above (I-II, Q. 62, A. 3). Now by charity we love not only God, who is the sovereign Good, but also our neighbor. Therefore the object of Faith is not only the First Truth.

On the contrary, Dionysius says (Div. Nom. vii) that "faith is about the simple and everlasting truth." Now this is the First Truth. Therefore the object of faith is the First Truth.

I answer that, The object of every cognitive habit includes two things: first, that which is known materially, and is the material object, so to speak, and, secondly, that whereby it is known, which is the formal aspect of the object. Thus in the science of geometry, the conclusions are what is known materially, while the formal aspect of the science is the mean of demonstration, through which the conclusions are known.

Accordingly if we consider, in faith, the formal aspect of the object, it is nothing else than the First Truth. For the faith of which we are speaking, does not assent to anything, except because it is revealed by God. Hence the mean on which faith is based is the Divine Truth. If, however, we consider materially the things to which faith assents, they include not only God, but also many other things, which, nevertheless, do not come under the assent of faith, except as bearing some relation to God, in as much as, to wit, through certain effects of the Divine operation, man is helped on his journey towards the enjoyment of God. Consequently from this point of view also the object of faith is, in a way, the First Truth, in as much as nothing comes under faith except in relation to God, even as the object of the medical art is health, for it considers nothing save in relation to health.

Reply Obj. 1: Things concerning Christ's human nature, and the sacraments of the Church, or any creatures whatever, come under faith, in so far as by them we are directed to God, and in as much as we assent to them on account of the Divine Truth.

Reply Obj. 2: The same answer applies to the Second Objection, as regards all things contained in Holy Writ.

Reply Obj. 3: Charity also loves our neighbor on account of God, so that its object, properly speaking, is God, as we shall show further on (Q. 25, A. 1).

* * * * *

SECOND ARTICLE [II-II, Q. 1, Art. 2]

Whether the Object of Faith Is Something Complex, by Way of a Proposition?

Objection 1: It would seem that the object of faith is not something complex by way of a proposition. For the object of faith is the First Truth, as stated above (A. 1). Now the First Truth is something simple. Therefore the object of faith is not something complex.

Obj. 2: Further, the exposition of faith is contained in the symbol. Now the symbol does not contain propositions, but things: for it is not stated therein that God is almighty, but: "I believe in God . . . almighty." Therefore the object of faith is not a proposition but a thing.

Obj. 3: Further, faith is succeeded by vision, according to 1 Cor. 13:12: "We see now through a glass in a dark manner; but then face to face. Now I know in part; but then I shall know even as I am known." But the object of the heavenly vision is something simple, for it is the Divine Essence. Therefore the faith of the wayfarer is also.

On the contrary, Faith is a mean between science and opinion. Now the mean is in the same genus as the extremes. Since, then, science and opinion are about propositions, it seems that faith is likewise about propositions; so that its object is something complex.

I answer that, The thing known is in the knower according to the mode of the knower. Now the mode proper to the human intellect is to know the truth by synthesis and analysis, as stated in the First Part (Q. 85, A. 5). Hence things that are simple in themselves, are known by the intellect with a certain amount of complexity, just as on the other hand, the Divine intellect knows, without any complexity, things that are complex in themselves.

Accordingly the object of faith may be considered in two ways. First, as regards the thing itself which is believed, and thus the object of faith is something simple, namely the thing itself about which we have faith. Secondly, on the part of the believer, and in this respect the object of faith is something complex by way of a proposition.

Hence in the past both opinions have been held with a certain amount of truth.

Reply Obj. 1: This argument considers the object of faith on the part of the thing believed.

Reply Obj. 2: The symbol mentions the things about which faith is, in so far as the act of the believer is terminated in them, as is evident from the manner of speaking about them. Now the act of the believer does not terminate in a proposition, but in a thing. For as in science we do not form propositions, except in order to have knowledge about things through their means, so is it in faith.

Reply Obj. 3: The object of the heavenly vision will be the First Truth seen in itself, according to 1 John 3:2: "We know that when He shall appear, we shall be like to Him: because we shall see Him as He is": hence that vision will not be by way of a proposition but by way of a simple understanding. On the other hand, by faith, we do not apprehend the First Truth as it is in itself. Hence the comparison fails.

* * * * *

THIRD ARTICLE [II-II, Q. 1, Art. 3]

Whether Anything False Can Come Under Faith?

Objection 1: It would seem that something false can come under faith. For faith is condivided with hope and charity. Now something false can come under hope, since many hope to have eternal life, who will not obtain it. The same may be said of charity, for many are loved as being good, who, nevertheless, are not good. Therefore something false can be the object of faith.

Obj. 2: Further, Abraham believed that Christ would be born, according to John 8:56: "Abraham your father rejoiced that he might see My day: he saw it, and was glad." But after the time of Abraham, God might not have taken flesh, for it was merely because He willed that He did, so that what Abraham believed about Christ would have been false. Therefore the object of faith can be something false.

Obj. 3: Further, the ancients believed in the future birth of Christ, and many continued so to believe, until they heard the preaching of the Gospel. Now, when once Christ was born, even before He began to preach, it was false that Christ was yet to be born. Therefore something false can come under faith.

Obj. 4: Further, it is a matter of faith, that one should believe that the true Body of Christ is contained in the Sacrament of the altar. But it might happen that the bread was not rightly consecrated, and that there was not Christ's true Body there, but only bread. Therefore something false can come under faith.

On the contrary, No virtue that perfects the intellect is related to the false, considered as the evil of the intellect, as the Philosopher declares (Ethic. vi, 2). Now faith is a virtue that perfects the intellect, as we shall show further on (Q. 4, AA. 2, 5). Therefore nothing false can come under it.

I answer that, Nothing comes under any power, habit or act, except by means of the formal aspect of the object: thus color cannot be seen except by means of light, and a conclusion cannot be known save through the mean of demonstration. Now it has been stated (A. 1) that the formal aspect of the object of faith is the First Truth; so that nothing can come under faith, save in so far as it stands under the First Truth, under which nothing false can stand, as neither can non-being stand under being, nor evil under goodness. It follows therefore that nothing false can come under faith.

Reply Obj. 1: Since the true is the good of the intellect, but not of the appetitive power, it follows that all virtues which perfect the intellect, exclude the false altogether, because it belongs to the nature of a virtue to bear relation to the good alone. On the other hand those virtues which perfect the appetitive faculty, do not entirely exclude the false, for it is possible to act in accordance with justice or temperance, while having a false opinion about what one is doing. Therefore, as faith perfects the intellect, whereas hope and charity perfect the appetitive part, the comparison between them fails.

Nevertheless neither can anything false come under hope, for a man hopes to obtain eternal life, not by his own power (since this would be an act of presumption), but with the help of grace; and if he perseveres therein he will obtain eternal life surely and infallibly.

In like manner it belongs to charity to love God, wherever He may be; so that it matters not to charity, whether God be in the individual whom we love for God's sake.

Reply Obj. 2: That "God would not take flesh," considered in itself was possible even after Abraham's time, but in so far as it stands in God's foreknowledge, it has a certain necessity of infallibility, as explained in the First Part (Q. 14, AA. 13, 15): and it is thus that it comes under faith. Hence in so far as it comes under faith, it cannot be false.

Reply Obj. 3: After Christ's birth, to believe in Him, was to believe in Christ's birth at some time or other. The fixing of the time, wherein some were deceived was not due to their faith, but to a human conjecture. For it is possible for a believer to have a false opinion through a human conjecture, but it is quite impossible for a false opinion to be the outcome of faith.

Reply Obj. 4: The faith of the believer is not directed to such and such accidents of bread, but to the fact that the true body of Christ is under the appearances of sensible bread, when it is rightly consecrated. Hence if it be not rightly consecrated, it does not follow that anything false comes under faith.

* * * * *

FOURTH ARTICLE [II-II, Q. 1, Art. 4]

Whether the Object of Faith Can Be Something Seen?

Objection 1: It would seem that the object of faith is something seen. For Our Lord said to Thomas (John 20:29): "Because thou hast seen Me, Thomas, thou hast believed." Therefore vision and faith regard the same object.

Obj. 2: Further, the Apostle, while speaking of the knowledge of faith, says (1 Cor. 13:12): "We see now through a glass in a dark manner." Therefore what is believed is seen.

Obj. 3: Further, faith is a spiritual light. Now something is seen under every light. Therefore faith is of things seen.

Obj. 4: Further, "Every sense is a kind of sight," as Augustine states (De Verb. Domini, Serm. xxxiii). But faith is of things heard, according to Rom. 10:17: "Faith . . . cometh by hearing." Therefore faith is of things seen.

On the contrary, The Apostle says (Heb. 11:1) that "faith is the evidence of things that appear not."

I answer that, Faith implies assent of the intellect to that which is believed. Now the intellect assents to a thing in two ways. First, through being moved to assent by its very object, which is known either by itself (as in the case of first principles, which are held by the habit of understanding), or through something else already known (as in the case of conclusions which are held by the habit of science). Secondly the intellect assents to something, not through being sufficiently moved to this assent by its proper object, but through an act of choice, whereby it turns voluntarily to one side rather than to the other: and if this be accompanied by doubt or fear of the opposite side, there will be opinion, while, if there be certainty and no fear of the other side, there will be faith.

Now those things are said to be seen which, of themselves, move the intellect or the senses to knowledge of them. Wherefore it is evident that neither faith nor opinion can be of things seen either by the senses or by the intellect.

Reply Obj. 1: Thomas "saw one thing, and believed another"[1]: he saw the Man, and believing Him to be God, he made profession of his faith, saying: "My Lord and my God."

Reply Obj. 2: Those things which come under faith can be considered in two ways. First, in particular; and thus they cannot be seen and believed at the same time, as shown above. Secondly, in general, that is, under the common aspect of credibility; and in this way they are seen by the believer. For he would not believe unless, on the evidence of signs, or of something similar, he saw that they ought to be believed.

---

1   St. Gregory: Hom. xxvi in Evang.

Reply Obj. 3: The light of faith makes us see what we believe. For just as, by the habits of the other virtues, man sees what is becoming to him in respect of that habit, so, by the habit of faith, the human mind is directed to assent to such things as are becoming to a right faith, and not to assent to others.

Reply Obj. 4: Hearing is of words signifying what is of faith, but not of the things themselves that are believed; hence it does not follow that these things are seen.

* * * * *

FIFTH ARTICLE [II-II, Q. 1, Art. 5]

Whether Those Things That Are of Faith Can Be an Object of Science[1]?

Objection 1: It would seem that those things that are of faith can be an object of science. For where science is lacking there is ignorance, since ignorance is the opposite of science. Now we are not in ignorance of those things we have to believe, since ignorance of such things savors of unbelief, according to 1 Tim. 1:13: "I did it ignorantly in unbelief." Therefore things that are of faith can be an object of science.

Obj. 2: Further, science is acquired by reasons. Now sacred writers employ reasons to inculcate things that are of faith. Therefore such things can be an object of science.

Obj. 3: Further, things which are demonstrated are an object of science, since a "demonstration is a syllogism that produces science." Now certain matters of faith have been demonstrated by the philosophers, such as the Existence and Unity of God, and so forth. Therefore things that are of faith can be an object of science.

Obj. 4: Further, opinion is further from science than faith is, since faith is said to stand between opinion and science. Now opinion and science can, in a way, be about the same object, as stated in Poster. i. Therefore faith and science can be about the same object also.

On the contrary, Gregory says (Hom. xxvi in Evang.) that "when a thing is manifest, it is the object, not of faith, but of perception." Therefore things that are of faith are not the object of perception, whereas what is an object of science is the object of perception.

---

[1] Science is certain knowledge of a demonstrated conclusion through its demonstration

Therefore there can be no faith about things which are an object of science.

I answer that, All science is derived from self-evident and therefore "seen" principles; wherefore all objects of science must needs be, in a fashion, seen.

Now as stated above (A. 4), it is impossible that one and the same thing should be believed and seen by the same person. Hence it is equally impossible for one and the same thing to be an object of science and of belief for the same person. It may happen, however, that a thing which is an object of vision or science for one, is believed by another: since we hope to see some day what we now believe about the Trinity, according to 1 Cor. 13:12: "We see now through a glass in a dark manner; but then face to face": which vision the angels possess already; so that what we believe, they see. In like manner it may happen that what is an object of vision or scientific knowledge for one man, even in the state of a wayfarer, is, for another man, an object of faith, because he does not know it by demonstration.

Nevertheless that which is proposed to be believed equally by all, is equally unknown by all as an object of science: such are the things which are of faith simply. Consequently faith and science are not about the same things.

Reply Obj. 1: Unbelievers are in ignorance of things that are of faith, for neither do they see or know them in themselves, nor do they know them to be credible. The faithful, on the other hand, know them, not as by demonstration, but by the light of faith which makes them see that they ought to believe them, as stated above (A. 4, ad 2, 3).

Reply Obj. 2: The reasons employed by holy men to prove things that are of faith, are not demonstrations; they are either persuasive arguments showing that what is proposed to our faith is not impossible, or else they are proofs drawn from the principles of faith, i.e. from the authority of Holy Writ, as Dionysius declares (Div. Nom. ii). Whatever is based on these principles is as well proved in the eyes of the faithful, as a conclusion drawn from self-evident principles is in the eyes of all. Hence again, theology is a science, as we stated at the outset of this work (P. I, Q. 1, A. 2).

Reply Obj. 3: Things which can be proved by demonstration are reckoned among the articles of faith, not because they are believed simply by all, but because they are a necessary presupposition to matters of faith, so that those who do not known them by demonstration must know them first of all by faith.

Reply Obj. 4: As the Philosopher says (Poster. i), "science and opinion about the same object can certainly be in different men," as we have stated above about science and faith; yet it is possible for one and the same man to have science and faith about the same thing relatively, i.e. in relation to the object, but not in the same respect. For it is possible for the same person, about one and the same object, to know one thing and to think another: and, in like manner, one may know by demonstration the unity of the Godhead, and, by faith, the Trinity. On the other hand, in one and the same man, about the same object, and in the same respect, science is incompatible with either opinion or faith, yet for different reasons. Because science is incompatible with opinion about the same object simply, for the reason that science demands that its object should be deemed impossible to be otherwise, whereas it is essential to opinion, that its object should be deemed possible to be otherwise. Yet that which is the object of faith, on account of the certainty of faith, is also deemed impossible to be otherwise; and the reason why science and faith cannot be about the same object and in the same respect is because the object of science is something seen whereas the object of faith is the unseen, as stated above.

* * * * *

SIXTH ARTICLE [II-II, Q. 1, Art. 6]

Whether Those Things That Are of Faith Should Be Divided into Certain Articles?

Objection 1: It would seem that those things that are of faith should not be divided into certain articles. For all things contained in Holy Writ are matters of faith. But these, by reason of their multitude, cannot be reduced to a certain number. Therefore it seems superfluous to distinguish certain articles of faith.

Obj. 2: Further, material differences can be multiplied indefinitely, and therefore art should take no notice of them. Now the formal aspect of the object of faith is one and indivisible, as stated above (A. 1), viz. the First Truth, so that matters of faith cannot be distinguished in respect of their formal object. Therefore no notice should be taken of a material division of matters of faith into articles.

Obj. 3: Further, it has been said by some[1] that "an article is an indivisible truth concerning God, exacting [arctans] our belief." Now belief is a voluntary act, since, as Augustine says (Tract. xxvi in Joan.), "no man believes against his will." Therefore it seems that matters of faith should not be divided into articles.

On the contrary, Isidore says: "An article is a glimpse of Divine truth, tending thereto." Now we can only get a glimpse of Divine truth by way of analysis, since things which in God are one, are manifold in our intellect. Therefore matters of faith should be divided into articles.

I answer that, the word "article" is apparently derived from the Greek; for the Greek *arthron*[2] which the Latin renders "articulus," signifies a fitting together of distinct parts: wherefore the small parts of the body which fit together are called the articulations of the limbs. Likewise, in the Greek grammar, articles are parts of speech which are affixed to words to show their gender, number or case. Again in rhetoric, articles are parts that fit together in a sentence, for Tully says (Rhet. iv) that an article is composed of words each pronounced singly and separately, thus: "Your passion, your voice, your look, have struck terror into your foes."

Hence matters of Christian faith are said to contain distinct articles, in so far as they are divided into parts, and fit together. Now the object of faith is something unseen in connection with God, as stated above (A. 4). Consequently any matter that, for a special reason, is unseen, is a special article; whereas when several matters are known or not known, under the same aspect, we are not to distinguish various articles. Thus one encounters one difficulty in seeing that God suffered, and another in seeing that He rose again from the dead, wherefore the article of the Resurrection is distinct from the article of the Passion. But that He suffered, died and was buried, present the same difficulty, so that if one be accepted, it is not difficult to accept the others; wherefore all these belong to one article.

---

1 Cf. William of Auxerre, Summa Aurea
2 Cf. William of Auxerre, Summa Aurea

Reply Obj. 1: Some things are proposed to our belief are in themselves of faith, while others are of faith, not in themselves but only in relation to others: even as in sciences certain propositions are put forward on their own account, while others are put forward in order to manifest others. Now, since the chief object of faith consists in those things which we hope to see, according to Heb. 11:2: "Faith is the substance of things to be hoped for," it follows that those things are in themselves of faith, which order us directly to eternal life. Such are the Trinity of Persons in Almighty God[1], the mystery of Christ's Incarnation, and the like: and these are distinct articles of faith. On the other hand certain things in Holy Writ are proposed to our belief, not chiefly on their own account, but for the manifestation of those mentioned above: for instance, that Abraham had two sons, that a dead man rose again at the touch of Eliseus' bones, and the like, which are related in Holy Writ for the purpose of manifesting the Divine mystery or the Incarnation of Christ: and such things should not form distinct articles.

Reply Obj. 2: The formal aspect of the object of faith can be taken in two ways: first, on the part of the thing believed, and thus there is one formal aspect of all matters of faith, viz. the First Truth: and from this point of view there is no distinction of articles. Secondly, the formal aspect of matters of faith, can be considered from our point of view; and thus the formal aspect of a matter of faith is that it is something unseen; and from this point of view there are various distinct articles of faith, as we saw above.

Reply Obj. 3: This definition of an article is taken from an etymology of the word as derived from the Latin, rather than in accordance with its real meaning, as derived from the Greek: hence it does not carry much weight. Yet even then it could be said that although faith is exacted of no man by a necessity of coercion, since belief is a voluntary act, yet it is exacted of him by a necessity of end, since "he that cometh to God must believe that He is," and "without faith it is impossible to please God," as the Apostle declares (Heb. 11:6).

* * * * *

---

[1] The Leonine Edition reads: The Three Persons, the omnipotence of God, etc.

SEVENTH ARTICLE [II-II, Q. 1, Art. 7]

Whether the Articles of Faith Have Increased in Course of Time?

Objection 1: It would seem that the articles of faith have not increased in course of time. Because, as the Apostle says (Heb. 11:1), "faith is the substance of things to be hoped for." Now the same things are to be hoped for at all times. Therefore, at all times, the same things are to be believed.

Obj. 2: Further, development has taken place, in sciences devised by man, on account of the lack of knowledge in those who discovered them, as the Philosopher observes (Metaph. ii). Now the doctrine of faith was not devised by man, but was delivered to us by God, as stated in Eph. 2:8: "It is the gift of God." Since then there can be no lack of knowledge in God, it seems that knowledge of matters of faith was perfect from the beginning and did not increase as time went on.

Obj. 3: Further, the operation of grace proceeds in orderly fashion no less than the operation of nature. Now nature always makes a beginning with perfect things, as Boethius states (De Consol. iii). Therefore it seems that the operation of grace also began with perfect things, so that those who were the first to deliver the faith, knew it most perfectly.

Obj. 4: Further, just as the faith of Christ was delivered to us through the apostles, so too, in the Old Testament, the knowledge of faith was delivered by the early fathers to those who came later, according to Deut. 32:7: "Ask thy father, and he will declare to thee." Now the apostles were most fully instructed about the mysteries, for "they received them more fully than others, even as they received them earlier," as a gloss says on Rom. 8:23: "Ourselves also who have the first fruits of the Spirit." Therefore it seems that knowledge of matters of faith has not increased as time went on.

On the contrary, Gregory says (Hom. xvi in Ezech.) that "the knowledge of the holy fathers increased as time went on ... and the nearer they were to Our Savior's coming, the more fully did they receive the mysteries of salvation."

I answer that, The articles of faith stand in the same relation to the doctrine of faith, as self-evident principles to a teaching based on natural reason. Among these principles there is a certain order, so that some are contained implicitly in others; thus all principles are reduced, as to their first principle, to this one: "The same thing cannot be affirmed and denied at the same time," as the Philosopher states (Metaph. iv, text. 9). In like manner all the articles are contained implicitly in certain primary matters of faith, such as God's existence, and His providence over the salvation of man, according to Heb. 11: "He that cometh to God, must believe that He is, and is a rewarder to them that seek Him." For the existence of God includes all that we believe to exist in God eternally, and in these our happiness consists; while belief in His providence includes all those things which God dispenses in time, for man's salvation, and which are the way to that happiness: and in this way, again, some of those articles which follow from these are contained in others: thus faith in the Redemption of mankind includes belief in the Incarnation of Christ, His Passion and so forth.

Accordingly we must conclude that, as regards the substance of the articles of faith, they have not received any increase as time went on: since whatever those who lived later have believed, was contained, albeit implicitly, in the faith of those Fathers who preceded them. But there was an increase in the number of articles believed explicitly, since to those who lived in later times some were known explicitly which were not known explicitly by those who lived before them. Hence the Lord said to Moses (Ex. 6:2, 3): "I am the God of Abraham, the God of Isaac, the God of Jacob[1] . . . and My name Adonai I did not show them": David also said (Ps. 118:100): "I have had understanding above ancients": and the Apostle says (Eph. 3:5) that the mystery of Christ, "in other generations was not known, as it is now revealed to His holy apostles and prophets."

Reply Obj. 1: Among men the same things were always to be hoped for from Christ. But as they did not acquire this hope save through Christ, the further they were removed from Christ in point of time, the further they were from obtaining what they hoped for. Hence the Apostle says (Heb. 11:13): "All these died according to faith, not having received the promises, but beholding them afar off." Now the further off a thing is the less distinctly is it seen; wherefore those who were nigh to Christ's advent had a more distinct knowledge of the good things to be hoped for.

---

[1] Vulg.: 'I am the Lord that appeared to Abraham, to Isaac, and to Jacob'

Reply Obj. 2: Progress in knowledge occurs in two ways. First, on the part of the teacher, be he one or many, who makes progress in knowledge as time goes on: and this is the kind of progress that takes place in sciences devised by man. Secondly, on the part of the learner; thus the master, who has perfect knowledge of the art, does not deliver it all at once to his disciple from the very outset, for he would not be able to take it all in, but he condescends to the disciple's capacity and instructs him little by little. It is in this way that men made progress in the knowledge of faith as time went on. Hence the Apostle (Gal. 3:24) compares the state of the Old Testament to childhood.

Reply Obj. 3: Two causes are requisite before actual generation can take place, an agent, namely, and matter. In the order of the active cause, the more perfect is naturally first; and in this way nature makes a beginning with perfect things, since the imperfect is not brought to perfection, except by something perfect already in existence. On the other hand, in the order of the material cause, the imperfect comes first, and in this way nature proceeds from the imperfect to the perfect. Now in the manifestation of faith, God is the active cause, having perfect knowledge from all eternity; while man is likened to matter in receiving the influx of God's action. Hence, among men, the knowledge of faith had to proceed from imperfection to perfection; and, although some men have been after the manner of active causes, through being doctors of faith, nevertheless the manifestation of the Spirit is given to such men for the common good, according to 1 Cor. 12:7; so that the knowledge of faith was imparted to the Fathers who were instructors in the faith, so far as was necessary at the time for the instruction of the people, either openly or in figures.

Reply Obj. 4: The ultimate consummation of grace was effected by Christ, wherefore the time of His coming is called the "time of fulness[1]" (Gal. 4:4). Hence those who were nearest to Christ, whether before, like John the Baptist, or after, like the apostles, had a fuller knowledge of the mysteries of faith; for even with regard to man's state we find that the perfection of manhood comes in youth, and that a man's state is all the more perfect, whether before or after, the nearer it is to the time of his youth.

---

1   Vulg.: 'fulness of time'

* * * * *

EIGHTH ARTICLE [II-II, Q. 1, Art. 8]

Whether the Articles of Faith Are Suitably Formulated?

Objection 1: It would seem that the articles of faith are unsuitably formulated. For those things, which can be known by demonstration, do not belong to faith as to an object of belief for all, as stated above (A. 5). Now it can be known by demonstration that there is one God; hence the Philosopher proves this (Metaph. xii, text. 52) and many other philosophers demonstrated the same truth. Therefore that "there is one God" should not be set down as an article of faith.

Obj. 2: Further, just as it is necessary to faith that we should believe God to be almighty, so is it too that we should believe Him to be "all-knowing" and "provident for all," about both of which points some have erred. Therefore, among the articles of faith, mention should have been made of God's wisdom and providence, even as of His omnipotence.

Obj. 3: Further, to know the Father is the same things as to know the Son, according to John 14:9: "He that seeth Me, seeth the Father also." Therefore there ought to be but one article about the Father and Son, and, for the same reason, about the Holy Ghost.

Obj. 4: Further, the Person of the Father is no less than the Person of the Son, and of the Holy Ghost. Now there are several articles about the Person of the Holy Ghost, and likewise about the Person of the Son. Therefore there should be several articles about the Person of the Father.

Obj. 5: Further, just as certain things are said by appropriation, of the Person of the Father and of the Person of the Holy Ghost, so too is something appropriated to the Person of the Son, in respect of His Godhead. Now, among the articles of faith, a place is given to a work appropriated to the Father, viz. the creation, and likewise, a work appropriated to the Holy Ghost, viz. that "He spoke by the prophets." Therefore the articles of faith should contain some work appropriated to the Son in respect of His Godhead.

Obj. 6: Further, the sacrament of the Eucharist presents a special difficulty over and above the other articles. Therefore it should have been mentioned in a special article: and consequently it seems that there is not a sufficient number of articles.

On the contrary stands the authority of the Church who formulates the articles thus.

I answer that, As stated above (AA. 4, 6), to faith those things in themselves belong, the sight of which we shall enjoy in eternal life, and by which we are brought to eternal life. Now two things are proposed to us to be seen in eternal life: viz. the secret of the Godhead, to see which is to possess happiness; and the mystery of Christ's Incarnation, "by Whom we have access" to the glory of the sons of God, according to Rom. 5:2. Hence it is written (John 17:3): "This is eternal life: that they may know Thee, the . . . true God, and Jesus Christ Whom Thou hast sent." Wherefore the first distinction in matters of faith is that some concern the majesty of the Godhead, while others pertain to the mystery of Christ's human nature, which is the "mystery of godliness" (1 Tim. 3:16).

Now with regard to the majesty of the Godhead, three things are proposed to our belief: first, the unity of the Godhead, to which the first article refers; secondly, the trinity of the Persons, to which three articles refer, corresponding to the three Persons; and thirdly, the works proper to the Godhead, the first of which refers to the order of nature, in relation to which the article about the creation is proposed to us; the second refers to the order of grace, in relation to which all matters concerning the sanctification of man are included in one article; while the third refers to the order of glory, and in relation to this another article is proposed to us concerning the resurrection of the dead and life everlasting. Thus there are seven articles referring to the Godhead.

In like manner, with regard to Christ's human nature, there are seven articles, the first of which refers to Christ's incarnation or conception; the second, to His virginal birth; the third, to His Passion, death and burial; the fourth, to His descent into hell; the fifth, to His resurrection; the sixth, to His ascension; the seventh, to His coming for the judgment, so that in all there are fourteen articles.

Some, however, distinguish twelve articles, six pertaining to the Godhead, and six to the humanity. For they include in one article the three about the three Persons; because we have one knowledge of the three Persons: while they divide the article referring to the work of glorification into two, viz. the resurrection of the body, and the glory of the soul. Likewise they unite the conception and nativity into one article.

Reply Obj. 1: By faith we hold many truths about God, which the philosophers were unable to discover by natural reason, for instance His providence and omnipotence, and that He alone is to be worshiped, all of which are contained in the one article of the unity of God.

Reply Obj. 2: The very name of the Godhead implies a kind of watching over things, as stated in the First Part (Q. 13, A. 8). Now in beings having an intellect, power does not work save by the will and knowledge. Hence God's omnipotence includes, in a way, universal knowledge and providence. For He would not be able to do all He wills in things here below, unless He knew them, and exercised His providence over them.

Reply Obj. 3: We have but one knowledge of the Father, Son, and Holy Ghost, as to the unity of the Essence, to which the first article refers: but, as to the distinction of the Persons, which is by the relations of origin, knowledge of the Father does indeed, in a way, include knowledge of the Son, for He would not be Father, had He not a Son; the bond whereof being the Holy Ghost. From this point of view, there was a sufficient motive for those who referred one article to the three Persons. Since, however, with regard to each Person, certain points have to be observed, about which some happen to fall into error, looking at it in this way, we may distinguish three articles about the three Persons. For Arius believed in the omnipotence and eternity of the Father, but did not believe the Son to be co-equal and consubstantial with the Father; hence the need for an article about the Person of the Son in order to settle this point. In like manner it was necessary to appoint a third article about the Person of the Holy Ghost, against Macedonius. In the same way Christ's conception and birth, just as the resurrection and life everlasting, can from one point of view be united together in one article, in so far as they are ordained to one end; while, from another point of view, they can be distinct articles, in as much as each one separately presents a special difficulty.

Reply Obj. 4: It belongs to the Son and Holy Ghost to be sent to sanctify the creature; and about this several things have to be believed. Hence it is that there are more articles about the Persons of the Son and Holy Ghost than about the Person of the Father, Who is never sent, as we stated in the First Part (Q. 43, A. 4).

Reply Obj. 5: The sanctification of a creature by grace, and its consummation by glory, is also effected by the gift of charity, which is appropriated to the Holy Ghost, and by the gift of wisdom, which is appropriated to the Son: so that each work belongs by appropriation, but under different aspects, both to the Son and to the Holy Ghost.

Reply Obj. 6: Two things may be considered in the sacrament of the Eucharist. One is the fact that it is a sacrament, and in this respect it is like the other effects of sanctifying grace. The other is that Christ's body is miraculously contained therein and thus it is included under God's omnipotence, like all other miracles which are ascribed to God's almighty power.

* * * * *

NINTH ARTICLE [II-II, Q. 1, Art. 9]

Whether It Is Suitable for the Articles of Faith to Be Embodied in a Symbol?

Objection 1: It would seem that it is unsuitable for the articles of faith to be embodied in a symbol. Because Holy Writ is the rule of faith, to which no addition or subtraction can lawfully be made, since it is written (Deut. 4:2): "You shall not add to the word that I speak to you, neither shall you take away from it." Therefore it was unlawful to make a symbol as a rule of faith, after the Holy Writ had once been published.

Obj. 2: Further, according to the Apostle (Eph. 4:5) there is but "one faith." Now the symbol is a profession of faith. Therefore it is not fitting that there should be more than one symbol.

Obj. 3: Further, the confession of faith, which is contained in the symbol, concerns all the faithful. Now the faithful are not all competent to believe in God, but only those who have living faith. Therefore it is unfitting for the symbol of faith to be expressed in the words: "I believe in one God."

Obj. 4: Further, the descent into hell is one of the articles of faith, as stated above (A. 8). But the descent into hell is not mentioned in the symbol of the Fathers. Therefore the latter is expressed inadequately.

Obj. 5: Further, Augustine (Tract. xxix in Joan.) expounding the passage, "You believe in God, believe also in Me" (John 14:1) says: "We believe Peter or Paul, but we speak only of believing 'in' God." Since then the Catholic Church is merely a created being, it seems unfitting to say: "In the One, Holy, Catholic and Apostolic Church."

Obj. 6: Further, a symbol is drawn up that it may be a rule of faith. Now a rule of faith ought to be proposed to all, and that publicly. Therefore every symbol, besides the symbol of the Fathers, should be sung at Mass. Therefore it seems unfitting to publish the articles of faith in a symbol.

On the contrary, The universal Church cannot err, since she is governed by the Holy Ghost, Who is the Spirit of truth: for such was Our Lord's promise to His disciples (John 16:13): "When He, the Spirit of truth, is come, He will teach you all truth." Now the symbol is published by the authority of the universal Church. Therefore it contains nothing defective.

I answer that, As the Apostle says (Heb. 11:6), "he that cometh to God, must believe that He is." Now a man cannot believe, unless the truth be proposed to him that he may believe it. Hence the need for the truth of faith to be collected together, so that it might the more easily be proposed to all, lest anyone might stray from the truth through ignorance of the faith. It is from its being a collection of maxims of faith that the symbol[1] takes its name.

Reply Obj. 1: The truth of faith is contained in Holy Writ, diffusely, under various modes of expression, and sometimes obscurely, so that, in order to gather the truth of faith from Holy Writ, one needs long study and practice, which are unattainable by all those who require to know the truth of faith, many of whom have no time for study, being busy with other affairs. And so it was necessary to gather together a clear summary from the sayings of Holy Writ, to be proposed to the belief of all. This indeed was no addition to Holy Writ, but something taken from it.

Reply Obj. 2: The same doctrine of faith is taught in all the symbols. Nevertheless, the people need more careful instruction about the truth of faith, when errors arise, lest the faith of simple-minded persons be corrupted by heretics. It was this that gave rise to the necessity of formulating several symbols, which nowise differ

---

1   The Greek *symballein*

from one another, save that on account of the obstinacy of heretics, one contains more explicitly what another contains implicitly.

Reply Obj. 3: The confession of faith is drawn up in a symbol in the person, as it were, of the whole Church, which is united together by faith. Now the faith of the Church is living faith; since such is the faith to be found in all those who are of the Church not only outwardly but also by merit. Hence the confession of faith is expressed in a symbol, in a manner that is in keeping with living faith, so that even if some of the faithful lack living faith, they should endeavor to acquire it.

Reply Obj. 4: No error about the descent into hell had arisen among heretics, so that there was no need to be more explicit on that point. For this reason it is not repeated in the symbol of the Fathers, but is supposed as already settled in the symbol of the Apostles. For a subsequent symbol does not cancel a preceding one; rather does it expound it, as stated above (ad 2).

Reply Obj. 5: If we say: "'In' the holy Catholic Church," this must be taken as verified in so far as our faith is directed to the Holy Ghost, Who sanctifies the Church; so that the sense is: "I believe in the Holy Ghost sanctifying the Church." But it is better and more in keeping with the common use, to omit the 'in,' and say simply, "the holy Catholic Church," as Pope Leo[1] observes.

Reply Obj. 6: Since the symbol of the Fathers is an explanation of the symbol of the Apostles, and was drawn up after the faith was already spread abroad, and when the Church was already at peace, it is sung publicly in the Mass. On the other hand the symbol of the Apostles, which was drawn up at the time of persecution, before the faith was made public, is said secretly at Prime and Compline, as though it were against the darkness of past and future errors.

* * * * *

TENTH ARTICLE [II-II, Q. 1, Art. 10]

Whether It Belongs to the Sovereign Pontiff to Draw Up a Symbol of Faith?

Objection 1: It would seem that it does not belong to the Sovereign Pontiff to draw up a symbol of faith. For a new edition

---

[1] Rufinus, Comm. in Sym. Apost.

of the symbol becomes necessary in order to explain the articles of faith, as stated above (A. 9). Now, in the Old Testament, the articles of faith were more and more explained as time went on, by reason of the truth of faith becoming clearer through greater nearness to Christ, as stated above (A. 7). Since then this reason ceased with the advent of the New Law, there is no need for the articles of faith to be more and more explicit. Therefore it does not seem to belong to the authority of the Sovereign Pontiff to draw up a new edition of the symbol.

Obj. 2: Further, no man has the power to do what is forbidden under pain of anathema by the universal Church. Now it was forbidden under pain of anathema by the universal Church, to make a new edition of the symbol. For it is stated in the acts of the first[1] council of Ephesus (P. ii, Act. 6) that "after the symbol of the Nicene council had been read through, the holy synod decreed that it was unlawful to utter, write or draw up any other creed, than that which was defined by the Fathers assembled at Nicaea together with the Holy Ghost," and this under pain of anathema. The same was repeated in the acts of the council of Chalcedon (P. ii, Act. 5). Therefore it seems that the Sovereign Pontiff has no authority to publish a new edition of the symbol.

Obj. 3: Further, Athanasius was not the Sovereign Pontiff, but patriarch of Alexandria, and yet he published a symbol which is sung in the Church. Therefore it does not seem to belong to the Sovereign Pontiff any more than to other bishops, to publish a new edition of the symbol.

On the contrary, The symbol was drawn up by a general council. Now such a council cannot be convoked otherwise than by the authority of the Sovereign Pontiff, as stated in the Decretals[2]. Therefore it belongs to the authority of the Sovereign Pontiff to draw up a symbol.

I answer that, As stated above (Obj. 1), a new edition of the symbol becomes necessary in order to set aside the errors that may arise. Consequently to publish a new edition of the symbol belongs to that authority which is empowered to decide matters of faith finally, so that they may be held by all with unshaken faith. Now

---

[1] St. Thomas wrote 'first' (expunged by Nicolai) to distinguish it from the other council, A.D. 451, known as the "Latrocinium" and condemned by the Pope.

[2] Dist. xvii, Can. 4, 5

this belongs to the authority of the Sovereign Pontiff, "to whom the more important and more difficult questions that arise in the Church are referred," as stated in the Decretals[1]. Hence our Lord said to Peter whom he made Sovereign Pontiff (Luke 22:32): "I have prayed for thee," Peter, "that thy faith fail not, and thou, being once converted, confirm thy brethren." The reason of this is that there should be but one faith of the whole Church, according to 1 Cor. 1:10: "That you all speak the same thing, and that there be no schisms among you": and this could not be secured unless any question of faith that may arise be decided by him who presides over the whole Church, so that the whole Church may hold firmly to his decision. Consequently it belongs to the sole authority of the Sovereign Pontiff to publish a new edition of the symbol, as do all other matters which concern the whole Church, such as to convoke a general council and so forth.

Reply Obj. 1: The truth of faith is sufficiently explicit in the teaching of Christ and the apostles. But since, according to 2 Pet. 3:16, some men are so evil-minded as to pervert the apostolic teaching and other doctrines and Scriptures to their own destruction, it was necessary as time went on to express the faith more explicitly against the errors which arose.

Reply Obj. 2: This prohibition and sentence of the council was intended for private individuals, who have no business to decide matters of faith: for this decision of the general council did not take away from a subsequent council the power of drawing up a new edition of the symbol, containing not indeed a new faith, but the same faith with greater explicitness. For every council has taken into account that a subsequent council would expound matters more fully than the preceding council, if this became necessary through some heresy arising. Consequently this belongs to the Sovereign Pontiff, by whose authority the council is convoked, and its decision confirmed.

Reply Obj. 3: Athanasius drew up a declaration of faith, not under the form of a symbol, but rather by way of an exposition of doctrine, as appears from his way of speaking. But since it contained briefly the whole truth of faith, it was accepted by the authority of the Sovereign Pontiff, so as to be considered as a rule of faith. Since it contained briefly the whole truth of faith, it was accepted by the authority of the Sovereign Pontiff, so as to be considered as a rule of faith.

---

[1] Dist. xvii, Can. 5

2. OF THE ACT OF FAITH (In Ten Articles)

We must now consider the act of faith, and (1) the internal act; (2) the external act.

Under the first head there are ten points of inquiry:

(1) What is "to believe," which is the internal act of faith?
(2) In how many ways is it expressed?
(3) Whether it is necessary for salvation to believe in anything above natural reason?
(4) Whether it is necessary to believe those things that are attainable by natural reason?
(5) Whether it is necessary for salvation to believe certain things explicitly?
(6) Whether all are equally bound to explicit faith?
(7) Whether explicit faith in Christ is always necessary for salvation?
(8) Whether it is necessary for salvation to believe in the Trinity explicitly?
(9) Whether the act of faith is meritorious?
(10) Whether human reason diminishes the merit of faith?.

* * * * *

FIRST ARTICLE [II-II, Q. 2, Art. 1]

Whether to Believe Is to Think with Assent?

Objection 1: It would seem that to believe is not to think with assent. Because the Latin word "cogitatio" [thought] implies a research, for "cogitare" [to think] seems to be equivalent to "coagitare," i.e. "to discuss together." Now Damascene says (De Fide Orth. iv) that faith is "an assent without research." Therefore thinking has no place in the act of faith.

Obj. 2: Further, faith resides in the reason, as we shall show further on (Q. 4, A. 2). Now to think is an act of the cogitative power, which belongs to the sensitive faculty, as stated in the First Part (Q. 78, A. 4). Therefore thought has nothing to do with faith.

Obj. 3: Further, to believe is an act of the intellect, since its object is truth. But assent seems to be an act not of the intellect, but of the will, even as consent is, as stated above (I-II, Q. 15, A. 1, ad 3). Therefore to believe is not to think with assent.

On the contrary, This is how "to believe" is defined by Augustine (De Praedest. Sanct. ii).

I answer that, "To think" can be taken in three ways. First, in a general way for any kind of actual consideration of the intellect, as Augustine observes (De Trin. xiv, 7): "By understanding I mean now the faculty whereby we understand when thinking." Secondly, "to think" is more strictly taken for that consideration of the intellect, which is accompanied by some kind of inquiry, and which precedes the intellect's arrival at the stage of perfection that comes with the certitude of sight. In this sense Augustine says (De Trin. xv, 16) that "the Son of God is not called the Thought, but the Word of God. When our thought realizes what we know and takes form therefrom, it becomes our word. Hence the Word of God must be understood without any thinking on the part of God, for there is nothing there that can take form, or be unformed." In this way thought is, properly speaking, the movement of the mind while yet deliberating, and not yet perfected by the clear sight of truth. Since, however, such a movement of the mind may be one of deliberation either about universal notions, which belongs to the intellectual faculty, or about particular matters, which belongs to the sensitive part, hence it is that "to think" is taken secondly for an act of the deliberating intellect, and thirdly for an act of the cogitative power.

Accordingly, if "to think" be understood broadly according to the first sense, then "to think with assent," does not express completely what is meant by "to believe": since, in this way, a man thinks with assent even when he considers what he knows by science[1], or understands. If, on the other hand, "to think" be understood in the second way, then this expresses completely the nature of the act of believing. For among the acts belonging to the intellect, some have a firm assent without any such kind of thinking, as when a man considers the things that he knows by science, or understands, for this consideration is already formed.

---

1 Science is certain knowledge of a demonstrated conclusion through its demonstration.

But some acts of the intellect have unformed thought devoid of a firm assent, whether they incline to neither side, as in one who "doubts"; or incline to one side rather than the other, but on account of some slight motive, as in one who "suspects"; or incline to one side yet with fear of the other, as in one who "opines." But this act "to believe," cleaves firmly to one side, in which respect belief has something in common with science and understanding; yet its knowledge does not attain the perfection of clear sight, wherein it agrees with doubt, suspicion and opinion. Hence it is proper to the believer to think with assent: so that the act of believing is distinguished from all the other acts of the intellect, which are about the true or the false.

Reply Obj. 1: Faith has not that research of natural reason which demonstrates what is believed, but a research into those things whereby a man is induced to believe, for instance that such things have been uttered by God and confirmed by miracles.

Reply Obj. 2: "To think" is not taken here for the act of the cogitative power, but for an act of the intellect, as explained above.

Reply Obj. 3: The intellect of the believer is determined to one object, not by the reason, but by the will, wherefore assent is taken here for an act of the intellect as determined to one object by the will.

* * * * *

SECOND ARTICLE [II-II, Q. 2, Art. 2]

Whether the Act of Faith Is Suitably Distinguished As Believing God, Believing in a God and Believing in God?

Objection 1: It would seem that the act of faith is unsuitably distinguished as believing God, believing in a God, and believing in God. For one habit has but one act. Now faith is one habit since it is one virtue. Therefore it is unreasonable to say that there are three acts of faith.

Obj. 2: Further, that which is common to all acts of faith should not be reckoned as a particular kind of act of faith. Now "to believe God" is common to all acts of faith, since faith is founded on the First Truth. Therefore it seems unreasonable to distinguish it from certain other acts of faith.

Obj. 3: Further, that which can be said of unbelievers, cannot be called an act of faith. Now unbelievers can be said to believe in a God. Therefore it should not be reckoned an act of faith.

Obj. 4: Further, movement towards the end belongs to the will, whose object is the good and the end. Now to believe is an act, not of the will, but of the intellect. Therefore "to believe in God," which implies movement towards an end, should not be reckoned as a species of that act.

On the contrary is the authority of Augustine who makes this distinction (De Verb. Dom., Serm. lxi—Tract. xxix in Joan.).

I answer that, The act of any power or habit depends on the relation of that power or habit to its object. Now the object of faith can be considered in three ways. For, since "to believe" is an act of the intellect, in so far as the will moves it to assent, as stated above (A. 1, ad 3), the object of faith can be considered either on the part of the intellect, or on the part of the will that moves the intellect.

If it be considered on the part of the intellect, then two things can be observed in the object of faith, as stated above (Q. 1, A. 1). One of these is the material object of faith, and in this way an act of faith is "to believe in a God"; because, as stated above (ibid.) nothing is proposed to our belief, except in as much as it is referred to God. The other is the formal aspect of the object, for it is the medium on account of which we assent to such and such a point of faith; and thus an act of faith is "to believe God," since, as stated above (ibid.) the formal object of faith is the First Truth, to Which man gives his adhesion, so as to assent for Its sake to whatever he believes.

Thirdly, if the object of faith be considered in so far as the intellect is moved by the will, an act of faith is "to believe in God." For the First Truth is referred to the will, through having the aspect of an end.

Reply Obj. 1: These three do not denote different acts of faith, but one and the same act having different relations to the object of faith.

This suffices for the Reply to the Second Objection.

Reply Obj. 3: Unbelievers cannot be said "to believe in a God" as we understand it in relation to the act of faith. For they do not believe that God exists under the conditions that faith determines; hence they do not truly imply believe in a God, since,

39

as the Philosopher observes (Metaph. ix, text. 22) "to know simple things defectively is not to know them at all."

Reply Obj. 4: As stated above (I-II, Q. 9, A. 1) the will moves the intellect and the other powers of the soul to the end: and in this respect an act of faith is "to believe in God.".

* * * * *

THIRD ARTICLE [II-II, Q. 2, Art. 3]

Whether It Is Necessary for Salvation to Believe Anything Above the Natural Reason?

Objection 1: It would seem unnecessary for salvation to believe anything above the natural reason. For the salvation and perfection of a thing seem to be sufficiently insured by its natural endowments. Now matters of faith, surpass man's natural reason, since they are things unseen as stated above (Q. 1, A. 4). Therefore to believe seems unnecessary for salvation.

Obj. 2: Further, it is dangerous for man to assent to matters, wherein he cannot judge whether that which is proposed to him be true or false, according to Job 12:11: "Doth not the ear discern words?" Now a man cannot form a judgment of this kind in matters of faith, since he cannot trace them back to first principles, by which all our judgments are guided. Therefore it is dangerous to believe in such matters. Therefore to believe is not necessary for salvation.

Obj. 3: Further, man's salvation rests on God, according to Ps. 36:39: "But the salvation of the just is from the Lord." Now "the invisible things" of God "are clearly seen, being understood by the things that are made; His eternal power also and Divinity," according to Rom. 1:20: and those things which are clearly seen by the understanding are not an object of belief. Therefore it is not necessary for man's salvation, that he should believe certain things.

On the contrary, It is written (Heb. 11:6): "Without faith it is impossible to please God."

I answer that, Wherever one nature is subordinate to another, we find that two things concur towards the perfection of the lower nature, one of which is in respect of that nature's proper movement, while the other is in respect of the movement of the higher nature. Thus water by its proper movement moves towards the centre (of the earth), while according to the movement of the moon, it moves round the centre by ebb and flow. In like manner the planets have their proper movements from west to east, while in accordance with the movement of the first heaven, they have a movement from east to west. Now the created rational nature alone is immediately subordinate to God, since other creatures do not attain to the universal, but only to something particular, while they partake of the Divine goodness either in *being* only, as inanimate things, or also in *living,* and in *knowing singulars,* as plants and animals; whereas the rational nature, in as much as it apprehends the universal notion of good and being, is immediately related to the universal principle of being.

Consequently the perfection of the rational creature consists not only in what belongs to it in respect of its nature, but also in that which it acquires through a supernatural participation of Divine goodness. Hence it was said above (I-II, Q. 3, A. 8) that man's ultimate happiness consists in a supernatural vision of God: to which vision man cannot attain unless he be taught by God, according to John 6:45: "Every one that hath heard of the Father and hath learned cometh to Me." Now man acquires a share of this learning, not indeed all at once, but by little and little, according to the mode of his nature: and every one who learns thus must needs believe, in order that he may acquire science in a perfect degree; thus also the Philosopher remarks (De Soph. Elench. i, 2) that "it behooves a learner to believe."

Hence in order that a man arrive at the perfect vision of heavenly happiness, he must first of all believe God, as a disciple believes the master who is teaching him.

Reply Obj. 1: Since man's nature is dependent on a higher nature, natural knowledge does not suffice for its perfection, and some supernatural knowledge is necessary, as stated above.

Reply Obj. 2: Just as man assents to first principles, by the natural light of his intellect, so does a virtuous man, by the habit of virtue, judge aright of things concerning that virtue; and in this way, by the light of faith which God bestows on him, a man assents to matters of faith and not to those which are against faith. Consequently "there is no" danger or "condemnation to them that are in Christ Jesus," and whom He has enlightened by faith.

Reply Obj. 3: In many respects faith perceives the invisible things of God in a higher way than natural reason does in proceeding to God from His creatures. Hence it is written (Ecclus. 3:25): "Many things are shown to thee above the understandings of man.".

* * * * *

FOURTH ARTICLE [II-II, Q. 2, Art. 4]

Whether It Is Necessary to Believe Those Things Which Can Be Proved by Natural Reason?

Objection 1: It would seem unnecessary to believe those things which can be proved by natural reason. For nothing is superfluous in God's works, much less even than in the works of nature. Now it is superfluous to employ other means, where one already suffices. Therefore it would be superfluous to receive by faith, things that can be known by natural reason.

Obj. 2: Further, those things must be believed, which are the object of faith. Now science and faith are not about the same object, as stated above (Q. 1, AA. 4, 5). Since therefore all things that can be known by natural reason are an object of science, it seems that there is no need to believe what can be proved by natural reason.

Obj. 3: Further, all things knowable scientifically[1] would seem to come under one head: so that if some of them are proposed to man as objects of faith, in like manner the others should also be believed. But this is not true. Therefore it is not necessary to believe those things which can be proved by natural reason.

On the contrary, It is necessary to believe that God is one and incorporeal: which things philosophers prove by natural reason.

I answer that, It is necessary for man to accept by faith not only things which are above reason, but also those which can be known by reason: and this for three motives. First, in order that man may arrive more quickly at the knowledge of Divine truth. Because the science to whose province it belongs to prove the existence of God, is the last of all to offer itself to human research, since it presupposes many other sciences: so that it would not by until late in life that man would arrive at the knowledge of God. The second reason is, in order that the knowledge of God may be more general. For many are unable to make progress in the study

---

[1] Science is certain knowledge of a demonstrated conclusion through its demonstration

of science, either through dullness of mind, or through having a number of occupations, and temporal needs, or even through laziness in learning, all of whom would be altogether deprived of the knowledge of God, unless Divine things were brought to their knowledge under the guise of faith. The third reason is for the sake of certitude. For human reason is very deficient in things concerning God. A sign of this is that philosophers in their researches, by natural investigation, into human affairs, have fallen into many errors, and have disagreed among themselves. And consequently, in order that men might have knowledge of God, free of doubt and uncertainty, it was necessary for Divine matters to be delivered to them by way of faith, being told to them, as it were, by God Himself Who cannot lie.

Reply Obj. 1: The researches of natural reason do not suffice mankind for the knowledge of Divine matters, even of those that can be proved by reason: and so it is not superfluous if these others be believed.

Reply Obj. 2: Science and faith cannot be in the same subject and about the same object: but what is an object of science for one, can be an object of faith for another, as stated above (Q. 1, A. 5).

Reply Obj. 3: Although all things that can be known by science are of one common scientific aspect, they do not all alike lead man to beatitude: hence they are not all equally proposed to our belief.

* * * * *

FIFTH ARTICLE [II-II, Q. 2, Art. 5]

Whether Man Is Bound to Believe Anything Explicitly?

Objection 1: It would seem that man is not bound to believe anything explicitly. For no man is bound to do what is not in his power. Now it is not in man's power to believe a thing explicitly, for it is written (Rom. 10:14, 15): "How shall they believe Him, of whom they have not heard? And how shall they hear without a preacher? And how shall they preach unless they be sent?" Therefore man is not bound to believe anything explicitly.

Obj. 2: Further, just as we are directed to God by faith, so are we by charity. Now man is not bound to keep the precepts of charity, and it is enough if he be ready to fulfil them: as is evidenced by the precept of Our Lord (Matt. 5:39): "If one strike thee on one [Vulg.: 'thy right'] cheek, turn to him also the other"; and by others of the same kind, according to Augustine's exposition (De Serm. Dom. in Monte xix). Therefore neither is man bound to believe anything explicitly, and it is enough if he be ready to believe whatever God proposes to be believed.

Obj. 3: Further, the good of faith consists in obedience, according to Rom. 1:5: "For obedience to the faith in all nations." Now the virtue of obedience does not require man to keep certain fixed precepts, but it is enough that his mind be ready to obey, according to Ps. 118:60: "I am ready and am not troubled; that I may keep Thy commandments." Therefore it seems enough for faith, too, that man should be ready to believe whatever God may propose, without his believing anything explicitly.

On the contrary, It is written (Heb. 11:6): "He that cometh to God, must believe that He is, and is a rewarder to them that seek Him."

I answer that, The precepts of the Law, which man is bound to fulfil, concern acts of virtue which are the means of attaining salvation. Now an act of virtue, as stated above (I-II, Q. 60, A. 5) depends on the relation of the habit to its object. Again two things may be considered in the object of any virtue; namely, that which is the proper and direct object of that virtue, and that which is accidental and consequent to the object properly so called. Thus it belongs properly and directly to the object of fortitude, to face the dangers of death, and to charge at the foe with danger to oneself, for the sake of the common good: yet that, in a just war, a man be armed, or strike another with his sword, and so forth, is reduced to the object of fortitude, but indirectly.

Accordingly, just as a virtuous act is required for the fulfilment of a precept, so is it necessary that the virtuous act should terminate in its proper and direct object: but, on the other hand, the fulfilment of the precept does not require that a virtuous act should terminate in those things which have an accidental or secondary relation to the proper and direct object of that virtue, except in certain places and at certain times. We must, therefore, say that the direct object of faith is that whereby man is made one of the Blessed, as stated above (Q. 1, A. 8): while the indirect and secondary object comprises all things delivered by God to us in Holy Writ, for instance that Abraham had two sons, that David was the son of Jesse, and so forth.

Therefore, as regards the primary points or articles of faith, man is bound to believe them, just as he is bound to have faith; but as to other points of faith, man is not bound to believe them explicitly, but only implicitly, or to be ready to believe them, in so far as he is prepared to believe whatever is contained in the Divine Scriptures. Then alone is he bound to believe such things explicitly, when it is clear to him that they are contained in the doctrine of faith.

Reply Obj. 1: If we understand those things alone to be in a man's power, which we can do without the help of grace, then we are bound to do many things which we cannot do without the aid of healing grace, such as to love God and our neighbor, and likewise to believe the articles of faith. But with the help of grace we can do this, for this help "to whomsoever it is given from above it is mercifully given; and from whom it is withheld it is justly withheld, as a punishment of a previous, or at least of original, sin," as Augustine states (De Corr. et Grat. v, vi[1]).

Reply Obj. 2: Man is bound to love definitely those lovable things which are properly and directly the objects of charity, namely, God and our neighbor. The objection refers to those precepts of charity which belong, as a consequence, to the objects of charity.

Reply Obj. 3: The virtue of obedience is seated, properly speaking, in the will; hence promptness of the will subject to authority, suffices for the act of obedience, because it is the proper and direct object of obedience. But this or that precept is accidental or consequent to that proper and direct object.

* * * * *

SIXTH ARTICLE [II-II, Q. 2, Art. 6]

Whether All Are Equally Bound to Have Explicit Faith?

Objection 1: It would seem that all are equally bound to have explicit faith. For all are bound to those things which are necessary for salvation, as is evidenced by the precepts of charity. Now it is necessary for salvation that certain things should be believed explicitly. Therefore all are equally bound to have explicit faith.

---

1   Cf. Ep. cxc; De Praed. Sanct. viii.

Obj. 2: Further, no one should be put to test in matters that he is not bound to believe. But simple persons are sometimes tested in reference to the slightest articles of faith. Therefore all are bound to believe everything explicitly.

Obj. 3: Further, if the simple are bound to have, not explicit but only implicit faith, their faith must needs be implied in the faith of the learned. But this seems unsafe, since it is possible for the learned to err. Therefore it seems that the simple should also have explicit faith; so that all are, therefore, equally bound to have explicit faith.

On the contrary, It is written (Job 1:14): "The oxen were ploughing, and the asses feeding beside them," because, as Gregory expounds this passage (Moral. ii, 17), the simple, who are signified by the asses, ought, in matters of faith, to stay by the learned, who are denoted by the oxen.

I answer that, The unfolding of matters of faith is the result of Divine revelation: for matters of faith surpass natural reason. Now Divine revelation reaches those of lower degree through those who are over them, in a certain order; to men, for instance, through the angels, and to the lower angels through the higher, as Dionysius explains (Coel. Hier. iv, vii). In like manner therefore the unfolding of faith must needs reach men of lower degree through those of higher degree. Consequently, just as the higher angels, who enlighten those who are below them, have a fuller knowledge of Divine things than the lower angels, as Dionysius states (Coel. Hier. xii), so too, men of higher degree, whose business it is to teach others, are under obligation to have fuller knowledge of matters of faith, and to believe them more explicitly.

Reply Obj. 1: The unfolding of the articles of faith is not equally necessary for the salvation of all, since those of higher degree, whose duty it is to teach others, are bound to believe explicitly more things than others are.

Reply Obj. 2: Simple persons should not be put to the test about subtle questions of faith, unless they be suspected of having been corrupted by heretics, who are wont to corrupt the faith of simple people in such questions. If, however, it is found that they are free from obstinacy in their heterodox sentiments, and that it is due to their simplicity, it is no fault of theirs.

Reply Obj. 3: The simple have no faith implied in that of the learned, except in so far as the latter adhere to the Divine teaching.

Hence the Apostle says (1 Cor. 4:16): "Be ye followers of me, as I also am of Christ." Hence it is not human knowledge, but the Divine truth that is the rule of faith: and if any of the learned stray from this rule, he does not harm the faith of the simple ones, who think that the learned believe aright; unless the simple hold obstinately to their individual errors, against the faith of the universal Church, which cannot err, since Our Lord said (Luke 22:32): "I have prayed for thee," Peter, "that thy faith fail not.".

* * * * *

SEVENTH ARTICLE [II-II, Q. 2, Art. 7]

Whether It Is Necessary for the Salvation of All, That They Should Believe Explicitly in the Mystery of Christ?

Objection 1: It would seem that it is not necessary for the salvation of all that they should believe explicitly in the mystery of Christ. For man is not bound to believe explicitly what the angels are ignorant about: since the unfolding of faith is the result of Divine revelation, which reaches man by means of the angels, as stated above (A. 6; I, Q. 111, A. 1). Now even the angels were in ignorance of the mystery of the Incarnation: hence, according to the commentary of Dionysius (Coel. Hier. vii), it is they who ask (Ps. 23:8): "Who is this king of glory?" and (Isa. 63:1): "Who is this that cometh from Edom?" Therefore men were not bound to believe explicitly in the mystery of Christ's Incarnation.

Obj. 2: Further, it is evident that John the Baptist was one of the teachers, and most nigh to Christ, Who said of him (Matt. 11:11) that "there hath not risen among them that are born of women, a greater than" he. Now John the Baptist does not appear to have known the mystery of Christ explicitly, since he asked Christ (Matt. 11:3): "Art Thou He that art to come, or look we for another?" Therefore even the teachers were not bound to explicit faith in Christ.

Obj. 3: Further, many gentiles obtained salvation through the ministry of the angels, as Dionysius states (Coel. Hier. ix). Now it would seem that the gentiles had neither explicit nor implicit faith in Christ, since they received no revelation. Therefore it seems that it was not necessary for the salvation of all to believe explicitly in the mystery of Christ.

On the contrary, Augustine says (De Corr. et Gratia vii; Ep. cxc): "Our faith is sound if we believe that no man, old or young is delivered from the contagion of death and the bonds of sin, except by the one Mediator of God and men, Jesus Christ."

I answer that, As stated above (A. 5; Q. 1, A. 8), the object of faith includes, properly and directly, that thing through which man obtains beatitude. Now the mystery of Christ's Incarnation and Passion is the way by which men obtain beatitude; for it is written (Acts 4:12): "There is no other name under heaven given to men, whereby we must be saved." Therefore belief of some kind in the mystery of Christ's Incarnation was necessary at all times and for all persons, but this belief differed according to differences of times and persons. The reason of this is that before the state of sin, man believed, explicitly in Christ's Incarnation, in so far as it was intended for the consummation of glory, but not as it was intended to deliver man from sin by the Passion and Resurrection, since man had no foreknowledge of his future sin. He does, however, seem to have had foreknowledge of the Incarnation of Christ, from the fact that he said (Gen. 2:24): "Wherefore a man shall leave father and mother, and shall cleave to his wife," of which the Apostle says (Eph. 5:32) that "this is a great sacrament . . . in Christ and the Church," and it is incredible that the first man was ignorant about this sacrament.

But after sin, man believed explicitly in Christ, not only as to the Incarnation, but also as to the Passion and Resurrection, whereby the human race is delivered from sin and death: for they would not, else, have foreshadowed Christ's Passion by certain sacrifices both before and after the Law, the meaning of which sacrifices was known by the learned explicitly, while the simple folk, under the veil of those sacrifices, believed them to be ordained by God in reference to Christ's coming, and thus their knowledge was covered with a veil, so to speak. And, as stated above (Q. 1, A. 7), the nearer they were to Christ, the more distinct was their knowledge of Christ's mysteries.

After grace had been revealed, both learned and simple folk are bound to explicit faith in the mysteries of Christ, chiefly as regards those which are observed throughout the Church, and publicly proclaimed, such as the articles which refer to the Incarnation, of which we have spoken above (Q. 1, A. 8). As to other minute points in reference to the articles of the Incarnation, men have been bound to believe them more or less explicitly according to each one's state and office.

Reply Obj. 1: The mystery of the Kingdom of God was not entirely hidden from the angels, as Augustine observes (Gen. ad lit. v, 19), yet certain aspects thereof were better known to them when Christ revealed them to them.

Reply Obj. 2: It was not through ignorance that John the Baptist inquired of Christ's advent in the flesh, since he had clearly professed his belief therein, saying: "I saw, and I gave testimony, that this is the Son of God" (John 1:34). Hence he did not say: "Art Thou He that hast come?" but "Art Thou He that art to come?" thus saying about the future, not about the past. Likewise it is not to be believed that he was ignorant of Christ's future Passion, for he had already said (John 1:39): "Behold the Lamb of God, behold Him who taketh away the sins [Vulg.: 'sin'] of the world," thus foretelling His future immolation; and since other prophets had foretold it, as may be seen especially in Isaias 53. We may therefore say with Gregory (Hom. xxvi in Evang.) that he asked this question, being in ignorance as to whether Christ would descend into hell in His own Person. But he did not ignore the fact that the power of Christ's Passion would be extended to those who were detained in Limbo, according to Zech. 9:11: "Thou also, by the blood of Thy testament hast sent forth Thy prisoners out of the pit, wherein there is no water"; nor was he bound to believe explicitly, before its fulfilment, that Christ was to descend thither Himself.

It may also be replied that, as Ambrose observes in his commentary on Luke 7:19, he made this inquiry, not from doubt or ignorance but from devotion: or again, with Chrysostom (Hom. xxxvi in Matth.), that he inquired, not as though ignorant himself, but because he wished his disciples to be satisfied on that point, through Christ: hence the latter framed His answer so as to instruct the disciples, by pointing to the signs of His works.

Reply Obj. 3: Many of the gentiles received revelations of Christ, as is clear from their predictions. Thus we read (Job 19:25): "I know that my Redeemer liveth." The Sibyl too foretold certain things about Christ, as Augustine states (Contra Faust. xiii, 15). Moreover, we read in the history of the Romans, that at the time of Constantine Augustus and his mother Irene a tomb was discovered, wherein lay a man on whose breast was a golden plate with the inscription: "Christ shall be born of a virgin, and in Him, I believe. O sun, during the lifetime of Irene and Constantine, thou shalt see me again"[1]. If, however, some were saved without receiving any revelation, they were not saved without faith in a Mediator, for, though they did not believe in Him explicitly, they did, nevertheless, have implicit faith through believing in Divine providence, since they believed that God would deliver mankind in whatever way was pleasing to Him, and according to the revelation of the Spirit to those who knew the truth, as stated in Job 35:11: "Who teacheth us more than the beasts of the earth.".

* * * * *

EIGHTH ARTICLE [II-II, Q. 2, Art. 8]

Whether It Is Necessary for Salvation to Believe Explicitly in the Trinity?

Objection 1: It would seem that it was not necessary for salvation to believe explicitly in the Trinity. For the Apostle says (Heb. 11:6): "He that cometh to God must believe that He is, and is a rewarder to them that seek Him." Now one can believe this without believing in the Trinity. Therefore it was not necessary to believe explicitly in the Trinity.

Obj. 2: Further our Lord said (John 17:5, 6): "Father, I have manifested Thy name to men," which words Augustine expounds (Tract. cvi) as follows: "Not the name by which Thou art called God, but the name whereby Thou art called My Father," and further on he adds: "In that He made this world, God is known to all nations; in that He is not to be worshipped together with false gods, 'God is known in Judea'; but, in that He is the Father of this Christ, through Whom He takes away the sin of the world, He now makes known to men this name of His, which hitherto they knew not." Therefore before the coming of Christ it was not known that Paternity and Filiation were in the Godhead: and so the Trinity was not believed explicitly.

Obj. 3: Further, that which we are bound to believe explicitly of God is the object of heavenly happiness. Now the object of heavenly happiness is the sovereign good, which can be understood

---

1   Cf. Baron, Annal., A.D. 780

to be in God, without any distinction of Persons. Therefore it was not necessary to believe explicitly in the Trinity.

On the contrary, In the Old Testament the Trinity of Persons is expressed in many ways; thus at the very outset of Genesis it is written in manifestation of the Trinity: "Let us make man to Our image and likeness" (Gen. 1:26). Therefore from the very beginning it was necessary for salvation to believe in the Trinity.

I answer that, It is impossible to believe explicitly in the mystery of Christ, without faith in the Trinity, since the mystery of Christ includes that the Son of God took flesh; that He renewed the world through the grace of the Holy Ghost; and again, that He was conceived by the Holy Ghost. Wherefore just as, before Christ, the mystery of Christ was believed explicitly by the learned, but implicitly and under a veil, so to speak, by the simple, so too was it with the mystery of the Trinity. And consequently, when once grace had been revealed, all were bound to explicit faith in the mystery of the Trinity: and all who are born again in Christ, have this bestowed on them by the invocation of the Trinity, according to Matt. 28:19: "Going therefore teach ye all nations, baptizing them in the name of the Father, and of the Son and of the Holy Ghost."

Reply Obj. 1: Explicit faith in those two things was necessary at all times and for all people: but it was not sufficient at all times and for all people.

Reply Obj. 2: Before Christ's coming, faith in the Trinity lay hidden in the faith of the learned, but through Christ and the apostles it was shown to the world.

Reply Obj. 3: God's sovereign goodness as we understand it now through its effects, can be understood without the Trinity of Persons: but as understood in itself, and as seen by the Blessed, it cannot be understood without the Trinity of Persons. Moreover the mission of the Divine Persons brings us to heavenly happiness.

* * * * *

NINTH ARTICLE [II-II, Q. 2, Art. 9]

Whether to Believe Is Meritorious?

Objection 1: It would seem that to believe is not meritorious. For the principle of all merit is charity, as stated above (I-II, Q. 114,

A. 4). Now faith, like nature, is a preamble to charity. Therefore, just as an act of nature is not meritorious, since we do not merit by our natural gifts, so neither is an act of faith.

Obj. 2: Further, belief is a mean between opinion and scientific knowledge or the consideration of things scientifically known[1]. Now the considerations of science are not meritorious, nor on the other hand is opinion. Therefore belief is not meritorious.

Obj. 3: Further, he who assents to a point of faith, either has a sufficient motive for believing, or he has not. If he has a sufficient motive for his belief, this does not seem to imply any merit on his part, since he is no longer free to believe or not to believe: whereas if he has not a sufficient motive for believing, this is a mark of levity, according to Ecclus. 19:4: "He that is hasty to give credit, is light of heart," so that, seemingly, he gains no merit thereby. Therefore to believe is by no means meritorious.

On the contrary, It is written (Heb. 11:33) that the saints "by faith ... obtained promises," which would not be the case if they did not merit by believing. Therefore to believe is meritorious.

I answer that, As stated above (I-II, Q. 114, AA. 3, 4), our actions are meritorious in so far as they proceed from the free-will moved with grace by God. Therefore every human act proceeding from the free-will, if it be referred to God, can be meritorious. Now the act of believing is an act of the intellect assenting to the Divine truth at the command of the will moved by the grace of God, so that it is subject to the free-will in relation to God; and consequently the act of faith can be meritorious.

Reply Obj. 1: Nature is compared to charity which is the principle of merit, as matter to form: whereas faith is compared to charity as the disposition which precedes the ultimate form. Now it is evident that the subject or the matter cannot act save by virtue of the form, nor can a preceding disposition, before the advent of the form: but after the advent of the form, both the subject and the preceding disposition act by virtue of the form, which is the chief principle of action, even as the heat of fire acts by virtue of the substantial form of fire. Accordingly neither nature nor faith can, without charity, produce a meritorious act; but, when accompanied

---

1 Science is a certain knowledge of a demonstrated conclusion through its demonstration.

by charity, the act of faith is made meritorious thereby, even as an act of nature, and a natural act of the free-will.

Reply Obj. 2: Two things may be considered in science: namely the scientist's assent to a scientific fact and his consideration of that fact. Now the assent of science is not subject to free-will, because the scientist is obliged to assent by force of the demonstration, wherefore scientific assent is not meritorious. But the actual consideration of what a man knows scientifically is subject to his free-will, for it is in his power to consider or not to consider. Hence scientific consideration may be meritorious if it be referred to the end of charity, i.e. to the honor of God or the good of our neighbor. On the other hand, in the case of faith, both these things are subject to the free-will so that in both respects the act of faith can be meritorious: whereas in the case of opinion, there is no firm assent, since it is weak and infirm, as the Philosopher observes (Poster. i, 33), so that it does not seem to proceed from a perfect act of the will: and for this reason, as regards the assent, it does not appear to be very meritorious, though it can be as regards the actual consideration.

Reply Obj. 3: The believer has sufficient motive for believing, for he is moved by the authority of Divine teaching confirmed by miracles, and, what is more, by the inward instinct of the Divine invitation: hence he does not believe lightly. He has not, however, sufficient reason for scientific knowledge, hence he does not lose the merit.

* * * * *

TENTH ARTICLE [II-II, Q. 2, Art. 10]

Whether Reasons in Support of What We Believe Lessen the Merit of Faith?

Objection 1: It would seem that reasons in support of what we believe lessen the merit of faith. For Gregory says (Hom. xxvi in Evang.) that "there is no merit in believing what is shown by reason." If, therefore, human reason provides sufficient proof, the merit of faith is altogether taken away. Therefore it seems that any kind of human reasoning in support of matters of faith, diminishes the merit of believing.

Obj. 2: Further, whatever lessens the measure of virtue, lessens the amount of merit, since "happiness is the reward of virtue," as the Philosopher states (Ethic. i, 9). Now human reasoning seems to diminish the measure of the virtue of faith, since it is essential to faith to be about the unseen, as stated above (Q. 1, AA. 4, 5). Now the more a thing is supported by reasons the less is it unseen. Therefore human reasons in support of matters of faith diminish the merit of faith.

Obj. 3: Further, contrary things have contrary causes. Now an inducement in opposition to faith increases the merit of faith whether it consist in persecution inflicted by one who endeavors to force a man to renounce his faith, or in an argument persuading him to do so. Therefore reasons in support of faith diminish the merit of faith.

On the contrary, It is written (1 Pet. 3:15): "Being ready always to satisfy every one that asketh you a reason of that faith[1] and hope which is in you." Now the Apostle would not give this advice, if it would imply a diminution in the merit of faith. Therefore reason does not diminish the merit of faith.

I answer that, As stated above (A. 9), the act of faith can be meritorious, in so far as it is subject to the will, not only as to the use, but also as to the assent. Now human reason in support of what we believe, may stand in a twofold relation to the will of the believer. First, as preceding the act of the will; as, for instance, when a man either has not the will, or not a prompt will, to believe, unless he be moved by human reasons: and in this way human reason diminishes the merit of faith. In this sense it has been said above (I-II, Q. 24, A. 3, ad 1; Q. 77, A. 6, ad 2) that, in moral virtues, a passion which precedes choice makes the virtuous act less praiseworthy. For just as a man ought to perform acts of moral virtue, on account of the judgment of his reason, and not on account of a passion, so ought he to believe matters of faith, not on account of human reason, but on account of the Divine authority. Secondly, human reasons may be consequent to the will of the believer. For when a man's will is ready to believe, he loves the truth he believes, he thinks out and

---

[1] Vulg.: 'Of that hope which is in you.' St. Thomas' reading is apparently taken from Bede.

takes to heart whatever reasons he can find in support thereof; and in this way human reason does not exclude the merit of faith but is a sign of greater merit. Thus again, in moral virtues a consequent passion is the sign of a more prompt will, as stated above (I-II, Q. 24, A. 3, ad 1). We have an indication of this in the words of the Samaritans to the woman, who is a type of human reason: "We now believe, not for thy saying" (John 4:42).

Reply Obj. 1: Gregory is referring to the case of a man who has no will to believe what is of faith, unless he be induced by reasons. But when a man has the will to believe what is of faith on the authority of God alone, although he may have reasons in demonstration of some of them, e.g. of the existence of God, the merit of his faith is not, for that reason, lost or diminished.

Reply Obj. 2: The reasons which are brought forward in support of the authority of faith, are not demonstrations which can bring intellectual vision to the human intellect, wherefore they do not cease to be unseen. But they remove obstacles to faith, by showing that what faith proposes is not impossible; wherefore such reasons do not diminish the merit or the measure of faith. On the other hand, though demonstrative reasons in support of the preambles of faith[1], but not of the articles of faith, diminish the measure of faith, since they make the thing believed to be seen, yet they do not diminish the measure of charity, which makes the will ready to believe them, even if they were unseen; and so the measure of merit is not diminished.

Reply Obj. 3: Whatever is in opposition to faith, whether it consist in a man's thoughts, or in outward persecution, increases the merit of faith, in so far as the will is shown to be more prompt and firm in believing. Hence the martyrs had more merit of faith, through not renouncing faith on account of persecution; and even the wise have greater merit of faith, through not renouncing their faith on account of the reasons brought forward by philosophers or heretics in opposition to faith. On the other hand things that are favorable to faith, do not always diminish the promptness of the will to believe, and therefore they do not always diminish the merit of faith.

---

[1] The Leonine Edition reads: 'in support of matters of faith which are however, preambles to the articles of faith, diminish,' etc.

3. OF THE OUTWARD ACT OF FAITH
(In Two Articles)

We must now consider the outward act, viz. the confession of faith: under which head there are two points of inquiry:

(1) Whether confession is an act of faith?
(2) Whether confession of faith is necessary for salvation?.

* * * * *

FIRST ARTICLE [II-II, Q. 3, Art. 1]

Whether Confession Is an Act of Faith?

Objection 1: It would seem that confession is not an act of faith. For the same act does not belong to different virtues. Now confession belongs to penance of which it is a part. Therefore it is not an act of faith.

Obj. 2: Further, man is sometimes deterred by fear or some kind of confusion, from confessing his faith: wherefore the Apostle (Eph. 6:19) asks for prayers that it may be granted him "with confidence, to make known the mystery of the gospel." Now it belongs to fortitude, which moderates daring and fear, not to be deterred from doing good on account of confusion or fear. Therefore it seems that confession is not an act of faith, but rather of fortitude or constancy.

Obj. 3: Further, just as the ardor of faith makes one confess one's faith outwardly, so does it make one do other external good works, for it is written (Gal. 5:6) that "faith . . . worketh by charity." But other external works are not reckoned acts of faith. Therefore neither is confession an act of faith.

On the contrary, A gloss explains the words of 2 Thess. 1:11, "and the work of faith in power" as referring to "confession which is a work proper to faith."

I answer that, Outward actions belong properly to the virtue to whose end they are specifically referred: thus fasting is referred specifically to the end of abstinence, which is to tame the flesh, and consequently it is an act of abstinence.

Now confession of those things that are of faith is referred specifically as to its end, to that which concerns faith, according to 2 Cor. 4:13: "Having the same spirit of faith . . . we believe, and therefore we speak also." For the outward utterance is intended to signify the inward thought. Wherefore, just as the inward thought of matters of faith is properly an act of faith, so too is the outward confession of them.

Reply Obj. 1: A threefold confession is commended by the Scriptures. One is the confession of matters of faith, and this is a proper act of faith, since it is referred to the end of faith as stated above. Another is the confession of thanksgiving or praise, and this is an act of "latria," for its purpose is to give outward honor to God, which is the end of "latria." The third is the confession of sins, which is ordained to the blotting out of sins, which is the end of penance, to which virtue it therefore belongs.

Reply Obj. 2: That which removes an obstacle is not a direct, but an indirect, cause, as the Philosopher proves (Phys. viii, 4). Hence fortitude which removes an obstacle to the confession of faith, viz. fear or shame, is not the proper and direct cause of confession, but an indirect cause so to speak.

Reply Obj. 3: Inward faith, with the aid of charity, causes all outward acts of virtue, by means of the other virtues, commanding, but not eliciting them; whereas it produces the act of confession as its proper act, without the help of any other virtue.

* * * * *

SECOND ARTICLE [II-II, Q. 3, Art. 2]

Whether Confession of Faith Is Necessary for Salvation?

Objection 1: It would seem that confession of faith is not necessary for salvation. For, seemingly, a thing is sufficient for salvation, if it is a means of attaining the end of virtue. Now the proper end of faith is the union of the human mind with Divine truth, and this can be realized without any outward confession. Therefore confession of faith is not necessary for salvation.

Obj. 2: Further, by outward confession of faith, a man reveals his faith to another man. But this is unnecessary save for those who have to instruct others in the faith. Therefore it seems that the simple folk are not bound to confess the faith.

Obj. 3: Further, whatever may tend to scandalize and disturb others, is not necessary for salvation, for the Apostle says (1 Cor. 10:32): "Be without offense to the Jews and to the gentiles and to the Church of God." Now confession of faith sometimes causes a disturbance among unbelievers. Therefore it is not necessary for salvation.

On the contrary, The Apostle says (Rom. 10:10): "With the heart we believe unto justice; but with the mouth, confession is made unto salvation."

I answer that, Things that are necessary for salvation come under the precepts of the Divine law. Now since confession of faith is something affirmative, it can only fall under an affirmative precept. Hence its necessity for salvation depends on how it falls under an affirmative precept of the Divine law. Now affirmative precepts as stated above (I-II, Q. 71, A. 5, ad 3; I-II, Q. 88, A. 1, ad 2) do not bind for always, although they are always binding; but they bind as to place and time according to other due circumstances, in respect of which human acts have to be regulated in order to be acts of virtue.

Thus then it is not necessary for salvation to confess one's faith at all times and in all places, but in certain places and at certain times, when, namely, by omitting to do so, we would deprive God of due honor, or our neighbor of a service that we ought to render him: for instance, if a man, on being asked about his faith, were to remain silent, so as to make people believe either that he is without faith, or that the faith is false, or so as to turn others away from the faith; for in such cases as these, confession of faith is necessary for salvation.

Reply Obj. 1: The end of faith, even as of the other virtues, must be referred to the end of charity, which is the love of God and our neighbor. Consequently when God's honor and our neighbor's good demand, man should not be contented with being united by faith to God's truth, but ought to confess his faith outwardly.

Reply Obj. 2: In cases of necessity where faith is in danger, every one is bound to proclaim his faith to others, either to give good example and encouragement to the rest of the faithful, or to check the attacks of unbelievers: but at other times it is not the duty of all the faithful to instruct others in the faith.

Reply Obj. 3: There is nothing commendable in making a public confession of one's faith, if it causes a disturbance among unbelievers, without any profit either to the faith or to the faithful. Hence Our Lord said (Matt. 7:6): "Give not that which is holy to dogs, neither cast ye your pearls before swine . . . lest turning upon you, they tear you." Yet, if there is hope of profit to the faith, or if there be urgency, a man should disregard the disturbance of unbelievers, and confess his faith in public. Hence it is written (Matt. 15:12) that when the disciples had said to Our Lord that "the Pharisee, when they heard this word, were scandalized," He answered: "Let them alone, they are blind, and leaders of the blind.".

4. OF THE VIRTUE ITSELF OF FAITH
(In Eight Articles)

We must now consider the virtue itself of faith, and, in the first place, faith itself; secondly, those who have faith; thirdly, the cause of faith; fourthly, its effects.

Under the first head there are eight points of inquiry:

(1) What is faith?
(2) In what power of the soul does it reside?
(3) Whether its form is charity?
(4) Whether living *(formata)* faith and lifeless *(informis)* faith are one identically?
(5) Whether faith is a virtue?
(6) Whether it is one virtue?
(7) Of its relation to the other virtues;
(8) Of its certitude as compared with the certitude of the intellectual virtues.

* * * * *

FIRST ARTICLE [II-II, Q. 4, Art. 1]

Whether This Is a Fitting Definition of Faith: "Faith Is the Substance of Things to Be Hoped For, the Evidence of Things That Appear Not?"

Objection 1: It would seem that the Apostle gives an unfitting definition of faith (Heb. 11:1) when he says: "Faith is the substance of things to be hoped for, the evidence of things that appear not." For no quality is a substance: whereas faith is a quality, since it is a theological virtue, as stated above (I-II, Q. 62, A. 3). Therefore it is not a substance.

Obj. 2: Further, different virtues have different objects. Now things to be hoped for are the object of hope. Therefore they should not be included in a definition of faith, as though they were its object.

Obj. 3: Further, faith is perfected by charity rather than by hope, since charity is the form of faith, as we shall state further on (A. 3). Therefore the definition of faith should have included the thing to be loved rather than the thing to be hoped for.

Obj. 4: Further, the same thing should not be placed in different genera. Now "substance" and "evidence" are different genera, and neither is subalternate to the other. Therefore it is unfitting to state that faith is both "substance" and "evidence."

Obj. 5: Further, evidence manifests the truth of the matter for which it is adduced. Now a thing is said to be apparent when its truth is already manifest. Therefore it seems to imply a contradiction to speak of "evidence of things that appear not": and so faith is unfittingly defined.

On the contrary, The authority of the Apostle suffices.

I answer that, Though some say that the above words of the Apostle are not a definition of faith, yet if we consider the matter aright, this definition overlooks none of the points in reference to which faith can be defined, albeit the words themselves are not arranged in the form of a definition, just as the philosophers touch on the principles of the syllogism, without employing the syllogistic form.

In order to make this clear, we must observe that since habits are known by their acts, and acts by their objects, faith, being a habit, should be defined by its proper act in relation to its proper object. Now the act of faith is to believe, as stated above (Q. 2, AA.

2, 3), which is an act of the intellect determinate to one object of the will's command. Hence an act of faith is related both to the object of the will, i.e. to the good and the end, and to the object of the intellect, i.e. to the true. And since faith, through being a theological virtue, as stated above (I-II, Q. 62, A. 2), has one same thing for object and end, its object and end must, of necessity, be in proportion to one another. Now it has been already stated (Q. 1, AA. 1, 4) that the object of faith is the First Truth, as unseen, and whatever we hold on account thereof: so that it must needs be under the aspect of something unseen that the First Truth is the end of the act of faith, which aspect is that of a thing hoped for, according to the Apostle (Rom. 8:25): "We hope for that which we see not": because to see the truth is to possess it. Now one hopes not for what one has already, but for what one has not, as stated above (I-II, Q. 67, A. 4). Accordingly the relation of the act of faith to its end which is the object of the will, is indicated by the words: "Faith is the substance of things to be hoped for." For we are wont to call by the name of substance, the first beginning of a thing, especially when the whole subsequent thing is virtually contained in the first beginning; for instance, we might say that the first self-evident principles are the substance of science, because, to wit, these principles are in us the first beginnings of science, the whole of which is itself contained in them virtually. In this way then faith is said to be the "substance of things to be hoped for," for the reason that in us the first beginning of things to be hoped for is brought about by the assent of faith, which contains virtually all things to be hoped for. Because we hope to be made happy through seeing the unveiled truth to which our faith cleaves, as was made evident when we were speaking of happiness (I-II, Q. 3, A. 8; I-II, Q. 4, A. 3).

The relationship of the act of faith to the object of the intellect, considered as the object of faith, is indicated by the words, "evidence of things that appear not," where "evidence" is taken for the result of evidence. For evidence induces the intellect to adhere to a truth, wherefore the firm adhesion of the intellect to the non-apparent truth of faith is called "evidence" here. Hence another reading has "conviction," because to wit, the intellect of the believer is convinced by Divine authority, so as to assent to what it sees not. Accordingly if anyone would reduce the foregoing words to the form of a definition, he may say that "faith is a habit of the mind, whereby eternal life is begun in us, making the intellect assent to what is non-apparent."

In this way faith is distinguished from all other things pertaining to the intellect. For when we describe it as "evidence," we distinguish it from opinion, suspicion, and doubt, which do not make the intellect adhere to anything firmly; when we go on to say, "of things that appear not," we distinguish it from science and understanding, the object of which is something apparent; and when we say that it is "the substance of things to be hoped for," we distinguish the virtue of faith from faith commonly so called, which has no reference to the beatitude we hope for.

Whatever other definitions are given of faith, are explanations of this one given by the Apostle. For when Augustine says (Tract. xl in Joan.: QQ. Evang. ii, qu. 39) that "faith is a virtue whereby we believe what we do not see," and when Damascene says (De Fide Orth. iv, 11) that "faith is an assent without research," and when others say that "faith is that certainty of the mind about absent things which surpasses opinion but falls short of science," these all amount to the same as the Apostle's words: "Evidence of things that appear not"; and when Dionysius says (Div. Nom. vii) that "faith is the solid foundation of the believer, establishing him in the truth, and showing forth the truth in him," comes to the same as "substance of things to be hoped for."

Reply Obj. 1: "Substance" here does not stand for the supreme genus condivided with the other genera, but for that likeness to substance which is found in each genus, inasmuch as the first thing in a genus contains the others virtually and is said to be the substance thereof.

Reply Obj. 2: Since faith pertains to the intellect as commanded by the will, it must needs be directed, as to its end, to the objects of those virtues which perfect the will, among which is hope, as we shall prove further on (Q. 18, A. 1). For this reason the definition of faith includes the object of hope.

Reply Obj. 3: Love may be of the seen and of the unseen, of the present and of the absent. Consequently a thing to be loved is not so adapted to faith, as a thing to be hoped for, since hope is always of the absent and the unseen.

Reply Obj. 4: "Substance" and "evidence" as included in the definition of faith, do not denote various genera of faith, nor different acts, but different relationships of one act to different objects, as is clear from what has been said.

Reply Obj. 5: Evidence taken from the proper principles of a thing, make[s] it apparent, whereas evidence taken from Divine authority does not make a thing apparent in itself, and such is the evidence referred to in the definition of faith.

* * * * *

SECOND ARTICLE [II-II, Q. 4, Art. 2]

Whether Faith Resides in the Intellect?

Objection 1: It would seem that faith does not reside in the intellect. For Augustine says (De Praedest. Sanct. v) that "faith resides in the believer's will." Now the will is a power distinct from the intellect. Therefore faith does not reside in the intellect.

Obj. 2: Further, the assent of faith to believe anything, proceeds from the will obeying God. Therefore it seems that faith owes all its praise to obedience. Now obedience is in the will. Therefore faith is in the will, and not in the intellect.

Obj. 3: Further, the intellect is either speculative or practical. Now faith is not in the speculative intellect, since this is not concerned with things to be sought or avoided, as stated in De Anima iii, 9, so that it is not a principle of operation, whereas "faith . . . worketh by charity" (Gal. 5:6). Likewise, neither is it in the practical intellect, the object of which is some true, contingent thing, that can be made or done. For the object of faith is the Eternal Truth, as was shown above (Q. 1, A. 1). Therefore faith does not reside in the intellect.

On the contrary, Faith is succeeded by the heavenly vision, according to 1 Cor. 13:12: "We see now through a glass in a dark manner; but then face to face." Now vision is in the intellect. Therefore faith is likewise.

I answer that, Since faith is a virtue, its act must needs be perfect. Now, for the perfection of an act proceeding from two active principles, each of these principles must be perfect: for it is not possible for a thing to be sawn well, unless the sawyer possess the art, and the saw be well fitted for sawing. Now, in a power of the soul, which is related to opposite objects, a disposition to act well is a habit, as stated above (I-II, Q. 49, A. 4, ad 1, 2, 3). Wherefore an act that proceeds from two such powers must be perfected by a habit residing in each of them. Again, it has been stated above (Q. 2, AA. 1, 2) that to believe is an act of the intellect inasmuch as the will moves it to assent. And this act proceeds from the will and the intellect, both of which have a natural aptitude to be perfected in this way. Consequently, if the act of faith is to be perfect, there needs to be a habit in the will as well as in the intellect: even as there needs to be the habit of prudence in the reason, besides the habit of temperance in the concupiscible faculty, in order that the act of that faculty be perfect. Now, to believe is immediately an act of the intellect, because the object of that act is "the true," which pertains properly to the intellect. Consequently faith, which is the proper principle of that act, must needs reside in the intellect.

Reply Obj. 1: Augustine takes faith for the act of faith, which is described as depending on the believer's will, in so far as his intellect assents to matters of faith at the command of the will.

Reply Obj. 2: Not only does the will need to be ready to obey but also the intellect needs to be well disposed to follow the command of the will, even as the concupiscible faculty needs to be well disposed in order to follow the command of reason; hence there needs to be a habit of virtue not only in the commanding will but also in the assenting intellect.

Reply Obj. 3: Faith resides in the speculative intellect, as evidenced by its object. But since this object, which is the First Truth, is the end of all our desires and actions, as Augustine proves (De Trin. i, 8), it follows that faith worketh by charity just as "the speculative intellect becomes practical by extension" (De Anima iii, 10).

* * * * *

THIRD ARTICLE [II-II, Q. 4, Art. 3]

Whether Charity Is the Form of Faith?

Objection 1: It would seem that charity is not the form of faith. For each thing derives its species from its form. When therefore two things are opposite members of a division, one cannot be the form of the other. Now faith and charity are stated to be opposite members of a division, as different species of virtue (1 Cor. 13:13). Therefore charity is not the form of faith.

Obj. 2: Further, a form and the thing of which it is the form are in one subject, since together they form one simply. Now faith is in the intellect, while charity is in the will. Therefore charity is not the form of faith.

Obj. 3: Further, the form of a thing is a principle thereof. Now obedience, rather than charity, seems to be the principle of believing, on the part of the will, according to Rom. 1:5: "For obedience to the faith in all nations." Therefore obedience rather than charity, is the form of faith.

On the contrary, Each thing works through its form. Now faith works through charity. Therefore the love of charity is the form of faith.

I answer that, As appears from what has been said above (I-II, Q. 1, A. 3; I-II, Q. 18, A. 6), voluntary acts take their species from their end which is the will's object. Now that which gives a thing its species, is after the manner of a form in natural things. Wherefore the form of any voluntary act is, in a manner, the end to which that act is directed, both because it takes its species therefrom, and because the mode of an action should correspond proportionately to the end. Now it is evident from what has been said (A. 1), that the act of faith is directed to the object of the will, i.e. the good, as to its end: and this good which is the end of faith, viz. the Divine Good, is the proper object of charity. Therefore charity is called the form of faith in so far as the act of faith is perfected and formed by charity.

Reply Obj. 1: Charity is called the form of faith because it quickens the act of faith. Now nothing hinders one act from being quickened by different habits, so as to be reduced to various species in a certain order, as stated above (I-II, Q. 18, AA. 6, 7; I-II, Q. 61, A. 2) when we were treating of human acts in general.

Reply Obj. 2: This objection is true of an intrinsic form. But it is not thus that charity is the form of faith, but in the sense that it quickens the act of faith, as explained above.

Reply Obj. 3: Even obedience, and hope likewise, and whatever other virtue might precede the act of faith, is quickened by charity, as we shall show further on (Q. 23, A. 8), and consequently charity is spoken of as the form of faith.

* * * * *

FOURTH ARTICLE [II-II, Q. 4, Art. 4]

Whether Lifeless Faith Can Become Living, or Living Faith, Lifeless?

Objection 1: It would seem that lifeless faith does not become living, or living faith lifeless. For, according to 1 Cor. 13:10, "when that which is perfect is come, that which is in part shall be done away." Now lifeless faith is imperfect in comparison with living faith. Therefore when living faith comes, lifeless faith is done away, so that they are not one identical habit.

Obj. 2: Further, a dead thing does not become a living thing. Now lifeless faith is dead, according to James 2:20: "Faith without works is dead." Therefore lifeless faith cannot become living.

Obj. 3: Further, God's grace, by its advent, has no less effect in a believer than in an unbeliever. Now by coming to an unbeliever it causes the habit of faith. Therefore when it comes to a believer, who hitherto had the habit of lifeless faith, it causes another habit of faith in him.

Obj. 4: Further, as Boethius says (In Categ. Arist. i), "accidents cannot be altered." Now faith is an accident. Therefore the same faith cannot be at one time living, and at another, lifeless.

On the contrary, A gloss on the words, "Faith without works is dead" (James 2:20) adds, "by which it lives once more." Therefore faith which was lifeless and without form hitherto, becomes formed and living.

I answer that, There have been various opinions on this question. For some[1] have said that living and lifeless faith are distinct habits, but that when living faith comes, lifeless faith is done away, and that, in like manner, when a man sins mortally after having living faith, a new habit of lifeless faith is infused into him by God. But it seems unfitting that grace should deprive man of a gift of God by coming to him, and that a gift of God should be infused into man, on account of a mortal sin.

Consequently others[2] have said that living and lifeless faith are indeed distinct habits, but that, all the same, when living faith comes the habit of lifeless faith is not taken away, and that it remains together with the habit of living faith in the same subject. Yet again

---

1 William of Auxerre, Sum. Aur. III, iii, 15
2 Alexander of Hales, Sum. Theol. iii, 64

it seems unreasonable that the habit of lifeless faith should remain inactive in a person having living faith.

We must therefore hold differently that living and lifeless faith are one and the same habit. The reason is that a habit is differentiated by that which directly pertains to that habit. Now since faith is a perfection of the intellect, that pertains directly to faith, which pertains to the intellect. Again, what pertains to the will, does not pertain directly to faith, so as to be able to differentiate the habit of faith. But the distinction of living from lifeless faith is in respect of something pertaining to the will, i.e. charity, and not in respect of something pertaining to the intellect. Therefore living and lifeless faith are not distinct habits.

Reply Obj. 1: The saying of the Apostle refers to those imperfect things from which imperfection is inseparable, for then, when the perfect comes the imperfect must needs be done away. Thus with the advent of clear vision, faith is done away, because it is essentially "of the things that appear not." When, however, imperfection is not inseparable from the imperfect thing, the same identical thing which was imperfect becomes perfect. Thus childhood is not essential to man and consequently the same identical subject who was a child, becomes a man. Now lifelessness is not essential to faith, but is accidental thereto as stated above. Therefore lifeless faith itself becomes living.

Reply Obj. 2: That which makes an animal live is inseparable from an animal, because it is its substantial form, viz. the soul: consequently a dead thing cannot become a living thing, and a living and a dead thing differ specifically. On the other hand that which gives faith its form, or makes it live, is not essential to faith. Hence there is no comparison.

Reply Obj. 3: Grace causes faith not only when faith begins anew to be in a man, but also as long as faith lasts. For it has been said above (I, Q. 104, A. 1; I-II, Q. 109, A. 9) that God is always working man's justification, even as the sun is always lighting up the air. Hence grace is not less effective when it comes to a believer than when it comes to an unbeliever: since it causes faith in both, in the former by confirming and perfecting it, in the latter by creating it anew.

We might also reply that it is accidental, namely on account of the disposition of the subject, that grace does not cause faith in one who has it already: just as, on the other hand, a second mortal sin does not take away grace from one who has already lost it through a previous mortal sin.

Reply Obj. 4: When living faith becomes lifeless, faith is not changed, but its subject, the soul, which at one time has faith without charity, and at another time, with charity.

* * * * *

FIFTH ARTICLE [II-II, Q. 4, Art. 5]

Whether Faith Is a Virtue?

Objection 1: It would seem that faith is not a virtue. For virtue is directed to the good, since "it is virtue that makes its subject good," as the Philosopher states (Ethic. ii, 6). But faith is directed to the true. Therefore faith is not a virtue.

Obj. 2: Further, infused virtue is more perfect than acquired virtue. Now faith, on account of its imperfection, is not placed among the acquired intellectual virtues, as the Philosopher states (Ethic. vi, 3). Much less, therefore, can it be considered an infused virtue.

Obj. 3: Further, living and lifeless faith are the same species, as stated above (A. 4). Now lifeless faith is not a virtue, since it is not connected with the other virtues. Therefore neither is living faith a virtue.

Obj. 4: Further, the gratuitous graces and the fruits are distinct from the virtues. But faith is numbered among the gratuitous graces (1 Cor. 12:9) and likewise among the fruits (Gal. 5:23). Therefore faith is not a virtue.

On the contrary, Man is justified by the virtues, since "justice is all virtue," as the Philosopher states (Ethic. v, 1). Now man is justified by faith according to Rom. 5:1: "Being justified therefore by faith let us have peace," etc. Therefore faith is a virtue.

I answer that, As shown above, it is by human virtue that human acts are rendered good; hence, any habit that is always the principle of a good act, may be called a human virtue. Such a habit is living faith. For since to believe is an act of the intellect assenting to the truth at the command of the will, two things are required that this act may be perfect: one of which is that the intellect should infallibly tend to its object, which is the true; while the other is that the will should be infallibly directed to the last end, on account of which it assents to the true: and both of these are to be found in the act of living faith. For it belongs to the very essence of faith that the intellect should ever tend to the true, since nothing false can be the object of faith, as proved above (Q. 1, A. 3): while the effect of charity, which is the form of faith, is that the soul ever has its will directed to a good end. Therefore living faith is a virtue.

On the other hand, lifeless faith is not a virtue, because, though the act of lifeless faith is duly perfect on the part of the intellect, it has not its due perfection as regards the will: just as if temperance be in the concupiscible, without prudence being in the rational part, temperance is not a virtue, as stated above (I-II, Q. 65, A. 1), because the act of temperance requires both an act of reason, and an act of the concupiscible faculty, even as the act of faith requires an act of the will, and an act of the intellect.

Reply Obj. 1: The truth is itself the good of the intellect, since it is its perfection: and consequently faith has a relation to some good in so far as it directs the intellect to the true. Furthermore, it has a relation to the good considered as the object of the will, inasmuch as it is formed by charity.

Reply Obj. 2: The faith of which the Philosopher speaks is based on human reasoning in a conclusion which does not follow, of necessity, from its premisses; and which is subject to be false: hence such like faith is not a virtue. On the other hand, the faith of which we are speaking is based on the Divine Truth, which is infallible, and consequently its object cannot be anything false; so that faith of this kind can be a virtue.

Reply Obj. 3: Living and lifeless faith do not differ specifically, as though they belonged to different species. But they differ as perfect and imperfect within the same species. Hence lifeless faith, being imperfect, does not satisfy the conditions of a perfect virtue, for "virtue is a kind of perfection" (Phys. vii, text. 18).

Reply Obj. 4: Some say that faith which is numbered among the gratuitous graces is lifeless faith. But this is said without reason, since the gratuitous graces, which are mentioned in that passage, are not common to all the members of the Church: wherefore the Apostle says: "There are diversities of graces," and again, "To one is given" this grace and "to another" that. Now lifeless faith is common to all members of the Church, because its lifelessness is not part of its substance, if we consider it as a gratuitous gift.

We must, therefore, say that in that passage, faith denotes a certain excellency of faith, for instance, "constancy in faith," according to a gloss, or the "word of faith."

Faith is numbered among the fruits, in so far as it gives a certain pleasure in its act by reason of its certainty, wherefore the gloss on the fifth chapter to the Galatians, where the fruits are enumerated, explains faith as being "certainty about the unseen.".

* * * * *

SIXTH ARTICLE [II-II, Q. 4, Art. 6]

Whether Faith Is One Virtue?

Objection 1: It would seem that faith is not one. For just as faith is a gift of God according to Eph. 2:8, so also wisdom and knowledge are numbered among God's gifts according to Isa. 11:2. Now wisdom and knowledge differ in this, that wisdom is about eternal things, and knowledge about temporal things, as Augustine states (De Trin. xii, 14, 15). Since, then, faith is about eternal things, and also about some temporal things, it seems that faith is not one virtue, but divided into several parts.

Obj. 2: Further, confession is an act of faith, as stated above (Q. 3, A. 1). Now confession of faith is not one and the same for all: since what we confess as past, the fathers of old confessed as yet to come, as appears from Isa. 7:14: "Behold a virgin shall conceive." Therefore faith is not one.

Obj. 3: Further, faith is common to all believers in Christ. But one accident cannot be in many subjects. Therefore all cannot have one faith.

On the contrary, The Apostle says (Eph. 4:5): "One Lord, one faith."

I answer that, If we take faith as a habit, we can consider it in two ways. First on the part of the object, and thus there is one faith. Because the formal object of faith is the First Truth, by adhering to which we believe whatever is contained in the faith. Secondly, on the part of the subject, and thus faith is differentiated according as it is in various subjects. Now it is evident that faith, just as any other habit, takes its species from the formal aspect of its object, but is individualized by its subject. Hence if we take faith for the habit whereby we believe, it is one specifically, but differs numerically according to its various subjects.

If, on the other hand, we take faith for that which is believed, then, again, there is one faith, since what is believed by all is one same thing: for though the things believed, which all agree in believing, be diverse from one another, yet they are all reduced to one.

Reply Obj. 1: Temporal matters which are proposed to be believed, do not belong to the object of faith, except in relation to something eternal, viz. the First Truth, as stated above (Q. 1, A. 1). Hence there is one faith of things both temporal and eternal. It is different with wisdom and knowledge, which consider temporal and eternal matters under their respective aspects.

Reply Obj. 2: This difference of past and future arises, not from any difference in the thing believed, but from the different relationships of believers to the one thing believed, as also we have mentioned above (I-II, Q. 103, A. 4; I-II, Q. 107, A. 1, ad 1).

Reply Obj. 3: This objection considers numerical diversity of faith.

* * * * *

SEVENTH ARTICLE [II-II, Q. 4, Art. 7]

Whether Faith Is the First of the Virtues?

Objection 1: It would seem that faith is not the first of the virtues. For a gloss on Luke 12:4, "I say to you My friends," says that fortitude is the foundation of faith. Now the foundation precedes that which is founded thereon. Therefore faith is not the first of the virtues.

Obj. 2: Further, a gloss on Ps. 36, "Be not emulous," says that hope "leads on to faith." Now hope is a virtue, as we shall state further on (Q. 17, A. 1). Therefore faith is not the first of the virtues.

Obj. 3: Further, it was stated above (A. 2) that the intellect of the believer is moved, out of obedience to God, to assent to matters of faith. Now obedience also is a virtue. Therefore faith is not the first virtue.

Obj. 4: Further, not lifeless but living faith is the foundation, as a gloss remarks on 1 Cor. 3:11[1]. Now faith is formed by charity, as

---

[1] Augustine, De Fide et Oper. xvi.

stated above (A. 3). Therefore it is owing to charity that faith is the foundation: so that charity is the foundation yet more than faith is (for the foundation is the first part of a building) and consequently it seems to precede faith.

Obj. 5: Further, the order of habits is taken from the order of acts. Now, in the act of faith, the act of the will which is perfected by charity, precedes the act of the intellect, which is perfected by faith, as the cause which precedes its effect. Therefore charity precedes faith. Therefore faith is not the first of the virtues.

On the contrary, The Apostle says (Heb. 11:1) that "faith is the substance of things to be hoped for." Now the substance of a thing is that which comes first. Therefore faith is first among the virtues.

I answer that, One thing can precede another in two ways: first, by its very nature; secondly, by accident. Faith, by its very nature, precedes all other virtues. For since the end is the principle in matters of action, as stated above (I-II, Q. 13, A. 3; I-II, Q. 34, A. 4, ad 1), the theological virtues, the object of which is the last end, must needs precede all the others. Again, the last end must of necessity be present to the intellect before it is present to the will, since the will has no inclination for anything except in so far as it is apprehended by the intellect. Hence, as the last end is present in the will by hope and charity, and in the intellect, by faith, the first of all the virtues must, of necessity, be faith, because natural knowledge cannot reach God as the object of heavenly bliss, which is the aspect under which hope and charity tend towards Him.

On the other hand, some virtues can precede faith accidentally. For an accidental cause precedes its effect accidentally. Now that which removes an obstacle is a kind of accidental cause, according to the Philosopher (Phys. viii, 4): and in this sense certain virtues may be said to precede faith accidentally, in so far as they remove obstacles to belief. Thus fortitude removes the inordinate fear that hinders faith; humility removes pride, whereby a man refuses to submit himself to the truth of faith. The same may be said of some other virtues, although there are no real virtues, unless faith be presupposed, as Augustine states (Contra Julian. iv, 3).

This suffices for the Reply to the First Objection.

Reply Obj. 2: Hope cannot lead to faith absolutely. For one cannot hope to obtain eternal happiness, unless one believes this possible, since hope does not tend to the impossible, as stated above (I-II, Q. 40, A. 1). It is, however, possible for one to be led by hope to persevere in faith, or to hold firmly to faith; and it is in this sense that hope is said to lead to faith.

Reply Obj. 3: Obedience is twofold: for sometimes it denotes the inclination of the will to fulfil God's commandments. In this way it is not a special virtue, but is a general condition of every virtue; since all acts of virtue come under the precepts of the Divine law, as stated above (I-II, Q. 100, A. 2); and thus it is requisite for faith. In another way, obedience denotes an inclination to fulfil the commandments considered as a duty. In this way it is a special virtue, and a part of justice: for a man does his duty by his superior when he obeys him: and thus obedience follows faith, whereby man knows that God is his superior, Whom he must obey.

Reply Obj. 4: To be a foundation a thing requires not only to come first, but also to be connected with the other parts of the building: since the building would not be founded on it unless the other parts adhered to it. Now the connecting bond of the spiritual edifice is charity, according to Col. 3:14: "Above all ... things have charity which is the bond of perfection." Consequently faith without charity cannot be the foundation: and yet it does not follow that charity precedes faith.

Reply Obj. 5: Some act of the will is required before faith, but not an act of the will quickened by charity. This latter act presupposes faith, because the will cannot tend to God with perfect love, unless the intellect possesses right faith about Him.

* * * * *

EIGHTH ARTICLE [II-II, Q. 4, Art. 8]

Whether Faith Is More Certain Than Science and the Other Intellectual Virtues?

Objection 1: It would seem that faith is not more certain than science and the other intellectual virtues. For doubt is opposed to certitude, wherefore a thing would seem to be the more certain, through being less doubtful, just as a thing is the whiter, the less it has of an admixture of black. Now understanding, science and also wisdom are free of any doubt about their objects; whereas the believer may sometimes suffer a movement of doubt, and doubt about matters of faith. Therefore faith is no more certain than the intellectual virtues.

Obj. 2: Further, sight is more certain than hearing. But "faith is through hearing" according to Rom. 10:17; whereas understanding, science and wisdom imply some kind of intellectual sight. Therefore science and understanding are more certain than faith.

Obj. 3: Further, in matters concerning the intellect, the more perfect is the more certain. Now understanding is more perfect than faith, since faith is the way to understanding, according to another version[1] of Isa. 7:9: "If you will not believe, you shall not understand [Vulg.: 'continue']": and Augustine says (De Trin. xiv, 1) that "faith is strengthened by science." Therefore it seems that science or understanding is more certain than faith.

On the contrary, The Apostle says (1 Thess. 2:15): "When you had received of us the word of the hearing," i.e. by faith ... "you received it not as the word of men, but, as it is indeed, the word of God." Now nothing is more certain than the word of God. Therefore science is not more certain than faith; nor is anything else.

I answer that, As stated above (I-II, Q. 57, A. 4, ad 2) two of the intellectual virtues are about contingent matter, viz. prudence and art; to which faith is preferable in point of certitude, by reason of its matter, since it is about eternal things, which never change, whereas the other three intellectual virtues, viz. wisdom, science[2] and understanding, are about necessary things, as stated above (I-II, Q. 57, A. 5, ad 3). But it must be observed that wisdom, science and understanding may be taken in two ways: first, as intellectual virtues, according to the Philosopher (Ethic. vi, 2, 3); secondly, for the gifts of the Holy Ghost. If we consider them in the first way, we must note that certitude can be looked at in two ways. First, on the part of its cause, and thus a thing which has a more certain cause, is itself more certain. In this way faith is more certain than those three virtues, because it is founded on the Divine truth, whereas the aforesaid three virtues are based on human reason. Secondly, certitude may be considered on the part of the subject, and thus the more a man's intellect lays hold of a thing, the more certain it is. In this way, faith is less certain, because matters of faith are above the human intellect, whereas the objects

---

1   The Septuagint
2   In English the corresponding 'gift' is called knowledge

of the aforesaid three virtues are not. Since, however, a thing is judged simply with regard to its cause, but relatively, with respect to a disposition on the part of the subject, it follows that faith is more certain simply, while the others are more certain relatively, i.e. for us. Likewise if these three be taken as gifts received in this present life, they are related to faith as to their principle which they presuppose: so that again, in this way, faith is more certain.

Reply Obj. 1: This doubt is not on the side of the cause of faith, but on our side, in so far as we do not fully grasp matters of faith with our intellect.

Reply Obj. 2: Other things being equal sight is more certain than hearing; but if (the authority of) the person from whom we hear greatly surpasses that of the seer's sight, hearing is more certain than sight: thus a man of little science is more certain about what he hears on the authority of an expert in science, than about what is apparent to him according to his own reason: and much more is a man certain about what he hears from God, Who cannot be deceived, than about what he sees with his own reason, which can be mistaken.

Reply Obj. 3: The gifts of understanding and knowledge are more perfect than the knowledge of faith in the point of their greater clearness, but not in regard to more certain adhesion: because the whole certitude of the gifts of understanding and knowledge, arises from the certitude of faith, even as the certitude of the knowledge of conclusions arises from the certitude of premisses. But in so far as science, wisdom and understanding are intellectual virtues, they are based upon the natural light of reason, which falls short of the certitude of God's word, on which faith is founded.

5. OF THOSE WHO HAVE FAITH
(In Four Articles)

We must now consider those who have faith: under which head there are four points of inquiry:

(1) Whether there was faith in the angels, or in man, in their original state?

(2) Whether the demons have faith?
(3) Whether those heretics who err in one article, have faith in others?
(4) Whether among those who have faith, one has it more than another?.

* * * * *

FIRST ARTICLE [II-II, Q. 5, Art. 1]

Whether There Was Faith in the Angels, or in Man, in Their Original State?

Objection 1: It would seem that there was no faith, either in the angels, or in man, in their original state. For Hugh of S. Victor says in his Sentences (De Sacram. i, 10) that "man cannot see God or things that are in God, because he closes his eyes to contemplation." Now the angels, in their original state, before they were either confirmed in grace, or had fallen from it, had their eyes opened to contemplation, since "they saw things in the Word," according to Augustine (Gen. ad lit. ii, 8). Likewise the first man, while in the state of innocence, seemingly had his eyes open to contemplation; for Hugh St. Victor says (De Sacram. i, 6) that "in his original state man knew his Creator, not by the mere outward perception of hearing, but by inward inspiration, not as now believers seek an absent God by faith, but by seeing Him clearly present to their contemplation." Therefore there was no faith in the angels and man in their original state.

Obj. 2: Further, the knowledge of faith is dark and obscure, according to 1 Cor. 13:13: "We see now through a glass in a dark manner." Now in their original state there was not obscurity either in the angels or in man, because it is a punishment of sin. Therefore there could be no faith in the angels or in man, in their original state.

Obj. 3: Further, the Apostle says (Rom. 10:17) that "faith . . . cometh by hearing." Now this could not apply to angels and man in their original state; for then they could not hear anything from another. Therefore, in that state, there was no faith either in man or in the angels.

On the contrary, It is written (Heb. 11:6): "He that cometh to God, must believe." Now the original state of angels and man was one of approach to God. Therefore they had need of faith.

I answer that, Some say that there was no faith in the angels before they were confirmed in grace or fell from it, and in man before he sinned, by reason of the manifest contemplation that they had of Divine things. Since, however, "faith is the evidence of things that appear not," according to the Apostle (Heb. 11:2), and since "by faith we believe what we see not," according to Augustine (Tract. xl in Joan.; QQ. Evang. ii, qu. 39), that manifestation alone excludes faith, which renders apparent or seen the principal object of faith. Now the principal object of faith is the First Truth, the sight of which gives the happiness of heaven and takes the place of faith. Consequently, as the angels before their confirmation in grace, and man before sin, did not possess the happiness whereby God is seen in His Essence, it is evident that the knowledge they possessed was not such as to exclude faith.

It follows then, that the absence of faith in them could only be explained by their being altogether ignorant of the object of faith. And if man and the angels were created in a purely natural state, as some[1] hold, perhaps one might hold that there was no faith in the angels before their confirmation in grace, or in man before sin, because the knowledge of faith surpasses not only a man's but even an angel's natural knowledge about God.

Since, however, we stated in the First Part (Q. 62, A. 3; Q. 95, A. 1) that man and the angels were created with the gift of grace, we must needs say that there was in them a certain beginning of hoped-for happiness, by reason of grace received but not yet consummated, which happiness was begun in their will by hope and charity, and in the intellect by faith, as stated above (Q. 4, A. 7). Consequently we must hold that the angels had faith before they were confirmed, and man, before he sinned. Nevertheless we must observe that in the object of faith, there is something formal, as it were, namely the First Truth surpassing all the natural knowledge of a creature, and something material, namely, the thing to which we assent while adhering to the First Truth. With regard to the former, before obtaining the happiness to come, faith is common to all who have knowledge of God, by adhering to the First Truth: whereas with regard to the things which are proposed as the material object of faith, some are believed by one, and known manifestly by

---

1   St. Bonaventure, Sent. ii, D, 29

another, even in the present state, as we have shown above (Q. 1, A. 5; Q. 2, A. 4, ad 2). In this respect, too, it may be said that the angels before being confirmed, and man, before sin, possessed manifest knowledge about certain points in the Divine mysteries, which now we cannot know except by believing them.

Reply Obj. 1: Although the words of Hugh of S. Victor are those of a master, and have the force of an authority, yet it may be said that the contemplation which removes the need of faith is heavenly contemplation, whereby the supernatural truth is seen in its essence. Now the angels did not possess this contemplation before they were confirmed, nor did man before he sinned: yet their contemplation was of a higher order than ours, for by its means they approached nearer to God, and had manifest knowledge of more of the Divine effects and mysteries than we can have knowledge of. Hence faith was not in them so that they sought an absent God as we seek Him: since by the light of wisdom He was more present to them than He is to us, although He was not so present to them as He is to the Blessed by the light of glory.

Reply Obj. 2: There was no darkness of sin or punishment in the original state of man and the angels, but there was a certain natural obscurity in the human and angelic intellect, in so far as every creature is darkness in comparison with the immensity of the Divine light: and this obscurity suffices for faith.

Reply Obj. 3: In the original state there was no hearing anything from man speaking outwardly, but there was from God inspiring inwardly: thus the prophets heard, as expressed by the Ps. 84:9: "I will hear what the Lord God will speak in me.".

* * * * *

SECOND ARTICLE [II-II, Q. 5, Art. 2]

Whether in the Demons There Is Faith?

Objection 1: It would seem that the demons have no faith. For Augustine says (De Praedest. Sanct. v) that "faith depends on the believer's will": and this is a good will, since by it man wishes to believe in God. Since then no deliberate will of the demons is good, as stated above (I, Q. 64, A. 2, ad 5), it seems that in the demons there is no faith.

Obj. 2: Further, faith is a gift of Divine grace, according to Eph. 2:8: "By grace you are saved through faith . . . for it is the gift of God." Now, according to a gloss on Osee 3:1, "They look to strange gods, and love the husks of the grapes," the demons lost their gifts of grace by sinning. Therefore faith did not remain in the demons after they sinned.

Obj. 3: Further, unbelief would seem to be graver than other sins, as Augustine observes (Tract. lxxxix in Joan.) on John 15:22, "If I had not come and spoken to them, they would not have sin: but now they have no excuse for their sin." Now the sin of unbelief is in some men. Consequently, if the demons have faith, some men would be guilty of a sin graver than that of the demons, which seems unreasonable. Therefore in the demons there is no faith.

On the contrary, It is written (James 2:19): "The devils . . . believe and tremble."

I answer that, As stated above (Q. 1, A. 4; Q. 2, A. 1), the believer's intellect assents to that which he believes, not because he sees it either in itself, or by resolving it to first self-evident principles, but because his will commands his intellect to assent. Now, that the will moves the intellect to assent, may be due to two causes. First, through the will being directed to the good, and in this way, to believe is a praiseworthy action. Secondly, because the intellect is convinced that it ought to believe what is said, though that conviction is not based on objective evidence. Thus if a prophet, while preaching the word of God, were to foretell something, and were to give a sign, by raising a dead person to life, the intellect of a witness would be convinced so as to recognize clearly that God, Who lieth not, was speaking, although the thing itself foretold would not be evident in itself, and consequently the essence of faith would not be removed.

Accordingly we must say that faith is commended in the first sense in the faithful of Christ: and in this way faith is not in the demons, but only in the second way, for they see many evident signs, whereby they recognize that the teaching of the Church is from God, although they do not see the things themselves that the Church teaches, for instance that there are three Persons in God, and so forth.

Reply Obj. 1: The demons are, in a way, compelled to believe, by the evidence of signs, and so their will deserves no praise for their belief.

Reply Obj. 2: Faith, which is a gift of grace, inclines man to believe, by giving him a certain affection for the good, even when that faith is lifeless. Consequently the faith which the demons have, is not a gift of grace. Rather are they compelled to believe through their natural intellectual acumen.

Reply Obj. 3: The very fact that the signs of faith are so evident, that the demons are compelled to believe, is displeasing to them, so that their malice is by no means diminished by their belief.

* * * * *

THIRD ARTICLE [II-II, Q. 5, Art. 3]

Whether a Man Who Disbelieves One Article of Faith, Can Have Lifeless Faith in the Other Articles?

Objection 1: It would seem that a heretic who disbelieves one article of faith, can have lifeless faith in the other articles. For the natural intellect of a heretic is not more able than that of a catholic. Now a catholic's intellect needs the aid of the gift of faith in order to believe any article whatever of faith. Therefore it seems that heretics cannot believe any articles of faith without the gift of lifeless faith.

Obj. 2: Further, just as faith contains many articles, so does one science, viz. geometry, contain many conclusions. Now a man may possess the science of geometry as to some geometrical conclusions, and yet be ignorant of other conclusions. Therefore a man can believe some articles of faith without believing the others.

Obj. 3: Further, just as man obeys God in believing the articles of faith, so does he also in keeping the commandments of the Law. Now a man can obey some commandments, and disobey others. Therefore he can believe some articles, and disbelieve others.

On the contrary, Just as mortal sin is contrary to charity, so is disbelief in one article of faith contrary to faith. Now charity does not remain in a man after one mortal sin. Therefore neither does faith, after a man disbelieves one article.

I answer that, Neither living nor lifeless faith remains in a heretic who disbelieves one article of faith.

The reason of this is that the species of every habit depends on the formal aspect of the object, without which the species of the habit cannot remain. Now the formal object of faith is the First Truth, as manifested in Holy Writ and the teaching of the Church, which proceeds from the First Truth. Consequently whoever does not adhere, as to an infallible and Divine rule, to the teaching of the Church, which proceeds from the First Truth manifested in Holy Writ, has not the habit of faith, but holds that which is of faith otherwise than by faith. Even so, it is evident that a man whose mind holds a conclusion without knowing how it is proved, has not scientific knowledge, but merely an opinion about it. Now it is manifest that he who adheres to the teaching of the Church, as to an infallible rule, assents to whatever the Church teaches; otherwise, if, of the things taught by the Church, he holds what he chooses to hold, and rejects what he chooses to reject, he no longer adheres to the teaching of the Church as to an infallible rule, but to his own will. Hence it is evident that a heretic who obstinately disbelieves one article of faith, is not prepared to follow the teaching of the Church in all things; but if he is not obstinate, he is no longer in heresy but only in error. Therefore it is clear that such a heretic with regard to one article has no faith in the other articles, but only a kind of opinion in accordance with his own will.

Reply Obj. 1: A heretic does not hold the other articles of faith, about which he does not err, in the same way as one of the faithful does, namely by adhering simply to the Divine Truth, because in order to do so, a man needs the help of the habit of faith; but he holds the things that are of faith, by his own will and judgment.

Reply Obj. 2: The various conclusions of a science have their respective means of demonstration, one of which may be known without another, so that we may know some conclusions of a science without knowing the others. On the other hand faith adheres to all the articles of faith by reason of one mean, viz. on account of the First Truth proposed to us in Scriptures, according to the teaching of the Church who has the right understanding of them. Hence whoever abandons this mean is altogether lacking in faith.

Reply Obj. 3: The various precepts of the Law may be referred either to their respective proximate motives, and thus one can be kept without another; or to their primary motive, which is perfect obedience to God, in which a man fails whenever he breaks one commandment, according to James 2:10: "Whosoever shall . . . offend in one point is become guilty of all.".

* * * * *

FOURTH ARTICLE [II-II, Q. 5, Art. 4]

Whether Faith Can Be Greater in One Man Than in Another?

Objection 1: It would seem that faith cannot be greater in one man than in another. For the quantity of a habit is taken from its object. Now whoever has faith believes everything that is of faith, since by failing in one point, a man loses his faith altogether, as stated above (A. 3). Therefore it seems that faith cannot be greater in one than in another.

Obj. 2: Further, those things which consist in something supreme cannot be "more" or "less." Now faith consists in something supreme, because it requires that man should adhere to the First Truth above all things. Therefore faith cannot be "more" or "less."

Obj. 3: Further, faith is to knowledge by grace, as the understanding of principles is to natural knowledge, since the articles of faith are the first principles of knowledge by grace, as was shown above (Q. 1, A. 7). Now the understanding of principles is possessed in equal degree by all men. Therefore faith is possessed in equal degree by all the faithful.

On the contrary, Wherever we find great and little, there we find more or less. Now in the matter of faith we find great and little, for Our Lord said to Peter (Matt. 14:31): "O thou of little faith, why didst thou doubt?" And to the woman he said (Matt. 15: 28): "O woman, great is thy faith!" Therefore faith can be greater in one than in another.

I answer that, As stated above (I-II, Q. 52, AA. 1, 2; I-II, Q. 112, A. 4), the quantity of a habit may be considered from two points of view: first, on the part of the object; secondly, on the part of its participation by the subject.

Now the object of faith may be considered in two ways: first, in respect of its formal aspect; secondly, in respect of the material object which is proposed to be believed. Now the formal object of faith is one and simple, namely the First Truth, as stated above (Q. 1, A. 1). Hence in this respect there is no diversity of faith among believers, but it is specifically one in all, as stated above (Q. 4, A. 6).

But the things which are proposed as the matter of our belief are many and can be received more or less explicitly; and in this respect one man can believe explicitly more things than another, so that faith can be greater in one man on account of its being more explicit.

If, on the other hand, we consider faith from the point of view of its participation by the subject, this happens in two ways, since the act of faith proceeds both from the intellect and from the will, as stated above (Q. 2, AA. 1, 2; Q. 4, A. 2). Consequently a man's faith may be described as being greater, in one way, on the part of his intellect, on account of its greater certitude and firmness, and, in another way, on the part of his will, on account of his greater promptitude, devotion, or confidence.

Reply Obj. 1: A man who obstinately disbelieves a thing that is of faith, has not the habit of faith, and yet he who does not explicitly believe all, while he is prepared to believe all, has that habit. In this respect, one man has greater faith than another, on the part of the object, in so far as he believes more things, as stated above.

Reply Obj. 2: It is essential to faith that one should give the first place to the First Truth. But among those who do this, some submit to it with greater certitude and devotion than others; and in this way faith is greater in one than in another.

Reply Obj. 3: The understanding of principles results from man's very nature, which is equally shared by all: whereas faith results from the gift of grace, which is not equally in all, as explained above (I-II, Q. 112, A. 4). Hence the comparison fails.

Nevertheless the truth of principles is more known to one than to another, according to the greater capacity of intellect.

6. OF THE CAUSE OF FAITH (In Two Articles)

We must now consider the cause of faith, under which head there are two points of inquiry:

(1) Whether faith is infused into man by God?
(2) Whether lifeless faith is a gift of God?.

* * * * *

FIRST ARTICLE [II-II, Q. 6, Art. 1]

Whether Faith Is Infused into Man by God?

Objection 1: It would seem that faith is not infused into man by God. For Augustine says (De Trin. xiv) that "science begets faith in us, and nourishes, defends and strengthens it." Now those things which science begets in us seem to be acquired rather than infused. Therefore faith does not seem to be in us by Divine infusion.

Obj. 2: Further, that to which man attains by hearing and seeing, seems to be acquired by him. Now man attains to belief, both by seeing miracles, and by hearing the teachings of faith: for it is written (John 4:53): "The father . . . knew that it was at the same hour, that Jesus said to him, Thy son liveth; and himself believed, and his whole house"; and (Rom. 10:17) it is said that "faith is through hearing." Therefore man attains to faith by acquiring it.

Obj. 3: Further, that which depends on a man's will can be acquired by him. But "faith depends on the believer's will," according to Augustine (De Praedest. Sanct. v). Therefore faith can be acquired by man.

On the contrary, It is written (Eph. 2:8, 9): "By grace you are saved through faith, and that not of yourselves . . . that no man may glory . . . for it is the gift of God."

I answer that, Two things are requisite for faith. First, that the things which are of faith should be proposed to man: this is necessary in order that man believe anything explicitly. The second thing requisite for faith is the assent of the believer to the things which are proposed to him. Accordingly, as regards the first of these, faith must needs be from God. Because those things which are of faith surpass human reason, hence they do not come to man's knowledge, unless God reveal them. To some, indeed, they are revealed by God immediately, as those things which were revealed to the apostles and prophets, while to some they are proposed by God in sending preachers of the faith, according to Rom. 10:15: "How shall they preach, unless they be sent?"

As regards the second, viz. man's assent to the things which are of faith, we may observe a twofold cause, one of external inducement, such as seeing a miracle, or being persuaded by someone to embrace the faith: neither of which is a sufficient cause, since of those who see the same miracle, or who hear the same sermon, some believe, and some do not. Hence we must assert another internal cause, which moves man inwardly to assent to matters of faith.

The Pelagians held that this cause was nothing else than man's free-will: and consequently they said that the beginning of faith is from ourselves, inasmuch as, to wit, it is in our power to be ready to assent to things which are of faith, but that the consummation of faith is from God, Who proposes to us the things we have to believe. But this is false, for, since man, by assenting to matters of faith, is raised above his nature, this must needs accrue to him from some supernatural principle moving him inwardly; and this is God. Therefore faith, as regards the assent which is the chief act of faith, is from God moving man inwardly by grace.

Reply Obj. 1: Science begets and nourishes faith, by way of external persuasion afforded by science; but the chief and proper cause of faith is that which moves man inwardly to assent.

Reply Obj. 2: This argument again refers to the cause that proposes outwardly the things that are of faith, or persuades man to believe by words or deeds.

Reply Obj. 3: To believe does indeed depend on the will of the believer: but man's will needs to be prepared by God with grace, in order that he may be raised to things which are above his nature, as stated above (Q. 2, A. 3).

* * * * *

SECOND ARTICLE [II-II, Q. 6, Art. 2]

Whether Lifeless Faith Is a Gift of God?

Objection 1: It would seem that lifeless faith is not a gift of God. For it is written (Deut. 32:4) that "the works of God are perfect." Now lifeless faith is something imperfect. Therefore it is not the work of God.

Obj. 2: Further, just as an act is said to be deformed through lacking its due form, so too is faith called lifeless (informis) when it lacks the form due to it. Now the deformed act of sin is not from God, as stated above (I-II, Q. 79, A. 2, ad 2). Therefore neither is lifeless faith from God.

Obj. 3: Further, whomsoever God heals, He heals wholly: for it is written (John 7:23): "If a man receive circumcision on the sabbath-day, that the law of Moses may not be broken; are you angry at Me because I have healed the whole man on the sabbath-day?" Now faith heals man from unbelief. Therefore whoever receives from God the gift of faith, is at the same time healed from all his sins. But this is not done except by living faith. Therefore living faith alone is a gift of God: and consequently lifeless faith is not from God.

On the contrary, A gloss on 1 Cor. 13:2 says that "the faith which lacks charity is a gift of God." Now this is lifeless faith. Therefore lifeless faith is a gift of God.

I answer that, Lifelessness is a privation. Now it must be noted that privation is sometimes essential to the species, whereas sometimes it is not, but supervenes in a thing already possessed of its proper species: thus privation of the due equilibrium of the humors is essential to the species of sickness, while darkness is not essential to a diaphanous body, but supervenes in it. Since, therefore, when we assign the cause of a thing, we intend to assign the cause of that thing as existing in its proper species, it follows that what is not the cause of privation, cannot be assigned as the cause of the thing to which that privation belongs as being essential to its species. For we cannot assign as the cause of a sickness, something which is not the cause of a disturbance in the humors: though we can assign as cause of a diaphanous body, something which is not the cause of the darkness, which is not essential to the diaphanous body.

Now the lifelessness of faith is not essential to the species of faith, since faith is said to be lifeless through lack of an extrinsic form, as stated above (Q. 4, A. 4). Consequently the cause of lifeless faith is that which is the cause of faith strictly so called: and this is God, as stated above (A. 1). It follows, therefore, that lifeless faith is a gift of God.

Reply Obj. 1: Lifeless faith, though it is not simply perfect with the perfection of a virtue, is, nevertheless, perfect with a perfection that suffices for the essential notion of faith.

Reply Obj. 2: The deformity of an act is essential to the act's species, considered as a moral act, as stated above (I, Q. 48, A. 1, ad 2; I-II, Q. 18, A. 5): for an act is said to be deformed through being deprived of an intrinsic form, viz. the due commensuration of the act's circumstances. Hence we cannot say that God is the cause of a deformed act, for He is not the cause of its deformity, though He is the cause of the act as such.

We may also reply that deformity denotes not only privation of a due form, but also a contrary disposition, wherefore deformity is compared to the act, as falsehood is to faith. Hence, just as the deformed act is not from God, so neither is a false faith; and as lifeless faith is from God, so too, acts that are good generically, though not quickened by charity, as is frequently the case in sinners, are from God.

Reply Obj. 3: He who receives faith from God without charity, is healed from unbelief, not entirely (because the sin of his previous unbelief is not removed) but in part, namely, in the point of ceasing from committing such and such a sin. Thus it happens frequently that a man desists from one act of sin, through God causing him thus to desist, without desisting from another act of sin, through the instigation of his own malice. And in this way sometimes it is granted by God to a man to believe, and yet he is not granted the gift of charity: even so the gift of prophecy, or the like, is given to some without charity.

7. OF THE EFFECTS OF FAITH
(In Two Articles)

We must now consider the effects of faith: under which head there are two points of inquiry:

(1) Whether fear is an effect of faith?
(2) Whether the heart is purified by faith?.

* * * * *

FIRST ARTICLE [II-II, Q. 7, Art. 1]
Whether Fear Is an Effect of Faith?

Objection 1: It would seem that fear is not an effect of faith. For an effect does not precede its cause. Now fear precedes faith: for it is written (Ecclus. 2:8): "Ye that fear the Lord, believe in Him." Therefore fear is not an effect of faith.

Obj. 2: Further, the same thing is not the cause of contraries. Now fear and hope are contraries, as stated above (I-II, Q. 23, A. 2): and faith begets hope, as a gloss observes on Matt. 1:2. Therefore fear is not an effect of faith.

Obj. 3: Further, one contrary does not cause another. Now the object of faith is a good, which is the First Truth, while the object of fear is an evil, as stated above (I-II, Q. 42, A. 1). Again, acts take their species from the object, according to what was stated above (I-II, Q. 18, A. 2). Therefore faith is not a cause of fear.

On the contrary, It is written (James 2:19): "The devils ... believe and tremble."

I answer that, Fear is a movement of the appetitive power, as stated above (I-II, Q. 41, A. 1). Now the principle of all appetitive movements is the good or evil apprehended: and consequently the principle of fear and of every appetitive movement must be an apprehension. Again, through faith there arises in us an apprehension of certain penal evils, which are inflicted in accordance with the Divine judgment. In this way, then, faith is a cause of the fear whereby one dreads to be punished by God; and this is servile fear.

It is also the cause of filial fear, whereby one dreads to be separated from God, or whereby one shrinks from equalling oneself to Him, and holds Him in reverence, inasmuch as faith makes us appreciate God as an unfathomable and supreme good, separation from which is the greatest evil, and to which it is wicked to wish to be equalled. Of the first fear, viz. servile fear, lifeless faith is the cause, while living faith is the cause of the second, viz. filial fear, because it makes man adhere to God and to be subject to Him by charity.

Reply Obj. 1: Fear of God cannot altogether precede faith, because if we knew nothing at all about Him, with regard to rewards and punishments, concerning which faith teaches us, we should nowise fear Him. If, however, faith be presupposed in reference to certain articles of faith, for example the Divine excellence, then reverential fear follows, the result of which is that man submits his intellect to God, so as to believe in all the Divine promises. Hence the text quoted continues: "And your reward shall not be made void."

Reply Obj. 2: The same thing in respect of contraries can be the cause of contraries, but not under the same aspect. Now faith begets hope, in so far as it enables us to appreciate the prize which God awards to the just, while it is the cause of fear, in so far as it makes us appreciate the punishments which He intends to inflict on sinners.

Reply Obj. 3: The primary and formal object of faith is the good which is the First Truth; but the material object of faith includes also certain evils; for instance, that it is an evil either not to submit to God, or to be separated from Him, and that sinners will suffer penal evils from God: in this way faith can be the cause of fear.

* * * * *

SECOND ARTICLE [II-II, Q. 7, Art. 2]

Whether Faith Has the Effect of Purifying the Heart?

Objection 1: It would seem that faith does not purify the heart. For purity of the heart pertains chiefly to the affections, whereas faith is in the intellect. Therefore faith has not the effect of purifying the heart.

Obj. 2: Further, that which purifies the heart is incompatible with impurity. But faith is compatible with the impurity of sin, as may be seen in those who have lifeless faith. Therefore faith does not purify the heart.

Obj. 3: Further, if faith were to purify the human heart in any way, it would chiefly purify the intellect of man. Now it does not purify the intellect from obscurity, since it is a veiled knowledge. Therefore faith nowise purifies the heart.

On the contrary, Peter said (Acts 15:9): "Purifying their hearts by faith."

I answer that, A thing is impure through being mixed with baser things: for silver is not called impure, when mixed with gold, which betters it, but when mixed with lead or tin. Now it is evident that the rational creature is more excellent than all transient and corporeal creatures; so that it becomes impure through subjecting itself to transient things by loving them. From this impurity the rational creature is purified by means of a contrary movement, namely, by tending to that which is above it, viz. God. The first beginning of this movement is faith: since "he that cometh to God must believe that He is," according to Heb. 11:6. Hence the first beginning of the heart's purifying is faith; and if this be perfected through being quickened by charity, the heart will be perfectly purified thereby.

Reply Obj. 1: Things that are in the intellect are the principles of those which are in the appetite, in so far as the apprehended good moves the appetite.

Reply Obj. 2: Even lifeless faith excludes a certain impurity which is contrary to it, viz. that of error, and which consists in the human intellect, adhering inordinately to things below itself, through wishing to measure Divine things by the rule of sensible objects. But when it is quickened by charity, then it is incompatible with any kind of impurity, because "charity covereth all sins" (Prov. 10:12).

Reply Obj. 3: The obscurity of faith does not pertain to the impurity of sin, but rather to the natural defect of the human intellect, according to the present state of life.

8. OF THE GIFT OF UNDERSTANDING
(In Eight Articles)

We must now consider the gifts of understanding and knowledge, which respond to the virtue of faith. With regard to the gift of understanding there are eight points of inquiry:

(1) Whether understanding is a gift of the Holy Ghost?
(2) Whether it can be together with faith in the same person?
(3) Whether the understanding which is a gift of the Holy Ghost, is only speculative, or practical also?
(4) Whether all who are in a state of grace have the gift of understanding?
(5) Whether this gift is to be found in those who are without grace?
(6) Of the relationship of the gift of understanding to the other gifts.
(7) Which of the beatitudes corresponds to this gift?
(8) Which of the fruits?.

* * * * *

FIRST ARTICLE [II-II, Q. 8, Art. 1]

Whether Understanding Is a Gift of the Holy Ghost?

Objection 1: It would seem that understanding is not a gift of the Holy Ghost. For the gifts of grace are distinct from the gifts of nature, since they are given in addition to the latter. Now understanding is a natural habit of the soul, whereby self-evident principles are known, as stated in Ethic. vi, 6. Therefore it should not be reckoned among the gifts of the Holy Ghost.

Obj. 2: Further, the Divine gifts are shared by creatures according to their capacity and mode, as Dionysius states (Div. Nom. iv). Now the mode of human nature is to know the truth, not simply (which is a sign of understanding), but discursively (which is a sign of reason), as Dionysius explains (Div. Nom. vii). Therefore the Divine knowledge which is bestowed on man, should be called a gift of reason rather than a gift of understanding.

Obj. 3: Further, in the powers of the soul the understanding is condivided with the will (De Anima iii, 9, 10). Now no gift of the Holy Ghost is called after the will. Therefore no gift of the Holy Ghost should receive the name of understanding.

On the contrary, It is written (Isa. 11:2): "The Spirit of the Lord shall rest upon him, the Spirit of wisdom of understanding."

I answer that, Understanding implies an intimate knowledge, for "intelligere" [to understand] is the same as "intus legere" [to read inwardly]. This is clear to anyone who considers the difference between intellect and sense, because sensitive knowledge is concerned with external sensible qualities, whereas intellective knowledge penetrates into the very essence of a thing, because the object of the intellect is "what a thing is," as stated in *De Anima* iii, 6.

Now there are many kinds of things that are hidden within, to find which human knowledge has to penetrate within so to speak. Thus, under the accidents lies hidden the nature of the substantial reality, under words lies hidden their meaning; under likenesses and figures the truth they denote lies hidden (because the intelligible world is enclosed within as compared with the sensible world, which is perceived externally), and effects lie hidden in their causes, and vice versa. Hence we may speak of understanding with regard to all these things.

Since, however, human knowledge begins with the outside of things as it were, it is evident that the stronger the light of the understanding, the further can it penetrate into the heart of things. Now the natural light of our understanding is of finite power; wherefore it can reach to a certain fixed point. Consequently man needs a supernatural light in order to penetrate further still so as to know what it cannot know by its natural light: and this supernatural light which is bestowed on man is called the gift of understanding.

Reply Obj. 1: The natural light instilled within us, manifests only certain general principles, which are known naturally. But since man is ordained to supernatural happiness, as stated above (Q. 2, A. 3; I-II, Q. 3, A. 8), man needs to reach to certain higher truths, for which he requires the gift of understanding.

Reply Obj. 2: The discourse of reason always begins from an understanding and ends at an understanding; because we reason by proceeding from certain understood principles, and the discourse of reason is perfected when we come to understand what hitherto we ignored. Hence the act of reasoning proceeds from something previously understood. Now a gift of grace does not proceed from the light of nature, but is added thereto as perfecting it. Wherefore this addition is not called "reason" but "understanding," since the additional light is in comparison with what we know supernaturally, what the natural light is in regard to those things which we know from the first.

Reply Obj. 3: "Will" denotes simply a movement of the appetite without indicating any excellence; whereas "understanding" denotes a certain excellence of a knowledge that penetrates into the heart of things. Hence the supernatural gift is called after the understanding rather than after the will.

* * * * *

SECOND ARTICLE [II-II, Q. 8, Art. 2]

Whether the Gift of Understanding Is Compatible with Faith?

Objection 1: It would seem that the gift of understanding is incompatible with faith. For Augustine says (QQ. lxxxiii, qu. 15) that "the thing which is understood is bounded by the comprehension of him who understands it." But the thing which is believed is not comprehended, according to the word of the Apostle to the Philippians 3:12: "Not as though I had already comprehended [Douay: 'attained'], or were already perfect." Therefore it seems that faith and understanding are incompatible in the same subject.

Obj. 2: Further, whatever is understood is seen by the understanding. But faith is of things that appear not, as stated above (Q. 1, A. 4; Q. 4, A. 1). Therefore faith is incompatible with understanding in the same subject.

Obj. 3: Further, understanding is more certain than science. But science and faith are incompatible in the same subject, as stated above (Q. 1, AA. 4, 5). Much less, therefore, can understanding and faith be in the same subject.

On the contrary, Gregory says (Moral. i, 15) that "understanding enlightens the mind concerning the things it has heard." Now one who has faith can be enlightened in his mind concerning what he has heard; thus it is written (Luke 24:27, 32) that Our Lord opened the scriptures to His disciples, that they might understand them. Therefore understanding is compatible with faith.

I answer that, We need to make a twofold distinction here: one on the side of faith, the other on the part of understanding.

On the side of faith the distinction to be made is that certain things, of themselves, come directly under faith, such as the mystery to three Persons in one God, and the incarnation of God the Son; whereas other things come under faith, through being subordinate, in one way or another, to those just mentioned, for instance, all that is contained in the Divine Scriptures.

On the part of understanding the distinction to be observed is that there are two ways in which we may be said to understand. In one way, we understand a thing perfectly, when we arrive at knowing the essence of the thing we understand, and the very truth considered in itself of the proposition understood. In this way, so long as the state of faith lasts, we cannot understand those things which are the direct object of faith: although certain other things that are subordinate to faith can be understood even in this way.

In another way we understand a thing imperfectly, when the essence of a thing or the truth of a proposition is not known as to its quiddity or mode of being, and yet we know that whatever be the outward appearances, they do not contradict the truth, in so far as we understand that we ought not to depart from matters of faith, for the sake of things that appear externally. In this way, even during the state of faith, nothing hinders us from understanding even those things which are the direct object of faith.

This suffices for the Replies to the Objections: for the first three argue in reference to perfect understanding, while the last refers to the understanding of matters subordinate to faith.

* * * * *

THIRD ARTICLE [II-II, Q. 8, Art. 3]

Whether the Gift of Understanding Is Merely Speculative or Also Practical?

Objection 1: It would seem that understanding, considered as a gift of the Holy Ghost, is not practical, but only speculative. For, according to Gregory (Moral. i, 32), "understanding penetrates certain more exalted things." But the practical intellect is occupied, not with exalted, but with inferior things, viz. singulars, about which actions are concerned. Therefore understanding, considered as a gift, is not practical.

Obj. 2: Further, the gift of understanding is something more excellent than the intellectual virtue of understanding. But the intellectual virtue of understanding is concerned with none but necessary things, according to the Philosopher (Ethic. vi, 6). Much more, therefore, is the gift of understanding concerned with none but necessary matters. Now the practical intellect is not about necessary things, but about things which may be otherwise than they are, and which may result from man's activity. Therefore the gift of understanding is not practical.

Obj. 3: Further, the gift of understanding enlightens the mind in matters which surpass natural reason. Now human activities, with which the practical intellect is concerned, do not surpass natural reason, which is the directing principle in matters of action, as was made clear above (I-II, Q. 58, A. 2; I-II, Q. 71, A. 6). Therefore the gift of understanding is not practical.

On the contrary, It is written (Ps. 110:10): "A good understanding to all that do it."

I answer that, As stated above (A. 2), the gift of understanding is not only about those things which come under faith first and principally, but also about all things subordinate to faith. Now good actions have a certain relationship to faith: since "faith worketh through charity," according to the Apostle (Gal. 5:6). Hence the gift of understanding extends also to certain actions, not as though these were its principal object, but in so far as the rule of our actions is the eternal law, to which the higher reason, which is perfected by the gift of understanding, adheres by contemplating and consulting it, as Augustine states (De Trin. xii, 7).

Reply Obj. 1: The things with which human actions are concerned are not surpassingly exalted considered in themselves, but, as referred to the rule of the eternal law, and to the end of Divine happiness, they are exalted so that they can be the matter of understanding.

Reply Obj. 2: The excellence of the gift of understanding consists precisely in its considering eternal or necessary matters, not only as they are rules of human actions, because a cognitive virtue is the more excellent, according to the greater extent of its object.

Reply Obj. 3: The rule of human actions is the human reason and the eternal law, as stated above (I-II, Q. 71, A. 6). Now the eternal law surpasses human reason: so that the knowledge of human actions, as ruled by the eternal law, surpasses the natural reason, and requires the supernatural light of a gift of the Holy Ghost.

* * * * *

FOURTH ARTICLE [II-II, Q. 8, Art. 4]

Whether the Gift of Understanding Is in All Who Are in a State of Grace?

Objection 1: It would seem that the gift of understanding is not in all who are in a state of grace. For Gregory says (Moral. ii, 49) that "the gift of understanding is given as a remedy against dulness of mind." Now many who are in a state of grace suffer from dulness of mind. Therefore the gift of understanding is not in all who are in a state of grace.

Obj. 2: Further, of all the things that are connected with knowledge, faith alone seems to be necessary for salvation, since by faith Christ dwells in our hearts, according to Eph. 3:17. Now the gift of understanding is not in everyone that has faith; indeed, those who have faith ought to pray that they may understand, as

Augustine says (De Trin. xv, 27). Therefore the gift of understanding is not necessary for salvation: and, consequently, is not in all who are in a state of grace.

Obj. 3: Further, those things which are common to all who are in a state of grace, are never withdrawn from them. Now the grace of understanding and of the other gifts sometimes withdraws itself profitably, for, at times, "when the mind is puffed up with understanding sublime things, it becomes sluggish and dull in base and vile things," as Gregory observes (Moral. ii, 49). Therefore the gift of understanding is not in all who are in a state of grace.

On the contrary, It is written (Ps. 81:5): "They have not known or understood, they walk on in darkness." But no one who is in a state of grace walks in darkness, according to John 8:12: "He that followeth Me, walketh not in darkness." Therefore no one who is in a state of grace is without the gift of understanding.

I answer that, In all who are in a state of grace, there must needs be rectitude of the will, since grace prepares man's will for good, according to Augustine (Contra Julian. Pelag. iv, 3). Now the will cannot be rightly directed to good, unless there be already some knowledge of the truth, since the object of the will is good understood, as stated in *De Anima* iii, 7. Again, just as the Holy Ghost directs man's will by the gift of charity, so as to move it directly to some supernatural good; so also, by the gift of understanding, He enlightens the human mind, so that it knows some supernatural truth, to which the right will needs to tend.

Therefore, just as the gift of charity is in all of those who have sanctifying grace, so also is the gift of understanding.

Reply Obj. 1: Some who have sanctifying grace may suffer dulness of mind with regard to things that are not necessary for salvation; but with regard to those that are necessary for salvation, they are sufficiently instructed by the Holy Ghost, according to 1 John 2:27: "His unction teacheth you of all things."

Reply Obj. 2: Although not all who have faith understand fully the things that are proposed to be believed, yet they understand that they ought to believe them, and that they ought nowise to deviate from them.

Reply Obj. 3: With regard to things necessary for salvation, the gift of understanding never withdraws from holy persons: but, in order that they may have no incentive to pride, it does withdraw sometimes with regard to other things, so that their mind is unable to penetrate all things clearly.

* * * * *

FIFTH ARTICLE [II-II, Q. 8, Art. 5]

Whether the Gift of Understanding Is Found Also in Those Who Have Not Sanctifying Grace?

Objection 1: It would seem that the gift of understanding is found also in those who have not sanctifying grace. For Augustine, in expounding the words of Ps. 118:20: "My soul hath coveted to long for Thy justifications," says: "Understanding flies ahead, and man's will is weak and slow to follow." But in all who have sanctifying grace, the will is prompt on account of charity. Therefore the gift of understanding can be in those who have not sanctifying grace.

Obj. 2: Further, it is written (Dan. 10:1) that "there is need of understanding in a" prophetic "vision," so that, seemingly, there is no prophecy without the gift of understanding. But there can be prophecy without sanctifying grace, as evidenced by Matt. 7:22, where those who say: "We have prophesied in Thy name[1]," are answered with the words: "I never knew you." Therefore the gift of understanding can be without sanctifying grace.

Obj. 3: Further, the gift of understanding responds to the virtue of faith, according to Isa. 7:9, following another reading[2]: "If you will not believe you shall not understand." Now faith can be without sanctifying grace. Therefore the gift of understanding can be without it.

On the contrary, Our Lord said (John 6:45): "Every one that hath heard of the Father, and hath learned, cometh to Me." Now it is by the intellect, as Gregory observes (Moral. i, 32), that we learn or understand what we hear. Therefore whoever has the gift of understanding, cometh to Christ, which is impossible without sanctifying grace. Therefore the gift of understanding cannot be without sanctifying grace.

I answer that, As stated above (I-II, Q. 68, AA. 1, 2) the gifts of the Holy Ghost perfect the soul, according as it is amenable to

---

1 Vulg.: 'Have we not prophesied in Thy name?'
2 The Septuagint

the motion of the Holy Ghost. Accordingly then, the intellectual light of grace is called the gift of understanding, in so far as man's understanding is easily moved by the Holy Ghost, the consideration of which movement depends on a true apprehension of the end. Wherefore unless the human intellect be moved by the Holy Ghost so far as to have a right estimate of the end, it has not yet obtained the gift of understanding, however much the Holy Ghost may have enlightened it in regard to other truths that are preambles to the faith.

Now to have a right estimate about the last end one must not be in error about the end, and must adhere to it firmly as to the greatest good: and no one can do this without sanctifying grace; even as in moral matters a man has a right estimate about the end through a habit of virtue. Therefore no one has the gift of understanding without sanctifying grace.

Reply Obj. 1: By understanding Augustine means any kind of intellectual light, that, however, does not fulfil all the conditions of a gift, unless the mind of man be so far perfected as to have a right estimate about the end.

Reply Obj. 2: The understanding that is requisite for prophecy, is a kind of enlightenment of the mind with regard to the things revealed to the prophet: but it is not an enlightenment of the mind with regard to a right estimate about the last end, which belongs to the gift of understanding.

Reply Obj. 3: Faith implies merely assent to what is proposed but understanding implies a certain perception of the truth, which perception, except in one who has sanctifying grace, cannot regard the end, as stated above. Hence the comparison fails between understanding and faith.

* * * * *

SIXTH ARTICLE [II-II, Q. 8, Art. 6]

Whether the Gift of Understanding Is Distinct from the Other Gifts?

Objection 1: It would seem that the gift of understanding is not distinct from the other gifts. For there is no distinction between things whose opposites are not distinct. Now "wisdom is contrary to folly, understanding is contrary to dulness, counsel is contrary to rashness, knowledge is contrary to ignorance," as Gregory states

(Moral. ii, 49). But there would seem to be no difference between folly, dulness, ignorance and rashness. Therefore neither does understanding differ from the other gifts.

Obj. 2: Further, the intellectual virtue of understanding differs from the other intellectual virtues in that it is proper to it to be about self-evident principles. But the gift of understanding is not about any self-evident principles, since the natural habit of first principles suffices in respect of those matters which are naturally self-evident: while faith is sufficient in respect of such things as are supernatural, since the articles of faith are like first principles in supernatural knowledge, as stated above (Q. 1, A. 7). Therefore the gift of understanding does not differ from the other intellectual gifts.

Obj. 3: Further, all intellectual knowledge is either speculative or practical. Now the gift of understanding is related to both, as stated above (A. 3). Therefore it is not distinct from the other intellectual gifts, but comprises them all.

On the contrary, When several things are enumerated together they must be, in some way, distinct from one another, because distinction is the origin of number. Now the gift of understanding is enumerated together with the other gifts, as appears from Isa. 11:2. Therefore the gift of understanding is distinct from the other gifts.

I answer that, The difference between the gift of understanding and three of the others, viz. piety, fortitude, and fear, is evident, since the gift of understanding belongs to the cognitive power, while the three belong to the appetitive power.

But the difference between this gift of understanding and the remaining three, viz. wisdom, knowledge, and counsel, which also belong to the cognitive power, is not so evident. To some[1], it seems that the gift of understanding differs from the gifts of knowledge and counsel, in that these two belong to practical knowledge, while the gift of understanding belongs to speculative knowledge; and that it differs from the gift of wisdom, which also belongs to speculative knowledge, in that wisdom is concerned with judgment, while understanding renders the mind apt to grasp the things that are proposed, and to penetrate into their very heart. And in this sense we have assigned the number of the gifts, above (I-II, Q. 68, A. 4).

---

1   William of Auxerre, Sum. Aur. III, iii, 8

But if we consider the matter carefully, the gift of understanding is concerned not only with speculative, but also with practical matters, as stated above (A. 3), and likewise, the gift of knowledge regards both matters, as we shall show further on (Q. 9, A. 3), and consequently, we must take their distinction in some other way. For all these four gifts are ordained to supernatural knowledge, which, in us, takes its foundation from faith. Now "faith is through hearing" (Rom. 10:17). Hence some things must be proposed to be believed by man, not as seen, but as heard, to which he assents by faith. But faith, first and principally, is about the First Truth, secondarily, about certain considerations concerning creatures, and furthermore extends to the direction of human actions, in so far as it works through charity, as appears from what has been said above (Q. 4, A. 2, ad 3).

Accordingly on the part of the things proposed to faith for belief, two things are requisite on our part: first that they be penetrated or grasped by the intellect, and this belongs to the gift of understanding. Secondly, it is necessary that man should judge these things aright, that he should esteem that he ought to adhere to these things, and to withdraw from their opposites: and this judgment, with regard to Divine things belong to the gift of wisdom, but with regard to created things, belongs to the gift of knowledge, and as to its application to individual actions, belongs to the gift of counsel.

Reply Obj. 1: The foregoing difference between those four gifts is clearly in agreement with the distinction of those things which Gregory assigns as their opposites. For dulness is contrary to sharpness, since an intellect is said, by comparison, to be sharp, when it is able to penetrate into the heart of the things that are proposed to it. Hence it is dulness of mind that renders the mind unable to pierce into the heart of a thing. A man is said to be a fool if he judges wrongly about the common end of life, wherefore folly is properly opposed to wisdom, which makes us judge aright about the universal cause. Ignorance implies a defect in the mind, even about any particular things whatever, so that it is contrary to knowledge, which gives man a right judgment about particular causes, viz. about creatures. Rashness is clearly opposed to counsel, whereby man does not proceed to action before deliberating with his reason.

Reply Obj. 2: The gift of understanding is about the first principles of that knowledge which is conferred by grace; but otherwise than faith, because it belongs to faith to assent to them, while it belongs to the gift of understanding to pierce with the mind the things that are said.

Reply Obj. 3: The gift of understanding is related to both kinds of knowledge, viz. speculative and practical, not as to the judgment, but as to apprehension, by grasping what is said.

* * * * *

SEVENTH ARTICLE [II-II, Q. 8, Art. 7]

Whether the Sixth Beatitude, "Blessed Are the Clean of Heart," etc., Responds to the Gift of Understanding?

Objection 1: It would seem that the sixth beatitude, "Blessed are the clean of heart, for they shall see God," does not respond to the gift of understanding. Because cleanness of heart seems to belong chiefly to the appetite. But the gift of understanding belongs, not to the appetite, but rather to the intellectual power. Therefore the aforesaid beatitude does not respond to the gift of understanding.

Obj. 2: Further, it is written (Acts 15:9): "Purifying their hearts by faith." Now cleanness of heart is acquired by the heart being purified. Therefore the aforesaid beatitude is related to the virtue of faith rather than to the gift of understanding.

Obj. 3: Further, the gifts of the Holy Ghost perfect man in the present state of life. But the sight of God does not belong to the present life, since it is that which gives happiness to the Blessed, as stated above (I-II, Q. 3, A. 8). Therefore the sixth beatitude which comprises the sight of God, does not respond to the gift of understanding.

On the contrary, Augustine says (De Serm. Dom. in Monte i, 4): "The sixth work of the Holy Ghost which is understanding, is applicable to the clean of heart, whose eye being purified, they can see what eye hath not seen."

I answer that, Two things are contained in the sixth beatitude, as also in the others, one by way of merit, viz. cleanness of heart; the other by way of reward, viz. the sight of God, as stated above (I-II, Q. 69, AA. 2, 4), and each of these, in some way, responds to the gift of understanding.

For cleanness is twofold. One is a preamble and a disposition to seeing God, and consists in the heart being cleansed of inordinate affections: and this cleanness of heart is effected by the virtues and gifts belonging to the appetitive power. The other cleanness of heart is a kind of complement to the sight of God; such is the cleanness of the mind that is purged of phantasms and errors, so as to receive the truths which are proposed to it about God, no longer by way of corporeal phantasms, nor infected with heretical misrepresentations: and this cleanness is the result of the gift of understanding.

Again, the sight of God is twofold. One is perfect, whereby God's Essence is seen: the other is imperfect, whereby, though we see not what God is, yet we see what He is not; and whereby, the more perfectly do we know God in this life, the more we understand that He surpasses all that the mind comprehends. Each of these visions of God belongs to the gift of understanding; the first, to the gift of understanding in its state of perfection, as possessed in heaven; the second, to the gift of understanding in its state of inchoation, as possessed by wayfarers.

This suffices for the Replies to the Objections: for the first two arguments refer to the first kind of cleanness; while the third refers to the perfect vision of God. Moreover the gifts both perfect us in this life by way of inchoation, and will be fulfilled, as stated above (I-II, Q. 69, A. 2).

* * * * *

EIGHTH ARTICLE [II-II, Q. 8, Art. 8]

Whether Faith, Among the Fruits, Responds to the Gift of Understanding?

Objection 1: It would seem that, among the fruits, faith does not respond to the gift of understanding. For understanding is the fruit of faith, since it is written (Isa. 7:9) according to another reading[1]: "If you will not believe you shall not understand," where our version has: "If you will not believe, you shall not continue." Therefore fruit is not the fruit of understanding.

Obj. 2: Further, that which precedes is not the fruit of what follows. But faith seems to precede understanding, since it is the foundation of the entire spiritual edifice, as stated above (Q. 4, AA. 1, 7). Therefore faith is not the fruit of understanding.

---

1 The Septuagint

Obj. 3: Further, more gifts pertain to the intellect than to the appetite. Now, among the fruits, only one pertains to the intellect; namely, faith, while all the others pertain to the appetite. Therefore faith, seemingly, does not pertain to understanding more than to wisdom, knowledge or counsel.

On the contrary, The end of a thing is its fruit. Now the gift of understanding seems to be ordained chiefly to the certitude of faith, which certitude is reckoned a fruit. For a gloss on Gal. 5:22 says that the "faith which is a fruit, is certitude about the unseen." Therefore faith, among the fruits, responds to the gift of understanding.

I answer that, The fruits of the Spirit, as stated above (I-II, Q. 70, A. 1), when we were discussing them, are so called because they are something ultimate and delightful, produced in us by the power of the Holy Ghost. Now the ultimate and delightful has the nature of an end, which is the proper object of the will: and consequently that which is ultimate and delightful with regard to the will, must be, after a fashion, the fruit of all the other things that pertain to the other powers.

Accordingly, therefore, to this kind of gift of virtue that perfects a power, we may distinguish a double fruit: one, belonging to the same power; the other, the last of all as it were, belonging to the will. In this way we must conclude that the fruit which properly responds to the gift of understanding is faith, i.e. the certitude of faith; while the fruit that responds to it last of all is joy, which belongs to the will.

Reply Obj. 1: Understanding is the fruit of faith, taken as a virtue. But we are not taking faith in this sense here, but for a kind of certitude of faith, to which man attains by the gift of understanding.

Reply Obj. 2: Faith cannot altogether precede understanding, for it would be impossible to assent by believing what is proposed to be believed, without understanding it in some way. However, the perfection of understanding follows the virtue of faith: which perfection of understanding is itself followed by a kind of certainty of faith.

Reply Obj. 3: The fruit of practical knowledge cannot consist in that very knowledge, since knowledge of that kind is known not for its own sake, but for the sake of something else. On the other hand, speculative knowledge has its fruit in its very self, which fruit is the certitude about the thing known. Hence the gift of counsel, which belongs only to practical knowledge, has no corresponding fruit of its own: while the gifts of wisdom, understanding and knowledge, which can belongs also to speculative knowledge, have but one corresponding fruit, which is certainly denoted by the name of faith. The reason why there are several fruits pertaining to the appetitive faculty, is because, as already stated, the character of end, which the word fruit implies, pertains to the appetitive rather than to the intellective part.

9. OF THE GIFT OF KNOWLEDGE
(In Four Articles)

We must now consider the gift of knowledge, under which head there are four points of inquiry:

(1) Whether knowledge is a gift?
(2) Whether it is about Divine things?
(3) Whether it is speculative or practical?
(4) Which beatitude responds to it?.

* * * * *

FIRST ARTICLE [II-II, Q. 9, Art. 1]
Whether Knowledge Is a Gift?

Objection 1: It would seem that knowledge is not a gift. For the gifts of the Holy Ghost surpass the natural faculty. But knowledge implies an effect of natural reason: for the Philosopher says (Poster. i, 2) that a "demonstration is a syllogism which produces knowledge." Therefore knowledge is not a gift of the Holy Ghost.

Obj. 2: Further, the gifts of the Holy Ghost are common to all holy persons, as stated above (Q. 8, A. 4; I-II, Q. 68, A. 5). Now Augustine says (De Trin. xiv, 1) that "many of the faithful lack knowledge though they have faith." Therefore knowledge is not a gift.

Obj. 3: Further, the gifts are more perfect than the virtues, as stated above (I-II, Q. 68, A. 8). Therefore one gift suffices for the perfection of one virtue. Now the gift of understanding responds to the virtue of faith, as stated above (Q. 8, A. 2). Therefore the gift of knowledge does not respond to that virtue, nor does it appear to which other virtue it can respond. Since, then, the gifts are perfections of virtues, as stated above (I-II, Q. 68, AA. 1, 2), it seems that knowledge is not a gift.

On the contrary, Knowledge is reckoned among the seven gifts (Isa. 11:2).

I answer that, Grace is more perfect than nature, and, therefore, does not fail in those things wherein man can be perfected by nature. Now, when a man, by his natural reason, assents by his intellect to some truth, he is perfected in two ways in respect of that truth: first, because he grasps it; secondly, because he forms a sure judgment on it.

Accordingly, two things are requisite in order that the human intellect may perfectly assent to the truth of the faith: one of these is that he should have a sound grasp of the things that are proposed to be believed, and this pertains to the gift of understanding, as stated above (Q. 8, A. 6): while the other is that he should have a sure and right judgment on them, so as to discern what is to be believed, from what is not to be believed, and for this the gift of knowledge is required.

Reply Obj. 1: Certitude of knowledge varies in various natures, according to the various conditions of each nature. Because man forms a sure judgment about a truth by the discursive process of his reason: and so human knowledge is acquired by means of demonstrative reasoning. On the other hand, in God, there is a sure judgment of truth, without any discursive process, by simple intuition, as was stated in the First Part (Q. 14, A. 7); wherefore God's knowledge is not discursive, or argumentative, but absolute and simple, to which that knowledge is likened which is a gift of the Holy Ghost, since it is a participated likeness thereof.

Reply Obj. 2: A twofold knowledge may be had about matters of belief. One is the knowledge of what one ought to believe by discerning things to be believed from things not to be believed: in this way knowledge is a gift and is common to all holy persons. The other is a knowledge about matters of belief, whereby one knows not only what one ought to believe, but also how to make the faith known, how to induce others to believe, and confute those who deny the faith. This knowledge is numbered among the gratuitous graces, which are not given to all, but to some. Hence Augustine, after the words quoted, adds: "It is one thing for a man merely to know what he ought to believe, and another to know how to dispense what he believes to the godly, and to defend it against the ungodly."

Reply Obj. 3: The gifts are more perfect than the moral and intellectual virtues; but they are not more perfect than the theological virtues; rather are all the gifts ordained to the perfection of the theological virtues, as to their end. Hence it is not unreasonable if several gifts are ordained to one theological virtue.

* * * * *

SECOND ARTICLE [II-II, Q. 9, Art. 2]

Whether the Gift of Knowledge Is About Divine Things?

Objection 1: It would seem that the gift of knowledge is about Divine things. For Augustine says (De Trin. xiv, 1) that "knowledge begets, nourishes and strengthens faith." Now faith is about Divine things, because its object is the First Truth, as stated above (Q. 1, A. 1). Therefore the gift of knowledge also is about Divine things.

Obj. 2: Further, the gift of knowledge is more excellent than acquired knowledge. But there is an acquired knowledge about Divine things, for instance, the science of metaphysics. Much more therefore is the gift of knowledge about Divine things.

Obj. 3: Further, according to Rom. 1:20, "the invisible things of God ... are clearly seen, being understood by the things that are made." If therefore there is knowledge about created things, it seems that there is also knowledge of Divine things.

On the contrary, Augustine says (De Trin. xiv, 1): "The knowledge of Divine things may be properly called wisdom, and the knowledge of human affairs may properly receive the name of knowledge."

I answer that, A sure judgment about a thing is formed chiefly from its cause, and so the order of judgments should be according to the order of causes. For just as the first cause is the cause of the second, so ought the judgment about the second cause to be formed through the first cause: nor is it possible to judge of the first cause through any other cause; wherefore the judgment which is formed through the first cause, is the first and most perfect judgment.

Now in those things where we find something most perfect, the common name of the genus is appropriated for those things which fall short of the most perfect, and some special name is adapted to the most perfect thing, as is the case in Logic. For in the genus of convertible terms, that which signifies "what a thing is," is given the special name of "definition," but the convertible terms which fall short of this, retain the common name, and are called "proper" terms.

Accordingly, since the word knowledge implies certitude of judgment as stated above (A. 1), if this certitude of the judgment is derived from the highest cause, the knowledge has a special name, which is wisdom: for a wise man in any branch of knowledge is one who knows the highest cause of that kind of knowledge, and is able to judge of all matters by that cause: and a wise man "absolutely," is one who knows the cause which is absolutely highest, namely God. Hence the knowledge of Divine things is called "wisdom," while the knowledge of human things is called "knowledge," this being the common name denoting certitude of judgment, and appropriated to the judgment which is formed through second causes. Accordingly, if we take knowledge in this way, it is a distinct gift from the gift of wisdom, so that the gift of knowledge is only about human or created things.

Reply Obj. 1: Although matters of faith are Divine and eternal, yet faith itself is something temporal in the mind of the believer. Hence to know what one ought to believe, belongs to the gift of knowledge, but to know in themselves the very things we believe, by a kind of union with them, belongs to the gift of wisdom. Therefore the gift of wisdom corresponds more to charity which unites man's mind to God.

Reply Obj. 2: This argument takes knowledge in the generic acceptation of the term: it is not thus that knowledge is a special gift, but according as it is restricted to judgments formed through created things.

Reply Obj. 3: As stated above (Q. 1, A. 1), every cognitive habit regards formally the mean through which things are known, and materially, the things that are known through the mean. And since that which is formal, is of most account, it follows that those sciences which draw conclusions about physical matter from mathematical principles, are reckoned rather among the mathematical sciences, though, as to their matter they have more in common with physical sciences: and for this reason it is stated in Phys. ii, 2 that they are more akin to physics. Accordingly, since man knows God through His creatures, this seems to pertain to "knowledge," to which it belongs formally, rather than to "wisdom," to which it belongs materially: and, conversely, when we judge of creatures according to Divine things, this pertains to "wisdom" rather than to "knowledge.".

* * * * *

THIRD ARTICLE [II-II, Q. 9, Art. 3]

Whether the Gift of Knowledge Is Practical Knowledge?

Objection 1: It would seem that the knowledge, which is numbered among the gifts, is practical knowledge. For Augustine says (De Trin. xii, 14) that "knowledge is concerned with the actions in which we make use of external things." But the knowledge which is concerned about actions is practical. Therefore the gift of knowledge is practical.

Obj. 2: Further, Gregory says (Moral. i, 32): "Knowledge is nought if it hath not its use for piety . . . and piety is very useless if it lacks the discernment of knowledge." Now it follows from this authority that knowledge directs piety. But this cannot apply to a speculative science. Therefore the gift of knowledge is not speculative but practical.

Obj. 3: Further, the gifts of the Holy Ghost are only in the righteous, as stated above (Q. 9, A. 5). But speculative knowledge can be also in the unrighteous, according to James 4:17: "To him . . . who knoweth to do good, and doth it not, to him it is a sin." Therefore the gift of knowledge is not speculative but practical.

On the contrary, Gregory says (Moral. i, 32): "Knowledge on her own day prepares a feast, because she overcomes the fast of ignorance in the mind." Now ignorance is not entirely removed, save by both kinds of knowledge, viz. speculative and practical. Therefore the gift of knowledge is both speculative and practical.

I answer that, As stated above (Q. 9, A. 8), the gift of knowledge, like the gift of understanding, is ordained to the certitude of faith. Now faith consists primarily and principally in speculation, in as much as it is founded on the First Truth. But since the First Truth is also the last end for the sake of which our works are done, hence it is that faith extends to works, according to Gal. 5:6: "Faith . . . worketh by charity."

The consequence is that the gift of knowledge also, primarily and principally indeed, regards speculation, in so far as man knows what he ought to hold by faith; yet, secondarily, it extends to works, since we are directed in our actions by the knowledge of matters of faith, and of conclusions drawn therefrom.

Reply Obj. 1: Augustine is speaking of the gift of knowledge, in so far as it extends to works; for action is ascribed to knowledge, yet not action solely, nor primarily: and in this way it directs piety.

Hence the Reply to the Second Objection is clear.

Reply Obj. 3: As we have already stated (Q. 8, A. 5) about the gift of understanding, not everyone who understands, has the gift of understanding, but only he that understands through a habit of grace: and so we must take note, with regard to the gift of knowledge, that they alone have the gift of knowledge, who judge aright about matters of faith and action, through the grace bestowed on them, so as never to wander from the straight path of justice. This is the knowledge of holy things, according to Wis. 10:10: "She conducted the just . . . through the right ways . . . and gave him the knowledge of holy things.".

* * * * *

FOURTH ARTICLE [II-II, Q. 9, Art. 4]

Whether the Third Beatitude, "Blessed Are They That Mourn," etc. Corresponds to the Gift of Knowledge?

Objection 1: It would seem that the third beatitude, "Blessed are they that mourn," does not correspond to the gift of knowledge. For, even as evil is the cause of sorrow and grief, so is good the cause of joy. Now knowledge brings good to light rather than evil, since the latter is known through evil: for "the straight line rules both itself and the crooked line" (De Anima i, 5). Therefore the aforesaid beatitude does not suitably correspond to the gift of knowledge.

Obj. 2: Further, consideration of truth is an act of knowledge. Now there is no sorrow in the consideration of truth; rather is there joy, since it is written (Wis. 8:16): "Her conversation hath no bitterness, nor her company any tediousness, but joy and gladness." Therefore the aforesaid beatitude does not suitably correspond with the gift of knowledge.

Obj. 3: Further, the gift of knowledge consists in speculation, before operation. Now, in so far as it consists in speculation, sorrow does not correspond to it, since "the speculative intellect is not concerned about things to be sought or avoided" (De Anima iii, 9). Therefore the aforesaid beatitude is not suitably reckoned to correspond with the gift of knowledge.

On the contrary, Augustine says (De Serm. Dom. in Monte iv): "Knowledge befits the mourner, who has discovered that he has been mastered by the evil which he coveted as though it were good."

I answer that, Right judgment about creatures belongs properly to knowledge. Now it is through creatures that man's aversion from God is occasioned, according to Wis. 14:11: "Creatures . . . are turned to an abomination . . . and a snare to the feet of the unwise," of those, namely, who do not judge aright about creatures, since they deem the perfect good to consist in them. Hence they sin by placing their last end in them, and lose the true good. It is by forming a right judgment of creatures that man becomes aware of the loss (of which they may be the occasion), which judgment he exercises through the gift of knowledge.

Hence the beatitude of sorrow is said to correspond to the gift of knowledge.

Reply Obj. 1: Created goods do not cause spiritual joy, except in so far as they are referred to the Divine good, which is the proper cause of spiritual joy. Hence spiritual peace and the resulting joy correspond directly to the gift of wisdom: but to the gift of knowledge there corresponds, in the first place, sorrow for past errors, and, in consequence, consolation, since, by his right judgment, man directs creatures to the Divine good. For this reason sorrow is set forth in this beatitude, as the merit, and the resulting consolation, as the reward; which is begun in this life, and is perfected in the life to come.

Reply Obj. 2: Man rejoices in the very consideration of truth; yet he may sometimes grieve for the thing, the truth of which he considers: it is thus that sorrow is ascribed to knowledge.

Reply Obj. 3: No beatitude corresponds to knowledge, in so far as it consists in speculation, because man's beatitude consists, not in considering creatures, but in contemplating God. But man's beatitude does consist somewhat in the right use of creatures, and in well-ordered love of them: and this I say with regard to the beatitude of a wayfarer. Hence beatitude relating to contemplation is not ascribed to knowledge, but to understanding and wisdom, which are about Divine things.

10. OF UNBELIEF IN GENERAL
(In Twelve Articles)

In due sequence we must consider the contrary vices: first, unbelief, which is contrary to faith; secondly, blasphemy, which is opposed to confession of faith; thirdly, ignorance and dulness of mind, which are contrary to knowledge and understanding.

As to the first, we must consider (1) unbelief in general; (2) heresy; (3) apostasy from the faith.

Under the first head there are twelve points of inquiry:

(1) Whether unbelief is a sin?
(2) What is its subject?
(3) Whether it is the greatest of sins?
(4) Whether every action of unbelievers is a sin?
(5) Of the species of unbelief;
(6) Of their comparison, one with another;
(7) Whether we ought to dispute about faith with unbelievers?
(8) Whether they ought to be compelled to the faith?
(9) Whether we ought to have communications with them?
(10) Whether unbelievers can have authority over Christians?
(11) Whether the rites of unbelievers should be tolerated?
(12) Whether the children of unbelievers are to be baptized against their parents' will?.

* * * * *

FIRST ARTICLE [II-II, Q. 10, Art. 1]

Whether Unbelief Is a Sin?

Objection 1: It would seem that unbelief is not a sin. For every sin is contrary to nature, as Damascene proves (De Fide Orth. ii, 4). Now unbelief seems not to be contrary to nature; for Augustine says (De Praedest. Sanct. v) that "to be capable to having faith, just as to be capable of having charity, is natural to all men; whereas to have faith, even as to have charity, belongs to the grace of the faithful." Therefore not to have faith, which is to be an unbeliever, is not a sin.

Obj. 2: Further, no one sins that which he cannot avoid, since every sin is voluntary. Now it is not in a man's power to avoid unbelief, for he cannot avoid it unless he have faith, because the Apostle says (Rom. 10:14): "How shall they believe in Him, of Whom they have not heard? And how shall they hear without a preacher?" Therefore unbelief does not seem to be a sin.

Obj. 3: Further, as stated above (I-II, Q. 84, A. 4), there are seven capital sins, to which all sins are reduced. But unbelief does not seem to be comprised under any of them. Therefore unbelief is not a sin.

On the contrary, Vice is opposed to virtue. Now faith is a virtue, and unbelief is opposed to it. Therefore unbelief is a sin.

I answer that, Unbelief may be taken in two ways: first, by way of pure negation, so that a man be called an unbeliever, merely because he has not the faith. Secondly, unbelief may be taken by way of opposition to the faith; in which sense a man refuses to hear the faith, or despises it, according to Isa. 53:1: "Who hath believed our report?" It is this that completes the notion of unbelief, and it is in this sense that unbelief is a sin.

If, however, we take it by way of pure negation, as we find it in those who have heard nothing about the faith, it bears the character, not of sin, but of punishment, because such like ignorance of Divine things is a result of the sin of our first parent. If such like unbelievers are damned, it is on account of other sins, which cannot be taken away without faith, but not on account of their sin of unbelief. Hence Our Lord said (John 15:22) "If I had not come, and spoken to them, they would not have sin"; which Augustine expounds (Tract. lxxxix in Joan.) as "referring to the sin whereby they believed not in Christ."

Reply Obj. 1: To have the faith is not part of human nature, but it is part of human nature that man's mind should not thwart his inner instinct, and the outward preaching of the truth. Hence, in this way, unbelief is contrary to nature.

Reply Obj. 2: This argument takes unbelief as denoting a pure negation.

Reply Obj. 3: Unbelief, in so far as it is a sin, arises from pride, through which man is unwilling to subject his intellect to the rules of faith, and to the sound interpretation of the Fathers. Hence Gregory says (Moral. xxxi, 45) that "presumptuous innovations arise from vainglory."

It might also be replied that just as the theological virtues are not reduced to the cardinal virtues, but precede them, so too, the vices opposed to the theological virtues are not reduced to the capital vices.

* * * * *

SECOND ARTICLE [II-II, Q. 10, Art. 2]

Whether Unbelief Is in the Intellect As Its Subject?

Objection 1: It would seem that unbelief is not in the intellect as its subject. For every sin is in the will, according to Augustine (De Duabus Anim. x, xi). Now unbelief is a sin, as stated above (A. 1). Therefore unbelief resides in the will and not in the intellect.

Obj. 2: Further, unbelief is sinful through contempt of the preaching of the faith. But contempt pertains to the will. Therefore unbelief is in the will.

Obj. 3: Further, a gloss[1] on 2 Cor. 11:14 "Satan . . . transformeth himself into an angel of light," says that if "a wicked angel pretend to be a good angel, and be taken for a good angel, it is not a dangerous or an unhealthy error, if he does or says what is becoming to a good angel." This seems to be because of the rectitude of the will of the man who adheres to the angel, since his intention is to adhere to a good angel. Therefore the sin of unbelief seems to consist entirely in a perverse will: and, consequently, it does not reside in the intellect.

On the contrary, Things which are contrary to one another are in the same subject. Now faith, to which unbelief is opposed, resides in the intellect. Therefore unbelief also is in the intellect.

I answer that, As stated above (I-II, Q. 74, AA. 1, 2), sin is said to be in the power which is the principle of the sinful act. Now a sinful act may have two principles: one is its first and universal principle, which commands all acts of sin; and this is the will, because every sin is voluntary. The other principle of the sinful

---

1   Augustine, Enchiridion lx.

act is the proper and proximate principle which elicits the sinful act: thus the concupiscible is the principle of gluttony and lust, wherefore these sins are said to be in the concupiscible. Now dissent, which is the act proper to unbelief, is an act of the intellect, moved, however, by the will, just as assent is.

Therefore unbelief, like faith, is in the intellect as its proximate subject. But it is in the will as its first moving principle, in which way every sin is said to be in the will.

Hence the Reply to the First Objection is clear.

Reply Obj. 2: The will's contempt causes the intellect's dissent, which completes the notion of unbelief. Hence the cause of unbelief is in the will, while unbelief itself is in the intellect.

Reply Obj. 3: He that believes a wicked angel to be a good one, does not dissent from a matter of faith, because "his bodily senses are deceived, while his mind does not depart from a true and right judgment" as the gloss observes[1]. But, according to the same authority, to adhere to Satan when he begins to invite one to his abode, i.e. wickedness and error, is not without sin.

* * * * *

THIRD ARTICLE [II-II, Q. 10, Art. 3]

Whether Unbelief Is the Greatest of Sins?

Objection 1: It would seem that unbelief is not the greatest of sins. For Augustine says (De Bapt. contra Donat. iv, 20): "I should hesitate to decide whether a very wicked Catholic ought to be preferred to a heretic, in whose life one finds nothing reprehensible beyond the fact that he is a heretic." But a heretic is an unbeliever. Therefore we ought not to say absolutely that unbelief is the greatest of sins.

Obj. 2: Further, that which diminishes or excuses a sin is not, seemingly, the greatest of sins. Now unbelief excuses or diminishes sin: for the Apostle says (1 Tim. 1:12, 13): "I ... before was a blasphemer, and a persecutor and contumelious; but I obtained ... mercy ... because I did it ignorantly in unbelief." Therefore unbelief is not the greatest of sins.

---

[1] Augustine, Enchiridion lx

Obj. 3: Further, the greater sin deserves the greater punishment, according to Deut. 25:2: "According to the measure of the sin shall the measure also of the stripes be." Now a greater punishment is due to believers than to unbelievers, according to Heb. 10:29: "How much more, do you think, he deserveth worse punishments, who hath trodden under foot the Son of God, and hath esteemed the blood of the testament unclean, by which he was sanctified?" Therefore unbelief is not the greatest of sins.

On the contrary, Augustine, commenting on John 15:22, "If I had not come, and spoken to them, they would not have sin," says (Tract. lxxxix in Joan.): "Under the general name, He refers to a singularly great sin. For this," viz. infidelity, "is the sin to which all others may be traced." Therefore unbelief is the greatest of sins.

I answer that, Every sin consists formally in aversion from God, as stated above (I-II, Q. 71, A. 6; I-II, Q. 73, A. 3). Hence the more a sin severs man from God, the graver it is. Now man is more than ever separated from God by unbelief, because he has not even true knowledge of God: and by false knowledge of God, man does not approach Him, but is severed from Him.

Nor is it possible for one who has a false opinion of God, to know Him in any way at all, because the object of his opinion is not God. Therefore it is clear that the sin of unbelief is greater than any sin that occurs in the perversion of morals. This does not apply to the sins that are opposed to the theological virtues, as we shall state further on (Q. 20, A. 3; Q. 34, A. 2, ad 2; Q. 39, A. 2, ad 3).

Reply Obj. 1: Nothing hinders a sin that is more grave in its genus from being less grave in respect of some circumstances. Hence Augustine hesitated to decide between a bad Catholic, and a heretic not sinning otherwise, because although the heretic's sin is more grave generically, it can be lessened by a circumstance, and conversely the sin of the Catholic can, by some circumstance, be aggravated.

Reply Obj. 2: Unbelief includes both ignorance, as an accessory thereto, and resistance to matters of faith, and in the latter respect it is a most grave sin. In respect, however, of this ignorance, it has a certain reason for excuse, especially when a man sins not from malice, as was the case with the Apostle.

Reply Obj. 3: An unbeliever is more severely punished for his sin of unbelief than another sinner is for any sin whatever, if we consider the kind of sin. But in the case of another sin, e.g. adultery, committed by a believer, and by an unbeliever, the believer, other things being equal, sins more gravely than the unbeliever, both on account of his knowledge of the truth through faith, and on account of the sacraments of faith with which he has been satiated, and which he insults by committing sin.

* * * * *

FOURTH ARTICLE [II-II, Q. 10, Art. 4]

Whether Every Act of an Unbeliever Is a Sin?

Objection 1: It would seem that each act of an unbeliever is a sin. Because a gloss on Rom. 14:23, "All that is not of faith is sin," says: "The whole life of unbelievers is a sin." Now the life of unbelievers consists of their actions. Therefore every action of an unbeliever is a sin.

Obj. 2: Further, faith directs the intention. Now there can be no good save what comes from a right intention. Therefore, among unbelievers, no action can be good.

Obj. 3: Further, when that which precedes is corrupted, that which follows is corrupted also. Now an act of faith precedes the acts of all the virtues. Therefore, since there is no act of faith in unbelievers, they can do no good work, but sin in every action of theirs.

On the contrary, It is said of Cornelius, while yet an unbeliever (Acts 10:4, 31), that his alms were acceptable to God. Therefore not every action of an unbeliever is a sin, but some of his actions are good.

I answer that, As stated above (I-II, Q. 85, AA. 2, 4) mortal sin takes away sanctifying grace, but does not wholly corrupt the good of nature. Since therefore, unbelief is a mortal sin, unbelievers are without grace indeed, yet some good of nature remains in them. Consequently it is evident that unbelievers cannot do those good works which proceed from grace, viz. meritorious works; yet they can, to a certain extent, do those good works for which the good of nature suffices.

Hence it does not follow that they sin in everything they do; but whenever they do anything out of their unbelief, then they sin. For even as one who has the faith, can commit an actual sin, venial or even mortal, which he does not refer to the end of faith, so too, an unbeliever can do a good deed in a matter which he does not refer to the end of his unbelief.

Reply Obj. 1: The words quoted must be taken to mean either that the life of unbelievers cannot be sinless, since without faith no sin is taken away, or that whatever they do out of unbelief, is a sin. Hence the same authority adds: "Because every one that lives or acts according to his unbelief, sins grievously."

Reply Obj. 2: Faith directs the intention with regard to the supernatural last end: but even the light of natural reason can direct the intention in respect of a connatural good.

Reply Obj. 3: Unbelief does not so wholly destroy natural reason in unbelievers, but that some knowledge of the truth remains in them, whereby they are able to do deeds that are generically good. With regard, however, to Cornelius, it is to be observed that he was not an unbeliever, else his works would not have been acceptable to God, whom none can please without faith. Now he had implicit faith, as the truth of the Gospel was not yet made manifest: hence Peter was sent to him to give him fuller instruction in the faith.

* * * * *

FIFTH ARTICLE [II-II, Q. 10, Art. 5]

Whether There Are Several Species of Unbelief?

Objection 1: It would seem that there are not several species of unbelief. For, since faith and unbelief are contrary to one another, they must be about the same thing. Now the formal object of faith is the First Truth, whence it derives its unity, although its matter contains many points of belief. Therefore the object of unbelief also is the First Truth; while the things which an unbeliever disbelieves are the matter of his unbelief. Now the specific difference depends not on material but on formal principles. Therefore there are not several species of unbelief, according to the various points which the unbeliever disbelieves.

Obj. 2: Further, it is possible to stray from the truth of faith in an infinite number of ways. If therefore the various species of unbelief correspond to the number of various errors, it would seem to follow that there is an infinite number of species of unbelief, and consequently, that we ought not to make these species the object of our consideration.

Obj. 3: Further, the same thing does not belong to different species. Now a man may be an unbeliever through erring about different points of truth. Therefore diversity of errors does not make a diversity of species of unbelief: and so there are not several species of unbelief.

On the contrary, Several species of vice are opposed to each virtue, because "good happens in one way, but evil in many ways," according to Dionysius (Div. Nom. iv) and the Philosopher (Ethic. ii, 6). Now faith is a virtue. Therefore several species of vice are opposed to it.

I answer that, As stated above (I-II, Q. 55, A. 4; I-II, Q. 64, A. 1), every virtue consists in following some rule of human knowledge or operation. Now conformity to a rule happens one way in one matter, whereas a breach of the rule happens in many ways, so that many vices are opposed to one virtue. The diversity of the vices that are opposed to each virtue may be considered in two ways, first, with regard to their different relations to the virtue: and in this way there are determinate species of vices contrary to a virtue: thus to a moral virtue one vice is opposed by exceeding the virtue, and another, by falling short of the virtue. Secondly, the diversity of vices opposed to one virtue may be considered in respect of the corruption of the various conditions required for that virtue. In this way an infinite number of vices are opposed to one virtue, e.g. temperance or fortitude, according to the infinite number of ways in which the various circumstances of a virtue may be corrupted, so that the rectitude of virtue is forsaken. For this reason the Pythagoreans held evil to be infinite.

Accordingly we must say that if unbelief be considered in comparison to faith, there are several species of unbelief, determinate in number. For, since the sin of unbelief consists in resisting the faith, this may happen in two ways: either the faith is resisted before it has been accepted, and such is the unbelief of pagans or heathens; or the Christian faith is resisted after it has been accepted, and this either in the figure, and such is the unbelief of the Jews, or in the very manifestation of truth, and such is the unbelief of heretics. Hence we may, in a general way, reckon these three as species of unbelief.

If, however, the species of unbelief be distinguished according to the various errors that occur in matters of faith, there are not determinate species of unbelief: for errors can be multiplied indefinitely, as Augustine observes (De Haeresibus).

Reply Obj. 1: The formal aspect of a sin can be considered in two ways. First, according to the intention of the sinner, in which case the thing to which the sinner turns is the formal object of his sin, and determines the various species of that sin. Secondly, it may be considered as an evil, and in this case the good which is forsaken is the formal object of the sin; which however does not derive its species from this point of view, in fact it is a privation. We must therefore reply that the object of unbelief is the First Truth considered as that which unbelief forsakes, but its formal aspect, considered as that to which unbelief turns, is the false opinion that it follows: and it is from this point of view that unbelief derives its various species. Hence, even as charity is one, because it adheres to the Sovereign Good, while there are various species of vice opposed to charity, which turn away from the Sovereign Good by turning to various temporal goods, and also in respect of various inordinate relations to God, so too, faith is one virtue through adhering to the one First Truth, yet there are many species of unbelief, because unbelievers follow many false opinions.

Reply Obj. 2: This argument considers the various species of unbelief according to various points in which errors occur.

Reply Obj. 3: Since faith is one because it believes in many things in relation to one, so may unbelief, although it errs in many things, be one in so far as all those things are related to one. Yet nothing hinders one man from erring in various species of unbelief, even as one man may be subject to various vices, and to various bodily diseases.

* * * * *

SIXTH ARTICLE [II-II, Q. 10, Art. 6]

Whether the Unbelief of Pagans or Heathens Is Graver Than Other Kinds?

Objection 1: It would seem that the unbelief of heathens or pagans is graver than other kinds. For just as bodily disease is graver according as it endangers the health of a more important member of the body, so does sin appear to be graver, according as it is opposed to that which holds a more important place in virtue. Now that which is most important in faith, is belief in the unity of God, from which the heathens deviate by believing in many gods. Therefore their unbelief is the gravest of all.

Obj. 2: Further, among heresies, the more detestable are those which contradict the truth of faith in more numerous and more important points: thus, the heresy of Arius, who severed the Godhead, was more detestable than that of Nestorius who severed the humanity of Christ from the Person of God the Son. Now the heathens deny the faith in more numerous and more important points than Jews and heretics; since they do not accept the faith at all. Therefore their unbelief is the gravest.

Obj. 3: Further, every good diminishes evil. Now there is some good in the Jews, since they believe in the Old Testament as being from God, and there is some good in heretics, since they venerate the New Testament. Therefore they sin less grievously than heathens, who receive neither Testament.

On the contrary, It is written (2 Pet. 2:21): "It had been better for them not to have known the way of justice, than after they have known it, to turn back." Now the heathens have not known the way of justice, whereas heretics and Jews have abandoned it after knowing it in some way. Therefore theirs is the graver sin.

I answer that, As stated above (A. 5), two things may be considered in unbelief. One of these is its relation to faith: and from this point of view, he who resists the faith after accepting it, sins more grievously against faith, than he who resists it without having accepted it, even as he who fails to fulfil what he has promised, sins more grievously than if he had never promised it. In this way the unbelief of heretics, who confess their belief in the Gospel, and resist that faith by corrupting it, is a more grievous sin than that of the Jews, who have never accepted the Gospel faith. Since, however, they accepted the figure of that faith in the Old Law, which they corrupt by their false interpretations, their unbelief is a more grievous sin than that of the heathens, because the latter have not accepted the Gospel faith in any way at all.

The second thing to be considered in unbelief is the corruption of matters of faith. In this respect, since heathens err on more points than Jews, and these in more points than heretics, the unbelief of heathens is more grievous than the unbelief of the Jews, and that of the Jews than that of the heretics, except in such cases as that of the Manichees, who, in matters of faith, err even more than heathens do.

Of these two gravities the first surpasses the second from the point of view of guilt; since, as stated above (A. 1) unbelief has the character of guilt, from its resisting faith rather than from the mere absence of faith, for the latter as was stated (A. 1) seems rather to bear the character of punishment. Hence, speaking absolutely, the unbelief of heretics is the worst.

This suffices for the Replies to the Objections.

* * * * *

SEVENTH ARTICLE [II-II, Q. 10, Art. 7]

Whether One Ought to Dispute with Unbelievers in Public?

Objection 1: It would seem that one ought not to dispute with unbelievers in public. For the Apostle says (2 Tim. 2:14): "Contend not in words, for it is to no profit, but to the subverting of the hearers." But it is impossible to dispute with unbelievers publicly without contending in words. Therefore one ought not to dispute publicly with unbelievers.

Obj. 2: Further, the law of Martianus Augustus confirmed by the canons[1] expresses itself thus: "It is an insult to the judgment of the most religious synod, if anyone ventures to debate or dispute in public about matters which have once been judged and disposed of." Now all matters of faith have been decided by the holy councils. Therefore it is an insult to the councils, and consequently a grave sin to presume to dispute in public about matters of faith.

Obj. 3: Further, disputations are conducted by means of arguments. But an argument is a reason in settlement of a dubious matter: whereas things that are of faith, being most certain, ought not to be a matter of doubt. Therefore one ought not to dispute in public about matters of faith.

---

[1] De Sum. Trin. Cod. lib. i, leg. Nemo

On the contrary, It is written (Acts 9:22, 29) that "Saul increased much more in strength, and confounded the Jews," and that "he spoke . . . to the gentiles and disputed with the Greeks."

I answer that, In disputing about the faith, two things must be observed: one on the part of the disputant; the other on the part of his hearers. On the part of the disputant, we must consider his intention. For if he were to dispute as though he had doubts about the faith, and did not hold the truth of faith for certain, and as though he intended to probe it with arguments, without doubt he would sin, as being doubtful of the faith and an unbeliever. On the other hand, it is praiseworthy to dispute about the faith in order to confute errors, or for practice.

On the part of the hearers we must consider whether those who hear the disputation are instructed and firm in the faith, or simple and wavering. As to those who are well instructed and firm in the faith, there can be no danger in disputing about the faith in their presence. But as to simple-minded people, we must make a distinction; because either they are provoked and molested by unbelievers, for instance, Jews or heretics, or pagans who strive to corrupt the faith in them, or else they are not subject to provocation in this matter, as in those countries where there are no unbelievers. In the first case it is necessary to dispute in public about the faith, provided there be those who are equal and adapted to the task of confuting errors; since in this way simple people are strengthened in the faith, and unbelievers are deprived of the opportunity to deceive, while if those who ought to withstand the perverters of the truth of faith were silent, this would tend to strengthen error. Hence Gregory says (Pastor. ii, 4): "Even as a thoughtless speech gives rise to error, so does an indiscreet silence leave those in error who might have been instructed." On the other hand, in the second case it is dangerous to dispute in public about the faith, in the presence of simple people, whose faith for this very reason is more firm, that they have never heard anything differing from what they believe. Hence it is not expedient for them to hear what unbelievers have to say against the faith.

Reply Obj. 1: The Apostle does not entirely forbid disputations, but such as are inordinate, and consist of contentious words rather than of sound speeches.

Reply Obj. 2: That law forbade those public disputations about the faith, which arise from doubting the faith, but not those which are for the safeguarding thereof.

Reply Obj. 3: One ought to dispute about matters of faith, not as though one doubted about them, but in order to make the truth known, and to confute errors. For, in order to confirm the faith, it is necessary sometimes to dispute with unbelievers, sometimes by defending the faith, according to 1 Pet. 3:15: "Being ready always to satisfy everyone that asketh you a reason of that hope and faith which is in you[1]." Sometimes again, it is necessary, in order to convince those who are in error, according to Titus 1:9: "That he may be able to exhort in sound doctrine and to convince the gainsayers.".

* * * * *

EIGHTH ARTICLE [II-II, Q. 10, Art. 8]

Whether Unbelievers Ought to Be Compelled to the Faith?

Objection 1: It would seem that unbelievers ought by no means to be compelled to the faith. For it is written (Matt. 13:28) that the servants of the householder, in whose field cockle had been sown, asked him: "Wilt thou that we go and gather it up?" and that he answered: "No, lest perhaps gathering up the cockle, you root up the wheat also together with it": on which passage Chrysostom says (Hom. xlvi in Matth.): "Our Lord says this so as to forbid the slaying of men. For it is not right to slay heretics, because if you do you will necessarily slay many innocent persons." Therefore it seems that for the same reason unbelievers ought not to be compelled to the faith.

Obj. 2: Further, we read in the Decretals (Dist. xlv can., De Judaeis): "The holy synod prescribes, with regard to the Jews, that for the future, none are to be compelled to believe." Therefore, in like manner, neither should unbelievers be compelled to the faith.

Obj. 3: Further, Augustine says (Tract. xxvi in Joan.) that "it is possible for a man to do other things against his will, but he cannot

---

[1] Vulg.: 'Of that hope which is in you'; St. Thomas' reading is apparently taken from Bede

believe unless he is willing." Therefore it seems that unbelievers ought not to be compelled to the faith.

Obj. 4: It is said in God's person (Ezech. 18:32[1]): "I desire not the death of the sinner [Vulg.: 'of him that dieth']." Now we ought to conform our will to the Divine will, as stated above (I-II, Q. 19, AA. 9, 10). Therefore we should not even wish unbelievers to be put to death.

On the contrary, It is written (Luke 14:23): "Go out into the highways and hedges; and compel them to come in." Now men enter into the house of God, i.e. into Holy Church, by faith. Therefore some ought to be compelled to the faith.

I answer that, Among unbelievers there are some who have never received the faith, such as the heathens and the Jews: and these are by no means to be compelled to the faith, in order that they may believe, because to believe depends on the will: nevertheless they should be compelled by the faithful, if it be possible to do so, so that they do not hinder the faith, by their blasphemies, or by their evil persuasions, or even by their open persecutions. It is for this reason that Christ's faithful often wage war with unbelievers, not indeed for the purpose of forcing them to believe, because even if they were to conquer them, and take them prisoners, they should still leave them free to believe, if they will, but in order to prevent them from hindering the faith of Christ.

On the other hand, there are unbelievers who at some time have accepted the faith, and professed it, such as heretics and all apostates: such should be submitted even to bodily compulsion, that they may fulfil what they have promised, and hold what they, at one time, received.

Reply Obj. 1: Some have understood the authority quoted to forbid, not the excommunication but the slaying of heretics, as appears from the words of Chrysostom. Augustine too, says (Ep. ad Vincent. xciii) of himself: "It was once my opinion that none should be compelled to union with Christ, that we should deal in words, and fight with arguments. However this opinion of mine is undone, not by words of contradiction, but by convincing examples. Because fear of the law was so profitable, that many say: Thanks be to the Lord Who has broken our chains asunder." Accordingly

---

[1] Ezech. 33:11

the meaning of Our Lord's words, "Suffer both to grow until the harvest," must be gathered from those which precede, "lest perhaps gathering up the cockle, you root the wheat also together with it." For, Augustine says (Contra Ep. Parmen. iii, 2) "these words show that when this is not to be feared, that is to say, when a man's crime is so publicly known, and so hateful to all, that he has no defenders, or none such as might cause a schism, the severity of discipline should not slacken."

Reply Obj. 2: Those Jews who have in no way received the faith, ought not by no means to be compelled to the faith: if, however, they have received it, they ought to be compelled to keep it, as is stated in the same chapter.

Reply Obj. 3: Just as taking a vow is a matter of will, and keeping a vow, a matter of obligation, so acceptance of the faith is a matter of the will, whereas keeping the faith, when once one has received it, is a matter of obligation. Wherefore heretics should be compelled to keep the faith. Thus Augustine says to the Count Boniface (Ep. clxxxv): "What do these people mean by crying out continually: 'We may believe or not believe just as we choose. Whom did Christ compel?' They should remember that Christ at first compelled Paul and afterwards taught Him."

Reply Obj. 4: As Augustine says in the same letter, "none of us wishes any heretic to perish. But the house of David did not deserve to have peace, unless his son Absalom had been killed in the war which he had raised against his father. Thus if the Catholic Church gathers together some of the perdition of others, she heals the sorrow of her maternal heart by the delivery of so many nations.".

* * * * *

NINTH ARTICLE [II-II, Q. 10, Art. 9]

Whether It Is Lawful to Communicate with Unbelievers?

Objection 1: It would seem that it is lawful to communicate with unbelievers. For the Apostle says (1 Cor. 10:27): "If any of them that believe not, invite you, and you be willing to go, eat of anything that is set before you." And Chrysostom says (Hom. xxv super Epist. ad Heb.): "If you wish to go to dine with pagans, we permit it without any reservation." Now to sit at table with anyone is to communicate with him. Therefore it is lawful to communicate with unbelievers.

Obj. 2: Further, the Apostle says (1 Cor. 5:12): "What have I to do to judge them that are without?" Now unbelievers are without. When, therefore, the Church forbids the faithful to communicate with certain people, it seems that they ought not to be forbidden to communicate with unbelievers.

Obj. 3: Further, a master cannot employ his servant, unless he communicate with him, at least by word, since the master moves his servant by command. Now Christians can have unbelievers, either Jews, or pagans, or Saracens, for servants. Therefore they can lawfully communicate with them.

On the contrary, It is written (Deut. 7:2, 3): "Thou shalt make no league with them, nor show mercy to them; neither shalt thou make marriages with them": and a gloss on Lev. 15:19, "The woman who at the return of the month," etc. says: "It is so necessary to shun idolatry, that we should not come in touch with idolaters or their disciples, nor have any dealings with them."

I answer that, Communication with a particular person is forbidden to the faithful, in two ways: first, as a punishment of the person with whom they are forbidden to communicate; secondly, for the safety of those who are forbidden to communicate with others. Both motives can be gathered from the Apostle's words (1 Cor. 5:6). For after he had pronounced sentence of excommunication, he adds as his reason: "Know you not that a little leaven corrupts the whole lump?" and afterwards he adds the reason on the part of the punishment inflicted by the sentence of the Church when he says (1 Cor. 5:12): "Do not you judge them that are within?"

Accordingly, in the first way the Church does not forbid the faithful to communicate with unbelievers, who have not in any way received the Christian faith, viz. with pagans and Jews, because she has not the right to exercise spiritual judgment over them, but only temporal judgment, in the case when, while dwelling among Christians they are guilty of some misdemeanor, and are condemned by the faithful to some temporal punishment. On the other hand, in this way, i.e. as a punishment, the Church forbids the faithful to communicate with those unbelievers who have forsaken the faith they once received, either by corrupting the faith, as heretics, or by entirely renouncing the faith, as apostates, because the Church pronounces sentence of excommunication on both.

With regard to the second way, it seems that one ought to distinguish according to the various conditions of persons, circumstances and time. For some are firm in the faith; and so it is to be hoped that their communicating with unbelievers will lead to the conversion of the latter rather than to the aversion of the faithful from the faith. These are not to be forbidden to communicate with unbelievers who have not received the faith, such as pagans or Jews, especially if there be some urgent necessity for so doing. But in the case of simple people and those who are weak in the faith, whose perversion is to be feared as a probable result, they should be forbidden to communicate with unbelievers, and especially to be on very familiar terms with them, or to communicate with them without necessity.

This suffices for the Reply to the First Objection.

Reply Obj. 2: The Church does not exercise judgment against unbelievers in the point of inflicting spiritual punishment on them: but she does exercise judgment over some of them in the matter of temporal punishment. It is under this head that sometimes the Church, for certain special sins, withdraws the faithful from communication with certain unbelievers.

Reply Obj. 3: There is more probability that a servant who is ruled by his master's commands, will be converted to the faith of his master who is a believer, than if the case were the reverse: and so the faithful are not forbidden to have unbelieving servants. If, however, the master were in danger, through communicating with such a servant, he should send him away, according to Our Lord's command (Matt. 18:8): "If . . . thy foot scandalize thee, cut it off, and cast it from thee."

With regard to the argument in the contrary[1] sense the reply is that the Lord gave this command in reference to those nations into whose territory the Jews were about to enter. For the latter were inclined to idolatry, so that it was to be feared lest, through frequent dealings with those nations, they should be estranged from the faith: hence the text goes on (Deut. 7:4): "For she will turn away thy son from following Me.".

* * * * *

---

1   The Leonine Edition gives this solution before the Reply Obj. 2

TENTH ARTICLE [II-II, Q. 10, Art. 10]

Whether Unbelievers May Have Authority or Dominion Over the Faithful?

Objection 1: It would seem that unbelievers may have authority or dominion over the faithful. For the Apostle says (1 Tim. 6:1): "Whosoever are servants under the yoke, let them count their masters worthy of all honor": and it is clear that he is speaking of unbelievers, since he adds (1 Tim. 6:2): "But they that have believing masters, let them not despise them." Moreover it is written (1 Pet. 2:18): "Servants be subject to your masters with all fear, not only to the good and gentle, but also to the froward." Now this command would not be contained in the apostolic teaching unless unbelievers could have authority over the faithful. Therefore it seems that unbelievers can have authority over the faithful.

Obj. 2: Further, all the members of a prince's household are his subjects. Now some of the faithful were members of unbelieving princes' households, for we read in the Epistle to the Philippians (4:22): "All the saints salute you, especially they that are of Caesar's household," referring to Nero, who was an unbeliever. Therefore unbelievers can have authority over the faithful.

Obj. 3: Further, according to the Philosopher (Polit. i, 2) a slave is his master's instrument in matters concerning everyday life, even as a craftsman's laborer is his instrument in matters concerning the working of his art. Now, in such matters, a believer can be subject to an unbeliever, for he may work on an unbeliever's farm. Therefore unbelievers may have authority over the faithful even as to dominion.

On the contrary, Those who are in authority can pronounce judgment on those over whom they are placed. But unbelievers cannot pronounce judgment on the faithful, for the Apostle says (1 Cor. 6:1): "Dare any of you, having a matter against another, go to be judged before the unjust," i.e. unbelievers, "and not before the saints?" Therefore it seems that unbelievers cannot have authority over the faithful.

I answer that, That this question may be considered in two ways. First, we may speak of dominion or authority of unbelievers over the faithful as of a thing to be established for the first time. This ought by no means to be allowed, since it would provoke scandal and endanger the faith, for subjects are easily influenced by their superiors to comply with their commands, unless the subjects are of great virtue: moreover unbelievers hold the faith in contempt, if they see the faithful fall away. Hence the Apostle forbade the faithful to go to law before an unbelieving judge. And so the Church altogether forbids unbelievers to acquire dominion over believers, or to have authority over them in any capacity whatever.

Secondly, we may speak of dominion or authority, as already in force: and here we must observe that dominion and authority are institutions of human law, while the distinction between faithful and unbelievers arises from the Divine law. Now the Divine law which is the law of grace, does not do away with human law which is the law of natural reason. Wherefore the distinction between faithful and unbelievers, considered in itself, does not do away with dominion and authority of unbelievers over the faithful.

Nevertheless this right of dominion or authority can be justly done away with by the sentence or ordination of the Church who has the authority of God: since unbelievers in virtue of their unbelief deserve to forfeit their power over the faithful who are converted into children of God.

This the Church does sometimes, and sometimes not. For among those unbelievers who are subject, even in temporal matters, to the Church and her members, the Church made the law that if the slave of a Jew became a Christian, he should forthwith receive his freedom, without paying any price, if he should be a "vernaculus," i.e. born in slavery; and likewise if, when yet an unbeliever, he had been bought for his service: if, however, he had been bought for sale, then he should be offered for sale within three months. Nor does the Church harm them in this, because since those Jews themselves are subject to the Church, she can dispose of their possessions, even as secular princes have enacted many laws to be observed by their subjects, in favor of liberty. On the other hand, the Church has not applied the above law to those unbelievers who are not subject to her or her members, in temporal matters, although she has the right to do so: and this, in order to avoid scandal, for as Our Lord showed (Matt. 17:25, 26) that He could be excused from paying the tribute, because "the children are free," yet He ordered the tribute to be paid in order to avoid giving scandal. Thus Paul too, after saying that servants should honor their masters, adds, "lest the name of the Lord and His doctrine be blasphemed."

This suffices for the Reply to the First Objection.

Reply Obj. 2: The authority of Caesar preceded the distinction of faithful from unbelievers. Hence it was not cancelled by the conversion of some to the faith. Moreover it was a good thing that there should be a few of the faithful in the emperor's household, that they might defend the rest of the faithful. Thus the Blessed Sebastian encouraged those whom he saw faltering under torture, and, the while, remained hidden under the military cloak in the palace of Diocletian.

Reply Obj. 3: Slaves are subject to their masters for their whole lifetime, and are subject to their overseers in everything: whereas the craftsman's laborer is subject to him for certain special works. Hence it would be more dangerous for unbelievers to have dominion or authority over the faithful, than that they should be allowed to employ them in some craft. Wherefore the Church permits Christians to work on the land of Jews, because this does not entail their living together with them. Thus Solomon besought the King of Tyre to send master workmen to hew the trees, as related in 3 Kings 5:6. Yet, if there be reason to fear that the faithful will be perverted by such communications and dealings, they should be absolutely forbidden.

* * * * *

ELEVENTH ARTICLE [II-II, Q. 10, Art. 11]

Whether the Rites of Unbelievers Ought to Be Tolerated?

Objection 1: It would seem that rites of unbelievers ought not to be tolerated. For it is evident that unbelievers sin in observing their rites: and not to prevent a sin, when one can, seems to imply consent therein, as a gloss observes on Rom. 1:32: "Not only they that do them, but they also that consent to them that do them." Therefore it is a sin to tolerate their rites.

Obj. 2: Further, the rites of the Jews are compared to idolatry, because a gloss on Gal. 5:1, "Be not held again under the yoke of bondage," says: "The bondage of that law was not lighter than that of idolatry." But it would not be allowable for anyone to observe the rites of idolatry, in fact Christian princes at first caused the temples of idols to be closed, and afterwards, to be destroyed, as Augustine relates (De Civ. Dei xviii, 54). Therefore it follows that even the rites of Jews ought not to be tolerated.

Obj. 3: Further, unbelief is the greatest of sins, as stated above (A. 3). Now other sins such as adultery, theft and the like, are not tolerated, but are punishable by law. Therefore neither ought the rites of unbelievers to be tolerated.

On the contrary, Gregory[1] says, speaking of the Jews: "They should be allowed to observe all their feasts, just as hitherto they and their fathers have for ages observed them."

I answer that, Human government is derived from the Divine government, and should imitate it. Now although God is all-powerful and supremely good, nevertheless He allows certain evils to take place in the universe, which He might prevent, lest, without them, greater goods might be forfeited, or greater evils ensue. Accordingly in human government also, those who are in authority, rightly tolerate certain evils, lest certain goods be lost, or certain greater evils be incurred: thus Augustine says (De Ordine ii, 4): "If you do away with harlots, the world will be convulsed with lust." Hence, though unbelievers sin in their rites, they may be tolerated, either on account of some good that ensues therefrom, or because of some evil avoided. Thus from the fact that the Jews observe their rites, which, of old, foreshadowed the truth of the faith which we hold, there follows this good—that our very enemies bear witness to our faith, and that our faith is represented in a figure, so to speak. For this reason they are tolerated in the observance of their rites.

On the other hand, the rites of other unbelievers, which are neither truthful nor profitable are by no means to be tolerated, except perchance in order to avoid an evil, e.g. the scandal or disturbance that might ensue, or some hindrance to the salvation of those who if they were unmolested might gradually be converted to the faith. For this reason the Church, at times, has tolerated the rites even of heretics and pagans, when unbelievers were very numerous.

This suffices for the Replies to the Objections.

* * * * *

---

1   Regist. xi, Ep. 15: cf. Decret., dist. xlv, can., Qui sincera

TWELFTH ARTICLE [II-II, Q. 10, Art. 12]

Whether the Children of Jews and Other Unbelievers Ought to Be Baptized Against Their Parents' Will?

Objection 1: It would seem that the children of Jews and of other unbelievers ought to be baptized against their parents' will. For the bond of marriage is stronger than the right of parental authority over children, since the right of parental authority can be made to cease, when a son is set at liberty; whereas the marriage bond cannot be severed by man, according to Matt. 19:6: "What . . . God hath joined together let no man put asunder." And yet the marriage bond is broken on account of unbelief: for the Apostle says (1 Cor. 7:15): "If the unbeliever depart, let him depart. For a brother or sister is not under servitude in such cases": and a canon[1] says that "if the unbelieving partner is unwilling to abide with the other, without insult to their Creator, then the other partner is not bound to cohabitation." Much more, therefore, does unbelief abrogate the right of unbelieving parents' authority over their children: and consequently their children may be baptized against their parents' will.

Obj. 2: Further, one is more bound to succor a man who is in danger of everlasting death, than one who is in danger of temporal death. Now it would be a sin, if one saw a man in danger of temporal death and failed to go to his aid. Since, then, the children of Jews and other unbelievers are in danger of everlasting death, should they be left to their parents who would imbue them with their unbelief, it seems that they ought to be taken away from them and baptized, and instructed in the faith.

Obj. 3: Further, the children of a bondsman are themselves bondsmen, and under the power of his master. Now the Jews are bondsmen of kings and princes: therefore their children are also. Consequently kings and princes have the power to do what they will with Jewish children. Therefore no injustice is committed if they baptize them against their parents' wishes.

Obj. 4: Further, every man belongs more to God, from Whom he has his soul, than to his carnal father, from whom he has his

---

[1] Can. Uxor legitima, and Idololatria, qu. i

body. Therefore it is not unjust if Jewish children be taken away from their parents, and consecrated to God in Baptism.

Obj. 5: Further, Baptism avails for salvation more than preaching does, since Baptism removes forthwith the stain of sin and the debt of punishment, and opens the gate of heaven. Now if danger ensue through not preaching, it is imputed to him who omitted to preach, according to the words of Ezech. 33:6 about the man who "sees the sword coming and sounds not the trumpet." Much more therefore, if Jewish children are lost through not being baptized are they accounted guilty of sin, who could have baptized them and did not.

On the contrary, Injustice should be done to no man. Now it would be an injustice to Jews if their children were to be baptized against their will, since they would lose the rights of parental authority over their children as soon as these were Christians. Therefore these should not be baptized against their parents' will.

I answer that, The custom of the Church has very great authority and ought to be jealously observed in all things, since the very doctrine of catholic doctors derives its authority from the Church. Hence we ought to abide by the authority of the Church rather than by that of an Augustine or a Jerome or of any doctor whatever. Now it was never the custom of the Church to baptize the children of the Jews against the will of their parents, although at times past there have been many very powerful catholic princes like Constantine and Theodosius, with whom most holy bishops have been on most friendly terms, as Sylvester with Constantine, and Ambrose with Theodosius, who would certainly not have failed to obtain this favor from them if it had been at all reasonable. It seems therefore hazardous to repeat this assertion, that the children of Jews should be baptized against their parents' wishes, in contradiction to the Church's custom observed hitherto.

There are two reasons for this custom. One is on account of the danger to the faith. For children baptized before coming to the use of reason, afterwards when they come to perfect age, might easily be persuaded by their parents to renounce what they had unknowingly embraced; and this would be detrimental to the faith.

The other reason is that it is against natural justice. For a child is by nature part of its father: thus, at first, it is not distinct from its parents as to its body, so long as it is enfolded within its mother's womb; and later on after birth, and before it has the use of its free-will, it is enfolded in the care of its parents, which is like a spiritual womb, for so long as man has not the use of reason, he differs not from an irrational animal; so that even as an ox or a horse belongs to someone who, according to the civil law, can use them when he likes, as his own instrument, so, according to the natural law, a son, before coming to the use of reason, is under his father's care. Hence it would be contrary to natural justice, if a child, before coming to the use of reason, were to be taken away from its parents' custody, or anything done to it against its parents' wish. As soon, however, as it begins to have the use of its free-will, it begins to belong to itself, and is able to look after itself, in matters concerning the Divine or the natural law, and then it should be induced, not by compulsion but by persuasion, to embrace the faith: it can then consent to the faith, and be baptized, even against its parents' wish; but not before it comes to the use of reason. Hence it is said of the children of the fathers of old that they were saved in the faith of their parents; whereby we are given to understand that it is the parents' duty to look after the salvation of their children, especially before they come to the use of reason.

Reply Obj. 1: In the marriage bond, both husband and wife have the use of the free-will, and each can assent to the faith without the other's consent. But this does not apply to a child before it comes to the use of reason: yet the comparison holds good after the child has come to the use of reason, if it is willing to be converted.

Reply Obj. 2: No one should be snatched from natural death against the order of civil law: for instance, if a man were condemned by the judge to temporal death, nobody ought to rescue him by violence: hence no one ought to break the order of the natural law, whereby a child is in the custody of its father, in order to rescue it from the danger of everlasting death.

Reply Obj. 3: Jews are bondsmen of princes by civil bondage, which does not exclude the order of natural or Divine law.

Reply Obj. 4: Man is directed to God by his reason, whereby he can know Him. Hence a child before coming to the use of reason, in the natural order of things, is directed to God by its parents' reason, under whose care it lies by nature: and it is for them to dispose of the child in all matters relating to God.

Reply Obj. 5: The peril that ensues from the omission of preaching, threatens only those who are entrusted with the duty of preaching. Hence it had already been said (Ezech. 3:17): "I have made thee a watchman to the children [Vulg.: 'house'] of Israel." On the other hand, to provide the sacraments of salvation for the children of unbelievers is the duty of their parents. Hence it is they whom the danger threatens, if through being deprived of the sacraments their children fail to obtain salvation.

11. OF HERESY (In Four Articles)

We must now consider heresy: under which head there are four points of inquiry:

(1) Whether heresy is a kind of unbelief?
(2) Of the matter about which it is;
(3) Whether heretics should be tolerated?
(4) Whether converts should be received?.

* * * * *

FIRST ARTICLE [II-II, Q. 11, Art. 1]

Whether Heresy Is a Species of Unbelief?

Objection 1: It would seem that heresy is not a species of unbelief. For unbelief is in the understanding, as stated above (Q. 10, A. 2). Now heresy would seem not to pertain to the understanding, but rather to the appetitive power; for Jerome says on Gal. 5:19:[1] "The works of the flesh are manifest: Heresy is derived from a Greek word meaning choice, whereby a man makes choice of that school which he deems best." But choice is an act of the appetitive power, as stated above (I-II, Q. 13, A. 1). Therefore heresy is not a species of unbelief.

Obj. 2: Further, vice takes its species chiefly from its end; hence the Philosopher says (Ethic. v, 2) that "he who commits adultery that he may steal, is a thief rather than an adulterer." Now

---
1 Cf. Decretals xxiv, qu. iii, cap. 27

the end of heresy is temporal profit, especially lordship and glory, which belong to the vice of pride or covetousness: for Augustine says (De Util. Credendi i) that "a heretic is one who either devises or follows false and new opinions, for the sake of some temporal profit, especially that he may lord and be honored above others." Therefore heresy is a species of pride rather than of unbelief.

Obj. 3: Further, since unbelief is in the understanding, it would seem not to pertain to the flesh. Now heresy belongs to the works of the flesh, for the Apostle says (Gal. 5:19): "The works of the flesh are manifest, which are fornication, uncleanness," and among the others, he adds, "dissensions, sects," which are the same as heresies. Therefore heresy is not a species of unbelief.

On the contrary, Falsehood is contrary to truth. Now a heretic is one who devises or follows false or new opinions. Therefore heresy is opposed to the truth, on which faith is founded; and consequently it is a species of unbelief.

I answer that, The word heresy as stated in the first objection denotes a choosing. Now choice as stated above (I-II, Q. 13, A. 3) is about things directed to the end, the end being presupposed. Now, in matters of faith, the will assents to some truth, as to its proper good, as was shown above (Q. 4, A. 3): wherefore that which is the chief truth, has the character of last end, while those which are secondary truths, have the character of being directed to the end.

Now, whoever believes, assents to someone's words; so that, in every form of unbelief, the person to whose words assent is given seems to hold the chief place and to be the end as it were; while the things by holding which one assents to that person hold a secondary place. Consequently he that holds the Christian faith aright, assents, by his will, to Christ, in those things which truly belong to His doctrine.

Accordingly there are two ways in which a man may deviate from the rectitude of the Christian faith. First, because he is unwilling to assent to Christ: and such a man has an evil will, so to say, in respect of the very end. This belongs to the species of unbelief in pagans and Jews. Secondly, because, though he intends to assent to Christ, yet he fails in his choice of those things wherein he assents to Christ, because he chooses not what Christ really taught, but the suggestions of his own mind.

Therefore heresy is a species of unbelief, belonging to those who profess the Christian faith, but corrupt its dogmas.

Reply Obj. 1: Choice regards unbelief in the same way as the will regards faith, as stated above.

Reply Obj. 2: Vices take their species from their proximate end, while, from their remote end, they take their genus and cause. Thus in the case of adultery committed for the sake of theft, there is the species of adultery taken from its proper end and object; but the ultimate end shows that the act of adultery is both the result of the theft, and is included under it, as an effect under its cause, or a species under its genus, as appears from what we have said about acts in general (I-II, Q. 18, A. 7). Wherefore, as to the case in point also, the proximate end of heresy is adherence to one's own false opinion, and from this it derives its species, while its remote end reveals its cause, viz. that it arises from pride or covetousness.

Reply Obj. 3: Just as heresy is so called from its being a choosing[1], so does sect derive its name from its being a cutting off (secando), as Isidore states (Etym. viii, 3). Wherefore heresy and sect are the same thing, and each belongs to the works of the flesh, not indeed by reason of the act itself of unbelief in respect of its proximate object, but by reason of its cause, which is either the desire of an undue end in which way it arises from pride or covetousness, as stated in the second objection, or some illusion of the imagination (which gives rise to error, as the Philosopher states in Metaph. iv; Ed. Did. iii, 5), for this faculty has a certain connection with the flesh, in as much as its act is independent on a bodily organ.

* * * * *

SECOND ARTICLE [II-II, Q. 11, Art. 2]

Whether Heresy Is Properly About Matters of Faith?

Objection 1: It would seem that heresy is not properly about matters of faith. For just as there are heresies and sects among Christians, so were there among the Jews, and Pharisees, as Isidore observes (Etym. viii, 3, 4, 5). Now their dissensions were not about matters of faith. Therefore heresy is not about matters of faith, as though they were its proper matter.

---

1 From the Greek hairein, to cut off

Obj. 2: Further, the matter of faith is the thing believed. Now heresy is not only about things, but also about works, and about interpretations of Holy Writ. For Jerome says on Gal. 5:20 that "whoever expounds the Scriptures in any sense but that of the Holy Ghost by Whom they were written, may be called a heretic, though he may not have left the Church": and elsewhere he says that "heresies spring up from words spoken amiss."[1] Therefore heresy is not properly about the matter of faith.

Obj. 3: Further, we find the holy doctors differing even about matters pertaining to the faith, for example Augustine and Jerome, on the question about the cessation of the legal observances: and yet this was without any heresy on their part. Therefore heresy is not properly about the matter of faith.

On the contrary, Augustine says against the Manichees[2]: "In Christ's Church, those are heretics, who hold mischievous and erroneous opinions, and when rebuked that they may think soundly and rightly, offer a stubborn resistance, and, refusing to mend their pernicious and deadly doctrines, persist in defending them." Now pernicious and deadly doctrines are none but those which are contrary to the dogmas of faith, whereby "the just man liveth" (Rom. 1:17). Therefore heresy is about matters of faith, as about its proper matter.

I answer that, We are speaking of heresy now as denoting a corruption of the Christian faith. Now it does not imply a corruption of the Christian faith, if a man has a false opinion in matters that are not of faith, for instance, in questions of geometry and so forth, which cannot belong to the faith by any means; but only when a person has a false opinion about things belonging to the faith.

Now a thing may be of the faith in two ways, as stated above (I, Q. 32, A. 4; I-II, Q. 1, A. 6, ad 1; I-II, Q. 2, A. 5), in one way, directly and principally, e.g. the articles of faith; in another way, indirectly and secondarily, e.g. those matters, the denial of which leads to the corruption of some article of faith; and there may be heresy in either way, even as there can be faith.

---

1   St. Thomas quotes this saying elsewhere, in Sent. iv, D, 13, and III, Q. 16, A. 8, but it is not to be found in St. Jerome's works.

2   Cf. De Civ. Dei xviii, 51

Reply Obj. 1: Just as the heresies of the Jews and Pharisees were about opinions relating to Judaism or Pharisaism, so also heresies among Christians are about matter touching the Christian faith.

Reply Obj. 2: A man is said to expound Holy Writ in another sense than that required by the Holy Ghost, when he so distorts the meaning of Holy Writ, that it is contrary to what the Holy Ghost has revealed. Hence it is written (Ezech. 13:6) about the false prophets: "They have persisted to confirm what they have said," viz. by false interpretations of Scripture. Moreover a man professes his faith by the words that he utters, since confession is an act of faith, as stated above (Q. 3, A. 1). Wherefore inordinate words about matters of faith may lead to corruption of the faith; and hence it is that Pope Leo says in a letter to Proterius, Bishop of Alexandria: "The enemies of Christ's cross lie in wait for our every deed and word, so that, if we but give them the slightest pretext, they may accuse us mendaciously of agreeing with Nestorius."

Reply Obj. 3: As Augustine says (Ep. xliii) and we find it stated in the Decretals (xxiv, qu. 3, can. Dixit Apostolus): "By no means should we accuse of heresy those who, however false and perverse their opinion may be, defend it without obstinate fervor, and seek the truth with careful anxiety, ready to mend their opinion, when they have found the truth," because, to wit, they do not make a choice in contradiction to the doctrine of the Church. Accordingly, certain doctors seem to have differed either in matters the holding of which in this or that way is of no consequence, so far as faith is concerned, or even in matters of faith, which were not as yet defined by the Church; although if anyone were obstinately to deny them after they had been defined by the authority of the universal Church, he would be deemed a heretic. This authority resides chiefly in the Sovereign Pontiff. For we read[1]: "Whenever a question of faith is in dispute, I think, that all our brethren and fellow bishops ought to refer the matter to none other than Peter, as being the source of their name and honor, against whose authority neither Jerome nor Augustine nor any of the holy doctors defended their opinion." Hence Jerome says (Exposit. Symbol[2]): "This, most blessed Pope, is the faith that we have been taught in

---

1 Decret. xxiv, qu. 1, can. Quoties
2 Among the supposititious works of St. Jerome

the Catholic Church. If anything therein has been incorrectly or carelessly expressed, we beg that it may be set aright by you who hold the faith and see of Peter. If however this, our profession, be approved by the judgment of your apostleship, whoever may blame me, will prove that he himself is ignorant, or malicious, or even not a catholic but a heretic.".

* * * * *

THIRD ARTICLE [II-II, Q. 11, Art. 3]

Whether Heretics Ought to Be Tolerated?

Objection 1: It seems that heretics ought to be tolerated. For the Apostle says (2 Tim. 2:24, 25): "The servant of the Lord must not wrangle . . . with modesty admonishing them that resist the truth, if peradventure God may give them repentance to know the truth, and they may recover themselves from the snares of the devil." Now if heretics are not tolerated but put to death, they lose the opportunity of repentance. Therefore it seems contrary to the Apostle's command.

Obj. 2: Further, whatever is necessary in the Church should be tolerated. Now heresies are necessary in the Church, since the Apostle says (1 Cor. 11:19): "There must be . . . heresies, that they . . . who are reproved, may be manifest among you." Therefore it seems that heretics should be tolerated.

Obj. 3: Further, the Master commanded his servants (Matt. 13:30) to suffer the cockle "to grow until the harvest," i.e. the end of the world, as a gloss explains it. Now holy men explain that the cockle denotes heretics. Therefore heretics should be tolerated.

On the contrary, The Apostle says (Titus 3:10, 11): "A man that is a heretic, after the first and second admonition, avoid: knowing that he, that is such an one, is subverted."

I answer that, With regard to heretics two points must be observed: one, on their own side; the other, on the side of the Church. On their own side there is the sin, whereby they deserve not only to be separated from the Church by excommunication, but also to be severed from the world by death. For it is a much graver matter to corrupt the faith which quickens the soul, than to forge money, which supports temporal life. Wherefore if forgers of money and other evil-doers are forthwith condemned to death by the secular authority, much more reason is there for heretics, as soon as they are convicted of heresy, to be not only excommunicated but even put to death.

On the part of the Church, however, there is mercy which looks to the conversion of the wanderer, wherefore she condemns not at once, but "after the first and second admonition," as the Apostle directs: after that, if he is yet stubborn, the Church no longer hoping for his conversion, looks to the salvation of others, by excommunicating him and separating him from the Church, and furthermore delivers him to the secular tribunal to be exterminated thereby from the world by death. For Jerome commenting on Gal. 5:9, "A little leaven," says: "Cut off the decayed flesh, expel the mangy sheep from the fold, lest the whole house, the whole paste, the whole body, the whole flock, burn, perish, rot, die. Arius was but one spark in Alexandria, but as that spark was not at once put out, the whole earth was laid waste by its flame."

Reply Obj. 1: This very modesty demands that the heretic should be admonished a first and second time: and if he be unwilling to retract, he must be reckoned as already "subverted," as we may gather from the words of the Apostle quoted above.

Reply Obj. 2: The profit that ensues from heresy is beside the intention of heretics, for it consists in the constancy of the faithful being put to the test, and "makes us shake off our sluggishness, and search the Scriptures more carefully," as Augustine states (De Gen. cont. Manich. i, 1). What they really intend is the corruption of the faith, which is to inflict very great harm indeed. Consequently we should consider what they directly intend, and expel them, rather than what is beside their intention, and so, tolerate them.

Reply Obj. 3: According to Decret. (xxiv, qu. iii, can. Notandum), "to be excommunicated is not to be uprooted." A man is excommunicated, as the Apostle says (1 Cor. 5:5) that his "spirit may be saved in the day of Our Lord." Yet if heretics be altogether uprooted by death, this is not contrary to Our Lord's command, which is to be understood as referring to the case when the cockle cannot be plucked up without plucking up the wheat, as we explained above (Q. 10, A. 8, ad 1), when treating of unbelievers in general.

* * * * *

FOURTH ARTICLE [II-II, Q. 11, Art. 4]

Whether the Church Should Receive Those Who Return from Heresy?

Objection 1: It would seem that the Church ought in all cases to receive those who return from heresy. For it is written (Jer. 3:1) in the person of the Lord: "Thou hast prostituted thyself to many lovers; nevertheless return to Me saith the Lord." Now the sentence of the Church is God's sentence, according to Deut. 1:17: "You shall hear the little as well as the great: neither shall you respect any man's person, because it is the judgment of God." Therefore even those who are guilty of the prostitution of unbelief which is spiritual prostitution, should be received all the same.

Obj. 2: Further, Our Lord commanded Peter (Matt. 18:22) to forgive his offending brother "not" only "till seven times, but till seventy times seven times," which Jerome expounds as meaning that "a man should be forgiven, as often as he has sinned." Therefore he ought to be received by the Church as often as he has sinned by falling back into heresy.

Obj. 3: Further, heresy is a kind of unbelief. Now other unbelievers who wish to be converted are received by the Church. Therefore heretics also should be received.

On the contrary, The Decretal Ad abolendam (De Haereticis, cap. ix) says that "those who are found to have relapsed into the error which they had already abjured, must be left to the secular tribunal." Therefore they should not be received by the Church.

I answer that, In obedience to Our Lord's institution, the Church extends her charity to all, not only to friends, but also to foes who persecute her, according to Matt. 5:44: "Love your enemies; do good to them that hate you." Now it is part of charity that we should both wish and work our neighbor's good. Again, good is twofold: one is spiritual, namely the health of the soul, which good is chiefly the object of charity, since it is this chiefly that we should wish for one another. Consequently, from this point of view, heretics who return after falling no matter how often, are admitted by the Church to Penance whereby the way of salvation is opened to them.

The other good is that which charity considers secondarily, viz. temporal good, such as life of the body, worldly possessions, good repute, ecclesiastical or secular dignity, for we are not bound by charity to wish others this good, except in relation to the eternal salvation of them and of others. Hence if the presence of one of these goods in one individual might be an obstacle to eternal salvation in many, we are not bound out of charity to wish such a good to that person, rather should we desire him to be without it, both because eternal salvation takes precedence of temporal good, and because the good of the many is to be preferred to the good of one. Now if heretics were always received on their return, in order to save their lives and other temporal goods, this might be prejudicial to the salvation of others, both because they would infect others if they relapsed again, and because, if they escaped without punishment, others would feel more assured in lapsing into heresy. For it is written (Eccles. 8:11): "For because sentence is not speedily pronounced against the evil, the children of men commit evils without any fear."

For this reason the Church not only admits to Penance those who return from heresy for the first time, but also safeguards their lives, and sometimes by dispensation, restores them to the ecclesiastical dignities which they may have had before, should their conversion appear to be sincere: we read of this as having frequently been done for the good of peace. But when they fall again, after having been received, this seems to prove them to be inconstant in faith, wherefore when they return again, they are admitted to Penance, but are not delivered from the pain of death.

Reply Obj. 1: In God's tribunal, those who return are always received, because God is a searcher of hearts, and knows those who return in sincerity. But the Church cannot imitate God in this, for she presumes that those who relapse after being once received, are not sincere in their return; hence she does not debar them from the way of salvation, but neither does she protect them from the sentence of death.

Reply Obj. 2: Our Lord was speaking to Peter of sins committed against oneself, for one should always forgive such offenses and spare our brother when he repents. These words are not to be applied to sins committed against one's neighbor or against God, for it is not left to our discretion to forgive such offenses, as Jerome says on Matt. 18:15, "If thy brother shall offend against thee." Yet even in this matter the law prescribes limits according as God's honor or our neighbor's good demands.

Reply Obj. 3: When other unbelievers, who have never received the faith are converted, they do not as yet show signs of inconstancy in faith, as relapsed heretics do; hence the comparison fails.

12. OF APOSTASY (In Two Articles)

We must now consider apostasy: about which there are two points of inquiry:

(1) Whether apostasy pertains to unbelief?
(2) Whether, on account of apostasy from the faith, subjects are absolved from allegiance to an apostate prince?.

* * * * *

FIRST ARTICLE [II-II, Q. 12, Art. 1]

Whether Apostasy Pertains to Unbelief?

Objection 1: It would seem that apostasy does not pertain to unbelief. For that which is the origin of all sins, does not, seemingly, pertain to unbelief, since many sins there are without unbelief. Now apostasy seems to be the origin of every sin, for it is written (Ecclus. 10:14): "The beginning of the pride of man is apostasy [Douay: 'to fall off'] from God," and further on, (Ecclus. 10:15): "Pride is the beginning of all sin." Therefore apostasy does not pertain to unbelief.

Obj. 2: Further, unbelief is an act of the understanding: whereas apostasy seems rather to consist in some outward deed or utterance, or even in some inward act of the will, for it is written (Prov. 6:12-14): "A man that is an apostate, an unprofitable man walketh with a perverse mouth. He winketh with the eyes, presseth with the foot, speaketh with the finger. With a wicked heart he deviseth evil, and at all times he soweth discord." Moreover if anyone were to have himself circumcised, or to worship at the tomb of Mahomet, he would be deemed an apostate. Therefore apostasy does not pertain to unbelief.

Obj. 3: Further, heresy, since it pertains to unbelief, is a determinate species of unbelief. If then, apostasy pertained to unbelief, it would follow that it is a determinate species of unbelief, which does not seem to agree with what has been said (Q. 10, A. 5). Therefore apostasy does not pertain to unbelief.

On the contrary, It is written (John 6:67): "Many of his disciples went back," i.e. apostatized, of whom Our Lord had said previously (John 6:65): "There are some of you that believe not." Therefore apostasy pertains to unbelief.

I answer that, Apostasy denotes a backsliding from God. This may happen in various ways according to the different kinds of union between man and God. For, in the first place, man is united to God by faith; secondly, by having his will duly submissive in obeying His commandments; thirdly, by certain special things pertaining to supererogation such as the religious life, the clerical state, or Holy Orders. Now if that which follows be removed, that which precedes, remains, but the converse does not hold. Accordingly a man may apostatize from God, by withdrawing from the religious life to which he was bound by profession, or from the Holy Order which he had received: and this is called "apostasy from religious life" or "Orders." A man may also apostatize from God, by rebelling in his mind against the Divine commandments: and though man may apostatize in both the above ways, he may still remain united to God by faith.

But if he give up the faith, then he seems to turn away from God altogether: and consequently, apostasy simply and absolutely is that whereby a man withdraws from the faith, and is called "apostasy of perfidy." In this way apostasy, simply so called, pertains to unbelief.

Reply Obj. 1: This objection refers to the second kind of apostasy, which denotes an act of the will in rebellion against God's commandments, an act that is to be found in every mortal sin.

Reply Obj. 2: It belongs to faith not only that the heart should believe, but also that external words and deeds should bear witness to the inward faith, for confession is an act of faith. In this way too, certain external words or deeds pertain to unbelief, in so far as they are signs of unbelief, even as a sign of health is said itself to be healthy. Now although the authority quoted may be understood as referring to every kind of apostate, yet it applies most truly to an apostate from the faith. For since faith is the first foundation of things to be hoped for, and since, without faith it is "impossible to please God"; when once faith is removed, man retains nothing that may be useful for the obtaining of eternal salvation, for which reason it is written (Prov. 6:12): "A man that is an apostate, an unprofitable man": because faith is the life of the soul, according to Rom. 1:17: "The just man liveth by faith." Therefore, just as when the life of the body is taken away, man's every member and part loses its due disposition, so when the life of justice, which is by faith, is done away, disorder appears in all his members. First, in his mouth, whereby chiefly his mind stands revealed; secondly, in his eyes; thirdly, in the instrument of movement; fourthly, in his will, which tends to evil. The result is that "he sows discord," endeavoring to sever others from the faith even as he severed himself.

Reply Obj. 3: The species of a quality or form are not diversified by the fact of its being the term wherefrom or whereto of movement: on the contrary, it is the movement that takes its species from the terms. Now apostasy regards unbelief as the term whereto of the movement of withdrawal from the faith; wherefore apostasy does not imply a special kind of unbelief, but an aggravating circumstance thereof, according to 2 Pet. 2:21: "It had been better for them not to know the truth [Vulg.: 'the way of justice'], than after they had known it, to turn back.".

* * * * *

SECOND ARTICLE [II-II, Q. 12, Art. 2]

Whether a Prince Forfeits His Dominion Over His Subjects,
on Account of Apostasy from the Faith,
So That They No Longer Owe Him Allegiance?

Objection 1: It would seem that a prince does not so forfeit his dominion over his subjects, on account of apostasy from the faith, that they no longer owe him allegiance. For Ambrose[1] says that the Emperor Julian, though an apostate, nevertheless had under him Christian soldiers, who when he said to them, "Fall into line for the defense of the republic," were bound to obey. Therefore subjects are not absolved from their allegiance to their prince on account of his apostasy.

Obj. 2: Further, an apostate from the faith is an unbeliever. Now we find that certain holy men served unbelieving masters;

---

1   St. Augustine, Super Ps. 124:3

thus Joseph served Pharaoh, Daniel served Nabuchodonosor, and Mardochai served Assuerus. Therefore apostasy from the faith does not release subjects from allegiance to their sovereign.

Obj. 3: Further, just as by apostasy from the faith, a man turns away from God, so does every sin. Consequently if, on account of apostasy from the faith, princes were to lose their right to command those of their subjects who are believers, they would equally lose it on account of other sins: which is evidently not the case. Therefore we ought not to refuse allegiance to a sovereign on account of his apostatizing from the faith.

On the contrary, Gregory VII says (Council, Roman V): "Holding to the institutions of our holy predecessors, we, by our apostolic authority, absolve from their oath those who through loyalty or through the sacred bond of an oath owe allegiance to excommunicated persons: and we absolutely forbid them to continue their allegiance to such persons, until these shall have made amends." Now apostates from the faith, like heretics, are excommunicated, according to the Decretal[1]. Therefore princes should not be obeyed when they have apostatized from the faith.

I answer that, As stated above (Q. 10, A. 10), unbelief, in itself, is not inconsistent with dominion, since dominion is a device of the law of nations which is a human law: whereas the distinction between believers and unbelievers is of Divine right, which does not annul human right. Nevertheless a man who sins by unbelief may be sentenced to the loss of his right of dominion, as also, sometimes, on account of other sins.

Now it is not within the competency of the Church to punish unbelief in those who have never received the faith, according to the saying of the Apostle (1 Cor. 5:12): "What have I to do to judge them that are without?" She can, however, pass sentence of punishment on the unbelief of those who have received the faith: and it is fitting that they should be punished by being deprived of the allegiance of their subjects: for this same allegiance might conduce to great corruption of the faith, since, as was stated above (A. 1, Obj. 2), "a man that is an apostate . . . with a wicked heart deviseth evil, and . . . soweth discord," in order to sever others from the faith. Consequently, as soon as sentence of excommunication is

---

[1] Extra, De Haereticis, cap. Ad abolendam

passed on a man on account of apostasy from the faith, his subjects are "ipso facto" absolved from his authority and from the oath of allegiance whereby they were bound to him.

Reply Obj. 1: At that time the Church was but recently instituted, and had not, as yet, the power of curbing earthly princes; and so she allowed the faithful to obey Julian the apostate, in matters that were not contrary to the faith, in order to avoid incurring a yet greater danger.

Reply Obj. 2: As stated in the article, it is not a question of those unbelievers who have never received the faith.

Reply Obj. 3: Apostasy from the faith severs man from God altogether, as stated above (A. 1), which is not the case in any other sin.

13. OF THE SIN OF BLASPHEMY, IN GENERAL (In Four Articles)

We must now consider the sin of blasphemy, which is opposed to the confession of faith; and (1) blasphemy in general, (2) that blasphemy which is called the sin against the Holy Ghost.

Under the first head there are four points of inquiry:

(1) Whether blasphemy is opposed to the confession of faith?
(2) Whether blasphemy is always a mortal sin?
(3) Whether blasphemy is the most grievous sin?
(4) Whether blasphemy is in the damned?.

* * * * *

FIRST ARTICLE [II-II, Q. 13, Art. 1]

Whether Blasphemy Is Opposed to the Confession of Faith?

Objection 1: It would seem that blasphemy is not opposed to the confession of faith. Because to blaspheme is to utter an affront or insult against the Creator. Now this pertains to ill-will against God rather than to unbelief. Therefore blasphemy is not opposed to the confession of faith.

Obj. 2: Further, on Eph. 4:31, "Let blasphemy . . . be put away from you," a gloss says, "that which is committed against God or the saints." But confession of faith, seemingly, is not about other things than those pertaining to God, Who is the object of faith. Therefore blasphemy is not always opposed to the confession of faith.

Obj. 3: Further, according to some, there are three kinds of blasphemy. The first of these is when something unfitting is affirmed of God; the second is when something fitting is denied of Him; and the third, when something proper to God is ascribed to a creature, so that, seemingly, blasphemy is not only about God, but also about His creatures. Now the object of faith is God. Therefore blasphemy is not opposed to confession of faith.

On the contrary, The Apostle says (1 Tim. 1:12, 13): "I . . . before was a blasphemer and a persecutor," and afterwards, "I did it ignorantly in" my "unbelief." Hence it seems that blasphemy pertains to unbelief.

I answer that, The word blasphemy seems to denote the disparagement of some surpassing goodness, especially that of God. Now God, as Dionysius says (Div. Nom. i), is the very essence of true goodness. Hence whatever befits God, pertains to His goodness, and whatever does not befit Him, is far removed from the perfection of goodness which is His Essence. Consequently whoever either denies anything befitting God, or affirms anything unbefitting Him, disparages the Divine goodness.

Now this may happen in two ways. In the first way it may happen merely in respect of the opinion in the intellect; in the second way this opinion is united to a certain detestation in the affections, even as, on the other hand, faith in God is perfected by love of Him. Accordingly this disparagement of the Divine goodness is either in the intellect alone, or in the affections also. If it is in thought only, it is blasphemy of the heart, whereas if it betrays itself outwardly in speech it is blasphemy of the tongue. It is in this sense that blasphemy is opposed to confession of faith.

Reply Obj. 1: He that speaks against God, with the intention of reviling Him, disparages the Divine goodness, not only in respect of the falsehood in his intellect, but also by reason of the wickedness of his will, whereby he detests and strives to hinder the honor due to God, and this is perfect blasphemy.

Reply Obj. 2: Even as God is praised in His saints, in so far as praise is given to the works which God does in His saints, so does blasphemy against the saints, redound, as a consequence, against God.

Reply Obj. 3: Properly speaking, the sin of blasphemy is not in this way divided into three species: since to affirm unfitting things, or to deny fitting things of God, differ merely as affirmation and negation. For this diversity does not cause distinct species of habits, since the falsehood of affirmations and negations is made known by the same knowledge, and it is the same ignorance which errs in either way, since negatives are proved by affirmatives, according to Poster. i, 25. Again to ascribe to creatures things that are proper to God, seems to amount to the same as affirming something unfitting of Him, since whatever is proper to God is God Himself: and to ascribe to a creature, that which is proper to God, is to assert that God is the same as a creature.

* * * * *

SECOND ARTICLE [II-II, Q. 13, Art. 2]

Whether Blasphemy Is Always a Mortal Sin?

Objection 1: It would seem that blasphemy is not always a mortal sin. Because a gloss on the words, "Now lay you also all away," etc. (Col. 3:8) says: "After prohibiting greater crimes he forbids lesser sins": and yet among the latter he includes blasphemy. Therefore blasphemy is comprised among the lesser, i.e. venial, sins.

Obj. 2: Further, every mortal sin is opposed to one of the precepts of the decalogue. But, seemingly, blasphemy is not contrary to any of them. Therefore blasphemy is not a mortal sin.

Obj. 3: Further, sins committed without deliberation, are not mortal: hence first movements are not mortal sins, because they precede the deliberation of the reason, as was shown above (I-II, Q. 74, AA. 3, 10). Now blasphemy sometimes occurs without deliberation of the reason. Therefore it is not always a mortal sin.

On the contrary, It is written (Lev. 24:16): "He that blasphemeth the name of the Lord, dying let him die." Now the death punishment is not inflicted except for a mortal sin. Therefore blasphemy is a mortal sin.

I answer that, As stated above (I-II, Q. 72, A. 5), a mortal sin is one whereby a man is severed from the first principle of spiritual life, which principle is the charity of God. Therefore whatever things are contrary to charity, are mortal sins in respect of their genus. Now blasphemy, as to its genus, is opposed to Divine charity, because, as stated above (A. 1), it disparages the Divine goodness, which is the object of charity. Consequently blasphemy is a mortal sin, by reason of its genus.

Reply Obj. 1: This gloss is not to be understood as meaning that all the sins which follow, are mortal, but that whereas all those mentioned previously are more grievous sins, some of those mentioned afterwards are less grievous; and yet among the latter some more grievous sins are included.

Reply Obj. 2: Since, as stated above (A. 1), blasphemy is contrary to the confession of faith, its prohibition is comprised under the prohibition of unbelief, expressed by the words: "I am the Lord thy God," etc. (Ex. 20:1). Or else, it is forbidden by the words: "Thou shalt not take the name of ... God in vain" (Ex. 20:7). Because he who asserts something false about God, takes His name in vain even more than he who uses the name of God in confirmation of a falsehood.

Reply Obj. 3: There are two ways in which blasphemy may occur unawares and without deliberation. In the first way, by a man failing to advert to the blasphemous nature of his words, and this may happen through his being moved suddenly by passion so as to break out into words suggested by his imagination, without heeding to the meaning of those words: this is a venial sin, and is not a blasphemy properly so called. In the second way, by adverting to the meaning of his words, and to their blasphemous nature: in which case he is not excused from mortal sin, even as neither is he who, in a sudden movement of anger, kills one who is sitting beside him.

* * * * *

THIRD ARTICLE [II-II, Q. 13, Art. 3]

Whether the Sin of Blasphemy Is the Greatest Sin?

Objection 1: It would seem that the sin of blasphemy is not the greatest sin. For, according to Augustine (Enchiridion xii), a thing is said to be evil because it does harm. Now the sin of murder, since it destroys a man's life, does more harm than the sin of blasphemy, which can do no harm to God. Therefore the sin of murder is more grievous than that of blasphemy.

Obj. 2: Further, a perjurer calls upon God to witness to a falsehood, and thus seems to assert that God is false. But not every blasphemer goes so far as to say that God is false. Therefore perjury is a more grievous sin than blasphemy.

Obj. 3: Further, on Ps. 74:6, "Lift not up your horn on high," a gloss says: "To excuse oneself for sin is the greatest sin of all." Therefore blasphemy is not the greatest sin.

On the contrary, On Isa. 18:2, "To a terrible people," etc. a gloss says: "In comparison with blasphemy, every sin is slight."

I answer that, As stated above (A. 1), blasphemy is opposed to the confession of faith, so that it contains the gravity of unbelief: while the sin is aggravated if the will's detestation is added thereto, and yet more, if it breaks out into words, even as love and confession add to the praise of faith.

Therefore, since, as stated above (Q. 10, A. 3), unbelief is the greatest of sins in respect of its genus, it follows that blasphemy also is a very great sin, through belonging to the same genus as unbelief and being an aggravated form of that sin.

Reply Obj. 1: If we compare murder and blasphemy as regards the objects of those sins, it is clear that blasphemy, which is a sin committed directly against God, is more grave than murder, which is a sin against one's neighbor. On the other hand, if we compare them in respect of the harm wrought by them, murder is the graver sin, for murder does more harm to one's neighbor, than blasphemy does to God. Since, however, the gravity of a sin depends on the intention of the evil will, rather than on the effect of the deed, as was shown above (I-II, Q. 73, A. 8), it follows that, as the blasphemer intends to do harm to God's honor, absolutely speaking, he sins more grievously that the murderer. Nevertheless murder takes precedence, as to punishment, among sins committed against our neighbor.

Reply Obj. 2: A gloss on the words, "Let ... blasphemy be put away from you" (Eph. 4:31) says: "Blasphemy is worse than perjury." The reason is that the perjurer does not say or think something false about God, as the blasphemer does: but he calls God to witness to a falsehood, not that he deems God a false witness, but in the hope, as it were, that God will not testify to the matter by some evident sign.

Reply Obj. 3: To excuse oneself for sin is a circumstance that aggravates every sin, even blasphemy itself: and it is called the most grievous sin, for as much as it makes every sin more grievous.

* * * * *

FOURTH ARTICLE [II-II, Q. 13, Art. 4]

Whether the Damned Blaspheme?

Objection 1: It would seem that the damned do not blaspheme. Because some wicked men are deterred from blaspheming now, on account of the fear of future punishment. But the damned are undergoing these punishments, so that they abhor them yet more. Therefore, much more are they restrained from blaspheming.

Obj. 2: Further, since blasphemy is a most grievous sin, it is most demeritorious. Now in the life to come there is no state of meriting or demeriting. Therefore there will be no place for blasphemy.

Obj. 3: Further, it is written (Eccles. 11:3) that "the tree . . . in what place soever it shall fall, there shall it be": whence it clearly follows that, after this life, man acquires neither merit nor sin, which he did not already possess in this life. Now many will be damned who were not blasphemous in this life. Neither, therefore, will they blaspheme in the life to come.

On the contrary, It is written (Apoc. 16:9): "The men were scorched with great heat, and they blasphemed the name of God, Who hath power over these plagues," and a gloss on these words says that "those who are in hell, though aware that they are deservedly punished, will nevertheless complain that God is so powerful as to torture them thus." Now this would be blasphemy in their present state: and consequently it will also be in their future state.

I answer that, As stated above (AA. 1, 3), detestation of the Divine goodness is a necessary condition of blasphemy. Now those who are in hell retain their wicked will which is turned away from God's justice, since they love the things for which they are punished, would wish to use them if they could, and hate the punishments inflicted on them for those same sins. They regret indeed the sins which they have committed, not because they hate them, but because they are punished for them. Accordingly this detestation of the Divine justice is, in them, the interior blasphemy of the heart: and it is credible that after the resurrection they will blaspheme God with the tongue, even as the saints will praise Him with their voices.

Reply Obj. 1: In the present life men are deterred from blasphemy through fear of punishment which they think they can escape: whereas, in hell, the damned have no hope of escape, so that, in despair, they are borne towards whatever their wicked will suggests to them.

Reply Obj. 2: Merit and demerit belong to the state of a wayfarer, wherefore good is meritorious in them, while evil is demeritorious. In the blessed, on the other hand, good is not meritorious, but is part of their blissful reward, and, in like manner, in the damned, evil is not demeritorious, but is part of the punishment of damnation.

Reply Obj. 3: Whoever dies in mortal sin, bears with him a will that detests the Divine justice with regard to a certain thing, and in this respect there can be blasphemy in him.

14. OF BLASPHEMY AGAINST THE HOLY GHOST (In Four Articles)

We must now consider in particular blasphemy against the Holy Ghost: under which head there are four points of inquiry:

(1) Whether blasphemy or the sin against the Holy Ghost is the same as the sin committed through certain malice?
(2) Of the species of this sin;
(3) Whether it can be forgiven?
(4) Whether it is possible to begin by sinning against the Holy Ghost before committing other sins?.

* * * * *

FIRST ARTICLE [II-II, Q. 14, Art. 1]

Whether the Sin Against the Holy Ghost Is the Same As the Sin Committed Through Certain Malice?

Objection 1: It would seem that the sin against the Holy Ghost is not the same as the sin committed through certain malice. Because the sin against the Holy Ghost is the sin of blasphemy, according to Matt. 12:32. But not every sin committed through certain malice is a sin of blasphemy: since many other kinds of sin may be committed through certain malice. Therefore the sin against the Holy Ghost is not the same as the sin committed through certain malice.

Obj. 2: Further, the sin committed through certain malice is condivided with sin committed through ignorance, and sin committed through weakness: whereas the sin against the Holy Ghost is condivided with the sin against the Son of Man (Matt. 12:32). Therefore the sin against the Holy Ghost is not the same as the sin committed through certain malice, since things whose opposites differ, are themselves different.

Obj. 3: Further, the sin against the Holy Ghost is itself a generic sin, having its own determinate species: whereas sin committed through certain malice is not a special kind of sin, but a condition or general circumstance of sin, which can affect any kind of sin at all. Therefore the sin against the Holy Ghost is not the same as the sin committed through certain malice.

On the contrary, The Master says (Sent. ii, D, 43) that "to sin against the Holy Ghost is to take pleasure in the malice of sin for its own sake." Now this is to sin through certain malice. Therefore it seems that the sin committed through certain malice is the same as the sin against the Holy Ghost.

I answer that, Three meanings have been given to the sin against the Holy Ghost. For the earlier doctors, viz. Athanasius (Super Matth. xii, 32), Hilary (Can. xii in Matth.), Ambrose (Super Luc. xii, 10), Jerome (Super Matth. xii), and Chrysostom (Hom. xli in Matth.), say that the sin against the Holy Ghost is literally to utter a blasphemy against the Holy Spirit, whether by Holy Spirit we understand the essential name applicable to the whole Trinity, each Person of which is a Spirit and is holy, or the personal name of one of the Persons of the Trinity, in which sense blasphemy against the Holy Ghost is distinct from the blasphemy against the Son of Man (Matt. 12:32), for Christ did certain things in respect of His human nature, by eating, drinking, and such like actions, while He did others in respect of His Godhead, by casting out devils, raising the dead, and the like: which things He did both by the power of His own Godhead and by the operation of the Holy Ghost, of Whom He was full, according to his human nature. Now the Jews began by speaking blasphemy against the Son of Man, when they said (Matt. 11:19) that He was "a glutton . . . a wine drinker," and a "friend of publicans": but afterwards they blasphemed against the Holy Ghost, when they ascribed to the prince of devils those works which Christ did by the power of His own Divine Nature and by the operation of the Holy Ghost.

Augustine, however (De Verb. Dom., Serm. lxxi), says that blasphemy or the sin against the Holy Ghost, is final impenitence when, namely, a man perseveres in mortal sin until death, and that it is not confined to utterance by word of mouth, but extends to words in thought and deed, not to one word only, but to many. Now this word, in this sense, is said to be uttered against the Holy Ghost, because it is contrary to the remission of sins, which is the work of the Holy Ghost, Who is the charity both of the Father and of the Son. Nor did Our Lord say this to the Jews, as though they had sinned against the Holy Ghost, since they were not yet guilty of final impenitence, but He warned them, lest by similar utterances they should come to sin against the Holy Ghost: and it is in this sense that we are to understand Mark 3:29, 30, where after Our Lord had said: "But he that shall blaspheme against the Holy Ghost," etc. the Evangelist adds, "because they said: He hath an unclean spirit."

But others understand it differently, and say that the sin of blasphemy against the Holy Ghost, is a sin committed against that good which is appropriated to the Holy Ghost: because goodness is appropriated to the Holy Ghost, just a power is appropriated to the Father, and wisdom to the Son. Hence they say that when a man sins through weakness, it is a sin "against the Father"; that when he sins through ignorance, it is a sin "against the Son"; and that when he sins through certain malice, i.e. through the very choosing of evil, as explained above (I-II, Q. 78, AA. 1, 3), it is a sin "against the Holy Ghost."

Now this may happen in two ways. First by reason of the very inclination of a vicious habit which we call malice, and, in this way, to sin through malice is not the same as to sin against the Holy Ghost. In another way it happens that by reason of contempt, that which might have prevented the choosing of evil, is rejected or removed; thus hope is removed by despair, and fear by presumption, and so on, as we shall explain further on (QQ. 20, 21). Now all these things which prevent the choosing of sin are effects of the Holy Ghost in us; so that, in this sense, to sin through malice is to sin against the Holy Ghost.

Reply Obj. 1: Just as the confession of faith consists in a protestation not only of words but also of deeds, so blasphemy against the Holy Ghost can be uttered in word, thought and deed.

Reply Obj. 2: According to the third interpretation, blasphemy against the Holy Ghost is condivided with blasphemy against the Son of Man, forasmuch as He is also the Son of God, i.e. the "power of God and the wisdom of God" (1 Cor. 1:24). Wherefore, in this sense, the sin against the Son of Man will be that which is committed through ignorance, or through weakness.

Reply Obj. 3: Sin committed through certain malice, in so far as it results from the inclination of a habit, is not a special sin, but a general condition of sin: whereas, in so far as it results from a special contempt of an effect of the Holy Ghost in us, it has the character of a special sin. According to this interpretation the sin against the Holy Ghost is a special kind of sin, as also according to the first interpretation: whereas according to the second, it is not a species of sin, because final impenitence may be a circumstance of any kind of sin.

* * * * *

SECOND ARTICLE [II-II, Q. 14, Art. 2]

Whether It Is Fitting to Distinguish Six Kinds of Sin Against the Holy Ghost?

Obj. 2: Further, impenitence, seemingly, regards past sins, while obstinacy regards future sins. Now past and future time do not diversify the species of virtues or vices, since it is the same faith whereby we believe that Christ was born, and those of old believed that He would be born. Therefore obstinacy and impenitence should not be reckoned as two species of sin against the Holy Ghost.

Obj. 3: Further, "grace and truth came by Jesus Christ" (John 1:17). Therefore it seem that resistance of the known truth, and envy of a brother's spiritual good, belong to blasphemy against the Son rather than against the Holy Ghost.

Obj. 4: Further, Bernard says (De Dispens. et Praecept. xi) that "to refuse to obey is to resist the Holy Ghost." Moreover a gloss on Lev. 10:16, says that "a feigned repentance is a blasphemy against the Holy Ghost." Again, schism is, seemingly, directly opposed to the Holy Ghost by Whom the Church is united together. Therefore it seems that the species of sins against the Holy Ghost are insufficiently enumerated.

On the contrary, Augustine[1] (De Fide ad Petrum iii) says that "those who despair of pardon for their sins, or who without merits presume on God's mercy, sin against the Holy Ghost," and (Enchiridion lxxxiii) that "he who dies in a state of obstinacy is guilty of the sin against the Holy Ghost," and (De Verb. Dom., Serm. lxxi) that "impenitence is a sin against the Holy Ghost," and (De Serm. Dom. in Monte xxii), that "to resist fraternal goodness with the brands of envy is to sin against the Holy Ghost," and in his book De unico Baptismo (De Bap. contra Donat. vi, 35) he says that "a man who spurns the truth, is either envious of his brethren to whom the truth is revealed, or ungrateful to God, by Whose inspiration the Church is taught," and therefore, seemingly, sins against the Holy Ghost.

I answer that, The above species are fittingly assigned to the sin against the Holy Ghost taken in the third sense, because they are distinguished in respect of the removal or contempt of those things whereby a man can be prevented from sinning through choice. These things are either on the part of God's judgment, or on the part of His gifts, or on the part of sin. For, by consideration of the Divine judgment, wherein justice is accompanied with mercy, man is hindered from sinning through choice, both by hope, arising from the consideration of the mercy that pardons sins and rewards good deeds, which hope is removed by "despair"; and by fear, arising from the consideration of the Divine justice that punishes sins, which fear is removed by "presumption," when, namely, a man presumes that he can obtain glory without merits, or pardon without repentance.

God's gifts whereby we are withdrawn from sin, are two: one is the acknowledgment of the truth, against which there is the "resistance of the known truth," when, namely, a man resists the truth which he has acknowledged, in order to sin more freely: while the other is the assistance of inward grace, against which there is "envy of a brother's spiritual good," when, namely, a man is envious not only of his brother's person, but also of the increase of Divine grace in the world.

---

1 Fulgentius

On the part of sin, there are two things which may withdraw man therefrom: one is the inordinateness and shamefulness of the act, the consideration of which is wont to arouse man to repentance for the sin he has committed, and against this there is "impenitence," not as denoting permanence in sin until death, in which sense it was taken above (for thus it would not be a special sin, but a circumstance of sin), but as denoting the purpose of not repenting. The other thing is the smallness or brevity of the good which is sought in sin, according to Rom. 6:21: "What fruit had you therefore then in those things, of which you are now ashamed?" The consideration of this is wont to prevent man's will from being hardened in sin, and this is removed by "obstinacy," whereby man hardens his purpose by clinging to sin. Of these two it is written (Jer. 8:6): "There is none that doth penance for his sin, saying: What have I done?" as regards the first; and, "They are all turned to their own course, as a horse rushing to the battle," as regards the second.

Reply Obj. 1: The sins of despair and presumption consist, not in disbelieving in God's justice and mercy, but in contemning them.

Reply Obj. 2: Obstinacy and impenitence differ not only in respect of past and future time, but also in respect of certain formal aspects by reason of the diverse consideration of those things which may be considered in sin, as explained above.

Reply Obj. 3: Grace and truth were the work of Christ through the gifts of the Holy Ghost which He gave to men.

Reply Obj. 4: To refuse to obey belongs to obstinacy, while a feigned repentance belongs to impenitence, and schism to the envy of a brother's spiritual good, whereby the members of the Church are united together.

* * * * *

THIRD ARTICLE [II-II, Q. 14, Art. 3]

Whether the Sin Against the Holy Ghost Can Be Forgiven?

Objection 1: It would seem that the sin against the Holy Ghost can be forgiven. For Augustine says (De Verb. Dom., Serm. lxxi): "We should despair of no man, so long as Our Lord's patience brings him back to repentance." But if any sin cannot be forgiven, it would be possible to despair of some sinners. Therefore the sin against the Holy Ghost can be forgiven.

Obj. 2: Further, no sin is forgiven, except through the soul being healed by God. But "no disease is incurable to an all-powerful physician," as a gloss says on Ps. 102:3, "Who healeth all thy diseases." Therefore the sin against the Holy Ghost can be forgiven.

Obj. 3: Further, the free-will is indifferent to either good or evil. Now, so long as man is a wayfarer, he can fall away from any virtue, since even an angel fell from heaven, wherefore it is written (Job 4:18, 19): "In His angels He found wickedness: how much more shall they that dwell in houses of clay?" Therefore, in like manner, a man can return from any sin to the state of justice. Therefore the sin against the Holy Ghost can be forgiven.

On the contrary, It is written (Matt. 12:32): "He that shall speak against the Holy Ghost, it shall not be forgiven him, neither in this world, nor in the world to come": and Augustine says (De Serm. Dom. in Monte i, 22) that "so great is the downfall of this sin that it cannot submit to the humiliation of asking for pardon."

I answer that, According to the various interpretations of the sin against the Holy Ghost, there are various ways in which it may be said that it cannot be forgiven. For if by the sin against the Holy Ghost we understand final impenitence, it is said to be unpardonable, since in no way is it pardoned: because the mortal sin wherein a man perseveres until death will not be forgiven in the life to come, since it was not remitted by repentance in this life.

According to the other two interpretations, it is said to be unpardonable, not as though it is nowise forgiven, but because, considered in itself, it deserves not to be pardoned: and this in two ways. First, as regards the punishment, since he that sins through ignorance or weakness, deserves less punishment, whereas he that sins through certain malice, can offer no excuse in alleviation of his punishment. Likewise those who blasphemed against the Son of Man before His Godhead was revealed, could have some excuse, on account of the weakness of the flesh which they perceived in Him, and hence, they deserved less punishment; whereas those who blasphemed against His very Godhead, by ascribing to the devil the works of the Holy Ghost, had no excuse in diminution of their punishment. Wherefore, according to Chrysostom's commentary

(Hom. xlii in Matth.), the Jews are said not to be forgiven this sin, neither in this world nor in the world to come, because they were punished for it, both in the present life, through the Romans, and in the life to come, in the pains of hell. Thus also Athanasius adduces the example of their forefathers who, first of all, wrangled with Moses on account of the shortage of water and bread; and this the Lord bore with patience, because they were to be excused on account of the weakness of the flesh: but afterwards they sinned more grievously when, by ascribing to an idol the favors bestowed by God Who had brought them out of Egypt, they blasphemed, so to speak, against the Holy Ghost, saying (Ex. 32:4): "These are thy gods, O Israel, that have brought thee out of the land of Egypt." Therefore the Lord both inflicted temporal punishment on them, since "there were slain on that day about three and twenty thousand men" (Ex. 32:28), and threatened them with punishment in the life to come, saying, (Ex. 32:34): "I, in the day of revenge, will visit this sin . . . of theirs."

Secondly, this may be understood to refer to the guilt: thus a disease is said to be incurable in respect of the nature of the disease, which removes whatever might be a means of cure, as when it takes away the power of nature, or causes loathing for food and medicine, although God is able to cure such a disease. So too, the sin against the Holy Ghost is said to be unpardonable, by reason of its nature, in so far as it removes those things which are a means towards the pardon of sins. This does not, however, close the way of forgiveness and healing to an all-powerful and merciful God, Who, sometimes, by a miracle, so to speak, restores spiritual health to such men.

Reply Obj. 1: We should despair of no man in this life, considering God's omnipotence and mercy. But if we consider the circumstances of sin, some are called (Eph. 2:2) "children of despair"[1].

Reply Obj. 2: This argument considers the question on the part of God's omnipotence, not on that of the circumstances of sin.

Reply Obj. 3: In this life the free-will does indeed ever remain subject to change: yet sometimes it rejects that whereby, so far as it is concerned, it can be turned to good. Hence considered in itself this sin is unpardonable, although God can pardon it.

---

1 Filios diffidentiae, which the Douay version renders "children of unbelief."

* * * * *

FOURTH ARTICLE [II-II, Q. 14, Art. 4]

Whether a Man Can Sin First of All Against the Holy Ghost?

Objection 1: It would seem that a man cannot sin first of all against the Holy Ghost, without having previously committed other sins. For the natural order requires that one should be moved to perfection from imperfection. This is evident as regards good things, according to Prov. 4:18: "The path of the just, as a shining light, goeth forwards and increases even to perfect day." Now, in evil things, the perfect is the greatest evil, as the Philosopher states (Metaph. v, text. 21). Since then the sin against the Holy Ghost is the most grievous sin, it seems that man comes to commit this sin through committing lesser sins.

Obj. 2: Further, to sin against the Holy Ghost is to sin through certain malice, or through choice. Now man cannot do this until he has sinned many times; for the Philosopher says (Ethic. v, 6, 9) that "although a man is able to do unjust deeds, yet he cannot all at once do them as an unjust man does," viz. from choice. Therefore it seems that the sin against the Holy Ghost cannot be committed except after other sins.

Obj. 3: Further, repentance and impenitence are about the same object. But there is no repentance, except about past sins. Therefore the same applies to impenitence which is a species of the sin against the Holy Ghost. Therefore the sin against the Holy Ghost presupposes other sins.

On the contrary, "It is easy in the eyes of God on a sudden to make a poor man rich" (Ecclus. 11:23). Therefore, conversely, it is possible for a man, according to the malice of the devil who tempts him, to be led to commit the most grievous of sins which is that against the Holy Ghost.

I answer that, As stated above (A. 1), in one way, to sin against the Holy Ghost is to sin through certain malice. Now one may sin through certain malice in two ways, as stated in the same place: first, through the inclination of a habit; but this is not, properly speaking, to sin against the Holy Ghost, nor does a man come to commit this sin all at once, in as much as sinful acts must precede so as to cause the habit that induces to sin. Secondly, one may sin through certain malice, by contemptuously rejecting the things whereby a man is withdrawn from sin. This is, properly speaking, to sin against the Holy Ghost, as stated above (A. 1); and this also, for the most part, presupposes other sins, for it is written (Prov. 18:3) that "the wicked man, when he is come into the depth of sins, contemneth."

Nevertheless it is possible for a man, in his first sinful act, to sin against the Holy Ghost by contempt, both on account of his free-will, and on account of the many previous dispositions, or again, through being vehemently moved to evil, while but feebly attached to good. Hence never or scarcely ever does it happen that the perfect sin all at once against the Holy Ghost: wherefore Origen says (Peri Archon. i, 3): "I do not think that anyone who stands on the highest step of perfection, can fail or fall suddenly; this can only happen by degrees and bit by bit."

The same applies, if the sin against the Holy Ghost be taken literally for blasphemy against the Holy Ghost. For such blasphemy as Our Lord speaks of, always proceeds from contemptuous malice.

If, however, with Augustine (De Verb. Dom., Serm. lxxi) we understand the sin against the Holy Ghost to denote final impenitence, it does not regard the question in point, because this sin against the Holy Ghost requires persistence in sin until the end of life.

Reply Obj. 1: Movement both in good and in evil is made, for the most part, from imperfect to perfect, according as man progresses in good or evil: and yet in both cases, one man can begin from a greater (good or evil) than another man does. Consequently, that from which a man begins can be perfect in good or evil according to its genus, although it may be imperfect as regards the series of good or evil actions whereby a man progresses in good or evil.

Reply Obj. 2: This argument considers the sin which is committed through certain malice, when it proceeds from the inclination of a habit.

Reply Obj. 3: If by impenitence we understand with Augustine (De Verb. Dom., Serm. lxxi) persistence in sin until the end, it is clear that it presupposes sin, just as repentance does. If, however, we take it for habitual impenitence, in which sense it is a sin against the Holy Ghost, it is evident that it can precede sin: for it is possible for a man who has never sinned to have the purpose either of repenting or of not repenting, if he should happen to sin.

15. OF THE VICES OPPOSED TO KNOWLEDGE AND UNDERSTANDING
(In Three Articles)

We must now consider the vices opposed to knowledge and understanding. Since, however, we have treated of ignorance which is opposed to knowledge, when we were discussing the causes of sins (I-II, Q. 76), we must now inquire about blindness of mind and dulness of sense, which are opposed to the gift of understanding; and under this head there are three points of inquiry:

(1) Whether blindness of mind is a sin?
(2) Whether dulness of sense is a sin distinct from blindness of mind?
(3) Whether these vices arise from sins of the flesh?.

* * * * *

FIRST ARTICLE [II-II, Q. 15, Art. 1]
Whether Blindness of Mind Is a Sin?

Objection 1: It would seem that blindness of mind is not a sin. Because, seemingly, that which excuses from sin is not itself a sin. Now blindness of mind excuses from sin; for it is written (John 9:41): "If you were blind, you should not have sin." Therefore blindness of mind is not a sin.

Obj. 2: Further, punishment differs from guilt. But blindness of mind is a punishment as appears from Isa. 6:10, "Blind the heart of this people," for, since it is an evil, it could not be from God, were it not a punishment. Therefore blindness of mind is not a sin.

Obj. 3: Further, every sin is voluntary, according to Augustine (De Vera Relig. xiv). Now blindness of mind is not voluntary, since, as Augustine says (Confess. x), "all love to know the resplendent truth," and as we read in Eccles. 11:7, "the light is sweet and it is delightful for the eyes to see the sun." Therefore blindness of mind is not a sin.

On the contrary, Gregory (Moral. xxxi, 45) reckons blindness of mind among the vices arising from lust.

I answer that, Just as bodily blindness is the privation of the principle of bodily sight, so blindness of mind is the privation of the principle of mental or intellectual sight. Now this has a threefold principle. One is the light of natural reason, which light, since it pertains to the species of the rational soul, is never forfeit from the soul, and yet, at times, it is prevented from exercising its proper act, through being hindered by the lower powers which the human intellect needs in order to understand, for instance in the case of imbeciles and madmen, as stated in the First Part (Q. 84, AA. 7, 8).

Another principle of intellectual sight is a certain habitual light superadded to the natural light of reason, which light is sometimes forfeit from the soul. This privation is blindness, and is a punishment, in so far as the privation of the light of grace is a punishment. Hence it is written concerning some (Wis. 2:21): "Their own malice blinded them."

A third principle of intellectual sight is an intelligible principle, through which a man understands other things; to which principle a man may attend or not attend. That he does not attend thereto happens in two ways. Sometimes it is due to the fact that a man's will is deliberately turned away from the consideration of that principle, according to Ps. 35:4, "He would not understand, that he might do well": whereas sometimes it is due to the mind being more busy about things which it loves more, so as to be hindered thereby from considering this principle, according to Ps. 57:9, "Fire," i.e. of concupiscence, "hath fallen on them and they shall not see the sun." In either of these ways blindness of mind is a sin.

Reply Obj. 1: The blindness that excuses from sin is that which arises from the natural defect of one who cannot see.

Reply Obj. 2: This argument considers the second kind of blindness which is a punishment.

Reply Obj. 3: To understand the truth is, in itself, beloved by all; and yet, accidentally it may be hateful to someone, in so far as a man is hindered thereby from having what he loves yet more.

* * * * *

SECOND ARTICLE [II-II, Q. 15, Art. 2]

Whether Dulness of Sense Is a Sin Distinct from Blindness of Mind?

Objection 1: It seems that dulness of sense is not a distinct sin from blindness of mind. Because one thing has one contrary.

Now dulness is opposed to the gift of understanding, according to Gregory (Moral. ii, 49); and so is blindness of mind, since understanding denotes a principle of sight. Therefore dulness of sense is the same as blindness of mind.

Obj. 2: Further, Gregory (Moral. xxxi, 45) in speaking of dulness describes it as "dulness of sense in respect of understanding." Now dulness of sense in respect of understanding seems to be the same as a defect in understanding, which pertains to blindness of mind. Therefore dulness of sense is the same as blindness of mind.

Obj. 3: Further, if they differ at all, it seems to be chiefly in the fact that blindness of mind is voluntary, as stated above (A. 1), while dulness of sense is a natural defect. But a natural defect is not a sin: so that, accordingly, dulness of sense would not be a sin, which is contrary to what Gregory says (Moral. xxxi, 45), where he reckons it among the sins arising from gluttony.

On the contrary, Different causes produce different effects. Now Gregory says (Moral. xxxi, 45) that dulness of sense arises from gluttony, and that blindness of mind arises from lust. Now these others are different vices. Therefore those are different vices also.

I answer that, Dull is opposed to sharp: and a thing is said to be sharp because it can pierce; so that a thing is called dull through being obtuse and unable to pierce. Now a bodily sense, by a kind of metaphor, is said to pierce the medium, in so far as it perceives its object from a distance or is able by penetration as it were to perceive the smallest details or the inmost parts of a thing. Hence in corporeal things the senses are said to be acute when they can perceive a sensible object from afar, by sight, hearing, or scent, while on the other hand they are said to be dull, through being unable to perceive, except sensible objects that are near at hand, or of great power.

Now, by way of similitude to bodily sense, we speak of sense in connection with the intellect; and this latter sense is in respect of certain primals and extremes, as stated in *Ethic.* vi, even as the senses are cognizant of sensible objects as of certain principles of knowledge. Now this sense which is connected with understanding, does not perceive its object through a medium of corporeal distance, but through certain other media, as, for instance, when it perceives a thing's essence through a property thereof, and the cause through its effect. Consequently a man is said to have an acute sense in connection with his understanding, if, as soon as he apprehends a property or effect of a thing, he understands the nature or the thing itself, and if he can succeed in perceiving its slightest details: whereas a man is said to have a dull sense in connection with his understanding, if he cannot arrive at knowing the truth about a thing, without many explanations; in which case, moreover, he is unable to obtain a perfect perception of everything pertaining to the nature of that thing.

Accordingly dulness of sense in connection with understanding denotes a certain weakness of the mind as to the consideration of spiritual goods; while blindness of mind implies the complete privation of the knowledge of such things. Both are opposed to the gift of understanding, whereby a man knows spiritual goods by apprehending them, and has a subtle penetration of their inmost nature. This dulness has the character of sin, just as blindness of mind has, that is, in so far as it is voluntary, as evidenced in one who, owing to his affection for carnal things, dislikes or neglects the careful consideration of spiritual things.

This suffices for the Replies to the Objections.

* * * * *

THIRD ARTICLE [II-II, Q. 15, Art. 3]

Whether Blindness of Mind and Dulness of
Sense Arise from Sins of the Flesh?

Objection 1: It would seem that blindness of mind and dulness of sense do not arise from sins of the flesh. For Augustine (Retract. i, 4) retracts what he had said in his Soliloquies i, 1, "God Who didst wish none but the clean to know the truth," and says that one might reply that "many, even those who are unclean, know many truths." Now men become unclean chiefly by sins of the flesh. Therefore blindness of mind and dulness of sense are not caused by sins of the flesh.

Obj. 2: Further, blindness of mind and dulness of sense are defects in connection with the intellective part of the soul: whereas carnal sins pertain to the corruption of the flesh. But the flesh does not act on the soul, but rather the reverse. Therefore the sins of the flesh do not cause blindness of mind and dulness of sense.

Obj. 3: Further, all things are more passive to what is near them than to what is remote. Now spiritual vices are nearer the mind than carnal vices are. Therefore blindness of mind and dulness of sense are caused by spiritual rather than by carnal vices.

On the contrary, Gregory says (Moral. xxxi, 45) that dulness of sense arises from gluttony and blindness of mind from lust.

I answer that, The perfect intellectual operation in man consists in an abstraction from sensible phantasms, wherefore the more a man's intellect is freed from those phantasms, the more thoroughly will it be able to consider things intelligible, and to set in order all things sensible. Thus Anaxagoras stated that the intellect requires to be "detached" in order to command, and that the agent must have power over matter, in order to be able to move it. Now it is evident that pleasure fixes a man's attention on that which he takes pleasure in: wherefore the Philosopher says (Ethic. x, 4, 5) that we all do best that which we take pleasure in doing, while as to other things, we do them either not at all, or in a faint-hearted fashion.

Now carnal vices, namely gluttony and lust, are concerned with pleasures of touch in matters of food and sex; and these are the most impetuous of all pleasures of the body. For this reason these vices cause man's attention to be very firmly fixed on corporeal things, so that in consequence man's operation in regard to intelligible things is weakened, more, however, by lust than by gluttony, forasmuch as sexual pleasures are more vehement than those of the table. Wherefore lust gives rise to blindness of mind, which excludes almost entirely the knowledge of spiritual things, while dulness of sense arises from gluttony, which makes a man weak in regard to the same intelligible things. On the other hand, the contrary virtues, viz. abstinence and chastity, dispose man very much to the perfection of intellectual operation. Hence it is written (Dan. 1:17) that "to these children" on account of their abstinence and continency, "God gave knowledge and understanding in every book, and wisdom."

Reply Obj. 1: Although some who are the slaves of carnal vices are at times capable of subtle considerations about intelligible things, on account of the perfection of their natural genius, or of some habit superadded thereto, nevertheless, on account of the pleasures of the body, it must needs happen that their attention is frequently withdrawn from this subtle contemplation: wherefore the unclean can know some truths, but their uncleanness is a clog on their knowledge.

Reply Obj. 2: The flesh acts on the intellective faculties, not by altering them, but by impeding their operation in the aforesaid manner.

Reply Obj. 3: It is owing to the fact that the carnal vices are further removed from the mind, that they distract the mind's attention to more remote things, so that they hinder the mind's contemplation all the more.

16. OF THE PRECEPTS OF FAITH, KNOWLEDGE AND UNDERSTANDING
(In Two Articles)

We must now consider the precepts pertaining to the aforesaid, and under this head there are two points of inquiry:

(1) The precepts concerning faith;
(2) The precepts concerning the gifts of knowledge and understanding.

* * * * *

FIRST ARTICLE [II-II, Q. 16, Art. 1]

Whether in the Old Law There Should Have Been Given Precepts of Faith?

Objection 1: It would seem that, in the Old Law, there should have been given precepts of faith. Because a precept is about something due and necessary. Now it is most necessary for man that he should believe, according to Heb. 11:6, "Without faith it is impossible to please God." Therefore there was very great need for precepts of faith to be given.

Obj. 2: Further, the New Testament is contained in the Old, as the reality in the figure, as stated above (I-II, Q. 107, A. 3). Now the New Testament contains explicit precepts of faith, for instance John 14:1: "You believe in God; believe also in Me." Therefore it seems that some precepts of faith ought to have been given in the Old Law also.

Obj. 3: Further, to prescribe the act of a virtue comes to the same as to forbid the opposite vices. Now the Old Law contained many precepts forbidding unbelief: thus (Ex. 20:3): "Thou shalt not have strange gods before Me," and (Deut. 13:1-3) they were forbidden to hear the words of the prophet or dreamer who might wish to turn them away from their faith in God. Therefore precepts of faith should have been given in the Old Law also.

Obj. 4: Further, confession is an act of faith, as stated above (Q. 3, A. 1). Now the Old Law contained precepts about the confession and the promulgation of faith: for they were commanded (Ex. 12:27) that, when their children should ask them, they should tell them the meaning of the paschal observance, and (Deut. 13:9) they were commanded to slay anyone who disseminated doctrine contrary to faith. Therefore the Old Law should have contained precepts of faith.

Obj. 5: Further, all the books of the Old Testament are contained in the Old Law; wherefore Our Lord said (John 15:25) that it was written in the Law: "They have hated Me without cause," although this is found written in Ps. 34 and 68. Now it is written (Ecclus. 2:8): "Ye that fear the Lord, believe Him." Therefore the Old Law should have contained precepts of faith.

On the contrary, The Apostle (Rom. 3:27) calls the Old Law the "law of works" which he contrasts with the "law of faith." Therefore the Old Law ought not to have contained precepts of faith.

I answer that, A master does not impose laws on others than his subjects; wherefore the precepts of a law presuppose that everyone who receives the law is subject to the giver of the law. Now the primary subjection of man to God is by faith, according to Heb. 11:6: "He that cometh to God, must believe that He is." Hence faith is presupposed to the precepts of the Law: for which reason (Ex. 20:2) that which is of faith, is set down before the legal precepts, in the words, "I am the Lord thy God, Who brought thee out of the land of Egypt," and, likewise (Deut. 6:4), the words, "Hear, O Israel, the Lord thy [Vulg.: 'our'] God is one," precede the recording of the precepts.

Since, however, faith contains many things subordinate to the faith whereby we believe that God is, which is the first and chief of all articles of faith, as stated above (Q. 1, AA. 1, 7), it follows that, if we presuppose faith in God, whereby man's mind is subjected to Him, it is possible for precepts to be given about other articles of faith. Thus Augustine expounding the words: "This is

My commandment" (John 15:12) says (Tract. lxxxiii in Joan.) that we have received many precepts of faith. In the Old Law, however, the secret things of faith were not to be set before the people, wherefore, presupposing their faith in one God, no other precepts of faith were given in the Old Law.

Reply Obj. 1: Faith is necessary as being the principle of spiritual life, wherefore it is presupposed before the receiving of the Law.

Reply Obj. 2: Even then Our Lord both presupposed something of faith, namely belief in one God, when He said: "You believe in God," and commanded something, namely, belief in the Incarnation whereby one Person is God and man. This explanation of faith belongs to the faith of the New Testament, wherefore He added: "Believe also in Me."

Reply Obj. 3: The prohibitive precepts regard sins, which corrupt virtue. Now virtue is corrupted by any particular defect, as stated above (I-II, Q. 18, A. 4, ad 3; I-II, Q. 19, A. 6, ad 1, A. 7, ad 3). Therefore faith in one God being presupposed, prohibitive precepts had to be given in the Old Law, so that men might be warned off those particular defects whereby their faith might be corrupted.

Reply Obj. 4: Confession of faith and the teaching thereof also presuppose man's submission to God by faith: so that the Old Law could contain precepts relating to the confession and teaching of faith, rather than to faith itself.

Reply Obj. 5: In this passage again that faith is presupposed whereby we believe that God is; hence it begins, "Ye that fear the Lord," which is not possible without faith. The words which follow—"believe Him"—must be referred to certain special articles of faith, chiefly to those things which God promises to them that obey Him, wherefore the passage concludes—"and your reward shall not be made void.".

* * * * *

SECOND ARTICLE [II-II, Q. 16, Art. 2]

Whether the Precepts Referring to Knowledge and Understanding Were Fittingly Set Down in the Old Law?

Objection 1: It would seem that the precepts referring to knowledge and understanding were unfittingly set down in the

Old Law. For knowledge and understanding pertain to cognition. Now cognition precedes and directs action. Therefore the precepts referring to knowledge and understanding should precede the precepts of the Law referring to action. Since, then, the first precepts of the Law are those of the decalogue, it seems that precepts of knowledge and understanding should have been given a place among the precepts of the decalogue.

Obj. 2: Further, learning precedes teaching, for a man must learn from another before he teaches another. Now the Old Law contains precepts about teaching—both affirmative precepts as, for example, (Deut. 4:9), "Thou shalt teach them to thy sons"— and prohibitive precepts, as, for instance, (Deut. 4:2), "You shall not add to the word that I speak to you, neither shall you take away from it." Therefore it seems that man ought to have been given also some precepts directing him to learn.

Obj. 3: Further, knowledge and understanding seem more necessary to a priest than to a king, wherefore it is written (Malachi 2:7): "The lips of the priest shall keep knowledge, and they shall seek the law at his mouth," and (Osee 4:6): "Because thou hast rejected knowledge, I will reject thee, that thou shalt not do the office of priesthood to Me." Now the king is commanded to learn knowledge of the Law (Deut. 17:18, 19). Much more therefore should the Law have commanded the priests to learn the Law.

Obj. 4: Further, it is not possible while asleep to meditate on things pertaining to knowledge and understanding: moreover it is hindered by extraneous occupations. Therefore it is unfittingly commanded (Deut. 6:7): "Thou shalt meditate upon them sitting in thy house, and walking on thy journey, sleeping and rising." Therefore the precepts relating to knowledge and understanding are unfittingly set down in the Law.

On the contrary, It is written (Deut. 4:6): "That, hearing all these precepts, they may say, Behold a wise and understanding people."

I answer that, Three things may be considered in relation to knowledge and understanding: first, the reception thereof; secondly, the use; and thirdly, their preservation. Now the reception of knowledge or understanding, is by means of teaching and learning, and both are prescribed in the Law. For it is written (Deut. 6:6): "These words which I command thee ... shall be in thy heart." This refers to learning, since it is the duty of a disciple to apply his mind to what is said, while the words that follow—"and thou shalt tell them to thy children"—refer to teaching.

The use of knowledge and understanding is the meditation on those things which one knows or understands. In reference to this, the text goes on: "thou shalt meditate upon them sitting in thy house," etc.

Their preservation is effected by the memory, and, as regards this, the text continues—"and thou shalt bind them as a sign on thy hand, and they shall be and shall move between thy eyes. And thou shalt write them in the entry, and on the doors of thy house." Thus the continual remembrance of God's commandments is signified, since it is impossible for us to forget those things which are continually attracting the notice of our senses, whether by touch, as those things we hold in our hands, or by sight, as those things which are ever before our eyes, or to which we are continually returning, for instance, to the house door. Moreover it is clearly stated (Deut. 4:9): "Forget not the words that thy eyes have seen and let them not go out of thy heart all the days of thy life."

We read of these things also being commanded more notably in the New Testament, both in the teaching of the Gospel and in that of the apostles.

Reply Obj. 1: According to Deut. 4:6, "this is your wisdom and understanding in the sight of the nations." By this we are given to understand that the wisdom and understanding of those who believe in God consist in the precepts of the Law. Wherefore the precepts of the Law had to be given first, and afterwards men had to be led to know and understand them, and so it was not fitting that the aforesaid precepts should be placed among the precepts of the decalogue which take the first place.

Reply Obj. 2: There are also in the Law precepts relating to learning, as stated above. Nevertheless teaching was commanded more expressly than learning, because it concerned the learned, who were not under any other authority, but were immediately under the law, and to them the precepts of the Law were given. On the other hand learning concerned the people of lower degree, and these the precepts of the Law have to reach through the learned.

Reply Obj. 3: Knowledge of the Law is so closely bound up with the priestly office that being charged with the office implies being charged to know the Law: hence there was no need for special precepts to be given about the training of the priests. On the other hand, the doctrine of God's law is not so bound up with the kingly office, because a king is placed over his people in temporal matters: hence it is especially commanded that the king should be instructed by the priests about things pertaining to the law of God.

Reply Obj. 4: That precept of the Law does not mean that man should meditate on God's law by sleeping, but during sleep, i.e. that he should meditate on the law of God when he is preparing to sleep, because this leads to his having better phantasms while asleep, in so far as our movements pass from the state of vigil to the state of sleep, as the Philosopher explains (Ethic. i, 13). In like manner we are commanded to meditate on the Law in every action of ours, not that we are bound to be always actually thinking about the Law, but that we should regulate all our actions according to it.

17. OF HOPE, CONSIDERED IN ITSELF
(In Eight Articles)

After treating of faith, we must consider hope and (1) hope itself; (2) the gift of fear; (3) the contrary vices; (4) the corresponding precepts. The first of these points gives rise to a twofold consideration: (1) hope, considered in itself; (2) its subject.

Under the first head there are eight points of inquiry:

(1) Whether hope is a virtue?
(2) Whether its object is eternal happiness?
(3) Whether, by the virtue of hope, one man may hope for another's happiness?
(4) Whether a man may lawfully hope in man?
(5) Whether hope is a theological virtue?
(6) Of its distinction from the other theological virtues?
(7) Of its relation to faith;
(8) Of its relation to charity.

* * * * *

FIRST ARTICLE [II-II, Q. 17, Art. 1]

Whether Hope Is a Virtue?

Objection 1: It would seem that hope is not a virtue. For "no man makes ill use of a virtue," as Augustine states (De Lib. Arb. ii, 18). But one may make ill use of hope, since the passion of hope, like the other passions, is subject to a mean and extremes. Therefore hope is not a virtue.

Obj. 2: Further, no virtue results from merits, since "God works virtue in us without us," as Augustine states (De Grat. et Lib. Arb. xvii). But hope is caused by grace and merits, according to the Master (Sent. iii, D, 26). Therefore hope is not a virtue.

Obj. 3: Further, "virtue is the disposition of a perfect thing" (Phys. vii, text. 17, 18). But hope is the disposition of an imperfect thing, of one, namely, that lacks what it hopes to have. Therefore hope is not a virtue.

On the contrary, Gregory says (Moral. i, 33) that the three daughters of Job signify these three virtues, faith, hope and charity. Therefore hope is a virtue.

I answer that, According to the Philosopher (Ethic. ii, 6) "the virtue of a thing is that which makes its subject good, and its work good likewise." Consequently wherever we find a good human act, it must correspond to some human virtue. Now in all things measured and ruled, the good is that which attains its proper rule: thus we say that a coat is good if it neither exceeds nor falls short of its proper measurement. But, as we stated above (Q. 8, A. 3, ad 3) human acts have a twofold measure; one is proximate and homogeneous, viz. the reason, while the other is remote and excelling, viz. God: wherefore every human act is good, which attains reason or God Himself. Now the act of hope, whereof we speak now, attains God. For, as we have already stated (I-II, Q. 40, A. 1), when we were treating of the passion of hope, the object of hope is a future good, difficult but possible to obtain. Now a thing is possible to us in two ways: first, by ourselves; secondly, by means of others, as stated in *Ethic.* iii. Wherefore, in so far as we hope for anything as being possible to us by means of the Divine assistance, our hope attains God Himself, on Whose help it leans. It is therefore evident that hope is a virtue, since it causes a human act to be good and to attain its due rule.

Reply Obj. 1: In the passions, the mean of virtue depends on right reason being attained, wherein also consists the essence of virtue. Wherefore in hope too, the good of virtue depends on a man's attaining, by hoping, the due rule, viz. God. Consequently man cannot make ill use of hope which attains God, as neither can he make ill use of moral virtue which attains the reason, because to attain thus is to make good use of virtue. Nevertheless, the hope of which we speak now, is not a passion but a habit of the mind, as we shall show further on (A. 5; Q. 18, A. 1).

Reply Obj. 2: Hope is said to arise from merits, as regards the thing hoped for, in so far as we hope to obtain happiness by means of grace and merits; or as regards the act of living hope. The habit itself of hope, whereby we hope to obtain happiness, does not flow from our merits, but from grace alone.

Reply Obj. 3: He who hopes is indeed imperfect in relation to that which he hopes to obtain, but has not as yet; yet he is perfect, in so far as he already attains his proper rule, viz. God, on Whose help he leans.

* * * * *

SECOND ARTICLE [II-II, Q. 17, Art. 2]

Whether Eternal Happiness Is the Proper Object of Hope?

Objection 1: It would seem that eternal happiness is not the proper object of hope. For a man does not hope for that which surpasses every movement of the soul, since hope itself is a movement of the soul. Now eternal happiness surpasses every movement of the human soul, for the Apostle says (1 Cor. 2:9) that it hath not "entered into the heart of man." Therefore happiness is not the proper object of hope.

Obj. 2: Further, prayer is an expression of hope, for it is written (Ps. 36:5): "Commit thy way to the Lord, and trust in Him, and He will do it." Now it is lawful for man to pray God not only for eternal happiness, but also for the goods, both temporal and spiritual, of the present life, and, as evidenced by the Lord's Prayer, to be delivered from evils which will no longer be in eternal happiness. Therefore eternal happiness is not the proper object of hope.

Obj. 3: Further, the object of hope is something difficult. Now many things besides eternal happiness are difficult to man. Therefore eternal happiness is not the proper object of hope.

On the contrary, The Apostle says (Heb. 6:19) that we have hope "which entereth in," i.e. maketh us to enter ... "within the veil," i.e. into the happiness of heaven, according to the interpretation of a gloss on these words. Therefore the object of hope is eternal happiness.

I answer that, As stated above (A. 1), the hope of which we speak now, attains God by leaning on His help in order to obtain the hoped for good. Now an effect must be proportionate to its cause. Wherefore the good which we ought to hope for from God properly and chiefly is the infinite good, which is proportionate to the power of our divine helper, since it belongs to an infinite power to lead anyone to an infinite good. Such a good is eternal life, which consists in the enjoyment of God Himself. For we should hope from Him for nothing less than Himself, since His goodness, whereby He imparts good things to His creature, is no less than His Essence. Therefore the proper and principal object of hope is eternal happiness.

Reply Obj. 1: Eternal happiness does not enter into the heart of man perfectly, i.e. so that it be possible for a wayfarer to know its nature and quality; yet, under the general notion of the perfect good, it is possible for it to be apprehended by a man, and it is in this way that the movement of hope towards it arises. Hence the Apostle says pointedly (Heb. 6:19) that hope "enters in, even within the veil," because that which we hope for is as yet veiled, so to speak.

Reply Obj. 2: We ought not to pray God for any other goods, except in reference to eternal happiness. Hence hope regards eternal happiness chiefly, and other things, for which we pray God, it regards secondarily and as referred to eternal happiness: just as faith regards God principally, and, secondarily, those things which are referred to God, as stated above (Q. 1, A. 1).

Reply Obj. 3: To him that longs for something great, all lesser things seem small; wherefore to him that hopes for eternal happiness, nothing else appears arduous, as compared with that hope; although, as compared with the capability of the man who hopes, other things besides may be arduous to him, so that he may have hope for such things in reference to its principal object.

* * * * *

THIRD ARTICLE [II-II, Q. 17, Art. 3]

Whether One Man May Hope for Another's Eternal Happiness?

Objection 1: It would seem that one may hope for another's eternal happiness. For the Apostle says (Phil. 1:6): "Being confident of this very thing, that He Who hath begun a good work in you, will perfect it unto the day of Jesus Christ." Now the perfection of that day will be eternal happiness. Therefore one man may hope for another's eternal happiness.

Obj. 2: Further, whatever we ask of God, we hope to obtain from Him. But we ask God to bring others to eternal happiness, according to James 5:16: "Pray for one another that you may be saved." Therefore we can hope for another's eternal happiness.

Obj. 3: Further, hope and despair are about the same object. Now it is possible to despair of another's eternal happiness, else Augustine would have no reason for saying (De Verb. Dom., Serm. lxxi) that we should not despair of anyone so long as he lives. Therefore one can also hope for another's eternal salvation.

On the contrary, Augustine says (Enchiridion viii) that "hope is only of such things as belong to him who is supposed to hope for them."

I answer that, We can hope for something in two ways: first, absolutely, and thus the object of hope is always something arduous and pertaining to the person who hopes. Secondly, we can hope for something, through something else being presupposed, and in this way its object can be something pertaining to someone else. In order to explain this we must observe that love and hope differ in this, that love denotes union between lover and beloved, while hope denotes a movement or a stretching forth of the appetite towards an arduous good. Now union is of things that are distinct, wherefore love can directly regard the other whom a man unites to himself by love, looking upon him as his other self: whereas movement is always towards its own term which is proportionate to the subject moved. Therefore hope regards directly one's own good, and not that which pertains to another. Yet if we presuppose the union of love with another, a man can hope for and desire something for another man, as for himself; and, accordingly, he can hope for another's eternal life, inasmuch as he is united to him by love, and just as it is the same virtue of charity whereby a man loves

God, himself, and his neighbor, so too it is the same virtue of hope, whereby a man hopes for himself and for another.

This suffices for the Replies to the Objections.

* * * * *

FOURTH ARTICLE [II-II, Q. 17, Art. 4]

Whether a Man Can Lawfully Hope in Man?

Objection 1: It would seem that one may lawfully hope in man. For the object of hope is eternal happiness. Now we are helped to obtain eternal happiness by the patronage of the saints, for Gregory says (Dial. i, 8) that "predestination is furthered by the saints' prayers." Therefore one may hope in man.

Obj. 2: Further, if a man may not hope in another man, it ought not to be reckoned a sin in a man, that one should not be able to hope in him. Yet this is reckoned a vice in some, as appears from Jer. 9:4: "Let every man take heed of his neighbor, and let him not trust in any brother of his." Therefore it is lawful to trust in a man.

Obj. 3: Further, prayer is the expression of hope, as stated above (A. 2, Obj. 2). But it is lawful to pray to a man for something. Therefore it is lawful to trust in him.

On the contrary, It is written (Jer. 17:5): "Cursed be the man that trusteth in man."

I answer that, Hope, as stated above (A. 1; I-II, Q. 40, A. 7), regards two things, viz. the good which it intends to obtain, and the help by which that good is obtained. Now the good which a man hopes to obtain, has the aspect of a final cause, while the help by which one hopes to obtain that good, has the character of an efficient cause. Now in each of these kinds of cause we find a principal and a secondary cause. For the principal end is the last end, while the secondary end is that which is referred to an end. In like manner the principal efficient cause is the first agent, while the secondary efficient cause is the secondary and instrumental agent. Now hope regards eternal happiness as its last end, and the Divine assistance as the first cause leading to happiness.

Accordingly, just as it is not lawful to hope for any good save happiness, as one's last end, but only as something referred to final happiness, so too, it is unlawful to hope in any man, or any creature, as though it were the first cause of movement towards happiness. It is, however, lawful to hope in a man or a creature as being the secondary and instrumental agent through whom one is helped to obtain any goods that are ordained to happiness. It is in this way that we turn to the saints, and that we ask men also for certain things; and for this reason some are blamed in that they cannot be trusted to give help.

This suffices for the Replies to the Objections.

* * * * *

FIFTH ARTICLE [II-II, Q. 17, Art. 5]

Whether Hope Is a Theological Virtue?

Objection 1: It would seem that hope is not a theological virtue. For a theological virtue is one that has God for its object. Now hope has for its object not only God but also other goods which we hope to obtain from God. Therefore hope is not a theological virtue.

Obj. 2: Further, a theological virtue is not a mean between two vices, as stated above (I-II, Q. 64, A. 4). But hope is a mean between presumption and despair. Therefore hope is not a theological virtue.

Obj. 3: Further, expectation belongs to longanimity which is a species of fortitude. Since, then, hope is a kind of expectation, it seems that hope is not a theological, but a moral virtue.

Obj. 4: Further, the object of hope is something arduous. But it belongs to magnanimity, which is a moral virtue, to tend to the arduous. Therefore hope is a moral, and not a theological virtue.

On the contrary, Hope is enumerated (1 Cor. 13) together with faith and charity, which are theological virtues.

I answer that, Since specific differences, by their very nature, divide a genus, in order to decide under what division we must place hope, we must observe whence it derives its character of virtue.

Now it has been stated above (A. 1) that hope has the character of virtue from the fact that it attains the supreme rule of human actions: and this it attains both as its first efficient cause, in as much as it leans on its assistance, and as its last final cause, in as much as it expects happiness in the enjoyment thereof. Hence it is evident that

God is the principal object of hope, considered as a virtue. Since, then, the very idea of a theological virtue is one that has God for its object, as stated above (I-II, Q. 62, A. 1), it is evident that hope is a theological virtue.

Reply Obj. 1: Whatever else hope expects to obtain, it hopes for it in reference to God as the last end, or as the first efficient cause, as stated above (A. 4).

Reply Obj. 2: In things measured and ruled the mean consists in the measure or rule being attained; if we go beyond the rule, there is excess, if we fall short of the rule, there is deficiency. But in the rule or measure itself there is no such thing as a mean or extremes. Now a moral virtue is concerned with things ruled by reason, and these things are its proper object; wherefore it is proper to it to follow the mean as regards its proper object. On the other hand, a theological virtue is concerned with the First Rule not ruled by another rule, and that Rule is its proper object. Wherefore it is not proper for a theological virtue, with regard to its proper object, to follow the mean, although this may happen to it accidentally with regard to something that is referred to its principal object. Thus faith can have no mean or extremes in the point of trusting to the First Truth, in which it is impossible to trust too much; whereas on the part of the things believed, it may have a mean and extremes; for instance one truth is a mean between two falsehoods. So too, hope has no mean or extremes, as regards its principal object, since it is impossible to trust too much in the Divine assistance; yet it may have a mean and extremes, as regards those things a man trusts to obtain, in so far as he either presumes above his capability, or despairs of things of which he is capable.

Reply Obj. 3: The expectation which is mentioned in the definition of hope does not imply delay, as does the expectation which belongs to longanimity. It implies a reference to the Divine assistance, whether that which we hope for be delayed or not.

Reply Obj. 4: Magnanimity tends to something arduous in the hope of obtaining something that is within one's power, wherefore its proper object is the doing of great things. On the other hand hope, as a theological virtue, regards something arduous, to be obtained by another's help, as stated above (A. 1).

* * * * *

SIXTH ARTICLE [II-II, Q. 17, Art. 6]

Whether Hope Is Distinct from the Other Theological Virtues?

Objection 1: It would seem that hope is not distinct from the other theological virtues. For habits are distinguished by their objects, as stated above (I-II, Q. 54, A. 2). Now the object of hope is the same as of the other theological virtues. Therefore hope is not distinct from the other theological virtues.

Obj. 2: Further, in the symbol of faith, whereby we make profession of faith, we say: "I expect the resurrection of the dead and the life of the world to come." Now expectation of future happiness belongs to hope, as stated above (A. 5). Therefore hope is not distinct from faith.

Obj. 3: Further, by hope man tends to God. But this belongs properly to charity. Therefore hope is not distinct from charity.

On the contrary, There cannot be number without distinction. Now hope is numbered with the other theological virtues: for Gregory says (Moral. i, 16) that the three virtues are faith, hope, and charity. Therefore hope is distinct from the theological virtues.

I answer that, A virtue is said to be theological from having God for the object to which it adheres. Now one may adhere to a thing in two ways: first, for its own sake; secondly, because something else is attained thereby. Accordingly charity makes us adhere to God for His own sake, uniting our minds to God by the emotion of love.

On the other hand, hope and faith make man adhere to God as to a principle wherefrom certain things accrue to us. Now we derive from God both knowledge of truth and the attainment of perfect goodness. Accordingly faith makes us adhere to God, as the source whence we derive the knowledge of truth, since we believe that what God tells us is true: while hope makes us adhere to God, as the source whence we derive perfect goodness, i.e. in so far as, by hope, we trust to the Divine assistance for obtaining happiness.

Reply Obj. 1: God is the object of these virtues under different aspects, as stated above: and a different aspect of the object suffices for the distinction of habits, as stated above (I-II, Q. 54, A. 2).

Reply Obj. 2: Expectation is mentioned in the symbol of faith, not as though it were the proper act of faith, but because the act of hope presupposes the act of faith, as we shall state further on (A. 7). Hence an act of faith is expressed in the act of hope.

Reply Obj. 3: Hope makes us tend to God, as to a good to be obtained finally, and as to a helper strong to assist: whereas charity, properly speaking, makes us tend to God, by uniting our affections to Him, so that we live, not for ourselves, but for God.

* * * * *

SEVENTH ARTICLE [II-II, Q. 17, Art. 7]

Whether Hope Precedes Faith?

Objection 1: It would seem that hope precedes faith. Because a gloss on Ps. 36:3, "Trust in the Lord, and do good," says: "Hope is the entrance to faith and the beginning of salvation." But salvation is by faith whereby we are justified. Therefore hope precedes faith.

Obj. 2: Further, that which is included in a definition should precede the thing defined and be more known. But hope is included in the definition of faith (Heb. 11:1): "Faith is the substance of things to be hoped for." Therefore hope precedes faith.

Obj. 3: Further, hope precedes a meritorious act, for the Apostle says (1 Cor. 9:10): "He that plougheth should plough in hope . . . to receive fruit." But the act of faith is meritorious. Therefore hope precedes faith.

On the contrary, It is written (Matt. 1:2): "Abraham begot Isaac," i.e. "Faith begot hope," according to a gloss.

I answer that, Absolutely speaking, faith precedes hope. For the object of hope is a future good, arduous but possible to obtain. In order, therefore, that we may hope, it is necessary for the object of hope to be proposed to us as possible. Now the object of hope is, in one way, eternal happiness, and in another way, the Divine assistance, as explained above (A. 2; A. 6, ad 3): and both of these are proposed to us by faith, whereby we come to know that we are able to obtain eternal life, and that for this purpose the Divine assistance is ready for us, according to Heb. 11:6: "He that cometh to God, must believe that He is, and is a rewarder to them that seek Him." Therefore it is evident that faith precedes hope.

Reply Obj. 1: As the same gloss observes further on, "hope" is called "the entrance" to faith, i.e. of the thing believed, because by hope we enter in to see what we believe. Or we may reply that it is called the "entrance to faith," because thereby man begins to be established and perfected in faith.

Reply Obj. 2: The thing to be hoped for is included in the definition of faith, because the proper object of faith, is something not apparent in itself. Hence it was necessary to express it in a circumlocution by something resulting from faith.

Reply Obj. 3: Hope does not precede every meritorious act; but it suffices for it to accompany or follow it.

* * * * *

EIGHTH ARTICLE [II-II, Q. 17, Art. 8]

Whether Charity Precedes Hope?

Objection 1: It would seem that charity precedes hope. For Ambrose says on Luke 27:6, "If you had faith like to a grain of mustard seed," etc.: "Charity flows from faith, and hope from charity." But faith precedes charity. Therefore charity precedes hope.

Obj. 2: Further, Augustine says (De Civ. Dei xiv, 9) that "good emotions and affections proceed from love and holy charity." Now to hope, considered as an act of hope, is a good emotion of the soul. Therefore it flows from charity.

Obj. 3: Further, the Master says (Sent. iii, D, 26) that hope proceeds from merits, which precede not only the thing hoped for, but also hope itself, which, in the order of nature, is preceded by charity. Therefore charity precedes hope.

On the contrary, The Apostle says (1 Tim. 1:5): "The end of the commandment is charity from a pure heart, and a good conscience," i.e. "from hope," according to a gloss. Therefore hope precedes charity.

I answer that, Order is twofold. One is the order of generation and of matter, in respect of which the imperfect precedes the perfect: the other is the order of perfection and form, in respect of which the perfect naturally precedes the imperfect. In respect of the first order hope precedes charity: and this is clear from the fact that hope and all movements of the appetite flow from love, as stated above (I-II, Q. 27, A. 4; I-II, Q. 28, A. 6, ad 2; I-II, Q. 40, A. 7) in the treatise on the passions.

Now there is a perfect, and an imperfect love. Perfect love is that whereby a man is loved in himself, as when someone wishes a person some good for his own sake; thus a man loves his friend. Imperfect love is that whereby a man love something, not for its own sake, but that he may obtain that good for himself; thus a man loves what he desires. The first love of God pertains to charity, which adheres to God for His own sake; while hope pertains to the second love, since he that hopes, intends to obtain possession of something for himself.

Hence in the order of generation, hope precedes charity. For just as a man is led to love God, through fear of being punished by Him for his sins, as Augustine states (In primam canon. Joan. Tract. ix), so too, hope leads to charity, in as much as a man through hoping to be rewarded by God, is encouraged to love God and obey His commandments. On the other hand, in the order of perfection charity naturally precedes hope, wherefore, with the advent of charity, hope is made more perfect, because we hope chiefly in our friends. It is in this sense that Ambrose states (Obj. 1) that charity flows from hope: so that this suffices for the Reply to the First Objection.

Reply Obj. 2: Hope and every movement of the appetite proceed from some kind of love, whereby the expected good is loved. But not every kind of hope proceeds from charity, but only the movement of living hope, viz. that whereby man hopes to obtain good from God, as from a friend.

Reply Obj. 3: The Master is speaking of living hope, which is naturally preceded by charity and the merits caused by charity.

18. OF THE SUBJECT OF HOPE
(In Four Articles)

We must now consider the subject of hope, under which head there are four points of inquiry:

(1) Whether the virtue of hope is in the will as its subject?
(2) Whether it is in the blessed?
(3) Whether it is in the damned?
(4) Whether there is certainty in the hope of the wayfarer?.

* * * * *

FIRST ARTICLE [II-II, Q. 18, Art. 1]

Whether Hope Is in the Will As Its Subject?

Objection 1: It would seem that hope is not in the will as its subject. For the object of hope is an arduous good, as stated above (Q. 17, A. 1; I-II, Q. 40, A. 1). Now the arduous is the object, not of the will, but of the irascible. Therefore hope is not in the will but in the irascible.

Obj. 2: Further, where one suffices it is superfluous to add another. Now charity suffices for the perfecting of the will, which is the most perfect of the virtues. Therefore hope is not in the will.

Obj. 3: Further, the one same power cannot exercise two acts at the same time; thus the intellect cannot understand many things simultaneously. Now the act of hope can be at the same time as an act of charity. Since, then, the act of charity evidently belongs to the will, it follows that the act of hope does not belong to that power: so that, therefore, hope is not in the will.

On the contrary, The soul is not apprehensive of God save as regards the mind in which is memory, intellect and will, as Augustine declares (De Trin. xiv, 3, 6). Now hope is a theological virtue having God for its object. Since therefore it is neither in the memory, nor in the intellect, which belong to the cognitive faculty, it follows that it is in the will as its subject.

I answer that, As shown above (I, Q. 87, A. 2), habits are known by their acts. Now the act of hope is a movement of the appetitive faculty, since its object is a good. And, since there is a twofold appetite in man, namely, the sensitive which is divided into irascible and concupiscible, and the intellective appetite, called the will, as stated in the First Part (Q. 82, A. 5), those movements which occur in the lower appetite, are with passion, while those in the higher appetite are without passion, as shown above (I, Q. 87, A. 2, ad 1; I-II, Q. 22, A. 3, ad 3). Now the act of the virtue of hope cannot belong to the sensitive appetite, since the good which is the principal object of this virtue, is not a sensible but a Divine good. Therefore hope resides in the higher appetite called the will, and not in the lower appetite, of which the irascible is a part.

Reply Obj. 1: The object of the irascible is an arduous sensible: whereas the object of the virtue of hope is an arduous intelligible, or rather superintelligible.

Reply Obj. 2: Charity perfects the will sufficiently with regard to one act, which is the act of loving: but another virtue is required in order to perfect it with regard to its other act, which is that of hoping.

Reply Obj. 3: The movement of hope and the movement of charity are mutually related, as was shown above (Q. 17, A. 8). Hence there is no reason why both movements should not belong at the same time to the same power: even as the intellect can understand many things at the same time if they be related to one another, as stated in the First Part (Q. 85, A. 4).

* * * * *

SECOND ARTICLE [II-II, Q. 18, Art. 2]

Whether in the Blessed There Is Hope?

Objection 1: It would seem that in the blessed there is hope. For Christ was a perfect comprehensor from the first moment of His conception. Now He had hope, since, according to a gloss, the words of Ps. 30:2, "In Thee, O Lord, have I hoped," are said in His person. Therefore in the blessed there can be hope.

Obj. 2: Further, even as the obtaining of happiness is an arduous good, so is its continuation. Now, before they obtain happiness, men hope to obtain it. Therefore, after they have obtained it, they can hope to continue in its possession.

Obj. 3: Further, by the virtue of hope, a man can hope for happiness, not only for himself, but also for others, as stated above (Q. 17, A. 3). But the blessed who are in heaven hope for the happiness of others, else they would not pray for them. Therefore there can be hope in them.

Obj. 4: Further, the happiness of the saints implies not only glory of the soul but also glory of the body. Now the souls of the saints in heaven, look yet for the glory of their bodies (Apoc. 6:10; Augustine, Gen. ad lit. xii, 35). Therefore in the blessed there can be hope.

On the contrary, The Apostle says (Rom. 8:24): "What a man seeth, why doth he hope for?" Now the blessed enjoy the sight of God. Therefore hope has no place in them.

I answer that, If what gives a thing its species be removed, the species is destroyed, and that thing cannot remain the same; just as when a natural body loses its form, it does not remain the same specifically. Now hope takes its species from its principal object, even as the other virtues do, as was shown above (Q. 17, AA. 5, 6; I-II, Q. 54, A. 2): and its principal object is eternal happiness as being possible to obtain by the assistance of God, as stated above (Q. 17, A. 2).

Since then the arduous possible good cannot be an object of hope except in so far as it is something future, it follows that when happiness is no longer future, but present, it is incompatible with the virtue of hope. Consequently hope, like faith, is voided in heaven, and neither of them can be in the blessed.

Reply Obj. 1: Although Christ was a comprehensor and therefore blessed as to the enjoyment of God, nevertheless He was, at the same time, a wayfarer, as regards the passibility of nature, to which He was still subject. Hence it was possible for Him to hope for the glory of impassibility and immortality, yet not so as to have the virtue of hope, the principal object of which is not the glory of the body but the enjoyment of God.

Reply Obj. 2: The happiness of the saints is called eternal life, because through enjoying God they become partakers, as it were, of God's eternity which surpasses all time: so that the continuation of happiness does not differ in respect of present, past and future. Hence the blessed do not hope for the continuation of their happiness (for as regards this there is no future), but are in actual possession thereof.

Reply Obj. 3: So long as the virtue of hope lasts, it is by the same hope that one hopes for one's own happiness, and for that of others. But when hope is voided in the blessed, whereby they hoped for their own happiness, they hope for the happiness of others indeed, yet not by the virtue of hope, but rather by the love of charity. Even so, he that has Divine charity, by that same charity loves his neighbor, without having the virtue of charity, but by some other love.

Reply Obj. 4: Since hope is a theological virtue having God for its object, its principal object is the glory of the soul, which consists in the enjoyment of God, and not the glory of the body. Moreover, although the glory of the body is something arduous in comparison with human nature, yet it is not so for one who has the glory of the soul; both because the glory of the body is a very small thing as compared with the glory of the soul, and because one who has the glory of the soul has already the sufficient cause of the glory of the body.

* * * * *

THIRD ARTICLE [II-II, Q. 18, Art. 3]

Whether Hope Is in the Damned?

Objection 1: It would seem that there is hope in the damned. For the devil is damned and prince of the damned, according to Matt. 25:41: "Depart . . . you cursed, into everlasting fire, which was prepared for the devil and his angels." But the devil has hope, according to Job 40:28, "Behold his hope shall fail him." Therefore it seems that the damned have hope.

Obj. 2: Further, just as faith is either living or dead, so is hope. But lifeless faith can be in the devils and the damned, according to James 2:19: "The devils . . . believe and tremble." Therefore it seems that lifeless hope also can be in the damned.

Obj. 3: Further, after death there accrues to man no merit or demerit that he had not before, according to Eccles. 11:3, "If the tree fall to the south, or to the north, in what place soever it shall fall, there shall it be." Now many who are damned, in this life hoped and never despaired. Therefore they will hope in the future life also.

On the contrary, Hope causes joy, according to Rom. 12:12, "Rejoicing in hope." Now the damned have no joy, but sorrow and grief, according to Isa. 65:14, "My servants shall praise for joyfulness of heart, and you shall cry for sorrow of heart, and shall howl for grief of spirit." Therefore no hope is in the damned.

I answer that, Just as it is a condition of happiness that the will should find rest therein, so is it a condition of punishment, that what is inflicted in punishment, should go against the will. Now that which is not known can neither be restful nor repugnant to the will: wherefore Augustine says (Gen. ad lit. xi, 17) that the angels could not be perfectly happy in their first state before their confirmation, or unhappy before their fall, since they had no foreknowledge of what would happen to them. For perfect and true happiness requires that one should be certain of being happy for ever, else the will would not rest.

In like manner, since the everlastingness of damnation is a necessary condition of the punishment of the damned, it would not be truly penal unless it went against the will; and this would be impossible if they were ignorant of the everlastingness of their damnation. Hence it belongs to the unhappy state of the damned, that they should know that they cannot by any means escape from damnation and obtain happiness. Wherefore it is written (Job 15:22): "He believeth not that he may return from darkness to light." It is, therefore, evident that they cannot apprehend happiness as a possible good, as neither can the blessed apprehend it as a future good. Consequently there is no hope either in the blessed or in the damned. On the other hand, hope can be in wayfarers, whether of this life or in purgatory, because in either case they apprehend happiness as a future possible thing.

Reply Obj. 1: As Gregory says (Moral. xxxiii, 20) this is said of the devil as regards his members, whose hope will fail utterly: or, if it be understood of the devil himself, it may refer to the hope whereby he expects to vanquish the saints, in which sense we read just before (Job 40:18): "He trusteth that the Jordan may run into his mouth": this is not, however, the hope of which we are speaking.

Reply Obj. 2: As Augustine says (Enchiridion viii), "faith is about things, bad or good, past, present, or future, one's own or another's; whereas hope is only about good things, future and concerning oneself." Hence it is possible for lifeless faith to be in the damned, but not hope, since the Divine goods are not for them future possible things, but far removed from them.

Reply Obj. 3: Lack of hope in the damned does not change their demerit, as neither does the voiding of hope in the blessed increase their merit: but both these things are due to the change in their respective states.

* * * * *

FOURTH ARTICLE [II-II, Q. 18, Art. 4]

Whether There Is Certainty in the Hope of a Wayfarer?

Objection 1: It would seem that there is no certainty in the hope of a wayfarer. For hope resides in the will. But certainty pertains not to the will but to the intellect. Therefore there is no certainty in hope.

Obj. 2: Further, hope is based on grace and merits, as stated above (Q. 17, A. 1). Now it is impossible in this life to know for certain that we are in a state of grace, as stated above (I-II, Q. 112, A. 5). Therefore there is no certainty in the hope of a wayfarer.

Obj. 3: Further, there can be no certainty about that which may fail. Now many a hopeful wayfarer fails to obtain happiness. Therefore wayfarer's hope has no certainty.

On the contrary, "Hope is the certain expectation of future happiness," as the Master states (Sent. iii, D, 26): and this may be gathered from 2 Tim. 1:12, "I know Whom I have believed, and I am certain that He is able to keep that which I have committed to Him."

I answer that, Certainty is found in a thing in two ways, essentially and by participation. It is found essentially in the cognitive power; by participation in whatever is moved infallibly to its end by the cognitive power. In this way we say that nature works with certainty, since it is moved by the Divine intellect which moves everything with certainty to its end. In this way too, the moral virtues are said to work with greater certainty than art, in as much as, like a second nature, they are moved to their acts by the reason: and thus too, hope tends to its end with certainty, as though sharing in the certainty of faith which is in the cognitive faculty.

This suffices for the Reply to the First Objection.

Reply Obj. 2: Hope does not trust chiefly in grace already received, but on God's omnipotence and mercy, whereby even he that has not grace, can obtain it, so as to come to eternal life. Now whoever has faith is certain of God's omnipotence and mercy.

Reply Obj. 3: That some who have hope fail to obtain happiness, is due to a fault of the free will in placing the obstacle of sin, but not to any deficiency in God's power or mercy, in which hope places its trust. Hence this does not prejudice the certainty of hope.

19. OF THE GIFT OF FEAR (In Twelve Articles)

We must now consider the gift of fear, about which there are twelve points of inquiry:

(1) Whether God is to be feared?
(2) Of the division of fear into filial, initial, servile and worldly;
(3) Whether worldly fear is always evil?

(4) Whether servile fear is good?
(5) Whether it is substantially the same as filial fear?
(6) Whether servile fear departs when charity comes?
(7) Whether fear is the beginning of wisdom?
(8) Whether initial fear is substantially the same as filial fear?
(9) Whether fear is a gift of the Holy Ghost?
(10) Whether it grows when charity grows?
(11) Whether it remains in heaven?
(12) Which of the beatitudes and fruits correspond to it?.

* * * * *

FIRST ARTICLE [II-II, Q. 19, Art. 1]

Whether God Can Be Feared?

Objection 1: It would seem that God cannot be feared. For the object of fear is a future evil, as stated above (I-II, Q. 41, AA. 2, 3). But God is free of all evil, since He is goodness itself. Therefore God cannot be feared.

Obj. 2: Further, fear is opposed to hope. Now we hope in God. Therefore we cannot fear Him at the same time.

Obj. 3: Further, as the Philosopher states (Rhet. ii, 5), "we fear those things whence evil comes to us." But evil comes to us, not from God, but from ourselves, according to Osee 13:9: "Destruction is thy own, O Israel: thy help is . . . in Me." Therefore God is not to be feared.

On the contrary, It is written (Jer. 10:7): "Who shall not fear Thee, O King of nations?" and (Malachi 1:6): "If I be a master, where is My fear?"

I answer that, Just as hope has two objects, one of which is the future good itself, that one expects to obtain, while the other is someone's help, through whom one expects to obtain what one hopes for, so, too, fear may have two objects, one of which is the very evil which a man shrinks from, while the other is that from which the evil may come. Accordingly, in the first way God, Who is goodness itself, cannot be an object of fear; but He can be an object of fear in the second way, in so far as there may come to us some evil either from Him or in relation to Him.

From Him there comes the evil of punishment, but this is evil not absolutely but relatively, and, absolutely speaking, is a good. Because, since a thing is said to be good through being ordered to an end, while evil implies lack of this order, that which excludes the order to the last end is altogether evil, and such is the evil of fault. On the other hand the evil of punishment is indeed an evil, in so far as it is the privation of some particular good, yet absolutely speaking, it is a good, in so far as it is ordained to the last end.

In relation to God the evil of fault can come to us, if we be separated from Him: and in this way God can and ought to be feared.

Reply Obj. 1: This objection considers the object of fear as being the evil which a man shuns.

Reply Obj. 2: In God, we may consider both His justice, in respect of which He punishes those who sin, and His mercy, in respect of which He sets us free: in us the consideration of His justice gives rise to fear, but the consideration of His mercy gives rise to hope, so that, accordingly, God is the object of both hope and fear, but under different aspects.

Reply Obj. 3: The evil of fault is not from God as its author but from us, in for far as we forsake God: while the evil of punishment is from God as its author, in so far as it has character of a good, since it is something just, through being inflicted on us justly; although originally this is due to the demerit of sin: thus it is written (Wis. 1:13, 16): "God made not death . . . but the wicked with works and words have called it to them.".

* * * * *

SECOND ARTICLE [II-II, Q. 19, Art. 2]

Whether Fear Is Fittingly Divided into Filial, Initial, Servile and Worldly Fear?

Objection 1: It would seem that fear is unfittingly divided into filial, initial, servile and worldly fear. For Damascene says (De Fide Orth. ii, 15) that there are six kinds of fear, viz. "laziness, shamefacedness," etc. of which we have treated above (I-II, Q. 41, A. 4), and which are not mentioned in the division in question. Therefore this division of fear seems unfitting.

Obj. 2: Further, each of these fears is either good or evil. But there is a fear, viz. natural fear, which is neither morally good, since it is in the demons, according to James 2:19, "The devils . . . believe and tremble," nor evil, since it is in Christ, according to Mk. 14:33, Jesus "began to fear and be heavy." Therefore the aforesaid division of fear is insufficient.

Obj. 3: Further, the relation of son to father differs from that of wife to husband, and this again from that of servant to master. Now filial fear, which is that of the son in comparison with his father, is distinct from servile fear, which is that of the servant in comparison with his master. Therefore chaste fear, which seems to be that of the wife in comparison with her husband, ought to be distinguished from all these other fears.

Obj. 4: Further, even as servile fear fears punishment, so do initial and worldly fear. Therefore no distinction should be made between them.

Obj. 5: Further, even as concupiscence is about some good, so is fear about some evil. Now "concupiscence of the eyes," which is the desire for things of this world, is distinct from "concupiscence of the flesh," which is the desire for one's own pleasure. Therefore "worldly fear," whereby one fears to lose external goods, is distinct from "human fear," whereby one fears harm to one's own person.

On the contrary stands the authority of the Master (Sent. iii, D, 34).

I answer that, We are speaking of fear now, in so far as it makes us turn, so to speak, to God or away from Him. For, since the object of fear is an evil, sometimes, on account of the evils he fears, man withdraws from God, and this is called human fear; while sometimes, on account of the evils he fears, he turns to God and adheres to Him. This latter evil is twofold, viz. evil of punishment, and evil of fault.

Accordingly if a man turn to God and adhere to Him, through fear of punishment, it will be servile fear; but if it be on account of fear of committing a fault, it will be filial fear, for it becomes a child to fear offending its father. If, however, it be on account of both, it will be initial fear, which is between both these fears. As to whether it is possible to fear the evil of fault, the question has been treated above (I-II, Q. 42, A. 3) when we were considering the passion of fear.

Reply Obj. 1: Damascene divides fear as a passion of the soul: whereas this division of fear is taken from its relation to God, as explained above.

Reply Obj. 2: Moral good consists chiefly in turning to God, while moral evil consists chiefly in turning away from Him: wherefore all the fears mentioned above imply either moral evil or moral good. Now natural fear is presupposed to moral good and evil, and so it is not numbered among these kinds of fear.

Reply Obj. 3: The relation of servant to master is based on the power which the master exercises over the servant; whereas, on the contrary, the relation of a son to his father or of a wife to her husband is based on the son's affection towards his father to whom he submits himself, or on the wife's affection towards her husband to whom she binds herself in the union of love. Hence filial and chaste fear amount to the same, because by the love of charity God becomes our Father, according to Rom. 8:15, "You have received the spirit of adoption of sons, whereby we cry: Abba (Father)"; and by this same charity He is called our spouse, according to 2 Cor. 11:2, "I have espoused you to one husband, that I may present you as a chaste virgin to Christ": whereas servile fear has no connection with these, since it does not include charity in its definition.

Reply Obj. 4: These three fears regard punishment but in different ways. For worldly or human fear regards a punishment which turns man away from God, and which God's enemies sometimes inflict or threaten: whereas servile and initial fear regard a punishment whereby men are drawn to God, and which is inflicted or threatened by God. Servile fear regards this punishment chiefly, while initial fear regards it secondarily.

Reply Obj. 5: It amounts to the same whether man turns away from God through fear of losing his worldly goods, or through fear of forfeiting the well-being of his body, since external goods belong to the body. Hence both these fears are reckoned as one here, although they fear different evils, even as they correspond to the desire of different goods. This diversity causes a specific diversity of sins, all of which alike however lead man away from God.

* * * * *

THIRD ARTICLE [II-II, Q. 19, Art. 3]

Whether Worldly Fear Is Always Evil?

Objection 1: It would seem that worldly fear is not always evil. Because regard for men seems to be a kind of human fear. Now some are blamed for having no regard for man, for instance, the unjust judge of whom we read (Luke 18:2) that he "feared not God, nor regarded man." Therefore it seems that worldly fear is not always evil.

Obj. 2: Further, worldly fear seems to have reference to the punishments inflicted by the secular power. Now such like punishments incite us to good actions, according to Rom. 13:3, "Wilt thou not be afraid of the power? Do that which is good, and thou shalt have praise from the same." Therefore worldly fear is not always evil.

Obj. 3: Further, it seems that what is in us naturally, is not evil, since our natural gifts are from God. Now it is natural to man to fear detriment to his body, and loss of his worldly goods, whereby the present life is supported. Therefore it seems that worldly fear is not always evil.

On the contrary, Our Lord said (Matt. 10:28): "Fear ye not them that kill the body," thus forbidding worldly fear. Now nothing but what is evil is forbidden by God. Therefore worldly fear is evil.

I answer that, As shown above (I-II, Q. 1, A. 3; I-II, Q. 18, A. 1; I-II, Q. 54, A. 2) moral acts and habits take their name and species from their objects. Now the proper object of the appetite's movement is the final good: so that, in consequence, every appetitive movement is both specified and named from its proper end. For if anyone were to describe covetousness as love of work because men work on account of covetousness, this description would be incorrect, since the covetous man seeks work not as end but as a means: the end that he seeks is wealth, wherefore covetousness is rightly described as the desire or the love of wealth, and this is evil. Accordingly worldly love is, properly speaking, the love whereby a man trusts in the world as his end, so that worldly love is always evil. Now fear is born of love, since man fears the loss of what he loves, as Augustine states (Qq. lxxxiii, qu. 33). Now worldly fear is that which arises from worldly love as from an evil root, for which reason worldly fear is always evil.

Reply Obj. 1: One may have regard for men in two ways. First in so far as there is in them something divine, for instance, the good of grace or of virtue, or at least of the natural image of God: and in this way those are blamed who have no regard for man. Secondly, one may have regard for men as being in opposition to God, and thus it is praiseworthy to have no regard for men, according as we read of Elias or Eliseus (Ecclus. 48:13): "In his days he feared not the prince."

Reply Obj. 2: When the secular power inflicts punishment in order to withdraw men from sin, it is acting as God's minister, according to Rom. 13:4, "For he is God's minister, an avenger to execute wrath upon him that doth evil." To fear the secular power in this way is part, not of worldly fear, but of servile or initial fear.

Reply Obj. 3: It is natural for man to shrink from detriment to his own body and loss of worldly goods, but to forsake justice on that account is contrary to natural reason. Hence the Philosopher says (Ethic. iii, 1) that there are certain things, viz. sinful deeds, which no fear should drive us to do, since to do such things is worse than to suffer any punishment whatever.

* * * * *

FOURTH ARTICLE [II-II, Q. 19, Art. 4]

Whether Servile Fear Is Good?

Objection 1: It would seem that servile fear is not good. For if the use of a thing is evil, the thing itself is evil. Now the use of servile fear is evil, for according to a gloss on Rom. 8:15, "if a man do anything through fear, although the deed be good, it is not well done." Therefore servile fear is not good.

Obj. 2: Further, no good grows from a sinful root. Now servile fear grows from a sinful root, because when commenting on Job 3:11, "Why did I not die in the womb?" Gregory says (Moral. iv, 25): "When a man dreads the punishment which confronts him for his sin and no longer loves the friendship of God which he has lost, his fear is born of pride, not of humility." Therefore servile fear is evil.

Obj. 3: Further, just as mercenary love is opposed to the love of charity, so is servile fear, apparently, opposed to chaste fear. But mercenary love is always evil. Therefore servile fear is also.

On the contrary, Nothing evil is from the Holy Ghost. But servile fear is from the Holy Ghost, since a gloss on Rom. 8:15, "You have not received the spirit of bondage," etc. says: "It is the one same spirit that bestows two fears, viz. servile and chaste fear." Therefore servile fear is not evil.

I answer that, It is owing to its servility that servile fear may be evil. For servitude is opposed to freedom. Since, then, "what is free is cause of itself" (Metaph. i, 2), a slave is one who does not act as cause of his own action, but as though moved from without. Now whoever does a thing through love, does it of himself so to speak, because it is by his own inclination that he is moved to act: so that it is contrary to the very notion of servility that one should act from love. Consequently servile fear as such is contrary to charity: so that if servility were essential to fear, servile fear would be evil simply, even as adultery is evil simply, because that which makes it contrary to charity belongs to its very species.

This servility, however, does not belong to the species of servile fear, even as neither does lifelessness to the species of lifeless faith. For the species of a moral habit or act is taken from the object. Now the object of servile fear is punishment, and it is by accident that, either the good to which the punishment is contrary, is loved as the last end, and that consequently the punishment is feared as the greatest evil, which is the case with one who is devoid of charity, or that the punishment is directed to God as its end, and that, consequently, it is not feared as the greatest evil, which is the case with one who has charity. For the species of a habit is not destroyed through its object or end being directed to a further end. Consequently servile fear is substantially good, but is servility is evil.

Reply Obj. 1: This saying of Augustine is to be applied to a man who does something through servile fear as such, so that he loves not justice, and fears nothing but the punishment.

Reply Obj. 2: Servile fear as to its substance is not born of pride, but its servility is, inasmuch as man is unwilling, by love, to subject his affections to the yoke of justice.

Reply Obj. 3: Mercenary love is that whereby God is loved for the sake of worldly goods, and this is, of itself, contrary to charity, so that mercenary love is always evil. But servile fear, as to its substance, implies merely fear of punishment, whether or not this be feared as the principal evil.

* * * * *

FIFTH ARTICLE [II-II, Q. 19, Art. 5]

Whether Servile Fear Is Substantially the Same As Filial Fear?

Objection 1: It would seem that servile fear is substantially the same as filial fear. For filial fear is to servile fear the same apparently as living faith is to lifeless faith, since the one is accompanied by mortal sin and the other not. Now living faith and lifeless faith are substantially the same. Therefore servile and filial fear are substantially the same.

Obj. 2: Further, habits are diversified by their objects. Now the same thing is the object of servile and of filial fear, since they both fear God. Therefore servile and filial fear are substantially the same.

Obj. 3: Further, just as man hopes to enjoy God and to obtain favors from Him, so does he fear to be separated from God and to be punished by Him. Now it is the same hope whereby we hope to enjoy God, and to receive other favors from Him, as stated above (Q. 17, A. 2, ad 2). Therefore filial fear, whereby we fear separation from God, is the same as servile fear whereby we fear His punishments.

On the contrary, Augustine (In prim. canon. Joan. Tract. ix) says that there are two fears, one servile, another filial or chaste fear.

I answer that, The proper object of fear is evil. And since acts and habits are diversified by their objects, as shown above (I-II, Q. 54, A. 2), it follows of necessity that different kinds of fear correspond to different kinds of evil.

Now the evil of punishment, from which servile fear shrinks, differs specifically from evil of fault, which filial fear shuns, as shown above (A. 2). Hence it is evident that servile and filial fear are not the same substantially but differ specifically.

Reply Obj. 1: Living and lifeless faith differ, not as regards the object, since each of them believes God and believes in a God, but in respect of something extrinsic, viz. the presence or absence of charity, and so they do not differ substantially. On the other hand, servile and filial fear differ as to their objects: and hence the comparison fails.

Reply Obj. 2: Servile fear and filial fear do not regard God in the same light. For servile fear looks upon God as the cause of the infliction of punishment, whereas filial fear looks upon Him, not as the active cause of guilt, but rather as the term wherefrom it shrinks to be separated by guilt. Consequently the identity of object, viz. God, does not prove a specific identity of fear, since also natural movements differ specifically according to their different relationships to some one term, for movement from whiteness is not specifically the same as movement towards whiteness.

Reply Obj. 3: Hope looks upon God as the principle not only of the enjoyment of God, but also of any other favor whatever. This cannot be said of fear; and so there is no comparison.

* * * * *

SIXTH ARTICLE [II-II, Q. 19, Art. 6]

Whether Servile Fear Remains with Charity?

Objection 1: It would seem that servile fear does not remain with charity. For Augustine says (In prim. canon. Joan. Tract. ix) that "when charity takes up its abode, it drives away fear which had prepared a place for it."

Obj. 2: Further, "The charity of God is poured forth in our hearts, by the Holy Ghost, Who is given to us" (Rom. 5:5). Now "where the Spirit of the Lord is, there is liberty" (2 Cor. 3:17). Since then freedom excludes servitude, it seems that servile fear is driven away when charity comes.

Obj. 3: Further, servile fear is caused by self-love, in so far as punishment diminishes one's own good. Now love of God drives away self-love, for it makes us despise ourselves: thus Augustine testifies (De Civ. Dei xiv, 28) that "the love of God unto the contempt of self builds up the city of God." Therefore it seems that servile fear is driven out when charity comes.

On the contrary, Servile fear is a gift of the Holy Ghost, as stated above (A. 4). Now the gifts of the Holy Ghost are not forfeited through the advent of charity, whereby the Holy Ghost dwells in us. Therefore servile fear is not driven out when charity comes.

I answer that, Servile fear proceeds from self-love, because it is fear of punishment which is detrimental to one's own good. Hence the fear of punishment is consistent with charity, in the same way as self-love is: because it comes to the same that a man love his own good and that he fear to be deprived of it.

Now self-love may stand in a threefold relationship to charity. In one way it is contrary to charity, when a man places his end in the love of his own good. In another way it is included in charity, when a man loves himself for the sake of God and in God. In a third way, it is indeed distinct from charity, but is not contrary thereto, as when a man loves himself from the point of view of his own good, yet not so as to place his end in this his own good: even as one may have another special love for one's neighbor, besides the love of charity which is founded on God, when we love him by reason of usefulness, consanguinity, or some other human consideration, which, however, is referable to charity.

Accordingly fear of punishment is, in one way, included in charity, because separation from God is a punishment, which charity shuns exceedingly; so that this belongs to chaste fear. In another way, it is contrary to charity, when a man shrinks from the punishment that is opposed to his natural good, as being the principal evil in opposition to the good which he loves as an end; and in this way fear of punishment is not consistent with charity. In another way fear of punishment is indeed substantially distinct from chaste fear, when, to wit, a man fears a penal evil, not because it separates him from God, but because it is hurtful to his own good, and yet he does not place his end in this good, so that neither does he dread this evil as being the principal evil. Such fear of punishment is consistent with charity; but it is not called servile, except when punishment is dreaded as a principal evil, as explained above (AA. 2, 4). Hence fear considered as servile, does not remain with charity, but the substance of servile fear can remain with charity, even as self-love can remain with charity.

Reply Obj. 1: Augustine is speaking of fear considered as servile: and such is the sense of the two other objections.

* * * * *

SIXTH ARTICLE [II-II, Q. 19, Art. 6]

Whether Fear Is the Beginning of Wisdom?

Objection 1: It would seem that fear is not the beginning of wisdom. For the beginning of a thing is a part thereof. But fear is not a part of wisdom, since fear is seated in the appetitive faculty, while wisdom is in the intellect. Therefore it seems that fear is not the beginning of wisdom.

Obj. 2: Further, nothing is the beginning of itself. "Now fear of the Lord, that is wisdom," according to Job 28:28. Therefore it seems that fear of God is not the beginning of wisdom.

Obj. 3: Further, nothing is prior to the beginning. But something is prior to fear, since faith precedes fear. Therefore it seems that fear is not the beginning of wisdom.

On the contrary, It is written in the Ps. 110:10: "The fear of the Lord is the beginning of wisdom."

I answer that, A thing may be called the beginning of wisdom in two ways: in one way because it is the beginning of wisdom itself as to its essence; in another way, as to its effect. Thus the beginning of an art as to its essence consists in the principles from which that art proceeds, while the beginning of an art as to its effect is that wherefrom it begins to operate: for instance we might say that the beginning of the art of building is the foundation because that is where the builder begins his work.

Now, since wisdom is the knowledge of Divine things, as we shall state further on (Q. 45, A. 1), it is considered by us in one way, and in another way by philosophers. For, seeing that our life is ordained to the enjoyment of God, and is directed thereto according to a participation of the Divine Nature, conferred on us through grace, wisdom, as we look at it, is considered not only as being cognizant of God, as it is with the philosophers, but also as directing human conduct; since this is directed not only by the human law, but also by the Divine law, as Augustine shows (De Trin. xii, 14). Accordingly the beginning of wisdom as to its essence consists in the first principles of wisdom, i.e. the articles of faith, and in this sense faith is said to be the beginning of wisdom. But as regards the effect, the beginning of wisdom is the point where wisdom begins to work, and in this way fear is the beginning of wisdom, yet servile fear in one way, and filial fear, in another. For servile fear is like a principle disposing a man to wisdom from without, in so far as he refrains from sin through fear of punishment, and is thus fashioned for the effect of wisdom, according to Ecclus. 1:27, "The fear of the Lord driveth out sin." On the other hand, chaste or filial fear is the beginning of wisdom, as being the first effect of wisdom. For since the regulation of human conduct by the Divine law belongs to wisdom, in order to make a beginning, man must first of all fear God and submit himself to Him: for the result will be that in all things he will be ruled by God.

Reply Obj. 1: This argument proves that fear is not the beginning of wisdom as to the essence of wisdom.

Reply Obj. 2: The fear of God is compared to a man's whole life that is ruled by God's wisdom, as the root to the tree: hence it is written (Ecclus. 1:25): "The root of wisdom is to fear the Lord, for [Vulg.: 'and'] the branches thereof are longlived." Consequently, as the root is said to be virtually the tree, so the fear of God is said to be wisdom.

Reply Obj. 3: As stated above, faith is the beginning of wisdom in one way, and fear, in another. Hence it is written (Ecclus. 25:16): "The fear of God is the beginning of love: and the beginning of faith is to be fast joined to it.".

* * * * *

SEVENTH ARTICLE [II-II, Q. 19, Art. 7]

Whether Initial Fear Differs Substantially from Filial Fear?

Objection 1: It would seem that initial fear differs substantially from filial fear. For filial fear is caused by love. Now initial fear is the beginning of love, according to Ecclus. 25:16, "The fear of God is the beginning of love." Therefore initial fear is distinct from filial fear.

Obj. 2: Further, initial fear dreads punishment, which is the object of servile fear, so that initial and servile fear would seem to be the same. But servile fear is distinct from filial fear. Therefore initial fear also is substantially distinct from initial fear.

Obj. 3: Further, a mean differs in the same ratio from both the extremes. Now initial fear is the mean between servile and filial fear. Therefore it differs from both filial and servile fear.

On the contrary, Perfect and imperfect do not diversify the substance of a thing. Now initial and filial fear differ in respect of perfection and imperfection of charity, as Augustine states (In prim. canon. Joan. Tract. ix). Therefore initial fear does not differ substantially from filial fear.

I answer that, Initial fear is so called because it is a beginning *(initium)*. Since, however, both servile and filial fear are, in some way, the beginning of wisdom, each may be called in some way, initial.

It is not in this sense, however, that we are to understand initial fear in so far as it is distinct from servile and filial fear, but in the sense according to which it belongs to the state of beginners, in whom there is a beginning of filial fear resulting from a beginning of charity, although they do not possess the perfection of filial fear, because they have not yet attained to the perfection of charity. Consequently initial fear stands in the same relation to filial fear as imperfect to perfect charity. Now perfect and imperfect charity differ, not as to essence but as to state. Therefore we must conclude that initial fear, as we understand it here, does not differ essentially from filial fear.

Reply Obj. 1: The fear which is a beginning of love is servile fear, which is the herald of charity, just as the bristle introduces the thread, as Augustine states (Tract. ix in Ep. i Joan.). Or else, if it be referred to initial fear, this is said to be the beginning of love, not absolutely, but relatively to the state of perfect charity.

Reply Obj. 2: Initial fear does not dread punishment as its proper object, but as having something of servile fear connected with it: for this servile fear, as to its substance, remains indeed, with charity, its servility being cast aside; whereas its act remains with imperfect charity in the man who is moved to perform good actions not only through love of justice, but also through fear of punishment, though this same act ceases in the man who has perfect charity, which "casteth out fear," according to 1 John 4:18.

Reply Obj. 3: Initial fear is a mean between servile and filial fear, not as between two things of the same genus, but as the imperfect is a mean between a perfect being and a non-being, as stated in Metaph. ii, for it is the same substantially as the perfect being, while it differs altogether from non-being.

* * * * *

NINTH ARTICLE [II-II, Q. 19, Art. 9]

Whether Fear Is a Gift of the Holy Ghost?

Objection 1: It would seem that fear is not a gift of the Holy Ghost. For no gift of the Holy Ghost is opposed to a virtue, which is also from the Holy Ghost; else the Holy Ghost would be in opposition to Himself. Now fear is opposed to hope, which is a virtue. Therefore fear is not a gift of the Holy Ghost.

Obj. 2: Further, it is proper to a theological virtue to have God for its object. But fear has God for its object, in so far as God is feared. Therefore fear is not a gift, but a theological virtue.

Obj. 3: Further, fear arises from love. But love is reckoned a theological virtue. Therefore fear also is a theological virtue, being connected with the same matter, as it were.

Obj. 4: Further, Gregory says (Moral. ii, 49) that "fear is bestowed as a remedy against pride." But the virtue of humility is opposed to pride. Therefore again, fear is a kind of virtue.

Obj. 5: Further, the gifts are more perfect than the virtues, since they are bestowed in support of the virtues as Gregory says (Moral. ii, 49). Now hope is more perfect than fear, since hope regards good, while fear regards evil. Since, then, hope is a virtue, it should not be said that fear is a gift.

On the contrary, The fear of the Lord is numbered among the seven gifts of the Holy Ghost (Isa. 11:3).

I answer that, Fear is of several kinds, as stated above (A. 2). Now it is not "human fear," according to Augustine (De Gratia et Lib. Arb. xviii), "that is a gift of God"—for it was by this fear that Peter denied Christ—but that fear of which it was said (Matt. 10:28): "Fear Him that can destroy both soul and body into hell."

Again servile fear is not to be reckoned among the seven gifts of the Holy Ghost, though it is from Him, because according to Augustine (De Nat. et Grat. lvii) it is compatible with the will to sin: whereas the gifts of the Holy Ghost are incompatible with the will to sin, as they are inseparable from charity, as stated above (I-II, Q. 68, A. 5).

It follows, therefore, that the fear of God, which is numbered among the seven gifts of the Holy Ghost, is filial or chaste fear. For it was stated above (I-II, Q. 68, AA. 1, 3) that the gifts of the Holy Ghost are certain habitual perfections of the soul's powers, whereby these are rendered amenable to the motion of the Holy Ghost, just as, by the moral virtues, the appetitive powers are rendered amenable to the motion of reason. Now for a thing to be amenable to the motion of a certain mover, the first condition required is that it be a non-resistant subject of that mover, because resistance of the movable subject to the mover hinders the movement. This is what filial or chaste fear does, since thereby we revere God and avoid separating ourselves from Him. Hence, according to Augustine (De

Serm. Dom. in Monte i, 4) filial fear holds the first place, as it were, among the gifts of the Holy Ghost, in the ascending order, and the last place, in the descending order.

Reply Obj. 1: Filial fear is not opposed to the virtue of hope: since thereby we fear, not that we may fail of what we hope to obtain by God's help, but lest we withdraw ourselves from this help. Wherefore filial fear and hope cling together, and perfect one another.

Reply Obj. 2: The proper and principal object of fear is the evil shunned, and in this way, as stated above (A. 1), God cannot be an object of fear. Yet He is, in this way, the object of hope and the other theological virtues, since, by the virtue of hope, we trust in God's help, not only to obtain any other goods, but, chiefly, to obtain God Himself, as the principal good. The same evidently applies to the other theological virtues.

Reply Obj. 3: From the fact that love is the origin of fear, it does not follow that the fear of God is not a distinct habit from charity which is the love of God, since love is the origin of all the emotions, and yet we are perfected by different habits in respect of different emotions. Yet love is more of a virtue than fear is, because love regards good, to which virtue is principally directed by reason of its own nature, as was shown above (I-II, Q. 55, AA. 3, 4); for which reason hope is also reckoned as a virtue; whereas fear principally regards evil, the avoidance of which it denotes, wherefore it is something less than a theological virtue.

Reply Obj. 4: According to Ecclus. 10:14, "the beginning of the pride of man is to fall off from God," that is to refuse submission to God, and this is opposed to filial fear, which reveres God. Thus fear cuts off the source of pride for which reason it is bestowed as a remedy against pride. Yet it does not follow that it is the same as the virtue of humility, but that it is its origin. For the gifts of the Holy Ghost are the origin of the intellectual and moral virtues, as stated above (I-II, Q. 68, A. 4), while the theological virtues are the origin of the gifts, as stated above (I-II, Q. 69, A. 4, ad 3).

This suffices for the Reply to the Fifth Objection.

* * * * *

TENTH ARTICLE [II-II, Q. 19, Art. 10]

Whether Fear Decreases When Charity Increases?

Objection 1: It seems that fear decreases when charity increases. For Augustine says (In prim. canon. Joan. Tract. ix): "The more charity increases, the more fear decreases."

Obj. 2: Further, fear decreases when hope increases. But charity increases when hope increases, as stated above (Q. 17, A. 8). Therefore fear decreases when charity increases.

Obj. 3: Further, love implies union, whereas fear implies separation. Now separation decreases when union increases. Therefore fear decreases when the love of charity increases.

On the contrary, Augustine says (Qq. lxxxiii, qu. 36) that "the fear of God not only begins but also perfects wisdom, whereby we love God above all things, and our neighbor as ourselves."

I answer that, Fear is twofold, as stated above (AA. 2, 4); one is filial fear, whereby a son fears to offend his father or to be separated from him; the other is servile fear, whereby one fears punishment.

Now filial fear must needs increase when charity increases, even as an effect increases with the increase of its cause. For the more one loves a man, the more one fears to offend him and to be separated from him.

On the other hand servile fear, as regards its servility, is entirely cast out when charity comes, although the fear of punishment remains as to its substance, as stated above (A. 6). This fear decreases as charity increases, chiefly as regards its act, since the more a man loves God, the less he fears punishment; first, because he thinks less of his own good, to which punishment is opposed; secondly, because, the faster he clings, the more confident he is of the reward, and, consequently the less fearful of punishment.

Reply Obj. 1: Augustine speaks there of the fear of punishment.

Reply Obj. 2: It is fear of punishment that decreases when hope increases; but with the increase of the latter filial fear increases, because the more certainly a man expects to obtain a good by another's help, the more he fears to offend him or to be separated from him.

Reply Obj. 3: Filial fear does not imply separation from God, but submission to Him, and shuns separation from that submission. Yet, in a way, it implies separation, in the point of not presuming to equal oneself to Him, and of submitting to Him, which separation is to be observed even in charity, in so far as a man loves God more than himself and more than aught else. Hence the increase of the love of charity implies not a decrease but an increase in the reverence of fear.

* * * * *

ELEVENTH ARTICLE [II-II, Q. 19, Art. 11]

Whether Fear Remains in Heaven?

Objection 1: It would seem that fear does not remain in heaven. For it is written (Prov. 1:33): "He ... shall enjoy abundance, without fear of evils," which is to be understood as referring to those who already enjoy wisdom in everlasting happiness. Now every fear is about some evil, since evil is the object of fear, as stated above (AA. 2, 5; I-II, Q. 42, A. 1). Therefore there will be no fear in heaven.

Obj. 2: Further, in heaven men will be conformed to God, according to 1 John 3:2, "When He shall appear, we shall be like to Him." But God fears nothing. Therefore, in heaven, men will have no fear.

Obj. 3: Further, hope is more perfect than fear, since hope regards good, and fear, evil. Now hope will not be in heaven. Therefore neither will there be fear in heaven.

On the contrary, It is written (Ps. 18:10): "The fear of the Lord is holy, enduring for ever and ever."

I answer that, Servile fear, or fear of punishment, will by no means be in heaven, since such a fear is excluded by the security which is essential to everlasting happiness, as stated above (I-II, Q. 5, A. 4).

But with regard to filial fear, as it increases with the increase of charity, so is it perfected when charity is made perfect; hence, in heaven, it will not have quite the same act as it has now.

In order to make this clear, we must observe that the proper object of fear is a possible evil, just as the proper object of hope is a possible good: and since the movement of fear is like one of avoidance, fear implies avoidance of a possible arduous evil, for little evils inspire no fear. Now as a thing's good consists in its staying in its own order, so a thing's evil consists in forsaking its order. Again, the order of a rational creature is that it should be under God and above other creatures. Hence, just as it is an evil for a rational creature to submit, by love, to a lower creature, so too is it an evil for it, if it submit not to God, but presumptuously revolt against Him or contemn Him. Now this evil is possible to a rational creature considered as to its nature on account of the natural flexibility of the free-will; whereas in the blessed, it becomes impossible, by reason of the perfection of glory. Therefore the avoidance of this evil that consists in non-subjection to God, and is possible to nature, but impossible in the state of bliss, will be in heaven; while in this life there is avoidance of this evil as of something altogether possible. Hence Gregory, expounding the words of Job (26:11), "The pillars of heaven tremble, and dread at His beck," says (Moral. xvii, 29): "The heavenly powers that gaze on Him without ceasing, tremble while contemplating: but their awe, lest it should be of a penal nature, is one not of fear but of wonder," because, to wit, they wonder at God's supereminence and incomprehensibility. Augustine also (De Civ. Dei xiv, 9) in this sense, admits fear in heaven, although he leaves the question doubtful. "If," he says, "this chaste fear that endureth for ever and ever is to be in the future life, it will not be a fear that is afraid of an evil which might possibly occur, but a fear that holds fast to a good which we cannot lose. For when we love the good which we have acquired, with an unchangeable love, without doubt, if it is allowable to say so, our fear is sure of avoiding evil. Because chaste fear denotes a will that cannot consent to sin, and whereby we avoid sin without trembling lest, in our weakness, we fall, and possess ourselves in the tranquillity born of charity. Else, if no kind of fear is possible there, perhaps fear is said to endure for ever and ever, because that which fear will lead us to, will be everlasting."

Reply Obj. 1: The passage quoted excludes from the blessed, the fear that denotes solicitude, and anxiety about evil, but not the fear which is accompanied by security.

Reply Obj. 2: As Dionysius says (Div. Nom. ix) "the same things are both like and unlike God. They are like by reason of a variable imitation of the Inimitable"—that is, because, so far as they can, they imitate God Who cannot be imitated perfectly— "they are unlike because they are the effects of a Cause of Whom they fall short infinitely and immeasurably." Hence, if there be no fear in God (since there is none above Him to whom He may be subject) it does not follow that there is none in the blessed, whose happiness consists in perfect subjection to God.

Reply Obj. 3: Hope implies a certain defect, namely the futurity of happiness, which ceases when happiness is present: whereas fear implies a natural defect in a creature, in so far as it is infinitely distant from God, and this defect will remain even in heaven. Hence fear will not be cast out altogether.

* * * * *

TWELFTH ARTICLE [II-II, Q. 19, Art. 12]

Whether Poverty of Spirit Is the Beatitude Corresponding to the Gift of Fear?

Objection 1: It would seem that poverty of spirit is not the beatitude corresponding to the gift of fear. For fear is the beginning of the spiritual life, as explained above (A. 7): whereas poverty belongs to the perfection of the spiritual life, according to Matt. 19:21, "If thou wilt be perfect, go sell what thou hast, and give to the poor." Therefore poverty of spirit does not correspond to the gift of fear.

Obj. 2: Further, it is written (Ps. 118:120): "Pierce Thou my flesh with Thy fear," whence it seems to follow that it belongs to fear to restrain the flesh. But the curbing of the flesh seems to belong rather to the beatitude of mourning. Therefore the beatitude of mourning corresponds to the gift of fear, rather than the beatitude of poverty.

Obj. 3: Further, the gift of fear corresponds to the virtue of hope, as stated above (A. 9, ad 1). Now the last beatitude which is, "Blessed are the peacemakers, for they shall be called the children of God," seems above all to correspond to hope, because according to Rom. 5:2, "we ... glory in the hope of the glory of the sons of God." Therefore that beatitude corresponds to the gift of fear, rather than poverty of spirit.

Obj. 4: Further, it was stated above (I-II, Q. 70, A. 2) that the fruits correspond to the beatitudes. Now none of the fruits correspond to the gift of fear. Neither, therefore, does any of the beatitudes.

On the contrary, Augustine says (De Serm. Dom. in Monte i, 4): "The fear of the Lord is befitting the humble of whom it is said: Blessed are the poor in spirit."

I answer that, Poverty of spirit properly corresponds to fear. Because, since it belongs to filial fear to show reverence and submission to God, whatever results from this submission belongs to the gift of fear. Now from the very fact that a man submits to God, it follows that he ceases to seek greatness either in himself or in another but seeks it only in God. For that would be inconsistent with perfect subjection to God, wherefore it is written (Ps. 19:8): "Some trust in chariots and some in horses; but we will call upon the name of . . . our God." It follows that if a man fear God perfectly, he does not, by pride, seek greatness either in himself or in external goods, viz. honors and riches. In either case, this proceeds from poverty of spirit, in so far as the latter denotes either the voiding of a puffed up and proud spirit, according to Augustine's interpretation (De Serm. Dom. in Monte i, 4), or the renunciation of worldly goods which is done in spirit, i.e. by one's own will, through the instigation of the Holy Spirit, according to the expounding of Ambrose on Luke 6:20 and Jerome on Matt. 5:3.

Reply Obj. 1: Since a beatitude is an act of perfect virtue, all the beatitudes belong to the perfection of spiritual life. And this perfection seems to require that whoever would strive to obtain a perfect share of spiritual goods, needs to begin by despising earthly goods, wherefore fear holds the first place among the gifts. Perfection, however, does not consist in the renunciation itself of temporal goods; since this is the way to perfection: whereas filial fear, to which the beatitude of poverty corresponds, is consistent with the perfection of wisdom, as stated above (AA. 7, 10).

Reply Obj. 2: The undue exaltation of man either in himself or in another is more directly opposed to that submission to God which is the result of filial fear, than is external pleasure. Yet this is, in consequence, opposed to fear, since whoever fears God and is subject to Him, takes no delight in things other than God. Nevertheless, pleasure is not concerned, as exaltation is, with the arduous character of a thing which fear regards: and so the beatitude of poverty corresponds to fear directly, and the beatitude of mourning, consequently.

Reply Obj. 3: Hope denotes a movement by way of a relation of tendency to a term, whereas fear implies movement by way of a relation of withdrawal from a term: wherefore the last beatitude which is the term of spiritual perfection, fittingly corresponds to hope, by way of ultimate object; while the first beatitude, which implies withdrawal from external things which hinder submission to God, fittingly corresponds to fear.

Reply Obj. 4: As regards the fruits, it seems that those things correspond to the gift of fear, which pertain to the moderate use of temporal things or to abstinence therefrom; such are modesty, continency and chastity.

20. OF DESPAIR (In Four Articles)

We must now consider the contrary vices; (1) despair; (2) presumption. Under the first head there are four points of inquiry:

(1) Whether despair is a sin?
(2) Whether it can be without unbelief?
(3) Whether it is the greatest of sins?
(4) Whether it arises from sloth?.

* * * * *

FIRST ARTICLE [II-II, Q. 20, Art. 1]

Whether Despair Is a Sin?

Objection 1: It would seem that despair is not a sin. For every sin includes conversion to a mutable good, together with aversion from the immutable good, as Augustine states (De Lib. Arb. ii, 19). But despair includes no conversion to a mutable good. Therefore it is not a sin.

Obj. 2: Further, that which grows from a good root, seems to be no sin, because "a good tree cannot bring forth evil fruit" (Matt. 7:18). Now despair seems to grow from a good root, viz. fear of God, or from horror at the greatness of one's own sins. Therefore despair is not a sin.

Obj. 3: Further, if despair were a sin, it would be a sin also for the damned to despair. But this is not imputed to them as their fault but as part of their damnation. Therefore neither is it imputed to wayfarers as their fault, so that it is not a sin.

On the contrary, That which leads men to sin, seems not only to be a sin itself, but a source of sins. Now such is despair, for the Apostle says of certain men (Eph. 4:19): "Who, despairing, have given themselves up to lasciviousness, unto the working of all uncleanness and [Vulg.: 'unto'] covetousness." Therefore despair is not only a sin but also the origin of other sins.

I answer that, According to the Philosopher (Ethic. vi, 2) affirmation and negation in the intellect correspond to search and avoidance in the appetite; while truth and falsehood in the intellect correspond to good and evil in the appetite. Consequently every appetitive movement which is conformed to a true intellect, is good in itself, while every appetitive movement which is conformed to a false intellect is evil in itself and sinful. Now the true opinion of the intellect about God is that from Him comes salvation to mankind, and pardon to sinners, according to Ezech. 18:23, "I desire not the death of the sinner, but that he should be converted, and live"[1]: while it is a false opinion that He refuses pardon to the repentant sinner, or that He does not turn sinners to Himself by sanctifying grace. Therefore, just as the movement of hope, which is in conformity with the true opinion, is praiseworthy and virtuous, so the contrary movement of despair, which is in conformity with the false opinion about God, is vicious and sinful.

Reply Obj. 1: In every mortal sin there is, in some way, aversion from the immutable good, and conversion to a mutable good, but not always in the same way. Because, since the theological virtues have God for their object, the sins which are contrary to them, such as hatred of God, despair and unbelief, consist principally in aversion from the immutable good; but, consequently, they imply conversion to a mutable good, in so far as the soul that is a deserter from God, must necessarily turn to other things. Other sins, however, consist principally in conversion to a mutable good, and, consequently, in aversion from the immutable good: because the fornicator intends, not to depart from God, but to enjoy carnal pleasure, the result of which is that he departs from God.

Reply Obj. 2: A thing may grow from a virtuous root in two ways: first, directly and on the part of the virtue itself; even as an

---

[1] Vulg.: 'Is it My will that a sinner should die . . . and not that he should be converted and live?' Cf. Ezech. 33:11

act proceeds from a habit: and in this way no sin can grow from a virtuous root, for in this sense Augustine declared (De Lib. Arb. ii, 18, 19) that "no man makes evil use of virtue." Secondly, a thing proceeds from a virtue indirectly, or is occasioned by a virtue, and in this way nothing hinders a sin proceeding from a virtue: thus sometimes men pride themselves of their virtues, according to Augustine (Ep. ccxi): "Pride lies in wait for good works that they may die." In this way fear of God or horror of one's own sins may lead to despair, in so far as man makes evil use of those good things, by allowing them to be an occasion of despair.

Reply Obj. 3: The damned are outside the pale of hope on account of the impossibility of returning to happiness: hence it is not imputed to them that they hope not, but it is a part of their damnation. Even so, it would be no sin for a wayfarer to despair of obtaining that which he had no natural capacity for obtaining, or which was not due to be obtained by him; for instance, if a physician were to despair of healing some sick man, or if anyone were to despair of ever becoming rich.

* * * * *

SECOND ARTICLE [II-II, Q. 20, Art. 2]

Whether There Can Be Despair Without Unbelief?

Objection 1: It would seem that there can be no despair without unbelief. For the certainty of hope is derived from faith; and so long as the cause remains the effect is not done away. Therefore a man cannot lose the certainty of hope, by despairing, unless his faith be removed.

Obj. 2: Further, to prefer one's own guilt to God's mercy and goodness, is to deny the infinity of God's goodness and mercy, and so savors of unbelief. But whoever despairs, prefers his own guilt to the Divine mercy and goodness, according to Gen. 4:13: "My iniquity is greater than that I may deserve pardon." Therefore whoever despairs, is an unbeliever.

Obj. 3: Further, whoever falls into a condemned heresy, is an unbeliever. But he that despairs seems to fall into a condemned heresy, viz. that of the Novatians, who say that there is no pardon for sins after Baptism. Therefore it seems that whoever despairs, is an unbeliever.

On the contrary, If we remove that which follows, that which precedes remains. But hope follows faith, as stated above (Q. 17, A. 7). Therefore when hope is removed, faith can remain; so that, not everyone who despairs, is an unbeliever.

I answer that, Unbelief pertains to the intellect, but despair, to the appetite: and the intellect is about universals, while the appetite is moved in connection with particulars, since the appetitive movement is from the soul towards things, which, in themselves, are particular. Now it may happen that a man, while having a right opinion in the universal, is not rightly disposed as to his appetitive movement, his estimate being corrupted in a particular matter, because, in order to pass from the universal opinion to the appetite for a particular thing, it is necessary to have a particular estimate (De Anima iii, 2), just as it is impossible to infer a particular conclusion from an universal proposition, except through the holding of a particular proposition. Hence it is that a man, while having right faith, in the universal, fails in an appetitive movement, in regard to some particular, his particular estimate being corrupted by a habit or a passion, just as the fornicator, by choosing fornication as a good for himself at this particular moment, has a corrupt estimate in a particular matter, although he retains the true universal estimate according to faith, viz. that fornication is a mortal sin. In the same way, a man while retaining in the universal, the true estimate of faith, viz. that there is in the Church the power of forgiving sins, may suffer a movement of despair, to wit, that for him, being in such a state, there is no hope of pardon, his estimate being corrupted in a particular matter. In this way there can be despair, just as there can be other mortal sins, without belief.

Reply Obj. 1: The effect is done away, not only when the first cause is removed, but also when the secondary cause is removed. Hence the movement of hope can be done away, not only by the removal of the universal estimate of faith, which is, so to say, the first cause of the certainty of hope, but also by the removal of the particular estimate, which is the secondary cause, as it were.

Reply Obj. 2: If anyone were to judge, in universal, that God's mercy is not infinite, he would be an unbeliever. But he who despairs judges not thus, but that, for him in that state, on account of some particular disposition, there is no hope of the Divine mercy.

The same answer applies to the Third Objection, since the Novatians denied, in universal, that there is remission of sins in the Church.

* * * * *

THIRD ARTICLE [II-II, Q. 20, Art. 3]

Whether Despair Is the Greatest of Sins?

Objection 1: It would seem that despair is not the greatest of sins. For there can be despair without unbelief, as stated above (A. 2). But unbelief is the greatest of sins because it overthrows the foundation of the spiritual edifice. Therefore despair is not the greatest of sins.

Obj. 2: Further, a greater evil is opposed to a greater good, as the Philosopher states (Ethic. viii, 10). But charity is greater than hope, according to 1 Cor. 13:13. Therefore hatred of God is a greater sin than despair.

Obj. 3: Further, in the sin of despair there is nothing but inordinate aversion from God: whereas in other sins there is not only inordinate aversion from God, but also an inordinate conversion. Therefore the sin of despair is not more but less grave than other sins.

On the contrary, An incurable sin seems to be most grievous, according to Jer. 30:12: "Thy bruise is incurable, thy wound is very grievous." Now the sin of despair is incurable, according to Jer. 15:18: "My wound is desperate so as to refuse to be healed."[1] Therefore despair is a most grievous sin.

I answer that, Those sins which are contrary to the theological virtues are in themselves more grievous than others: because, since the theological virtues have God for their object, the sins which are opposed to them imply aversion from God directly and principally. Now every mortal sin takes its principal malice and gravity from the fact of its turning away from God, for if it were possible to turn to a mutable good, even inordinately, without turning away from God,

---

1   Vulg.: "Why is my wound," etc.

it would not be a mortal sin. Consequently a sin which, first and of its very nature, includes aversion from God, is most grievous among mortal sins.

Now unbelief, despair and hatred of God are opposed to the theological virtues: and among them, if we compare hatred of God and unbelief to despair, we shall find that, in themselves, that is, in respect of their proper species, they are more grievous. For unbelief is due to a man not believing God's own truth; while the hatred of God arises from man's will being opposed to God's goodness itself; whereas despair consists in a man ceasing to hope for a share of God's goodness. Hence it is clear that unbelief and hatred of God are against God as He is in Himself, while despair is against Him, according as His good is partaken of by us. Wherefore strictly speaking it is a more grievous sin to disbelieve God's truth, or to hate God, than not to hope to receive glory from Him.

If, however, despair be compared to the other two sins from our point of view, then despair is more dangerous, since hope withdraws us from evils and induces us to seek for good things, so that when hope is given up, men rush headlong into sin, and are drawn away from good works. Wherefore a gloss on Prov. 24:10, "If thou lose hope being weary in the day of distress, thy strength shall be diminished," says: "Nothing is more hateful than despair, for the man that has it loses his constancy both in the every day toils of this life, and, what is worse, in the battle of faith." And Isidore says (De Sum. Bono ii, 14): "To commit a crime is to kill the soul, but to despair is to fall into hell."

[And from this the response to the objections is evident.].

* * * * *

FOURTH ARTICLE [II-II, Q. 20, Art. 4]

Whether Despair Arises from Sloth?

Objection 1: It would seem that despair does not arise from sloth. Because different causes do not give rise to one same effect. Now despair of the future life arises from lust, according to Gregory (Moral. xxxi, 45). Therefore it does not arise from sloth.

Obj. 2: Further, just as despair is contrary to hope, so is sloth contrary to spiritual joy. But spiritual joy arises from hope, according to Rom. 12:12, "rejoicing in hope." Therefore sloth arises from despair, and not vice versa.

Obj. 3: Further, contrary effects have contrary causes. Now hope, the contrary of which is despair, seems to proceed from the consideration of Divine favors, especially the Incarnation, for Augustine says (De Trin. xiii, 10): "Nothing was so necessary to raise our hope, than that we should be shown how much God loves us. Now what greater proof could we have of this than that God's Son should deign to unite Himself to our nature?" Therefore despair arises rather from the neglect of the above consideration than from sloth.

On the contrary, Gregory (Moral. xxxi, 45) reckons despair among the effects of sloth.

I answer that, As stated above (Q. 17, A. 1; I-II, Q. 40, A. 1), the object of hope is a good, difficult but possible to obtain by oneself or by another. Consequently the hope of obtaining happiness may be lacking in a person in two ways: first, through his not deeming it an arduous good; secondly, through his deeming it impossible to obtain either by himself, or by another. Now, the fact that spiritual goods taste good to us no more, or seem to be goods of no great account, is chiefly due to our affections being infected with the love of bodily pleasures, among which, sexual pleasures hold the first place: for the love of those pleasures leads man to have a distaste for spiritual things, and not to hope for them as arduous goods. In this way despair is caused by lust.

On the other hand, the fact that a man deems an arduous good impossible to obtain, either by himself or by another, is due to his being over downcast, because when this state of mind dominates his affections, it seems to him that he will never be able to rise to any good. And since sloth is a sadness that casts down the spirit, in this way despair is born of sloth.

Now this is the proper object of hope—that the thing is possible, because the good and the arduous regard other passions also. Hence despair is born of sloth in a more special way: though it may arise from lust, for the reason given above.

This suffices for the Reply to the First Objection.

Reply Obj. 2: According to the Philosopher (Rhet. i, 11), just as hope gives rise to joy, so, when a man is joyful he has greater hope: and, accordingly, those who are sorrowful fall the more easily into despair, according to 2 Cor. 2:7: "Lest... such an one be swallowed up by overmuch sorrow." Yet, since the object of hope is good, to which the appetite tends naturally, and which it shuns, not naturally but only on account of some supervening obstacle, it follows that, more directly, hope gives birth to joy, while on the contrary despair is born of sorrow.

Reply Obj. 3: This very neglect to consider the Divine favors arises from sloth. For when a man is influenced by a certain passion he considers chiefly the things which pertain to that passion: so that a man who is full of sorrow does not easily think of great and joyful things, but only of sad things, unless by a great effort he turn his thoughts away from sadness.

21. OF PRESUMPTION (In Four Articles)

We must now consider presumption, under which head there are four points of inquiry:

(1)   What is the object in which presumption trusts?
(2)   Whether presumption is a sin?
(3)   To what is it opposed?
(4)   From what vice does it arise?.

* * * * *

FIRST ARTICLE [II-II, Q. 21, Art. 1]

Whether Presumption Trusts in God or in Our Own Power?

Objection 1: It would seem that presumption, which is a sin against the Holy Ghost, trusts, not in God, but in our own power. For the lesser the power, the more grievously does he sin who trusts in it too much. But man's power is less than God's. Therefore it is a more grievous sin to presume on human power than to presume on the power of God. Now the sin against the Holy Ghost is most grievous. Therefore presumption, which is reckoned a species of sin against the Holy Ghost, trusts to human rather than to Divine power.

Obj. 2: Further, other sins arise from the sin against the Holy Ghost, for this sin is called malice which is a source from which sins arise. Now other sins seem to arise from the presumption whereby man presumes on himself rather than from the presumption whereby he presumes on God, since self-love is the origin of sin, according to Augustine (De Civ. Dei xiv, 28). Therefore it seems that presumption which is a sin against the Holy Ghost, relies chiefly on human power.

Obj. 3: Further, sin arises from the inordinate conversion to a mutable good. Now presumption is a sin. Therefore it arises from turning to human power, which is a mutable good, rather than from turning to the power of God, which is an immutable good.

On the contrary, Just as, through despair, a man despises the Divine mercy, on which hope relies, so, through presumption, he despises the Divine justice, which punishes the sinner. Now justice is in God even as mercy is. Therefore, just as despair consists in aversion from God, so presumption consists in inordinate conversion to Him.

I answer that, Presumption seems to imply immoderate hope. Now the object of hope is an arduous possible good: and a thing is possible to a man in two ways: first by his own power; secondly, by the power of God alone. With regard to either hope there may be presumption owing to lack of moderation. As to the hope whereby a man relies on his own power, there is presumption if he tends to a good as though it were possible to him, whereas it surpasses his powers, according to Judith 6:15: "Thou humblest them that presume of themselves." This presumption is contrary to the virtue of magnanimity which holds to the mean in this kind of hope.

But as to the hope whereby a man relies on the power of God, there may be presumption through immoderation, in the fact that a man tends to some good as though it were possible by the power and mercy of God, whereas it is not possible, for instance, if a man hope to obtain pardon without repenting, or glory without merits. This presumption is, properly, the sin against the Holy Ghost, because, to wit, by presuming thus a man removes or despises the assistance of the Holy Spirit, whereby he is withdrawn from sin.

Reply Obj. 1: As stated above (Q. 20, A. 3; I-II, Q. 73, A. 3) a sin which is against God is, in its genus, graver than other sins. Hence presumption whereby a man relies on God inordinately, is a more grievous sin than the presumption of trusting in one's own power, since to rely on the Divine power for obtaining what is unbecoming to God, is to depreciate the Divine power, and it is evident that it is a graver sin to detract from the Divine power than to exaggerate one's own.

Reply Obj. 2: The presumption whereby a man presumes inordinately on God, includes self-love, whereby he loves his own good inordinately. For when we desire a thing very much, we think we can easily procure it through others, even though we cannot.

Reply Obj. 3: Presumption on God's mercy implies both conversion to a mutable good, in so far as it arises from an inordinate desire of one's own good, and aversion from the immutable good, in as much as it ascribes to the Divine power that which is unbecoming to it, for thus man turns away from God's power.

* * * * *

SECOND ARTICLE [II-II, Q. 21, Art. 2]

Whether Presumption Is a Sin?

Objection 1: It would seem that presumption is not a sin. For no sin is a reason why man should be heard by God. Yet, through presumption some are heard by God, for it is written (Judith 9:17): "Hear me a poor wretch making supplication to Thee, and presuming of Thy mercy." Therefore presumption on God's mercy is not a sin.

Obj. 2: Further, presumption denotes excessive hope. But there cannot be excess of that hope which is in God, since His power and mercy are infinite. Therefore it seems that presumption is not a sin.

Obj. 3: Further, that which is a sin does not excuse from sin: for the Master says (Sent. ii, D, 22) that "Adam sinned less, because he sinned in the hope of pardon," which seems to indicate presumption. Therefore presumption is not a sin.

On the contrary, It is reckoned a species of sin against the Holy Ghost.

I answer that, As stated above (Q. 20, A. 1) with regard to despair, every appetitive movement that is conformed to a false intellect, is evil in itself and sinful. Now presumption is an appetitive movement, since it denotes an inordinate hope. Moreover it is conformed to a false intellect, just as despair is: for just as it is false that God does not pardon the repentant, or that He does not turn sinners to repentance, so is it false that He grants forgiveness to those who persevere in their sins, and that He gives glory to those who cease from good works: and it is to this estimate that the movement of presumption is conformed.

Consequently presumption is a sin, but less grave than despair, since, on account of His infinite goodness, it is more proper to God to have mercy and to spare, than to punish: for the former becomes God in Himself, the latter becomes Him by reason of our sins.

Reply Obj. 1: Presumption sometimes stands for hope, because even the right hope which we have in God seems to be presumption, if it be measured according to man's estate: yet it is not, if we look at the immensity of the goodness of God.

Reply Obj. 2: Presumption does not denote excessive hope, as though man hoped too much in God; but through man hoping to obtain from God something unbecoming to Him; which is the same as to hope too little in Him, since it implies a depreciation of His power; as stated above (A. 1, ad 1).

Reply Obj. 3: To sin with the intention of persevering in sin and through the hope of being pardoned, is presumptuous, and this does not diminish, but increases sin. To sin, however, with the hope of obtaining pardon some time, and with the intention of refraining from sin and of repenting of it, is not presumptuous, but diminishes sin, because this seems to indicate a will less hardened in sin.

* * * * *

THIRD ARTICLE [II-II, Q. 21, Art. 3]

Whether Presumption Is More Opposed to Fear Than to Hope?

Objection 1: It would seem that presumption is more opposed to fear than to hope. Because inordinate fear is opposed to right fear. Now presumption seems to pertain to inordinate fear, for it is written (Wis. 17:10): "A troubled conscience always presumes [Douay: 'forecasteth'] grievous things," and (Wis. 17:11) that "fear is a help to presumption[1]." Therefore presumption is opposed to fear rather than to hope.

Obj. 2: Further, contraries are most distant from one another. Now presumption is more distant from fear than from hope, because presumption implies movement to something, just as hope

---

1   Vulg.: 'Fear is nothing else but a yielding up of the succours from thought.'

does, whereas fear denotes movement from a thing. Therefore presumption is contrary to fear rather than to hope.

Obj. 3: Further, presumption excludes fear altogether, whereas it does not exclude hope altogether, but only the rectitude of hope. Since therefore contraries destroy one another, it seems that presumption is contrary to fear rather than to hope.

On the contrary, When two vices are opposed to one another they are contrary to the same virtue, as timidity and audacity are opposed to fortitude. Now the sin of presumption is contrary to the sin of despair, which is directly opposed to hope. Therefore it seems that presumption also is more directly opposed to hope.

I answer that, As Augustine states (Contra Julian. iv, 3), "every virtue not only has a contrary vice manifestly distinct from it, as temerity is opposed to prudence, but also a sort of kindred vice, alike, not in truth but only in its deceitful appearance, as cunning is opposed to prudence." This agrees with the Philosopher who says (Ethic. ii, 8) that a virtue seems to have more in common with one of the contrary vices than with the other, as temperance with insensibility, and fortitude with audacity.

Accordingly presumption appears to be manifestly opposed to fear, especially servile fear, which looks at the punishment arising from God's justice, the remission of which presumption hopes for; yet by a kind of false likeness it is more opposed to hope, since it denotes an inordinate hope in God. And since things are more directly opposed when they belong to the same genus, than when they belong to different genera, it follows that presumption is more directly opposed to hope than to fear. For they both regard and rely on the same object, hope inordinately, presumption inordinately.

Reply Obj. 1: Just as hope is misused in speaking of evils, and properly applied in speaking of good, so is presumption: it is in this way that inordinate fear is called presumption.

Reply Obj. 2: Contraries are things that are most distant from one another within the same genus. Now presumption and hope denote a movement of the same genus, which can be either ordinate or inordinate. Hence presumption is more directly opposed to hope than to fear, since it is opposed to hope in respect of its specific difference, as an inordinate thing to an ordinate one, whereas it is opposed to fear, in respect of its generic difference, which is the movement of hope.

Reply Obj. 3: Presumption is opposed to fear by a generic contrariety, and to the virtue of hope by a specific contrariety. Hence presumption excludes fear altogether even generically, whereas it does not exclude hope except by reason of its difference, by excluding its ordinateness.

* * * * *

FOURTH ARTICLE [II-II, Q. 21, Art. 4]

Whether Presumption Arises from Vainglory?

Objection 1: It would seem that presumption does not arise from vainglory. For presumption seems to rely most of all on the Divine mercy. Now mercy (misericordia) regards unhappiness (miseriam) which is contrary to glory. Therefore presumption does not arise from vainglory.

Obj. 2: Further, presumption is opposed to despair. Now despair arises from sorrow, as stated above (Q. 20, A. 4, ad 2). Since therefore opposites have opposite causes, presumption would seem to arise from pleasure, and consequently from sins of the flesh, which give the most absorbing pleasure.

Obj. 3: Further, the vice of presumption consists in tending to some impossible good, as though it were possible. Now it is owing to ignorance that one deems an impossible thing to be possible. Therefore presumption arises from ignorance rather than from vainglory.

On the contrary, Gregory says (Moral. xxxi, 45) that "presumption of novelties is a daughter of vainglory."

I answer that, As stated above (A. 1), presumption is twofold; one whereby a man relies on his own power, when he attempts something beyond his power, as though it were possible to him. Such like presumption clearly arises from vainglory; for it is owing to a great desire for glory, that a man attempts things beyond his power, and especially novelties which call for greater admiration. Hence Gregory states explicitly that presumption of novelties is a daughter of vainglory.

The other presumption is an inordinate trust in the Divine mercy or power, consisting in the hope of obtaining glory without merits, or pardon without repentance. Such like presumption seems to arise directly from pride, as though man thought so much of himself as to esteem that God would not punish him or exclude him from glory, however much he might be a sinner.

This suffices for the Replies to the Objections.

22. OF THE PRECEPTS RELATING TO HOPE AND FEAR (In Two Articles)

We must now consider the precepts relating to hope and fear: under which head there are two points of inquiry:

(1) The precepts relating to hope;
(2) The precepts relating to fear.

* * * * *

FIRST ARTICLE [II-II, Q. 22, Art. 1]

Whether There Should Be a Precept of Hope?

Objection 1: It would seem that no precept should be given relating to the virtue of hope. For when an effect is sufficiently procured by one cause, there is no need to induce it by another. Now man is sufficiently induced by his natural inclination to hope for good. Therefore there is no need of a precept of the Law to induce him to do this.

Obj. 2: Further, since precepts are given about acts of virtue, the chief precepts are about the acts of the chief virtues. Now the chief of all the virtues are the three theological virtues, viz. hope, faith and charity. Consequently, as the chief precepts of the Law are those of the decalogue, to which all others may be reduced, as stated above (I-II, Q. 100, A. 3), it seems that if any precept of hope were given, it should be found among the precepts of the decalogue. But it is not to be found there. Therefore it seems that the Law should contain no precept of hope.

Obj. 3: Further, to prescribe an act of virtue is equivalent to a prohibition of the act of the opposite vice. Now no precept is to be found forbidding despair which is contrary to hope. Therefore it seems that the Law should contain no precept of hope.

On the contrary, Augustine says on John 15:12, "This is My commandment, that you love one another" (Tract. lxxxiii in Joan.): "How many things are commanded us about faith! How many relating to hope!" Therefore it is fitting that some precepts should be given about hope.

I answer that, Among the precepts contained in Holy Writ, some belong to the substance of the Law, others are preambles to the Law. The preambles to the Law are those without which no law is possible: such are the precepts relating to the act of faith and the act of hope, because the act of faith inclines man's mind so that he believes the Author of the Law to be One to Whom he owes submission, while, by the hope of a reward, he is induced to observe the precepts. The precepts that belong to the substance of the Law are those which relate to right conduct and are imposed on man already subject and ready to obey: wherefore when the Law was given these precepts were set forth from the very outset under the form of a command.

Yet the precepts of hope and faith were not to be given under the form of a command, since, unless man already believed and hoped, it would be useless to give him the Law: but, just as the precept of faith had to be given under the form of an announcement or reminder, as stated above (Q. 16, A. 1), so too, the precept of hope, in the first promulgation of the Law, had to be given under the form of a promise. For he who promises rewards to them that obey him, by that very fact, urges them to hope: hence all the promises contained in the Law are incitements to hope.

Since, however, when once the Law has been given, it is for a wise man to induce men not only to observe the precepts, but also, and much more, to safeguard the foundation of the Law, therefore, after the first promulgation of the Law, Holy Writ holds out to man many inducements to hope, even by way of warning or command, and not merely by way of promise, as in the Law; for instance, in the Ps. 61:9: "Hope [Douay: 'Trust'] in Him all ye congregation of the people," and in many other passages of the Scriptures.

Reply Obj. 1: Nature inclines us to hope for the good which is proportionate to human nature; but for man to hope for a supernatural good he had to be induced by the authority of the Divine law, partly by promises, partly by admonitions and commands. Nevertheless there was need for precepts of the Divine law to be given even for those things to which natural reason inclines us, such as the acts of the moral virtues, for sake of insuring a greater stability, especially since the natural reason of man was clouded by the lusts of sin.

Reply Obj. 2: The precepts of the law of the decalogue belong to the first promulgation of the Law: hence there was no need for a precept of hope among the precepts of the decalogue, and it was enough to induce men to hope by the inclusion of certain promises, as in the case of the first and fourth commandments.

Reply Obj. 3: In those observances to which man is bound as under a duty, it is enough that he receive an affirmative precept as to what he has to do, wherein is implied the prohibition of what he must avoid doing: thus he is given a precept concerning the honor due to parents, but not a prohibition against dishonoring them, except by the law inflicting punishment on those who dishonor their parents. And since in order to be saved it is man's duty to hope in God, he had to be induced to do so by one of the above ways, affirmatively, so to speak, wherein is implied the prohibition of the opposite.

* * * * *

SECOND ARTICLE [II-II, Q. 22, Art. 2]

Whether There Should Have Been Given a Precept of Fear?

Objection 1: It would seem that, in the Law, there should not have been given a precept of fear. For the fear of God is about things which are a preamble to the Law, since it is the "beginning of wisdom." Now things which are a preamble to the Law do not come under a precept of the Law. Therefore no precept of fear should be given in the Law.

Obj. 2: Further, given the cause, the effect is also given. Now love is the cause of fear, since "every fear proceeds from some kind of love," as Augustine states (Qq. lxxxiii, qu. 33). Therefore given the precept of love, it would have been superfluous to command fear.

Obj. 3: Further, presumption, in a way, is opposed to fear. But the Law contains no prohibition against presumption. Therefore it seems that neither should any precept of fear have been given.

On the contrary, It is written (Deut. 10:12): "And now, Israel, what doth the Lord thy God require of thee, but that thou fear the Lord thy God?" But He requires of us that which He commands us to do. Therefore it is a matter of precept that man should fear God.

I answer that, Fear is twofold, servile and filial. Now just as man is induced, by the hope of rewards, to observe precepts of law, so too is he induced thereto by the fear of punishment, which fear is servile.

And just as according to what has been said (A. 1), in the promulgation of the Law there was no need for a precept of the act of hope, and men were to be induced thereto by promises, so neither was there need for a precept, under form of command, of fear which regards punishment, and men were to be induced thereto by the threat of punishment: and this was realized both in the precepts of the decalogue, and afterwards, in due sequence, in the secondary precepts of the Law.

Yet, just as wise men and the prophets who, consequently, strove to strengthen man in the observance of the Law, delivered their teaching about hope under the form of admonition or command, so too did they in the matter of fear.

On the other hand filial fear which shows reverence to God, is a sort of genus in respect of the love of God, and a kind of principle of all observances connected with reverence for God. Hence precepts of filial fear are given in the Law, even as precepts of love, because each is a preamble to the external acts prescribed by the Law and to which the precepts of the decalogue refer. Hence in the passage quoted in the argument *On the contrary*, man is required "to have fear, to walk in God's ways," by worshipping Him, and "to love Him."

Reply Obj. 1: Filial fear is a preamble to the Law, not as though it were extrinsic thereto, but as being the beginning of the Law, just as love is. Hence precepts are given of both, since they are like general principles of the whole Law.

Reply Obj. 2: From love proceeds filial fear as also other good works that are done from charity. Hence, just as after the precept of charity, precepts are given of the other acts of virtue, so at the same time precepts are given of fear and of the love of charity, just as, in demonstrative sciences, it is not enough to lay down the first principles, unless the conclusions also are given which follow from them proximately or remotely.

Reply Obj. 3: Inducement to fear suffices to exclude presumption, even as inducement to hope suffices to exclude despair, as stated above (A. 1, ad 3).

23. OF CHARITY, CONSIDERED IN ITSELF
(In Eight Articles)

In proper sequence, we must consider charity; and (1) charity itself; (2) the corresponding gift of wisdom. The first consideration will be fivefold: (1) Charity itself; (2) The object of charity; (3) Its acts; (4) The opposite vices; (5) The precepts relating thereto.

The first of these considerations will be twofold: (1) Charity, considered as regards itself; (2) Charity, considered in its relation to its subject. Under the first head there are eight points of inquiry:

(1) Whether charity is friendship?
(2) Whether it is something created in the soul?
(3) Whether it is a virtue?
(4) Whether it is a special virtue?
(5) Whether it is one virtue?
(6) Whether it is the greatest of the virtues?
(7) Whether any true virtue is possible without it?
(8) Whether it is the form of the virtues?.

* * * * *

FIRST ARTICLE [II-II, Q. 23, Art. 1]

Whether Charity Is Friendship?

Objection 1: It would seem that charity is not friendship. For nothing is so appropriate to friendship as to dwell with one's friend, according to the Philosopher (Ethic. viii, 5). Now charity is of man towards God and the angels, "whose dwelling [Douay: 'conversation'] is not with men" (Dan. 2:11). Therefore charity is not friendship.

Obj. 2: Further, there is no friendship without return of love (Ethic. viii, 2). But charity extends even to one's enemies, according to Matt. 5:44: "Love your enemies." Therefore charity is not friendship.

Obj. 3: Further, according to the Philosopher (Ethic. viii, 3) there are three kinds of friendship, directed respectively towards the delightful, the useful, or the virtuous. Now charity is not the friendship for the useful or delightful; for Jerome says in his letter to Paulinus which is to be found at the beginning of the Bible: "True friendship cemented by Christ, is where men are drawn together, not by household interests, not by mere bodily presence, not by crafty and cajoling flattery, but by the fear of God, and the study of the Divine Scriptures." No more is it friendship for the virtuous, since by charity we love even sinners, whereas friendship based on the virtuous is only for virtuous men (Ethic. viii). Therefore charity is not friendship.

On the contrary, It is written (John 15:15): "I will not now call you servants . . . but My friends." Now this was said to them by reason of nothing else than charity. Therefore charity is friendship.

I answer that, According to the Philosopher (Ethic. viii, 2, 3) not every love has the character of friendship, but that love which is together with benevolence, when, to wit, we love someone so as to wish good to him. If, however, we do not wish good to what we love, but wish its good for ourselves, (thus we are said to love wine, or a horse, or the like), it is love not of friendship, but of a kind of concupiscence. For it would be absurd to speak of having friendship for wine or for a horse.

Yet neither does well-wishing suffice for friendship, for a certain mutual love is requisite, since friendship is between friend and friend: and this well-wishing is founded on some kind of communication.

Accordingly, since there is a communication between man and God, inasmuch as He communicates His happiness to us, some kind of friendship must needs be based on this same communication, of which it is written (1 Cor. 1:9): "God is faithful: by Whom you are called unto the fellowship of His Son." The love which is based on this communication, is charity: wherefore it is evident that charity is the friendship of man for God.

Reply Obj. 1: Man's life is twofold. There is his outward life in respect of his sensitive and corporeal nature: and with regard to this life there is no communication or fellowship between us and God or the angels. The other is man's spiritual life in respect of his mind, and with regard to this life there is fellowship between us and both God and the angels, imperfectly indeed in this present state of life, wherefore it is written (Phil. 3:20): "Our conversation is in heaven." But this "conversation" will be perfected in heaven, when "His servants shall serve Him, and they shall see His face" (Apoc. 22:3, 4). Therefore charity is imperfect here, but will be perfected in heaven.

Reply Obj. 2: Friendship extends to a person in two ways: first in respect of himself, and in this way friendship never extends but to one's friends: secondly, it extends to someone in respect of another, as, when a man has friendship for a certain person, for his sake he loves all belonging to him, be they children, servants, or connected with him in any way. Indeed so much do we love our friends, that for their sake we love all who belong to them, even if they hurt or hate us; so that, in this way, the friendship of charity extends even to our enemies, whom we love out of charity in relation to God, to Whom the friendship of charity is chiefly directed.

Reply Obj. 3: The friendship that is based on the virtuous is directed to none but a virtuous man as the principal person, but for his sake we love those who belong to him, even though they be not virtuous: in this way charity, which above all is friendship based on the virtuous, extends to sinners, whom, out of charity, we love for God's sake.

* * * * *

SECOND ARTICLE [II-II, Q. 23, Art. 2]

Whether Charity Is Something Created in the Soul?

Objection 1: It would seem that charity is not something created in the soul. For Augustine says (De Trin. viii, 7): "He that loveth his neighbor, consequently, loveth love itself." Now God is love. Therefore it follows that he loves God in the first place. Again he says (De Trin. xv, 17): "It was said: God is Charity, even as it was said: God is a Spirit." Therefore charity is not something created in the soul, but is God Himself.

Obj. 2: Further, God is the life of the soul spiritually just as the soul is the life of the body, according to Deut. 30:20: "He is thy life." Now the soul by itself quickens the body. Therefore God quickens the soul by Himself. But He quickens it by charity, according to 1 John 3:14: "We know that we have passed from death to life, because we love the brethren." Therefore God is charity itself.

Obj. 3: Further, no created thing is of infinite power; on the contrary every creature is vanity. But charity is not vanity, indeed it is opposed to vanity; and it is of infinite power, since it brings the human soul to the infinite good. Therefore charity is not something created in the soul.

On the charity, Augustine says (De Doctr. Christ. iii, 10): "By charity I mean the movement of the soul towards the enjoyment of God for His own sake." But a movement of the soul is something created in the soul. Therefore charity is something created in the soul.

I answer that, The Master looks thoroughly into this question in Q. 17 of the First Book, and concludes that charity is not something created in the soul, but is the Holy Ghost Himself dwelling in the mind. Nor does he mean to say that this movement of love whereby we love God is the Holy Ghost Himself, but that this movement is from the Holy Ghost without any intermediary habit, whereas other virtuous acts are from the Holy Ghost by means of the habits of other virtues, for instance the habit of faith or hope or of some other virtue: and this he said on account of the excellence of charity.

But if we consider the matter aright, this would be, on the contrary, detrimental to charity. For when the Holy Ghost moves the human mind the movement of charity does not proceed from this motion in such a way that the human mind be merely moved, without being the principle of this movement, as when a body is moved by some extrinsic motive power. For this is contrary to the nature of a voluntary act, whose principle needs to be in itself, as stated above (I-II, Q. 6, A. 1): so that it would follow that to love is not a voluntary act, which involves a contradiction, since love, of its very nature, implies an act of the will.

Likewise, neither can it be said that the Holy Ghost moves the will in such a way to the act of loving, as though the will were an instrument, for an instrument, though it be a principle of action, nevertheless has not the power to act or not to act, for then again the act would cease to be voluntary and meritorious, whereas it has been stated above (I-II, Q. 114, A. 4) that the love of charity is the root of merit: and, given that the will is moved by the Holy Ghost to the act of love, it is necessary that the will also should be the efficient cause of that act.

Now no act is perfectly produced by an active power, unless it be connatural to that power by reason of some form which is the principle of that action. Wherefore God, Who moves all things to their due ends, bestowed on each thing the form whereby it is inclined to the end appointed to it by Him; and in this way He "ordereth all things sweetly" (Wis. 8:1). But it is evident that the act of charity surpasses the nature of the power of the will, so that, therefore, unless some form be superadded to the natural power, inclining it to the act of love, this same act would be less perfect than the natural acts and the acts of the other powers; nor would it be easy and pleasurable to perform. And this is evidently untrue, since no virtue has such a strong inclination to its act as charity has, nor does any virtue perform its act with so great pleasure. Therefore it is most necessary that, for us to perform the act of charity, there should be in us some habitual form superadded to the natural power, inclining that power to the act of charity, and causing it to act with ease and pleasure.

Reply Obj. 1: The Divine Essence Itself is charity, even as It is wisdom and goodness. Wherefore just as we are said to be good with the goodness which is God, and wise with the wisdom which is God (since the goodness whereby we are formally good is a participation of Divine goodness, and the wisdom whereby we are formally wise, is a share of Divine wisdom), so too, the charity whereby formally we love our neighbor is a participation of Divine charity. For this manner of speaking is common among the Platonists, with whose doctrines Augustine was imbued; and the lack of adverting to this has been to some an occasion of error.

Reply Obj. 2: God is effectively the life both of the soul by charity, and of the body by the soul: but formally charity is the life of the soul, even as the soul is the life of the body. Consequently we may conclude from this that just as the soul is immediately united to the body, so is charity to the soul.

Reply Obj. 3: Charity works formally. Now the efficacy of a form depends on the power of the agent, who instills the form, wherefore it is evident that charity is not vanity. But because it produces an infinite effect, since, by justifying the soul, it unites it to God, this proves the infinity of the Divine power, which is the author of charity.

* * * * *

THIRD ARTICLE [II-II, Q. 23, Art. 3]

Whether Charity Is a Virtue?

Objection 1: It would seem that charity is not a virtue. For charity is a kind of friendship. Now philosophers do not reckon friendship a virtue, as may be gathered from Ethic. viii, 1; nor is it numbered among the virtues whether moral or intellectual. Neither, therefore, is charity a virtue.

Obj. 2: Further, "virtue is the ultimate limit of power" (De Coelo et Mundo i, 11). But charity is not something ultimate, this applies rather to joy and peace. Therefore it seems that charity is not a virtue, and that this should be said rather of joy and peace.

Obj. 3: Further, every virtue is an accidental habit. But charity is not an accidental habit, since it is a more excellent thing than the soul itself: whereas no accident is more excellent than its subject. Therefore charity is not a virtue.

On the contrary, Augustine says (De Moribus Eccl. xi): "Charity is a virtue which, when our affections are perfectly ordered, unites us to God, for by it we love Him."

I answer that, Human acts are good according as they are regulated by their due rule and measure. Wherefore human virtue which is the principle of all man's good acts consists in following the rule of human acts, which is twofold, as stated above (Q. 17, A. 1), viz. human reason and God.

Consequently just as moral virtue is defined as being "in accord with right reason," as stated in *Ethic.* ii, 6, so too, the nature of virtue consists in attaining God, as also stated above with regard to faith, (Q. 4, A. 5) and hope (Q. 17, A. 1). Wherefore, it follows that charity is a virtue, for, since charity attains God, it unites us to God, as evidenced by the authority of Augustine quoted above.

Reply Obj. 1: The Philosopher (Ethic. viii) does not deny that friendship is a virtue, but affirms that it is "either a virtue or with a virtue." For we might say that it is a moral virtue about works done in respect of another person, but under a different aspect from justice. For justice is about works done in respect of another person, under the aspect of the legal due, whereas friendship considers the aspect of a friendly and moral duty, or rather that of a gratuitous favor, as the Philosopher explains (Ethic. viii, 13). Nevertheless it may be admitted that it is not a virtue distinct of itself from the other virtues. For its praiseworthiness and virtuousness are derived merely from its object, in so far, to wit, as it is based on the moral goodness of the virtues. This is evident from the fact that not every friendship is praiseworthy and virtuous, as in the case of friendship based on pleasure or utility. Wherefore friendship for the virtuous is something consequent to virtue rather than a virtue. Moreover there is no comparison with charity since it is not founded principally on the virtue of a man, but on the goodness of God.

Reply Obj. 2: It belongs to the same virtue to love a man and to rejoice about him, since joy results from love, as stated above (I-II, Q. 25, A. 2) in the treatise on the passions: wherefore love is reckoned a virtue, rather than joy, which is an effect of love. And when virtue is described as being something ultimate, we mean that it is last, not in the order of effect, but in the order of excess, just as one hundred pounds exceed sixty.

Reply Obj. 3: Every accident is inferior to substance if we consider its being, since substance has being in itself, while an accident has its being in another: but considered as to its species, an accident which results from the principles of its subject is inferior to its subject, even as an effect is inferior to its cause; whereas an accident that results from a participation of some higher nature is superior to its subject, in so far as it is a likeness of that higher nature, even as light is superior to the diaphanous body. In this way charity is superior to the soul, in as much as it is a participation of the Holy Ghost.

* * * * *

FOURTH ARTICLE [II-II, Q. 23, Art. 4]

Whether Charity Is a Special Virtue?

Objection 1: It would seem that charity is not a special virtue. For Jerome says: "Let me briefly define all virtue as the charity whereby we love God"[1]: and Augustine says (De Moribus Eccl. xv)[2] that "virtue is the order of love." Now no special virtue is included in the definition of virtue in general. Therefore charity is not a special virtue.

---

1 The reference should be to Augustine, Ep. clxvii
2 De Civ. Dei xv, 22

Obj. 2: Further, that which extends to all works of virtue, cannot be a special virtue. But charity extends to all works of virtue, according to 1 Cor. 13:4: "Charity is patient, is kind," etc.; indeed it extends to all human actions, according to 1 Cor. 16:14: "Let all your things be done in charity." Therefore charity is not a special virtue.

Obj. 3: Further, the precepts of the Law refer to acts of virtue. Now Augustine says (De Perfect. Human. Justit. v) that, "Thou shalt love" is "a general commandment," and "Thou shalt not covet," "a general prohibition." Therefore charity is a general virtue.

On the contrary, Nothing general is enumerated together with what is special. But charity is enumerated together with special virtues, viz. hope and faith, according to 1 Cor. 13:13: "And now there remain faith, hope, charity, these three." Therefore charity is a special virtue.

I answer that, Acts and habits are specified by their objects, as shown above (I-II, Q. 18, A. 2; I-II, Q. 54, A. 2). Now the proper object of love is the good, as stated above (I-II, Q. 27, A. 1), so that wherever there is a special aspect of good, there is a special kind of love. But the Divine good, inasmuch as it is the object of happiness, has a special aspect of good, wherefore the love of charity, which is the love of that good, is a special kind of love. Therefore charity is a special virtue.

Reply Obj. 1: Charity is included in the definition of every virtue, not as being essentially every virtue, but because every virtue depends on it in a way, as we shall state further on (AA. 7, 8). In this way prudence is included in the definition of the moral virtues, as explained in Ethic. ii, vi, from the fact that they depend on prudence.

Reply Obj. 2: The virtue or art which is concerned about the last end, commands the virtues or arts which are concerned about other ends which are secondary, thus the military art commands the art of horse-riding (Ethic. i). Accordingly since charity has for its object the last end of human life, viz. everlasting happiness, it follows that it extends to the acts of a man's whole life, by commanding them, not by eliciting immediately all acts of virtue.

Reply Obj. 3: The precept of love is said to be a general command, because all other precepts are reduced thereto as to their end, according to 1 Tim. 1:5: "The end of the commandment is charity.".

* * * * *

FIFTH ARTICLE [II-II, Q. 23, Art. 5]

Whether Charity Is One Virtue?

Objection 1: It would seem that charity is not one virtue. For habits are distinct according to their objects. Now there are two objects of charity—God and our neighbor—which are infinitely distant from one another. Therefore charity is not one virtue.

Obj. 2: Further, different aspects of the object diversify a habit, even though that object be one in reality, as shown above (Q. 17, A. 6; I-II, Q. 54, A. 2, ad 1). Now there are many aspects under which God is an object of love, because we are debtors to His love by reason of each one of His favors. Therefore charity is not one virtue.

Obj. 3: Further, charity comprises friendship for our neighbor. But the Philosopher reckons several species of friendship (Ethic. viii, 3, 11, 12). Therefore charity is not one virtue, but is divided into a number of various species.

On the contrary, Just as God is the object of faith, so is He the object of charity. Now faith is one virtue by reason of the unity of the Divine truth, according to Eph. 4:5: "One faith." Therefore charity also is one virtue by reason of the unity of the Divine goodness.

I answer that, Charity, as stated above (A. 1) is a kind of friendship of man for God. Now the different species of friendship are differentiated, first of all, in respect of a diversity of end, and in this way there are three species of friendship, namely friendship for the useful, for the delightful, and for the virtuous; secondly, in respect of the different kinds of communion on which friendships are based; thus there is one species of friendship between kinsmen, and another between fellow citizens or fellow travellers, the former being based on natural communion, the latter on civil communion or on the comradeship of the road, as the Philosopher explains (Ethic. viii, 12).

Now charity cannot be differentiated in either of these ways: for its end is one, namely, the goodness of God; and the fellowship of everlasting happiness, on which this friendship is based, is also one. Hence it follows that charity is simply one virtue, and not divided into several species.

Reply Obj. 1: This argument would hold, if God and our neighbor were equally objects of charity. But this is not true: for

God is the principal object of charity, while our neighbor is loved out of charity for God's sake.

Reply Obj. 2: God is loved by charity for His own sake: wherefore charity regards principally but one aspect of lovableness, namely God's goodness, which is His substance, according to Ps. 105:1: "Give glory to the Lord for He is good." Other reasons that inspire us with love for Him, or which make it our duty to love Him, are secondary and result from the first.

Reply Obj. 3: Human friendship of which the Philosopher treats has various ends and various forms of fellowship. This does not apply to charity, as stated above: wherefore the comparison fails.

* * * * *

SIXTH ARTICLE [II-II, Q. 23, Art. 6]

Whether Charity Is the Most Excellent of the Virtues?

Objection 1: It would seem that charity is not the most excellent of the virtues. Because the higher power has the higher virtue even as it has a higher operation. Now the intellect is higher than the will, since it directs the will. Therefore, faith, which is in the intellect, is more excellent than charity which is in the will.

Obj. 2: Further, the thing by which another works seems the less excellent of the two, even as a servant, by whom his master works, is beneath his master. Now "faith . . . worketh by charity," according to Gal. 5:6. Therefore faith is more excellent than charity.

Obj. 3: Further, that which is by way of addition to another seems to be the more perfect of the two. Now hope seems to be something additional to charity: for the object of charity is good, whereas the object of hope is an arduous good. Therefore hope is more excellent than charity.

On the contrary, It is written (1 Cor. 13:13): "The greater of these is charity."

I answer that, Since good, in human acts, depends on their being regulated by the due rule, it must needs be that human virtue, which is a principle of good acts, consists in attaining the rule of human acts. Now the rule of human acts is twofold, as stated above (A. 3), namely, human reason and God: yet God is the first rule, whereby, even human reason must be regulated. Consequently the theological virtues, which consist in attaining this first rule, since their object is God, are more excellent than the moral, or the intellectual virtues, which consist in attaining human reason: and it follows that among the theological virtues themselves, the first place belongs to that which attains God most.

Now that which is of itself always ranks before that which is by another. But faith and hope attain God indeed in so far as we derive from Him the knowledge of truth or the acquisition of good, whereas charity attains God Himself that it may rest in Him, but not that something may accrue to us from Him. Hence charity is more excellent than faith or hope, and, consequently, than all the other virtues, just as prudence, which by itself attains reason, is more excellent than the other moral virtues, which attain reason in so far as it appoints the mean in human operations or passions.

Reply Obj. 1: The operation of the intellect is completed by the thing understood being in the intellectual subject, so that the excellence of the intellectual operation is assessed according to the measure of the intellect. On the other hand, the operation of the will and of every appetitive power is completed in the tendency of the appetite towards a thing as its term, wherefore the excellence of the appetitive operation is gauged according to the thing which is the object of the operation. Now those things which are beneath the soul are more excellent in the soul than they are in themselves, because a thing is contained according to the mode of the container (De Causis xii). On the other hand, things that are above the soul, are more excellent in themselves than they are in the soul. Consequently it is better to know than to love the things that are beneath us; for which reason the Philosopher gave the preference to the intellectual virtues over the moral virtues (Ethic. x, 7, 8): whereas the love of the things that are above us, especially of God, ranks before the knowledge of such things. Therefore charity is more excellent than faith.

Reply Obj. 2: Faith works by love, not instrumentally, as a master by his servant, but as by its proper form: hence the argument does not prove.

Reply Obj. 3: The same good is the object of charity and of hope: but charity implies union with that good, whereas hope implies distance therefrom. Hence charity does not regard that good as being arduous, as hope does, since what is already united has not the character of arduous: and this shows that charity is more perfect than hope.

* * * * *

SEVENTH ARTICLE [II-II, Q. 23, Art. 7]

Whether Any True Virtue Is Possible Without Charity?

Objection 1: It would seem that there can be true virtue without charity. For it is proper to virtue to produce a good act. Now those who have not charity, do some good actions, as when they clothe the naked, or feed the hungry and so forth. Therefore true virtue is possible without charity.

Obj. 2: Further, charity is not possible without faith, since it comes of "an unfeigned faith," as the Apostle says (1 Tim. 1:5). Now, in unbelievers, there can be true chastity, if they curb their concupiscences, and true justice, if they judge rightly. Therefore true virtue is possible without charity.

Obj. 3: Further, science and art are virtues, according to Ethic. vi. But they are to be found in sinners who lack charity. Therefore true virtue can be without charity.

On the contrary, The Apostle says (1 Cor. 13:3): "If I should distribute all my goods to the poor, and if I should deliver my body to be burned, and have not charity, it profiteth me nothing." And yet true virtue is very profitable, according to Wis. 8:7: "She teacheth temperance, and prudence, and justice, and fortitude, which are such things as men can have nothing more profitable in life." Therefore no true virtue is possible without charity.

I answer that, Virtue is ordered to the good, as stated above (I-II, Q. 55, A. 4). Now the good is chiefly an end, for things directed to the end are not said to be good except in relation to the end. Accordingly, just as the end is twofold, the last end, and the proximate end, so also, is good twofold, one, the ultimate and universal good, the other proximate and particular. The ultimate and principal good of man is the enjoyment of God, according to Ps. 72:28: "It is good for me to adhere to God," and to this good man is ordered by charity. Man's secondary and, as it were, particular good may be twofold: one is truly good, because, considered in itself, it can be directed to the principal good, which is the last end; while the other is good apparently and not truly, because it leads us away from the final good. Accordingly it is evident that simply true virtue is that which is directed to man's principal good; thus also the Philosopher says (Phys. vii, text. 17) that "virtue is the disposition of a perfect thing to that which is best": and in this way no true virtue is possible without charity.

If, however, we take virtue as being ordered to some particular end, then we speak of virtue being where there is no charity, in so far as it is directed to some particular good. But if this particular good is not a true, but an apparent good, it is not a true virtue that is ordered to such a good, but a counterfeit virtue. Even so, as Augustine says (Contra Julian. iv, 3), "the prudence of the miser, whereby he devises various roads to gain, is no true virtue; nor the miser's justice, whereby he scorns the property of another through fear of severe punishment; nor the miser's temperance, whereby he curbs his desire for expensive pleasures; nor the miser's fortitude, whereby as Horace, says, 'he braves the sea, he crosses mountains, he goes through fire, in order to avoid poverty'" (Epis. lib, 1; Ep. i, 45). If, on the other hand, this particular good be a true good, for instance the welfare of the state, or the like, it will indeed be a true virtue, imperfect, however, unless it be referred to the final and perfect good. Accordingly no strictly true virtue is possible without charity.

Reply Obj. 1: The act of one lacking charity may be of two kinds; one is in accordance with his lack of charity, as when he does something that is referred to that whereby he lacks charity. Such an act is always evil: thus Augustine says (Contra Julian. iv, 3) that the actions which an unbeliever performs as an unbeliever, are always sinful, even when he clothes the naked, or does any like thing, and directs it to his unbelief as end.

There is, however, another act of one lacking charity, not in accordance with his lack of charity, but in accordance with his possession of some other gift of God, whether faith, or hope, or even his natural good, which is not completely taken away by sin, as stated above (Q. 10, A. 4; I-II, Q. 85, A. 2). In this way it is possible for an act, without charity, to be generically good, but not perfectly good, because it lacks its due order to the last end.

Reply Obj. 2: Since the end is in practical matters, what the principle is in speculative matters, just as there can be no strictly true science, if a right estimate of the first indemonstrable principle be lacking, so, there can be no strictly true justice, or chastity, without that due ordering to the end, which is effected by charity, however rightly a man may be affected about other matters.

Reply Obj. 3: Science and art of their very nature imply a relation to some particular good, and not to the ultimate good of human life, as do the moral virtues, which make man good simply, as stated above (I-II, Q. 56, A. 3). Hence the comparison fails.

* * * * *

EIGHTH ARTICLE [II-II, Q. 23, Art. 8]

Whether Charity Is the Form of the Virtues?

Objection 1: It would seem that charity is not the true form of the virtues. Because the form of a thing is either exemplar or essential. Now charity is not the exemplar form of the other virtues, since it would follow that the other virtues are of the same species as charity: nor is it the essential form of the other virtues, since then it would not be distinct from them. Therefore it is in no way the form of the virtues.

Obj. 2: Further, charity is compared to the other virtues as their root and foundation, according to Eph. 3:17: "Rooted and founded in charity." Now a root or foundation is not the form, but rather the matter of a thing, since it is the first part in the making. Therefore charity is not the form of the virtues.

Obj. 3: Further, formal, final, and efficient causes do not coincide with one another (Phys. ii, 7). Now charity is called the end and the mother of the virtues. Therefore it should not be called their form.

On the contrary, Ambrose[1] says that charity is the form of the virtues.

I answer that, In morals the form of an act is taken chiefly from the end. The reason of this is that the principal of moral acts is the will, whose object and form, so to speak, are the end. Now the form of an act always follows from a form of the agent. Consequently, in morals, that which gives an act its order to the end, must needs give the act its form. Now it is evident, in accordance with what has been said (A. 7), that it is charity which directs the acts of all other virtues to the last end, and which, consequently, also gives the form to all other acts of

---

1   Lombard, Sent. iii, D, 23

virtue: and it is precisely in this sense that charity is called the form of the virtues, for these are called virtues in relation to "informed" acts.

Reply Obj. 1: Charity is called the form of the other virtues not as being their exemplar or their essential form, but rather by way of efficient cause, in so far as it sets the form on all, in the aforesaid manner.

Reply Obj. 2: Charity is compared to the foundation or root in so far as all other virtues draw their sustenance and nourishment therefrom, and not in the sense that the foundation and root have the character of a material cause.

Reply Obj. 3: Charity is said to be the end of other virtues, because it directs all other virtues to its own end. And since a mother is one who conceives within herself and by another, charity is called the mother of the other virtues, because, by commanding them, it conceives the acts of the other virtues, by the desire of the last end.

24. OF THE SUBJECT OF CHARITY
(In Twelve Articles)

We must now consider charity in relation to its subject, under which head there are twelve points of inquiry:

(1) Whether charity is in the will as its subject?
(2) Whether charity is caused in man by preceding acts or by a Divine infusion?
(3) Whether it is infused according to the capacity of our natural gifts?
(4) Whether it increases in the person who has it?
(5) Whether it increases by addition?
(6) Whether it increases by every act?
(7) Whether it increases indefinitely?
(8) Whether the charity of a wayfarer can be perfect?
(9) Of the various degrees of charity;
(10) Whether charity can diminish?
(11) Whether charity can be lost after it has been possessed?
(12) Whether it is lost through one mortal sin?.

* * * * *

FIRST ARTICLE [II-II, Q. 24, Art. 1]

Whether the Will Is the Subject of Charity?

Objection 1: It would seem that the will is not the subject of charity. For charity is a kind of love. Now, according to the Philosopher (Topic. ii, 3) love is in the concupiscible part. Therefore charity is also in the concupiscible and not in the will.

Obj. 2: Further, charity is the foremost of the virtues, as stated above (Q. 23, A. 6). But the reason is the subject of virtue. Therefore it seems that charity is in the reason and not in the will.

Obj. 3: Further, charity extends to all human acts, according to 1 Cor. 16:14: "Let all your things be done in charity." Now the principle of human acts is the free-will. Therefore it seems that charity is chiefly in the free-will as its subject and not in the will.

On the contrary, The object of charity is the good, which is also the object of the will. Therefore charity is in the will as its subject.

I answer that, Since, as stated in the First Part (Q. 80, A. 2), the appetite is twofold, namely the sensitive, and the intellective which is called the will, the object of each is the good, but in different ways: for the object of the sensitive appetite is a good apprehended by sense, whereas the object of the intellective appetite or will is good under the universal aspect of good, according as it can be apprehended by the intellect. Now the object of charity is not a sensible good, but the Divine good which is known by the intellect alone. Therefore the subject of charity is not the sensitive, but the intellective appetite, i.e. the will.

Reply Obj. 1: The concupiscible is a part of the sensitive, not of the intellective appetite, as proved in the First Part (Q. 81, A. 2): wherefore the love which is in the concupiscible, is the love of sensible good: nor can the concupiscible reach to the Divine good which is an intelligible good; the will alone can. Consequently the concupiscible cannot be the subject of charity.

Reply Obj. 2: According to the Philosopher (De Anima iii, 9), the will also is in the reason: wherefore charity is not excluded from the reason through being in the will. Yet charity is regulated, not by the reason, as human virtues are, but by God's wisdom, and transcends the rule of human reason, according to Eph. 3:19: "The charity of Christ, which surpasseth all knowledge." Hence it is not in the reason, either as its subject, like prudence is, or as its rule, like justice and temperance are, but only by a certain kinship of the will to the reason.

Reply Obj. 3: As stated in the First Part (Q. 83, A. 4), the free-will is not a distinct power from the will. Yet charity is not in the will considered as free-will, the act of which is to choose. For choice is of things directed to the end, whereas the will is of the end itself (Ethic. iii, 2). Hence charity, whose object is the last end, should be described as residing in the will rather than in the free-will.

* * * * *

SECOND ARTICLE [II-II, Q. 24, Art. 2]

Whether Charity Is Caused in Us by Infusion?

Objection 1: It would seem that charity is not caused in us by infusion. For that which is common to all creatures, is in man naturally. Now, according to Dionysius (Div. Nom. iv), the "Divine good," which is the object of charity, "is for all an object of dilection and love." Therefore charity is in us naturally, and not by infusion.

Obj. 2: Further, the more lovable a thing is the easier it is to love it. Now God is supremely lovable, since He is supremely good. Therefore it is easier to love Him than other things. But we need no infused habit in order to love other things. Neither, therefore, do we need one in order to love God.

Obj. 3: Further, the Apostle says (1 Tim. 1:5): "The end of the commandment is charity from a pure heart, and a good conscience, and an unfeigned faith." Now these three have reference to human acts. Therefore charity is caused in us from preceding acts, and not from infusion.

On the contrary, The Apostle says (Rom. 5:5): "The charity of God is poured forth in our hearts by the Holy Ghost, Who is given to us."

I answer that, As stated above (Q. 23, A. 1), charity is a friendship of man for God, founded upon the fellowship of everlasting happiness. Now this fellowship is in respect, not of natural, but of gratuitous gifts, for, according to Rom. 6:23, "the grace of God is life everlasting": wherefore charity itself surpasses our natural facilities. Now that which surpasses the faculty of nature, cannot be natural or acquired by the natural powers, since a natural effect does not transcend its cause.

Therefore charity can be in us neither naturally, nor through acquisition by the natural powers, but by the infusion of the Holy Ghost, Who is the love of the Father and the Son, and the participation of Whom in us is created charity, as stated above (Q. 23, A. 2).

Reply Obj. 1: Dionysius is speaking of the love of God, which is founded on the fellowship of natural goods, wherefore it is in all naturally. On the other hand, charity is founded on a supernatural fellowship, so the comparison fails.

Reply Obj. 2: Just as God is supremely knowable in Himself yet not to us, on account of a defect in our knowledge which depends on sensible things, so too, God is supremely lovable in Himself, in as much as He is the object of happiness. But He is not supremely lovable to us in this way, on account of the inclination of our appetite towards visible goods. Hence it is evident that for us to love God above all things in this way, it is necessary that charity be infused into our hearts.

Reply Obj. 3: When it is said that in us charity proceeds from "a pure heart, and a good conscience, and an unfeigned faith," this must be referred to the act of charity which is aroused by these things. Or again, this is said because the aforesaid acts dispose man to receive the infusion of charity. The same remark applies to the saying of Augustine (Tract. ix in prim. canon. Joan.): "Fear leads to charity," and of a gloss on Matt. 1:2: "Faith begets hope, and hope charity.".

* * * * *

THIRD ARTICLE [II-II, Q. 24, Art. 3]

Whether Charity Is Infused According to the Capacity of Our Natural Gifts?

Objection 1: It would seem that charity is infused according to the capacity of our natural gifts. For it is written (Matt. 25:15) that "He gave to every one according to his own virtue [Douay: 'proper ability']." Now, in man, none but natural virtue precedes charity, since there is no virtue without charity, as stated above (Q. 23, A. 7). Therefore God infuses charity into man according to the measure of his natural virtue.

Obj. 2: Further, among things ordained towards one another, the second is proportionate to the first: thus we find in natural things that the form is proportionate to the matter, and in gratuitous gifts, that glory is proportionate to grace. Now, since charity is a perfection of nature, it is compared to the capacity of nature as second to first. Therefore it seems that charity is infused according to the capacity of nature.

Obj. 3: Further, men and angels partake of happiness according to the same measure, since happiness is alike in both, according to Matt. 22:30 and Luke 20:36. Now charity and other gratuitous gifts are bestowed on the angels, according to their natural capacity, as the Master teaches (Sent. ii, D, 3). Therefore the same apparently applies to man.

On the contrary, It is written (John 3:8): "The Spirit breatheth where He will," and (1 Cor. 12:11): "All these things one and the same Spirit worketh, dividing to every one according as He will." Therefore charity is given, not according to our natural capacity, but according as the Spirit wills to distribute His gifts.

I answer that, The quantity of a thing depends on the proper cause of that thing, since the more universal cause produces a greater effect. Now, since charity surpasses the proportion of human nature, as stated above (A. 2) it depends, not on any natural virtue, but on the sole grace of the Holy Ghost Who infuses charity. Wherefore the quantity of charity depends neither on the condition of nature nor on the capacity of natural virtue, but only on the will of the Holy Ghost Who "divides" His gifts "according as He will." Hence the Apostle says (Eph. 4:7): "To every one of us is given grace according to the measure of the giving of Christ."

Reply Obj. 1: The virtue in accordance with which God gives His gifts to each one, is a disposition or previous preparation or effort of the one who receives grace. But the Holy Ghost forestalls even this disposition or effort, by moving man's mind either more or less, according as He will. Wherefore the Apostle says (Col. 1:12): "Who hath made us worthy to be partakers of the lot of the saints in light."

Reply Obj. 2: The form does not surpass the proportion of the matter. In like manner grace and glory are referred to the same genus, for grace is nothing else than a beginning of glory in us. But charity and nature do not belong to the same genus, so that the comparison fails.

Reply Obj. 3: The angel's is an intellectual nature, and it is consistent with his condition that he should be borne wholly whithersoever he is borne, as stated in the First Part (Q. 61, A. 6). Hence there was a greater effort in the higher angels, both for good in those who persevered, and for evil in those who fell, and consequently those of the higher angels who remained steadfast became better than the others, and those who fell became worse. But man's is a rational nature, with which it is consistent to be sometimes in potentiality and sometimes in act: so that it is not necessarily borne wholly whithersoever it is borne, and where there are greater natural gifts there may be less effort, and vice versa. Thus the comparison fails.

* * * * *

FOURTH ARTICLE [II-II, Q. 24, Art. 4]

Whether Charity Can Increase?

Objection 1: It would seem that charity cannot increase. For nothing increases save what has quantity. Now quantity is twofold, namely dimensive and virtual. The former does not befit charity which is a spiritual perfection, while virtual quantity regards the objects in respect of which charity does not increase, since the slightest charity loves all that is to be loved out of charity. Therefore charity does not increase.

Obj. 2: Further, that which consists in something extreme receives no increase. But charity consists in something extreme, being the greatest of the virtues, and the supreme love of the greatest good. Therefore charity cannot increase.

Obj. 3: Further, increase is a kind of movement. Therefore wherever there is increase there is movement, and if there be increase of essence there is movement of essence. Now there is no movement of essence save either by corruption or generation. Therefore charity cannot increase essentially, unless it happen to be generated anew or corrupted, which is unreasonable.

On the contrary, Augustine says (Tract. lxxiv in Joan.)[1] that "charity merits increase that by increase it may merit perfection."

I answer that, The charity of a wayfarer can increase. For we are called wayfarers by reason of our being on the way to God, Who is the last end of our happiness. In this way we advance as we get nigh to God, Who is approached, "not by steps of the body but by the affections of the soul"[2]: and this approach is the result of charity, since it unites man's mind to God. Consequently it is essential to the charity of a wayfarer that it can increase, for if it could not, all further advance along the way would cease. Hence the Apostle calls charity the way, when he says (1 Cor. 12:31): "I show unto you yet a more excellent way."

Reply Obj. 1: Charity is not subject to dimensive, but only to virtual quantity: and the latter depends not only on the number of objects, namely whether they be in greater number or of greater excellence, but also on the intensity of the act, namely whether a thing is loved more, or less; it is in this way that the virtual quantity of charity increases.

Reply Obj. 2: Charity consists in an extreme with regard to its object, in so far as its object is the Supreme Good, and from this it follows that charity is the most excellent of the virtues. Yet not every charity consists in an extreme, as regards the intensity of the act.

Reply Obj. 3: Some have said that charity does not increase in its essence, but only as to its radication in its subject, or according to its fervor.

But these people did not know what they were talking about. For since charity is an accident, its being is to be in something. So that an essential increase of charity means nothing else but that it is yet more in its subject, which implies a greater radication in its subject. Furthermore, charity is essentially a virtue ordained to act, so that an essential increase of charity implies ability to produce an act of more fervent love. Hence charity increases essentially, not by beginning anew, or ceasing to be in its subject, as the objection imagines, but by beginning to be more and more in its subject.

* * * * *

---

[1] Cf. Ep. clxxxv.
[2] St. Augustine, Tract. in Joan. xxxii

FIFTH ARTICLE [II-II, Q. 24, Art. 5]

Whether Charity Increases by Addition?

Objection 1: It would seem that charity increases by addition. For just as increase may be in respect of bodily quantity, so may it be according to virtual quantity. Now increase in bodily quantity results from addition; for the Philosopher says (De Gener. i, 5) that "increase is addition to pre-existing magnitude." Therefore the increase of charity which is according to virtual quantity is by addition.

Obj. 2: Further, charity is a kind of spiritual light in the soul, according to 1 John 2:10: "He that loveth his brother abideth in the light." Now light increases in the air by addition; thus the light in a house increases when another candle is lit. Therefore charity also increases in the soul by addition.

Obj. 3: Further, the increase of charity is God's work, even as the causing of it, according to 2 Cor. 9:10: "He will increase the growth of the fruits of your justice." Now when God first infuses charity, He puts something in the soul that was not there before. Therefore also, when He increases charity, He puts something there which was not there before. Therefore charity increases by addition.

On the contrary, Charity is a simple form. Now nothing greater results from the addition of one simple thing to another, as proved in Phys. iii, text. 59, and Metaph. ii, 4. Therefore charity does not increase by addition.

I answer that, Every addition is of something to something else: so that in every addition we must at least presuppose that the things added together are distinct before the addition. Consequently if charity be added to charity, the added charity must be presupposed as distinct from charity to which it is added, not necessarily by a distinction of reality, but at least by a distinction of thought. For God is able to increase a bodily quantity by adding a magnitude which did not exist before, but was created at that very moment; which magnitude, though not pre-existent in reality, is nevertheless capable of being distinguished from the quantity to which it is added. Wherefore if charity be added to charity we must presuppose the distinction, at least logical, of the one charity from the other.

Now distinction among forms is twofold: specific and numeric. Specific distinction of habits follows diversity of objects, while numeric distinction follows distinction of subjects. Consequently a habit may receive increase through extending to objects to which it did not extend before: thus the science of geometry increases in one who acquires knowledge of geometrical matters which he ignored hitherto. But this cannot be said of charity, for even the slightest charity extends to all that we have to love by charity. Hence the addition which causes an increase of charity cannot be understood, as though the added charity were presupposed to be distinct specifically from that to which it is added.

It follows therefore that if charity be added to charity, we must presuppose a numerical distinction between them, which follows a distinction of subjects: thus whiteness receives an increase when one white thing is added to another, although such an increase does not make a thing whiter. This, however, does not apply to the case in point, since the subject of charity is none other than the rational mind, so that such like an increase of charity could only take place by one rational mind being added to another; which is impossible. Moreover, even if it were possible, the result would be a greater lover, but not a more loving one. It follows, therefore, that charity can by no means increase by addition of charity to charity, as some have held to be the case.

Accordingly charity increases only by its subject partaking of charity more and more subject thereto. For this is the proper mode of increase in a form that is intensified, since the being of such a form consists wholly in its adhering to its subject. Consequently, since the magnitude of a thing follows on its being, to say that a form is greater is the same as to say that it is more in its subject, and not that another form is added to it: for this would be the case if the form, of itself, had any quantity, and not in comparison with its subject. Therefore charity increases by being intensified in its subject, and this is for charity to increase in its essence; and not by charity being added to charity.

Reply Obj. 1: Bodily quantity has something as quantity, and something else, in so far as it is an accidental form. As quantity, it is distinguishable in respect of position or number, and in this way we have the increase of magnitude by addition, as may be seen in animals. But in so far as it is an accidental form, it is distinguishable only in respect of its subject, and in this way it has its proper increase, like other accidental forms, by way of intensity in its subject, for instance in things subject to rarefaction, as is proved in Phys. iv, 9. In like manner science, as a habit, has its quantity from its objects, and accordingly it increases by addition, when a man knows more things; and again, as an accidental form, it has a certain quantity through being in its subject, and in this way it increases in a man who knows the same scientific truths with greater certainty now than before. In the same way charity has a twofold quantity; but with regard to that which it has from its object, it does not increase, as stated above: hence it follows that it increases solely by being intensified.

Reply Obj. 2: The addition of light to light can be understood through the light being intensified in the air on account of there being several luminaries giving light: but this distinction does not apply to the case in point, since there is but one luminary shedding forth the light of charity.

Reply Obj. 3: The infusion of charity denotes a change to the state of having charity from the state of not having it, so that something must needs come which was not there before. On the other hand, the increase of charity denotes a change to more having from less having, so that there is need, not for anything to be there that was not there before, but for something to be more there that previously was less there. This is what God does when He increases charity, that is He makes it to have a greater hold on the soul, and the likeness of the Holy Ghost to be more perfectly participated by the soul.

* * * * *

SIXTH ARTICLE

Whether Charity Increases Through Every Act of Charity?

Objection 1: It would seem that charity increases through every act of charity. For that which can do what is more, can do what is less. But every act of charity can merit everlasting life; and this is more than a simple addition of charity, since it includes the perfection of charity. Much more, therefore, does every act of charity increase charity.

Obj. 2: Further, just as the habits of acquired virtue are engendered by acts, so too an increase of charity is caused by an act of charity. Now each virtuous act conduces to the engendering of virtue. Therefore also each virtuous act of charity conduces to the increase of charity.

Obj. 3: Further, Gregory[1] says that "to stand still in the way to God is to go back." Now no man goes back when he is moved by an act of charity. Therefore whoever is moved by an act of charity goes forward in the way to God. Therefore charity increases through every act of charity.

On the contrary, The effect does not surpass the power of its cause. But an act of charity is sometimes done with tepidity or slackness. Therefore it does not conduce to a more excellent charity, rather does it dispose one to a lower degree.

I answer that, The spiritual increase of charity is somewhat like the increase of a body. Now bodily increase in animals and plants is not a continuous movement, so that, to wit, if a thing increase so much in so much time, it need to increase proportionally in each part of that time, as happens in local movement; but for a certain space of time nature works by disposing for the increase, without causing any actual increase, and afterwards brings into effect that to which it had disposed, by giving the animal or plant an actual increase. In like manner charity does not actually increase through every act of charity, but each act of charity disposes to an increase of charity, in so far as one act of charity makes man more ready to act again according to charity, and this readiness increasing, man breaks out into an act of more fervent love, and strives to advance in charity, and then his charity increases actually.

Reply Obj. 1: Every act of charity merits everlasting life, which, however, is not to be bestowed then and there, but at its proper time. In like manner every act of charity merits an increase of charity; yet this increase does not take place at once, but when we strive for that increase.

Reply Obj. 2: Even when an acquired virtue is being engendered, each act does not complete the formation of the virtue, but conduces towards that effect by disposing to it, while the last act, which is the most perfect, and acts in virtue of all those that preceded it, reduces the virtue into act, just as when many drops hollow out a stone.

Reply Obj. 3: Man advances in the way to God, not merely by actual increase of charity, but also by being disposed to that increase.

* * * * *

---

[1] St. Bernard, Serm. ii in Festo Purif.

SEVENTH ARTICLE [II-II, Q. 24, Art. 7]

Whether Charity Increases Indefinitely?

Objection 1: It would seem that charity does not increase indefinitely. For every movement is towards some end and term, as stated in Metaph. ii, text. 8, 9. But the increase of charity is a movement. Therefore it tends to an end and term. Therefore charity does not increase indefinitely.

Obj. 2: Further, no form surpasses the capacity of its subject. But the capacity of the rational creature who is the subject of charity is finite. Therefore charity cannot increase indefinitely.

Obj. 3: Further, every finite thing can, by continual increase, attain to the quantity of another finite thing however much greater, unless the amount of its increase be ever less and less. Thus the Philosopher states (Phys. iii, 6) that if we divide a line into an indefinite number of parts, and take these parts away and add them indefinitely to another line, we shall never arrive at any definite quantity resulting from those two lines, viz. the one from which we subtracted and the one to which we added what was subtracted. But this does not occur in the case in point: because there is no need for the second increase of charity to be less than the first, since rather is it probable that it would be equal or greater. As, therefore, the charity of the blessed is something finite, if the charity of the wayfarer can increase indefinitely, it would follow that the charity of the way can equal the charity of heaven; which is absurd. Therefore the wayfarer's charity cannot increase indefinitely.

On the contrary, The Apostle says (Phil. 3:12): "Not as though I had already attained, or were already perfect; but I follow after, if I may, by any means apprehend," on which words a gloss says: "Even if he has made great progress, let none of the faithful say: 'Enough.' For whosoever says this, leaves the road before coming to his destination." Therefore the wayfarer's charity can ever increase more and more.

I answer that, A term to the increase of a form may be fixed in three ways: first by reason of the form itself having a fixed measure, and when this has been reached it is no longer possible to go any further in that form, but if any further advance is made, another form is attained. An example of this is paleness, the bounds of which may, by continual alteration, be passed, either so that whiteness ensues, or so that blackness results. Secondly, on the part of the agent, whose power does not extend to a further increase of the form in its subject. Thirdly, on the part of the subject, which is not capable of ulterior perfection.

Now, in none of these ways, is a limit imposed to the increase of man's charity, while he is in the state of the wayfarer. For charity itself considered as such has no limit to its increase, since it is a participation of the infinite charity which is the Holy Ghost. In like manner the cause of the increase of charity, viz. God, is possessed of infinite power. Furthermore, on the part of its subject, no limit to this increase can be determined, because whenever charity increases, there is a corresponding increased ability to receive a further increase. It is therefore evident that it is not possible to fix any limits to the increase of charity in this life.

Reply Obj. 1: The increase of charity is directed to an end, which is not in this, but in a future life.

Reply Obj. 2: The capacity of the rational creature is increased by charity, because the heart is enlarged thereby, according to 2 Cor. 6:11: "Our heart is enlarged"; so that it still remains capable of receiving a further increase.

Reply Obj. 3: This argument holds good in those things which have the same kind of quantity, but not in those which have different kinds: thus however much a line may increase it does not reach the quantity of a superficies. Now the quantity of a wayfarer's charity which follows the knowledge of faith is not of the same kind as the quantity of the charity of the blessed, which follows open vision. Hence the argument does not prove.

* * * * *

EIGHTH ARTICLE [II-II, Q. 24, Art. 8]

Whether Charity Can Be Perfect in This Life?

Objection 1: It would seem that charity cannot be perfect in this life. For this would have been the case with the apostles before all others. Yet it was not so, since the Apostle says (Phil. 3:12): "Not as though I had already attained, or were already perfect." Therefore charity cannot be perfect in this life.

Obj. 2: Further, Augustine says (Qq. lxxxiii, qu. 36) that "whatever kindles charity quenches cupidity, but where charity is perfect, cupidity is done away altogether." But this cannot be in this world, wherein it is impossible to live without sin, according to 1 John 1:8: "If we say that we have no sin, we deceive ourselves." Now all sin arises from some inordinate cupidity. Therefore charity cannot be perfect in this life.

Obj. 3: Further, what is already perfect cannot be perfected any more. But in this life charity can always increase, as stated above (A. 7). Therefore charity cannot be perfect in this life.

On the contrary, Augustine says (In prim. canon. Joan. Tract. v) "Charity is perfected by being strengthened; and when it has been brought to perfection, it exclaims, 'I desire to be dissolved and to be with Christ.'" Now this is possible in this life, as in the case of Paul. Therefore charity can be perfect in this life.

I answer that, The perfection of charity may be understood in two ways: first with regard to the object loved, secondly with regard to the person who loves. With regard to the object loved, charity is perfect, if the object be loved as much as it is lovable. Now God is as lovable as He is good, and His goodness is infinite, wherefore He is infinitely lovable. But no creature can love Him infinitely since all created power is finite. Consequently no creature's charity can be perfect in this way; the charity of God alone can, whereby He loves Himself.

On the part of the person who loves, charity is perfect, when he loves as much as he can. This happens in three ways. First, so that a man's whole heart is always actually borne towards God: this is the perfection of the charity of heaven, and is not possible in this life, wherein, by reason of the weakness of human life, it is impossible to think always actually of God, and to be moved by love towards Him. Secondly, so that man makes an earnest endeavor to give his time to God and Divine things, while scorning other things except in so far as the needs of the present life demand. This is the perfection of charity that is possible to a wayfarer; but is not common to all who have charity. Thirdly, so that a man gives his whole heart to God habitually, viz. by neither thinking nor desiring anything contrary to the love of God; and this perfection is common to all who have charity.

Reply Obj. 1: The Apostle denies that he has the perfection of heaven, wherefore a gloss on the same passage says that "he was a perfect wayfarer, but had not yet achieved the perfection to which the way leads."

Reply Obj. 2: This is said on account of venial sins, which are contrary, not to the habit, but to the act of charity: hence they are incompatible, not with the perfection of the way, but with that of heaven.

Reply Obj. 3: The perfection of the way is not perfection simply, wherefore it can always increase.

* * * * *

NINTH ARTICLE [II-II, Q. 24, Art. 9]

Whether Charity Is Rightly Distinguished into Three Degrees, Beginning, Progress, and Perfection?

Objection 1: It would seem unfitting to distinguish three degrees of charity, beginning, progress, and perfection. For there are many degrees between the beginning of charity and its ultimate perfection. Therefore it is not right to put only one.

Obj. 2: Further, charity begins to progress as soon as it begins to be. Therefore we ought not to distinguish between charity as progressing and as beginning.

Obj. 3: Further, in this world, however perfect a man's charity may be, it can increase, as stated above (A. 7). Now for charity to increase is to progress. Therefore perfect charity ought not to be distinguished from progressing charity: and so the aforesaid degrees are unsuitably assigned to charity.

On the contrary, Augustine says (In prim. canon. Joan. Tract. v) "As soon as charity is born it takes food," which refers to beginners, "after taking food, it waxes strong," which refers to those who are progressing, "and when it has become strong it is perfected," which refers to the perfect. Therefore there are three degrees of charity.

I answer that, The spiritual increase of charity may be considered in respect of a certain likeness to the growth of the human body. For although this latter growth may be divided into many parts, yet it has certain fixed divisions according to those particular actions or pursuits to which man is brought by this same growth. Thus we speak of a man being an infant until he has the use of reason, after which we distinguish another state of man wherein he begins to speak and to use his reason, while there is again a third state, that of puberty when he begins to acquire the power of generation, and so on until he arrives at perfection.

In like manner the divers degrees of charity are distinguished according to the different pursuits to which man is brought by the increase of charity. For at first it is incumbent on man to occupy himself chiefly with avoiding sin and resisting his concupiscences, which move him in opposition to charity: this concerns beginners, in whom charity has to be fed or fostered lest it be destroyed: in the second place man's chief pursuit is to aim at progress in good, and this is the pursuit of the proficient, whose chief aim is to strengthen their charity by adding to it: while man's third pursuit is to aim chiefly at union with and enjoyment of God: this belongs to the perfect who "desire to be dissolved and to be with Christ."

In like manner we observe in local motion that at first there is withdrawal from one term, then approach to the other term, and thirdly, rest in this term.

Reply Obj. 1: All these distinct degrees which can be discerned in the increase of charity, are comprised in the aforesaid three, even as every division of continuous things is included in these three—the beginning, the middle, and the end, as the Philosopher states (De Coelo i, 1).

Reply Obj. 2: Although those who are beginners in charity may progress, yet the chief care that besets them is to resist the sins which disturb them by their onslaught. Afterwards, however, when they come to feel this onslaught less, they begin to tend to perfection with greater security; yet with one hand doing the work, and with the other holding the sword as related in 2 Esdr. 4:17 about those who built up Jerusalem.

Reply Obj. 3: Even the perfect make progress in charity: yet this is not their chief care, but their aim is principally directed towards union with God. And though both the beginner and the proficient seek this, yet their solicitude is chiefly about other things, with the beginner, about avoiding sin, with the proficient, about progressing in virtue.

* * * * *

TENTH ARTICLE [II-II, Q. 24, Art. 10]

Whether Charity Can Decrease?

Objection 1: It would seem that charity can decrease. For contraries by their nature affect the same subject. Now increase and decrease are contraries. Since then charity increases, as stated above (A. 4), it seems that it can also decrease.

Obj. 2: Further, Augustine, speaking to God, says (Confess. x) "He loves Thee less, who loves aught besides Thee": and (Qq. lxxxiii, qu. 36) he says that "what kindles charity quenches cupidity." From this it seems to follow that, on the contrary, what arouses cupidity quenches charity. But cupidity, whereby a man loves something besides God, can increase in man. Therefore charity can decrease.

Obj. 3: Further, as Augustine says (Gen. ad lit. viii, 12) "God makes the just man, by justifying him, but in such a way, that if the man turns away from God, he no longer retains the effect of the Divine operation." From this we may gather that when God preserves charity in man, He works in the same way as when He first infuses charity into him. Now at the first infusion of charity God infuses less charity into him that prepares himself less. Therefore also in preserving charity, He preserves less charity in him that prepares himself less. Therefore charity can decrease.

On the contrary, In Scripture, charity is compared to fire, according to Cant 8:6: "The lamps thereof," i.e. of charity, "are fire and flames." Now fire ever mounts upward so long as it lasts. Therefore as long as charity endures, it can ascend, but cannot descend, i.e. decrease.

I answer that, The quantity which charity has in comparison with its proper object, cannot decrease, even as neither can it increase, as stated above (A. 4, ad 2).

Since, however, it increases in that quantity which it has in comparison with its subject, here is the place to consider whether it can decrease in this way. Now, if it decrease, this must needs be either through an act, or by the mere cessation from act. It is true that virtues acquired through acts decrease and sometimes cease altogether through cessation from act, as stated above (I-II, Q. 53, A. 3). Wherefore the Philosopher says, in reference to friendship (Ethic. viii, 5) "that want of intercourse," i.e. the neglect to call upon or speak with one's friends, "has destroyed many a friendship." Now this is because the safe-keeping of a thing depends on its cause, and the cause of human virtue is a human act, so that when human acts cease, the virtue acquired thereby decreases and at last ceases altogether. Yet this does not occur to charity, because it is not the result of human acts, but is caused by God alone, as stated above (A. 2). Hence it follows that even when its act ceases, it does not for this reason decrease, or cease altogether, unless the cessation involves a sin.

The consequence is that a decrease of charity cannot be caused except either by God or by some sinful act. Now no defect is caused in us by God, except by way of punishment, in so far as He withdraws His grace in punishment of sin. Hence He does not diminish charity except by way of punishment: and this punishment is due on account of sin.

It follows, therefore, that if charity decrease, the cause of this decrease must be sin either effectively or by way of merit. But mortal sin does not diminish charity, in either of these ways, but destroys it entirely, both effectively, because every mortal sin is contrary to charity, as we shall state further on (A. 12), and by way of merit, since when, by sinning mortally, a man acts against charity, he deserves that God should withdraw charity from him.

In like manner, neither can venial sin diminish charity either effectively or by way of merit. Not effectively, because it does not touch charity, since charity is about the last end, whereas venial sin is a disorder about things directed to the end: and a man's love for the end is none the less through his committing an inordinate act as regards the things directed to the end. Thus sick people sometimes, though they love health much, are irregular in keeping to their diet: and thus again, in speculative sciences, the false opinions that are derived from the principles, do not diminish the certitude of the principles. So too, venial sin does not merit diminution of charity; for when a man offends in a small matter he does not deserve to be mulcted in a great matter. For God does not turn away from man, more than man turns away from Him: wherefore he that is out of order in respect of things directed to the end, does not deserve to be mulcted in charity whereby he is ordered to the last end.

The consequence is that charity can by no means be diminished, if we speak of direct causality, yet whatever disposes to its corruption may be said to conduce indirectly to its diminution, and such are venial sins, or even the cessation from the practice of works of charity.

Reply Obj. 1: Contraries affect the same subject when that subject stands in equal relation to both. But charity does not stand in equal relation to increase and decrease. For it can have a cause of increase, but not of decrease, as stated above. Hence the argument does not prove.

Reply Obj. 2: Cupidity is twofold, one whereby man places his end in creatures, and this kills charity altogether, since it is its poison, as Augustine states (Confess. x). This makes us love God less (i.e. less than we ought to love Him by charity), not indeed by diminishing charity but by destroying it altogether. It is thus that we must understand the saying: "He loves Thee less, who loves aught beside Thee," for he adds these words, "which he loveth not for Thee." This does not apply to venial sin, but only to mortal sin: since that which we love in venial sin, is loved for God's sake habitually though not actually. There is another cupidity, that of venial sin, which is always diminished by charity: and yet this cupidity cannot diminish charity, for the reason given above.

Reply Obj. 3: A movement of the free-will is requisite in the infusion of charity, as stated above (I-II, Q. 113, A. 3). Wherefore that which diminishes the intensity of the free-will conduces dispositively to a diminution in the charity to be infused. On the other hand, no movement of the free-will is required for the safe-keeping of charity, else it would not remain in us while we sleep. Hence charity does not decrease on account of an obstacle on the part of the intensity of the free-will's movement.

* * * * *

ELEVENTH ARTICLE [II-II, Q. 24, Art. 11]

Whether We Can Lose Charity When Once We Have It?

Objection 1: It would seem that we cannot lose charity when once we have it. For if we lose it, this can only be through sin. Now he who has charity cannot sin, for it is written (1 John 3:9): "Whosoever is born of God, committeth not sin; for His seed abideth in him, and he cannot sin, because he is born of God." But none save the children of God have charity, for it is this which distinguishes "the children of

God from the children of perdition," as Augustine says (De Trin. xv, 17). Therefore he that has charity cannot lose it.

Obj. 2: Further, Augustine says (De Trin. viii, 7) that "if love be not true, it should not be called love." Now, as he says again in a letter to Count Julian, "charity which can fail was never true."[1] Therefore it was no charity at all. Therefore, when once we have charity, we cannot lose it.

Obj. 3: Further, Gregory says in a homily for Pentecost (In Evang. xxx) that "God's love works great things where it is; if it ceases to work it is not charity." Now no man loses charity by doing great things. Therefore if charity be there, it cannot be lost.

Obj. 4: Further, the free-will is not inclined to sin unless by some motive for sinning. Now charity excludes all motives for sinning, both self-love and cupidity, and all such things. Therefore charity cannot be lost.

On the contrary, It is written (Apoc. 2:4): "I have somewhat against thee, because thou hast left thy first charity."

I answer that, The Holy Ghost dwells in us by charity, as shown above (A. 2; QQ. 23, 24). We can, accordingly, consider charity in three ways: first on the part of the Holy Ghost, Who moves the soul to love God, and in this respect charity is incompatible with sin through the power of the Holy Ghost, Who does unfailingly whatever He wills to do. Hence it is impossible for these two things to be true at the same time—that the Holy Ghost should will to move a certain man to an act of charity, and that this man, by sinning, should lose charity. For the gift of perseverance is reckoned among the blessings of God whereby "whoever is delivered, is most certainly delivered," as Augustine says in his book on the Predestination of the saints (De Dono Persev. xiv).

Secondly, charity may be considered as such, and thus it is incapable of anything that is against its nature. Wherefore charity cannot sin at all, even as neither can heat cool, nor unrighteousness do good, as Augustine says (De Serm. Dom. in Monte ii, 24).

Thirdly, charity can be considered on the part of its subject, which is changeable on account of the free-will. Moreover charity

---

1 The quotation is from De Salutaribus Documentis ad quemdam comitem, vii., among the works of Paul of Friuli, more commonly known as Paul the Deacon, a monk of Monte Cassino.

may be compared with this subject, both from the general point of view of form in comparison with matter, and from the specific point of view of habit as compared with power. Now it is natural for a form to be in its subject in such a way that it can be lost, when it does not entirely fill the potentiality of matter: this is evident in the forms of things generated and corrupted, because the matter of such things receives one form in such a way, that it retains the potentiality to another form, as though its potentiality were not completely satisfied with the one form. Hence the one form may be lost by the other being received. On the other hand the form of a celestial body which entirely fills the potentiality of its matter, so that the latter does not retain the potentiality to another form, is in its subject inseparably. Accordingly the charity of the blessed, because it entirely fills the potentiality of the rational mind, since every actual movement of that mind is directed to God, is possessed by its subject inseparably: whereas the charity of the wayfarer does not so fill the potentiality of its subject, because the latter is not always actually directed to God: so that when it is not actually directed to God, something may occur whereby charity is lost.

It is proper to a habit to incline a power to act, and this belongs to a habit, in so far as it makes whatever is suitable to it, to seem good, and whatever is unsuitable, to seem evil. For as the taste judges of savors according to its disposition, even so does the human mind judge of things to be done, according to its habitual disposition. Hence the Philosopher says (Ethic. iii, 5) that "such as a man is, so does the end appear to him." Accordingly charity is inseparable from its possessor, where that which pertains to charity cannot appear otherwise than good, and that is in heaven, where God is seen in His Essence, which is the very essence of goodness. Therefore the charity of heaven cannot be lost, whereas the charity of the way can, because in this state God is not seen in His Essence, which is the essence of goodness.

Reply Obj. 1: The passage quoted speaks from the point of view of the power of the Holy Ghost, by Whose safeguarding, those whom He wills to move are rendered immune from sin, as much as He wills.

Reply Obj. 2: The charity which can fail by reason of itself is no true charity; for this would be the case, were its love given only for a time, and afterwards were to cease, which would be inconsistent with true love. If, however, charity be lost through the changeableness of the subject, and against the purpose of charity included in its act, this is not contrary to true charity.

Reply Obj. 3: The love of God ever works great things in its purpose, which is essential to charity; but it does not always work great things in its act, on account of the condition of its subject.

Reply Obj. 4: Charity by reason of its act excludes every motive for sinning. But it happens sometimes that charity is not acting actually, and then it is possible for a motive to intervene for sinning, and if we consent to this motive, we lose charity.

* * * * *

TWELFTH ARTICLE [II-II, Q. 24, Art. 12]

Whether Charity Is Lost Through One Mortal Sin?

Objection 1: It would seem that charity is not lost through one mortal sin. For Origen says (Peri Archon i): "When a man who has mounted to the stage of perfection, is satiated, I do not think that he will become empty or fall away suddenly; but he must needs do so gradually and by little and little." But man falls away by losing charity. Therefore charity is not lost through only one mortal sin.

Obj. 2: Further, Pope Leo in a sermon on the Passion (lx) addresses Peter thus: "Our Lord saw in thee not a conquered faith, not an averted love, but constancy shaken. Tears abounded where love never failed, and the words uttered in trepidation were washed away by the fount of charity." From this Bernard[1] drew his assertion that "charity in Peter was not quenched, but cooled." But Peter sinned mortally in denying Christ. Therefore charity is not lost through one mortal sin.

Obj. 3: Further, charity is stronger than an acquired virtue. Now a habit of acquired virtue is not destroyed by one contrary sinful act. Much less, therefore, is charity destroyed by one contrary mortal sin.

Obj. 4: Further, charity denotes love of God and our neighbor. Now, seemingly, one may commit a mortal sin, and yet retain the love of God and one's neighbor; because an inordinate affection for things directed to the end, does not remove the love for the end, as stated above (A. 10). Therefore charity towards God can endure,

---

[1] William of St. Thierry, De Nat. et Dig. Amoris. vi.

though there be a mortal sin through an inordinate affection for some temporal good.

Obj. 5: Further, the object of a theological virtue is the last end. Now the other theological virtues, namely faith and hope, are not done away by one mortal sin, in fact they remain though lifeless. Therefore charity can remain without a form, even when a mortal sin has been committed.

On the contrary, By mortal sin man becomes deserving of eternal death, according to Rom. 6:23: "The wages of sin is death." On the other hand whoever has charity is deserving of eternal life, for it is written (John 14:21): "He that loveth Me, shall be loved by My Father: and I will love Him, and will manifest Myself to him," in which manifestation everlasting life consists, according to John 17:3: "This is eternal life; that they may know Thee the ... true God, and Jesus Christ Whom Thou hast sent." Now no man can be worthy, at the same time, of eternal life and of eternal death. Therefore it is impossible for a man to have charity with a mortal sin. Therefore charity is destroyed by one mortal sin.

I answer that, That one contrary is removed by the other contrary supervening. Now every mortal sin is contrary to charity by its very nature, which consists in man's loving God above all things, and subjecting himself to Him entirely, by referring all that is his to God. It is therefore essential to charity that man should so love God as to wish to submit to Him in all things, and always to follow the rule of His commandments; since whatever is contrary to His commandments is manifestly contrary to charity, and therefore by its very nature is capable of destroying charity.

If indeed charity were an acquired habit dependent on the power of its subject, it would not necessarily be removed by one mortal sin, for act is directly contrary, not to habit but to act. Now the endurance of a habit in its subject does not require the endurance of its act, so that when a contrary act supervenes the acquired habit is not at once done away. But charity, being an infused habit, depends on the action of God Who infuses it, Who stands in relation to the infusion and safekeeping of charity, as the sun does to the diffusion of light in the air, as stated above (A. 10, Obj. 3). Consequently, just as the light would cease at once in the air, were an obstacle placed to its being lit up by the sun, even so charity ceases at once to be in the soul through the placing of an obstacle to the outpouring of charity by God into the soul.

Now it is evident that through every mortal sin which is contrary to God's commandments, an obstacle is placed to the outpouring of charity, since from the very fact that a man chooses to prefer sin to God's friendship, which requires that we should obey His will, it follows that the habit of charity is lost at once through one mortal sin. Hence Augustine says (Gen. ad lit. viii, 12) that "man is enlightened by God's presence, but he is darkened at once by God's absence, because distance from Him is effected not by change of place but by aversion of the will."

Reply Obj. 1: This saying of Origen may be understood, in one way, that a man who is in the state of perfection, does not suddenly go so far as to commit a mortal sin, but is disposed thereto by some previous negligence, for which reason venial sins are said to be dispositions to mortal sin, as stated above (I-II, Q. 88, A. 3). Nevertheless he falls, and loses charity through the one mortal sin if he commits it.

Since, however, he adds: "If some slight slip should occur, and he recover himself quickly he does not appear to fall altogether," we may reply in another way, that when he speaks of a man being emptied and falling away altogether, he means one who falls so as to sin through malice; and this does not occur in a perfect man all at once.

Reply Obj. 2: Charity may be lost in two ways; first, directly, by actual contempt, and, in this way, Peter did not lose charity. Secondly, indirectly, when a sin is committed against charity, through some passion of desire or fear; it was by sinning against charity in this way, that Peter lost charity; yet he soon recovered it.

The Reply to the Third Objection is evident from what has been said.

Reply Obj. 4: Not every inordinate affection for things directed to the end, i.e., for created goods, constitutes a mortal sin, but only such as is directly contrary to the Divine will; and then the inordinate affection is contrary to charity, as stated.

Reply Obj. 5: Charity denotes union with God, whereas faith and hope do not. Now every mortal sin consists in aversion from God, as stated above (Gen. ad lit. viii, 12). Consequently every mortal sin is contrary to charity, but not to faith and hope, but only certain determinate sins, which destroy the habit of faith or of hope, even as charity is destroyed by every moral sin. Hence it is evident that charity cannot remain lifeless, since it is itself the ultimate form regarding God under the aspect of last end as stated above (Q. 23, A. 8).

25. OF THE OBJECT OF CHARITY (TWELVE ARTICLES)

We must now consider the object of charity; which consideration will be twofold: (1) The things we ought to love out of charity: (2) The order in which they ought to be loved. Under the first head there are twelve points of inquiry:

(1) Whether we should love God alone, out of charity, or should we love our neighbor also?
(2) Whether charity should be loved out of charity?
(3) Whether irrational creatures ought to be loved out of charity?
(4) Whether one may love oneself out of charity?
(5) Whether one's own body?
(6) Whether sinners should be loved out of charity?
(7) Whether sinners love themselves?
(8) Whether we should love our enemies out of charity?
(9) Whether we are bound to show them tokens of friendship?
(10) Whether we ought to love the angels out of charity?
(11) Whether we ought to love the demons?
(12) How to enumerate the things we are bound to love out of charity.

* * * * *

FIRST ARTICLE [II-II, Q. 25, Art. 1]

Whether the Love of Charity Stops at God, or Extends to Our Neighbor?

Objection 1: It would seem that the love of charity stops at God and does not extend to our neighbor. For as we owe God love, so do we owe Him fear, according Deut. 10:12: "And now Israel, what doth the Lord thy God require of thee, but that thou fear . . .

and love Him?" Now the fear with which we fear man, and which is called human fear, is distinct from the fear with which we fear God, and which is either servile or filial, as is evident from what has been stated above (Q. 10, A. 2). Therefore also the love with which we love God, is distinct from the love with which we love our neighbor.

Obj. 2: Further, the Philosopher says (Ethic. viii, 8) that "to be loved is to be honored." Now the honor due to God, which is known as latria, is distinct from the honor due to a creature, and known as dulia. Therefore again the love wherewith we love God, is distinct from that with which we love our neighbor.

Obj. 3: Further, hope begets charity, as a gloss states on Matt. 1:2. Now hope is so due to God that it is reprehensible to hope in man, according to Jer. 17:5: "Cursed be the man that trusteth in man." Therefore charity is so due to God, as not to extend to our neighbor.

On the contrary, It is written (1 John 4:21): "This commandment we have from God, that he, who loveth God, love also his brother."

I answer that, As stated above (Q. 17, A. 6; Q. 19, A. 3; I-II, Q. 54, A. 3) habits are not differentiated except their acts be of different species. For every act of the one species belongs to the same habit. Now since the species of an act is derived from its object, considered under its formal aspect, it follows of necessity that it is specifically the same act that tends to an aspect of the object, and that tends to the object under that aspect: thus it is specifically the same visual act whereby we see the light, and whereby we see the color under the aspect of light.

Now the aspect under which our neighbor is to be loved, is God, since what we ought to love in our neighbor is that he may be in God. Hence it is clear that it is specifically the same act whereby we love God, and whereby we love our neighbor. Consequently the habit of charity extends not only to the love of God, but also to the love of our neighbor.

Reply Obj. 1: We may fear our neighbor, even as we may love him, in two ways: first, on account of something that is proper to him, as when a man fears a tyrant on account of his cruelty, or loves him by reason of his own desire to get something from him. Such like human fear is distinct from the fear of God, and the same applies to love. Secondly, we fear a man, or love him on account of what he has of God; as when we fear the secular power by reason of its exercising the ministry of God for the punishment of evildoers, and love it for its justice: such like fear of man is not distinct from fear of God, as neither is such like love.

Reply Obj. 2: Love regards good in general, whereas honor regards the honored person's own good, for it is given to a person in recognition of his own virtue. Hence love is not differentiated specifically on account of the various degrees of goodness in various persons, so long as it is referred to one good common to all, whereas honor is distinguished according to the good belonging to individuals. Consequently we love all our neighbors with the same love of charity, in so far as they are referred to one good common to them all, which is God; whereas we give various honors to various people, according to each one's own virtue, and likewise to God we give the singular honor of latria on account of His singular virtue.

Reply Obj. 3: It is wrong to hope in man as though he were the principal author of salvation, but not, to hope in man as helping us ministerially under God. In like manner it would be wrong if a man loved his neighbor as though he were his last end, but not, if he loved him for God's sake; and this is what charity does.

* * * * *

SECOND ARTICLE [II-II, Q. 25, Art. 2]

Whether We Should Love Charity Out of Charity?

Objection 1: It would seem that charity need not be loved out of charity. For the things to be loved out of charity are contained in the two precepts of charity (Matt. 22:37-39): and neither of them includes charity, since charity is neither God nor our neighbor. Therefore charity need not be loved out of charity.

Obj. 2: Further, charity is founded on the fellowship of happiness, as stated above (Q. 23, A. 1). But charity cannot participate in happiness. Therefore charity need not be loved out of charity.

Obj. 3: Further, charity is a kind of friendship, as stated above (Q. 23, A. 1). But no man can have friendship for charity or for an accident, since such things cannot return love for love, which is essential to friendship, as stated in Ethic. viii. Therefore charity need not be loved out of charity.

On the contrary, Augustine says (De Trin. viii, 8): "He that loves his neighbor, must, in consequence, love love itself." But we love our neighbor out of charity. Therefore it follows that charity also is loved out of charity.

I answer that, Charity is love. Now love, by reason of the nature of the power whose act it is, is capable of reflecting on itself; for since the object of the will is the universal good, whatever has the aspect of good, can be the object of an act of the will: and since to will is itself a good, man can will himself to will. Even so the intellect, whose object is the true, understands that it understands, because this again is something true. Love, however, even by reason of its own species, is capable of reflecting on itself, because it is a spontaneous movement of the lover towards the beloved, wherefore from the moment a man loves, he loves himself to love.

Yet charity is not love simply, but has the nature of friendship, as stated above (Q. 23, A. 1). Now by friendship a thing is loved in two ways: first, as the friend for whom we have friendship, and to whom we wish good things: secondly, as the good which we wish to a friend. It is in the latter and not in the former way that charity is loved out of charity, because charity is the good which we desire for all those whom we love out of charity. The same applies to happiness, and to the other virtues.

Reply Obj. 1: God and our neighbor are those with whom we are friends, but love of them includes the loving of charity, since we love both God and our neighbor, in so far as we love ourselves and our neighbor to love God, and this is to love charity.

Reply Obj. 2: Charity is itself the fellowship of the spiritual life, whereby we arrive at happiness: hence it is loved as the good which we desire for all whom we love out of charity.

Reply Obj. 3: This argument considers friendship as referred to those with whom we are friends.

* * * * *

THIRD ARTICLE [II-II, Q. 25, Art. 3]

Whether Irrational Creatures Also Ought to Be Loved Out of Charity?

Objection 1: It would seem that irrational creatures also ought to be loved out of charity. For it is chiefly by charity that we are conformed to God. Now God loves irrational creatures out of charity, for He loves "all things that are" (Wis. 11:25), and whatever He loves, He loves by Himself Who is charity. Therefore we also should love irrational creatures out of charity.

Obj. 2: Further, charity is referred to God principally, and extends to other things as referable to God. Now just as the rational creature is referable to God, in as much as it bears the resemblance of image, so too, are the irrational creatures, in as much as they bear the resemblance of a trace[1]. Therefore charity extends also to irrational creatures.

Obj. 3: Further, just as the object of charity is God. so is the object of faith. Now faith extends to irrational creatures, since we believe that heaven and earth were created by God, that the fishes and birds were brought forth out of the waters, and animals that walk, and plants, out of the earth. Therefore charity extends also to irrational creatures.

On the contrary, The love of charity extends to none but God and our neighbor. But the word neighbor cannot be extended to irrational creatures, since they have no fellowship with man in the rational life. Therefore charity does not extend to irrational creatures.

I answer that, According to what has been stated above (Q. 13, A. 1) charity is a kind of friendship. Now the love of friendship is twofold: first, there is the love for the friend to whom our friendship is given, secondly, the love for those good things which we desire for our friend. With regard to the first, no irrational creature can be loved out of charity; and for three reasons. Two of these reasons refer in a general way to friendship, which cannot have an irrational creature for its object: first because friendship is towards one to whom we wish good things, while, properly speaking, we cannot wish good things to an irrational creature, because it is not competent, properly speaking, to possess good, this being proper to the rational creature which, through its free-will, is the master of its disposal of the good it possesses. Hence the Philosopher says (Phys. ii, 6) that we do not speak of good or evil befalling such like things, except metaphorically. Secondly, because all friendship is based on some fellowship in life; since "nothing is so proper to friendship as to live together," as the Philosopher proves (Ethic. viii, 5). Now irrational creatures can have no fellowship in human life which is regulated by reason. Hence friendship with irrational

---

[1] Cf. I, Q. 45, A. 7

creatures is impossible, except metaphorically speaking. The third reason is proper to charity, for charity is based on the fellowship of everlasting happiness, to which the irrational creature cannot attain. Therefore we cannot have the friendship of charity towards an irrational creature.

Nevertheless we can love irrational creatures out of charity, if we regard them as the good things that we desire for others, in so far, to wit, as we wish for their preservation, to God's honor and man's use; thus too does God love them out of charity.

Wherefore the Reply to the First Objection is evident.

Reply Obj. 2: The likeness by way of trace does not confer the capacity for everlasting life, whereas the likeness of image does: and so the comparison fails.

Reply Obj. 3: Faith can extend to all that is in any way true, whereas the friendship of charity extends only to such things as have a natural capacity for everlasting life; wherefore the comparison fails.

* * * * *

FOURTH ARTICLE [II-II, Q. 25, Art. 4]

Whether a Man Ought to Love Himself Out of Charity?

Objection 1: It would seem that a man is [not] bound to love himself out of charity. For Gregory says in a homily (In Evang. xvii) that there "can be no charity between less than two." Therefore no man has charity towards himself.

Obj. 2: Further, friendship, by its very nature, implies mutual love and equality (Ethic. viii, 2, 7), which cannot be of one man towards himself. But charity is a kind of friendship, as stated above (Q. 23, A. 1). Therefore a man cannot have charity towards himself.

Obj. 3: Further, anything relating to charity cannot be blameworthy, since charity "dealeth not perversely" (1 Cor. 23:4). Now a man deserves to be blamed for loving himself, since it is written (2 Tim. 3:1, 2): "In the last days shall come dangerous times, men shall be lovers of themselves." Therefore a man cannot love himself out of charity.

On the contrary, It is written (Lev. 19:18): "Thou shalt love thy friend as thyself." Now we love our friends out of charity. Therefore we should love ourselves too out of charity.

I answer that, Since charity is a kind of friendship, as stated above (Q. 23, A. 1), we may consider charity from two standpoints: first, under the general notion of friendship, and in this way we must hold that, properly speaking, a man is not a friend to himself, but something more than a friend, since friendship implies union, for Dionysius says (Div. Nom. iv) that "love is a unitive force," whereas a man is one with himself which is more than being united to another. Hence, just as unity is the principle of union, so the love with which a man loves himself is the form and root of friendship. For if we have friendship with others it is because we do unto them as we do unto ourselves, hence we read in *Ethic.* ix, 4, 8, that "the origin of friendly relations with others lies in our relations to ourselves." Thus too with regard to principles we have something greater than science, namely understanding.

Secondly, we may speak of charity in respect of its specific nature, namely as denoting man's friendship with God in the first place, and, consequently, with the things of God, among which things is man himself who has charity. Hence, among these other things which he loves out of charity because they pertain to God, he loves also himself out of charity.

Reply Obj. 1: Gregory speaks there of charity under the general notion of friendship: and the Second Objection is to be taken in the same sense.

Reply Obj. 3: Those who love themselves are to be blamed, in so far as they love themselves as regards their sensitive nature, which they humor. This is not to love oneself truly according to one's rational nature, so as to desire for oneself the good things which pertain to the perfection of reason: and in this way chiefly it is through charity that a man loves himself.

* * * * *

FIFTH ARTICLE [II-II, Q. 25, Art. 5]

Whether a Man Ought to Love His Body Out of Charity?

Objection 1: It would seem that a man ought not to love his body out of charity. For we do not love one with whom we are unwilling to associate. But those who have charity shun the society of the body, according to Rom. 7:24: "Who shall deliver me from the body of this death?" and Phil. 1:23: "Having a desire to be dissolved and to be with Christ." Therefore our bodies are not to be loved out of charity.

Obj. 2: Further, the friendship of charity is based on fellowship in the enjoyment of God. But the body can have no share in that enjoyment. Therefore the body is not to be loved out of charity.

Obj. 3: Further, since charity is a kind of friendship it is towards those who are capable of loving in return. But our body cannot love us out of charity. Therefore it should not be loved out of charity.

On the contrary, Augustine says (De Doctr. Christ. i, 23, 26) that there are four things that we should love out of charity, and among them he reckons our own body.

I answer that, Our bodies can be considered in two ways: first, in respect of their nature, secondly, in respect of the corruption of sin and its punishment.

Now the nature of our body was created, not by an evil principle, as the Manicheans pretend, but by God. Hence we can use it for God's service, according to Rom. 6:13: "Present . . . your members as instruments of justice unto God." Consequently, out of the love of charity with which we love God, we ought to love our bodies also, but we ought not to love the evil effects of sin and the corruption of punishment; we ought rather, by the desire of charity, to long for the removal of such things.

Reply Obj. 1: The Apostle did not shrink from the society of his body, as regards the nature of the body, in fact in this respect he was loth to be deprived thereof, according to 2 Cor. 5:4: "We would not be unclothed, but clothed over." He did, however, wish to escape from the taint of concupiscence, which remains in the body, and from the corruption of the body which weighs down the soul, so as to hinder it from seeing God. Hence he says expressly: "From the body of this death."

Reply Obj. 2: Although our bodies are unable to enjoy God by knowing and loving Him, yet by the works which we do through the body, we are able to attain to the perfect knowledge of God. Hence from the enjoyment in the soul there overflows a certain happiness into the body, viz., "the flush of health and incorruption," as Augustine states (Ep. ad Dioscor. cxviii). Hence, since the body has, in a fashion, a share of happiness, it can be loved with the love of charity.

Reply Obj. 3: Mutual love is found in the friendship which is for another, but not in that which a man has for himself, either in respect of his soul, or in respect of his body.

* * * * *

SIXTH ARTICLE [II-II, Q. 25, Art. 6]

Whether We Ought to Love Sinners Out of Charity?

Objection 1: It would seem that we ought not to love sinners out of charity. For it is written (Ps. 118:113): "I have hated the unjust." But David had perfect charity. Therefore sinners should be hated rather than loved, out of charity.

Obj. 2: Further, "love is proved by deeds" as Gregory says in a homily for Pentecost (In Evang. xxx). But good men do no works of the unjust: on the contrary, they do such as would appear to be works of hate, according to Ps. 100:8: "In the morning I put to death all the wicked of the land": and God commanded (Ex. 22:18): "Wizards thou shalt not suffer to live." Therefore sinners should not be loved out of charity.

Obj. 3: Further, it is part of friendship that one should desire and wish good things for one's friends. Now the saints, out of charity, desire evil things for the wicked, according to Ps. 9:18: "May the wicked be turned into hell[1]." Therefore sinners should not be loved out of charity.

Obj. 4: Further, it is proper to friends to rejoice in, and will the same things. Now charity does not make us will what sinners will, nor to rejoice in what gives them joy, but rather the contrary. Therefore sinners should not be loved out of charity.

Obj. 5: Further, it is proper to friends to associate together, according to Ethic. viii. But we ought not to associate with sinners, according to 2 Cor. 6:17: "Go ye out from among them." Therefore we should not love sinners out of charity.

On the contrary, Augustine says (De Doctr. Christ. i, 30) that "when it is said: 'Thou shalt love thy neighbor,' it is evident that we ought to look upon every man as our neighbor." Now sinners do

---

1   Douay and A. V.: 'The wicked shall be,' etc. See Reply to this Objection.

not cease to be men, for sin does not destroy nature. Therefore we ought to love sinners out of charity.

I answer that, Two things may be considered in the sinner: his nature and his guilt. According to his nature, which he has from God, he has a capacity for happiness, on the fellowship of which charity is based, as stated above (A. 3; Q. 23, AA. 1, 5), wherefore we ought to love sinners, out of charity, in respect of their nature.

On the other hand their guilt is opposed to God, and is an obstacle to happiness. Wherefore, in respect of their guilt whereby they are opposed to God, all sinners are to be hated, even one's father or mother or kindred, according to Luke 12:26. For it is our duty to hate, in the sinner, his being a sinner, and to love in him, his being a man capable of bliss; and this is to love him truly, out of charity, for God's sake.

Reply Obj. 1: The prophet hated the unjust, as such, and the object of his hate was their injustice, which was their evil. Such hatred is perfect, of which he himself says (Ps. 138:22): "I have hated them with a perfect hatred." Now hatred of a person's evil is equivalent to love of his good. Hence also this perfect hatred belongs to charity.

Reply Obj. 2: As the Philosopher observes (Ethic. ix, 3), when our friends fall into sin, we ought not to deny them the amenities of friendship, so long as there is hope of their mending their ways, and we ought to help them more readily to regain virtue than to recover money, had they lost it, for as much as virtue is more akin than money to friendship. When, however, they fall into very great wickedness, and become incurable, we ought no longer to show them friendliness. It is for this reason that both Divine and human laws command such like sinners to be put to death, because there is greater likelihood of their harming others than of their mending their ways. Nevertheless the judge puts this into effect, not out of hatred for the sinners, but out of the love of charity, by reason of which he prefers the public good to the life of the individual. Moreover the death inflicted by the judge profits the sinner, if he be converted, unto the expiation of his crime; and, if he be not converted, it profits so as to put an end to the sin, because the sinner is thus deprived of the power to sin any more.

Reply Obj. 3: Such like imprecations which we come across in Holy Writ, may be understood in three ways: first, by way of prediction, not by way of wish, so that the sense is: "May the wicked be," that is, "The wicked shall be, turned into hell." Secondly, by way of wish, yet so that the desire of the wisher is not referred to the man's punishment, but to the justice of the punisher, according to Ps. 57:11: "The just shall rejoice when he shall see the revenge," since, according to Wis. 1:13, not even God "hath pleasure in the destruction of the wicked [Vulg.: 'living']" when He punishes them, but He rejoices in His justice, according to Ps. 10:8: "The Lord is just and hath loved justice." Thirdly, so that this desire is referred to the removal of the sin, and not to the punishment itself, to the effect, namely, that the sin be destroyed, but that the man may live.

Reply Obj. 4: We love sinners out of charity, not so as to will what they will, or to rejoice in what gives them joy, but so as to make them will what we will, and rejoice in what rejoices us. Hence it is written (Jer. 15:19): "They shall be turned to thee, and thou shalt not to be turned to them."

Reply Obj. 5: The weak should avoid associating with sinners, on account of the danger in which they stand of being perverted by them. But it is commendable for the perfect, of whose perversion there is no fear, to associate with sinners that they may convert them. For thus did Our Lord eat and drink with sinners as related by Matt. 9:11-13. Yet all should avoid the society of sinners, as regards fellowship in sin; in this sense it is written (2 Cor. 6:17): "Go out from among them . . . and touch not the unclean thing," i.e. by consenting to sin.

* * * * *

SEVENTH ARTICLE [II-II, Q. 25, Art. 7]

Whether Sinners Love Themselves?

Objection 1: It would seem that sinners love themselves. For that which is the principle of sin, is most of all in the sinner. Now love of self is the principle of sin, since Augustine says (De Civ. Dei xiv, 28) that it "builds up the city of Babylon." Therefore sinners most of all love themselves.

Obj. 2: Further, sin does not destroy nature. Now it is in keeping with nature that every man should love himself: wherefore even irrational creatures naturally desire their own good, for instance, the preservation of their being, and so forth. Therefore sinners love themselves.

Obj. 3: Further, good is beloved by all, as Dionysius states (Div. Nom. iv). Now many sinners reckon themselves to be good. Therefore many sinners love themselves.

On the contrary, It is written (Ps. 10:6): "He that loveth iniquity, hateth his own soul."

I answer that, Love of self is common to all, in one way; in another way it is proper to the good; in a third way, it is proper to the wicked. For it is common to all for each one to love what he thinks himself to be. Now a man is said to be a thing, in two ways: first, in respect of his substance and nature, and, this way all think themselves to be what they are, that is, composed of a soul and body. In this way too, all men, both good and wicked, love themselves, in so far as they love their own preservation.

Secondly, a man is said to be something in respect of some predominance, as the sovereign of a state is spoken of as being the state, and so, what the sovereign does, the state is said to do. In this way, all do not think themselves to be what they are. For the reasoning mind is the predominant part of man, while the sensitive and corporeal nature takes the second place, the former of which the Apostle calls the "inward man," and the latter, the "outward man" (2 Cor. 4:16). Now the good look upon their rational nature or the inward man as being the chief thing in them, wherefore in this way they think themselves to be what they are. On the other hand, the wicked reckon their sensitive and corporeal nature, or the outward man, to hold the first place. Wherefore, since they know not themselves aright, they do not love themselves aright, but love what they think themselves to be. But the good know themselves truly, and therefore truly love themselves.

The Philosopher proves this from five things that are proper to friendship. For in the first place, every friend wishes his friend to be and to live; secondly, he desires good things for him; thirdly, he does good things to him; fourthly, he takes pleasure in his company; fifthly, he is of one mind with him, rejoicing and sorrowing in almost the same things. In this way the good love themselves, as to the inward man, because they wish the preservation thereof in its integrity, they desire good things for him, namely spiritual goods, indeed they do their best to obtain them, and they take pleasure in entering into their own hearts, because they find there good thoughts in the present, the memory of past good, and the hope of future good, all of which are sources of pleasure. Likewise they experience no clashing of wills, since their whole soul tends to one thing.

On the other hand, the wicked have no wish to be preserved in the integrity of the inward man, nor do they desire spiritual goods for him, nor do they work for that end, nor do they take pleasure in their own company by entering into their own hearts, because whatever they find there, present, past and future, is evil and horrible; nor do they agree with themselves, on account of the gnawings of conscience, according to Ps. 49:21: "I will reprove thee and set before thy face."

In the same manner it may be shown that the wicked love themselves, as regards the corruption of the outward man, whereas the good do not love themselves thus.

Reply Obj. 1: The love of self which is the principle of sin is that which is proper to the wicked, and reaches "to the contempt of God," as stated in the passage quoted, because the wicked so desire external goods as to despise spiritual goods.

Reply Obj. 2: Although natural love is not altogether forfeited by wicked men, yet it is perverted in them, as explained above.

Reply Obj. 3: The wicked have some share of self-love, in so far as they think themselves good. Yet such love of self is not true but apparent: and even this is not possible in those who are very wicked.

* * * * *

EIGHTH ARTICLE [II-II, Q. 25, Art. 8]

Whether Charity Requires That We Should Love Our Enemies?

Objection 1: It would seem that charity does not require us to love our enemies. For Augustine says (Enchiridion lxxiii) that "this great good," namely, the love of our enemies, is "not so universal in its application, as the object of our petition when we say: Forgive us our trespasses." Now no one is forgiven sin without he have charity, because, according to Prov. 10:12, "charity covereth all sins." Therefore charity does not require that we should love our enemies.

Obj. 2: Further, charity does not do away with nature. Now everything, even an irrational being, naturally hates its contrary, as a lamb hates a wolf, and water fire. Therefore charity does not make us love our enemies.

Obj. 3: Further, charity "doth nothing perversely" (1 Cor. 13:4). Now it seems perverse to love one's enemies, as it would be to hate one's friends: hence Joab upbraided David by saying (2 Kings 19:6): "Thou lovest them that hate thee, and thou hatest them that love thee." Therefore charity does not make us love our enemies.

On the contrary, Our Lord said (Matt. 4:44): "Love your enemies."

I answer that, Love of one's enemies may be understood in three ways. First, as though we were to love our enemies as such: this is perverse, and contrary to charity, since it implies love of that which is evil in another.

Secondly love of one's enemies may mean that we love them as to their nature, but in general: and in this sense charity requires that we should love our enemies, namely, that in loving God and our neighbor, we should not exclude our enemies from the love given to our neighbor in general.

Thirdly, love of one's enemies may be considered as specially directed to them, namely, that we should have a special movement of love towards our enemies. Charity does not require this absolutely, because it does not require that we should have a special movement of love to every individual man, since this would be impossible. Nevertheless charity does require this, in respect of our being prepared in mind, namely, that we should be ready to love our enemies individually, if the necessity were to occur. That man should actually do so, and love his enemy for God's sake, without it being necessary for him to do so, belongs to the perfection of charity. For since man loves his neighbor, out of charity, for God's sake, the more he loves God, the more does he put enmities aside and show love towards his neighbor: thus if we loved a certain man very much, we would love his children though they were unfriendly towards us. This is the sense in which Augustine speaks in the passage quoted in the First Objection, the Reply to which is therefore evident.

Reply Obj. 2: Everything naturally hates its contrary as such. Now our enemies are contrary to us, as enemies, wherefore this itself should be hateful to us, for their enmity should displease us. They are not, however, contrary to us, as men and capable of happiness: and it is as such that we are bound to love them.

Reply Obj. 3: It is wrong to love one's enemies as such: charity does not do this, as stated above.

* * * * *

NINTH ARTICLE [II-II, Q. 25, Art. 9]

Whether It Is Necessary for Salvation That We Should Show Our Enemies the Signs and Effects of Love?

Objection 1: It would seem that charity demands of a man to show his enemy the signs or effects of love. For it is written (1 John 3:18): "Let us not love in word nor in tongue, but in deed and in truth." Now a man loves in deed by showing the one he loves signs and effects of love. Therefore charity requires that a man show his enemies such signs and effects of love.

Obj. 2: Further, Our Lord said in the same breath (Matt. 5:44): "Love your enemies," and, "Do good to them that hate you." Now charity demands that we love our enemies. Therefore it demands also that we should "do good to them."

Obj. 3: Further, not only God but also our neighbor is the object of charity. Now Gregory says in a homily for Pentecost (In Evang. xxx), that "love of God cannot be idle for wherever it is it does great things, and if it ceases to work, it is no longer love." Hence charity towards our neighbor cannot be without producing works. But charity requires us to love our neighbor without exception, though he be an enemy. Therefore charity requires us to show the signs and effects of love towards our enemies.

On the contrary, A gloss on Matt. 5:44, "Do good to them that hate you," says: "To do good to one's enemies is the height of perfection"[1]. Now charity does not require us to do that which belongs to its perfection. Therefore charity does not require us to show the signs and effects of love to our enemies.

I answer that, The effects and signs of charity are the result of inward love, and are in proportion with it. Now it is absolutely necessary, for the fulfilment of the precept, that we should inwardly love our enemies in general, but not individually, except as regards the mind being prepared to do so, as explained above (A. 8).

---

1   Augustine, Enchiridion lxxiii

We must accordingly apply this to the showing of the effects and signs of love. For some of the signs and favors of love are shown to our neighbors in general, as when we pray for all the faithful, or for a whole people, or when anyone bestows a favor on a whole community: and the fulfilment of the precept requires that we should show such like favors or signs of love towards our enemies. For if we did not so, it would be a proof of vengeful spite, and contrary to what is written (Lev. 19:18): "Seek not revenge, nor be mindful of the injury of thy citizens." But there are other favors or signs of love, which one shows to certain persons in particular: and it is not necessary for salvation that we show our enemies such like favors and signs of love, except as regards being ready in our minds, for instance to come to their assistance in a case of urgency, according to Prov. 25:21: "If thy enemy be hungry, give him to eat; if he thirst, give him . . . drink." Outside cases of urgency, to show such like favors to an enemy belongs to the perfection of charity, whereby we not only beware, as in duty bound, of being overcome by evil, but also wish to overcome evil by good[1], which belongs to perfection: for then we not only beware of being drawn into hatred on account of the hurt done to us, but purpose to induce our enemy to love us on account of our kindliness.

This suffices for the Replies to the Objections.

* * * * *

TENTH ARTICLE [II-II, Q. 25, Art. 10]

Whether We Ought to Love the Angels Out of Charity?

Objection 1: It would seem that we are not bound to love the angels out of charity. For, as Augustine says (De Doctr. Christ. i), charity is a twofold love: the love of God and of our neighbor. Now love of the angels is not contained in the love of God, since they are created substances; nor is it, seemingly, contained in the love of our neighbor, since they do not belong with us to a common species. Therefore we are not bound to love them out of charity.

Obj. 2: Further, dumb animals have more in common with us than the angels have, since they belong to the same proximate genus

---

[1] Rom. 12:21

as we do. But we have not charity towards dumb animals, as stated above (A. 3). Neither, therefore, have we towards the angels.

Obj. 3: Further, nothing is so proper to friends as companionship with one another (Ethic. viii, 5). But the angels are not our companions; we cannot even see them. Therefore we are unable to give them the friendship of charity.

On the contrary, Augustine says (De Doctr. Christ. i, 30): "If the name of neighbor is given either to those whom we pity, or to those who pity us, it is evident that the precept binding us to love our neighbor includes also the holy angels from whom we receive many merciful favors."

I answer that, As stated above (Q. 23, A. 1), the friendship of charity is founded upon the fellowship of everlasting happiness, in which men share in common with the angels. For it is written (Matt. 22:30) that "in the resurrection . . . men shall be as the angels of God in heaven." It is therefore evident that the friendship of charity extends also to the angels.

Reply Obj. 1: Our neighbor is not only one who is united to us in a common species, but also one who is united to us by sharing in the blessings pertaining to everlasting life, and it is on the latter fellowship that the friendship of charity is founded.

Reply Obj. 2: Dumb animals are united to us in the proximate genus, by reason of their sensitive nature; whereas we are partakers of everlasting happiness, by reason not of our sensitive nature but of our rational mind wherein we associate with the angels.

Reply Obj. 3: The companionship of the angels does not consist in outward fellowship, which we have in respect of our sensitive nature; it consists in a fellowship of the mind, imperfect indeed in this life, but perfect in heaven, as stated above (Q. 23, A. 1, ad 1).

* * * * *

ELEVENTH ARTICLE [II-II, Q. 25, Art. 11]

Whether We Are Bound to Love the Demons Out of Charity?

Objection 1: It would seem that we ought to love the demons out of charity. For the angels are our neighbors by reason of their fellowship with us in a rational mind. But the demons also share in our fellowship thus, since natural gifts, such as life and understanding, remain in them unimpaired, as Dionysius states (Div. Nom. iv). Therefore we ought to love the demons out of charity.

Obj. 2: Further, the demons differ from the blessed angels in the matter of sin, even as sinners from just men. Now the just man loves the sinner out of charity. Therefore he ought to love the demons also out of charity.

Obj. 3: Further, we ought, out of charity, to love, as being our neighbors, those from whom we receive favors, as appears from the passage of Augustine quoted above (A. 9). Now the demons are useful to us in many things, for "by tempting us they work crowns for us," as Augustine says (De Civ. Dei xi, 17). Therefore we ought to love the demons out of charity.

On the contrary, It is written (Isa. 28:18): "Your league with death shall be abolished, and your covenant with hell shall not stand." Now the perfection of a peace and covenant is through charity. Therefore we ought not to have charity for the demons who live in hell and compass death.

I answer that, As stated above (A. 6), in the sinner, we are bound, out of charity, to love his nature, but to hate his sin. But the name of demon is given to designate a nature deformed by sin, wherefore demons should not be loved out of charity. Without however laying stress on the word, the question as to whether the spirits called demons ought to be loved out of charity, must be answered in accordance with the statement made above (AA. 2, 3), that a thing may be loved out of charity in two ways. First, a thing may be loved as the person who is the object of friendship, and thus we cannot have the friendship of charity towards the demons. For it is an essential part of friendship that one should be a well-wisher towards one's friend; and it is impossible for us, out of charity, to desire the good of everlasting life, to which charity is referred, for those spirits whom God has condemned eternally, since this would be in opposition to our charity towards God whereby we approve of His justice.

Secondly, we love a thing as being that which we desire to be enduring as another's good. In this way we love irrational creatures out of charity, in as much as we wish them to endure, to give glory to God and be useful to man, as stated above (A. 3): and in this way too we can love the nature of the demons even out of charity, in as much as we desire those spirits to endure, as to their natural gifts, unto God's glory.

Reply Obj. 1: The possession of everlasting happiness is not impossible for the angelic mind as it is for the mind of a demon; consequently the friendship of charity which is based on the fellowship of everlasting life, rather than on the fellowship of nature, is possible towards the angels, but not towards the demons.

Reply Obj. 2: In this life, men who are in sin retain the possibility of obtaining everlasting happiness: not so those who are lost in hell, who, in this respect, are in the same case as the demons.

Reply Obj. 3: That the demons are useful to us is due not to their intention but to the ordering of Divine providence; hence this leads us to be friends, not with them, but with God, Who turns their perverse intention to our profit.

* * * * *

TWELFTH ARTICLE [II-II, Q. 25, Art. 12]

Whether Four Things Are Rightly Reckoned As to Be Loved Out of Charity, Viz. God, Our Neighbor, Our Body and Ourselves?

Objection 1: It would seem that these four things are not rightly reckoned as to be loved out of charity, to wit: God, our neighbor, our body, and ourselves. For, as Augustine states (Tract. super Joan. lxxxiii), "he that loveth not God, loveth not himself." Hence love of oneself is included in the love of God. Therefore love of oneself is not distinct from the love of God.

Obj. 2: Further, a part ought not to be condivided with the whole. But our body is part of ourselves. Therefore it ought not to be condivided with ourselves as a distinct object of love.

Obj. 3: Further, just as a man has a body, so has his neighbor. Since then the love with which a man loves his neighbor, is distinct from the love with which a man loves himself, so the love with which a man loves his neighbor's body, ought to be distinct from the love with which he loves his own body. Therefore these four things are not rightly distinguished as objects to be loved out of charity.

On the contrary, Augustine says (De Doctr. Christ. i, 23): "There are four things to be loved; one which is above us," namely God, "another, which is ourselves, a third which is nigh to us," namely our neighbor, "and a fourth which is beneath us," namely our own body.

I answer that, As stated above (Q. 23, AA. 1, 5), the friendship of charity is based on the fellowship of happiness. Now, in this fellowship, one thing is considered as the principle from which happiness flows, namely God; a second is that which directly partakes of happiness, namely men and angels; a third is a thing to which happiness comes by a kind of overflow, namely the human body.

Now the source from which happiness flows is lovable by reason of its being the cause of happiness: that which is a partaker of happiness, can be an object of love for two reasons, either through being identified with ourselves, or through being associated with us in partaking of happiness, and in this respect, there are two things to be loved out of charity, in as much as man loves both himself and his neighbor.

Reply Obj. 1: The different relations between a lover and the various things loved make a different kind of lovableness. Accordingly, since the relation between the human lover and God is different from his relation to himself, these two are reckoned as distinct objects of love, for the love of the one is the cause of the love of the other, so that the former love being removed the latter is taken away.

Reply Obj. 2: The subject of charity is the rational mind that can be capable of obtaining happiness, to which the body does not reach directly, but only by a kind of overflow. Hence, by his reasonable mind which holds the first place in him, man, out of charity, loves himself in one way, and his own body in another.

Reply Obj. 3: Man loves his neighbor, both as to his soul and as to his body, by reason of a certain fellowship in happiness. Wherefore, on the part of his neighbor, there is only one reason for loving him; and our neighbor's body is not reckoned as a special object of love.

26. OF THE ORDER OF CHARITY
(In Thirteen Articles)

We must now consider the order of charity, under which head there are thirteen points of inquiry:

(1) Whether there is an order in charity?
(2) Whether man ought to love God more than his neighbor?

(3) Whether more than himself?
(4) Whether he ought to love himself more than his neighbor?
(5) Whether man ought to love his neighbor more than his own body?
(6) Whether he ought to love one neighbor more than another?
(7) Whether he ought to love more, a neighbor who is better, or one who is more closely united to him?
(8) Whether he ought to love more, one who is akin to him by blood, or one who is united to him by other ties?
(9) Whether, out of charity, a man ought to love his son more than his father?
(10) Whether he ought to love his mother more than his father?
(11) Whether he ought to love his wife more than his father or mother?
(12) Whether we ought to love those who are kind to us more than those whom we are kind to?
(13) Whether the order of charity endures in heaven?.

* * * * *

FIRST ARTICLE [II-II, Q. 26, Art. 1]

Whether There Is Order in Charity?

Objection 1: It would seem that there is no order in charity. For charity is a virtue. But no order is assigned to the other virtues. Neither, therefore, should any order be assigned to charity.

Obj. 2: Further, just as the object of faith is the First Truth, so is the object of charity the Sovereign Good. Now no order is appointed for faith, but all things are believed equally. Neither, therefore, ought there to be any order in charity.

Obj. 3: Further, charity is in the will: whereas ordering belongs, not to the will, but to the reason. Therefore no order should be ascribed to charity.

On the contrary, It is written (Cant 2:4): "He brought me into the cellar of wine, he set in order charity in me."

I answer that, As the Philosopher says (Metaph. v, text. 16), the terms "before" and "after" are used in reference to some principle. Now order implies that certain things are, in some way, before or after. Hence wherever there is a principle, there must needs be also order of some kind. But it has been said above (Q. 23, A. 1; Q. 25, A. 12) that the love of charity tends to God as to the principle of happiness, on the fellowship of which the friendship of charity is based. Consequently there must needs be some order in things loved out of charity, which order is in reference to the first principle of that love, which is God.

Reply Obj. 1: Charity tends towards the last end considered as last end: and this does not apply to any other virtue, as stated above (Q. 23, A. 6). Now the end has the character of principle in matters of appetite and action, as was shown above (Q. 23, A. 7, ad 2; I-II, A. 1, ad 1). Wherefore charity, above all, implies relation to the First Principle, and consequently, in charity above all, we find an order in reference to the First Principle.

Reply Obj. 2: Faith pertains to the cognitive power, whose operation depends on the thing known being in the knower. On the other hand, charity is in an appetitive power, whose operation consists in the soul tending to things themselves. Now order is to be found in things themselves, and flows from them into our knowledge. Hence order is more appropriate to charity than to faith.

And yet there is a certain order in faith, in so far as it is chiefly about God, and secondarily about things referred to God.

Reply Obj. 3: Order belongs to reason as the faculty that orders, and to the appetitive power as to the faculty which is ordered. It is in this way that order is stated to be in charity.

* * * * *

SECOND ARTICLE [II-II, Q. 26, Art. 2]

Whether God Ought to Be Loved More Than Our Neighbor?

Objection 1: It would seem that God ought not to be loved more than our neighbor. For it is written (1 John 4:20): "He that loveth not his brother whom he seeth, how can he love God, Whom he seeth not?" Whence it seems to follow that the more a thing is visible the more lovable it is, since loving begins with seeing, according to Ethic. ix, 5, 12. Now God is less visible than our neighbor. Therefore He is less lovable, out of charity, than our neighbor.

Obj. 2: Further, likeness causes love, according to Ecclus. 13:19: "Every beast loveth its like." Now man bears more likeness to his neighbor than to God. Therefore man loves his neighbor, out of charity, more than he loves God.

Obj. 3: Further, what charity loves in a neighbor, is God, according to Augustine (De Doctr. Christ. i, 22, 27). Now God is not greater in Himself than He is in our neighbor. Therefore He is not more to be loved in Himself than in our neighbor. Therefore we ought not to love God more than our neighbor.

On the contrary, A thing ought to be loved more, if others ought to be hated on its account. Now we ought to hate our neighbor for God's sake, if, to wit, he leads us astray from God, according to Luke 14:26: "If any man come to Me and hate not his father, and mother, and wife, end children, and brethren, and sisters ... he cannot be My disciple." Therefore we ought to love God, out of charity, more than our neighbor.

I answer that, Each kind of friendship regards chiefly the subject in which we chiefly find the good on the fellowship of which that friendship is based: thus civil friendship regards chiefly the ruler of the state, on whom the entire common good of the state depends; hence to him before all, the citizens owe fidelity and obedience. Now the friendship of charity is based on the fellowship of happiness, which consists essentially in God, as the First Principle, whence it flows to all who are capable of happiness.

Therefore God ought to be loved chiefly and before all out of charity: for He is loved as the cause of happiness, whereas our neighbor is loved as receiving together with us a share of happiness from Him.

Reply Obj. 1: A thing is a cause of love in two ways: first, as being the reason for loving. In this way good is the cause of love, since each thing is loved according to its measure of goodness. Secondly, a thing causes love, as being a way to acquire love. It is in this way that seeing is the cause of loving, not as though a thing were lovable according as it is visible, but because by seeing a thing we are led to love it. Hence it does not follow that what is more visible is more lovable, but that as an object of love we meet with it before others: and that is the sense of the Apostle's argument. For, since our neighbor is more visible to us, he is the first lovable object we meet with, because "the soul learns, from those things it knows, to love what it knows not," as Gregory says in a homily (In Evang. xi). Hence it can be argued that, if any man loves not his neighbor, neither does he love God, not because his neighbor is more lovable, but because he is the first thing to demand our love: and God is more lovable by reason of His greater goodness.

Reply Obj. 2: The likeness we have to God precedes and causes the likeness we have to our neighbor: because from the very fact that we share along with our neighbor in something received from God, we become like to our neighbor. Hence by reason of this likeness we ought to love God more than we love our neighbor.

Reply Obj. 3: Considered in His substance, God is equally in all, in whomsoever He may be, for He is not lessened by being in anything. And yet our neighbor does not possess God's goodness equally with God, for God has it essentially, and our neighbor by participation.

* * * * *

THIRD ARTICLE [II-II, Q. 26, Art. 3]

Whether Out of Charity, Man Is Bound to Love God More Than Himself?

Objection 1: It would seem that man is not bound, out of charity, to love God more than himself. For the Philosopher says (Ethic. ix, 8) that "a man's friendly relations with others arise from his friendly relations with himself." Now the cause is stronger than its effect. Therefore man's friendship towards himself is greater than his friendship for anyone else. Therefore he ought to love himself more than God.

Obj. 2: Further, one loves a thing in so far as it is one's own good. Now the reason for loving a thing is more loved than the thing itself which is loved for that reason, even as the principles which are the reason for knowing a thing are more known. Therefore man loves himself more than any other good loved by him. Therefore he does not love God more than himself.

Obj. 3: Further, a man loves God as much as he loves to enjoy God. But a man loves himself as much as he loves to enjoy God;

since this is the highest good a man can wish for himself. Therefore man is not bound, out of charity, to love God more than himself.

On the contrary, Augustine says (De Doctr. Christ. i, 22): "If thou oughtest to love thyself, not for thy own sake, but for the sake of Him in Whom is the rightest end of thy love, let no other man take offense if him also thou lovest for God's sake." Now "the cause of a thing being such is yet more so." Therefore man ought to love God more than himself.

I answer that, The good we receive from God is twofold, the good of nature, and the good of grace. Now the fellowship of natural goods bestowed on us by God is the foundation of natural love, in virtue of which not only man, so long as his nature remains unimpaired, loves God above all things and more than himself, but also every single creature, each in its own way, i.e. either by an intellectual, or by a rational, or by an animal, or at least by a natural love, as stones do, for instance, and other things bereft of knowledge, because each part naturally loves the common good of the whole more than its own particular good. This is evidenced by its operation, since the principal inclination of each part is towards common action conducive to the good of the whole. It may also be seen in civic virtues whereby sometimes the citizens suffer damage even to their own property and persons for the sake of the common good. Wherefore much more is this realized with regard to the friendship of charity which is based on the fellowship of the gifts of grace.

Therefore man ought, out of charity, to love God, Who is the common good of all, more than himself: since happiness is in God as in the universal and fountain principle of all who are able to have a share of that happiness.

Reply Obj. 1: The Philosopher is speaking of friendly relations towards another person in whom the good, which is the object of friendship, resides in some restricted way; and not of friendly relations with another in whom the aforesaid good resides in totality.

Reply Obj. 2: The part does indeed love the good of the whole, as becomes a part, not however so as to refer the good of the whole to itself, but rather itself to the good of the whole.

Reply Obj. 3: That a man wishes to enjoy God pertains to that love of God which is love of concupiscence. Now we love God with the love of friendship more than with the love of concupiscence, because the Divine good is greater in itself, than our share of good in enjoying Him. Hence, out of charity, man simply loves God more than himself.

* * * * *

FOURTH ARTICLE [II-II, Q. 26, Art. 4]

Whether Out of Charity, Man Ought to Love Himself More Than His Neighbor?

Objection 1: It would seem that a man ought not, out of charity, to love himself more than his neighbor. For the principal object of charity is God, as stated above (A. 2; Q. 25, AA. 1, 12). Now sometimes our neighbor is more closely united to God than we are ourselves. Therefore we ought to love such a one more than ourselves.

Obj. 2: Further, the more we love a person, the more we avoid injuring him. Now a man, out of charity, submits to injury for his neighbor's sake, according to Prov. 12:26: "He that neglecteth a loss for the sake of a friend, is just." Therefore a man ought, out of charity, to love his neighbor more than himself.

Obj. 3: Further, it is written (1 Cor. 13:5) "charity seeketh not its own." Now the thing we love most is the one whose good we seek most. Therefore a man does not, out of charity, love himself more than his neighbor.

On the contrary, It is written (Lev. 19:18, Matt. 22:39): "Thou shalt love thy neighbor (Lev. 19:18: 'friend') as thyself." Whence it seems to follow that man's love for himself is the model of his love for another. But the model exceeds the copy. Therefore, out of charity, a man ought to love himself more than his neighbor.

I answer that, There are two things in man, his spiritual nature and his corporeal nature. And a man is said to love himself by reason of his loving himself with regard to his spiritual nature, as stated above (Q. 25, A. 7): so that accordingly, a man ought, out of charity, to love himself more than he loves any other person.

This is evident from the very reason for loving: since, as stated above (Q. 25, AA. 1, 12), God is loved as the principle of good, on which the love of charity is founded; while man, out of charity, loves himself by reason of his being a partaker of the aforesaid good, and loves his neighbor by reason of his fellowship in that good. Now fellowship is a reason for love according to a certain union in relation to God. Wherefore just as unity surpasses union, the fact that man himself has a share of the Divine good, is a more potent reason for loving than that another should be a partner with him in that share. Therefore man, out of charity, ought to love himself more than his neighbor: in sign whereof, a man ought not to give way to any evil of sin, which counteracts his share of happiness, not even that he may free his neighbor from sin.

Reply Obj. 1: The love of charity takes its quantity not only from its object which is God, but also from the lover, who is the man that has charity, even as the quantity of any action depends in some way on the subject. Wherefore, though a better neighbor is nearer to God, yet because he is not as near to the man who has charity, as this man is to himself, it does not follow that a man is bound to love his neighbor more than himself.

Reply Obj. 2: A man ought to bear bodily injury for his friend's sake, and precisely in so doing he loves himself more as regards his spiritual mind, because it pertains to the perfection of virtue, which is a good of the mind. In spiritual matters, however, man ought not to suffer injury by sinning, in order to free his neighbor from sin, as stated above.

Reply Obj. 3: As Augustine says in his Rule (Ep. ccxi), the saying, "'charity seeks not her own,' means that it prefers the common to the private good." Now the common good is always more lovable to the individual than his private good, even as the good of the whole is more lovable to the part, than the latter's own partial good, as stated above (A. 3).

* * * * *

FIFTH ARTICLE [II-II, Q. 26, Art. 5]

Whether a Man Ought to Love His Neighbor More Than His Own Body?

Objection 1: It would seem that a man is not bound to love his neighbor more than his own body. For his neighbor includes his neighbor's body. If therefore a man ought to love his neighbor more than his own body, it follows that he ought to love his neighbor's body more than his own.

Obj. 2: Further, a man ought to love his own soul more than his neighbor's, as stated above (A. 4). Now a man's own body is nearer to his soul than his neighbor. Therefore we ought to love our body more than our neighbor.

Obj. 3: Further, a man imperils that which he loves less for the sake of what he loves more. Now every man is not bound to imperil his own body for his neighbor's safety: this belongs to the perfect, according to John 15:13: "Greater love than this no man hath, that a man lay down his life for his friends." Therefore a man is not bound, out of charity, to love his neighbor more than his own body.

On the contrary, Augustine says (De Doctr. Christ. i, 27) that "we ought to love our neighbor more than our own body."

I answer that, Out of charity we ought to love more that which has more fully the reason for being loved out of charity, as stated above (A. 2; Q. 25, A. 12). Now fellowship in the full participation of happiness which is the reason for loving one's neighbor, is a greater reason for loving, than the participation of happiness by way of overflow, which is the reason for loving one's own body. Therefore, as regards the welfare of the soul we ought to love our neighbor more than our own body.

Reply Obj. 1: According to the Philosopher (Ethic. ix, 8) a thing seems to be that which is predominant in it: so that when we say that we ought to love our neighbor more than our own body, this refers to his soul, which is his predominant part.

Reply Obj. 2: Our body is nearer to our soul than our neighbor, as regards the constitution of our own nature: but as regards the participation of happiness, our neighbor's soul is more closely associated with our own soul, than even our own body is.

Reply Obj. 3: Every man is immediately concerned with the care of his own body, but not with his neighbor's welfare, except perhaps in cases of urgency: wherefore charity does not necessarily require a man to imperil his own body for his neighbor's welfare, except in a case where he is under obligation to do so; and if a man of his own accord offer himself for that purpose, this belongs to the perfection of charity.

* * * * *

SIXTH ARTICLE [II-II, Q. 26, Art. 6]

Whether We Ought to Love One Neighbor More Than Another?

Objection 1: It would seem that we ought not to love one neighbor more than another. For Augustine says (De Doctr. Christ. i, 28): "One ought to love all men equally. Since, however, one cannot do good to all, we ought to consider those chiefly who by reason of place, time or any other circumstance, by a kind of chance, are more closely united to us." Therefore one neighbor ought not to be loved more than another.

Obj. 2: Further, where there is one and the same reason for loving several, there should be no inequality of love. Now there is one and the same reason for loving all one's neighbors, which reason is God, as Augustine states (De Doctr. Christ. i, 27). Therefore we ought to love all our neighbors equally.

Obj. 3: Further, to love a man is to wish him good things, as the Philosopher states (Rhet. ii, 4). Now to all our neighbors we wish an equal good, viz. everlasting life. Therefore we ought to love all our neighbors equally.

On the contrary, One's obligation to love a person is proportionate to the gravity of the sin one commits in acting against that love. Now it is a more grievous sin to act against the love of certain neighbors, than against the love of others. Hence the commandment (Lev. 10:9), "He that curseth his father or mother, dying let him die," which does not apply to those who cursed others than the above. Therefore we ought to love some neighbors more than others.

I answer that, There have been two opinions on this question: for some have said that we ought, out of charity, to love all our neighbors equally, as regards our affection, but not as regards the outward effect. They held that the order of love is to be understood as applying to outward favors, which we ought to confer on those who are connected with us in preference to those who are unconnected, and not to the inward affection, which ought to be given equally to all including our enemies.

But this is unreasonable. For the affection of charity, which is the inclination of grace, is not less orderly than the natural appetite, which is the inclination of nature, for both inclinations flow from Divine wisdom. Now we observe in the physical order that the natural inclination in each thing is proportionate to the act or movement that is becoming to the nature of that thing: thus in earth the inclination of gravity is greater than in water, because it is becoming to earth to be beneath water. Consequently the inclination also of grace which is the effect of charity, must needs be proportionate to those actions which have to be performed outwardly, so that, to wit, the affection of our charity be more intense towards those to whom we ought to behave with greater kindness.

We must, therefore, say that, even as regards the affection we ought to love one neighbor more than another. The reason is that, since the principle of love is God, and the person who loves, it must needs be that the affection of love increases in proportion to the nearness to one or the other of those principles. For as we stated above (A. 1), wherever we find a principle, order depends on relation to that principle.

Reply Obj. 1: Love can be unequal in two ways: first on the part of the good we wish our friend. In this respect we love all men equally out of charity: because we wish them all one same generic good, namely everlasting happiness. Secondly love is said to be greater through its action being more intense: and in this way we ought not to love all equally.

Or we may reply that we have unequal love for certain persons in two ways: first, through our loving some and not loving others. As regards beneficence we are bound to observe this inequality, because we cannot do good to all: but as regards benevolence, love ought not to be thus unequal. The other inequality arises from our loving some more than others: and Augustine does not mean to exclude the latter inequality, but the former, as is evident from what he says of beneficence.

Reply Obj. 2: Our neighbors are not all equally related to God; some are nearer to Him, by reason of their greater goodness, and those we ought, out of charity, to love more than those who are not so near to Him.

Reply Obj. 3: This argument considers the quantity of love on the part of the good which we wish our friends.

* * * * *

SEVENTH ARTICLE [II-II, Q. 26, Art. 7]

Whether We Ought to Love Those Who Are Better More Than Those Who Are More Closely United Us?

Objection 1: It would seem that we ought to love those who are better more than those who are more closely united to us. For that which is in no way hateful seems more lovable than that which is hateful for some reason: just as a thing is all the whiter for having less black mixed with it. Now those who are connected with us are hateful for some reason, according to Luke 14:26: "If any man come to Me, and hate not his father," etc. On the other hand good men are not hateful for any reason. Therefore it seems that we ought to love those who are better more than those who are more closely connected with us.

Obj. 2: Further, by charity above all, man is likened to God. But God loves more the better man. Therefore man also, out of charity, ought to love the better man more than one who is more closely united to him.

Obj. 3: Further, in every friendship, that ought to be loved most which has most to do with the foundation of that friendship: for, by natural friendship we love most those who are connected with us by nature, our parents for instance, or our children. Now the friendship of charity is founded upon the fellowship of happiness, which has more to do with better men than with those who are more closely united to us. Therefore, out of charity, we ought to love better men more than those who are more closely connected with us.

On the contrary, It is written (1 Tim. 5:8): "If any man have not care of his own and especially of those of his house, he hath denied the faith, and is worse than an infidel." Now the inward affection of charity ought to correspond to the outward effect. Therefore charity regards those who are nearer to us before those who are better.

I answer that, Every act should be proportionate both to its object and to the agent. But from its object it takes its species, while, from the power of the agent it takes the mode of its intensity: thus movement has its species from the term to which it tends, while the intensity of its speed arises from the disposition of the thing moved and the power of the mover. Accordingly love takes its species from its object, but its intensity is due to the lover.

Now the object of charity's love is God, and man is the lover. Therefore the specific diversity of the love which is in accordance with charity, as regards the love of our neighbor, depends on his relation to God, so that, out of charity, we should wish a greater good to one who is nearer to God; for though the good which charity wishes to all, viz. everlasting happiness, is one in itself, yet it has various degrees according to various shares of happiness, and it belongs to charity to wish God's justice to be maintained, in accordance with which better men have a fuller share of happiness. And this regards the species of love; for there are different species of love according to the different goods that we wish for those whom we love.

On the other hand, the intensity of love is measured with regard to the man who loves, and accordingly man loves those who are more closely united to him, with more intense affection as to the good he wishes for them, than he loves those who are better as to the greater good he wishes for them.

Again a further difference must be observed here: for some neighbors are connected with us by their natural origin, a connection which cannot be severed, since that origin makes them to be what they are. But the goodness of virtue, wherein some are close to God, can come and go, increase and decrease, as was shown above (Q. 24, AA. 4, 10, 11). Hence it is possible for one, out of charity, to wish this man who is more closely united to one, to be better than another, and so reach a higher degree of happiness.

Moreover there is yet another reason for which, out of charity, we love more those who are more nearly connected with us, since we love them in more ways. For, towards those who are not connected with us we have no other friendship than charity, whereas for those who are connected with us, we have certain other friendships, according to the way in which they are connected. Now since the good on which every other friendship of the virtuous is based, is directed, as to its end, to the good on which charity is based, it follows that charity commands each act of another friendship, even as the art which is about the end commands the art which is about the means. Consequently this very act of loving someone because he is akin or connected with us, or because he is a fellow-countryman or for any like reason that is referable to the end of charity, can be commanded by charity, so that, out of charity both eliciting and commanding, we love in more ways those who are more nearly connected with us.

Reply Obj. 1: We are commanded to hate, in our kindred, not their kinship, but only the fact of their being an obstacle between us and God. In this respect they are not akin but hostile to us, according to Micah 7:6: "A men's enemies are they of his own household."

Reply Obj. 2: Charity conforms man to God proportionately, by making man comport himself towards what is his, as God does towards what is His. For we may, out of charity, will certain things as becoming to us which God does not will, because it becomes Him not to will them, as stated above (I-II, Q. 19, A. 10), when we were treating of the goodness of the will.

Reply Obj. 3: Charity elicits the act of love not only as regards the object, but also as regards the lover, as stated above. The result is that the man who is more nearly united to us is more loved.

* * * * *

EIGHTH ARTICLE [II-II, Q. 26, Art. 8]

Whether We Ought to Love More Those Who Are Connected with Us by Ties of Blood?

Objection 1: It would seem that we ought not to love more those who are more closely united to us by ties of blood. For it is written (Prov. 18:24): "A man amiable in society, shall be more friendly than a brother." Again, Valerius Maximus says (Fact. et Dict. Memor. iv 7): "The ties of friendship are most strong and in no way yield to the ties of blood." Moreover it is quite certain and undeniable, that as to the latter, the lot of birth is fortuitous, whereas we contract the former by an untrammelled will, and a solid pledge. Therefore we ought not to love more than others those who are united to us by ties of blood.

Obj. 2: Further, Ambrose says (De Officiis i, 7): "I love not less you whom I have begotten in the Gospel, than if I had begotten you in wedlock, for nature is no more eager to love than grace." Surely we ought to love those whom we expect to be with us for ever more than those who will be with us only in this world. Therefore we should not love our kindred more than those who are otherwise connected with us.

Obj. 3: Further, "Love is proved by deeds," as Gregory states (Hom. in Evang. xxx). Now we are bound to do acts of love to others than our kindred: thus in the army a man must obey his officer rather than his father. Therefore we are not bound to love our kindred most of all.

On the contrary, The commandments of the decalogue contain a special precept about the honor due to our parents (Ex. 20:12). Therefore we ought to love more specially those who are united to us by ties of blood.

I answer that, As stated above (A. 7), we ought out of charity to love those who are more closely united to us more, both because our love for them is more intense, and because there are more reasons for loving them. Now intensity of love arises from the union of lover and beloved: and therefore we should measure the love of different persons according to the different kinds of union, so that a man is more loved in matters touching that particular union in respect of which he is loved. And, again, in comparing love to love we should compare one union with another. Accordingly we must say that friendship among blood relations is based upon their connection by natural origin, the friendship of fellow-citizens on their civic fellowship, and the friendship of those who are fighting side by side on the comradeship of battle. Wherefore in matters pertaining to nature we should love our kindred most, in matters concerning relations between citizens, we should prefer our fellow-citizens, and on the battlefield our fellow-soldiers. Hence the Philosopher says (Ethic. ix, 2) that "it is our duty to render to each class of people such respect as is natural and appropriate. This is in fact the principle upon which we seem to act, for we invite our relations to a wedding . . . It would seem to be a special duty to afford our parents the means of living . . . and to honor them."

The same applies to other kinds of friendship.

If however we compare union with union, it is evident that the union arising from natural origin is prior to, and more stable than, all others, because it is something affecting the very substance, whereas other unions supervene and may cease altogether. Therefore the friendship of kindred is more stable, while other friendships may be stronger in respect of that which is proper to each of them.

Reply Obj. 1: In as much as the friendship of comrades originates through their own choice, love of this kind takes precedence of the love of kindred in matters where we are free to do as we choose, for instance in matters of action. Yet the friendship of kindred is more stable, since it is more natural, and preponderates over others in matters touching nature: consequently we are more beholden to them in the providing of necessaries.

Reply Obj. 2: Ambrose is speaking of love with regard to favors respecting the fellowship of grace, namely, moral instruction. For in this matter, a man ought to provide for his spiritual children whom he has begotten spiritually, more than for the sons of his body, whom he is bound to support in bodily sustenance.

Reply Obj. 3: The fact that in the battle a man obeys his officer rather than his father proves, that he loves his father less, not simply [but] relatively, i.e. as regards the love which is based on fellowship in battle.

* * * * *

NINTH ARTICLE [II-II, Q. 26, Art. 9]

Whether a Man Ought, Out of Charity, to Love His Children More Than His Father?

Objection 1: It seems that a man ought, out of charity, to love his children more than his father. For we ought to love those more to whom we are more bound to do good. Now we are more bound to do good to our children than to our parents, since the Apostle says (2 Cor. 12:14): "Neither ought the children to lay up for the parents, but the parents for the children." Therefore a man ought to love his children more than his parents.

Obj. 2: Further, grace perfects nature. But parents naturally love their children more than these love them, as the Philosopher states (Ethic. viii, 12). Therefore a man ought to love his children more than his parents.

Obj. 3: Further, man's affections are conformed to God by charity. But God loves His children more than they love Him. Therefore we also ought to love our children more than our parents.

On the contrary, Ambrose[1] says: "We ought to love God first, then our parents, then our children, and lastly those of our household."

I answer that, As stated above (A. 4, ad 1; A. 7), the degrees of love may be measured from two standpoints. First, from that of the object. In this respect the better a thing is, and the more like to God, the more is it to be loved: and in this way a man ought to love his father more than his children, because, to wit, he loves his father as his principle, in which respect he is a more exalted good and more like God.

Secondly, the degrees of love may be measured from the standpoint of the lover, and in this respect a man loves more that which is more closely connected with him, in which way a man's children are more lovable to him than his father, as the Philosopher states (Ethic. viii). First, because parents love their children as being part of themselves, whereas the father is not part of his son, so that the love of a father for his children, is more like a man's love for himself. Secondly, because parents know better that so and so is their child than vice versa. Thirdly, because children are nearer to their parents, as being part of them, than their parents are to them to whom they stand in the relation of a principle. Fourthly, because parents have loved longer, for the father begins to love his child at once, whereas the child begins to love his father after a lapse of time; and the longer love lasts, the stronger it is, according to Ecclus. 9:14: "Forsake not an old friend, for the new will not be like to him."

Reply Obj. 1: The debt due to a principle is submission of respect and honor, whereas that due to the effect is one of influence and care. Hence the duty of children to their parents consists chiefly in honor: while that of parents to their children is especially one of care.

Reply Obj. 2: It is natural for a man as father to love his children more, if we consider them as closely connected with him: but if we consider which is the more exalted good, the son naturally loves his father more.

Reply Obj. 3: As Augustine says (De Doctr. Christ. i, 32), God loves us for our good and for His honor. Wherefore since

---

[1] Origen, Hom. ii in Cant.

our father is related to us as principle, even as God is, it belongs properly to the father to receive honor from his children, and to the children to be provided by their parents with what is good for them. Nevertheless in cases of necessity the child is bound out of the favors received to provide for his parents before all.

* * * * *

TENTH ARTICLE [II-II, Q. 26, Art. 10]

Whether a Man Ought to Love His Mother More Than His Father?

Objection 1: It would seem that a man ought to love his mother more than his father. For, as the Philosopher says (De Gener. Animal. i, 20), "the female produces the body in generation." Now man receives his soul, not from his father, but from God by creation, as stated in the First Part (Q. 90, A. 2; Q. 118). Therefore a man receives more from his mother than from his father: and consequently he ought to love her more than him.

Obj. 2: Further, where greater love is given, greater love is due. Now a mother loves her child more than the father does: for the Philosopher says (Ethic. ix, 7) that "mothers have greater love for their children. For the mother labors more in child-bearing, and she knows more surely than the father who are her children."

Obj. 3: Further, love should be more fond towards those who have labored for us more, according to Rom. 16:6: "Salute Mary, who hath labored much among you." Now the mother labors more than the father in giving birth and education to her child; wherefore it is written (Ecclus. 7:29): "Forget not the groanings of thy mother." Therefore a man ought to love his mother more than his father.

On the contrary, Jerome says on Ezech. 44:25 that "man ought to love God the Father of all, and then his own father," and mentions the mother afterwards.

I answer that, In making such comparisons as this, we must take the answer in the strict sense, so that the present question is whether the father as father, ought to be loved more than the mother as mother. The reason is that virtue and vice may make such a difference in such like matters, that friendship may be diminished or destroyed, as the Philosopher remarks (Ethic. viii, 7). Hence Ambrose[1] says: "Good servants should be preferred to wicked children."

Strictly speaking, however, the father should be loved more than the mother. For father and mother are loved as principles of our natural origin. Now the father is principle in a more excellent way than the mother, because he is the active principle, while the mother is a passive and material principle. Consequently, strictly speaking, the father is to be loved more.

Reply Obj. 1: In the begetting of man, the mother supplies the formless matter of the body; and the latter receives its form through the formative power that is in the semen of the father. And though this power cannot create the rational soul, yet it disposes the matter of the body to receive that form.

Reply Obj. 2: This applies to another kind of love. For the friendship between lover and lover differs specifically from the friendship between child and parent: while the friendship we are speaking of here, is that which a man owes his father and mother through being begotten of them.

The Reply to the Third Objection is evident.

* * * * *

ELEVENTH ARTICLE [II-II, Q. 26, Art. 11]

Whether a Man Ought to Love His Wife More Than His Father and Mother?

Objection 1: It would seem that a man ought to love his wife more than his father and mother. For no man leaves a thing for another unless he love the latter more. Now it is written (Gen. 2:24) that "a man shell leave father and mother" on account of his wife. Therefore a man ought to love his wife more than his father and mother.

Obj. 2: Further, the Apostle says (Eph. 5:33) that a husband should "love his wife as himself." Now a man ought to love himself more than his parents. Therefore he ought to love his wife also more than his parents.

---

[1] Origen, Hom. ii in Cant.

Obj. 2: Further, love should be greater where there are more reasons for loving. Now there are more reasons for love in the friendship of a man towards his wife. For the Philosopher says (Ethic. viii, 12) that "in this friendship there are the motives of utility, pleasure, and also of virtue, if husband and wife are virtuous." Therefore a man's love for his wife ought to be greater than his love for his parents.

On the contrary, According to Eph. 5:28, "men ought to love their wives as their own bodies." Now a man ought to love his body less than his neighbor, as stated above (A. 5): and among his neighbors he should love his parents most. Therefore he ought to love his parents more than his wife.

I answer that, As stated above (A. 9), the degrees of love may be taken from the good (which is loved), or from the union between those who love. On the part of the good which is the object loved, a man should love his parents more than his wife, because he loves them as his principles and considered as a more exalted good.

But on the part of the union, the wife ought to be loved more, because she is united with her husband, as one flesh, according to Matt. 19:6: "Therefore now they are not two, but one flesh." Consequently a man loves his wife more intensely, but his parents with greater reverence.

Reply Obj. 1: A man does not in all respects leave his father and mother for the sake of his wife: for in certain cases a man ought to succor his parents rather than his wife. He does however leave all his kinsfolk, and cleaves to his wife as regards the union of carnal connection and co-habitation.

Reply Obj. 2: The words of the Apostle do not mean that a man ought to love his wife equally with himself, but that a man's love for himself is the reason for his love of his wife, since she is one with him.

Reply Obj. 3: There are also several reasons for a man's love for his father; and these, in a certain respect, namely, as regards good, are more weighty than those for which a man loves his wife; although the latter outweigh the former as regards the closeness of the union.

As to the argument in the contrary sense, it must be observed that in the words quoted, the particle "as" denotes not equality of love but the motive of love. For the principal reason why a man loves his wife is her being united to him in the flesh.

* * * * *

TWELFTH ARTICLE [II-II, Q. 26, Art. 12]

Whether a Man Ought to Love More His Benefactor Than One He Has Benefited?

Objection 1: It would seem that a man ought to love his benefactor more than one he has benefited. For Augustine says (De Catech. Rud. iv): "Nothing will incite another more to love you than that you love him first: for he must have a hard heart indeed, who not only refuses to love, but declines to return love already given." Now a man's benefactor forestalls him in the kindly deeds of charity. Therefore we ought to love our benefactors above all.

Obj. 2: Further, the more grievously we sin by ceasing to love a man or by working against him, the more ought we to love him. Now it is a more grievous sin to cease loving a benefactor or to work against him, than to cease loving one to whom one has hitherto done kindly actions. Therefore we ought to love our benefactors more than those to whom we are kind.

Obj. 3: Further, of all things lovable, God is to be loved most, and then one's father, as Jerome says[1]. Now these are our greatest benefactors. Therefore a benefactor should be loved above all others.

On the contrary, The Philosopher says (Ethic. ix, 7), that "benefactors seem to love recipients of their benefactions, rather than vice versa."

I answer that, As stated above (AA. 9, 11), a thing is loved more in two ways: first because it has the character of a more excellent good, secondly by reason of a closer connection. In the first way we ought to love our benefactor most, because, since he is a principle of good to the man he has benefited, he has the character of a more excellent good, as stated above with regard to one's father (A. 9).

In the second way, however, we love those more who have received benefactions from us, as the Philosopher proves (Ethic. ix, 7) by four arguments. First because the recipient of benefactions

---

1 Comment. in Ezechiel xliv, 25

is the handiwork of the benefactor, so that we are wont to say of a man: "He was made by so and so." Now it is natural to a man to love his own work (thus it is to be observed that poets love their own poems): and the reason is that we love *to be* and *to live,* and these are made manifest in our *action*. Secondly, because we all naturally love that in which we see our own good. Now it is true that the benefactor has some good of his in the recipient of his benefaction, and the recipient some good in the benefactor; but the benefactor sees his virtuous good in the recipient, while the recipient sees his useful good in the benefactor. Now it gives more pleasure to see one's virtuous good than one's useful good, both because it is more enduring,—for usefulness quickly flits by, and the pleasure of calling a thing to mind is not like the pleasure of having it present—and because it is more pleasant to recall virtuous goods than the profit we have derived from others. Thirdly, because is it the lover's part to act, since he wills and works the good of the beloved, while the beloved takes a passive part in receiving good, so that to love surpasses being loved, for which reason the greater love is on the part of the benefactor. Fourthly because it is more difficult to give than to receive favors: and we are most fond of things which have cost us most trouble, while we almost despise what comes easy to us.

Reply Obj. 1: It is some thing in the benefactor that incites the recipient to love him: whereas the benefactor loves the recipient, not through being incited by him, but through being moved thereto of his own accord: and what we do of our own accord surpasses what we do through another.

Reply Obj. 2: The love of the beneficiary for the benefactor is more of a duty, wherefore the contrary is the greater sin. On the other hand, the love of the benefactor for the beneficiary is more spontaneous, wherefore it is quicker to act.

Reply Obj. 3: God also loves us more than we love Him, and parents love their children more than these love them. Yet it does not follow that we love all who have received good from us, more than any of our benefactors. For we prefer such benefactors as God and our parents, from whom we have received the greatest favors, to those on whom we have bestowed lesser benefits.

* * * * *

THIRTEENTH ARTICLE [II-II, Q. 26, Art. 13]

Whether the Order of Charity Endures in Heaven?

Objection 1: It would seem that the order of charity does not endure in heaven. For Augustine says (De Vera Relig. xlviii): "Perfect charity consists in loving greater goods more, and lesser goods less." Now charity will be perfect in heaven. Therefore a man will love those who are better more than either himself or those who are connected with him.

Obj. 2: Further, we love more him to whom we wish a greater good. Now each one in heaven wishes a greater good for those who have more good, else his will would not be conformed in all things to God's will: and there to be better is to have more good. Therefore in heaven each one loves more those who are better, and consequently he loves others more than himself, and one who is not connected with him, more than one who is.

Obj. 3: Further, in heaven love will be entirely for God's sake, for then will be fulfilled the words of 1 Cor. 15:28: "That God may be all in all." Therefore he who is nearer God will be loved more, so that a man will love a better man more than himself, and one who is not connected with him, more than one who is.

On the contrary, Nature is not done away, but perfected, by glory. Now the order of charity given above (AA. 2, 3, 4) is derived from nature: since all things naturally love themselves more than others. Therefore this order of charity will endure in heaven.

I answer that, The order of charity must needs remain in heaven, as regards the love of God above all things. For this will be realized simply when man shall enjoy God perfectly. But, as regards the order between man himself and other men, a distinction would seem to be necessary, because, as we stated above (AA. 7, 9), the degrees of love may be distinguished either in respect of the good which a man desires for another, or according to the intensity of love itself. In the first way a man will love better men more than himself, and those who are less good, less than himself: because, by reason of the perfect conformity of the human to the Divine will, each of the blessed will desire everyone to have what is due to him according to Divine justice. Nor will that be a time for advancing by means of merit to a yet greater reward, as happens now while it is possible for a man to desire both the virtue and the reward of a better man, whereas then the will of each one will rest within the limits determined by God. But in the second way a man will love himself more than even his better neighbors, because the intensity of the act of love arises on the part of the person who loves, as stated above (AA. 7, 9). Moreover it is for this that the gift of charity is bestowed by God on each one, namely, that he may first of all direct his mind to God, and this pertains to a man's love for himself, and that, in the second place, he may wish other things to be directed to God, and even work for that end according to his capacity.

As to the order to be observed among our neighbors, a man will simply love those who are better, according to the love of charity. Because the entire life of the blessed consists in directing their minds to God, wherefore the entire ordering of their love will be ruled with respect to God, so that each one will love more and reckon to be nearer to himself those who are nearer to God. For then one man will no longer succor another, as he needs to in the present life, wherein each man has to succor those who are closely connected with him rather than those who are not, no matter what be the nature of their distress: hence it is that in this life, a man, by the inclination of charity, loves more those who are more closely united to him, for he is under a greater obligation to bestow on them the effect of charity. It will however be possible in heaven for a man to love in several ways one who is connected with him, since the causes of virtuous love will not be banished from the mind of the blessed. Yet all these reasons are incomparably surpassed by that which is taken from nighness to God.

Reply Obj. 1: This argument should be granted as to those who are connected together; but as regards man himself, he ought to love himself so much the more than others, as his charity is more perfect, since perfect entire reason of his love, for God is man's charity directs man to God perfectly, and this belongs to love of oneself, as stated above.

Reply Obj. 2: This argument considers the order of charity in respect of the degree of good one wills the person one loves.

Reply Obj. 3: God will be to each one the entire reason of his love, for God is man's entire good. For if we make the impossible supposition that God were not man's good, He would not be man's reason for loving. Hence it is that in the order of love man should love himself more than all else after God.

27. OF THE PRINCIPAL ACT OF CHARITY, WHICH IS TO LOVE (In Eight Articles)

We must now consider the act of charity, and (1) the principal act of charity, which is to love, (2) the other acts or effects which follow from that act.

Under the first head there are eight points of inquiry:

(1) Which is the more proper to charity, to love or to be loved?
(2) Whether to love considered as an act of charity is the same as goodwill?
(3) Whether God should be loved for His own sake?
(4) Whether God can be loved immediately in this life?
(5) Whether God can be loved wholly?
(6) Whether the love of God is according to measure?
(7) Which is the better, to love one's friend, or one's enemy?
(8) Which is the better, to love God, or one's neighbor?.

* * * * *

FIRST ARTICLE [II-II, Q. 27, Art. 1]

Whether to Be Loved Is More Proper to Charity Than to Love?

Objection 1: It would seem that it is more proper to charity to be loved than to love. For the better charity is to be found in those who are themselves better. But those who are better should be more loved. Therefore to be loved is more proper to charity.

Obj. 2: Further, that which is to be found in more subjects seems to be more in keeping with nature, and, for that reason, better. Now, as the Philosopher says (Ethic. viii, 8), "many would rather be loved than love, and lovers of flattery always abound." Therefore it is better to be loved than to love, and consequently it is more in keeping with charity.

Obj. 3: Further, "the cause of anything being such is yet more so." Now men love because they are loved, for Augustine says (De Catech. Rud. iv) that "nothing incites another more to love you than that you love him first." Therefore charity consists in being loved rather than in loving.

On the contrary, The Philosopher says (Ethic. viii, 8) that friendship consists in loving rather than in being loved. Now charity is a kind of friendship. Therefore it consists in loving rather than in being loved.

I answer that, To love belongs to charity as charity. For, since charity is a virtue, by its very essence it has an inclination to its proper act. Now to be loved is not the act of the charity of the person loved; for this act is to love: and to be loved is competent to him as coming under the common notion of good, in so far as another tends towards his good by an act of charity. Hence it is clear that to love is more proper to charity than to be loved: for that which befits a thing by reason of itself and its essence is more competent to it than that which is befitting to it by reason of something else. This can be exemplified in two ways. First, in the fact that friends are more commended for loving than for being loved, indeed, if they be loved and yet love not, they are blamed. Secondly, because a mother, whose love is the greatest, seeks rather to love than to be loved: for "some women," as the Philosopher observes (Ethic. viii, 8) "entrust their children to a nurse; they do love them indeed, yet seek not to be loved in return, if they happen not to be loved."

Reply Obj. 1: A better man, through being better, is more lovable; but through having more perfect charity, loves more. He loves more, however, in proportion to the person he loves. For a better man does not love that which is beneath him less than it ought to be loved: whereas he who is less good fails to love one who is better, as much as he ought to be loved.

Reply Obj. 2: As the Philosopher says (Ethic. viii, 8), "men wish to be loved in as much as they wish to be honored." For just as honor is bestowed on a man in order to bear witness to the good which is in him, so by being loved a man is shown to have some good, since good alone is lovable. Accordingly men seek to be loved and to be honored, for the sake of something else, viz. to make known the good which is in the person loved. On the other hand, those who have charity seek to love for the sake of loving, as though this were itself the good of charity, even as the act of any virtue is that virtue's good. Hence it is more proper to charity to wish to love than to wish to be loved.

Reply Obj. 3: Some love on account of being loved, not so that to be loved is the end of their loving, but because it is a kind of way leading a man to love.

* * * * *

SECOND ARTICLE [II-II, Q. 27, Art. 2]

Whether to Love Considered As an Act of Charity Is the Same As Goodwill?

Objection 1: It would seem that to love, considered as an act of charity, is nothing else than goodwill. For the Philosopher says (Rhet. ii, 4) that "to love is to wish a person well"; and this is goodwill. Therefore the act of charity is nothing but goodwill.

Obj. 2: Further, the act belongs to the same subject as the habit. Now the habit of charity is in the power of the will, as stated above (Q. 24, A. 1). Therefore the act of charity is also an act of the will. But it tends to good only, and this is goodwill. Therefore the act of charity is nothing else than goodwill.

Obj. 3: Further, the Philosopher reckons five things pertaining to friendship (Ethic. ix, 4), the first of which is that a man should wish his friend well; the second, that he should wish him to be and to live; the third, that he should take pleasure in his company; the fourth, that he should make choice of the same things; the fifth, that he should grieve and rejoice with him. Now the first two pertain to goodwill. Therefore goodwill is the first act of charity.

On the contrary, The Philosopher says (Ethic. ix, 5) that "goodwill is neither friendship nor love, but the beginning of friendship." Now charity is friendship, as stated above (Q. 23, A. 1). Therefore goodwill is not the same as to love considered as an act of charity.

I answer that, Goodwill properly speaking is that act of the will whereby we wish well to another. Now this act of the will differs from actual love, considered not only as being in the sensitive appetite but also as being in the intellective appetite or will. For the love which is in the sensitive appetite is a passion. Now every passion seeks its object with a certain eagerness. And the passion of love is not aroused suddenly, but is born of an earnest consideration of the object loved; wherefore the Philosopher, showing the difference between goodwill and the love which is a passion, says (Ethic. ix, 5) that goodwill does not imply impetuosity or desire, that is to say, has not an eager inclination, because it is by the sole judgment of his reason that one man wishes another well. Again such like love arises from previous acquaintance, whereas goodwill sometimes arises suddenly, as happens to us if we look on at a boxing-match, and we wish one of the boxers to win. But the love, which is in the intellective appetite, also differs from goodwill, because it denotes a certain union of affections between the lover and the beloved, in as much as the lover deems the beloved as somewhat united to him, or belonging to him, and so tends towards him. On the other hand, goodwill is a simple act of the will, whereby we wish a person well, even without presupposing the aforesaid union of the affections with him. Accordingly, to love, considered as an act of charity, includes goodwill, but such dilection or love adds union of affections, wherefore the Philosopher says (Ethic. ix, 5) that "goodwill is a beginning of friendship."

Reply Obj. 1: The Philosopher, by thus defining "to love," does not describe it fully, but mentions only that part of its definition in which the act of love is chiefly manifested.

Reply Obj. 2: To love is indeed an act of the will tending to the good, but it adds a certain union with the beloved, which union is not denoted by goodwill.

Reply Obj. 3: These things mentioned by the Philosopher belong to friendship because they arise from a man's love for himself, as he says in the same passage, in so far as a man does all these things in respect of his friend, even as he does them to himself: and this belongs to the aforesaid union of the affections.

* * * * *

THIRD ARTICLE [II-II, Q. 27, Art. 3]

Whether Out of Charity God Ought to Be Loved for Himself?

Objection 1: It would seem that God is loved out of charity, not for Himself but for the sake of something else. For Gregory says in a homily (In Evang. xi): "The soul learns from the things it knows, to love those it knows not," where by things unknown he means the intelligible and the Divine, and by things known he indicates the objects of the senses. Therefore God is to be loved for the sake of something else.

Obj. 2: Further, love follows knowledge. But God is known through something else, according to Rom. 1:20: "The invisible things of God are clearly seen, being understood by the things that are made." Therefore He is also loved on account of something else and not for Himself.

Obj. 3: Further, "hope begets charity" as a gloss says on Matt. 1:1, and "fear leads to charity," according to Augustine in his commentary on the First Canonical Epistle of John (In prim. canon. Joan. Tract. ix). Now hope looks forward to obtain something from God, while fear shuns something which can be inflicted by God. Therefore it seems that God is to be loved on account of some good we hope for, or some evil to be feared. Therefore He is not to be loved for Himself.

On the contrary, According to Augustine (De Doctr. Christ. i), to enjoy is to cleave to something for its own sake. Now "God is to be enjoyed" as he says in the same book. Therefore God is to be loved for Himself.

I answer that, The preposition "for" denotes a relation of causality. Now there are four kinds of cause, viz., final, formal, efficient, and material, to which a material disposition also is to be reduced, though it is not a cause simply but relatively. According to these four different causes one thing is said to be loved for another. In respect of the final cause, we love medicine, for instance, for health; in respect of the formal cause, we love a man for his virtue, because, to wit, by his virtue he is formally good and therefore lovable; in respect of the efficient cause, we love certain men because, for instance, they are the sons of such and such a father; and in respect of the disposition which is reducible to the genus of a material cause, we speak of loving something for that which disposed us to love it, e.g. we love a man for the favors received from him, although after we have begun to love our friend, we no longer love him for his favors, but for his virtue. Accordingly, as regards the first three ways, we love God, not for anything else, but for Himself. For He is not directed to anything else as to an end, but is Himself the last end of all things; nor does He require to receive any form in order to be good, for His very substance is His goodness, which is itself the exemplar of all other good things; nor again does goodness accrue to Him from aught else, but from Him to all other things. In the fourth way, however, He can be loved for something else, because we are disposed by certain things to advance in His love, for instance, by favors bestowed by Him, by the rewards we hope to receive from Him, or even by the punishments which we are minded to avoid through Him.

Reply Obj. 1: From the things it knows the soul learns to love what it knows not, not as though the things it knows were the reason for its loving things it knows not, through being the formal, final, or efficient cause of this love, but because this knowledge disposes man to love the unknown.

Reply Obj. 2: Knowledge of God is indeed acquired through other things, but after He is known, He is no longer known through them, but through Himself, according to John 4:42: "We now believe, not for thy saying: for we ourselves have heard Him, and know that this is indeed the Saviour of the world."

Reply Obj. 3: Hope and fear lead to charity by way of a certain disposition, as was shown above (Q. 17, A. 8; Q. 19, AA. 4, 7, 10).

* * * * *

FOURTH ARTICLE [II-II, Q. 27, Art. 4]

Whether God Can Be Loved Immediately in This Life?

Objection 1: It would seem that God cannot be loved immediately in this life. For the "unknown cannot be loved" as Augustine says (De Trin. x, 1). Now we do not know God immediately in this life, since "we see now through a glass, in a dark manner" (1 Cor. 13:12). Neither, therefore, do we love Him immediately.

Obj. 2: Further, he who cannot do what is less, cannot do what is more. Now it is more to love God than to know Him, since "he who is joined" to God by love, is "one spirit with Him" (1 Cor. 6:17). But man cannot know God immediately. Therefore much less can he love Him immediately.

Obj. 3: Further, man is severed from God by sin, according to Isa. 59:2: "Your iniquities have divided between you and your God." Now sin is in the will rather than in the intellect. Therefore man is less able to love God immediately than to know Him immediately.

On the contrary, Knowledge of God, through being mediate, is said to be "enigmatic," and "falls away" in heaven, as stated in 1 Cor. 13:12.

But charity "does not fall away" as stated in the same passage (1 Cor. 13:12). Therefore the charity of the way adheres to God immediately.

I answer that, As stated above (I, Q. 82, A. 3; Q. 84, A. 7), the act of a cognitive power is completed by the thing known being in the knower, whereas the act of an appetitive power consists in the appetite being inclined towards the thing in itself. Hence it follows that the movement of the appetitive power is towards things in respect of their own condition, whereas the act of a cognitive power follows the mode of the knower.

Now in itself the very order of things is such, that God is knowable and lovable for Himself, since He is essentially truth and goodness itself, whereby other things are known and loved: but with regard to us, since our knowledge is derived through the senses, those things are knowable first which are nearer to our senses, and the last term of knowledge is that which is most remote from our senses.

Accordingly, we must assert that to love which is an act of the appetitive power, even in this state of life, tends to God first, and flows on from Him to other things, and in this sense charity loves God immediately, and other things through God. On the other hand, with regard to knowledge, it is the reverse, since we know God through other things, either as a cause through its effects, or by way of pre-eminence or negation as Dionysius states (Div. Nom. i; cf. I, Q. 12, A. 12).

Reply Obj. 1: Although the unknown cannot be loved, it does not follow that the order of knowledge is the same as the order of love, since love is the term of knowledge, and consequently, love can begin at once where knowledge ends, namely in the thing itself which is known through another thing.

Reply Obj. 2: Since to love God is something greater than to know Him, especially in this state of life, it follows that love of God presupposes knowledge of God. And because this knowledge does not rest in creatures, but, through them, tends to something else, love begins there, and thence goes on to other things by a circular movement so to speak; for knowledge begins from creatures, tends to God, and love begins with God as the last end, and passes on to creatures.

Reply Obj. 3: Aversion from God, which is brought about by sin, is removed by charity, but not by knowledge alone: hence charity, by loving God, unites the soul immediately to Him with a chain of spiritual union.

* * * * *

FIFTH ARTICLE [II-II, Q. 27, Art. 5]

Whether God can be loved wholly?[1]

Objection 1: It would seem that God cannot be loved wholly. For love follows knowledge. Now God cannot be wholly known by us, since this would imply comprehension of Him. Therefore He cannot be wholly loved by us.

Obj. 2: Further, love is a kind of union, as Dionysius shows (Div. Nom. iv). But the heart of man cannot be wholly united to God, because "God is greater than our heart" (1 John 3:20). Therefore God cannot be loved wholly.

Obj. 3: Further, God loves Himself wholly. If therefore He be loved wholly by another, this one will love Him as much as God loves Himself. But this is unreasonable. Therefore God cannot be wholly loved by a creature.

On the contrary, It is written (Deut. 6:5): "Thou shalt love the Lord thy God with thy whole heart."

I answer that, Since love may be considered as something between lover and beloved, when we ask whether God can be wholly loved, the question may be understood in three ways, first so that the qualification "wholly" be referred to the thing loved, and thus God is to be loved wholly, since man should love all that pertains to God.

Secondly, it may be understood as though "wholly" qualified the lover: and thus again God ought to be loved wholly, since man ought to love God with all his might, and to refer all he has to the love of God, according to Deut. 6:5: "Thou shalt love the Lord thy God with thy whole heart."

Thirdly, it may be understood by way of comparison of the lover to the thing loved, so that the mode of the lover equal the mode of the thing loved. This is impossible: for, since a thing is lovable in proportion to its goodness, God is infinitely lovable, since His goodness is infinite. Now no creature can love God infinitely, because all power of creatures, whether it be natural or infused, is finite.

---

[1] Cf. Q. 184, A. 2

This suffices for the Replies to the Objections, because the first three objections consider the question in this third sense, while the last takes it in the second sense.

* * * * *

SIXTH ARTICLE [II-II, Q. 27, Art. 6]

Whether in Loving God We Ought to Observe Any Mode?

Objection 1: It would seem that we ought to observe some mode in loving God. For the notion of good consists in mode, species and order, as Augustine states (De Nat. Boni iii, iv). Now the love of God is the best thing in man, according to Col. 3:14: "Above all . . . things, have charity." Therefore there ought to be a mode of the love of God.

Obj. 2: Further, Augustine says (De Morib. Eccl. viii): "Prithee, tell me which is the mode of love. For I fear lest I burn with the desire and love of my Lord, more or less than I ought." But it would be useless to seek the mode of the Divine love, unless there were one. Therefore there is a mode of the love of God.

Obj. 3: Further, as Augustine says (Gen. ad lit. iv, 3), "the measure which nature appoints to a thing, is its mode." Now the measure of the human will, as also of external action, is the reason. Therefore just as it is necessary for the reason to appoint a mode to the exterior effect of charity, according to Rom. 12:1: "Your reasonable service," so also the interior love of God requires a mode.

On the contrary, Bernard says (De Dilig. Deum 1) that "God is the cause of our loving God; the measure is to love Him without measure."

I answer that, As appears from the words of Augustine quoted above (Obj. 3) mode signifies a determination of measure; which determination is to be found both in the measure and in the thing measured, but not in the same way. For it is found in the measure essentially, because a measure is of itself the determining and modifying rule of other things; whereas in the things measured, it is found relatively, that is in so far as they attain to the measure. Hence there can be nothing unmodified in the measure whereas the thing measured is unmodified if it fails to attain to the measure, whether by deficiency or by excess.

Now in all matters of appetite and action the measure is the end, because the proper reason for all that we desire or do should be taken from the end, as the Philosopher proves (Phys. ii, 9). Therefore the end has a mode by itself, while the means take their mode from being proportionate to the end. Hence, according to the Philosopher (Polit. i, 3), "in every art, the desire for the end is endless and unlimited," whereas there is a limit to the means: thus the physician does not put limits to health, but makes it as perfect as he possibly can; but he puts a limit to medicine, for he does not give as much medicine as he can, but according as health demands so that if he give too much or too little, the medicine would be immoderate.

Again, the end of all human actions and affections is the love of God, whereby principally we attain to our last end, as stated above (Q. 23, A. 6), wherefore the mode in the love of God, must not be taken as in a thing measured where we find too much or too little, but as in the measure itself, where there cannot be excess, and where the more the rule is attained the better it is, so that the more we love God the better our love is.

Reply Obj. 1: That which is so by its essence takes precedence of that which is so through another, wherefore the goodness of the measure which has the mode essentially, takes precedence of the goodness of the thing measured, which has its mode through something else; and so too, charity, which has a mode as a measure has, stands before the other virtues, which have a mode through being measured.

Reply Obj. 2: As Augustine adds in the same passage, "the measure of our love for God is to love Him with our whole heart," that is to love Him as much as He can be loved, and this belongs to the mode which is proper to the measure.

Reply Obj. 3: An affection, whose object is subject to reason's judgment, should be measured by reason. But the object of the Divine love which is God surpasses the judgment of reason, wherefore it is not measured by reason but transcends it. Nor is there parity between the interior act and external acts of charity. For the interior act of charity has the character of an end, since man's ultimate good consists in his soul cleaving to God, according to Ps. 72:28: "It is good for me to adhere to my God"; whereas the exterior acts are as means to the end, and so have to be measured both according to charity and according to reason.

* * * * *

SEVENTH ARTICLE [II-II, Q. 27, Art. 7]

Whether It Is More Meritorious to Love an Enemy Than to Love a Friend?

Objection 1: It would seem more meritorious to love an enemy than to love a friend. For it is written (Matt. 5:46): "If you love them that love you, what reward shall you have?" Therefore it is not deserving of reward to love one's friend: whereas, as the same passage proves, to love one's enemy is deserving of a reward. Therefore it is more meritorious to love one's enemy than to love one's friend.

Obj. 2: Further, an act is the more meritorious through proceeding from a greater charity. But it belongs to the perfect children of God to love their enemies, whereas those also who have imperfect charity love their friends. Therefore it is more meritorious to love one's enemy than to love one's friend.

Obj. 3: Further, where there is more effort for good, there seems to be more merit, since "every man shall receive his own reward according to his own labor" (1 Cor. 3:8). Now a man has to make a greater effort to love his enemy than to love his friend, because it is more difficult. Therefore it seems more meritorious to love one's enemy than to love one's friend.

On the contrary, The better an action is, the more meritorious it is. Now it is better to love one's friend, since it is better to love a better man, and the friend who loves you is better than the enemy who hates you. Therefore it is more meritorious to love one's friend than to love one's enemy.

I answer that, God is the reason for our loving our neighbor out of charity, as stated above (Q. 25, A. 1). When therefore it is asked which is better or more meritorious, to love one's friend or one's enemy, these two loves may be compared in two ways, first, on the part of our neighbor whom we love, secondly, on the part of the reason for which we love him.

In the first way, love of one's friend surpasses love of one's enemy, because a friend is both better and more closely united to us, so that he is a more suitable matter of love and consequently the act of love that passes over this matter, is better, and therefore its opposite is worse, for it is worse to hate a friend than an enemy.

In the second way, however, it is better to love one's enemy than one's friend, and this for two reasons. First, because it is possible to love one's friend for another reason than God, whereas God is the only reason for loving one's enemy. Secondly, because if we suppose that both are loved for God, our love for God is proved to be all the stronger through carrying a man's affections to things which are furthest from him, namely, to the love of his enemies, even as the power of a furnace is proved to be the stronger, according as it throws its heat to more distant objects. Hence our love for God is proved to be so much the stronger, as the more difficult are the things we accomplish for its sake, just as the power of fire is so much the stronger, as it is able to set fire to a less inflammable matter.

Yet just as the same fire acts with greater force on what is near than on what is distant, so too, charity loves with greater fervor those who are united to us than those who are far removed; and in this respect the love of friends, considered in itself, is more ardent and better than the love of one's enemy.

Reply Obj. 1: The words of Our Lord must be taken in their strict sense: because the love of one's friends is not meritorious in God's sight when we love them merely because they are our friends: and this would seem to be the case when we love our friends in such a way that we love not our enemies. On the other hand the love of our friends is meritorious, if we love them for God's sake, and not merely because they are our friends.

The Reply to the other Objections is evident from what has been said in the article, because the two arguments that follow consider the reason for loving, while the last considers the question on the part of those who are loved.

* * * * *

EIGHTH ARTICLE [II-II, Q. 27, Art. 8]

Whether It Is More Meritorious to Love One's Neighbor Than to Love God?

Objection 1: It would seem that it is more meritorious to love one's neighbor than to love God. For the more meritorious thing would seem to be what the Apostle preferred. Now the Apostle preferred the love of our neighbor to the love of God, according to Rom. 9:3: "I wished myself to be an anathema from Christ for my brethren." Therefore it is more meritorious to love one's neighbor than to love God.

Obj. 2: Further, in a certain sense it seems to be less meritorious to love one's friend, as stated above (A. 7). Now God is our chief friend, since "He hath first loved us" (1 John 4:10). Therefore it seems less meritorious to love God.

Obj. 3: Further, whatever is more difficult seems to be more virtuous and meritorious since "virtue is about that which is difficult and good" (Ethic. ii, 3). Now it is easier to love God than to love one's neighbor, both because all things love God naturally, and because there is nothing unlovable in God, and this cannot be said of one's neighbor. Therefore it is more meritorious to love one's neighbor than to love God.

On the contrary, That on account of which a thing is such, is yet more so. Now the love of one's neighbor is not meritorious, except by reason of his being loved for God's sake. Therefore the love of God is more meritorious than the love of our neighbor.

I answer that, This comparison may be taken in two ways. First, by considering both loves separately: and then, without doubt, the love of God is the more meritorious, because a reward is due to it for its own sake, since the ultimate reward is the enjoyment of God, to Whom the movement of the Divine love tends: hence a reward is promised to him that loves God (John 14:21): "He that loveth Me, shall be loved of My Father, and I will . . . manifest Myself to him." Secondly, the comparison may be understood to be between the love of God alone on the one side, and the love of one's neighbor for God's sake, on the other. In this way love of our neighbor includes love of God, while love of God does not include love of our neighbor. Hence the comparison will be between perfect love of God, extending also to our neighbor, and inadequate and imperfect love of God, for "this commandment we have from God, that he, who loveth God, love also his brother" (1 John 4:21).

Reply Obj. 1: According to one gloss, the Apostle did not desire this, viz. to be severed from Christ for his brethren, when he was in a state of grace, but had formerly desired it when he was in a state of unbelief, so that we should not imitate him in this respect.

We may also reply, with Chrysostom (De Compunct. i, 8)[1] that this does not prove the Apostle to have loved his neighbor more than God, but that he loved God more than himself. For he wished to be deprived for a time of the Divine fruition which pertains to love of one self, in order that God might be honored in his neighbor, which pertains to the love of God.

Reply Obj. 2: A man's love for his friends is sometimes less meritorious in so far as he loves them for their sake, so as to fall short of the true reason for the friendship of charity, which is God. Hence that God be loved for His own sake does not diminish the merit, but is the entire reason for merit.

Reply Obj. 3: The good has, more than the difficult, to do with the reason of merit and virtue. Therefore it does not follow that whatever is more difficult is more meritorious, but only what is more difficult, and at the same time better.

28. OF JOY (In Four Articles)

We must now consider the effects which result from the principal act of charity which is love, and (1) the interior effects, (2) the exterior effects. As to the first, three things have to be considered: (1) Joy, (2) Peace, (3) Mercy.

Under the first head there are four points of inquiry:

(1) Whether joy is an effect of charity?
(2) Whether this kind of joy is compatible with sorrow?
(3) Whether this joy can be full?
(4) Whether it is a virtue?.

* * * * *

FIRST ARTICLE [II-II, Q. 28, Art. 1]

Whether Joy Is Effected in Us by Charity?

Objection 1: It would seem that joy is not effected in us by charity. For the absence of what we love causes sorrow rather than

---

[1] Hom. xvi in Ep. ad Rom.

joy. But God, Whom we love by charity, is absent from us, so long as we are in this state of life, since "while we are in the body, we are absent from the Lord" (2 Cor. 5:6). Therefore charity causes sorrow in us rather than joy.

Obj. 2: Further, it is chiefly through charity that we merit happiness. Now mourning, which pertains to sorrow, is reckoned among those things whereby we merit happiness, according to Matt. 5:5: "Blessed are they that mourn, for they shall be comforted." Therefore sorrow, rather than joy, is an effect of charity.

Obj. 3: Further, charity is a virtue distinct from hope, as shown above (Q. 17, A. 6). Now joy is the effect of hope, according to Rom. 12:12: "Rejoicing in hope." Therefore it is not the effect of charity.

On the contrary, It is written (Rom. 5:5): "The charity of God is poured forth in our hearts by the Holy Ghost, Who is given to us." But joy is caused in us by the Holy Ghost according to Rom. 14:17: "The kingdom of God is not meat and drink, but justice and peace, and joy in the Holy Ghost." Therefore charity is a cause of joy.

I answer that, As stated above (I-II, Q. 25, AA. 1, 2, 3), when we were treating of the passions, joy and sorrow proceed from love, but in contrary ways. For joy is caused by love, either through the presence of the thing loved, or because the proper good of the thing loved exists and endures in it; and the latter is the case chiefly in the love of benevolence, whereby a man rejoices in the well-being of his friend, though he be absent. On the other hand sorrow arises from love, either through the absence of the thing loved, or because the loved object to which we wish well, is deprived of its good or afflicted with some evil. Now charity is love of God, Whose good is unchangeable, since He is His goodness, and from the very fact that He is loved, He is in those who love Him by His most excellent effect, according to 1 John 4:16: "He that abideth in charity, abideth in God, and God in him." Therefore spiritual joy, which is about God, is caused by charity.

Reply Obj. 1: So long as we are in the body, we are said to be "absent from the Lord," in comparison with that presence whereby He is present to some by the vision of "sight"; wherefore the Apostle goes on to say (2 Cor. 5:6): "For we walk by faith and not by sight." Nevertheless, even in this life, He is present to those who love Him, by the indwelling of His grace.

Reply Obj. 2: The mourning that merits happiness, is about those things that are contrary to happiness. Wherefore it amounts to the same that charity causes this mourning, and this spiritual joy about God, since to rejoice in a certain good amounts to the same as to grieve for things that are contrary to it.

Reply Obj. 3: There can be spiritual joy about God in two ways. First, when we rejoice in the Divine good considered in itself; secondly, when we rejoice in the Divine good as participated by us. The former joy is the better, and proceeds from charity chiefly: while the latter joy proceeds from hope also, whereby we look forward to enjoy the Divine good, although this enjoyment itself, whether perfect or imperfect, is obtained according to the measure of one's charity.

* * * * *

SECOND ARTICLE [II-II, Q. 28, Art. 2]

Whether the Spiritual Joy, Which Results from Charity, Is Compatible with an Admixture of Sorrow?

Objection 1: It would seem that the spiritual joy that results from charity is compatible with an admixture of sorrow. For it belongs to charity to rejoice in our neighbor's good, according to 1 Cor. 13:4, 6: "Charity . . . rejoiceth not in iniquity, but rejoiceth with the truth." But this joy is compatible with an admixture of sorrow, according to Rom. 12:15: "Rejoice with them that rejoice, weep with them that weep." Therefore the spiritual joy of charity is compatible with an admixture of sorrow.

Obj. 2: Further, according to Gregory (Hom. in Evang. xxxiv), "penance consists in deploring past sins, and in not committing again those we have deplored." But there is no true penance without charity. Therefore the joy of charity has an admixture of sorrow.

Obj. 3: Further, it is through charity that man desires to be with Christ according to Phil. 1:23: "Having a desire to be dissolved and to be with Christ." Now this desire gives rise, in man, to a certain sadness, according to Ps. 119:5: "Woe is me that my sojourning is prolonged!" Therefore the joy of charity admits of a seasoning of sorrow.

On the contrary, The joy of charity is joy about the Divine wisdom. Now such like joy has no admixture of sorrow, according to Wis. 8:16: "Her conversation hath no bitterness." Therefore the joy of charity is incompatible with an admixture of sorrow.

I answer that, As stated above (A. 1, ad 3), a twofold joy in God arises from charity. One, the more excellent, is proper to charity; and with this joy we rejoice in the Divine good considered in itself. This joy of charity is incompatible with an admixture of sorrow, even as the good which is its object is incompatible with any admixture of evil: hence the Apostle says (Phil. 4:4): "Rejoice in the Lord always."

The other is the joy of charity whereby we rejoice in the Divine good as participated by us. This participation can be hindered by anything contrary to it, wherefore, in this respect, the joy of charity is compatible with an admixture of sorrow, in so far as a man grieves for that which hinders the participation of the Divine good, either in us or in our neighbor, whom we love as ourselves.

Reply Obj. 1: Our neighbor does not weep save on account of some evil. Now every evil implies lack of participation in the sovereign good: hence charity makes us weep with our neighbor in so far as he is hindered from participating in the Divine good.

Reply Obj. 2: Our sins divide between us and God, according to Isa. 59:2; wherefore this is the reason why we grieve for our past sins, or for those of others, in so far as they hinder us from participating in the Divine good.

Reply Obj. 3: Although in this unhappy abode we participate, after a fashion, in the Divine good, by knowledge and love, yet the unhappiness of this life is an obstacle to a perfect participation in the Divine good: hence this very sorrow, whereby a man grieves for the delay of glory, is connected with the hindrance to a participation of the Divine good.

* * * * *

THIRD ARTICLE [II-II, Q. 28, Art. 3]

Whether the Spiritual Joy Which Proceeds from Charity, Can Be Filled?

Objection 1: It would seem that the spiritual joy which proceeds from charity cannot be filled. For the more we rejoice in

God, the more is our joy in Him filled. But we can never rejoice in Him as much as it is meet that we should rejoice in God, since His goodness which is infinite, surpasses the creature's joy which is finite. Therefore joy in God can never be filled.

Obj. 2: Further, that which is filled cannot be increased. But the joy, even of the blessed, can be increased, since one's joy is greater than another's. Therefore joy in God cannot be filled in a creature.

Obj. 3: Further, comprehension seems to be nothing else than the fulness of knowledge. Now, just as the cognitive power of a creature is finite, so is its appetitive power. Since therefore God cannot be comprehended by any creature, it seems that no creature's joy in God can be filled.

On the contrary, Our Lord said to His disciples (John 15:11): "That My joy may be in you, and your joy may be filled."

I answer that, Fulness of joy can be understood in two ways; first, on the part of the thing rejoiced in, so that one rejoice in it as much as it is meet that one should rejoice in it, and thus God's joy alone in Himself is filled, because it is infinite; and this is condignly due to the infinite goodness of God: but the joy of any creature must needs be finite. Secondly, fulness of joy may be understood on the part of the one who rejoices. Now joy is compared to desire, as rest to movement, as stated above (I-II, Q. 25, AA. 1, 2), when we were treating of the passions: and rest is full when there is no more movement. Hence joy is full, when there remains nothing to be desired. But as long as we are in this world, the movement of desire does not cease in us, because it still remains possible for us to approach nearer to God by grace, as was shown above (Q. 24, AA. 4, 7). When once, however, perfect happiness has been attained, nothing will remain to be desired, because then there will be full enjoyment of God, wherein man will obtain whatever he had desired, even with regard to other goods, according to Ps. 102:5: "Who satisfieth thy desire with good things." Hence desire will be at rest, not only our desire for God, but all our desires: so that the joy of the blessed is full to perfection—indeed over-full, since they will obtain more than they were capable of desiring: for "neither hath it entered into the heart of man, what things God hath prepared for them that love Him" (1 Cor. 2:9). This is what is meant by the words of Luke 6:38: "Good measure and pressed down, and shaken together, and running over shall they give into your bosom." Yet, since no creature is capable of the joy condignly due to God, it follows that this perfectly full joy is not taken into man, but, on the contrary, man enters into it, according to Matt. 25:21: "Enter into the joy of thy Lord."

Reply Obj. 1: This argument takes the fulness of joy in reference to the thing in which we rejoice.

Reply Obj. 2: When each one attains to happiness he will reach the term appointed to him by Divine predestination, and nothing further will remain to which he may tend, although by reaching that term, some will approach nearer to God than others. Hence each one's joy will be full with regard to himself, because his desire will be fully set at rest; yet one's joy will be greater than another's, on account of a fuller participation of the Divine happiness.

Reply Obj. 3: Comprehension denotes fulness of knowledge in respect of the thing known, so that it is known as much as it can be. There is however a fulness of knowledge in respect of the knower, just as we have said of joy. Wherefore the Apostle says (Col. 1:9): "That you may be filled with the knowledge of His will, in all wisdom and spiritual understanding.".

* * * * *

FOURTH ARTICLE [II-II, Q. 28, Art. 4]

Whether Joy Is a Virtue?

Objection 1: It would seem that joy is a virtue. For vice is contrary to virtue. Now sorrow is set down as a vice, as in the case of sloth and envy. Therefore joy also should be accounted a virtue.

Obj. 2: Further, as love and hope are passions, the object of which is good, so also is joy. Now love and hope are reckoned to be virtues. Therefore joy also should be reckoned a virtue.

Obj. 3: Further, the precepts of the Law are about acts of virtue. But we are commanded to rejoice in the Lord, according to Phil. 4:4: "Rejoice in the Lord always." Therefore joy is a virtue.

On the contrary, It is not numbered among the theological virtues, nor among the moral, nor among the intellectual virtues, as is evident from what has been said above (I-II, QQ. 57, 60, 62).

I answer that, As stated above (I-II, Q. 55, AA. 2, 4), virtue is an operative habit, wherefore by its very nature it has an inclination to a certain act. Now it may happen that from the same habit there proceed several ordinate and homogeneous acts, each of which follows from another. And since the subsequent acts do not proceed from the virtuous habit except through the preceding act, hence it is that the virtue is defined and named in reference to that preceding act, although those other acts also proceed from the virtue. Now it is evident from what we have said about the passions (I-II, Q. 25, AA. 2, 4) that love is the first affection of the appetitive power, and that desire and joy follow from it. Hence the same virtuous habit inclines us to love and desire the beloved good, and to rejoice in it. But in as much as love is the first of these acts, that virtue takes its name, not from joy, nor from desire, but from love, and is called charity. Hence joy is not a virtue distinct from charity, but an act, or effect, of charity: for which reason it is numbered among the Fruits (Gal. 5:22).

Reply Obj. 1: The sorrow which is a vice is caused by inordinate self-love, and this is not a special vice, but a general source of the vices, as stated above (I-II, Q. 77, A. 4); so that it was necessary to account certain particular sorrows as special vices, because they do not arise from a special, but from a general vice. On the other hand love of God is accounted a special virtue, namely charity, to which joy must be referred, as its proper act, as stated above (here and A. 2).

Reply Obj. 2: Hope proceeds from love even as joy does, but hope adds, on the part of the object, a special character, viz. difficult, and possible to obtain; for which reason it is accounted a special virtue. On the other hand joy does not add to love any special aspect, that might cause a special virtue.

Reply Obj. 3: The Law prescribes joy, as being an act of charity, albeit not its first act.

29. OF PEACE (Four Articles)

We must now consider Peace, under which head there are four points of inquiry:

(1) Whether peace is the same as concord?
(2) Whether all things desire peace?

(3) Whether peace is an effect of charity?
(4) Whether peace is a virtue?.

* * * * *

FIRST ARTICLE [II-II, Q. 29, Art. 1]

Whether Peace Is the Same As Concord?

Objection 1: It would seem that peace is the same as concord. For Augustine says (De Civ. Dei xix, 13): "Peace among men is well ordered concord." Now we are speaking here of no other peace than that of men. Therefore peace is the same as concord.

Obj. 2: Further, concord is union of wills. Now the nature of peace consists in such like union, for Dionysius says (Div. Nom. xi) that peace unites all, and makes them of one mind. Therefore peace is the same as concord.

Obj. 3: Further, things whose opposites are identical are themselves identical. Now the one same thing is opposed to concord and peace, viz. dissension; hence it is written (1 Cor. 16:33): "God is not the God of dissension but of peace." Therefore peace is the same as concord.

On the contrary, There can be concord in evil between wicked men. But "there is no peace to the wicked" (Isa. 48:22). Therefore peace is not the same as concord.

I answer that, Peace includes concord and adds something thereto. Hence wherever peace is, there is concord, but there is not peace, wherever there is concord, if we give peace its proper meaning.

For concord, properly speaking, is between one man and another, in so far as the wills of various hearts agree together in consenting to the same thing. Now the heart of one man may happen to tend to diverse things, and this in two ways. First, in respect of the diverse appetitive powers: thus the sensitive appetite tends sometimes to that which is opposed to the rational appetite, according to Gal. 5:17: "The flesh lusteth against the spirit." Secondly, in so far as one and the same appetitive power tends to diverse objects of appetite, which it cannot obtain all at the same time: so that there must needs be a clashing of the movements of the appetite. Now the union of such movements is essential to peace, because man's heart is not at peace, so long as he has not what he wants, or if, having what he wants, there still remains something for him to want, and which he cannot have at the same time. On the other hand this union is not essential to concord: wherefore concord denotes union of appetites among various persons, while peace denotes, in addition to this union, the union of the appetites even in one man.

Reply Obj. 1: Augustine is speaking there of that peace which is between one man and another, and he says that this peace is concord, not indeed any kind of concord, but that which is well ordered, through one man agreeing with another in respect of something befitting to both of them. For if one man concord with another, not of his own accord, but through being forced, as it were, by the fear of some evil that besets him, such concord is not really peace, because the order of each concordant is not observed, but is disturbed by some fear-inspiring cause. For this reason he premises that "peace is tranquillity of order," which tranquillity consists in all the appetitive movements in one man being set at rest together.

Reply Obj. 2: If one man consent to the same thing together with another man, his consent is nevertheless not perfectly united to himself, unless at the same time all his appetitive movements be in agreement.

Reply Obj. 3: A twofold dissension is opposed to peace, namely dissension between a man and himself, and dissension between one man and another. The latter alone is opposed to concord.

* * * * *

SECOND ARTICLE [II-II, Q. 29, Art. 2]

Whether All Things Desire Peace?

Objection 1: It would seem that not all things desire peace. For, according to Dionysius (Div. Nom. xi), peace "unites consent." But there cannot be unity of consent in things which are devoid of knowledge. Therefore such things cannot desire peace.

Obj. 2: Further, the appetite does not tend to opposite things at the same time. Now many desire war and dissension. Therefore all men do not desire peace.

Obj. 3: Further, good alone is an object of appetite. But a certain peace is, seemingly, evil, else Our Lord would not have said

(Matt. 10:34): "I came not to send peace." Therefore all things do not desire peace.

Obj. 4: Further, that which all desire is, seemingly, the sovereign good which is the last end. But this is not true of peace, since it is attainable even by a wayfarer; else Our Lord would vainly command (Mk. 9:49): "Have peace among you." Therefore all things do not desire peace.

On the contrary, Augustine says (De Civ. Dei xix, 12, 14) that "all things desire peace": and Dionysius says the same (Div. Nom. xi).

I answer that, From the very fact that a man desires a certain thing it follows that he desires to obtain what he desires, and, in consequence, to remove whatever may be an obstacle to his obtaining it. Now a man may be hindered from obtaining the good he desires, by a contrary desire either of his own or of some other, and both are removed by peace, as stated above. Hence it follows of necessity that whoever desires anything desires peace, in so far as he who desires anything, desires to attain, with tranquillity and without hindrance, to that which he desires: and this is what is meant by peace which Augustine defines (De Civ. Dei xix, 13) "the tranquillity of order."

Reply Obj. 1: Peace denotes union not only of the intellective or rational appetite, or of the animal appetite, in both of which consent may be found, but also of the natural appetite. Hence Dionysius says that "peace is the cause of consent and of connaturalness," where "consent" denotes the union of appetites proceeding from knowledge, and "connaturalness," the union of natural appetites.

Reply Obj. 2: Even those who seek war and dissension, desire nothing but peace, which they deem themselves not to have. For as we stated above, there is no peace when a man concords with another man counter to what he would prefer. Consequently men seek by means of war to break this concord, because it is a defective peace, in order that they may obtain peace, where nothing is contrary to their will. Hence all wars are waged that men may find a more perfect peace than that which they had heretofore.

Reply Obj. 3: Peace gives calm and unity to the appetite. Now just as the appetite may tend to what is good simply, or to what is good apparently, so too, peace may be either true or apparent. There can be no true peace except where the appetite is directed to what is truly good, since every evil, though it may appear good in a way, so as to calm the appetite in some respect, has, nevertheless many defects, which cause the appetite to remain restless and disturbed. Hence true peace is only in good men and about good things. The peace of the wicked is not a true peace but a semblance thereof, wherefore it is written (Wis. 14:22): "Whereas they lived in a great war of ignorance, they call so many and so great evils peace."

Reply Obj. 4: Since true peace is only about good things, as the true good is possessed in two ways, perfectly and imperfectly, so there is a twofold true peace. One is perfect peace. It consists in the perfect enjoyment of the sovereign good, and unites all one's desires by giving them rest in one object. This is the last end of the rational creature, according to Ps. 147:3: "Who hath placed peace in thy borders." The other is imperfect peace, which may be had in this world, for though the chief movement of the soul finds rest in God, yet there are certain things within and without which disturb the peace.

* * * * *

THIRD ARTICLE [II-II, Q. 29, Art. 3]

Whether Peace Is the Proper Effect of Charity?

Objection 1: It would seem that peace is not the proper effect of charity. For one cannot have charity without sanctifying grace. But some have peace who have not sanctifying grace, thus heathens sometimes have peace. Therefore peace is not the effect of charity.

Obj. 2: Further, if a certain thing is caused by charity, its contrary is not compatible with charity. But dissension, which is contrary to peace, is compatible with charity, for we find that even holy doctors, such as Jerome and Augustine, dissented in some of their opinions. We also read that Paul and Barnabas dissented from one another (Acts 15). Therefore it seems that peace is not the effect of charity.

Obj. 3: Further, the same thing is not the proper effect of different things. Now peace is the effect of justice, according to Isa. 32:17: "And the work of justice shall be peace." Therefore it is not the effect of charity.

On the contrary, It is written (Ps. 118:165): "Much peace have they that love Thy Law."

I answer that, Peace implies a twofold union, as stated above (A. 1). The first is the result of one's own appetites being directed to one object; while the other results from one's own appetite being united with the appetite of another: and each of these unions is effected by charity—the first, in so far as man loves God with his whole heart, by referring all things to Him, so that all his desires tend to one object—the second, in so far as we love our neighbor as ourselves, the result being that we wish to fulfil our neighbor's will as though it were ours: hence it is reckoned a sign of friendship if people "make choice of the same things" (Ethic. ix, 4), and Tully says (De Amicitia) that friends "like and dislike the same things" (Sallust, Catilin.)

Reply Obj. 1: Without sin no one falls from a state of sanctifying grace, for it turns man away from his due end by making him place his end in something undue: so that his appetite does not cleave chiefly to the true final good, but to some apparent good. Hence, without sanctifying grace, peace is not real but merely apparentapparent.

Reply Obj. 2: As the Philosopher says (Ethic. ix, 6) friends need not agree in opinion, but only upon such goods as conduce to life, and especially upon such as are important; because dissension in small matters is scarcely accounted dissension. Hence nothing hinders those who have charity from holding different opinions. Nor is this an obstacle to peace, because opinions concern the intellect, which precedes the appetite that is united by peace. In like manner if there be concord as to goods of importance, dissension with regard to some that are of little account is not contrary to charity: for such a dissension proceeds from a difference of opinion, because one man thinks that the particular good, which is the object of dissension, belongs to the good about which they agree, while the other thinks that it does not. Accordingly such like dissension about very slight matters and about opinions is inconsistent with a state of perfect peace, wherein the truth will be known fully, and every desire fulfilled; but it is not inconsistent with the imperfect peace of the wayfarer.

Reply Obj. 3: Peace is the "work of justice" indirectly, in so far as justice removes the obstacles to peace: but it is the work of charity directly, since charity, according to its very nature, causes peace. For love is "a unitive force" as Dionysius says (Div. Nom. iv): and peace is the union of the appetite's inclinations.

* * * * *

FOURTH ARTICLE [II-II, Q. 29, Art. 4]

Whether Peace Is a Virtue?

Objection 1: It would seem that peace is a virtue. For nothing is a matter of precept, unless it be an act of virtue. But there are precepts about keeping peace, for example: "Have peace among you" (Mk. 9:49). Therefore peace is a virtue.

Obj. 2: Further, we do not merit except by acts of virtue. Now it is meritorious to keep peace, according to Matt. 5:9: "Blessed are the peacemakers, for they shall be called the children of God." Therefore peace is a virtue.

Obj. 3: Further, vices are opposed to virtues. But dissensions, which are contrary to peace, are numbered among the vices (Gal. 5:20). Therefore peace is a virtue.

On the contrary, Virtue is not the last end, but the way thereto. But peace is the last end, in a sense, as Augustine says (De Civ. Dei xix, 11). Therefore peace is not a virtue.

I answer that, As stated above (Q. 28, A. 4), when a number of acts all proceeding uniformly from an agent, follow one from the other, they all arise from the same virtue, nor do they each have a virtue from which they proceed, as may be seen in corporeal things. For, though fire by heating, both liquefies and rarefies, there are not two powers in fire, one of liquefaction, the other of rarefaction: and fire produces all such actions by its own power of calefaction.

Since then charity causes peace precisely because it is love of God and of our neighbor, as shown above (A. 3), there is no other virtue except charity whose proper act is peace, as we have also said in reference to joy (Q. 28, A. 4).

Reply Obj. 1: We are commanded to keep peace because it is an act of charity; and for this reason too it is a meritorious act. Hence it is placed among the beatitudes, which are acts of perfect virtue, as stated above (I-II, Q. 69, AA. 1, 3). It is also numbered among the fruits, in so far as it is a final good, having spiritual sweetness.

This suffices for the Reply to the Second Objection.

Reply Obj. 3: Several vices are opposed to one virtue in respect of its various acts: so that not only is hatred opposed to charity, in respect of its act which is love, but also sloth and envy, in respect of joy, and dissension in respect of peace.

30. OF MERCY[1] (In Four Articles)

We must now go on to consider Mercy, under which head there are four points of inquiry:

(1) Whether evil is the cause of mercy on the part of the person pitied?
(2) To whom does it belong to pity?
(3) Whether mercy is a virtue?
(4) Whether it is the greatest of virtues?.

* * * * *

FIRST ARTICLE [II-II, Q. 30, Art. 1]

Whether Evil Is Properly the Motive of Mercy?

Objection 1: It would seem that, properly speaking, evil is not the motive of mercy. For, as shown above (Q. 19, A. 1; I-II, Q. 79, A. 1, ad 4; I, Q. 48, A. 6), fault is an evil rather than punishment. Now fault provokes indignation rather than mercy. Therefore evil does not excite mercy.

Obj. 2: Further, cruelty and harshness seem to excel other evils. Now the Philosopher says (Rhet. ii, 8) that "harshness does not call for pity but drives it away." Therefore evil, as such, is not the motive of mercy.

Obj. 3: Further, signs of evils are not true evils. But signs of evils excite one to mercy, as the Philosopher states (Rhet. ii, 8). Therefore evil, properly speaking, is not an incentive to mercy.

On the contrary, Damascene says (De Fide Orth. ii, 2) that mercy is a kind of sorrow. Now evil is the motive of sorrow. Therefore it is the motive of mercy.

I answer that, As Augustine says (De Civ. Dei ix, 5), mercy is heartfelt sympathy for another's distress, impelling us to succor him if we can. For mercy takes its name *misericordia* from denoting a man's compassionate heart *(miserum cor)* for another's unhappiness. Now

---

[1] The one Latin word "misericordia" signifies either pity or mercy. The distinction between these two is that pity may stand either for the act or for the virtue, whereas mercy stands only for the virtue.

unhappiness is opposed to happiness: and it is essential to beatitude or happiness that one should obtain what one wishes; for, according to Augustine (De Trin. xiii, 5), "happy is he who has whatever he desires, and desires nothing amiss." Hence, on the other hand, it belongs to unhappiness that a man should suffer what he wishes not.

Now a man wishes a thing in three ways: first, by his natural appetite; thus all men naturally wish to be and to live: secondly, a man wishes a thing from deliberate choice: thirdly, a man wishes a thing, not in itself, but in its cause, thus, if a man wishes to eat what is bad for him, we say that, in a way, he wishes to be ill.

Accordingly the motive of *mercy,* being something pertaining to *misery,* is, in the first way, anything contrary to the will's natural appetite, namely corruptive or distressing evils, the contrary of which man desires naturally, wherefore the Philosopher says (Rhet. ii, 8) that "pity is sorrow for a visible evil, whether corruptive or distressing." Secondly, such like evils are yet more provocative of pity if they are contrary to deliberate choice, wherefore the Philosopher says (Rhet. ii, 8) that evil excites our pity "when it is the result of an accident, as when something turns out ill, whereas we hoped well of it." Thirdly, they cause yet greater pity, if they are entirely contrary to the will, as when evil befalls a man who has always striven to do well: wherefore the Philosopher says (Rhet. ii, 8) that "we pity most the distress of one who suffers undeservedly."

Reply Obj. 1: It is essential to fault that it be voluntary; and in this respect it deserves punishment rather than mercy. Since, however, fault may be, in a way, a punishment, through having something connected with it that is against the sinner's will, it may, in this respect, call for mercy. It is in this sense that we pity and commiserate sinners. Thus Gregory says in a homily (Hom. in Evang. xxxiv) that "true godliness is not disdainful but compassionate," and again it is written (Matt. 9:36) that Jesus "seeing the multitudes, had compassion on them: because they were distressed, and lying like sheep that have no shepherd."

Reply Obj. 2: Since pity is sympathy for another's distress, it is directed, properly speaking, towards another, and not to oneself, except figuratively, like justice, according as a man is considered to have various parts (Ethic. v, 11). Thus it is written (Ecclus. 30:24): "Have pity on thy own soul, pleasing God"[1].

---

1   Cf. Q. 106, A. 3, ad 1

Accordingly just as, properly speaking, a man does not pity himself, but suffers in himself, as when we suffer cruel treatment in ourselves, so too, in the case of those who are so closely united to us, as to be part of ourselves, such as our children or our parents, we do not pity their distress, but suffer as for our own sores; in which sense the Philosopher says that "harshness drives pity away."

Reply Obj. 3: Just as pleasure results from hope and memory of good things, so does sorrow arise from the prospect or the recollection of evil things; though not so keenly as when they are present to the senses. Hence the signs of evil move us to pity, in so far as they represent as present, the evil that excites our pity.

* * * * *

SECOND ARTICLE [II-II, Q. 30, Art. 2]

Whether the Reason for Taking Pity Is a Defect in the Person Who Pities?

Objection 1: It would seem that the reason for taking pity is not a defect in the person who takes pity. For it is proper to God to be merciful, wherefore it is written (Ps. 144:9): "His tender mercies are over all His works." But there is no defect in God. Therefore a defect cannot be the reason for taking pity.

Obj. 2: Further, if a defect is the reason for taking pity, those in whom there is most defect, must needs take most pity. But this is false: for the Philosopher says (Rhet. ii, 8) that "those who are in a desperate state are pitiless." Therefore it seems that the reason for taking pity is not a defect in the person who pities.

Obj. 3: Further, to be treated with contempt is to be defective. But the Philosopher says (Rhet. ii, 8) that "those who are disposed to contumely are pitiless." Therefore the reason for taking pity, is not a defect in the person who pities.

On the contrary, Pity is a kind of sorrow. But a defect is the reason of sorrow, wherefore those who are in bad health give way to sorrow more easily, as we shall say further on (Q. 35, A. 1, ad 2). Therefore the reason why one takes pity is a defect in oneself.

I answer that, Since pity is grief for another's distress, as stated above (A. 1), from the very fact that a person takes pity on anyone, it follows that another's distress grieves him. And since sorrow or grief is about one's own ills, one grieves or sorrows for another's distress, in so far as one looks upon another's distress as one's own.

Now this happens in two ways: first, through union of the affections, which is the effect of love. For, since he who loves another looks upon his friend as another self, he counts his friend's hurt as his own, so that he grieves for his friend's hurt as though he were hurt himself. Hence the Philosopher (Ethic. ix, 4) reckons "grieving with one's friend" as being one of the signs of friendship, and the Apostle says (Rom. 12:15): "Rejoice with them that rejoice, weep with them that weep."

Secondly, it happens through real union, for instance when another's evil comes near to us, so as to pass to us from him. Hence the Philosopher says (Rhet. ii, 8) that men pity such as are akin to them, and the like, because it makes them realize that the same may happen to themselves. This also explains why the old and the wise who consider that they may fall upon evil times, as also feeble and timorous persons, are more inclined to pity: whereas those who deem themselves happy, and so far powerful as to think themselves in no danger of suffering any hurt, are not so inclined to pity.

Accordingly a defect is always the reason for taking pity, either because one looks upon another's defect as one's own, through being united to him by love, or on account of the possibility of suffering in the same way.

Reply Obj. 1: God takes pity on us through love alone, in as much as He loves us as belonging to Him.

Reply Obj. 2: Those who are already in infinite distress, do not fear to suffer more, wherefore they are without pity. In like manner this applies to those also who are in great fear, for they are so intent on their own passion, that they pay no attention to the suffering of others.

Reply Obj. 3: Those who are disposed to contumely, whether through having been contemned, or because they wish to contemn others, are incited to anger and daring, which are manly passions and arouse the human spirit to attempt difficult things. Hence they make a man think that he is going to suffer something in the future, so that while they are disposed in that way they are pitiless, according to Prov. 27:4: "Anger hath no mercy, nor fury when it breaketh forth." For the same reason the proud are without pity, because they despise others, and think them wicked, so that they account them as suffering deservedly whatever they suffer. Hence Gregory says (Hom. in Evang. xxxiv) that "false godliness," i.e. of the proud, "is not compassionate but disdainful.".

* * * * *

THIRD ARTICLE [II-II, Q. 30, Art. 3]

Whether Mercy Is a Virtue?

Objection 1: It would seem that mercy is not a virtue. For the chief part of virtue is choice as the Philosopher states (Ethic. ii, 5). Now choice is "the desire of what has been already counselled" (Ethic. iii, 2). Therefore whatever hinders counsel cannot be called a virtue. But mercy hinders counsel, according to the saying of Sallust (Catilin.): "All those that take counsel about matters of doubt, should be free from ... anger ... and mercy, because the mind does not easily see aright, when these things stand in the way." Therefore mercy is not a virtue.

Obj. 2: Further, nothing contrary to virtue is praiseworthy. But nemesis is contrary to mercy, as the Philosopher states (Rhet. ii, 9), and yet it is a praiseworthy passion (Rhet. ii, 9). Therefore mercy is not a virtue.

Obj. 3: Further, joy and peace are not special virtues, because they result from charity, as stated above (Q. 28, A. 4; Q. 29, A. 4). Now mercy, also, results from charity; for it is out of charity that we weep with them that weep, as we rejoice with them that rejoice. Therefore mercy is not a special virtue.

Obj. 4: Further, since mercy belongs to the appetitive power, it is not an intellectual virtue, and, since it has not God for its object, neither is it a theological virtue. Moreover it is not a moral virtue, because neither is it about operations, for this belongs to justice; nor is it about passions, since it is not reduced to one of the twelve means mentioned by the Philosopher (Ethic. ii, 7). Therefore mercy is not a virtue.

On the contrary, Augustine says (De Civ. Dei ix, 5): "Cicero in praising Caesar expresses himself much better and in a fashion at once more humane and more in accordance with religious feeling, when he says: 'Of all thy virtues none is more marvelous or more graceful than thy mercy.'" Therefore mercy is a virtue.

I answer that, Mercy signifies grief for another's distress. Now this grief may denote, in one way, a movement of the sensitive appetite, in which case mercy is not a virtue but a passion; whereas, in another way, it may denote a movement of the intellective appetite, in as much as one person's evil is displeasing to another. This movement may be ruled in accordance with reason, and in accordance with this movement regulated by reason, the movement of the lower appetite may be regulated. Hence Augustine says (De Civ. Dei ix, 5) that "this movement of the mind" (viz. mercy) "obeys the reason, when mercy is vouchsafed in such a way that justice is safeguarded, whether we give to the needy or forgive the repentant." And since it is essential to human virtue that the movements of the soul should be regulated by reason, as was shown above (I-II, Q. 59, AA. 4, 5), it follows that mercy is a virtue.

Reply Obj. 1: The words of Sallust are to be understood as applying to the mercy which is a passion unregulated by reason: for thus it impedes the counselling of reason, by making it wander from justice.

Reply Obj. 2: The Philosopher is speaking there of pity and nemesis, considered, both of them, as passions. They are contrary to one another on the part of their respective estimation of another's evils, for which pity grieves, in so far as it esteems someone to suffer undeservedly, whereas nemesis rejoices, in so far as it esteems someone to suffer deservedly, and grieves, if things go well with the undeserving: "both of these are praiseworthy and come from the same disposition of character" (Rhet. ii, 9). Properly speaking, however, it is envy which is opposed to pity, as we shall state further on (Q. 36, A. 3).

Reply Obj. 3: Joy and peace add nothing to the aspect of good which is the object of charity, wherefore they do not require any other virtue besides charity. But mercy regards a certain special aspect, namely the misery of the person pitied.

Reply Obj. 4: Mercy, considered as a virtue, is a moral virtue having relation to the passions, and it is reduced to the mean called nemesis, because "they both proceed from the same character" (Rhet. ii, 9). Now the Philosopher proposes these means not as virtues, but as passions, because, even as passions, they are praiseworthy. Yet nothing prevents them from proceeding from some elective habit, in which case they assume the character of a virtue.

* * * * *

FOURTH ARTICLE [II-II, Q. 30, Art. 4]

Whether Mercy Is the Greatest of the Virtues?

Objection 1: It would seem that mercy is the greatest of the virtues. For the worship of God seems a most virtuous act. But mercy is preferred before the worship of God, according to Osee 6:6 and Matt. 12:7: "I have desired mercy and not sacrifice." Therefore mercy is the greatest virtue.

Obj. 2: Further, on the words of 1 Tim. 4:8: "Godliness is profitable to all things," a gloss says: "The sum total of a Christian's rule of life consists in mercy and godliness." Now the Christian rule of life embraces every virtue. Therefore the sum total of all virtues is contained in mercy.

Obj. 3: Further, "Virtue is that which makes its subject good," according to the Philosopher. Therefore the more a virtue makes a man like God, the better is that virtue: since man is the better for being more like God. Now this is chiefly the result of mercy, since of God is it said (Ps. 144:9) that "His tender mercies are over all His works," and (Luke 6:36) Our Lord said: "Be ye ... merciful, as your Father also is merciful." Therefore mercy is the greatest of virtues.

On the contrary, The Apostle after saying (Col. 3:12): "Put ye on ... as the elect of God ... the bowels of mercy," etc., adds (Col. 3:14): "Above all things have charity." Therefore mercy is not the greatest of virtues.

I answer that, A virtue may take precedence of others in two ways: first, in itself; secondly, in comparison with its subject. In itself, mercy takes precedence of other virtues, for it belongs to mercy to be bountiful to others, and, what is more, to succor others in their wants, which pertains chiefly to one who stands above. Hence mercy is accounted as being proper to God: and therein His omnipotence is declared to be chiefly manifested[1].

On the other hand, with regard to its subject, mercy is not the greatest virtue, unless that subject be greater than all others, surpassed by none and excelling all: since for him that has anyone above him it is better to be united to that which is above than to

---

1 Collect, Tenth Sunday after Pentecost

supply the defect of that which is beneath.[1] Hence, as regards man, who has God above him, charity which unites him to God, is greater than mercy, whereby he supplies the defects of his neighbor. But of all the virtues which relate to our neighbor, mercy is the greatest, even as its act surpasses all others, since it belongs to one who is higher and better to supply the defect of another, in so far as the latter is deficient.

Reply Obj. 1: We worship God by external sacrifices and gifts, not for His own profit, but for that of ourselves and our neighbor. For He needs not our sacrifices, but wishes them to be offered to Him, in order to arouse our devotion and to profit our neighbor. Hence mercy, whereby we supply others' defects is a sacrifice more acceptable to Him, as conducing more directly to our neighbor's well-being, according to Heb. 13:16: "Do not forget to do good and to impart, for by such sacrifices God's favor is obtained."

Reply Obj. 2: The sum total of the Christian religion consists in mercy, as regards external works: but the inward love of charity, whereby we are united to God preponderates over both love and mercy for our neighbor.

Reply Obj. 3: Charity likens us to God by uniting us to Him in the bond of love: wherefore it surpasses mercy, which likens us to God as regards similarity of works.

31. OF BENEFICENCE (In Four Articles)

We must now consider the outward acts or effects of charity, (1) Beneficence, (2) Almsdeeds, which are a part of beneficence, (3) Fraternal correction, which is a kind of alms.

Under the first head there are four points of inquiry:

(1) Whether beneficence is an act of charity?
(2) Whether we ought to be beneficent to all?

---

[1] "The quality of mercy is not strained./'Tis mightiest in the mightiest: it becomes/The throned monarch better than his crown." Merchant of Venice, Act IV, Scene i.

(3) Whether we ought to be more beneficent to those who are more closely united to us?
(4) Whether beneficence is a special virtue?.

* * * * *

FIRST ARTICLE [II-II, Q. 31, Art. 1]

Whether Beneficence Is an Act of Charity?

Objection 1: It would seem that beneficence is not an act of charity. For charity is chiefly directed to God. Now we cannot benefit God, according to Job 35:7: "What shalt thou give Him? or what shall He receive of thy hand?" Therefore beneficence is not an act of charity.

Obj. 2: Further, beneficence consists chiefly in making gifts. But this belongs to liberality. Therefore beneficence is an act of liberality and not of charity.

Obj. 3: Further, what a man gives, he gives either as being due, or as not due. But a benefit conferred as being due belongs to justice while a benefit conferred as not due, is gratuitous, and in this respect is an act of mercy. Therefore every benefit conferred is either an act of justice, or an act of mercy. Therefore it is not an act of charity.

On the contrary, Charity is a kind of friendship, as stated above (Q. 23, A. 1). Now the Philosopher reckons among the acts of friendship (Ethic. ix, 1) "doing good," i.e. being beneficent, "to one's friends." Therefore it is an act of charity to do good to others.

I answer that, Beneficence simply means doing good to someone. This good may be considered in two ways, first under the general aspect of good, and this belongs to beneficence in general, and is an act of friendship, and, consequently, of charity: because the act of love includes goodwill whereby a man wishes his friend well, as stated above (Q. 23, A. 1; Q. 27, A. 2). Now the will carries into effect if possible, the things it wills, so that, consequently, the result of an act of love is that a man is beneficent to his friend. Therefore beneficence in its general acceptation is an act of friendship or charity.

But if the good which one man does another, be considered under some special aspect of good, then beneficence will assume a special character and will belong to some special virtue.

Reply Obj. 1: According to Dionysius (Div. Nom. iv), "love moves those, whom it unites, to a mutual relationship: it turns the inferior to the superior to be perfected thereby; it moves the superior to watch over the inferior:" and in this respect beneficence is an effect of love. Hence it is not for us to benefit God, but to honor Him by obeying Him, while it is for Him, out of His love, to bestow good things on us.

Reply Obj. 2: Two things must be observed in the bestowal of gifts. One is the thing given outwardly, while the other is the inward passion that a man has in the delight of riches. It belongs to liberality to moderate this inward passion so as to avoid excessive desire and love for riches; for this makes a man more ready to part with his wealth. Hence, if a man makes some great gift, while yet desiring to keep it for himself, his is not a liberal giving. On the other hand, as regards the outward gift, the act of beneficence belongs in general to friendship or charity. Hence it does not detract from a man's friendship, if, through love, he give his friend something he would like to keep for himself; rather does this prove the perfection of his friendship.

Reply Obj. 3: Just as friendship or charity sees, in the benefit bestowed, the general aspect of good, so does justice see therein the aspect of debt, while pity considers the relieving of distress or defect.

* * * * *

SECOND ARTICLE [II-II, Q. 31, Art. 2]

Whether We Ought to Do Good to All?

Objection 1: It would seem that we are not bound to do good to all. For Augustine says (De Doctr. Christ. i, 28) that we "are unable to do good to everyone." Now virtue does not incline one to the impossible. Therefore it is not necessary to do good to all.

Obj. 2: Further, it is written (Ecclus. 12:5) "Give to the good, and receive not a sinner." But many men are sinners. Therefore we need not do good to all.

Obj. 3: Further, "Charity dealeth not perversely" (1 Cor. 13:4). Now to do good to some is to deal perversely: for instance if one were to do good to an enemy of the common weal, or if one were to do good to an excommunicated person, since, by doing so, he would be holding communion with him. Therefore, since beneficence is an act of charity, we ought not to do good to all.

On the contrary, The Apostle says (Gal. 6:10): "Whilst we have time, let us work good to all men."

I answer that, As stated above (A. 1, ad 1), beneficence is an effect of love in so far as love moves the superior to watch over the inferior. Now degrees among men are not unchangeable as among angels, because men are subject to many failings, so that he who is superior in one respect, is or may be inferior in another. Therefore, since the love of charity extends to all, beneficence also should extend to all, but according as time and place require: because all acts of virtue must be modified with a view to their due circumstances.

Reply Obj. 1: Absolutely speaking it is impossible to do good to every single one: yet it is true of each individual that one may be bound to do good to him in some particular case. Hence charity binds us, though not actually doing good to someone, to be prepared in mind to do good to anyone if we have time to spare. There is however a good that we can do to all, if not to each individual, at least to all in general, as when we pray for all, for unbelievers as well as for the faithful.

Reply Obj. 2: In a sinner there are two things, his guilt and his nature. Accordingly we are bound to succor the sinner as to the maintenance of his nature, but not so as to abet his sin, for this would be to do evil rather than good.

Reply Obj. 3: The excommunicated and the enemies of the common weal are deprived of all beneficence, in so far as this prevents them from doing evil deeds. Yet if their nature be in urgent need of succor lest it fail, we are bound to help them: for instance, if they be in danger of death through hunger or thirst, or suffer some like distress, unless this be according to the order of justice.

* * * * *

THIRD ARTICLE [II-II, Q. 31, Art. 3]

Whether We Ought to Do Good to Those Rather Who Are More Closely United to Us?

Objection 1: It would seem that we are not bound to do good to those rather who are more closely united to us. For it is written (Luke 14:12): "When thou makest a dinner or a supper, call not thy friends, nor thy brethren, nor thy kinsmen." Now these are the most closely united to us. Therefore we are not bound to do good to those rather who are more closely united to us, but preferably to strangers and to those who are in want: hence the text goes on: "But, when thou makest a feast, call the poor, the maimed," etc.

Obj. 2: Further, to help another in the battle is an act of very great goodness. But a soldier on the battlefield is bound to help a fellow-soldier who is a stranger rather than a kinsman who is a foe. Therefore in doing acts of kindness we are not bound to give the preference to those who are most closely united to us.

Obj. 3: Further, we should pay what is due before conferring gratuitous favors. But it is a man's duty to be good to those who have been good to him. Therefore we ought to do good to our benefactors rather than to those who are closely united to us.

Obj. 4: Further, a man ought to love his parents more than his children, as stated above (Q. 26, A. 9). Yet a man ought to be more beneficent to his children, since "neither ought the children to lay up for the parents," according to 2 Cor. 12:14. Therefore we are not bound to be more beneficent to those who are more closely united to us.

On the contrary, Augustine says (De Doctr. Christ. i, 28): "Since one cannot do good to all, we ought to consider those chiefly who by reason of place, time or any other circumstance, by a kind of chance are more closely united to us."

I answer that, Grace and virtue imitate the order of nature, which is established by Divine wisdom. Now the order of nature is such that every natural agent pours forth its activity first and most of all on the things which are nearest to it: thus fire heats most what is next to it. In like manner God pours forth the gifts of His goodness first and most plentifully on the substances which are nearest to Him, as Dionysius declares (Coel. Hier. vii). But the bestowal of benefits is an act of charity towards others. Therefore we ought to be most beneficent towards those who are most closely connected with us.

Now one man's connection with another may be measured in reference to the various matters in which men are engaged together;

(thus the intercourse of kinsmen is in natural matters, that of fellow-citizens is in civic matters, that of the faithful is in spiritual matters, and so forth): and various benefits should be conferred in various ways according to these various connections, because we ought in preference to bestow on each one such benefits as pertain to the matter in which, speaking simply, he is most closely connected with us. And yet this may vary according to the various requirements of time, place, or matter in hand: because in certain cases one ought, for instance, to succor a stranger, in extreme necessity, rather than one's own father, if he is not in such urgent need.

Reply Obj. 1: Our Lord did not absolutely forbid us to invite our friends and kinsmen to eat with us, but to invite them so that they may invite us in return, since that would be an act not of charity but of cupidity. The case may occur, however, that one ought rather to invite strangers, on account of their greater want. For it must be understood that, other things being equal, one ought to succor those rather who are most closely connected with us. And if of two, one be more closely connected, and the other in greater want, it is not possible to decide, by any general rule, which of them we ought to help rather than the other, since there are various degrees of want as well as of connection: and the matter requires the judgment of a prudent man.

Reply Obj. 2: The common good of many is more Godlike than the good of an individual. Wherefore it is a virtuous action for a man to endanger even his own life, either for the spiritual or for the temporal common good of his country. Since therefore men engage together in warlike acts in order to safeguard the common weal, the soldier who with this in view succors his comrade, succors him not as a private individual, but with a view to the welfare of his country as a whole: wherefore it is not a matter for wonder if a stranger be preferred to one who is a blood relation.

Reply Obj. 3: A thing may be due in two ways. There is one which should be reckoned, not among the goods of the debtor, but rather as belonging to the person to whom it is due: for instance, a man may have another's goods, whether in money or in kind, either because he has stolen them, or because he has received them on loan or in deposit or in some other way. In this case a man ought to pay what he owes, rather than benefit his connections out of it, unless perchance the case be so urgent that it would be lawful for him to take another's property in order to relieve the one who is in need. Yet, again, this would not apply if the creditor were in equal distress: in which case, however, the claims on either side would have to be weighed with regard to such other conditions as a prudent man would take into consideration, because, on account of the different particular cases, as the Philosopher states (Ethic. ix, 2), it is impossible to lay down a general rule.

The other kind of due is one which is reckoned among the goods of the debtor and not of the creditor; for instance, a thing may be due, not because justice requires it, but on account of a certain moral equity, as in the case of benefits received gratis. Now no benefactor confers a benefit equal to that which a man receives from his parents: wherefore in paying back benefits received, we should give the first place to our parents before all others, unless, on the other side, there be such weightier motives, as need or some other circumstance, for instance the common good of the Church or state. In other cases we must take to account the connection and the benefit received; and here again no general rule can laid down.

Reply Obj. 4: Parents are like superiors, and so a parent's love tends to conferring benefits, while the children's love tends to honor their parents. Nevertheless in a case of extreme urgency it would be lawful to abandon one's children rather than one's parents, to abandon whom it is by no means lawful, on account of the obligation we lie under towards them for the benefits we have received from them, as the Philosopher states (Ethic. iii, 14).

* * * * *

FOURTH ARTICLE [II-II, Q. 31, Art. 4]

Whether Beneficence Is a Special Virtue?

Objection 1: It would seem that beneficence is a special virtue. For precepts are directed to virtue, since lawgivers purpose to make men virtuous (Ethic. i 9, 13; ii, 1). Now beneficence and love are prescribed as distinct from one another, for it is written (Matt. 4:44): "Love your enemies, do good to them that hate you." Therefore beneficence is a virtue distinct from charity.

Obj. 2: Further, vices are opposed to virtues. Now there are opposed to beneficence certain vices whereby a hurt is inflicted on our neighbor, for instance, rapine, theft and so forth. Therefore beneficence is a special virtue.

Obj. 3: Further, charity is not divided into several species: whereas there would seem to be several kinds of beneficence, according to the various kinds of benefits. Therefore beneficence is a distinct virtue from charity.

On the contrary, The internal and the external act do not require different virtues. Now beneficence and goodwill differ only as external and internal act, since beneficence is the execution of goodwill. Therefore as goodwill is not a distinct virtue from charity, so neither is beneficence.

I answer that, Virtues differ according to the different aspects of their objects. Now the formal aspect of the object of charity and of beneficence is the same, since both virtues regard the common aspect of good, as explained above (A. 1). Wherefore beneficence is not a distinct virtue from charity, but denotes an act of charity.

Reply Obj. 1: Precepts are given, not about habits but about acts of virtue: wherefore distinction of precept denotes distinction, not of habits, but of acts.

Reply Obj. 2: Even as all benefits conferred on our neighbor, if we consider them under the common aspect of good, are to be traced to love, so all hurts considered under the common aspect of evil, are to be traced to hatred. But if we consider these same things under certain special aspects of good or of evil, they are to be traced to certain special virtues or vices, and in this way also there are various kinds of benefits.

Hence the Reply to the Third Objection is evident.

32. OF ALMSDEEDS (In Ten Articles)

We must now consider almsdeeds, under which head there are ten points of inquiry:

(1) Whether almsgiving is an act of charity?
(2) Of the different kinds of alms;
(3) Which alms are of greater account, spiritual or corporal?
(4) Whether corporal alms have a spiritual effect?

(5) Whether the giving of alms is a matter of precept?
(6) Whether corporal alms should be given out of the things we need?
(7) Whether corporal alms should be given out of ill-gotten goods?
(8) Who can give alms?
(9) To whom should we give alms?
(10) How should alms be given?.

* * * * *

FIRST ARTICLE [II-II, Q. 32, Art. 1]

Whether Almsgiving Is an Act of Charity?

Objection 1: It would seem that almsgiving is not an act of charity. For without charity one cannot do acts of charity. Now it is possible to give alms without having charity, according to 1 Cor. 13:3: "If I should distribute all my goods to feed the poor . . . and have not charity, it profiteth me nothing." Therefore almsgiving is not an act of charity.

Obj. 2: Further, almsdeeds are reckoned among works of satisfaction, according to Dan. 4:24: "Redeem thou thy sins with alms." Now satisfaction is an act of justice. Therefore almsgiving is an act of justice and not of charity.

Obj. 3: Further, the offering of sacrifices to God is an act of religion. But almsgiving is offering a sacrifice to God, according to Heb. 13:16: "Do not forget to do good and to impart, for by such sacrifices God's favor is obtained." Therefore almsgiving is not an act of charity, but of religion.

Obj. 4: Further, the Philosopher says (Ethic. iv, 1) that to give for a good purpose is an act of liberality. Now this is especially true of almsgiving. Therefore almsgiving is not an act of charity.

On the contrary, It is written 2 John 3:17: "He that hath the substance of this world, and shall see his brother in need, and shall put up his bowels from him, how doth the charity of God abide in him?"

I answer that, External acts belong to that virtue which regards the motive for doing those acts. Now the motive for giving alms is to relieve one who is in need. Wherefore some have defined alms as being "a deed whereby something is given to the needy, out of compassion and for God's sake," which motive belongs to mercy, as stated above (Q. 30, AA. 1, 2). Hence it is clear that almsgiving is, properly speaking, an act of mercy. This appears in its very name, for in Greek (eleemosyne) it is derived from having mercy (eleein) even as the Latin miseratio is. And since mercy is an effect of charity, as shown above (Q. 30, A. 2, A. 3, Obj. 3), it follows that almsgiving is an act of charity through the medium of mercy.

Reply Obj. 1: An act of virtue may be taken in two ways: first materially, thus an act of justice is to do what is just; and such an act of virtue can be without the virtue, since many, without having the habit of justice, do what is just, led by the natural light of reason, or through fear, or in the hope of gain. Secondly, we speak of a thing being an act of justice formally, and thus an act of justice is to do what is just, in the same way as a just man, i.e. with readiness and delight, and such an act of virtue cannot be without the virtue.

Accordingly almsgiving can be materially without charity, but to give alms formally, i.e. for God's sake, with delight and readiness, and altogether as one ought, is not possible without charity.

Reply Obj. 2: Nothing hinders the proper elicited act of one virtue being commanded by another virtue as commanding it and directing it to this other virtue's end. It is in this way that almsgiving is reckoned among works of satisfaction in so far as pity for the one in distress is directed to the satisfaction for his sin; and in so far as it is directed to placate God, it has the character of a sacrifice, and thus it is commanded by religion.

Wherefore the Reply to the Third Objection is evident.

Reply Obj. 4: Almsgiving belongs to liberality, in so far as liberality removes an obstacle to that act, which might arise from excessive love of riches, the result of which is that one clings to them more than one ought.

* * * * *

SECOND ARTICLE [II-II, Q. 32, Art. 2]

Whether the Different Kinds of Almsdeeds Are Suitably Enumerated?

Objection 1: It would seem that the different kinds of almsdeeds are unsuitably enumerated. For we reckon seven corporal almsdeeds, namely, to feed the hungry, to give drink to the thirsty, to clothe the naked, to harbor the harborless, to visit the sick, to ransom the captive, to bury the dead; all of which are expressed in the following verse: "To visit, to quench, to feed, to ransom, clothe, harbor or bury."

Again we reckon seven spiritual alms, namely, to instruct the ignorant, to counsel the doubtful, to comfort the sorrowful, to reprove the sinner, to forgive injuries, to bear with those who trouble and annoy us, and to pray for all, which are all contained in the following verse: "To counsel, reprove, console, to pardon, forbear, and to pray," yet so that counsel includes both advice and instruction.

And it seems that these various almsdeeds are unsuitably enumerated. For the purpose of almsdeeds is to succor our neighbor. But a dead man profits nothing by being buried, else Our Lord would not have spoken truly when He said (Matt. 10:28): "Be not afraid of them who kill the body, and after that have no more that they can do."[1] This explains why Our Lord, in enumerating the works of mercy, made no mention of the burial of the dead (Matt. 25:35, 36). Therefore it seems that these almsdeeds are unsuitably enumerated.

Obj. 2: Further, as stated above (A. 1), the purpose of giving alms is to relieve our neighbor's need. Now there are many needs of human life other than those mentioned above, for instance, a blind man needs a leader, a lame man needs someone to lean on, a poor man needs riches. Therefore these almsdeeds are unsuitably enumerated.

Obj. 3: Further, almsgiving is a work of mercy. But the reproof of the wrong-doer savors, apparently, of severity rather than of mercy. Therefore it ought not to be reckoned among the spiritual almsdeeds.

Obj. 4: Further, almsgiving is intended for the supply of a defect. But no man is without the defect of ignorance in some matter or other. Therefore, apparently, each one ought to instruct anyone who is ignorant of what he knows himself.

On the contrary, Gregory says (Nom. in Evang. ix): "Let him that hath understanding beware lest he withhold his knowledge; let him that hath abundance of wealth, watch lest he slacken his merciful bounty; let him who is a servant to art be most solicitous to share his skill and profit with his neighbor; let him who has an

---

1 The quotation is from Luke 12:4.

opportunity of speaking with the wealthy, fear lest he be condemned for retaining his talent, if when he has the chance he plead not with him the cause of the poor." Therefore the aforesaid almsdeeds are suitably enumerated in respect of those things whereof men have abundance or insufficiency.

I answer that, The aforesaid distinction of almsdeeds is suitably taken from the various needs of our neighbor: some of which affect the soul, and are relieved by spiritual almsdeeds, while others affect the body, and are relieved by corporal almsdeeds. For corporal need occurs either during this life or afterwards. If it occurs during this life, it is either a common need in respect of things needed by all, or it is a special need occurring through some accident supervening. In the first case, the need is either internal or external. Internal need is twofold: one which is relieved by solid food, viz. hunger, in respect of which we have *to feed the hungry;* while the other is relieved by liquid food, viz. thirst, and in respect of this we have *to give drink to the thirsty.* The common need with regard to external help is twofold; one in respect of clothing, and as to this we have *to clothe the naked:* while the other is in respect of a dwelling place, and as to this we have *to harbor the harborless.* Again if the need be special, it is either the result of an internal cause, like sickness, and then we have *to visit the sick,* or it results from an external cause, and then we have *to ransom the captive.* After this life we give *burial to the dead.*

In like manner spiritual needs are relieved by spiritual acts in two ways, first by asking for help from God, and in this respect we have *prayer,* whereby one man prays for others; secondly, by giving human assistance, and this in three ways. First, in order to relieve a deficiency on the part of the intellect, and if this deficiency be in the speculative intellect, the remedy is applied by *instructing,* and if in the practical intellect, the remedy is applied by *counselling.* Secondly, there may be a deficiency on the part of the appetitive power, especially by way of sorrow, which is remedied by *comforting.* Thirdly, the deficiency may be due to an inordinate act; and this may be the subject of a threefold consideration. First, in respect of the sinner, inasmuch as the sin proceeds from his inordinate will, and thus the remedy takes the form of *reproof.* Secondly, in respect of the person sinned against; and if the sin be committed against ourselves, we apply the remedy by *pardoning the injury,* while, if it be committed against God or our neighbor, it is not in our power to pardon, as Jerome observes (Super Matth. xviii, 15). Thirdly, in respect of the result of the inordinate act, on account of which the sinner is an annoyance to those who live with him, even beside his intention; in which case the remedy is applied by *bearing with him,* especially with regard to those who sin out of weakness, according to Rom. 15:1: "We that are stronger, ought to bear the infirmities of the weak," and not only as regards their being infirm and consequently troublesome on account of their unruly actions, but also by bearing any other burdens of theirs with them, according to Gal. 6:2: "Bear ye one another's burdens."

Reply Obj. 1: Burial does not profit a dead man as though his body could be capable of perception after death. In this sense Our Lord said that those who kill the body "have no more that they can do"; and for this reason He did not mention the burial of the dead with the other works of mercy, but those only which are more clearly necessary. Nevertheless it does concern the deceased what is done with his body: both that he may live in the memory of man whose respect he forfeits if he remain without burial, and as regards a man's fondness for his own body while he was yet living, a fondness which kindly persons should imitate after his death. It is thus that some are praised for burying the dead, as Tobias, and those who buried Our Lord; as Augustine says (De Cura pro Mort. iii).

Reply Obj. 2: All other needs are reduced to these, for blindness and lameness are kinds of sickness, so that to lead the blind, and to support the lame, come to the same as visiting the sick. In like manner to assist a man against any distress that is due to an extrinsic cause comes to the same as the ransom of captives. And the wealth with which we relieve the poor is sought merely for the purpose of relieving the aforesaid needs: hence there was no reason for special mention of this particular need.

Reply Obj. 3: The reproof of the sinner, as to the exercise of the act of reproving, seems to imply the severity of justice, but, as to the intention of the reprover, who wishes to free a man from the evil of sin, it is an act of mercy and lovingkindness, according to Prov. 27:6: "Better are the wounds of a friend, than the deceitful kisses of an enemy."

Reply Obj. 4: Nescience is not always a defect, but only when it is about what one ought to know, and it is a part of almsgiving to supply this defect by instruction. In doing this however we should observe the due circumstances of persons, place and time, even as in other virtuous acts.

* * * * *

THIRD ARTICLE [II-II, Q. 32, Art. 3]

Whether Corporal Alms Are of More Account Than Spiritual Alms?

Objection 1: It would seem that corporal alms are of more account than spiritual alms. For it is more praiseworthy to give an alms to one who is in greater want, since an almsdeed is to be praised because it relieves one who is in need. Now the body which is relieved by corporal alms, is by nature more needy than the spirit which is relieved by spiritual alms. Therefore corporal alms are of more account.

Obj. 2: Further, an alms is less praiseworthy and meritorious if the kindness is compensated, wherefore Our Lord says (Luke 14:12): "When thou makest a dinner or a supper, call not thy neighbors who are rich, lest perhaps they also invite thee again." Now there is always compensation in spiritual almsdeeds, since he who prays for another, profits thereby, according to Ps. 34:13: "My prayer shall be turned into my bosom": and he who teaches another, makes progress in knowledge, which cannot be said of corporal almsdeeds. Therefore corporal almsdeeds are of more account than spiritual almsdeeds.

Obj. 3: Further, an alms is to be commended if the needy one is comforted by it: wherefore it is written (Job 31:20): "If his sides have not blessed me," and the Apostle says to Philemon (verse 7): "The bowels of the saints have been refreshed by thee, brother." Now a corporal alms is sometimes more welcome to a needy man than a spiritual alms. Therefore bodily almsdeeds are of more account than spiritual almsdeeds.

On the contrary, Augustine says (De Serm. Dom. in Monte i, 20) on the words, "Give to him that asketh of thee" (Matt. 5:42): "You should give so as to injure neither yourself nor another, and when you refuse what another asks you must not lose sight of the claims of justice, and send him away empty; at times indeed you will give what is better than what is asked for, if you reprove him that asks unjustly." Now reproof is a spiritual alms. Therefore spiritual almsdeeds are preferable to corporal almsdeeds.

I answer that, There are two ways of comparing these almsdeeds. First, simply; and in this respect, spiritual almsdeeds hold the first place, for three reasons. First, because the offering is more excellent, since it is a spiritual gift, which surpasses a corporal gift, according to Prov. 4:2: "I will give you a good gift, forsake not My Law." Secondly, on account of the object succored, because the spirit is more excellent than the body, wherefore, even as a man in looking after himself, ought to look to his soul more than to his body, so ought he in looking after his neighbor, whom he ought to love as himself. Thirdly, as regards the acts themselves by which our neighbor is succored, because spiritual acts are more excellent than corporal acts, which are, in a fashion, servile.

Secondly, we may compare them with regard to some particular case, when some corporal alms excels some spiritual alms: for instance, a man in hunger is to be fed rather than instructed, and as the Philosopher observes (Topic. iii, 2), for a needy man "money is better than philosophy," although the latter is better simply.

Reply Obj. 1: It is better to give to one who is in greater want, other things being equal, but if he who is less needy is better, and is in want of better things, it is better to give to him: and it is thus in the case in point.

Reply Obj. 2: Compensation does not detract from merit and praise if it be not intended, even as human glory, if not intended, does not detract from virtue. Thus Sallust says of Cato (Catilin.), that "the less he sought fame, the more he became famous": and thus it is with spiritual almsdeeds.

Nevertheless the intention of gaining spiritual goods does not detract from merit, as the intention of gaining corporal goods.

Reply Obj. 3: The merit of an almsgiver depends on that in which the will of the recipient rests reasonably, and not on that in which it rests when it is inordinate.

* * * * *

FOURTH ARTICLE [II-II, Q. 32, Art. 4]

Whether Corporal Almsdeeds Have a Spiritual Effect?

Objection 1: It would seem that corporal almsdeeds have not a spiritual effect. For no effect exceeds its cause. But spiritual goods exceed corporal goods. Therefore corporal almsdeeds have no spiritual effect.

Obj. 2: Further, the sin of simony consists in giving the corporal for the spiritual, and it is to be utterly avoided. Therefore one ought not to give alms in order to receive a spiritual effect.

Obj. 3: Further, to multiply the cause is to multiply the effect. If therefore corporal almsdeeds cause a spiritual effect, the greater the alms, the greater the spiritual profit, which is contrary to what we read (Luke 21:3) of the widow who cast two brass mites into the treasury, and in Our Lord's own words "cast in more than . . . all." Therefore bodily almsdeeds have no spiritual effect.

On the contrary, It is written (Ecclus. 17:18): "The alms of a man . . . shall preserve the grace of a man as the apple of the eye."

I answer that, Corporal almsdeeds may be considered in three ways. First, with regard to their substance, and in this way they have merely a corporal effect, inasmuch as they supply our neighbor's corporal needs. Secondly, they may be considered with regard to their cause, in so far as a man gives a corporal alms out of love for God and his neighbor, and in this respect they bring forth a spiritual fruit, according to Ecclus. 29:13, 14: "Lose thy money for thy brother . . . place thy treasure in the commandments of the Most High, and it shall bring thee more profit than gold."

Thirdly, with regard to the effect, and in this way again, they have a spiritual fruit, inasmuch as our neighbor, who is succored by a corporal alms, is moved to pray for his benefactor; wherefore the above text goes on (Ecclus. 29:15): "Shut up alms in the heart of the poor, and it shall obtain help for thee from all evil."

Reply Obj. 1: This argument considers corporal almsdeeds as to their substance.

Reply Obj. 2: He who gives an alms does not intend to buy a spiritual thing with a corporal thing, for he knows that spiritual things infinitely surpass corporal things, but he intends to merit a spiritual fruit through the love of charity.

Reply Obj. 3: The widow who gave less in quantity, gave more in proportion; and thus we gather that the fervor of her charity, whence corporal almsdeeds derive their spiritual efficacy, was greater.

* * * * *

FIFTH ARTICLE [II-II, Q. 32, Art. 5]

Whether Almsgiving Is a Matter of Precept?

Objection 1: It would seem that almsgiving is not a matter of precept. For the counsels are distinct from the precepts. Now almsgiving is a matter of counsel, according to Dan. 4:24: "Let my counsel be acceptable to the King; [Vulg.: 'to thee, and'] redeem thou thy sins with alms." Therefore almsgiving is not a matter of precept.

Obj. 2: Further, it is lawful for everyone to use and to keep what is his own. Yet by keeping it he will not give alms. Therefore it is lawful not to give alms: and consequently almsgiving is not a matter of precept.

Obj. 3: Further, whatever is a matter of precept binds the transgressor at some time or other under pain of mortal sin, because positive precepts are binding for some fixed time. Therefore, if almsgiving were a matter of precept, it would be possible to point to some fixed time when a man would commit a mortal sin unless he gave an alms. But it does not appear how this can be so, because it can always be deemed probable that the person in need can be relieved in some other way, and that what we would spend in almsgiving might be needful to ourselves either now or in some future time. Therefore it seems that almsgiving is not a matter of precept.

Obj. 4: Further, every commandment is reducible to the precepts of the Decalogue. But these precepts contain no reference to almsgiving. Therefore almsgiving is not a matter of precept.

On the contrary, No man is punished eternally for omitting to do what is not a matter of precept. But some are punished eternally for omitting to give alms, as is clear from Matt. 25:41-43. Therefore almsgiving is a matter of precept.

I answer that, As love of our neighbor is a matter of precept, whatever is a necessary condition to the love of our neighbor is a matter of precept also. Now the love of our neighbor requires that not only should we be our neighbor's well-wishers, but also his well-doers, according to 1 John 3:18: "Let us not love in word, nor in tongue, but in deed, and in truth." And in order to be a person's well-wisher and well-doer, we ought to succor his needs: this is done by almsgiving. Therefore almsgiving is a matter of precept.

Since, however, precepts are about acts of virtue, it follows that all almsgiving must be a matter of precept, in so far as it is necessary to virtue, namely, in so far as it is demanded by right reason. Now right reason demands that we should take into consideration something on the part of the giver, and something on the part of the recipient. On the part of the giver, it must be noted that he should give of his surplus, according to Luke 11:41: "That which remaineth, give alms." This surplus is to be taken in reference not only to himself, so as to denote what is unnecessary to the individual, but also in reference to those of whom he has charge (in which case we have the expression "necessary to the person"[1] taking the word "person" as expressive of dignity). Because each one must first of all look after himself and then after those over whom he has charge, and afterwards with what remains relieve the needs of others. Thus nature first, by its nutritive power, takes what it requires for the upkeep of one's own body, and afterwards yields the residue for the formation of another by the power of generation.

On the part of the recipient it is requisite that he should be in need, else there would be no reason for giving him alms: yet since it is not possible for one individual to relieve the needs of all, we are not bound to relieve all who are in need, but only those who could not be succored if we not did succor them. For in such cases the words of Ambrose apply, "Feed him that dies of hunger: if thou hast not fed him, thou hast slain him"[2]. Accordingly we are bound to give alms of our surplus, as also to give alms to one whose need is extreme: otherwise almsgiving, like any other greater good, is a matter of counsel.

Reply Obj. 1: Daniel spoke to a king who was not subject to God's Law, wherefore such things as were prescribed by the Law which he did not profess, had to be counselled to him. Or he may have been speaking in reference to a case in which almsgiving was not a matter of precept.

Reply Obj. 2: The temporal goods which God grants us, are ours as to the ownership, but as to the use of them, they belong not to us alone but also to such others as we are able to succor out of what we

---

1 The official necessities of a person in position
2 Cf. Canon *Pasce,* dist. lxxxvi, whence the words, as quoted, are taken

have over and above our needs. Hence Basil says[1]: "If you acknowledge them," viz. your temporal goods, "as coming from God, is He unjust because He apportions them unequally? Why are you rich while another is poor, unless it be that you may have the merit of a good stewardship, and he the reward of patience? It is the hungry man's bread that you withhold, the naked man's cloak that you have stored away, the shoe of the barefoot that you have left to rot, the money of the needy that you have buried underground: and so you injure as many as you might help." Ambrose expresses himself in the same way.

Reply Obj. 3: There is a time when we sin mortally if we omit to give alms; on the part of the recipient when we see that his need is evident and urgent, and that he is not likely to be succored otherwise—on the part of the giver, when he has superfluous goods, which he does not need for the time being, as far as he can judge with probability. Nor need he consider every case that may possibly occur in the future, for this would be to think about the morrow, which Our Lord forbade us to do (Matt. 6:34), but he should judge what is superfluous and what necessary, according as things probably and generally occur.

Reply Obj. 4: All succor given to our neighbor is reduced to the precept about honoring our parents. For thus does the Apostle interpret it (1 Tim. 4:8) where he says: "Dutifulness[2] [Douay: 'Godliness'] is profitable to all things, having promise of the life that now is, and of that which is to come," and he says this because the precept about honoring our parents contains the promise, "that thou mayest be longlived upon the land" (Ex. 20:12): and dutifulness comprises all kinds of almsgiving.

* * * * *

SIXTH ARTICLE [II-II, Q. 32, Art. 6]

Whether One Ought to Give Alms Out of What One Needs?

Objection 1: It would seem that one ought not to give alms out of what one needs. For the order of charity should be observed not only as regards the effect of our benefactions but also as regards our interior affections. Now it is a sin to contravene the order of

---

1 Hom. super Luc. xii, 18
2 Pietas, whence our English word "Piety." Cf. also inf. Q. 101, A. 2.

charity, because this order is a matter of precept. Since, then, the order of charity requires that a man should love himself more than his neighbor, it seems that he would sin if he deprived himself of what he needed, in order to succor his neighbor.

Obj. 2: Further, whoever gives away what he needs himself, squanders his own substance, and that is to be a prodigal, according to the Philosopher (Ethic. iv, 1). But no sinful deed should be done. Therefore we should not give alms out of what we need.

Obj. 3: Further, the Apostle says (1 Tim. 5:8): "If any man have not care of his own, and especially of those of his house, he hath denied the faith, and is worse than an infidel." Now if a man gives of what he needs for himself or for his charge, he seems to detract from the care he should have for himself or his charge. Therefore it seems that whoever gives alms from what he needs, sins gravely.

On the contrary, Our Lord said (Matt. 19:21): "If thou wilt be perfect, go, sell what thou hast, and give to the poor." Now he that gives all he has to the poor, gives not only what he needs not, but also what he needs. Therefore a man may give alms out of what he needs.

I answer that, A thing is necessary in two ways: first, because without it something is impossible, and it is altogether wrong to give alms out of what is necessary to us in this sense; for instance, if a man found himself in the presence of a case of urgency, and had merely sufficient to support himself and his children, or others under his charge, he would be throwing away his life and that of others if he were to give away in alms, what was then necessary to him. Yet I say this without prejudice to such a case as might happen, supposing that by depriving himself of necessaries a man might help a great personage, and a support of the Church or State, since it would be a praiseworthy act to endanger one's life and the lives of those who are under our charge for the delivery of such a person, since the common good is to be preferred to one's own.

Secondly, a thing is said to be necessary, if a man cannot without it live in keeping with his social station, as regards either himself or those of whom he has charge. The "necessary" considered thus is not an invariable quantity, for one might add much more to a man's property, and yet not go beyond what he needs in this way, or one might take much from him, and he would still have sufficient for the decencies of life in keeping with his own position. Accordingly it is good to give alms of this kind of "necessary"; and it is a matter not of precept but of counsel. Yet it would be inordinate to deprive oneself of one's own, in order to give to others to such an extent that the residue would be insufficient for one to live in keeping with one's station and the ordinary occurrences of life: for no man ought to live unbecomingly. There are, however, three exceptions to the above rule. The first is when a man changes his state of life, for instance, by entering religion, for then he gives away all his possessions for Christ's sake, and does the deed of perfection by transferring himself to another state. Secondly, when that which he deprives himself of, though it be required for the decencies of life, can nevertheless easily be recovered, so that he does not suffer extreme inconvenience. Thirdly, when he is in presence of extreme indigence in an individual, or great need on the part of the common weal. For in such cases it would seem praiseworthy to forego the requirements of one's station, in order to provide for a greater need.

The objections may be easily solved from what has been said.

* * * * *

SEVENTH ARTICLE [II-II, Q. 32, Art. 7]

Whether One May Give Alms Out of Ill-gotten Goods?

Objection 1: It would seem that one may give alms out of ill-gotten goods. For it is written (Luke 16:9): "Make unto you friends of the mammon of iniquity." Now mammon signifies riches. Therefore it is lawful to make unto oneself spiritual friends by giving alms out of ill-gotten riches.

Obj. 2: Further, all filthy lucre seems to be ill-gotten. But the profits from whoredom are filthy lucre; wherefore it was forbidden (Deut. 23:18) to offer therefrom sacrifices or oblations to God: "Thou shalt not offer the hire of a strumpet . . . in the house of . . . thy God." In like manner gains from games of chance are ill-gotten, for, as the Philosopher says (Ethic. iv, 1), "we take such like gains from our friends to whom we ought rather to give." And most of all are the profits from simony ill-gotten, since thereby the Holy Ghost is wronged. Nevertheless out of such gains it is lawful to give alms. Therefore one may give alms out of ill-gotten goods.

Obj. 3: Further, greater evils should be avoided more than lesser evils. Now it is less sinful to keep back another's property than to commit murder, of which a man is guilty if he fails to succor one who is in extreme need, as appears from the words of Ambrose who says (Cf. Canon Pasce dist. lxxxvi, whence the words, as quoted, are taken): "Feed him that dies of hunger, if thou hast not fed him, thou hast slain him". Therefore, in certain cases, it is lawful to give alms of ill-gotten goods.

On the contrary, Augustine says (De Verb. Dom. xxxv, 2): "Give alms from your just labors. For you will not bribe Christ your judge, not to hear you with the poor whom you rob . . . Give not alms from interest and usury: I speak to the faithful to whom we dispense the Body of Christ."

I answer that, A thing may be ill-gotten in three ways. In the first place a thing is ill-gotten if it be due to the person from whom it is gotten, and may not be kept by the person who has obtained possession of it; as in the case of rapine, theft and usury, and of such things a man may not give alms since he is bound to restore them.

Secondly, a thing is ill-gotten, when he that has it may not keep it, and yet he may not return it to the person from whom he received it, because he received it unjustly, while the latter gave it unjustly. This happens in simony, wherein both giver and receiver contravene the justice of the Divine Law, so that restitution is to be made not to the giver, but by giving alms. The same applies to all similar cases of illegal giving and receiving.

Thirdly, a thing is ill-gotten, not because the taking was unlawful, but because it is the outcome of something unlawful, as in the case of a woman's profits from whoredom. This is filthy lucre properly so called, because the practice of whoredom is filthy and against the Law of God, yet the woman does not act unjustly or unlawfully in taking the money. Consequently it is lawful to keep and to give in alms what is thus acquired by an unlawful action.

Reply Obj. 1: As Augustine says (De Verb. Dom. 2), "Some have misunderstood this saying of Our Lord, so as to take another's property and give thereof to the poor, thinking that they are fulfilling the commandment by so doing. This interpretation must be amended. Yet all riches are called riches of iniquity, as stated in De Quaest. Ev. ii, 34, because "riches are not unjust save for those who are themselves unjust, and put all their trust in them. Or, according to Ambrose in his commentary on Luke 16:9, "Make unto yourselves friends," etc., "He calls mammon unjust, because it draws our affections by the various allurements of wealth." Or, because "among the many ancestors whose property you inherit, there is one who took the property of others unjustly, although you know nothing about it," as Basil says in a homily (Hom. super Luc. A, 5). Or, all riches are styled riches "of iniquity," i.e., of "inequality," because they are not distributed equally among all, one being in need, and another in affluence.

Reply Obj. 2: We have already explained how alms may be given out of the profits of whoredom. Yet sacrifices and oblations were not made therefrom at the altar, both on account of the scandal, and through reverence for sacred things. It is also lawful to give alms out of the profits of simony, because they are not due to him who paid, indeed he deserves to lose them. But as to the profits from games of chance, there would seem to be something unlawful as being contrary to the Divine Law, when a man wins from one who cannot alienate his property, such as minors, lunatics and so forth, or when a man, with the desire of making money out of another man, entices him to play, and wins from him by cheating. In these cases he is bound to restitution, and consequently cannot give away his gains in alms. Then again there would seem to be something unlawful as being against the positive civil law, which altogether forbids any such profits. Since, however, a civil law does not bind all, but only those who are subject to that law, and moreover may be abrogated through desuetude, it follows that all such as are bound by these laws are bound to make restitution of such gains, unless perchance the contrary custom prevail, or unless a man win from one who enticed him to play, in which case he is not bound to restitution, because the loser does not deserve to be paid back: and yet he cannot lawfully keep what he has won, so long as that positive law is in force, wherefore in this case he ought to give it away in alms.

Reply Obj. 3: All things are common property in a case of extreme necessity. Hence one who is in such dire straits may take another's goods in order to succor himself, if he can find no one who is willing to give him something. For the same reason a man may retain what belongs to another, and give alms thereof; or even take something if there be no other way of succoring the one who is in need. If however this be possible without danger, he must ask the owner's consent, and then succor the poor man who is in extreme necessity.

* * * * *

EIGHTH ARTICLE [II-II, Q. 32, Art. 8]

Whether One Who Is Under Another's Power Can Give Alms?

Objection 1: It would seem that one who is under another's power can give alms. For religious are under the power of their prelates to whom they have vowed obedience. Now if it were unlawful for them to give alms, they would lose by entering the state of religion, for as Ambrose[1] says on 1 Tim. 4:8: "'Dutifulness [Douay: 'godliness'] is profitable to all things': The sum total of the Christian religion consists in doing one's duty by all," and the most creditable way of doing this is to give alms. Therefore those who are in another's power can give alms.

Obj. 2: Further, a wife is under her husband's power (Gen. 3:16). But a wife can give alms since she is her husband's partner; hence it is related of the Blessed Lucy that she gave alms without the knowledge of her betrothed.[2] Therefore a person is not prevented from giving alms, by being under another's power.

Obj. 3: Further, the subjection of children to their parents is founded on nature, wherefore the Apostle says (Eph. 6:1): "Children, obey your parents in the Lord." But, apparently, children may give alms out of their parents' property. For it is their own, since they are the heirs; wherefore, since they can employ it for some bodily use, it seems that much more can they use it in giving alms so as to profit their souls. Therefore those who are under another's power can give alms.

Obj. 4: Further, servants are under their master's power, according to Titus 2:9: "Exhort servants to be obedient to their masters." Now they may lawfully do anything that will profit their masters: and this

---

[1] The quotation is from the works of Ambrosiaster. Cf. Index to ecclesiastical authorities quoted by St. Thomas

[2] Sponsus. The matrimonial institutions of the Romans were so entirely different from ours that sponsus is no longer accurately rendered either "husband" or "betrothed."

would be especially the case if they gave alms for them. Therefore those who are under another's power can give alms.

On the contrary, Alms should not be given out of another's property; and each one should give alms out of the just profit of his own labor as Augustine says (De Verb. Dom. xxxv, 2). Now if those who are subject to anyone were to give alms, this would be out of another's property. Therefore those who are under another's power cannot give alms.

I answer that, Anyone who is under another's power must, as such, be ruled in accordance with the power of his superior: for the natural order demands that the inferior should be ruled according to its superior. Therefore in those matters in which the inferior is subject to his superior, his ministrations must be subject to the superior's permission.

Accordingly he that is under another's power must not give alms of anything in respect of which he is subject to that other, except in so far as he has been commissioned by his superior. But if he has something in respect of which he is not under the power of his superior, he is no longer subject to another in its regard, being independent in respect of that particular thing, and he can give alms therefrom.

Reply Obj. 1: If a monk be dispensed through being commissioned by his superior, he can give alms from the property of his monastery, in accordance with the terms of his commission; but if he has no such dispensation, since he has nothing of his own, he cannot give alms without his abbot's permission either express or presumed for some probable reason: except in a case of extreme necessity, when it would be lawful for him to commit a theft in order to give an alms. Nor does it follow that he is worse off than before, because, as stated in De Eccles. Dogm. lxxi, "it is a good thing to give one's property to the poor little by little, but it is better still to give all at once in order to follow Christ, and being freed from care, to be needy with Christ."

Reply Obj. 2: A wife, who has other property besides her dowry which is for the support of the burdens of marriage, whether that property be gained by her own industry or by any other lawful means, can give alms, out of that property, without asking her husband's permission: yet such alms should be moderate, lest through giving too much she impoverish her husband. Otherwise she ought not to give alms without the express or presumed consent of her husband, except in cases of necessity as stated, in the case of a monk, in the preceding Reply. For though the wife be her husband's equal in the marriage act, yet in matters of housekeeping, the head of the woman is the man, as the Apostle says (1 Cor. 11:3). As regards Blessed Lucy, she had a betrothed, not a husband, wherefore she could give alms with her mother's consent.

Reply Obj. 3: What belongs to the children belongs also to the father: wherefore the child cannot give alms, except in such small quantity that one may presume the father to be willing: unless, perchance, the father authorize his child to dispose of any particular property. The same applies to servants. Hence the Reply to the Fourth Objection is clear.

* * * * *

NINTH ARTICLE [II-II, Q. 32, Art. 9]

Whether One Ought to Give Alms to Those Rather Who Are More Closely United to Us?

Objection 1: It would seem that one ought not to give alms to those rather who are more closely united to us. For it is written (Ecclus. 12:4, 6): "Give to the merciful and uphold not the sinner ... Do good to the humble and give not to the ungodly." Now it happens sometimes that those who are closely united to us are sinful and ungodly. Therefore we ought not to give alms to them in preference to others.

Obj. 2: Further, alms should be given that we may receive an eternal reward in return, according to Matt. 6:18: "And thy Father Who seeth in secret, will repay thee." Now the eternal reward is gained chiefly by the alms which are given to the saints, according to Luke 16:9: "Make unto you friends of the mammon of iniquity, that when you shall fail, they may receive you into everlasting dwellings," which passage Augustine expounds (De Verb. Dom. xxxv, 1): "Who shall have everlasting dwellings unless the saints of God? And who are they that shall be received by them into their dwellings, if not those who succor them in their needs?" Therefore alms should be given to the more holy persons rather than to those who are more closely united to us.

Obj. 3: Further, man is more closely united to himself. But a man cannot give himself an alms. Therefore it seems that we are not bound to give alms to those who are most closely united to us.

On the contrary, The Apostle says (1 Tim. 5:8): "If any man have not care of his own, and especially of those of his house, he hath denied the faith, and is worse than an infidel."

I answer that, As Augustine says (De Doctr. Christ. i, 28), "it falls to us by lot, as it were, to have to look to the welfare of those who are more closely united to us." Nevertheless in this matter we must employ discretion, according to the various degrees of connection, holiness and utility. For we ought to give alms to one who is much holier and in greater want, and to one who is more useful to the common weal, rather than to one who is more closely united to us, especially if the latter be not very closely united, and has no special claim on our care then and there, and who is not in very urgent need.

Reply Obj. 1: We ought not to help a sinner as such, that is by encouraging him to sin, but as man, that is by supporting his nature.

Reply Obj. 2: Almsdeeds deserve on two counts to receive an eternal reward. First because they are rooted in charity, and in this respect an almsdeed is meritorious in so far as it observes the order of charity, which requires that, other things being equal, we should, in preference, help those who are more closely connected with us. Wherefore Ambrose says (De Officiis i, 30): "It is with commendable liberality that you forget not your kindred, if you know them to be in need, for it is better that you should yourself help your own family, who would be ashamed to beg help from others." Secondly, almsdeeds deserve to be rewarded eternally, through the merit of the recipient, who prays for the giver, and it is in this sense that Augustine is speaking.

Reply Obj. 3: Since almsdeeds are works of mercy, just as a man does not, properly speaking, pity himself, but only by a kind of comparison, as stated above (Q. 30, AA. 1, 2), so too, properly speaking, no man gives himself an alms, unless he act in another's person; thus when a man is appointed to distribute alms, he can take something for himself, if he be in want, on the same ground as when he gives to others.

* * * * *

TENTH ARTICLE [II-II, Q. 32, Art. 10]

Whether Alms Should Be Given in Abundance?

Objection 1: It would seem that alms should not be given in abundance. For we ought to give alms to those chiefly who are most closely connected with us. But we ought not to give to them in such a way that they are likely to become richer thereby, as Ambrose says (De Officiis i, 30). Therefore neither should we give abundantly to others.

Obj. 2: Further, Ambrose says (De Officiis i, 30): "We should not lavish our wealth on others all at once, we should dole it out by degrees." But to give abundantly is to give lavishly. Therefore alms should not be given in abundance.

Obj. 3: Further, the Apostle says (2 Cor. 8:13): "Not that others should be eased," i.e. should live on you without working themselves, "and you burthened," i.e. impoverished. But this would be the result if alms were given in abundance. Therefore we ought not to give alms abundantly.

On the contrary, It is written (Tob. 4:93): "If thou have much, give abundantly."

I answer that, Alms may be considered abundant in relation either to the giver, or to the recipient: in relation to the giver, when that which a man gives is great as compared with his means. To give thus is praiseworthy, wherefore Our Lord (Luke 21:3, 4) commended the widow because "of her want, she cast in all the living that she had." Nevertheless those conditions must be observed which were laid down when we spoke of giving alms out of one's necessary goods (A. 9).

On the part of the recipient, an alms may be abundant in two ways; first, by relieving his need sufficiently, and in this sense it is praiseworthy to give alms: secondly, by relieving his need more than sufficiently; this is not praiseworthy, and it would be better to give to several that are in need, wherefore the Apostle says (1 Cor. 13:3): "If I should distribute ... to feed the poor," on which words a gloss comments: "Thus we are warned to be careful in giving alms, and to give, not to one only, but to many, that we may profit many."

Reply Obj. 1: This argument considers abundance of alms as exceeding the needs of the recipient.

Reply Obj. 2: The passage quoted considers abundance of alms on the part of the giver; but the sense is that God does not wish a man to lavish all his wealth at once, except when he changes his state of life, wherefore he goes on to say: "Except we imitate Eliseus who slew his oxen and fed the poor with what he had, so that no household cares might keep him back" (3 Kings 19:21).

Reply Obj. 3: In the passage quoted the words, "not that others should be eased or refreshed," refer to that abundance of alms which surpasses the need of the recipient, to whom one should give alms not that he may have an easy life, but that he may have relief. Nevertheless we must bring discretion to bear on the matter, on account of the various conditions of men, some of whom are more daintily nurtured, and need finer food and clothing. Hence Ambrose says (De Officiis i, 30): "When you give an alms to a man, you should take into consideration his age and his weakness; and sometimes the shame which proclaims his good birth; and again that perhaps he has fallen from riches to indigence through no fault of his own."

With regard to the words that follow, "and you burdened," they refer to abundance on the part of the giver. Yet, as a gloss says on the same passage, "he says this, not because it would be better to give in abundance, but because he fears for the weak, and he admonishes them so to give that they lack not for themselves.".

33. OF FRATERNAL CORRECTION
(In Eight Articles)

We must now consider Fraternal Correction, under which head there are eight points of inquiry:

(1) Whether fraternal correction is an act of charity?
(2) Whether it is a matter of precept?
(3) Whether this precept binds all, or only superiors?
(4) Whether this precept binds the subject to correct his superior?
(5) Whether a sinner may correct anyone?
(6) Whether one ought to correct a person who becomes worse through being corrected?
(7) Whether secret correction should precede denouncement?
(8) Whether witnesses should be called before denouncement?.

* * * * *

FIRST ARTICLE [II-II, Q. 33, Art. 1]

Whether Fraternal Correction Is an Act of Charity?

Objection 1: It would seem that fraternal correction is not an act of charity. For a gloss on Matt. 18:15, "If thy brother shall offend against thee," says that "a man should reprove his brother out of zeal for justice." But justice is a distinct virtue from charity. Therefore fraternal correction is an act, not of charity, but of justice.

Obj. 2: Further, fraternal correction is given by secret admonition. Now admonition is a kind of counsel, which is an act of prudence, for a prudent man is one who is of good counsel (Ethic. vi, 5). Therefore fraternal correction is an act, not of charity, but of prudence.

Obj. 3: Further, contrary acts do not belong to the same virtue. Now it is an act of charity to bear with a sinner, according to Gal. 6:2: "Bear ye one another's burdens, and so you shall fulfil the law of Christ," which is the law of charity. Therefore it seems that the correction of a sinning brother, which is contrary to bearing with him, is not an act of charity.

On the contrary, To correct the wrongdoer is a spiritual almsdeed. But almsdeeds are works of charity, as stated above (Q. 32, A. 1). Therefore fraternal correction is an act of charity.

I answer that, The correction of the wrongdoer is a remedy which should be employed against a man's sin. Now a man's sin may be considered in two ways, first as being harmful to the sinner, secondly as conducing to the harm of others, by hurting or scandalizing them, or by being detrimental to the common good, the justice of which is disturbed by that man's sin.

Consequently the correction of a wrongdoer is twofold, one which applies a remedy to the sin considered as an evil of the sinner himself. This is fraternal correction properly so called, which is directed to the amendment of the sinner. Now to do away with anyone's evil is the same as to procure his good: and to procure a person's good is an act of charity, whereby we wish and do our friend well. Consequently fraternal correction also is an act of charity, because thereby we drive out our brother's evil, viz. sin, the removal of which pertains to charity rather than the removal of an external loss, or of a bodily injury, in so much as the contrary good of virtue is more akin to charity than the good of the body or of external things. Therefore fraternal correction is an act of charity rather than the healing of a bodily infirmity, or the relieving of an external bodily need. There is another correction which applies a remedy to the sin of the wrongdoer, considered as hurtful to others, and especially to the common good. This correction is an act of justice, whose concern it is to safeguard the rectitude of justice between one man and another.

Reply Obj. 1: This gloss speaks of the second correction which is an act of justice. Or if it speaks of the first correction, then it takes justice as denoting a general virtue, as we shall state further on (Q. 58, A. 5), in which sense again all "sin is iniquity" (1 John 3:4), through being contrary to justice.

Reply Obj. 2: According to the Philosopher (Ethic. vi, 12), prudence regulates whatever is directed to the end, about which things counsel and choice are concerned. Nevertheless when, guided by prudence, we perform some action aright which is directed to the end of some virtue, such as temperance or fortitude, that action belongs chiefly to the virtue to whose end it is directed. Since, then, the admonition which is given in fraternal correction is directed to the removal of a brother's sin, which removal pertains to charity, it is evident that this admonition is chiefly an act of charity, which virtue commands it, so to speak, but secondarily an act of prudence, which executes and directs the action.

Reply Obj. 3: Fraternal correction is not opposed to forbearance with the weak, on the contrary it results from it. For a man bears with a sinner, in so far as he is not disturbed against him, and retains his goodwill towards him: the result being that he strives to make him do better.

* * * * *

SECOND ARTICLE [II-II, Q. 33, Art. 2]

Whether Fraternal Correction Is a Matter of Precept?

Objection 1: It would seem that fraternal correction is not a matter of precept. For nothing impossible is a matter of precept, according to the saying of Jerome[1]: "Accursed be he who says

---
1   Pelagius, Expos. Symb. ad Damas

that God has commanded anything impossible." Now it is written (Eccles. 7:14): "Consider the works of God, that no man can correct whom He hath despised." Therefore fraternal correction is not a matter of precept.

Obj. 2: Further, all the precepts of the Divine Law are reduced to the precepts of the Decalogue. But fraternal correction does not come under any precept of the Decalogue. Therefore it is not a matter of precept.

Obj. 3: Further, the omission of a Divine precept is a mortal sin, which has no place in a holy man. Yet holy and spiritual men are found to omit fraternal correction: since Augustine says (De Civ. Dei i, 9): "Not only those of low degree, but also those of high position, refrain from reproving others, moved by a guilty cupidity, not by the claims of charity." Therefore fraternal correction is not a matter of precept.

Obj. 4: Further, whatever is a matter of precept is something due. If, therefore, fraternal correction is a matter of precept, it is due to our brethren that we correct them when they sin. Now when a man owes anyone a material due, such as the payment of a sum of money, he must not be content that his creditor come to him, but he should seek him out, that he may pay him his due. Hence we should have to go seeking for those who need correction, in order that we might correct them; which appears to be inconvenient, both on account of the great number of sinners, for whose correction one man could not suffice, and because religious would have to leave the cloister in order to reprove men, which would be unbecoming. Therefore fraternal correction is not a matter of precept.

On the contrary, Augustine says (De Verb. Dom. xvi, 4): "You become worse than the sinner if you fail to correct him." But this would not be so unless, by this neglect, one omitted to observe some precept. Therefore fraternal correction is a matter of precept.

I answer that, Fraternal correction is a matter of precept. We must observe, however, that while the negative precepts of the Law forbid sinful acts, the positive precepts inculcate acts of virtue. Now sinful acts are evil in themselves, and cannot become good, no matter how, or when, or where, they are done, because of their very nature they are connected with an evil end, as stated in *Ethic.* ii, 6: wherefore negative precepts bind always and for all times. On the other hand, acts of virtue must not be done anyhow, but by observing the due circumstances, which are requisite in order that an act be virtuous; namely, that it be done where, when, and how it ought to be done. And since the disposition of whatever is directed to the end depends on the formal aspect of the end, the chief of these circumstances of a virtuous act is this aspect of the end, which in this case is the good of virtue. If therefore such a circumstance be omitted from a virtuous act, as entirely takes away the good of virtue, such an act is contrary to a precept. If, however, the circumstance omitted from a virtuous act be such as not to destroy the virtue altogether, though it does not perfectly attain the good of virtue, it is not against a precept. Hence the Philosopher (Ethic. ii, 9) says that if we depart but little from the mean, it is not contrary to the virtue, whereas if we depart much from the mean virtue is destroyed in its act. Now fraternal correction is directed to a brother's amendment: so that it is a matter of precept, in so far as it is necessary for that end, but not so as we have to correct our erring brother at all places and times.

Reply Obj. 1: In all good deeds man's action is not efficacious without the Divine assistance: and yet man must do what is in his power. Hence Augustine says (De Correp. et Gratia xv): "Since we ignore who is predestined and who is not, charity should so guide our feelings, that we wish all to be saved." Consequently we ought to do our brethren the kindness of correcting them, with the hope of God's help.

Reply Obj. 2: As stated above (Q. 32, A. 5, ad 4), all the precepts about rendering service to our neighbor are reduced to the precept about the honor due to parents.

Reply Obj. 3: Fraternal correction may be omitted in three ways.

First, meritoriously, when out of charity one omits to correct someone. For Augustine says (De Civ. Dei i, 9): "If a man refrains from chiding and reproving wrongdoers, because he awaits a suitable time for so doing, or because he fears lest, if he does so, they may become worse, or hinder, oppress, or turn away from the faith, others who are weak and need to be instructed in a life of goodness and virtue, this does not seem to result from covetousness, but to be counselled by charity."

Secondly, fraternal correction may be omitted in such a way that one commits a mortal sin, namely, "when" (as he says in the same passage) "one fears what people may think, or lest one may suffer grievous pain or death; provided, however, that the mind is so dominated by such things, that it gives them the preference to fraternal charity." This would seem to be the case when a man reckons that he might probably withdraw some wrongdoer from sin, and yet omits to do so, through fear or covetousness.

Thirdly, such an omission is a venial sin, when through fear or covetousness, a man is loth to correct his brother's faults, and yet not to such a degree, that if he saw clearly that he could withdraw him from sin, he would still forbear from so doing, through fear or covetousness, because in his own mind he prefers fraternal charity to these things. It is in this way that holy men sometimes omit to correct wrongdoers.

Reply Obj. 4: We are bound to pay that which is due to some fixed and certain person, whether it be a material or a spiritual good, without waiting for him to come to us, but by taking proper steps to find him. Wherefore just as he that owes money to a creditor should seek him, when the time comes, so as to pay him what he owes, so he that has spiritual charge of some person is bound to seek him out, in order to reprove him for a sin. On the other hand, we are not bound to seek someone on whom to bestow such favors as are due, not to any certain person, but to all our neighbors in general, whether those favors be material or spiritual goods, but it suffices that we bestow them when the opportunity occurs; because, as Augustine says (De Doctr. Christ. i, 28), we must look upon this as a matter of chance. For this reason he says (De Verb. Dom. xvi, 1) that "Our Lord warns us not to be listless in regard of one another's sins: not indeed by being on the lookout for something to denounce, but by correcting what we see": else we should become spies on the lives of others, which is against the saying of Prov. 24:19: "Lie not in wait, nor seek after wickedness in the house of the just, nor spoil his rest." It is evident from this that there is no need for religious to leave their cloister in order to rebuke evil-doers.

* * * * *

THIRD ARTICLE [II-II, Q. 33, Art. 3]

Whether Fraternal Correction Belongs Only to Prelates?

Objection 1: It would seem that fraternal correction belongs to prelates alone. For Jerome[1] says: "Let priests endeavor to fulfil

---

1   Origen, Hom. vii in Joan.

this saying of the Gospel: 'If thy brother sin against thee,'" etc. Now prelates having charge of others were usually designated under the name of priests. Therefore it seems that fraternal correction belongs to prelates alone.

Obj. 2: Further, fraternal correction is a spiritual alms. Now corporal almsgiving belongs to those who are placed above others in temporal matters, i.e. to the rich. Therefore fraternal correction belongs to those who are placed above others in spiritual matters, i.e. to prelates.

Obj. 3: Further, when one man reproves another he moves him by his rebuke to something better. Now in the physical order the inferior is moved by the superior. Therefore in the order of virtue also, which follows the order of nature, it belongs to prelates alone to correct inferiors.

On the contrary, It is written (Dist. xxiv, qu. 3, Can. Tam Sacerdotes): "Both priests and all the rest of the faithful should be most solicitous for those who perish, so that their reproof may either correct their sinful ways, or, if they be incorrigible, cut them off from the Church."

I answer that, As stated above (A. 1), correction is twofold. One is an act of charity, which seeks in a special way the recovery of an erring brother by means of a simple warning: such like correction belongs to anyone who has charity, be he subject or prelate.

But there is another correction which is an act of justice purposing the common good, which is procured not only by warning one's brother, but also, sometimes, by punishing him, that others may, through fear, desist from sin. Such a correction belongs only to prelates, whose business it is not only to admonish, but also to correct by means of punishments.

Reply Obj. 1: Even as regards that fraternal correction which is common to all, prelates have a grave responsibility, as Augustine says (De Civ. Dei i, 9): "for just as a man ought to bestow temporal favors on those especially of whom he has temporal care, so too ought he to confer spiritual favors, such as correction, teaching and the like, on those who are entrusted to his spiritual care." Therefore Jerome does not mean that the precept of fraternal correction concerns priests only, but that it concerns them chiefly.

Reply Obj. 2: Just as he who has the means wherewith to give corporal assistance is rich in this respect, so he whose reason is gifted with a sane judgment, so as to be able to correct another's wrong-doing, is, in this respect, to be looked on as a superior.

Reply Obj. 3: Even in the physical order certain things act mutually on one another, through being in some respect higher than one another, in so far as each is somewhat in act, and somewhat in potentiality with regard to another. In like manner one man can correct another in so far as he has a sane judgment in a matter wherein the other sins, though he is not his superior simply.

* * * * *

FOURTH ARTICLE [II-II, Q. 33, Art. 4]

Whether a Man Is Bound to Correct His Prelate?

Objection 1: It would seem that no man is bound to correct his prelate. For it is written (Ex. 19:12): "The beast that shall touch the mount shall be stoned,"[1] and (2 Kings 6:7) it is related that the Lord struck Oza for touching the ark. Now the mount and the ark signify our prelates. Therefore prelates should not be corrected by their subjects.

Obj. 2: Further, a gloss on Gal. 2:11, "I withstood him to the face," adds: "as an equal." Therefore, since a subject is not equal to his prelate, he ought not to correct him.

Obj. 3: Further, Gregory says (Moral. xxiii, 8) that "one ought not to presume to reprove the conduct of holy men, unless one thinks better of oneself." But one ought not to think better of oneself than of one's prelate. Therefore one ought not to correct one's prelate.

On the contrary, Augustine says in his Rule: "Show mercy not only to yourselves, but also to him who, being in the higher position among you, is therefore in greater danger." But fraternal correction is a work of mercy. Therefore even prelates ought to be corrected.

I answer that, A subject is not competent to administer to his prelate the correction which is an act of justice through the coercive nature of punishment: but the fraternal correction which is an act of charity is within the competency of everyone in respect of any person towards whom he is bound by charity, provided there be something in that person which requires correction.

---

1 Vulg.: 'Everyone that shall touch the mount, dying he shall die.'

Now an act which proceeds from a habit or power extends to whatever is contained under the object of that power or habit: thus vision extends to all things comprised in the object of sight. Since, however, a virtuous act needs to be moderated by due circumstances, it follows that when a subject corrects his prelate, he ought to do so in a becoming manner, not with impudence and harshness, but with gentleness and respect. Hence the Apostle says (1 Tim. 5:1): "An ancient man rebuke not, but entreat him as a father." Wherefore Dionysius finds fault with the monk Demophilus (Ep. viii), for rebuking a priest with insolence, by striking and turning him out of the church.

Reply Obj. 1: It would seem that a subject touches his prelate inordinately when he upbraids him with insolence, as also when he speaks ill of him: and this is signified by God's condemnation of those who touched the mount and the ark.

Reply Obj. 2: To withstand anyone in public exceeds the mode of fraternal correction, and so Paul would not have withstood Peter then, unless he were in some way his equal as regards the defense of the faith. But one who is not an equal can reprove privately and respectfully. Hence the Apostle in writing to the Colossians (4:17) tells them to admonish their prelate: "Say to Archippus: Fulfil thy ministry[1]." It must be observed, however, that if the faith were endangered, a subject ought to rebuke his prelate even publicly. Hence Paul, who was Peter's subject, rebuked him in public, on account of the imminent danger of scandal concerning faith, and, as the gloss of Augustine says on Gal. 2:11, "Peter gave an example to superiors, that if at any time they should happen to stray from the straight path, they should not disdain to be reproved by their subjects."

Reply Obj. 3: To presume oneself to be simply better than one's prelate, would seem to savor of presumptuous pride; but there is no presumption in thinking oneself better in some respect, because, in this life, no man is without some fault. We must also remember that when a man reproves his prelate charitably, it does not follow that he thinks himself any better, but merely that he offers his help to one who, "being in the higher position among you, is therefore in greater danger," as Augustine observes in his Rule quoted above.

---

1 Vulg.: 'Take heed to the ministry which thou hast received in the Lord, that thou fulfil it.' Cf. 2 Tim. 4:5

* * * * *

FIFTH ARTICLE [II-II, Q. 33, Art. 5]

Whether a Sinner Ought to Reprove a Wrongdoer?

Objection 1: It would seem that a sinner ought to reprove a wrongdoer. For no man is excused from obeying a precept by having committed a sin. But fraternal correction is a matter of precept, as stated above (A. 2). Therefore it seems that a man ought not to forbear from such like correction for the reason that he has committed a sin.

Obj. 2: Further, spiritual almsdeeds are of more account than corporal almsdeeds. Now one who is in sin ought not to abstain from administering corporal alms. Much less therefore ought he, on account of a previous sin, to refrain from correcting wrongdoers.

Obj. 3: Further, it is written (1 John 1:8): "If we say that we have no sin, we deceive ourselves." Therefore if, on account of a sin, a man is hindered from reproving his brother, there will be none to reprove the wrongdoer. But the latter proposition is unreasonable: therefore the former is also.

On the contrary, Isidore says (De Summo Bono iii, 32): "He that is subject to vice should not correct the vices of others." Again it is written (Rom. 2:1): "Wherein thou judgest another, thou condemnest thyself. For thou dost the same things which thou judgest."

I answer that, As stated above (A. 3, ad 2), to correct a wrongdoer belongs to a man, in so far as his reason is gifted with right judgment. Now sin, as stated above (I-II, Q. 85, AA. 1, 2), does not destroy the good of nature so as to deprive the sinner's reason of all right judgment, and in this respect he may be competent to find fault with others for committing sin. Nevertheless a previous sin proves somewhat of a hindrance to this correction, for three reasons. First because this previous sin renders a man unworthy to rebuke another; and especially is he unworthy to correct another for a lesser sin, if he himself has committed a greater. Hence Jerome says on the words, "Why seest thou the mote?" etc. (Matt. 7:3): "He is speaking of those who, while they are themselves guilty of mortal sin, have no patience with the lesser sins of their brethren."

Secondly, such like correction becomes unseemly, on account of the scandal which ensues therefrom, if the corrector's sin be well known, because it would seem that he corrects, not out of charity, but more for the sake of ostentation. Hence the words of Matt. 7:4, "How sayest thou to thy brother?" etc. are expounded by Chrysostom[1] thus: "That is—'With what object?' Out of charity, think you, that you may save your neighbor?" No, "because you would look after your own salvation first. What you want is, not to save others, but to hide your evil deeds with good teaching, and to seek to be praised by men for your knowledge."

Thirdly, on account of the rebuker's pride; when, for instance, a man thinks lightly of his own sins, and, in his own heart, sets himself above his neighbor, judging the latter's sins with harsh severity, as though he himself were a just man. Hence Augustine says (De Serm. Dom. in Monte ii, 19): "To reprove the faults of others is the duty of good and kindly men: when a wicked man rebukes anyone, his rebuke is the latter's acquittal." And so, as Augustine says (De Serm. Dom. in Monte ii, 19): "When we have to find fault with anyone, we should think whether we were never guilty of his sin; and then we must remember that we are men, and might have been guilty of it; or that we once had it on our conscience, but have it no longer: and then we should bethink ourselves that we are all weak, in order that our reproof may be the outcome, not of hatred, but of pity. But if we find that we are guilty of the same sin, we must not rebuke him, but groan with him, and invite him to repent with us." It follows from this that, if a sinner reprove a wrongdoer with humility, he does not sin, nor does he bring a further condemnation on himself, although thereby he proves himself deserving of condemnation, either in his brother's or in his own conscience, on account of his previous sin.

Hence the Replies to the Objections are clear.

* * * * *

SIXTH ARTICLE [II-II, Q. 33, Art. 6]

Whether One Ought to Forbear from Correcting Someone, Through Fear Lest He Become Worse?

Objection 1: It would seem that one ought not to forbear from correcting someone through fear lest he become worse. For

---

[1] Hom. xvii in the Opus Imperfectum falsely ascribed to St. John Chrysostom

sin is weakness of the soul, according to Ps. 6:3: "Have mercy on me, O Lord, for I am weak." Now he that has charge of a sick person, must not cease to take care of him, even if he be fractious or contemptuous, because then the danger is greater, as in the case of madmen. Much more, therefore should one correct a sinner, no matter how badly he takes it.

Obj. 2: Further, according to Jerome vital truths are not to be foregone on account of scandal. Now God's commandments are vital truths. Since, therefore, fraternal correction is a matter of precept, as stated above (A. 2), it seems that it should not be foregone for fear of scandalizing the person to be corrected.

Obj. 3: Further, according to the Apostle (Rom. 3:8) we should not do evil that good may come of it. Therefore, in like manner, good should not be omitted lest evil befall. Now fraternal correction is a good thing. Therefore it should not be omitted for fear lest the person corrected become worse.

On the contrary, It is written (Prov. 9:8): "Rebuke not a scorner lest he hate thee," where a gloss remarks: "You must not fear lest the scorner insult you when you rebuke him: rather should you bear in mind that by making him hate you, you may make him worse." Therefore one ought to forego fraternal correction, when we fear lest we may make a man worse.

I answer that, As stated above (A. 3) the correction of the wrongdoer is twofold. One, which belongs to prelates, and is directed to the common good, has coercive force. Such correction should not be omitted lest the person corrected be disturbed, both because if he is unwilling to amend his ways of his own accord, he should be made to cease sinning by being punished, and because, if he be incorrigible, the common good is safeguarded in this way, since the order of justice is observed, and others are deterred by one being made an example of. Hence a judge does not desist from pronouncing sentence of condemnation against a sinner, for fear of disturbing him or his friends.

The other fraternal correction is directed to the amendment of the wrongdoer, whom it does not coerce, but merely admonishes. Consequently when it is deemed probable that the sinner will not take the warning, and will become worse, such fraternal correction should be foregone, because the means should be regulated according to the requirements of the end.

Reply Obj. 1: The doctor uses force towards a madman, who is unwilling to submit to his treatment; and this may be compared with the correction administered by prelates, which has coercive power, but not with simple fraternal correction.

Reply Obj. 2: Fraternal correction is a matter of precept, in so far as it is an act of virtue, and it will be a virtuous act in so far as it is proportionate to the end. Consequently whenever it is a hindrance to the end, for instance when a man becomes worse through it, it is longer a vital truth, nor is it a matter of precept.

Reply Obj. 3: Whatever is directed to an end, becomes good through being directed to the end. Hence whenever fraternal correction hinders the end, namely the amendment of our brother, it is no longer good, so that when such a correction is omitted, good is not omitted lest evil should befall.

* * * * *

SEVENTH ARTICLE [II-II, Q. 33, Art. 7]

Whether the Precept of Fraternal Correction Demands That a Private Admonition Should Precede Denunciation?

Objection 1: It would seem that the precept of fraternal correction does not demand that a private admonition should precede denunciation. For, in works of charity, we should above all follow the example of God, according to Eph. 5:1, 2: "Be ye followers of God, as most dear children, and walk in love." Now God sometimes punishes a man for a sin, without previously warning him in secret. Therefore it seems that there is no need for a private admonition to precede denunciation.

Obj. 2: Further, according to Augustine (De Mendacio xv), we learn from the deeds of holy men how we ought to understand the commandments of Holy Writ. Now among the deeds of holy men we find that a hidden sin is publicly denounced, without any previous admonition in private. Thus we read (Gen. 37:2) that "Joseph accused his brethren to his father of a most wicked crime": and (Acts 5:4, 9) that Peter publicly denounced Ananias and Saphira who had secretly "by fraud kept back the price of the land," without beforehand admonishing them in private: nor do we read that Our Lord admonished Judas in secret before denouncing him. Therefore the precept does not require that secret admonition should precede public denunciation.

Obj. 3: Further, it is a graver matter to accuse than to denounce. Now one may go to the length of accusing a person publicly, without previously admonishing him in secret: for it is decided in the Decretal (Cap. Qualiter, xiv, De Accusationibus) that "nothing else need precede accusation except inscription."[1] Therefore it seems that the precept does not require that a secret admonition should precede public denunciation.

Obj. 4: Further, it does not seem probable that the customs observed by religious in general are contrary to the precepts of Christ. Now it is customary among religious orders to proclaim this or that one for a fault, without any previous secret admonition. Therefore it seems that this admonition is not required by the precept.

Obj. 5: Further, religious are bound to obey their prelates. Now a prelate sometimes commands either all in general, or someone in particular, to tell him if they know of anything that requires correction. Therefore it would seem that they are bound to tell them this, even before any secret admonition. Therefore the precept does not require secret admonition before public denunciation.

On the contrary, Augustine says (De Verb. Dom. xvi, 4) on the words, "Rebuke him between thee and him alone" (Matt. 18:15): "Aiming at his amendment, while avoiding his disgrace: since perhaps from shame he might begin to defend his sin; and him whom you thought to make a better man, you make worse." Now we are bound by the precept of charity to beware lest our brother become worse. Therefore the order of fraternal correction comes under the precept.

I answer that, With regard to the public denunciation of sins it is necessary to make a distinction: because sins may be either public or secret. In the case of public sins, a remedy is required not only for the sinner, that he may become better, but also for others, who know of his sin, lest they be scandalized. Wherefore such like sins should be denounced in public, according to the saying of the Apostle (1 Tim. 5:20): "Them that sin reprove before all, that the

---

1   The accuser was bound by Roman Law to endorse (se inscribere) the writ of accusation. The effect of this endorsement or inscription was that the accuser bound himself, if he failed to prove the accusation, to suffer the same punishment as the accused would have to suffer if proved guilty.

rest also may have fear," which is to be understood as referring to public sins, as Augustine states (De Verb. Dom. xvi, 7).

On the other hand, in the case of secret sins, the words of Our Lord seem to apply (Matt. 18:15): "If thy brother shall offend against thee," etc. For if he offend thee publicly in the presence of others, he no longer sins against thee alone, but also against others whom he disturbs. Since, however, a man's neighbor may take offense even at his secret sins, it seems that we must make yet a further distinction. For certain secret sins are hurtful to our neighbor either in his body or in his soul, as, for instance, when a man plots secretly to betray his country to its enemies, or when a heretic secretly turns other men away from the faith. And since he that sins thus in secret, sins not only against you in particular, but also against others, it is necessary to take steps to denounce him at once, in order to prevent him doing such harm, unless by chance you were firmly persuaded that this evil result would be prevented by admonishing him secretly. On the other hand there are other sins which injure none but the sinner, and the person sinned against, either because he alone is hurt by the sinner, or at least because he alone knows about his sin, and then our one purpose should be to succor our sinning brother: and just as the physician of the body restores the sick man to health, if possible, without cutting off a limb, but, if this be unavoidable, cuts off a limb which is least indispensable, in order to preserve the life of the whole body, so too he who desires his brother's amendment should, if possible, so amend him as regards his conscience, that he keep his good name.

For a good name is useful, first of all to the sinner himself, not only in temporal matters wherein a man suffers many losses, if he lose his good name, but also in spiritual matters, because many are restrained from sinning, through fear of dishonor, so that when a man finds his honor lost, he puts no curb on his sinning. Hence Jerome says on Matt. 18:15: "If he sin against thee, thou shouldst rebuke him in private, lest he persist in his sin if he should once become shameless or unabashed." Secondly, we ought to safeguard our sinning brother's good name, both because the dishonor of one leads to the dishonor of others, according to the saying of Augustine (Ep. ad pleb. Hipponens. lxxviii): "When a few of those who bear a name for holiness are reported falsely or proved in truth to have done anything wrong, people will seek by busily repeating it to make it believed of all": and also because when one man's sin is made public others are incited to sin likewise.

Since, however, one's conscience should be preferred to a good name, Our Lord wished that we should publicly denounce our brother and so deliver his conscience from sin, even though he should forfeit his good name. Therefore it is evident that the precept requires a secret admonition to precede public denunciation.

Reply Obj. 1: Whatever is hidden, is known to God, wherefore hidden sins are to the judgment of God, just what public sins are to the judgment of man. Nevertheless God does rebuke sinners sometimes by secretly admonishing them, so to speak, with an inward inspiration, either while they wake or while they sleep, according to Job 33:15-17: "By a dream in a vision by night, when deep sleep falleth upon men . . . then He openeth the ears of men, and teaching instructeth them in what they are to learn, that He may withdraw a man from the things he is doing."

Reply Obj. 2: Our Lord as God knew the sin of Judas as though it were public, wherefore He could have made it known at once. Yet He did not, but warned Judas of his sin in words that were obscure. The sin of Ananias and Saphira was denounced by Peter acting as God's executor, by Whose revelation he knew of their sin. With regard to Joseph it is probable that he warned his brethren, though Scripture does not say so. Or we may say that the sin was public with regard to his brethren, wherefore it is stated in the plural that he accused "his brethren."

Reply Obj. 3: When there is danger to a great number of people, those words of Our Lord do not apply, because then thy brother does not sin against thee alone.

Reply Obj. 4: Proclamations made in the chapter of religious are about little faults which do not affect a man's good name, wherefore they are reminders of forgotten faults rather than accusations or denunciations. If, however, they should be of such a nature as to injure our brother's good name, it would be contrary to Our Lord's precept, to denounce a brother's fault in this manner.

Reply Obj. 5: A prelate is not to be obeyed contrary to a Divine precept, according to Acts 5:29: "We ought to obey God rather then men." Therefore when a prelate commands anyone to tell him anything that he knows to need correction, the command rightly understood supports the safeguarding of the order of fraternal correction, whether the command be addressed to all in general, or to some particular individual. If, on the other hand, a prelate were to issue a command in express opposition to this order instituted by Our Lord, both would sin, the one commanding, and the one obeying him, as disobeying Our Lord's command. Consequently he ought not to be obeyed, because a prelate is not the judge of secret things, but God alone is, wherefore he has no power to command anything in respect of hidden matters, except in so far as they are made known through certain signs, as by ill-repute or suspicion; in which cases a prelate can command just as a judge, whether secular or ecclesiastical, can bind a man under oath to tell the truth.

* * * * *

EIGHTH ARTICLE [II-II, Q. 33, Art. 8]

Whether Before the Public Denunciation Witnesses Ought to Be Brought Forward?

Objection 1: It would seem that before the public denunciation witnesses ought not to be brought forward. For secret sins ought not to be made known to others, because by so doing "a man would betray his brother's sins instead of correcting them," as Augustine says (De Verb. Dom. xvi, 7). Now by bringing forward witnesses one makes known a brother's sin to others. Therefore in the case of secret sins one ought not to bring witnesses forward before the public denunciation.

Obj. 2: Further, man should love his neighbor as himself. Now no man brings in witnesses to prove his own secret sin. Neither therefore ought one to bring forward witnesses to prove the secret sin of our brother.

Obj. 3: Further, witnesses are brought forward to prove something. But witnesses afford no proof in secret matters. Therefore it is useless to bring witnesses forward in such cases.

Obj. 4: Further, Augustine says in his Rule that "before bringing it to the notice of witnesses ... it should be put before the superior." Now to bring a matter before a superior or a prelate is to tell the Church. Therefore witnesses should not be brought forward before the public denunciation.

On the contrary, Our Lord said (Matt. 18:16): "Take with thee one or two more, that in the mouth of two," etc.

I answer that, The right way to go from one extreme to another is to pass through the middle space. Now Our Lord wished the beginning of fraternal correction to be hidden, when one brother corrects another between this one and himself alone, while He wished the end to be public, when such a one would be denounced to the Church. Consequently it is befitting that a citation of witnesses should be placed between the two extremes, so that at first the brother's sin be indicated to a few, who will be of use without being a hindrance, and thus his sin be amended without dishonoring him before the public.

Reply Obj. 1: Some have understood the order of fraternal correction to demand that we should first of all rebuke our brother secretly, and that if he listens, it is well; but if he listen not, and his sin be altogether hidden, they say that we should go no further in the matter, whereas if it has already begun to reach the ears of several by various signs, we ought to prosecute the matter, according to Our Lord's command. But this is contrary to what Augustine says in his Rule that "we are bound to reveal" a brother's sin, if it "will cause a worse corruption in the heart." Wherefore we must say otherwise that when the secret admonition has been given once or several times, as long as there is probable hope of his amendment, we must continue to admonish him in private, but as soon as we are able to judge with any probability that the secret admonition is of no avail, we must take further steps, however secret the sin may be, and call witnesses, unless perhaps it were thought probable that this would not conduce to our brother's amendment, and that he would become worse: because on that account one ought to abstain altogether from correcting him, as stated above (A. 6).

Reply Obj. 2: A man needs no witnesses that he may amend his own sin: yet they may be necessary that we may amend a brother's sin. Hence the comparison fails.

Reply Obj. 3: There may be three reasons for citing witnesses. First, to show that the deed in question is a sin, as Jerome says: secondly, to prove that the deed was done, if repeated, as Augustine says (loc. cit.): thirdly, "to prove that the man who rebuked his brother, has done what he could," as Chrysostom says (Hom. in Matth. lx).

Reply Obj. 4: Augustine means that the matter ought to be made known to the prelate before it is stated to the witnesses, in so far as the prelate is a private individual who is able to be of more use than others, but not that it is to be told him as to the Church, i.e. as holding the position of judge.

34. OF HATRED (In Six Articles)

We must now consider the vices opposed to charity: (1) hatred, which is opposed to love; (2) sloth and envy, which are opposed to the joy of charity; (3) discord and schism, which are contrary to peace; (4) offense and scandal, which are contrary to beneficence and fraternal correction.

Under the first head there are six points of inquiry:

(1) Whether it is possible to hate God?
(2) Whether hatred of God is the greatest of sins?
(3) Whether hatred of one's neighbor is always a sin?
(4) Whether it is the greatest of all sins against our neighbor?
(5) Whether it is a capital sin?
(6) From what capital sin does it arise?.

* * * * *

FIRST ARTICLE [II-II, Q. 34, Art. 1]

Whether It Is Possible for Anyone to Hate God?

Objection 1: It would seem that no man can hate God. For Dionysius says (Div. Nom. iv) that "the first good and beautiful is an object of love and dilection to all." But God is goodness and beauty itself. Therefore He is hated by none.

Obj. 2: Further, in the Apocryphal books of 3 Esdras 4:36, 39 it is written that "all things call upon truth . . . and (all men) do well like of her works." Now God is the very truth according to John 14:6. Therefore all love God, and none can hate Him.

Obj. 3: Further, hatred is a kind of aversion. But according to Dionysius (Div. Nom. i) God draws all things to Himself. Therefore none can hate Him.

On the contrary, It is written (Ps. 73:23): "The pride of them that hate Thee ascendeth continually," and (John 15:24): "But now they have both seen and hated both Me and My Father."

I answer that, As shown above (I-II, Q. 29, A. 1), hatred is a movement of the appetitive power, which power is not set in motion save by something apprehended. Now God can be apprehended by man in two ways; first, in Himself, as when He is seen in His Essence; secondly, in His effects, when, to wit, "the invisible things" of God ... "are clearly seen, being understood by the things that are made" (Rom. 1:20). Now God in His Essence is goodness itself, which no man can hate—for it is natural to good to be loved. Hence it is impossible for one who sees God in His Essence, to hate Him.

Moreover some of His effects are such that they can nowise be contrary to the human will, since *to be, to live, to understand,* which are effects of God, are desirable and lovable to all. Wherefore again God cannot be an object of hatred if we consider Him as the Author of such like effects. Some of God's effects, however, are contrary to an inordinate will, such as the infliction of punishment, and the prohibition of sin by the Divine Law. Such like effects are repugnant to a will debased by sin, and as regards the consideration of them, God may be an object of hatred to some, in so far as they look upon Him as forbidding sin, and inflicting punishment.

Reply Obj. 1: This argument is true of those who see God's Essence, which is the very essence of goodness.

Reply Obj. 2: This argument is true in so far as God is apprehended as the cause of such effects as are naturally beloved of all, among which are the works of Truth who reveals herself to men.

Reply Obj. 3: God draws all things to Himself, in so far as He is the source of being, since all things, in as much as they are, tend to be like God, Who is Being itself.

* * * * *

SECOND ARTICLE [II-II, Q. 34, Art. 2]

Whether Hatred of God Is the Greatest of Sins?

Objection 1: It would seem that hatred of God is not the greatest of sins. For the most grievous sin is the sin against the Holy Ghost, since it cannot be forgiven, according to Matt. 12:32. Now hatred of

God is not reckoned among the various kinds of sin against the Holy Ghost, as may be seen from what has been said above (Q. 14, A. 2). Therefore hatred of God is not the most grievous sin.

Obj. 2: Further, sin consists in withdrawing oneself from God. Now an unbeliever who has not even knowledge of God seems to be further away from Him than a believer, who though he hate God, nevertheless knows Him. Therefore it seems that the sin of unbelief is graver than the sin of hatred against God.

Obj. 3: Further, God is an object of hatred, only by reason of those of His effects that are contrary to the will: the chief of which is punishment. But hatred of punishment is not the most grievous sin. Therefore hatred of God is not the most grievous sin.

On the contrary, The best is opposite to the worst, according to the Philosopher (Ethic. viii, 10). But hatred of God is contrary to the love of God, wherein man's best consists. Therefore hatred of God is man's worst sin.

I answer that, The defect in sin consists in its aversion from God, as stated above (Q. 10, A. 3): and this aversion would not have the character of guilt, were it not voluntary. Hence the nature of guilt consists in a voluntary aversion from God.

Now this voluntary aversion from God is directly implied in the hatred of God, but in other sins, by participation and indirectly. For just as the will cleaves directly to what it loves, so does it directly shun what it hates. Hence when a man hates God, his will is directly averted from God, whereas in other sins, fornication for instance, a man turns away from God, not directly, but indirectly, in so far, namely, as he desires an inordinate pleasure, to which aversion from God is connected. Now that which is so by itself, always takes precedence of that which is so by another. Wherefore hatred of God is more grievous than other sins.

Reply Obj. 1: According to Gregory (Moral. xxv, 11), "it is one thing not to do good things, and another to hate the giver of good things, even as it is one thing to sin indeliberately, and another to sin deliberately." This implies that to hate God, the giver of all good things, is to sin deliberately, and this is a sin against the Holy Ghost. Hence it is evident that hatred of God is chiefly a sin against the Holy Ghost, in so far as the sin against the Holy Ghost denotes a special kind of sin: and yet it is not reckoned among the kinds of sin against the Holy Ghost, because it is universally found in every kind of that sin.

Reply Obj. 2: Even unbelief is not sinful unless it be voluntary: wherefore the more voluntary it is, the more it is sinful. Now it becomes voluntary by the fact that a man hates the truth that is proposed to him. Wherefore it is evident that unbelief derives its sinfulness from hatred of God, Whose truth is the object of faith; and hence just as a cause is greater than its effect, so hatred of God is a greater sin than unbelief.

Reply Obj. 3: Not everyone who hates his punishment, hates God the author of punishments. For many hate the punishments inflicted on them, and yet they bear them patiently out of reverence for the Divine justice. Wherefore Augustine says (Confess. x) that God commands us to bear with penal evils, not to love them. On the other hand, to break out into hatred of God when He inflicts those punishments, is to hate God's very justice, and that is a most grievous sin. Hence Gregory says (Moral. xxv, 11): "Even as sometimes it is more grievous to love sin than to do it, so is it more wicked to hate justice than not to have done it.".

* * * * *

THIRD ARTICLE [II-II, Q. 34, Art. 3]

Whether hatred of one's neighbor is always a sin?

Objection 1: It would seem that hatred of one's neighbor is not always a sin. For no sin is commanded or counselled by God, according to Prov. 8:8: "All My words are just, there is nothing wicked nor perverse in them." Now, it is written (Luke 14:26): "If any man come to Me, and hate not his father and mother... he cannot be My disciple." Therefore hatred of one's neighbor is not always a sin.

Obj. 2: Further, nothing wherein we imitate God can be a sin. But it is in imitation of God that we hate certain people: for it is written (Rom. 1:30): "Detractors, hateful to God." Therefore it is possible to hate certain people without committing a sin.

Obj. 3: Further, nothing that is natural is a sin, for sin is a "wandering away from what is according to nature," according to Damascene (De Fide Orth. ii, 4, 30; iv, 20). Now it is natural to a thing to hate whatever is contrary to it, and to aim at its undoing. Therefore it seems that it is not a sin to hate one's I enemy.

On the contrary, It is written (1 John 2:9): "He that ... hateth his brother, is in darkness." Now spiritual darkness is sin. Therefore there cannot be hatred of one's neighbor without sin.

I answer that, Hatred is opposed to love, as stated above (I-II, Q. 29, A. 2); so that hatred of a thing is evil according as the love of that thing is good. Now love is due to our neighbor in respect of what he holds from God, i.e. in respect of nature and grace, but not in respect of what he has of himself and from the devil, i.e. in respect of sin and lack of justice.

Consequently it is lawful to hate the sin in one's brother, and whatever pertains to the defect of Divine justice, but we cannot hate our brother's nature and grace without sin. Now it is part of our love for our brother that we hate the fault and the lack of good in him, since desire for another's good is equivalent to hatred of his evil. Consequently the hatred of one's brother, if we consider it simply, is always sinful.

Reply Obj. 1: By the commandment of God (Ex. 20:12) we must honor our parents—as united to us in nature and kinship. But we must hate them in so far as they prove an obstacle to our attaining the perfection of Divine justice.

Reply Obj. 2: God hates the sin which is in the detractor, not his nature: so that we can hate detractors without committing a sin.

Reply Obj. 3: Men are not opposed to us in respect of the goods which they have received from God: wherefore, in this respect, we should love them. But they are opposed to us, in so far as they show hostility towards us, and this is sinful in them. In this respect we should hate them, for we should hate in them the fact that they are hostile to us.

* * * * *

FOURTH ARTICLE [II-II, Q. 34, Art. 4]

Whether Hatred of Our Neighbor Is the Most Grievous Sin Against Our Neighbor?

Objection 1: It would seem that hatred of our neighbor is the most grievous sin against our neighbor. For it is written (1 John 3:15): "Whosoever hateth his brother is a murderer." Now murder is the most grievous of sins against our neighbor. Therefore hatred is also.

Obj. 2: Further, worst is opposed to best. Now the best thing we give our neighbor is love, since all other things are referable to love. Therefore hatred is the worst.

On the contrary, A thing is said to be evil, because it hurts, as Augustine observes (Enchiridion xii). Now there are sins by which a man hurts his neighbor more than by hatred, e.g. theft, murder and adultery. Therefore hatred is not the most grievous sin.

Moreover, Chrysostom[1] commenting on Matt. 5:19, "He that shall break one of these least commandments," says: "The commandments of Moses, Thou shalt not kill, Thou shalt not commit adultery, count for little in their reward, but they count for much if they be disobeyed. On the other hand the commandments of Christ such as, Thou shalt not be angry, Thou shalt not desire, are reckoned great in their reward, but little in the transgression." Now hatred is an internal movement like anger and desire. Therefore hatred of one's brother is a less grievous sin than murder.

I answer that, Sins committed against our neighbor are evil on two counts; first by reason of the disorder in the person who sins, secondly by reason of the hurt inflicted on the person sinned against. On the first count, hatred is a more grievous sin than external actions that hurt our neighbor, because hatred is a disorder of man's will, which is the chief part of man, and wherein is the root of sin, so that if a man's outward actions were to be inordinate, without any disorder in his will, they would not be sinful, for instance, if he were to kill a man, through ignorance or out of zeal for justice: and if there be anything sinful in a man's outward sins against his neighbor, it is all to be traced to his inward hatred.

On the other hand, as regards the hurt inflicted on his neighbor, a man's outward sins are worse than his inward hatred. This suffices for the Replies to the Objections.

* * * * *

---

1   Hom. x in the Opus Imperfectum, falsely ascribed to St. John Chrysostom

FIFTH ARTICLE [II-II, Q. 34, Art. 5]

Whether Hatred Is a Capital Sin?

Objection 1: It would seem that hatred is a capital sin. For hatred is directly opposed to charity. Now charity is the foremost among the virtues, and the mother of all others. Therefore hatred is the chief of the capital sins, and the origin of all others.

Obj. 2: Further, sins arise in us on account of the inclinations of our passions, according to Rom. 7:5: "The passions of sins ... did work in our members to bring forth fruit unto death." Now all other passions of the soul seem to arise from love and hatred, as was shown above (I-II, Q. 25, AA. 1, 2). Therefore hatred should be reckoned one of the capital sins.

Obj. 3: Further, vice is a moral evil. Now hatred regards evil more than any other passion does. Therefore it seems that hatred should be reckoned a capital sin.

On the contrary, Gregory (Moral. xxxi) does not reckon hatred among the seven capital sins.

I answer that, As stated above (I-II, Q. 84, AA. 3, 4), a capital vice is one from which other vices arise most frequently. Now vice is contrary to man's nature, in as much as he is a rational animal: and when a thing acts contrary to its nature, that which is natural to it is corrupted little by little. Consequently it must first of all fail in that which is less in accordance with its nature, and last of all in that which is most in accordance with its nature, since what is first in construction is last in destruction. Now that which, first and foremost, is most natural to man, is the love of what is good, and especially love of the Divine good, and of his neighbor's good. Wherefore hatred, which is opposed to this love, is not the first but the last thing in the downfall of virtue resulting from vice: and therefore it is not a capital vice.

Reply Obj. 1: As stated in Phys. vii, text. 18, "the virtue of a thing consists in its being well disposed in accordance with its nature." Hence what is first and foremost in the virtues must be first and foremost in the natural order. Hence charity is reckoned the foremost of the virtues, and for the same reason hatred cannot be first among the vices, as stated above.

Reply Obj. 2: Hatred of the evil that is contrary to one's natural good, is the first of the soul's passions, even as love of one's natural good is. But hatred of one's connatural good cannot be first, but is something last, because such like hatred is a proof of an already corrupted nature, even as love of an extraneous good.

Reply Obj. 3: Evil is twofold. One is a true evil, for the reason that it is incompatible with one's natural good, and the hatred of such an evil may have priority over the other passions. There is, however, another which is not a true, but an apparent evil, which, namely, is a true and connatural good, and yet is reckoned evil on account of the corruption of nature: and the hatred of such an evil must needs come last. This hatred is vicious, but the former is not.

* * * * *

SIXTH ARTICLE [II-II, Q. 34, Art. 6]

Whether Hatred Arises from Envy?

Objection 1: It seems that hatred does not arise from envy. For envy is sorrow for another's good. Now hatred does not arise from sorrow, for, on the contrary, we grieve for the presence of the evil we hate. Therefore hatred does not arise from envy.

Obj. 2: Further, hatred is opposed to love. Now love of our neighbor is referred to our love of God, as stated above (Q. 25, A. 1; Q. 26, A. 2). Therefore hatred of our neighbor is referred to our hatred of God. But hatred of God does not arise from envy, for we do not envy those who are very far removed from us, but rather those who seem to be near us, as the Philosopher states (Rhet. ii). Therefore hatred does not arise from envy.

Obj. 3: Further, to one effect there is one cause. Now hatred is caused by anger, for Augustine says in his Rule that "anger grows into hatred." Therefore hatred does not arise from envy.

On the contrary, Gregory says (Moral. xxxi, 45) that "out of envy cometh hatred."

I answer that, As stated above (A. 5), hatred of his neighbor is a man's last step in the path of sin, because it is opposed to the love which he naturally has for his neighbor. Now if a man declines from that which is natural, it is because he intends to avoid that which is naturally an object to be shunned. Now every animal naturally avoids sorrow, just as it desires pleasure, as the Philosopher states (Ethic. vii, x).

Accordingly just as love arises from pleasure, so does hatred arise from sorrow. For just as we are moved to love whatever gives us pleasure, in as much as for that very reason it assumes the aspect of good; so we are moved to hate whatever displeases us, in so far as for this very reason it assumes the aspect of evil. Wherefore, since envy is sorrow for our neighbor's good, it follows that our neighbor's good becomes hateful to us, so that "out of envy cometh hatred."

Reply Obj. 1: Since the appetitive power, like the apprehensive power, reflects on its own acts, it follows that there is a kind of circular movement in the actions of the appetitive power. And so according to the first forward course of the appetitive movement, love gives rise to desire, whence follows pleasure when one has obtained what one desired. And since the very fact of taking pleasure in the good one loves is a kind of good, it follows that pleasure causes love. And in the same way sorrow causes hatred.

Reply Obj. 2: Love and hatred are essentially different, for the object of love is good, which flows from God to creatures, wherefore love is due to God in the first place, and to our neighbor afterwards. On the other hand, hatred is of evil, which has no place in God Himself, but only in His effects, for which reason it has been stated above (A. 1), that God is not an object of hatred, except in so far as He is considered in relation to His effects, and consequently hatred is directed to our neighbor before being directed to God. Therefore, since envy of our neighbor is the mother of hatred of our neighbor, it becomes, in consequence, the cause of hatred towards God.

Reply Obj. 3: Nothing prevents a thing arising from various causes in various respects, and accordingly hatred may arise both from anger and from envy. However it arises more directly from envy, which looks upon the very good of our neighbor as displeasing and therefore hateful, whereas hatred arises from anger by way of increase. For at first, through anger, we desire our neighbor's evil according to a certain measure, that is in so far as that evil has the aspect of vengeance: but afterwards, through the continuance of anger, man goes so far as absolutely to desire his neighbor's evil, which desire is part of hatred. Wherefore it is evident that hatred is caused by envy formally as regards the aspect of the object, but dispositively by anger.

35. OF SLOTH (In Four Articles)

We must now consider the vices opposed to the joy of charity. This joy is either about the Divine good, and then its contrary is sloth, or about our neighbor's good, and then its contrary is envy. Wherefore we must consider (1) Sloth and (2) Envy.

Under the first head there are four points of inquiry:

(1) Whether sloth is a sin?
(2) Whether it is a special vice?
(3) Whether it is a mortal sin?
(4) Whether it is a capital sin?.

* * * * *

FIRST ARTICLE [II-II, Q. 35, Art. 1]

Whether Sloth Is a Sin?

Objection 1: It would seem that sloth is not a sin. For we are neither praised nor blamed for our passions, according to the Philosopher (Ethic. ii, 5). Now sloth is a passion, since it is a kind of sorrow, according to Damascene (De Fide Orth. ii, 14), and as we stated above (I-II, Q. 35, A. 8). Therefore sloth is not a sin.

Obj. 2: Further, no bodily failing that occurs at fixed times is a sin. But sloth is like this, for Cassian says (De Instit. Monast. x,[1]): "The monk is troubled with sloth chiefly about the sixth hour: it is like an intermittent fever, and inflicts the soul of the one it lays low with burning fires at regular and fixed intervals." Therefore sloth is not a sin.

Obj. 3: Further, that which proceeds from a good root is, seemingly, no sin. Now sloth proceeds from a good root, for Cassian says (De Instit. Monast. x) that "sloth arises from the fact that we sigh at being deprived of spiritual fruit, and think that other monasteries and those which are a long way off are much better than the one we dwell in": all of which seems to point to humility. Therefore sloth is not a sin.

---

[1] De Institutione Caenobiorum

Obj. 4: Further, all sin is to be avoided, according to Ecclus. 21:2: "Flee from sins as from the face of a serpent." Now Cassian says (De Instit. Monast. x): "Experience shows that the onslaught of sloth is not to be evaded by flight but to be conquered by resistance." Therefore sloth is not a sin.

On the contrary, Whatever is forbidden in Holy Writ is a sin. Now such is sloth (acedia): for it is written (Ecclus. 6:26): "Bow down thy shoulder, and bear her," namely spiritual wisdom, "and be not grieved (acedieris) with her bands." Therefore sloth is a sin.

I answer that, Sloth, according to Damascene (De Fide Orth. ii, 14) is an oppressive sorrow, which, to wit, so weighs upon man's mind, that he wants to do nothing; thus acid things are also cold. Hence sloth implies a certain weariness of work, as appears from a gloss on Ps. 106:18, "Their soul abhorred all manner of meat," and from the definition of some who say that sloth is a "sluggishness of the mind which neglects to begin good."

Now this sorrow is always evil, sometimes in itself, sometimes in its effect. For sorrow is evil in itself when it is about that which is apparently evil but good in reality, even as, on the other hand, pleasure is evil if it is about that which seems to be good but is, in truth, evil. Since, then, spiritual good is a good in very truth, sorrow about spiritual good is evil in itself. And yet that sorrow also which is about a real evil, is evil in its effect, if it so oppresses man as to draw him away entirely from good deeds. Hence the Apostle (2 Cor. 2:7) did not wish those who repented to be "swallowed up with overmuch sorrow."

Accordingly, since sloth, as we understand it here, denotes sorrow for spiritual good, it is evil on two counts, both in itself and in point of its effect. Consequently it is a sin, for by sin we mean an evil movement of the appetite, as appears from what has been said above (Q. 10, A. 2; I-II, Q. 74, A. 4).

Reply Obj. 1: Passions are not sinful in themselves; but they are blameworthy in so far as they are applied to something evil, just as they deserve praise in so far as they are applied to something good. Wherefore sorrow, in itself, calls neither for praise nor for blame: whereas moderate sorrow for evil calls for praise, while sorrow for good, and again immoderate sorrow for evil, call for blame. It is in this sense that sloth is said to be a sin.

Reply Obj. 2: The passions of the sensitive appetite may either be venial sins in themselves, or incline the soul to mortal sin. And since the sensitive appetite has a bodily organ, it follows that on account of some bodily transmutation a man becomes apt to commit some particular sin. Hence it may happen that certain sins may become more insistent, through certain bodily transmutations occurring at certain fixed times. Now all bodily effects, of themselves, dispose one to sorrow; and thus it is that those who fast are harassed by sloth towards mid-day, when they begin to feel the want of food, and to be parched by the sun's heat.

Reply Obj. 3: It is a sign of humility if a man does not think too much of himself, through observing his own faults; but if a man contemns the good things he has received from God, this, far from being a proof of humility, shows him to be ungrateful: and from such like contempt results sloth, because we sorrow for things that we reckon evil and worthless. Accordingly we ought to think much of the goods of others, in such a way as not to disparage those we have received ourselves, because if we did they would give us sorrow.

Reply Obj. 4: Sin is ever to be shunned, but the assaults of sin should be overcome, sometimes by flight, sometimes by resistance; by flight when a continued thought increases the incentive to sin, as in lust; for which reason it is written (1 Cor. 6:18): "Fly fornication"; by resistance, when perseverance in the thought diminishes the incentive to sin, which incentive arises from some trivial consideration. This is the case with sloth, because the more we think about spiritual goods, the more pleasing they become to us, and forthwith sloth dies away.

* * * * *

SECOND ARTICLE [II-II, Q. 35, Art. 2]

Whether Sloth Is a Special Vice?

Objection 1: It would seem that sloth is not a special vice. For that which is common to all vices does not constitute a special kind of vice. But every vice makes a man sorrowful about the opposite spiritual good: for the lustful man is sorrowful about the good of continence, and the glutton about the good of abstinence. Since then sloth is sorrow for spiritual good, as stated above (A. 1), it seems that sloth is not a special sin.

Obj. 2: Further, sloth, through being a kind of sorrow, is opposed to joy. Now joy is not accounted one special virtue. Therefore sloth should not be reckoned a special vice.

Obj. 3: Further, since spiritual good is a general kind of object, which virtue seeks, and vice shuns, it does not constitute a special virtue or vice, unless it be determined by some addition. Now nothing, seemingly, except toil, can determine it to sloth, if this be a special vice; because the reason why a man shuns spiritual goods, is that they are toilsome, wherefore sloth is a kind of weariness: while dislike of toil, and love of bodily repose seem to be due to the same cause, viz. idleness. Hence sloth would be nothing but laziness, which seems untrue, for idleness is opposed to carefulness, whereas sloth is opposed to joy. Therefore sloth is not a special vice.

On the contrary, Gregory (Moral. xxxi, 45) distinguishes sloth from the other vices. Therefore it is a special vice.

I answer that, Since sloth is sorrow for spiritual good, if we take spiritual good in a general way, sloth will not be a special vice, because, as stated above (I-II, Q. 71, A. 1), every vice shuns the spiritual good of its opposite virtue. Again it cannot be said that sloth is a special vice, in so far as it shuns spiritual good, as toilsome, or troublesome to the body, or as a hindrance to the body's pleasure, for this again would not sever sloth from carnal vices, whereby a man seeks bodily comfort and pleasure.

Wherefore we must say that a certain order exists among spiritual goods, since all the spiritual goods that are in the acts of each virtue are directed to one spiritual good, which is the Divine good, about which there is a special virtue, viz. charity. Hence it is proper to each virtue to rejoice in its own spiritual good, which consists in its own act, while it belongs specially to charity to have that spiritual joy whereby one rejoices in the Divine good. In like manner the sorrow whereby one is displeased at the spiritual good which is in each act of virtue, belongs, not to any special vice, but to every vice, but sorrow in the Divine good about which charity rejoices, belongs to a special vice, which is called sloth. This suffices for the Replies to the Objections.

* * * * *

THIRD ARTICLE [II-II, Q. 35, Art. 3]

Whether Sloth Is a Mortal Sin?

Objection 1: It would seem that sloth is not a mortal sin. For every mortal sin is contrary to a precept of the Divine Law. But sloth seems contrary to no precept, as one may see by going through the precepts of the Decalogue. Therefore sloth is not a mortal sin.

Obj. 2: Further, in the same genus, a sin of deed is no less grievous than a sin of thought. Now it is not a mortal sin to refrain in deed from some spiritual good which leads to God, else it would be a mortal sin not to observe the counsels. Therefore it is not a mortal sin to refrain in thought from such like spiritual works. Therefore sloth is not a mortal sin.

Obj. 3: Further, no mortal sin is to be found in a perfect man. But sloth is to be found in a perfect man: for Cassian says (De Instit. Caenob. x, l) that "sloth is well known to the solitary, and is a most vexatious and persistent foe to the hermit." Therefore sloth is not always a mortal sin.

On the contrary, It is written (2 Cor. 7:20): "The sorrow of the world worketh death." But such is sloth; for it is not sorrow "according to God," which is contrasted with sorrow of the world. Therefore it is a mortal sin.

I answer that, As stated above (I-II, Q. 88, AA. 1, 2), mortal sin is so called because it destroys the spiritual life which is the effect of charity, whereby God dwells in us. Wherefore any sin which by its very nature is contrary to charity is a mortal sin by reason of its genus. And such is sloth, because the proper effect of charity is joy in God, as stated above (Q. 28, A. 1), while sloth is sorrow about spiritual good in as much as it is a Divine good. Therefore sloth is a mortal sin in respect of its genus. But it must be observed with regard to all sins that are mortal in respect of their genus, that they are not mortal, save when they attain to their perfection. Because the consummation of sin is in the consent of reason: for we are speaking now of human sins consisting in human acts, the principle of which is the reason. Wherefore if the sin be a mere beginning of sin in the sensuality alone, without attaining to the consent of reason, it is a venial sin on account of the imperfection of the act. Thus in the genus of adultery, the concupiscence that goes no further than the sensuality is a venial sin, whereas if it reach to the consent of reason, it is a mortal sin. So too, the movement of sloth is sometimes in the sensuality alone, by reason of the opposition of the flesh to the spirit, and then it is a venial sin; whereas sometimes it reaches to the reason, which consents in the dislike, horror and detestation of the Divine good, on account of the flesh utterly prevailing over the spirit. In this case it is evident that sloth is a mortal sin.

Reply Obj. 1: Sloth is opposed to the precept about hallowing the Sabbath day. For this precept, in so far as it is a moral precept, implicitly commands the mind to rest in God: and sorrow of the mind about the Divine good is contrary thereto.

Reply Obj. 2: Sloth is not an aversion of the mind from any spiritual good, but from the Divine good, to which the mind is obliged to adhere. Wherefore if a man is sorry because someone forces him to do acts of virtue that he is not bound to do, this is not a sin of sloth; but when he is sorry to have to do something for God's sake.

Reply Obj. 3: Imperfect movements of sloth are to be found in holy men, but they do not reach to the consent of reason.

* * * * *

FOURTH ARTICLE [II-II, Q. 35, Art. 4]

Whether Sloth Should Be Accounted a Capital Vice?

Objection 1: It would seem that sloth ought not to be accounted a capital vice. For a capital vice is one that moves a man to sinful acts, as stated above (Q. 34, A. 5). Now sloth does not move one to action, but on the contrary withdraws one from it. Therefore it should not be accounted a capital sin.

Obj. 2: Further, a capital sin is one to which daughters are assigned. Now Gregory (Moral. xxxi, 45) assigns six daughters to sloth, viz. "malice, spite, faint-heartedness, despair, sluggishness in regard to the commandments, wandering of the mind after unlawful things." Now these do not seem in reality to arise from sloth. For "spite" is, seemingly the same as hatred, which arises from envy, as stated above (Q. 34, A. 6); "malice" is a genus which contains all vices, and, in like manner, a "wandering" of the mind after unlawful things is to be found in every vice; "sluggishness" about the commandments seems to be the same as sloth, while "faint-heartedness" and "despair" may arise from any sin. Therefore sloth is not rightly accounted a capital sin.

Obj. 3: Further, Isidore distinguishes the vice of sloth from the vice of sorrow, saying (De Summo Bono ii, 37) that in so far as a man shirks his duty because it is distasteful and burdensome, it is sorrow, and in so far as he is inclined to undue repose, it is sloth: and of sorrow he says that it gives rise to "spite, faint-heartedness, bitterness, despair," whereas he states that from sloth seven things arise, viz. "idleness, drowsiness, uneasiness of the mind, restlessness of the body, instability, loquacity, curiosity." Therefore it seems that either Gregory or Isidore has wrongly assigned sloth as a capital sin together with its daughters.

On the contrary, The same Gregory (Moral. xxxi, 45) states that sloth is a capital sin, and has the daughters aforesaid.

I answer that, As stated above (I-II, Q. 84, AA. 3, 4), a capital vice is one which easily gives rise to others as being their final cause. Now just as we do many things on account of pleasure, both in order to obtain it, and through being moved to do something under the impulse of pleasure, so again we do many things on account of sorrow, either that we may avoid it, or through being exasperated into doing something under pressure thereof. Wherefore, since sloth is a kind of sorrow, as stated above (A. 2; I-II, Q. 85, A. 8), it is fittingly reckoned a capital sin.

Reply Obj. 1: Sloth by weighing on the mind, hinders us from doing things that cause sorrow: nevertheless it induces the mind to do certain things, either because they are in harmony with sorrow, such as weeping, or because they are a means of avoiding sorrow.

Reply Obj. 2: Gregory fittingly assigns the daughters of sloth. For since, according to the Philosopher (Ethic. viii, 5, 6) "no man can be a long time in company with what is painful and unpleasant," it follows that something arises from sorrow in two ways: first, that man shuns whatever causes sorrow; secondly, that he passes to other things that give him pleasure: thus those who find no joy in spiritual pleasures, have recourse to pleasures of the body, according to the Philosopher (Ethic. x, 6). Now in the avoidance of sorrow the order observed is that man at first flies from unpleasant objects, and secondly he even struggles against such things as cause sorrow. Now spiritual goods which are the object of the sorrow of sloth, are both end and means. Avoidance of the end is the result of "despair," while avoidance of those goods which are the means to the end, in matters of difficulty which come under the counsels, is the effect of "faint-heartedness," and in matters of common righteousness, is the effect of "sluggishness about the commandments." The struggle against spiritual goods that cause sorrow is sometimes with men who lead others to spiritual goods, and this is called "spite"; and sometimes it extends to the spiritual goods themselves, when a man goes so far as to detest them, and this is properly called "malice." In so far as a man has recourse to eternal objects of pleasure, the daughter of sloth is called "wandering after unlawful things." From this it is clear how to reply to the objections against each of the daughters: for "malice" does not denote here that which is generic to all vices, but must be understood as explained. Nor is "spite" taken as synonymous with hatred, but for a kind of indignation, as stated above: and the same applies to the others.

Reply Obj. 3: This distinction between sorrow and sloth is also given by Cassian (De Instit. Caenob. x, 1). But Gregory more fittingly (Moral. xxxi, 45) calls sloth a kind of sorrow, because, as stated above (A. 2), sorrow is not a distinct vice, in so far as a man shirks a distasteful and burdensome work, or sorrows on account of any other cause whatever, but only in so far as he is sorry on account of the Divine good, which sorrow belongs essentially to sloth; since sloth seeks undue rest in so far as it spurns the Divine good. Moreover the things which Isidore reckons to arise from sloth and sorrow, are reduced to those mentioned by Gregory: for "bitterness" which Isidore states to be the result of sorrow, is an effect of "spite." "Idleness" and "drowsiness" are reduced to "sluggishness about the precepts": for some are idle and omit them altogether, while others are drowsy and fulfil them with negligence. All the other five which he reckons as effects of sloth, belong to the "wandering of the mind after unlawful things." This tendency to wander, if it reside in the mind itself that is desirous of rushing after various things without rhyme or reason, is called "uneasiness of the mind," but if it pertains to the imaginative power, it is called "curiosity"; if it affect the speech it is called "loquacity"; and in so far as it affects a body that changes place, it is called "restlessness of the body," when, to wit, a man shows the unsteadiness of his mind, by the inordinate movements of members of his body; while if it causes the body to move from one place to another, it is called "instability"; or "instability" may denote changeableness of purpose.

36. OF ENVY (FOUR ARTICLES)

We must now consider envy, and under this head there are four points of inquiry:

(1) What is envy?
(2) Whether it is a sin?
(3) Whether it is a mortal sin?
(4) Whether it is a capital sin, and which are its daughters?.

* * * * *

FIRST ARTICLE [II-II, Q. 36, Art. 1]

Whether Envy Is a Kind of Sorrow?

Objection 1: It would seem that envy is not a kind of sorrow. For the object of envy is a good, for Gregory says (Moral. v, 46) of the envious man that "self-inflicted pain wounds the pining spirit, which is racked by the prosperity of another." Therefore envy is not a kind of sorrow.

Obj. 2: Further, likeness is a cause, not of sorrow but rather of pleasure. But likeness is a cause of envy: for the Philosopher says (Rhet. ii, 10): "Men are envious of such as are like them in genus, in knowledge, in stature, in habit, or in reputation." Therefore envy is not a kind of sorrow.

Obj. 3: Further, sorrow is caused by a defect, wherefore those who are in great defect are inclined to sorrow, as stated above (I-II, Q. 47, A. 3) when we were treating of the passions. Now those who lack little, and who love honors, and who are considered wise, are envious, according to the Philosopher (Rhet. ii, 10). Therefore envy is not a kind of sorrow.

Obj. 4: Further, sorrow is opposed to pleasure. Now opposite effects have not one and the same cause. Therefore, since the recollection of goods once possessed is a cause of pleasure, as stated above (I-II, Q. 32, A. 3) it will not be a cause of sorrow. But it is a cause of envy; for the Philosopher says (Rhet. ii, 10) that "we envy those who have or have had things that befitted ourselves, or which we possessed at some time." Therefore sloth is not a kind of sorrow.

On the contrary, Damascene (De Fide Orth. ii, 14) calls envy a species of sorrow, and says that "envy is sorrow for another's good."

I answer that, The object of a man's sorrow is his own evil. Now it may happen that another's good is apprehended as one's own evil, and in this way sorrow can be about another's good. But this happens in two ways: first, when a man is sorry about another's good, in so far as it threatens to be an occasion of harm to himself, as when a man grieves for his enemy's prosperity, for fear lest he may do him some harm: such like sorrow is not envy, but rather an effect of fear, as the Philosopher states (Rhet. ii, 9).

Secondly, another's good may be reckoned as being one's own evil, in so far as it conduces to the lessening of one's own good name or excellence. It is in this way that envy grieves for another's good: and consequently men are envious of those goods in which a good name consists, and about which men like to be honored and esteemed, as the Philosopher remarks (Rhet. ii, 10).

Reply Obj. 1: Nothing hinders what is good for one from being reckoned as evil for another: and in this way it is possible for sorrow to be about good, as stated above.

Reply Obj. 2: Since envy is about another's good name in so far as it diminishes the good name a man desires to have, it follows that a man is envious of those only whom he wishes to rival or surpass in reputation. But this does not apply to people who are far removed from one another: for no man, unless he be out of his mind, endeavors to rival or surpass in reputation those who are far above him. Thus a commoner does not envy the king, nor does the king envy a commoner whom he is far above. Wherefore a man envies not those who are far removed from him, whether in place, time, or station, but those who are near him, and whom he strives to rival or surpass. For it is against our will that these should be in better repute than we are, and that gives rise to sorrow. On the other hand, likeness causes pleasure in so far as it is in agreement with the will.

Reply Obj. 3: A man does not strive for mastery in matters where he is very deficient; so that he does not envy one who surpasses him in such matters, unless he surpass him by little, for then it seems to him that this is not beyond him, and so he makes an effort; wherefore, if his effort fails through the other's reputation surpassing his, he grieves. Hence it is that those who love to be honored are more envious; and in like manner the faint-hearted are envious, because all things are great to them, and whatever good may befall another, they reckon that they themselves have been bested in something great. Hence it is written (Job 5:2): "Envy slayeth the little one," and Gregory says (Moral. v, 46) that "we can envy those only whom we think better in some respect than ourselves."

Reply Obj. 4: Recollection of past goods in so far as we have had them, causes pleasure; in so far as we have lost them, causes sorrow; and in so far as others have them, causes envy, because that, above all, seems to belittle our reputation. Hence the Philosopher says (Rhet. ii) that the old envy the young, and those who have spent much in order to get something, envy those who have got it by spending little, because they grieve that they have lost their goods, and that others have acquired goods.

* * * * *

SECOND ARTICLE [II-II, Q. 36, Art. 2]

Whether Envy Is a Sin?

Objection 1: It would seem that envy is not a sin. For Jerome says to Laeta about the education of her daughter (Ep. cvii): "Let her have companions, so that she may learn together with them, envy them, and be nettled when they are praised." But no one should be advised to commit a sin. Therefore envy is not a sin.

Objection 2: Further, "Envy is sorrow for another's good," as Damascene says (De Fide Orth. ii, 14). But this is sometimes praiseworthy: for it is written (Prov. 29:2): "When the wicked shall bear rule, the people shall mourn." Therefore envy is not always a sin.

Obj. 3: Further, envy denotes a kind of zeal. But there is a good zeal, according to Ps. 68:10: "The zeal of Thy house hath eaten me up." Therefore envy is not always a sin.

Obj. 4: Further, punishment is condivided with fault. But envy is a kind of punishment: for Gregory says (Moral. v, 46): "When the foul sore of envy corrupts the vanquished heart, the very exterior itself shows how forcibly the mind is urged by madness. For paleness seizes the complexion, the eyes are weighed down, the spirit is inflamed, while the limbs are chilled, there is frenzy in the heart, there is gnashing with the teeth." Therefore envy is not a sin.

On the contrary, It is written (Gal. 5:26): "Let us not be made desirous of vainglory, provoking one another, envying one another."

I answer that, As stated above (A. 1), envy is sorrow for another's good. Now this sorrow may come about in four ways. First, when a man grieves for another's good, through fear that it may cause harm either to himself, or to some other goods. This sorrow is not envy, as stated above (A. 1), and may be void of sin. Hence Gregory says (Moral. xxii, 11): "It very often happens that without charity being lost, both the destruction of an enemy rejoices us, and again his glory, without any sin of envy, saddens us, since, when he falls, we believe that some are deservedly set up, and when he prospers, we dread lest many suffer unjustly."

Secondly, we may grieve over another's good, not because he has it, but because the good which he has, we have not: and this, properly speaking, is zeal, as the Philosopher says (Rhet. ii, 9). And if this zeal be about virtuous goods, it is praiseworthy, according to 1 Cor. 14:1: "Be zealous for spiritual gifts": while, if it be about temporal goods, it may be either sinful or sinless. Thirdly, one may grieve over another's good, because he who happens to have that good is unworthy of it. Such sorrow as this cannot be occasioned by virtuous goods, which make a man righteous, but, as the Philosopher states, is about riches, and those things which can accrue to the worthy and the unworthy; and he calls this sorrow *nemesis*[1], saying that it belongs to good morals. But he says this because he considered temporal goods in themselves, in so far as they may seem great to those who look not to eternal goods: whereas, according to the teaching of faith, temporal goods that accrue to those who are unworthy, are so disposed according to God's just ordinance, either for the correction of those men, or for their condemnation, and such goods are as nothing in comparison with the goods to come, which are prepared for good men. Wherefore sorrow of this kind is forbidden in Holy Writ, according to Ps. 36:1: "Be not emulous of evil doers, nor envy

---

1   The nearest equivalent is "indignation." The use of the word "nemesis" to signify "revenge" does not represent the original Greek.

them that work iniquity," and elsewhere (Ps. 72:2, 3): "My steps had well nigh slipped, for I was envious of the wicked, when I saw the prosperity of sinners[1]." Fourthly, we grieve over a man's good, in so far as his good surpasses ours; this is envy properly speaking, and is always sinful, as also the Philosopher states (Rhet. ii, 10), because to do so is to grieve over what should make us rejoice, viz. over our neighbor's good.

Reply Obj. 1: Envy there denotes the zeal with which we ought to strive to progress with those who are better than we are.

Reply Obj. 2: This argument considers sorrow for another's good in the first sense given above.

Reply Obj. 3: Envy differs from zeal, as stated above. Hence a certain zeal may be good, whereas envy is always evil.

Reply Obj. 4: Nothing hinders a sin from being penal accidentally, as stated above (I-II, Q. 87, A. 2) when we were treating of sins.

* * * * *

THIRD ARTICLE [II-II, Q. 36, Art. 3]

Whether Envy Is a Mortal Sin?

Objection 1: It would seem that envy is not a mortal sin. For since envy is a kind of sorrow, it is a passion of the sensitive appetite. Now there is no mortal sin in the sensuality, but only in the reason, as Augustine declares (De Trin. xii, 12)[2]. Therefore envy is not a mortal sin.

Obj. 2: Further, there cannot be mortal sin in infants. But envy can be in them, for Augustine says (Confess. i): "I myself have seen and known even a baby envious, it could not speak, yet it turned pale and looked bitterly on its foster-brother." Therefore envy is not a mortal sin.

Obj. 3: Further, every mortal sin is contrary to some virtue. But envy is contrary, not to a virtue but to nemesis, which is a passion, according to the Philosopher (Rhet. ii, 9). Therefore envy is not a mortal sin.

---

[1] Douay: 'because I had a zeal on occasion of the wicked, seeing the prosperity of sinners'

[2] Cf. I-II, Q. 74, A. 4

On the contrary, It is written (Job 5:2): "Envy slayeth the little one." Now nothing slays spiritually, except mortal sin. Therefore envy is a mortal sin.

I answer that, Envy is a mortal sin, in respect of its genus. For the genus of a sin is taken from its object; and envy according to the aspect of its object is contrary to charity, whence the soul derives its spiritual life, according to 1 John 3:14: "We know that we have passed from death to life, because we love the brethren." Now the object both of charity and of envy is our neighbor's good, but by contrary movements, since charity rejoices in our neighbor's good, while envy grieves over it, as stated above (A. 1). Therefore it is evident that envy is a mortal sin in respect of its genus.

Nevertheless, as stated above (Q. 35, A. 4; I-II, Q. 72, A. 5, ad 1), in every kind of mortal sin we find certain imperfect movements in the sensuality, which are venial sins: such are the first movement of concupiscence, in the genus of adultery, and the first movement of anger, in the genus of murder, and so in the genus of envy we find sometimes even in perfect men certain first movements, which are venial sins.

Reply Obj. 1: The movement of envy in so far as it is a passion of the sensuality, is an imperfect thing in the genus of human acts, the principle of which is the reason, so that envy of that kind is not a mortal sin. The same applies to the envy of little children who have not the use of reason: wherefore the Reply to the Second Objection is manifest.

Reply Obj. 3: According to the Philosopher (Rhet. ii, 9), envy is contrary both to nemesis and to pity, but for different reasons. For it is directly contrary to pity, their principal objects being contrary to one another, since the envious man grieves over his neighbor's good, whereas the pitiful man grieves over his neighbor's evil, so that the envious have no pity, as he states in the same passage, nor is the pitiful man envious. On the other hand, envy is contrary to nemesis on the part of the man whose good grieves the envious man, for nemesis is sorrow for the good of the undeserving according to Ps. 72:3: "I was envious of the wicked, when I saw the prosperity of sinners"[1], whereas the envious grieves over the

---

[1] Douay: "because I had a zeal on occasion of the wicked, seeing the prosperity of sinners"

good of those who are deserving of it. Hence it is clear that the former contrariety is more direct than the latter. Now pity is a virtue, and an effect proper to charity: so that envy is contrary to pity and charity.

* * * * *

FOURTH ARTICLE [II-II, Q. 36, Art. 4]

Whether Envy Is a Capital Vice?

Objection 1: It would seem that envy is not a capital vice. For the capital vices are distinct from their daughters. Now envy is the daughter of vainglory; for the Philosopher says (Rhet. ii, 10) that "those who love honor and glory are more envious." Therefore envy is not a capital vice.

Obj. 2: Further, the capital vices seem to be less grave than the other vices which arise from them. For Gregory says (Moral. xxxi, 45): "The leading vices seem to worm their way into the deceived mind under some kind of pretext, but those which follow them provoke the soul to all kinds of outrage, and confuse the mind with their wild outcry." Now envy is seemingly a most grave sin, for Gregory says (Moral. v, 46): "Though in every evil thing that is done, the venom of our old enemy is infused into the heart of man, yet in this wickedness the serpent stirs his whole bowels and discharges the bane of spite fitted to enter deep into the mind." Therefore envy is not a capital sin.

Obj. 3: Further, it seems that its daughters are unfittingly assigned by Gregory (Moral. xxxi, 45), who says that from envy arise "hatred, tale-bearing, detraction, joy at our neighbor's misfortunes, and grief for his prosperity." For joy at our neighbor's misfortunes and grief for his prosperity seem to be the same as envy, as appears from what has been said above (A. 3). Therefore these should not be assigned as daughters of envy.

On the contrary stands the authority of Gregory (Moral. xxxi, 45) who states that envy is a capital sin and assigns the aforesaid daughters thereto.

I answer that, Just as sloth is grief for a Divine spiritual good, so envy is grief for our neighbor's good. Now it has been stated above (Q. 35, A. 4) that sloth is a capital vice for the reason that it incites man to do certain things, with the purpose either of avoiding sorrow or of satisfying its demands. Wherefore envy is accounted a capital vice for the same reason.

Reply Obj. 1: As Gregory says (Moral. xxxi, 45), "the capital vices are so closely akin to one another that one springs from the other. For the first offspring of pride is vainglory, which by corrupting the mind it occupies begets envy, since while it craves for the power of an empty name, it repines for fear lest another should acquire that power." Consequently the notion of a capital vice does not exclude its originating from another vice, but it demands that it should have some principal reason for being itself the origin of several kinds of sin. However it is perhaps because envy manifestly arises from vainglory, that it is not reckoned a capital sin, either by Isidore (De Summo Bono) or by Cassian (De Instit. Caenob. v, 1).

Reply Obj. 2: It does not follow from the passage quoted that envy is the greatest of sins, but that when the devil tempts us to envy, he is enticing us to that which has its chief place in his heart, for as quoted further on in the same passage, "by the envy of the devil, death came into the world" (Wis. 2:24).

There is, however, a kind of envy which is accounted among the most grievous sins, viz. envy of another's spiritual good, which envy is a sorrow for the increase of God's grace, and not merely for our neighbor's good. Hence it is accounted a sin against the Holy Ghost, because thereby a man envies, as it were, the Holy Ghost Himself, Who is glorified in His works.

Reply Obj. 3: The number of envy's daughters may be understood for the reason that in the struggle aroused by envy there is something by way of beginning, something by way of middle, and something by way of term. The beginning is that a man strives to lower another's reputation, and this either secretly, and then we have tale-bearing, or openly, and then we have detraction. The middle consists in the fact that when a man aims at defaming another, he is either able to do so, and then we have joy at another's misfortune, or he is unable, and then we have grief at another's prosperity. The term is hatred itself, because just as good which delights causes love, so does sorrow cause hatred, as stated above (Q. 34, A. 6). Grief at another's prosperity is in one way the very same as envy, when, to wit, a man grieves over another's prosperity, in so far as it gives the latter a good name, but in another way it is a daughter of envy, in so far as the envious man sees his neighbor prosper notwithstanding his efforts to prevent it. On the other hand, joy at another's misfortune is not directly the same as envy, but is a result thereof, because grief over our neighbor's good which is envy, gives rise to joy in his evil.

37. OF DISCORD, WHICH IS CONTRARY TO PEACE (In Two Articles)

We must now consider the sins contrary to peace, and first we shall consider discord which is in the heart, secondly contention, which is on the lips, thirdly, those things which consist in deeds, viz. schism, quarrelling, war, and sedition. Under the first head there are two points of inquiry:

(1) Whether discord is a sin?
(2) Whether it is a daughter of vainglory?.

* * * * *

FIRST ARTICLE [II-II, Q. 37, Art. 1]

Whether Discord Is a Sin?

Objection 1: It would seem that discord is not a sin. For to disaccord with man is to sever oneself from another's will. But this does not seem to be a sin, because God's will alone, and not our neighbor's, is the rule of our own will. Therefore discord is not a sin.

Obj. 2: Further, whoever induces another to sin, sins also himself. But it appears not to be a sin to incite others to discord, for it is written (Acts 23:6) that Paul, knowing that the one part were Sadducees, and the other Pharisees, cried out in the council: "Men brethren, I am a Pharisee, the son of Pharisees, concerning the hope and resurrection of the dead I am called in question. And when he had so said, there arose a dissension between the Pharisees and the Sadducees." Therefore discord is not a sin.

Obj. 3: Further, sin, especially mortal sin, is not to be found in a holy man. But discord is to be found even among holy men, for it is written (Acts 15:39): "There arose a dissension" between Paul and Barnabas, "so that they departed one from another." Therefore discord is not a sin, and least of all a mortal sin.

On the contrary, "Dissensions," that is, discords, are reckoned among the works of the flesh (Gal. 5:20), of which it is said afterwards (Gal. 5:21) that "they who do such things shall not obtain the kingdom of God." Now nothing, save mortal sin, excludes man from the kingdom of God. Therefore discord is a mortal sin.

I answer that, Discord is opposed to concord. Now, as stated above (Q. 29, AA. 1, 3) concord results from charity, in as much as charity directs many hearts together to one thing, which is chiefly the Divine good, secondarily, the good of our neighbor. Wherefore discord is a sin, in so far as it is opposed to this concord.

But it must be observed that this concord is destroyed by discord in two ways: first, directly; secondly, accidentally. Now, human acts and movements are said to be direct when they are according to one's intention. Wherefore a man directly disaccords with his neighbor, when he knowingly and intentionally dissents from the Divine good and his neighbor's good, to which he ought to consent. This is a mortal sin in respect of its genus, because it is contrary to charity, although the first movements of such discord are venial sins by reason of their being imperfect acts.

The accidental in human acts is that which occurs beside the intention. Hence when several intend a good pertaining to God's honor, or our neighbor's profit, while one deems a certain thing good, and another thinks contrariwise, the discord is in this case accidentally contrary to the Divine good or that of our neighbor. Such like discord is neither sinful nor against charity, unless it be accompanied by an error about things necessary to salvation, or by undue obstinacy, since it has also been stated above (Q. 29, AA. 1, 3, ad 2) that the concord which is an effect of charity, is union of wills not of opinions. It follows from this that discord is sometimes the sin of one party only, for instance, when one wills a good which the other knowingly resists; while sometimes it implies sin in both parties, as when each dissents from the other's good, and loves his own.

Reply Obj. 1: One man's will considered in itself is not the rule of another man's will; but in so far as our neighbor's will adheres to God's will, it becomes in consequence, a rule regulated according to its proper measure. Wherefore it is a sin to disaccord with such a will, because by that very fact one disaccords with the Divine rule.

Reply Obj. 2: Just as a man's will that adheres to God is a right rule, to disaccord with which is a sin, so too a man's will that is opposed to God is a perverse rule, to disaccord with which is good. Hence to cause a discord, whereby a good concord resulting from charity is destroyed, is a grave sin: wherefore it is written (Prov. 6:16): "Six things there are, which the Lord hateth, and the seventh His soul detesteth," which seventh is stated (Prov. 6:19) to be "him that soweth discord among brethren." On the other hand, to arouse a discord whereby an evil concord (i.e. concord in an evil will) is destroyed, is praiseworthy. In this way Paul was to be commended for sowing discord among those who concorded together in evil, because Our Lord also said of Himself (Matt. 10:34): "I came not to send peace, but the sword."

Reply Obj. 3: The discord between Paul and Barnabas was accidental and not direct: because each intended some good, yet the one thought one thing good, while the other thought something else, which was owing to human deficiency: for that controversy was not about things necessary to salvation. Moreover all this was ordained by Divine providence, on account of the good which would ensue.

* * * * *

SECOND ARTICLE [II-II, Q. 37, Art. 2]

Whether Discord Is a Daughter of Vainglory?

Objection 1: It would seem that discord is not a daughter of vainglory. For anger is a vice distinct from vainglory. Now discord is apparently the daughter of anger, according to Prov. 15:18: "A passionate man stirreth up strifes." Therefore it is not a daughter of vainglory.

Obj. 2: Further, Augustine expounding the words of John 7:39, "As yet the Spirit was not given," says (Tract. xxxii) "Malice severs, charity unites." Now discord is merely a separation of wills. Therefore discord arises from malice, i.e. envy, rather than from vainglory.

Obj. 3: Further, whatever gives rise to many evils, would seem to be a capital vice. Now such is discord, because Jerome in commenting on Matt. 12:25, "Every kingdom divided against itself shall be made desolate," says: "Just as concord makes small things thrive, so discord brings the greatest things to ruin." Therefore discord should itself be reckoned a capital vice, rather than a daughter of vainglory.

On the contrary stands the authority of Gregory (Moral. xxxi, 45).

I answer that, Discord denotes a certain disunion of wills, in so far, to wit, as one man's will holds fast to one thing, while the other man's will holds fast to something else. Now if a man's will holds fast to its own ground, this is due to the act that he prefers what is his own to that which belongs to others, and if he do this inordinately, it is due to pride and vainglory. Therefore discord, whereby a man holds to his own way of thinking, and departs from that of others, is reckoned to be a daughter of vainglory.

Reply Obj. 1: Strife is not the same as discord, for strife consists in external deeds, wherefore it is becoming that it should arise from anger, which incites the mind to hurt one's neighbor; whereas discord consists in a divergence in the movements of wills, which arises from pride or vainglory, for the reason given above.

Reply Obj. 2: In discord we may consider that which is the term wherefrom, i.e. another's will from which we recede, and in this respect it arises from envy; and again we may consider that which is the term whither, i.e. something of our own to which we cling, and in this respect it is caused by vainglory. And since in every moment the term whither is more important than the term wherefrom (because the end is of more account than the beginning), discord is accounted a daughter of vainglory rather than of envy, though it may arise from both for different reasons, as stated.

Reply Obj. 3: The reason why concord makes small things thrive, while discord brings the greatest to ruin, is because "the more united a force is, the stronger it is, while the more disunited it is the weaker it becomes" (De Causis xvii). Hence it is evident that this is part of the proper effect of discord which is a disunion of wills, and in no way indicates that other vices arise from discord, as though it were a capital vice.

38. OF CONTENTION (In Two Articles)

We must now consider contention, in respect of which there are two points of inquiry:

(1) Whether contention is a mortal sin?
(2) Whether it is a daughter of vainglory?.

* * * * *

FIRST ARTICLE [II-II, Q. 38, Art. 1]

Whether Contention Is a Mortal Sin?

Objection 1: It would seem that contention is not a mortal sin. For there is no mortal sin in spiritual men: and yet contention is to be found in them, according to Luke 22:24: "And there was also a strife amongst" the disciples of Jesus, "which of them should . . . be the greatest." Therefore contention is not a mortal sin.

Obj. 2: Further, no well disposed man should be pleased that his neighbor commit a mortal sin. But the Apostle says (Phil. 1:17): "Some out of contention preach Christ," and afterwards he says (Phil. 1:18): "In this also I rejoice, yea, and will rejoice." Therefore contention is not a mortal sin.

Obj. 3: Further, it happens that people contend either in the courts or in disputations, without any spiteful purpose, and with a good intention, as, for example, those who contend by disputing with heretics. Hence a gloss on 1 Kings 14:1, "It came to pass one day," etc. says: "Catholics do not raise contentions with heretics, unless they are first challenged to dispute." Therefore contention is not a mortal sin.

Obj. 4: Further, Job seems to have contended with God, according to Job 39:32: "Shall he that contendeth with God be so easily silenced?" And yet Job was not guilty of mortal sin, since the Lord said of him (Job 42:7): "You have not spoken the thing that is right before me, as my servant Job hath." Therefore contention is not always a mortal sin.

On the contrary, It is against the precept of the Apostle who says (2 Tim. 2:14): "Contend not in words." Moreover (Gal. 5:20) contention is included among the works of the flesh, and as stated there (Gal. 5:21) "they who do such things shall not obtain the kingdom of God." Now whatever excludes a man from the kingdom of God and is against a precept, is a mortal sin. Therefore contention is a mortal sin.

I answer that, To contend is to tend against some one. Wherefore just as discord denotes a contrariety of wills, so contention signifies contrariety of speech. For this reason when a man contrasts various contrary things in a speech, this is called *contentio,* which Tully calls one of the rhetorical colors (De Rhet. ad Heren. iv), where he says that "it consists in developing a speech from contrary things," for instance: "Adulation has a pleasant beginning, and a most bitter end."

Now contrariety of speech may be looked at in two ways: first with regard to the intention of the contentious party, secondly, with regard to the manner of contending. As to the intention, we must consider whether he contends against the truth, and then he is to be blamed, or against falsehood, and then he should be praised. As to the manner, we must consider whether his manner of contending is in keeping with the persons and the matter in dispute, for then it would be praiseworthy, hence Tully says (De Rhet. ad Heren. iii) that "contention is a sharp speech suitable for proof and refutation"—or whether it exceeds the demands of the persons and matter in dispute, in which case it is blameworthy.

Accordingly if we take contention as denoting a disclaimer of the truth and an inordinate manner, it is a mortal sin. Thus Ambrose[1] defines contention: "Contention is a disclaimer of the truth with clamorous confidence." If, however, contention denote a disavowal of what is false, with the proper measure of acrimony, it is praiseworthy: whereas, if it denote a disavowal of falsehood, together with an inordinate manner, it can be a venial sin, unless the contention be conducted so inordinately, as to give scandal to others. Hence the Apostle after saying (2 Tim. 2:14): "Contend not in words," adds, "for it is to no profit, but to the subverting of the hearers."

Reply Obj. 1: The disciples of Christ contended together, not with the intention of disclaiming the truth, since each one stood up for what he thought was true. Yet there was inordinateness in their contention, because they contended about a matter which they ought not to have contended about, viz. the primacy of honor;

---

[1] Cf. Gloss. Ord. in Rom. i, 29

for they were not spiritual men as yet, as a gloss says on the same passage; and for this reason Our Lord checked them.

Reply Obj. 2: Those who preached Christ "out of contention," were to be blamed, because, although they did not gainsay the truth of faith, but preached it, yet they did gainsay the truth, by the fact that they thought they would "raise affliction" to the Apostle who was preaching the truth of faith. Hence the Apostle rejoiced not in their contention, but in the fruit that would result therefrom, namely that Christ would be made known—since evil is sometimes the occasion of good results.

Reply Obj. 3: Contention is complete and is a mortal sin when, in contending before a judge, a man gainsays the truth of justice, or in a disputation, intends to impugn the true doctrine. In this sense Catholics do not contend against heretics, but the reverse. But when, whether in court or in a disputation, it is incomplete, i.e. in respect of the acrimony of speech, it is not always a mortal sin.

Reply Obj. 4: Contention here denotes an ordinary dispute. For Job had said (13:3): "I will speak to the Almighty, and I desire to reason with God": yet he intended not to impugn the truth, but to defend it, and in seeking the truth thus, he had no wish to be inordinate in mind or in speech.

* * * * *

SECOND ARTICLE [II-II, Q. 38, Art. 2]

Whether Contention Is a Daughter of Vainglory?

Objection 1: It would seem that contention is not a daughter of vainglory. For contention is akin to zeal, wherefore it is written (1 Cor. 3:3): "Whereas there is among you zeal [Douay: 'envying'] and contention, are you not carnal, and walk according to men?" Now zeal pertains to envy. Therefore contention arises rather from envy.

Obj. 2: Further, contention is accompanied by raising of the voice. But the voice is raised on account of anger, as Gregory declares (Moral. xxxi, 14). Therefore contention too arises from anger.

Obj. 3: Further, among other things knowledge seems to be the matter of pride and vainglory, according to 1 Cor. 8:1: "Knowledge puffeth up." Now contention is often due to lack of knowledge, and by knowledge we do not impugn the truth, we know it. Therefore contention is not a daughter of vainglory.

On the contrary stands the authority of Gregory (Moral. xxxi, 14).

I answer that, As stated above (Q. 37, A. 2), discord is a daughter of vainglory, because each of the disaccording parties clings to his own opinion, rather than acquiesce with the other. Now it is proper to pride and vainglory to seek one's own glory. And just as people are discordant when they hold to their own opinion in their hearts, so are they contentious when each defends his own opinion by words. Consequently contention is reckoned a daughter of vainglory for the same reason as discord.

Reply Obj. 1: Contention, like discord, is akin to envy in so far as a man severs himself from the one with whom he is discordant, or with whom he contends, but in so far as a contentious man holds to something, it is akin to pride and vainglory, because, to wit, he clings to his own opinion, as stated above (Q. 37, A. 2, ad 1).

Reply Obj. 2: The contention of which we are speaking puts on a loud voice, for the purpose of impugning the truth, so that it is not the chief part of contention. Hence it does not follow that contention arises from the same source as the raising of the voice.

Reply Obj. 3: Pride and vainglory are occasioned chiefly by goods even those that are contrary to them, for instance, when a man is proud of his humility: for when a thing arises in this way, it does so not directly but accidentally, in which way nothing hinders one contrary from arising out of another. Hence there is no reason why the per se and direct effects of pride or vainglory, should not result from the contraries of those things which are the occasion of pride.

39. OF SCHISM (In Four Articles)

We must now consider the vices contrary to peace, which belong to deeds: such are schism, strife, sedition, and war. In the first place, then, about schism, there are four points of inquiry:

(1) Whether schism is a special sin?
(2) Whether it is graver than unbelief?

(3) Of the power exercised by schismatics;
(4) Of the punishment inflicted on them.

* * * * *

FIRST ARTICLE [II-II, Q. 39, Art. 1]

Whether Schism Is a Special Sin?

Objection 1: It would seem that schism is not a special sin. For "schism," as Pope Pelagius I says (Epist. ad Victor. et Pancrat.), "denotes a division." But every sin causes a division, according to Isa. 59: "Your sins have divided between you and your God." Therefore schism is not a special sin.

Obj. 2: Further, a man is apparently a schismatic if he disobeys the Church. But every sin makes a man disobey the commandments of the Church, because sin, according to Ambrose (De Parad. viii) "is disobedience against the heavenly commandments." Therefore every sin is a schism.

Obj. 3: Further, heresy also divides a man from the unity of faith. If, therefore, the word schism denotes a division, it would seem not to differ, as a special sin, from the sin of unbelief.

On the contrary, Augustine (Contra Faust. xx, 3; Contra Crescon. ii, 4) distinguishes between schism and heresy, for he says that a "schismatic is one who holds the same faith, and practises the same worship, as others, and takes pleasure in the mere disunion of the community, whereas a heretic is one who holds another faith from that of the Catholic Church." Therefore schism is not a generic sin.

I answer that, As Isidore says (Etym. viii, 3), schism takes its name "from being a scission of minds," and scission is opposed to unity. Wherefore the sin of schism is one that is directly and essentially opposed to unity. For in the moral, as in the physical order, the species is not constituted by that which is accidental. Now, in the moral order, the essential is that which is intended, and that which results beside the intention, is, as it were, accidental. Hence the sin of schism is, properly speaking, a special sin, for the reason that the schismatic intends to sever himself from that unity which is the effect of charity: because charity unites not only one person to another with the bond of spiritual love, but also the whole Church in unity of spirit.

Accordingly schismatics properly so called are those who, wilfully and intentionally separate themselves from the unity of the Church; for this is the chief unity, and the particular unity of several individuals among themselves is subordinate to the unity of the Church, even as the mutual adaptation of each member of a natural body is subordinate to the unity of the whole body. Now the unity of the Church consists in two things; namely, in the mutual connection or communion of the members of the Church, and again in the subordination of all the members of the Church to the one head, according to Col. 2:18, 19: "Puffed up by the sense of his flesh, and not holding the Head, from which the whole body, by joints and bands, being supplied with nourishment and compacted, groweth unto the increase of God." Now this Head is Christ Himself, Whose viceregent in the Church is the Sovereign Pontiff. Wherefore schismatics are those who refuse to submit to the Sovereign Pontiff, and to hold communion with those members of the Church who acknowledge his supremacy.

Reply Obj. 1: The division between man and God that results from sin is not intended by the sinner: it happens beside his intention as a result of his turning inordinately to a mutable good, and so it is not schism properly so called.

Reply Obj. 2: The essence of schism consists in rebelliously disobeying the commandments: and I say "rebelliously," since a schismatic both obstinately scorns the commandments of the Church, and refuses to submit to her judgment. But every sinner does not do this, wherefore not every sin is a schism.

Reply Obj. 3: Heresy and schism are distinguished in respect of those things to which each is opposed essentially and directly. For heresy is essentially opposed to faith, while schism is essentially opposed to the unity of ecclesiastical charity. Wherefore just as faith and charity are different virtues, although whoever lacks faith lacks charity, so too schism and heresy are different vices, although whoever is a heretic is also a schismatic, but not conversely. This is what Jerome says in his commentary on the Epistle to the Galatians[1]: "I consider the difference between schism and heresy to be that heresy holds false doctrine while schism severs a man from the Church." Nevertheless, just as the loss of charity is the

---

1   In Ep. ad Tit. iii, 10

road to the loss of faith, according to 1 Tim. 1:6: "From which things," i.e. charity and the like, "some going astray, are turned aside into vain babbling," so too, schism is the road to heresy. Wherefore Jerome adds (In Ep. ad Tit. iii, 10) that "at the outset it is possible, in a certain respect, to find a difference between schism and heresy: yet there is no schism that does not devise some heresy for itself, that it may appear to have had a reason for separating from the Church.".

* * * * *

SECOND ARTICLE [II-II, Q. 39, Art. 2]

Whether Schism Is a Graver Sin Than Unbelief?

Objection 1: It would seem that schism is a graver sin than unbelief. For the graver sin meets with a graver punishment, according to Deut. 25:2: "According to the measure of the sin shall the measure also of the stripes be." Now we find the sin of schism punished more severely than even the sin of unbelief or idolatry: for we read (Ex. 32:28) that some were slain by the swords of their fellow men on account of idolatry: whereas of the sin of schism we read (Num. 16:30): "If the Lord do a new thing, and the earth opening her mouth swallow them down, and all things that belong to them, and they go down alive into hell, you shall know that they have blasphemed the Lord God." Moreover the ten tribes who were guilty of schism in revolting from the rule of David were most severely punished (4 Kings 17). Therefore the sin of schism is graver than the sin of unbelief.

Obj. 2: Further, "The good of the multitude is greater and more godlike than the good of the individual," as the Philosopher states (Ethic. i, 2). Now schism is opposed to the good of the multitude, namely, ecclesiastical unity, whereas unbelief is contrary to the particular good of one man, namely the faith of an individual. Therefore it seems that schism is a graver sin than unbelief.

Obj. 3: Further, a greater good is opposed to a greater evil, according to the Philosopher (Ethic. viii, 10). Now schism is opposed to charity, which is a greater virtue than faith to which unbelief is opposed, as shown above (Q. 10, A. 2; Q. 23, A. 6). Therefore schism is a graver sin than unbelief.

On the contrary, That which results from an addition to something else surpasses that thing either in good or in evil. Now heresy results from something being added to schism, for it adds corrupt doctrine, as Jerome declares in the passage quoted above (A. 1, ad 3). Therefore schism is a less grievous sin than unbelief.

I answer that, The gravity of a sin can be considered in two ways: first, according to the species of that sin, secondly, according to its circumstances. And since particular circumstances are infinite in number, so too they can be varied in an infinite number of ways: wherefore if one were to ask in general which of two sins is the graver, the question must be understood to refer to the gravity derived from the sin's genus. Now the genus or species of a sin is taken from its object, as shown above (I-II, Q. 72, A. 1; I-II, Q. 73, A. 3). Wherefore the sin which is opposed to the greater good is, in respect of its genus, more grievous, for instance a sin committed against God is graver than a sin committed against one's neighbor.

Now it is evident that unbelief is a sin committed against God Himself, according as He is Himself the First Truth, on which faith is founded; whereas schism is opposed to ecclesiastical unity, which is a participated good, and a lesser good than God Himself. Wherefore it is manifest that the sin of unbelief is generically more grievous than the sin of schism, although it may happen that a particular schismatic sins more grievously than a particular unbeliever, either because his contempt is greater, or because his sin is a source of greater danger, or for some similar reason.

Reply Obj. 1: It had already been declared to that people by the law which they had received that there was one God, and that no other God was to be worshipped by them; and the same had been confirmed among them by many kinds of signs. Consequently there was no need for those who sinned against this faith by falling into idolatry, to be punished in an unwonted manner: it was enough that they should be punished in the usual way. On the other hand, it was not so well known among them that Moses was always to be their ruler, and so it behooved those who rebelled against his authority to be punished in a miraculous and unwonted manner.

We may also reply by saying that the sin of schism was sometimes more severely punished in that people, because they were inclined to seditions and schisms. For it is written (1 Esdra 4:15): "This city since days gone by has rebelled against its kings:

and seditions and wars were raised therein[1]." Now sometimes a more severe punishment is inflicted for an habitual sin (as stated above, I-II, Q. 105, A. 2, ad 9), because punishments are medicines intended to keep man away from sin: so that where there is greater proneness to sin, a more severe punishment ought to be inflicted. As regards the ten tribes, they were punished not only for the sin of schism, but also for that of idolatry as stated in the passage quoted.

Reply Obj. 2: Just as the good of the multitude is greater than the good of a unit in that multitude, so is it less than the extrinsic good to which that multitude is directed, even as the good of a rank in the army is less than the good of the commander-in-chief. In like manner the good of ecclesiastical unity, to which schism is opposed, is less than the good of Divine truth, to which unbelief is opposed.

Reply Obj. 3: Charity has two objects; one is its principal object and is the Divine goodness, the other is its secondary object and is our neighbor's good. Now schism and other sins against our neighbor, are opposed to charity in respect of its secondary good, which is less than the object of faith, for this is God Himself; and so these sins are less grievous than unbelief. On the other hand, hatred of God, which is opposed to charity in respect of its principal object, is not less grievous than unbelief. Nevertheless of all sins committed by man against his neighbor, the sin of schism would seem to be the greatest, because it is opposed to the spiritual good of the multitude.

* * * * *

THIRD ARTICLE [II-II, Q. 39, Art. 3]

Whether Schismatics Have Any Power?

Objection 1: It would seem that schismatics have some power. For Augustine says (Contra Donat. i, 1): "Just as those who come back to the Church after being baptized, are not baptized again, so those who return after being ordained, are not ordained again."

---

[1] Vulg.: 'This city is a rebellious city, and hurtful to the kings and provinces, and ... wars were raised therein of old'

Now Order is a kind of power. Therefore schismatics have some power since they retain their Orders.

Obj. 2: Further, Augustine says (De Unico Bapt.[1]): "One who is separated can confer a sacrament even as he can have it." But the power of conferring a sacrament is a very great power. Therefore schismatics who are separated from the Church, have a spiritual power.

Obj. 3: Further, Pope Urban II[2] says: "We command that persons consecrated by bishops who were themselves consecrated according to the Catholic rite, but have separated themselves by schism from the Roman Church, should be received mercifully and that their Orders should be acknowledged, when they return to the unity of the Church, provided they be of commendable life and knowledge." But this would not be so, unless spiritual power were retained by schismatics. Therefore schismatics have spiritual power.

On the contrary, Cyprian says in a letter (Ep. lii, quoted vii, qu. 1, can. Novatianus): "He who observes neither unity of spirit nor the concord of peace, and severs himself from the bonds of the Church, and from the fellowship of her priests, cannot have episcopal power or honor."

I answer that, Spiritual power is twofold, the one sacramental, the other a power of jurisdiction. The sacramental power is one that is conferred by some kind of consecration. Now all the consecrations of the Church are immovable so long as the consecrated thing remains: as appears even in inanimate things, since an altar, once consecrated, is not consecrated again unless it has been broken up. Consequently such a power as this remains, as to its essence, in the man who has received it by consecration, as long as he lives, even if he fall into schism or heresy: and this is proved from the fact that if he come back to the Church, he is not consecrated anew. Since, however, the lower power ought not to exercise its act, except in so far as it is moved by the higher power, as may be seen also in the physical order, it follows that such persons lose the use of their power, so that it is not lawful for them to use it. Yet if they use it, this power has its effect in sacramental acts, because therein man acts only as God's instrument, so that sacramental effects are

---

[1] De Bap. contra Donat. vi, 5
[2] Council of Piacenza, cap. x; cf. Can. Ordinationes, ix, qu. 1

not precluded on account of any fault whatever in the person who confers the sacrament.

On the other hand, the power of jurisdiction is that which is conferred by a mere human appointment. Such a power as this does not adhere to the recipient immovably: so that it does not remain in heretics and schismatics; and consequently they neither absolve nor excommunicate, nor grant indulgence, nor do anything of the kind, and if they do, it is invalid.

Accordingly when it is said that such like persons have no spiritual power, it is to be understood as referring either to the second power, or if it be referred to the first power, not as referring to the essence of the power, but to its lawful use.

This suffices for the Replies to the Objections.

* * * * *

FOURTH ARTICLE [II-II, Q. 39, Art. 4]

Whether It Is Right That Schismatics Should Be Punished with Excommunication?

Objection 1: It would seem that schismatics are not rightly punished with excommunication. For excommunication deprives a man chiefly of a share in the sacraments. But Augustine says (Contra Donat. vi, 5) that "Baptism can be received from a schismatic." Therefore it seems that excommunication is not a fitting punishment for schismatics.

Obj. 2: Further, it is the duty of Christ's faithful to lead back those who have gone astray, wherefore it is written against certain persons (Ezech. 34:4): "That which was driven away you have not brought again, neither have you sought that which was lost." Now schismatics are more easily brought back by such as may hold communion with them. Therefore it seems that they ought not to be excommunicated.

Obj. 3: Further, a double punishment is not inflicted for one and the same sin, according to Nahum 1:9: "God will not judge the same twice"[1] Now some receive a temporal punishment for the sin

---

1 Septuagint version.

of schism, according to 23, qu. 5[1], where it is stated: "Both divine and earthly laws have laid down that those who are severed from the unity of the Church, and disturb her peace, must be punished by the secular power." Therefore they ought not to be punished with excommunication.

On the contrary, It is written (Num. 16:26): "Depart from the tents of these wicked men," those, to wit, who had caused the schism, "and touch nothing of theirs, lest you be involved in their sins."

I answer that, According to Wis. 11:11, "By what things a man sinneth, by the same also he should be punished" [Vulg.: 'he is tormented']. Now a schismatic, as shown above (A. 1), commits a twofold sin: first by separating himself from communion with the members of the Church, and in this respect the fitting punishment for schismatics is that they be excommunicated. Secondly, they refuse submission to the head of the Church, wherefore, since they are unwilling to be controlled by the Church's spiritual power, it is just that they should be compelled by the secular power.

Reply Obj. 1: It is not lawful to receive Baptism from a schismatic, save in a case of necessity, since it is better for a man to quit this life, marked with the sign of Christ, no matter from whom he may receive it, whether from a Jew or a pagan, than deprived of that mark, which is bestowed in Baptism.

Reply Obj. 2: Excommunication does not forbid the intercourse whereby a person by salutary admonitions leads back to the unity of the Church those who are separated from her. Indeed this very separation brings them back somewhat, because through confusion at their separation, they are sometimes led to do penance.

Reply Obj. 3: The punishments of the present life are medicinal, and therefore when one punishment does not suffice to compel a man, another is added: just as physicians employ several bod[il]y medicines when one has no effect. In like manner the Church, when excommunication does not sufficiently restrain certain men, employs the compulsion of the secular arm. If, however, one punishment suffices, another should not be employed.

---

1 Gratianus, Decretum, P. II, causa XXIII, qu. 5, can. 44, Quali nos (RP I, 943)

40. OF WAR (In Four Articles)

We must now consider war, under which head there are four points of inquiry:

(1) Whether some kind of war is lawful?
(2) Whether it is lawful for clerics to fight?
(3) Whether it is lawful for belligerents to lay ambushes?
(4) Whether it is lawful to fight on holy days?.

* * * * *

FIRST ARTICLE [II-II, Q. 40, Art. 1]

Whether It Is Always Sinful to Wage War?

Objection 1: It would seem that it is always sinful to wage war. Because punishment is not inflicted except for sin. Now those who wage war are threatened by Our Lord with punishment, according to Matt. 26:52: "All that take the sword shall perish with the sword." Therefore all wars are unlawful.

Obj. 2: Further, whatever is contrary to a Divine precept is a sin. But war is contrary to a Divine precept, for it is written (Matt. 5:39): "But I say to you not to resist evil"; and (Rom. 12:19): "Not revenging yourselves, my dearly beloved, but give place unto wrath." Therefore war is always sinful.

Obj. 3: Further, nothing, except sin, is contrary to an act of virtue. But war is contrary to peace. Therefore war is always a sin.

Obj. 4: Further, the exercise of a lawful thing is itself lawful, as is evident in scientific exercises. But warlike exercises which take place in tournaments are forbidden by the Church, since those who are slain in these trials are deprived of ecclesiastical burial. Therefore it seems that war is a sin in itself.

On the contrary, Augustine says in a sermon on the son of the centurion[1]: "If the Christian Religion forbade war altogether, those who sought salutary advice in the Gospel would rather have been counselled to cast aside their arms, and to give up soldiering

---

1   Ep. ad Marcel. cxxxviii

altogether. On the contrary, they were told: 'Do violence to no man . . . and be content with your pay'[1]. If he commanded them to be content with their pay, he did not forbid soldiering."

I answer that, In order for a war to be just, three things are necessary. First, the authority of the sovereign by whose command the war is to be waged. For it is not the business of a private individual to declare war, because he can seek for redress of his rights from the tribunal of his superior. Moreover it is not the business of a private individual to summon together the people, which has to be done in wartime. And as the care of the common weal is committed to those who are in authority, it is their business to watch over the common weal of the city, kingdom or province subject to them. And just as it is lawful for them to have recourse to the sword in defending that common weal against internal disturbances, when they punish evil-doers, according to the words of the Apostle (Rom. 13:4): "He beareth not the sword in vain: for he is God's minister, an avenger to execute wrath upon him that doth evil"; so too, it is their business to have recourse to the sword of war in defending the common weal against external enemies. Hence it is said to those who are in authority (Ps. 81:4): "Rescue the poor: and deliver the needy out of the hand of the sinner"; and for this reason Augustine says (Contra Faust. xxii, 75): "The natural order conducive to peace among mortals demands that the power to declare and counsel war should be in the hands of those who hold the supreme authority."

Secondly, a just cause is required, namely that those who are attacked, should be attacked because they deserve it on account of some fault. Wherefore Augustine says (QQ. in Hept., qu. x, super Jos.): "A just war is wont to be described as one that avenges wrongs, when a nation or state has to be punished, for refusing to make amends for the wrongs inflicted by its subjects, or to restore what it has seized unjustly."

Thirdly, it is necessary that the belligerents should have a rightful intention, so that they intend the advancement of good, or the avoidance of evil. Hence Augustine says (De Verb. Dom.[2]):

---

[1] Luke 3:14
[2] The words quoted are to be found not in St. Augustine's works, but Can. Apud. Caus. xxiii, qu. 1

"True religion looks upon as peaceful those wars that are waged not for motives of aggrandizement, or cruelty, but with the object of securing peace, of punishing evil-doers, and of uplifting the good." For it may happen that the war is declared by the legitimate authority, and for a just cause, and yet be rendered unlawful through a wicked intention. Hence Augustine says (Contra Faust. xxii, 74): "The passion for inflicting harm, the cruel thirst for vengeance, an unpacific and relentless spirit, the fever of revolt, the lust of power, and such like things, all these are rightly condemned in war."

Reply Obj. 1: As Augustine says (Contra Faust. xxii, 70): "To take the sword is to arm oneself in order to take the life of anyone, without the command or permission of superior or lawful authority." On the other hand, to have recourse to the sword (as a private person) by the authority of the sovereign or judge, or (as a public person) through zeal for justice, and by the authority, so to speak, of God, is not to "take the sword," but to use it as commissioned by another, wherefore it does not deserve punishment. And yet even those who make sinful use of the sword are not always slain with the sword, yet they always perish with their own sword, because, unless they repent, they are punished eternally for their sinful use of the sword.

Reply Obj. 2: Such like precepts, as Augustine observes (De Serm. Dom. in Monte i, 19), should always be borne in readiness of mind, so that we be ready to obey them, and, if necessary, to refrain from resistance or self-defense. Nevertheless it is necessary sometimes for a man to act otherwise for the common good, or for the good of those with whom he is fighting. Hence Augustine says (Ep. ad Marcellin. cxxxviii): "Those whom we have to punish with a kindly severity, it is necessary to handle in many ways against their will. For when we are stripping a man of the lawlessness of sin, it is good for him to be vanquished, since nothing is more hopeless than the happiness of sinners, whence arises a guilty impunity, and an evil will, like an internal enemy."

Reply Obj. 3: Those who wage war justly aim at peace, and so they are not opposed to peace, except to the evil peace, which Our Lord "came not to send upon earth" (Matt. 10:34). Hence Augustine says (Ep. ad Bonif. clxxxix): "We do not seek peace in order to be at war, but we go to war that we may have peace. Be peaceful, therefore, in warring, so that you may vanquish those whom you war against, and bring them to the prosperity of peace."

Reply Obj. 4: Manly exercises in warlike feats of arms are not all forbidden, but those which are inordinate and perilous, and end in slaying or plundering. In olden times warlike exercises presented no such danger, and hence they were called "exercises of arms" or "bloodless wars," as Jerome states in an epistle[1].

* * * * *

SECOND ARTICLE [II-II, Q. 40, Art. 2]

Whether It Is Lawful for Clerics and Bishops to Fight?

Objection 1: It would seem lawful for clerics and bishops to fight. For, as stated above (A. 1), wars are lawful and just in so far as they protect the poor and the entire common weal from suffering at the hands of the foe. Now this seems to be above all the duty of prelates, for Gregory says (Hom. in Ev. xiv): "The wolf comes upon the sheep, when any unjust and rapacious man oppresses those who are faithful and humble. But he who was thought to be the shepherd, and was not, leaveth the sheep, and flieth, for he fears lest the wolf hurt him, and dares not stand up against his injustice." Therefore it is lawful for prelates and clerics to fight.

Obj. 2: Further, Pope Leo IV writes (xxiii, qu. 8, can. Igitur): "As untoward tidings had frequently come from the Saracen side, some said that the Saracens would come to the port of Rome secretly and covertly; for which reason we commanded our people to gather together, and ordered them to go down to the seashore." Therefore it is lawful for bishops to fight.

Obj. 3: Further, apparently, it comes to the same whether a man does a thing himself, or consents to its being done by another, according to Rom. 1:32: "They who do such things, are worthy of death, and not only they that do them, but they also that consent to them that do them." Now those, above all, seem to consent to a thing, who induce others to do it. But it is lawful for bishops and clerics to induce others to fight: for it is written (xxiii, qu. 8, can. Hortatu) that Charles went to war with the Lombards at the

---

1 Reference incorrect: cf. Veget., De Re Milit. i

instance and entreaty of Adrian, bishop of Rome. Therefore they also are allowed to fight.

Obj. 4: Further, whatever is right and meritorious in itself, is lawful for prelates and clerics. Now it is sometimes right and meritorious to make war, for it is written (xxiii, qu. 8, can. Omni timore) that if "a man die for the true faith, or to save his country, or in defense of Christians, God will give him a heavenly reward." Therefore it is lawful for bishops and clerics to fight.

On the contrary, It was said to Peter as representing bishops and clerics (Matt. 16:52): "Put up again thy sword into the scabbard [Vulg.: 'its place'][1]." Therefore it is not lawful for them to fight.

I answer that, Several things are requisite for the good of a human society: and a number of things are done better and quicker by a number of persons than by one, as the Philosopher observes (Polit. i, 1), while certain occupations are so inconsistent with one another, that they cannot be fittingly exercised at the same time; wherefore those who are deputed to important duties are forbidden to occupy themselves with things of small importance. Thus according to human laws, soldiers who are deputed to warlike pursuits are forbidden to engage in commerce[2].

Now warlike pursuits are altogether incompatible with the duties of a bishop and a cleric, for two reasons. The first reason is a general one, because, to wit, warlike pursuits are full of unrest, so that they hinder the mind very much from the contemplation of Divine things, the praise of God, and prayers for the people, which belong to the duties of a cleric. Wherefore just as commercial enterprises are forbidden to clerics, because they unsettle the mind too much, so too are warlike pursuits, according to 2 Tim. 2:4: "No man being a soldier to God, entangleth himself with secular business." The second reason is a special one, because, to wit, all the clerical Orders are directed to the ministry of the altar, on which the Passion of Christ is represented sacramentally, according to 1 Cor. 11:26: "As often as you shall eat this bread, and drink the chalice, you shall show the death of the Lord, until He come." Wherefore it is unbecoming for them to slay or shed blood, and it is

---

[1] "Scabbard" is the reading in John 18:11
[2] Cod. xii, 35, De Re Milit.

more fitting that they should be ready to shed their own blood for Christ, so as to imitate in deed what they portray in their ministry. For this reason it has been decreed that those who shed blood, even without sin, become irregular. Now no man who has a certain duty to perform, can lawfully do that which renders him unfit for that duty. Wherefore it is altogether unlawful for clerics to fight, because war is directed to the shedding of blood.

Reply Obj. 1: Prelates ought to withstand not only the wolf who brings spiritual death upon the flock, but also the pillager and the oppressor who work bodily harm; not, however, by having recourse themselves to material arms, but by means of spiritual weapons, according to the saying of the Apostle (2 Cor. 10:4): "The weapons of our warfare are not carnal, but mighty through God." Such are salutary warnings, devout prayers, and, for those who are obstinate, the sentence of excommunication.

Reply Obj. 2: Prelates and clerics may, by the authority of their superiors, take part in wars, not indeed by taking up arms themselves, but by affording spiritual help to those who fight justly, by exhorting and absolving them, and by other like spiritual helps. Thus in the Old Testament (Joshua 6:4) the priests were commanded to sound the sacred trumpets in the battle. It was for this purpose that bishops or clerics were first allowed to go to the front: and it is an abuse of this permission, if any of them take up arms themselves.

Reply Obj. 3: As stated above (Q. 23, A. 4, ad 2) every power, art or virtue that regards the end, has to dispose that which is directed to the end. Now, among the faithful, carnal wars should be considered as having for their end the Divine spiritual good to which clerics are deputed. Wherefore it is the duty of clerics to dispose and counsel other men to engage in just wars. For they are forbidden to take up arms, not as though it were a sin, but because such an occupation is unbecoming their personality.

Reply Obj. 4: Although it is meritorious to wage a just war, nevertheless it is rendered unlawful for clerics, by reason of their being deputed to works more meritorious still. Thus the marriage act may be meritorious; and yet it becomes reprehensible in those who have vowed virginity, because they are bound to a yet greater good.

* * * * *

THIRD ARTICLE [II-II, Q., 40, Art. 3]

Whether It Is Lawful to Lay Ambushes in War?

Objection 1: It would seem that it is unlawful to lay ambushes in war. For it is written (Deut. 16:20): "Thou shalt follow justly after that which is just." But ambushes, since they are a kind of deception, seem to pertain to injustice. Therefore it is unlawful to lay ambushes even in a just war.

Obj. 2: Further, ambushes and deception seem to be opposed to faithfulness even as lies are. But since we are bound to keep faith with all men, it is wrong to lie to anyone, as Augustine states (Contra Mend. xv). Therefore, as one is bound to keep faith with one's enemy, as Augustine states (Ep. ad Bonif. clxxxix), it seems that it is unlawful to lay ambushes for one's enemies.

Obj. 3: Further, it is written (Matt. 7:12): "Whatsoever you would that men should do to you, do you also to them": and we ought to observe this in all our dealings with our neighbor. Now our enemy is our neighbor. Therefore, since no man wishes ambushes or deceptions to be prepared for himself, it seems that no one ought to carry on war by laying ambushes.

On the contrary, Augustine says (QQ. in Hept. qu. x super Jos): "Provided the war be just, it is no concern of justice whether it be carried on openly or by ambushes": and he proves this by the authority of the Lord, Who commanded Joshua to lay ambushes for the city of Hai (Joshua 8:2).

I answer that, The object of laying ambushes is in order to deceive the enemy. Now a man may be deceived by another's word or deed in two ways. First, through being told something false, or through the breaking of a promise, and this is always unlawful. No one ought to deceive the enemy in this way, for there are certain "rights of war and covenants, which ought to be observed even among enemies," as Ambrose states (De Officiis i).

Secondly, a man may be deceived by what we say or do, because we do not declare our purpose or meaning to him. Now we are not always bound to do this, since even in the Sacred Doctrine many things have to be concealed, especially from unbelievers, lest they deride it, according to Matt. 7:6: "Give not that which is holy, to dogs." Wherefore much more ought the plan of campaign to be hidden from the enemy. For this reason among other things that a soldier has to learn is the art of concealing his purpose lest it come to the enemy's knowledge, as stated in the Book on *Strategy*[1] by Frontinus. Such like concealment is what is meant by an ambush which may be lawfully employed in a just war.

Nor can these ambushes be properly called deceptions, nor are they contrary to justice or to a well-ordered will. For a man would have an inordinate will if he were unwilling that others should hide anything from him.

This suffices for the Replies to the Objections.

* * * * *

FOURTH ARTICLE [II-II, Q. 40, Art. 4]

Whether It Is Lawful to Fight on Holy Days?

Objection 1: It would seem unlawful to fight on holy days. For holy days are instituted that we may give our time to the things of God. Hence they are included in the keeping of the Sabbath prescribed Ex. 20:8: for "sabbath" is interpreted "rest." But wars are full of unrest. Therefore by no means is it lawful to fight on holy days.

Obj. 2: Further, certain persons are reproached (Isa. 58:3) because on fast-days they exacted what was owing to them, were guilty of strife, and of smiting with the fist. Much more, therefore, is it unlawful to fight on holy days.

Obj. 3: Further, no ill deed should be done to avoid temporal harm. But fighting on a holy day seems in itself to be an ill deed. Therefore no one should fight on a holy day even through the need of avoiding temporal harm.

On the contrary, It is written (1 Mac. 2:41): The Jews rightly determined ... saying: "Whosoever shall come up against us to fight on the Sabbath-day, we will fight against him."

I answer that, The observance of holy days is no hindrance to those things which are ordained to man's safety, even that of his body. Hence Our Lord argued with the Jews, saying (John 7:23): "Are you angry at Me because I have healed the whole man on the Sabbath-day?" Hence physicians may lawfully

---

[1] Stratagematum i, 1

attend to their patients on holy days. Now there is much more reason for safeguarding the common weal (whereby many are saved from being slain, and innumerable evils both temporal and spiritual prevented), than the bodily safety of an individual. Therefore, for the purpose of safeguarding the common weal of the faithful, it is lawful to carry on a war on holy days, provided there be need for doing so: because it would be to tempt God, if notwithstanding such a need, one were to choose to refrain from fighting.

However, as soon as the need ceases, it is no longer lawful to fight on a holy day, for the reasons given: wherefore this suffices for the Replies to the Objections.

41. OF STRIFE (In Two Articles)[1]

We must now consider strife, under which head there are two points of inquiry:

(1) Whether strife is a sin?
(2) Whether it is a daughter of anger?.

* * * * *

FIRST ARTICLE [II-II, Q. 41, Art. 1]

Whether Strife Is Always a Sin?

Objection 1: It would seem that strife is not always a sin. For strife seems a kind of contention: hence Isidore says (Etym. x) that the word "rixosus [quarrelsome] is derived from the snarling [rictu] of a dog, because the quarrelsome man is ever ready to contradict; he delights in brawling, and provokes contention." Now contention is not always a sin. Neither, therefore, is strife.

Obj. 2: Further, it is related (Gen. 26:21) that the servants of Isaac "digged" another well, "and for that they quarrelled likewise." Now it is not credible that the household of Isaac quarrelled

---

[1] Strife here denotes fighting between individuals

publicly, without being reproved by him, supposing it were a sin. Therefore strife is not a sin.

Obj. 3: Further, strife seems to be a war between individuals. But war is not always sinful. Therefore strife is not always a sin.

On the contrary, Strifes[1] are reckoned among the works of the flesh (Gal. 5:20), and "they who do such things shall not obtain the kingdom of God." Therefore strifes are not only sinful, but they are even mortal sins.

I answer that, While contention implies a contradiction of words, strife denotes a certain contradiction of deeds. Wherefore a gloss on Gal. 5:20 says that "strifes are when persons strike one another through anger." Hence strife is a kind of private war, because it takes place between private persons, being declared not by public authority, but rather by an inordinate will. Therefore strife is always sinful. In fact it is a mortal sin in the man who attacks another unjustly, for it is not without mortal sin that one inflicts harm on another even if the deed be done by the hands. But in him who defends himself, it may be without sin, or it may sometimes involve a venial sin, or sometimes a mortal sin; and this depends on his intention and on his manner of defending himself. For if his sole intention be to withstand the injury done to him, and he defend himself with due moderation, it is no sin, and one cannot say properly that there is strife on his part. But if, on the other hand, his self-defense be inspired by vengeance and hatred, it is always a sin. It is a venial sin, if a slight movement of hatred or vengeance obtrude itself, or if he does not much exceed moderation in defending himself: but it is a mortal sin if he makes for his assailant with the fixed intention of killing him, or inflicting grievous harm on him.

Reply Obj. 1: Strife is not just the same as contention: and there are three things in the passage quoted from Isidore, which express the inordinate nature of strife. First, the quarrelsome man is always ready to fight, and this is conveyed by the words, "ever ready to contradict," that is to say, whether the other man says or does well or ill. Secondly, he delights in quarrelling itself, and so the passage proceeds, "and delights in brawling." Thirdly, "he" provokes others to quarrel, wherefore it goes on, "and provokes contention."

---

1   The Douay version has 'quarrels'

Reply Obj. 1: The sense of the text is not that the servants of Isaac quarrelled, but that the inhabitants of that country quarrelled with them: wherefore these sinned, and not the servants of Isaac, who bore the calumny[1].

Reply Obj. 3: In order for a war to be just it must be declared by authority of the governing power, as stated above (Q. 40, A. 1); whereas strife proceeds from a private feeling of anger or hatred. For if the servants of a sovereign or judge, in virtue of their public authority, attack certain men and these defend themselves, it is not the former who are said to be guilty of strife, but those who resist the public authority. Hence it is not the assailants in this case who are guilty of strife and commit sin, but those who defend themselves inordinately.

* * * * *

SECOND ARTICLE [II-II, Q. 41, Art. 2]

Whether Strife Is a Daughter of Anger?

Objection 1: It would seem that strife is not a daughter of anger. For it is written (James 4:1): "Whence are wars and contentions? Are they not . . . from your concupiscences, which war in your members?" But anger is not in the concupiscible faculty. Therefore strife is a daughter, not of anger, but of concupiscence.

Obj. 2: Further, it is written (Prov. 28:25): "He that boasteth and puffeth up himself, stirreth up quarrels." Now strife is apparently the same as quarrel. Therefore it seems that strife is a daughter of pride or vainglory which makes a man boast and puff himself up.

Obj. 3: Further, it is written (Prov. 18:6): "The lips of a fool intermeddle with strife." Now folly differs from anger, for it is opposed, not to meekness, but to wisdom or prudence. Therefore strife is not a daughter of anger.

Obj. 4: Further, it is written (Prov. 10:12): "Hatred stirreth up strifes." But hatred arises from envy, according to Gregory (Moral. xxxi, 17). Therefore strife is not a daughter of anger, but of envy.

---

[1] Cf. Gen. 26:20

Obj. 5: Further, it is written (Prov. 17:19): "He that studieth discords, soweth [Vulg.: 'loveth'] quarrels." But discord is a daughter of vainglory, as stated above (Q. 37, A. 2). Therefore strife is also.

On the contrary, Gregory says (Moral. xxxi, 17) that "anger gives rise to strife"; and it is written (Prov. 15:18; 29:22): "A passionate man stirreth up strifes."

I answer that, As stated above (A. 1), strife denotes an antagonism extending to deeds, when one man designs to harm another. Now there are two ways in which one man may intend to harm another. In one way it is as though he intended absolutely the other's hurt, which in this case is the outcome of hatred, for the intention of hatred is directed to the hurt of one's enemy either openly or secretly. In another way a man intends to hurt another who knows and withstands his intention. This is what we mean by strife, and belongs properly to anger which is the desire of vengeance: for the angry man is not content to hurt secretly the object of his anger, he even wishes him to feel the hurt and know that what he suffers is in revenge for what he has done, as may be seen from what has been said above about the passion of anger (I-II, Q. 46, A. 6, ad 2). Therefore, properly speaking, strife arises from anger.

Reply Obj. 1: As stated above (I-II, Q. 25, AA. 1, 2), all the irascible passions arise from those of the concupiscible faculty, so that whatever is the immediate outcome of anger, arises also from concupiscence as from its first root.

Reply Obj. 2: Boasting and puffing up of self which are the result of anger or vainglory, are not the direct but the occasional cause of quarrels or strife, because, when a man resents another being preferred to him, his anger is aroused, and then his anger results in quarrel and strife.

Reply Obj. 3: Anger, as stated above (I-II, Q. 48, A. 3) hinders the judgment of the reason, so that it bears a likeness to folly. Hence they have a common effect, since it is due to a defect in the reason that a man designs to hurt another inordinately.

Reply Obj. 4: Although strife sometimes arises from hatred, it is not the proper effect thereof, because when one man hates another it is beside his intention to hurt him in a quarrelsome and open manner, since sometimes he seeks to hurt him secretly. When, however, he sees himself prevailing, he endeavors to harm him with strife and quarrel. But to hurt a man in a quarrel is the proper effect of anger, for the reason given above.

Reply Obj. 5: Strifes give rise to hatred and discord in the hearts of those who are guilty of strife, and so he that "studies," i.e., intends to sow discord among others, causes them to quarrel among themselves. Even so any sin may command the act of another sin, by directing it to its own end. This does not, however, prove that strife is the daughter of vainglory properly and directly.

42. OF SEDITION (In Two Articles)

We must now consider sedition, under which head there are two points of inquiry:

(1) Whether it is a special sin?
(2) Whether it is a mortal sin?.

* * * * *

FIRST ARTICLE [II-II, Q. 42, Art. 1]

Whether Sedition Is a Special Sin Distinct from Other Sins?

Objection 1: It would seem that sedition is not a special sin distinct from other sins. For, according to Isidore (Etym. x), "a seditious man is one who sows dissent among minds, and begets discord." Now, by provoking the commission of a sin, a man sins by no other kind of sin than that which he provoked. Therefore it seems that sedition is not a special sin distinct from discord.

Obj. 2: Further, sedition denotes a kind of division. Now schism takes its name from scission, as stated above (Q. 39, A. 1). Therefore, seemingly, the sin of sedition is not distinct from that of schism.

Obj. 3: Further, every special sin that is distinct from other sins, is either a capital vice, or arises from some capital vice. Now sedition is reckoned neither among the capital vices, nor among those vices which arise from them, as appears from Moral. xxxi, 45, where both kinds of vice are enumerated. Therefore sedition is not a special sin, distinct from other sins.

On the contrary, Seditions are mentioned as distinct from other sins (2 Cor. 12:20).

I answer that, Sedition is a special sin, having something in common with war and strife, and differing somewhat from them. It has something in common with them, in so far as it implies a certain antagonism, and it differs from them in two points. First, because war and strife denote actual aggression on either side, whereas sedition may be said to denote either actual aggression, or the preparation for such aggression. Hence a gloss on 2 Cor. 12:20 says that "seditions are tumults tending to fight," when, to wit, a number of people make preparations with the intention of fighting. Secondly, they differ in that war is, properly speaking, carried on against external foes, being as it were between one people and another, whereas strife is between one individual and another, or between few people on one side and few on the other side, while sedition, in its proper sense, is between mutually dissentient parts of one people, as when one part of the state rises in tumult against another part. Wherefore, since sedition is opposed to a special kind of good, namely the unity and peace of a people, it is a special kind of sin.

Reply Obj. 1: A seditious man is one who incites others to sedition, and since sedition denotes a kind of discord, it follows that a seditious man is one who creates discord, not of any kind, but between the parts of a multitude. And the sin of sedition is not only in him who sows discord, but also in those who dissent from one another inordinately.

Reply Obj. 2: Sedition differs from schism in two respects. First, because schism is opposed to the spiritual unity of the multitude, viz. ecclesiastical unity, whereas sedition is contrary to the temporal or secular unity of the multitude, for instance of a city or kingdom. Secondly, schism does not imply any preparation for a material fight as sedition does, but only for a spiritual dissent.

Reply Obj. 3: Sedition, like schism, is contained under discord, since each is a kind of discord, not between individuals, but between the parts of a multitude.

* * * * *

SECOND ARTICLE [II-II, Q. 42, Art. 2]

Whether Sedition Is Always a Mortal Sin?

Objection 1: It would seem that sedition is not always a mortal sin. For sedition denotes "a tumult tending to fight," according to the gloss quoted above (A. 1). But fighting is not always a mortal sin, indeed it is sometimes just and lawful, as stated above (Q. 40, A. 1). Much more, therefore, can sedition be without a mortal sin.

Obj. 2: Further, sedition is a kind of discord, as stated above (A. 1, ad 3). Now discord can be without mortal sin, and sometimes without any sin at all. Therefore sedition can be also.

Obj. 3: Further, it is praiseworthy to deliver a multitude from a tyrannical rule. Yet this cannot easily be done without some dissension in the multitude, if one part of the multitude seeks to retain the tyrant, while the rest strive to dethrone him. Therefore there can be sedition without mortal sin.

On the contrary, The Apostle forbids seditions together with other things that are mortal sins (2 Cor. 12:20).

I answer that, As stated above (A. 1, ad 2), sedition is contrary to the unity of the multitude, viz. the people of a city or kingdom. Now Augustine says (De Civ. Dei ii, 21) that "wise men understand the word people to designate not any crowd of persons, but the assembly of those who are united together in fellowship recognized by law and for the common good." Wherefore it is evident that the unity to which sedition is opposed is the unity of law and common good: whence it follows manifestly that sedition is opposed to justice and the common good. Therefore by reason of its genus it is a mortal sin, and its gravity will be all the greater according as the common good which it assails surpasses the private good which is assailed by strife.

Accordingly the sin of sedition is first and chiefly in its authors, who sin most grievously; and secondly it is in those who are led by them to disturb the common good. Those, however, who defend the common good, and withstand the seditious party, are not themselves seditious, even as neither is a man to be called quarrelsome because he defends himself, as stated above (Q. 41, A. 1).

Reply Obj. 1: It is lawful to fight, provided it be for the common good, as stated above (Q. 40, A. 1). But sedition runs counter to the common good of the multitude, so that it is always a mortal sin.

Reply Obj. 2: Discord from what is not evidently good, may be without sin, but discord from what is evidently good, cannot be without sin: and sedition is discord of this kind, for it is contrary to the unity of the multitude, which is a manifest good.

Reply Obj. 3: A tyrannical government is not just, because it is directed, not to the common good, but to the private good of the ruler, as the Philosopher states (Polit. iii, 5; Ethic. viii, 10). Consequently there is no sedition in disturbing a government of this kind, unless indeed the tyrant's rule be disturbed so inordinately, that his subjects suffer greater harm from the consequent disturbance than from the tyrant's government. Indeed it is the tyrant rather that is guilty of sedition, since he encourages discord and sedition among his subjects, that he may lord over them more securely; for this is tyranny, being conducive to the private good of the ruler, and to the injury of the multitude.

43. OF SCANDAL (In Eight Articles)

It remains for us to consider the vices which are opposed to beneficence, among which some come under the head of injustice, those, to wit, whereby one harms one's neighbor unjustly. But scandal seems to be specially opposed to charity. Accordingly we must here consider scandal, under which head there are eight points of inquiry:

(1) What is scandal?
(2) Whether scandal is a sin?
(3) Whether it is a special sin?
(4) Whether it is a mortal sin?
(5) Whether the perfect can be scandalized?
(6) Whether they can give scandal?
(7) Whether spiritual goods are to be foregone on account of scandal?
(8) Whether temporal things are to be foregone on account of scandal?.

* * * * *

FIRST ARTICLE [II-II, Q. 43, Art. 1]

Whether Scandal Is Fittingly Defined As Being Something Less Rightly Said or Done That Occasions Spiritual Downfall?

Objection 1: It would seem that scandal is unfittingly defined as "something less rightly said or done that occasions spiritual downfall." For scandal is a sin as we shall state further on (A. 2). Now, according to Augustine (Contra Faust. xxii, 27), a sin is a "word, deed, or desire contrary to the law of God." Therefore the definition given above is insufficient, since it omits "thought" or "desire."

Obj. 2: Further, since among virtuous or right acts one is more virtuous or more right than another, that one alone which has perfect rectitude would not seem to be a "less" right one. If, therefore, scandal is something "less" rightly said or done, it follows that every virtuous act except the best of all, is a scandal.

Obj. 3: Further, an occasion is an accidental cause. But nothing accidental should enter a definition, because it does not specify the thing defined. Therefore it is unfitting, in defining scandal, to say that it is an "occasion."

Obj. 4: Further, whatever a man does may be the occasion of another's spiritual downfall, because accidental causes are indeterminate. Consequently, if scandal is something that occasions another's spiritual downfall, any deed or word can be a scandal: and this seems unreasonable.

Obj. 5: Further, a man occasions his neighbor's spiritual downfall when he offends or weakens him. Now scandal is condivided with offense and weakness, for the Apostle says (Rom. 14:21): "It is good not to eat flesh, and not to drink wine, nor anything whereby thy brother is offended or scandalized, or weakened." Therefore the aforesaid definition of scandal is unfitting.

On the contrary, Jerome in expounding Matt. 15:12, "Dost thou know that the Pharisees, when they heard this word," etc. says: "When we read 'Whosoever shall scandalize,' the sense is 'Whosoever shall, by deed or word, occasion another's spiritual downfall.'"

I answer that, As Jerome observes the Greek *skandalon* may be rendered offense, downfall, or a stumbling against something. For when a body, while moving along a path, meets with an obstacle, it may happen to stumble against it, and be disposed to fall down: such an obstacle is a *skandalon*.

In like manner, while going along the spiritual way, a man may be disposed to a spiritual downfall by another's word or deed, in so far, to wit, as one man by his injunction, inducement or example, moves another to sin; and this is scandal properly so called.

Now nothing by its very nature disposes a man to spiritual downfall, except that which has some lack of rectitude, since what is perfectly right, secures man against a fall, instead of conducing to his downfall. Scandal is, therefore, fittingly defined as "something less rightly done or said, that occasions another's spiritual downfall."

Reply Obj. 1: The thought or desire of evil lies hidden in the heart, wherefore it does not suggest itself to another man as an obstacle conducing to his spiritual downfall: hence it cannot come under the head of scandal.

Reply Obj. 2: A thing is said to be less right, not because something else surpasses it in rectitude, but because it has some lack of rectitude, either through being evil in itself, such as sin, or through having an appearance of evil. Thus, for instance, if a man were to "sit at meat in the idol's temple" (1 Cor. 8:10), though this is not sinful in itself, provided it be done with no evil intention, yet, since it has a certain appearance of evil, and a semblance of worshipping the idol, it might occasion another man's spiritual downfall. Hence the Apostle says (1 Thess. 5:22): "From all appearance of evil refrain yourselves." Scandal is therefore fittingly described as something done "less rightly," so as to comprise both whatever is sinful in itself, and all that has an appearance of evil.

Reply Obj. 3: As stated above (I-II, Q. 75, AA. 2, 3; I-II, Q. 80, A. 1), nothing can be a sufficient cause of a man's spiritual downfall, which is sin, save his own will. Wherefore another man's words or deeds can only be an imperfect cause, conducing somewhat to that downfall. For this reason scandal is said to afford not a cause, but an occasion, which is an imperfect, and not always an accidental cause. Nor is there any reason why certain definitions should not make mention of things that are accidental, since what is accidental to one, may be proper to something else: thus the accidental cause is mentioned in the definition of chance (Phys. ii, 5).

Reply Obj. 4: Another's words or deed may be the cause of another's sin in two ways, directly and accidentally. Directly, when a man either intends, by his evil word or deed, to lead another man into sin, or, if he does not so intend, when his deed is of such a nature as to lead another into sin: for instance, when a man publicly commits a sin or does something that has an appearance of sin. In this case he that does such an act does, properly speaking, afford an occasion of another's spiritual downfall, wherefore his act is called "active scandal." One man's word or deed is the accidental cause of another's sin, when he neither intends to lead him into sin, nor does what is of a nature to lead him into sin, and yet this other one, through being ill-disposed, is led into sin, for instance, into envy of another's good, and then he who does this righteous act, does not, so far as he is concerned, afford an occasion of the other's downfall, but it is this other one who takes the occasion according to Rom. 7:8: "Sin taking occasion by the commandment wrought in me all manner of concupiscence." Wherefore this is "passive," without "active scandal," since he that acts rightly does not, for his own part, afford the occasion of the other's downfall. Sometimes therefore it happens that there is active scandal in the one together with passive scandal in the other, as when one commits a sin being induced thereto by another; sometimes there is active without passive scandal, for instance when one, by word or deed, provokes another to sin, and the latter does not consent; and sometimes there is passive without active scandal, as we have already said.

Reply Obj. 5: "Weakness" denotes proneness to scandal; while "offense" signifies resentment against the person who commits a sin, which resentment may be sometimes without spiritual downfall; and "scandal" is the stumbling that results in downfall.

* * * * *

SECOND ARTICLE [II-II, Q. 43, Art. 2]

Whether Scandal Is a Sin?

Objection 1: It would seem that scandal is not a sin. For sins do not occur from necessity, since all sin is voluntary, as stated above (I-II, Q. 74, AA. 1, 2). Now it is written (Matt. 18:7): "It must needs be that scandals come." Therefore scandal is not a sin.

Obj. 2: Further, no sin arises from a sense of dutifulness, because "a good tree cannot bring forth evil fruit" (Matt. 7:18). But scandal may come from a sense of dutifulness, for Our Lord said to Peter (Matt. 16:23): "Thou art a scandal unto Me," in reference to which words Jerome says that "the Apostle's error was due to his sense of dutifulness, and such is never inspired by the devil." Therefore scandal is not always a sin.

Obj. 3: Further, scandal denotes a stumbling. But he that stumbles does not always fall. Therefore scandal, which is a spiritual fall, can be without sin.

On the contrary, Scandal is "something less rightly said or done." Now anything that lacks rectitude is a sin. Therefore scandal is always with sin.

I answer that, As already said (A. 1, ad 4), scandal is of two kinds, passive scandal in the person scandalized, and active scandal in the person who gives scandal, and so occasions a spiritual downfall. Accordingly passive scandal is always a sin in the person scandalized; for he is not scandalized except in so far as he succumbs to a spiritual downfall, and that is a sin.

Yet there can be passive scandal, without sin on the part of the person whose action has occasioned the scandal, as for instance, when a person is scandalized at another's good deed. In like manner active scandal is always a sin in the person who gives scandal, since either what he does is a sin, or if it only have the appearance of sin, it should always be left undone out of that love for our neighbor which binds each one to be solicitous for his neighbor's spiritual welfare; so that if he persist in doing it he acts against charity.

Yet there can be active scandal without sin on the part of the person scandalized, as stated above (A. 1, ad 4).

Reply Obj. 1: These words, "It must needs be that scandals come," are to be understood to convey, not the absolute, but the conditional necessity of scandal; in which sense it is necessary that whatever God foresees or foretells must happen, provided it be taken conjointly with such foreknowledge, as explained in the First Part (Q. 14, A. 13, ad 3; Q. 23, A. 6, ad 2).

Or we may say that the necessity of scandals occurring is a necessity of end, because they are useful in order that "they . . . who are reproved may be made manifest" (1 Cor. 11:19).

Or scandals must needs occur, seeing the condition of man who fails to shield himself from sin. Thus a physician on seeing a man partaking of unsuitable food might say that such a man must needs injure his health, which is to be understood on the condition that he does not change his diet. In like manner it must needs be that scandals come, so long as men fail to change their evil mode of living.

Reply Obj. 2: In that passage scandal denotes any kind of hindrance: for Peter wished to hinder Our Lord's Passion out of a sense of dutifulness towards Christ.

Reply Obj. 3: No man stumbles spiritually, without being kept back somewhat from advancing in God's way, and that is at least a venial sin.

* * * * *

THIRD ARTICLE [II-II, Q. 43, Art. 3]

Whether Scandal Is a Special Sin?

Objection 1: It would seem that scandal is not a special sin. For scandal is "something said or done less rightly." But this applies to every kind of sin. Therefore every sin is a scandal, and consequently, scandal is not a special sin.

Obj. 2: Further, every special kind of sin, or every special kind of injustice, may be found separately from other kinds, as stated in Ethic. v, 3, 5. But scandal is not to be found separately from other sins. Therefore it is not a special kind of sin.

Obj. 3: Further, every special sin is constituted by something which specifies the moral act. But the notion of scandal consists in its being something done in the presence of others: and the fact of a sin being committed openly, though it is an aggravating circumstance, does not seem to constitute the species of a sin. Therefore scandal is not a special sin.

On the contrary, A special virtue has a special sin opposed to it. But scandal is opposed to a special virtue, viz. charity. For it is written (Rom. 14:15): "If, because of thy meat, thy brother be grieved, thou walkest not now according to charity." Therefore scandal is a special sin.

I answer that, As stated above (A. 2), scandal is twofold, active and passive. Passive scandal cannot be a special sin, because through another's word or deed a man may fall into any kind of sin: and the fact that a man takes occasion to sin from another's word or deed, does not constitute a special kind of sin, because it does not imply a special deformity in opposition to a special virtue.

On the other hand, active scandal may be understood in two ways, directly and accidentally. The scandal is accidental when it is beside the agent's intention, as when a man does not intend, by his inordinate deed or word, to occasion another's spiritual downfall, but merely to satisfy his own will. In such a case even active scandal is not a special sin, because a species is not constituted by that which is accidental.

Active scandal is direct when a man intends, by his inordinate word or deed, to draw another into sin, and then it becomes a special kind of sin on account of the intention of a special kind of end, because moral actions take their species from their end, as stated above (I-II, Q. 1, A. 3; Q. 18, AA. 4, 6). Hence, just as theft and murder are special kinds of sin, on account of their denoting the intention of doing a special injury to one's neighbor: so too, scandal is a special kind of sin, because thereby a man intends a special harm to his neighbor, and it is directly opposed to fraternal correction, whereby a man intends the removal of a special kind of harm.

Reply Obj. 1: Any sin may be the matter of active scandal, but it may derive the formal aspect of a special sin from the end intended, as stated above.

Reply Obj. 2: Active scandal can be found separate from other sins, as when a man scandalizes his neighbor by a deed which is not a sin in itself, but has an appearance of evil.

Reply Obj. 3: Scandal does not derive the species of a special sin from the circumstance in question, but from the intention of the end, as stated above.

* * * * *

FOURTH ARTICLE [II-II, Q. 43, Art. 4]

Whether Scandal Is a Mortal Sin?

Objection 1: It would seem that scandal is a mortal sin. For every sin that is contrary to charity is a mortal sin, as stated above (Q. 24, A. 12; Q. 35, A. 3). But scandal is contrary to charity, as stated above (AA. 2, 3). Therefore scandal is a mortal sin.

Obj. 2: Further, no sin, save mortal sin, deserves the punishment of eternal damnation. But scandal deserves the punishment of eternal damnation, according to Matt. 18:6: "He that shall scandalize one of these little ones, that believe in Me, it were better for him that a mill-stone should be hanged about his neck, and that he should be drowned in the depth of the sea." For, as Jerome says on this passage, "it is much better to receive a brief punishment for a fault, than to await everlasting torments." Therefore scandal is a mortal sin.

Obj. 3: Further, every sin committed against God is a mortal sin, because mortal sin alone turns man away from God. Now scandal is a sin against God, for the Apostle says (1 Cor. 8:12): "When you wound the weak conscience of the brethren[1], you sin against Christ." Therefore scandal is always a mortal sin.

On the contrary, It may be a venial sin to lead a person into venial sin: and yet this would be to give scandal. Therefore scandal may be a venial sin.

I answer that, As stated above (A. 1), scandal denotes a stumbling whereby a person is disposed to a spiritual downfall. Consequently passive scandal may sometimes be a venial sin, when it consists in a stumbling and nothing more; for instance, when a person is disturbed by a movement of venial sin occasioned by another's inordinate word or deed: while sometimes it is a mortal sin, when the stumbling results in a downfall, for instance, when a person goes so far as to commit a mortal sin through another's inordinate word or deed.

Active scandal, if it be accidental, may sometimes be a venial sin; for instance, when, through a slight indiscretion, a person either commits a venial sin, or does something that is not a sin in itself, but has some appearance of evil. On the other hand, it is sometimes a mortal sin, either because a person commits a mortal sin, or because he has such contempt for his neighbor's spiritual welfare that he declines, for the sake of procuring it, to forego doing what he wishes to do. But in the case of active direct scandal, as when a person intends to lead another into sin, if he intends to lead him into mortal sin, his own sin will be mortal; and in like manner if he intends by committing a mortal sin himself, to lead another into

---

[1] Vulg.: 'When you sin thus against the brethren and wound their weak conscience'

venial sin; whereas if he intends, by committing a venial sin, to lead another into venial sin, there will be a venial sin of scandal.

And this suffices for the Replies to the Objections.

* * * * *

FIFTH ARTICLE [II-II, Q. 43, Art. 5]

Whether Passive Scandal May Happen Even to the Perfect?

Objection 1: It would seem that passive scandal may happen even to the perfect. For Christ was supremely perfect: and yet He said to Peter (Matt. 16:23): "Thou art a scandal to Me." Much more therefore can other perfect men suffer scandal.

Obj. 2: Further, scandal denotes an obstacle which is put in a person's spiritual way. Now even perfect men can be hindered in their progress along the spiritual way, according to 1 Thess. 2:18: "We would have come to you, I Paul indeed, once and again; but Satan hath hindered us." Therefore even perfect men can suffer scandal.

Obj. 3: Further, even perfect men are liable to venial sins, according to 1 John 1:8: "If we say that we have no sin, we deceive ourselves." Now passive scandal is not always a mortal sin, but is sometimes venial, as stated above (A. 4). Therefore passive scandal may be found in perfect men.

On the contrary, Jerome, in commenting on Matt. 18:6, "He that shall scandalize one of these little ones," says: "Observe that it is the little one that is scandalized, for the elders do not take scandal."

I answer that, Passive scandal implies that the mind of the person who takes scandal is unsettled in its adherence to good. Now no man can be unsettled, who adheres firmly to something immovable. The elders, i.e. the perfect, adhere to God alone, Whose goodness is unchangeable, for though they adhere to their superiors, they do so only in so far as these adhere to Christ, according to 1 Cor. 4:16: "Be ye followers of me, as I also am of Christ." Wherefore, however much others may appear to them to conduct themselves ill in word or deed, they themselves do not stray from their righteousness, according to Ps. 124:1: "They that trust in the Lord shall be as Mount Sion: he shall not be moved for ever that dwelleth in Jerusalem." Therefore scandal is not found in those who adhere to God perfectly by love, according to Ps. 118:165: "Much peace have they that love Thy law, and to them there is no stumbling-block *(scandalum).*"

Reply Obj. 1: As stated above (A. 2, ad 2), in this passage, scandal is used in a broad sense, to denote any kind of hindrance. Hence Our Lord said to Peter: "Thou art a scandal to Me," because he was endeavoring to weaken Our Lord's purpose of undergoing His Passion.

Reply Obj. 2: Perfect men may be hindered in the performance of external actions. But they are not hindered by the words or deeds of others, from tending to God in the internal acts of the will, according to Rom. 8:38, 39: "Neither death, nor life . . . shall be able to separate us from the love of God."

Reply Obj. 3: Perfect men sometimes fall into venial sins through the weakness of the flesh; but they are not scandalized (taking scandal in its true sense), by the words or deeds of others, although there can be an approach to scandal in them, according to Ps. 72:2: "My feet were almost moved.".

* * * * *

SIXTH ARTICLE [II-II, Q. 43, Art. 6]

Whether Active Scandal Can Be Found in the Perfect?

Objection 1: It would seem that active scandal can be found in the perfect. For passion is the effect of action. Now some are scandalized passively by the words or deeds of the perfect, according to Matt. 15:12: "Dost thou know that the Pharisees, when they heard this word, were scandalized?" Therefore active scandal can be found in the perfect.

Obj. 2: Further, Peter, after receiving the Holy Ghost, was in the state of the perfect. Yet afterwards he scandalized the gentiles: for it is written (Gal. 2:14): "When I saw that they walked not uprightly unto the truth of the Gospel, I said to Cephas," i.e. Peter, "before them all: If thou being a Jew, livest after the manner of the gentiles, and not as the Jews do, how dost thou compel the gentiles to live as do the Jews?" Therefore active scandal can be in the perfect.

Obj. 3: Further, active scandal is sometimes a venial sin. But venial sins may be in perfect men. Therefore active scandal may be in perfect men.

On the contrary, Active scandal is more opposed to perfection, than passive scandal. But passive scandal cannot be in the perfect. Much less, therefore, can active scandal be in them.

I answer that, Active scandal, properly so called, occurs when a man says or does a thing which in itself is of a nature to occasion another's spiritual downfall, and that is only when what he says or does is inordinate. Now it belongs to the perfect to direct all their actions according to the rule of reason, as stated in 1 Cor. 14:40: "Let all things be done decently and according to order"; and they are careful to do this in those matters chiefly wherein not only would they do wrong, but would also be to others an occasion of wrongdoing. And if indeed they fail in this moderation in such words or deeds as come to the knowledge of others, this has its origin in human weakness wherein they fall short of perfection. Yet they do not fall short so far as to stray far from the order of reason, but only a little and in some slight matter: and this is not so grave that anyone can reasonably take therefrom an occasion for committing sin.

Reply Obj. 1: Passive scandal is always due to some active scandal; yet this active scandal is not always in another, but in the very person who is scandalized, because, to wit, he scandalizes himself.

Reply Obj. 2: In the opinion of Augustine (Ep. xxviii, xl, lxxxii) and of Paul also, Peter sinned and was to be blamed, in withdrawing from the gentiles in order to avoid the scandal of the Jews, because he did this somewhat imprudently, so that the gentiles who had been converted to the faith were scandalized. Nevertheless Peter's action was not so grave a sin as to give others sufficient ground for scandal. Hence they were guilty of passive scandal, while there was no active scandal in Peter.

Reply Obj. 3: The venial sins of the perfect consist chiefly in sudden movements, which being hidden cannot give scandal. If, however, they commit any venial sins even in their external words or deeds, these are so slight as to be insufficient in themselves to give scandal.

* * * * *

SEVENTH ARTICLE [II-II, Q. 43, Art. 7]

Whether Spiritual Goods Should Be Foregone on Account of Scandal?

Objection 1: It would seem that spiritual goods ought to be foregone on account of scandal. For Augustine (Contra Ep. Parmen. iii, 2) teaches that "punishment for sin should cease, when the peril of schism is feared." But punishment of sins is a spiritual good, since it is an act of justice. Therefore a spiritual good is to be foregone on account of scandal.

Obj. 2: Further, the Sacred Doctrine is a most spiritual thing. Yet one ought to desist therefrom on account of scandal, according to Matt. 7:6: "Give not that which is holy to dogs, neither cast ye your pearls before swine lest . . . turning upon you, they tear you." Therefore a spiritual good should be foregone on account of scandal.

Obj. 3: Further, since fraternal correction is an act of charity, it is a spiritual good. Yet sometimes it is omitted out of charity, in order to avoid giving scandal to others, as Augustine observes (De Civ. Dei i, 9). Therefore a spiritual good should be foregone on account of scandal.

Obj. 4: Further, Jerome[1] says that in order to avoid scandal we should forego whatever it is possible to omit without prejudice to the threefold truth, i.e. "the truth of life, of justice and of doctrine." Now the observance of the counsels, and the bestowal of alms may often be omitted without prejudice to the aforesaid threefold truth, else whoever omitted them would always be guilty of sin, and yet such things are the greatest of spiritual works. Therefore spiritual works should be omitted on account of scandal.

Obj. 5: Further, the avoidance of any sin is a spiritual good, since any sin brings spiritual harm to the sinner. Now it seems that one ought sometimes to commit a venial sin in order to avoid scandalizing one's neighbor, for instance, when by sinning venially, one would prevent someone else from committing a mortal sin: because one is bound to hinder the damnation of one's neighbor as much as one can without prejudice to one's own salvation, which

---

[1] Hugh de S. Cher., In Matth. xviii; in Luc. xvii, 2

is not precluded by a venial sin. Therefore one ought to forego a spiritual good in order to avoid scandal.

On the contrary, Gregory says (Hom. Super Ezech. vii): "If people are scandalized at the truth, it is better to allow the birth of scandal, than to abandon the truth." Now spiritual goods belong, above all others, to the truth. Therefore spiritual goods are not to be foregone on account of scandal.

I answer that, Whereas scandal is twofold, active and passive, the present question does not apply to active scandal, for since active scandal is "something said or done less rightly," nothing ought to be done that implies active scandal. The question does, however, apply to passive scandal, and accordingly we have to see what ought to be foregone in order to avoid scandal. Now a distinction must be made in spiritual goods. For some of them are necessary for salvation, and cannot be foregone without mortal sin: and it is evident that no man ought to commit a mortal sin, in order to prevent another from sinning, because according to the order of charity, a man ought to love his own spiritual welfare more than another's. Therefore one ought not to forego that which is necessary for salvation, in order to avoid giving scandal.

Again a distinction seems necessary among spiritual things which are not necessary for salvation: because the scandal which arises from such things sometimes proceeds from malice, for instance when a man wishes to hinder those spiritual goods by stirring up scandal. This is the "scandal of the Pharisees," who were scandalized at Our Lord's teaching: and Our Lord teaches (Matt. 15:14) that we ought to treat such like scandal with contempt. Sometimes scandal proceeds from weakness or ignorance, and such is the "scandal of little ones." In order to avoid this kind of scandal, spiritual goods ought to be either concealed, or sometimes even deferred (if this can be done without incurring immediate danger), until the matter being explained the scandal cease. If, however, the scandal continue after the matter has been explained, it would seem to be due to malice, and then it would no longer be right to forego that spiritual good in order to avoid such like scandal.

Reply Obj. 1: In the infliction of punishment it is not the punishment itself that is the end in view, but its medicinal properties in checking sin; wherefore punishment partakes of the nature of justice, in so far as it checks sin. But if it is evident that the infliction of punishment will result in more numerous and more grievous sins being committed, the infliction of punishment will no longer be a part of justice. It is in this sense that Augustine is speaking, when, to wit, the excommunication of a few threatens to bring about the danger of a schism, for in that case it would be contrary to the truth of justice to pronounce excommunication.

Reply Obj. 2: With regard to a man's doctrine two points must be considered, namely, the truth which is taught, and the act of teaching. The first of these is necessary for salvation, to wit, that he whose duty it is to teach should not teach what is contrary to the truth, and that he should teach the truth according to the requirements of times and persons: wherefore on no account ought he to suppress the truth and teach error in order to avoid any scandal that might ensue. But the act itself of teaching is one of the spiritual almsdeeds, as stated above (Q. 32, A. 2), and so the same is to be said of it as of the other works of mercy, of which we shall speak further on (ad 4).

Reply Obj. 3: As stated above (Q. 33, A. 1), fraternal correction aims at the correction of a brother, wherefore it is to be reckoned among spiritual goods in so far as this end can be obtained, which is not the case if the brother be scandalized through being corrected. And so, if the correction be omitted in order to avoid scandal, no spiritual good is foregone.

Reply Obj. 4: The truth of life, of doctrine, and of justice comprises not only whatever is necessary for salvation, but also whatever is a means of obtaining salvation more perfectly, according to 1 Cor. 12:31: "Be zealous for the better gifts." Wherefore neither the counsels nor even the works of mercy are to be altogether omitted in order to avoid scandal; but sometimes they should be concealed or deferred, on account of the scandal of the little ones, as stated above. Sometimes, however, the observance of the counsels and the fulfilment of the works of mercy are necessary for salvation. This may be seen in the case of those who have vowed to keep the counsels, and of those whose duty it is to relieve the wants of others, either in temporal matters (as by feeding the hungry), or in spiritual matters (as by instructing the ignorant), whether such duties arise from their being enjoined as in the case of prelates, or from the need on the part of the person in want; and then the same applies to these things as to others that are necessary for salvation.

Reply Obj. 5: Some have said that one ought to commit a venial sin in order to avoid scandal. But this implies a contradiction, since if it ought to be done, it is no longer evil or sinful, for a sin cannot be a matter of choice. It may happen however that, on account of some circumstance, something is not a venial sin, though it would be were it not for that circumstance: thus an idle word is a venial sin, when it is uttered uselessly; yet if it be uttered for a reasonable cause, it is neither idle nor sinful. And though venial sin does not deprive a man of grace which is his means of salvation, yet, in so far as it disposes him to mortal sin, it tends to the loss of salvation.

* * * * *

EIGHTH ARTICLE [II-II, Q. 43, Art. 8]

Whether Temporal Goods Should Be Foregone on Account of Scandal?

Objection 1: It would seem that temporal goods should be foregone on account of scandal. For we ought to love our neighbor's spiritual welfare which is hindered by scandal, more than any temporal goods whatever. But we forego what we love less for the sake of what we love more. Therefore we should forego temporal goods in order to avoid scandalizing our neighbor.

Obj. 2: Further, according to Jerome's rule[1], whatever can be foregone without prejudice to the threefold truth, should be omitted in order to avoid scandal. Now temporal goods can be foregone without prejudice to the threefold truth. Therefore they should be foregone in order to avoid scandal.

Obj. 3: Further, no temporal good is more necessary than food. But we ought to forego taking food on account of scandal, according to Rom. 14:15: "Destroy not him with thy meat for whom Christ died." Much more therefore should all other temporal goods be foregone on account of scandal.

Obj. 4: Further, the most fitting way of safeguarding and recovering temporal goods is the court of justice. But it is unlawful to have recourse to justice, especially if scandal ensues: for it is

---

[1] Cf. A. 7, Obj. 4

written (Matt. 5:40): "If a man will contend with thee in judgment, and take away thy coat, let go thy cloak also unto him"; and (1 Cor. 6:7): "Already indeed there is plainly a fault among you, that you have lawsuits one with another. Why do you not rather take wrong? why do you not rather suffer yourselves to be defrauded?" Therefore it seems that we ought to forego temporal goods on account of scandal.

Obj. 5: Further, we ought, seemingly, to forego least of all those temporal goods which are connected with spiritual goods: and yet we ought to forego them on account of scandal. For the Apostle while sowing spiritual things did not accept a temporal stipend lest he "should give any hindrance to the Gospel of Christ" as we read 1 Cor. 9:12. For a like reason the Church does not demand tithes in certain countries, in order to avoid scandal. Much more, therefore, ought we to forego other temporal goods in order to avoid scandal.

On the contrary, Blessed Thomas of Canterbury demanded the restitution of Church property, notwithstanding that the king took scandal from his doing so.

I answer that, A distinction must be made in temporal goods: for either they are ours, or they are consigned to us to take care of them for someone else; thus the goods of the Church are consigned to prelates, and the goods of the community are entrusted to all such persons as have authority over the common weal. In this latter case the care of such things (as of things held in deposit) devolves of necessity on those persons to whom they are entrusted, wherefore, even as other things that are necessary for salvation, they are not to be foregone on account of scandal. On the other hand, as regards those temporalities of which we have the dominion, sometimes, on account of scandal, we are bound to forego them, and sometimes we are not so bound, whether we forego them by giving them up, if we have them in our possession, or by omitting to claim them, if they are in the possession of others. For if the scandal arise therefrom through the ignorance or weakness of others (in which case, as stated above, A. 7, it is scandal of the little ones) we must either forego such temporalities altogether, or the scandal must be abated by some other means, namely, by some kind of admonition. Hence Augustine says (De Serm. Dom. in Monte i, 20): "Thou shouldst give so as to injure neither thyself nor another, as much as thou canst lend, and if thou refusest what is asked, thou must yet be just to him, indeed thou wilt give him something better than he asks, if thou reprove him that asks unjustly." Sometimes, however, scandal arises from malice. This is scandal of the Pharisees: and we ought not to forego temporal goods for the sake of those who stir up scandals of this kind, for this would both be harmful to the common good, since it would give wicked men an opportunity of plunder, and would be injurious to the plunderers themselves, who would remain in sin as long as they were in possession of another's property. Hence Gregory says (Moral. xxxi, 13): "Sometimes we ought to suffer those who rob us of our temporalities, while sometimes we should resist them, as far as equity allows, in the hope not only that we may safeguard our property, but also lest those who take what is not theirs may lose themselves."

This suffices for the Reply to the First Objection.

Reply Obj. 2: If it were permissible for wicked men to rob other people of their property, this would tend to the detriment of the truth of life and justice. Therefore we are not always bound to forego our temporal goods in order to avoid scandal.

Reply Obj. 3: The Apostle had no intention of counselling total abstinence from food on account of scandal, because our welfare requires that we should take food: but he intended to counsel abstinence from a particular kind of food, in order to avoid scandal, according to 1 Cor. 8:13: "I will never eat flesh, lest I should scandalize my brother."

Reply Obj. 4: According to Augustine (De Serm. Dom. in Monte i, 19) this precept of Our Lord is to be understood of the preparedness of the mind, namely, that man should be prepared, if it be expedient, to suffer being harmed or defrauded, rather than go to law. But sometimes it is not expedient, as stated above (ad 2). The same applies to the saying of the Apostle.

Reply Obj. 5: The scandal which the Apostle avoided, arose from an error of the gentiles who were not used to this payment. Hence it behooved him to forego it for the time being, so that they might be taught first of all that such a payment was a duty. For a like reason the Church refrains from demanding tithes in those countries where it is not customary to pay them.

44. OF THE PRECEPTS OF CHARITY
(In Eight Articles)

We must now consider the Precepts of Charity, under which there are eight points of inquiry:

(1) Whether precepts should be given about charity?
(2) Whether there should be one or two?
(3) Whether two suffice?
(4) Whether it is fittingly prescribed that we should love God, "with thy whole heart"?
(5) Whether it is fittingly added: "With thy whole mind," etc.?
(6) Whether it is possible to fulfil this precept in this life?
(7) Of the precept: "Thou shalt love thy neighbor as thyself";
(8) Whether the order of charity is included in the precept?.

* * * * *

FIRST ARTICLE [II-II, Q. 44, Art. 1]

Whether Any Precept Should Be Given About Charity?

Objection 1: It would seem that no precept should be given about charity. For charity imposes the mode on all acts of virtue, since it is the form of the virtues as stated above (Q. 23, A. 8), while the precepts are about the virtues themselves. Now, according to the common saying, the mode is not included in the precept. Therefore no precepts should be given about charity.

Obj. 2: Further, charity, which "is poured forth in our hearts by the Holy Ghost" (Rom. 5:5), makes us free, since "where the Spirit of the Lord is, there is liberty" (2 Cor. 3:17). Now the obligation that arises from a precept is opposed to liberty, since it imposes a necessity. Therefore no precept should be given about charity.

Obj. 3: Further, charity is the foremost among all the virtues, to which the precepts are directed, as shown above (I-II, Q. 90, A. 2; Q. 100, A. 9). If, therefore, any precepts were given about charity, they should have a place among the chief precepts which are those of the decalogue. But they have no place there. Therefore no precepts should be given about charity.

On the contrary, Whatever God requires of us is included in a precept. Now God requires that man should love Him, according to Deut. 10:12. Therefore it behooved precepts to be given about the love of charity, which is the love of God.

I answer that, As stated above (Q. 16, A. 1; I-II, Q. 99, A. 1), a precept implies the notion of something due. Hence a thing is a matter of precept, in so far as it is something due. Now a thing is due in two ways, for its own sake, and for the sake of something else. In every affair, it is the end that is due for its own sake, because it has the character of a good for its own sake: while that which is directed to the end is due for the sake of something else: thus for a physician, it is due for its own sake, that he should heal, while it is due for the sake of something else that he should give a medicine in order to heal. Now the end of the spiritual life is that man be united to God, and this union is effected by charity, while all things pertaining to the spiritual life are ordained to this union, as to their end. Hence the Apostle says (1 Tim. 1:5): "The end of the commandment is charity from a pure heart, and a good conscience, and an unfeigned faith." For all the virtues, about whose acts the precepts are given, are directed either to the freeing of the heart from the whirl of the passions—such are the virtues that regulate the passions—or at least to the possession of a good conscience—such are the virtues that regulate operations—or to the having of a right faith—such are those which pertain to the worship of God: and these three things are required of man that he may love God. For an impure heart is withdrawn from loving God, on account of the passion that inclines it to earthly things; an evil conscience gives man a horror for God's justice, through fear of His punishments; and an untrue faith draws man's affections to an untrue representation of God, and separates him from the truth of God. Now in every genus that which is for its own sake takes precedence of that which is for the sake of another, wherefore the greatest precept is that of charity, as stated in Matt. 22:39.

Reply Obj. 1: As stated above (I-II, Q. 100, A. 10) when we were treating of the commandments, the mode of love does not come under those precepts which are about the other acts of virtue: for instance, this precept, "Honor thy father and thy mother," does not prescribe that this should be done out of charity. The act of love does, however, fall under special precepts.

Reply Obj. 2: The obligation of a precept is not opposed to liberty, except in one whose mind is averted from that which is prescribed, as may be seen in those who keep the precepts through fear alone. But the precept of love cannot be fulfilled save of one's own will, wherefore it is not opposed to charity.

Reply Obj. 3: All the precepts of the decalogue are directed to the love of God and of our neighbor: and therefore the precepts of charity had not to be enumerated among the precepts of the decalogue, since they are included in all of them.

* * * * *

SECOND ARTICLE [II-II, Q. 44, Art. 2]

Whether There Should Have Been Given Two Precepts of Charity?

Objection 1: It would seem that there should not have been given two precepts of charity. For the precepts of the Law are directed to virtue, as stated above (A. 1, Obj. 3). Now charity is one virtue, as shown above (Q. 33, A. 5). Therefore only one precept of charity should have been given.

Obj. 2: Further, as Augustine says (De Doctr. Christ. i, 22, 27), charity loves none but God in our neighbor. Now we are sufficiently directed to love God by the precept, "Thou shalt love the Lord thy God." Therefore there was no need to add the precept about loving our neighbor.

Obj. 3: Further, different sins are opposed to different precepts. But it is not a sin to put aside the love of our neighbor, provided we put not aside the love of God; indeed, it is written (Luke 15:26): "If any man come to Me, and hate not his father, and mother ... he cannot be My disciple." Therefore the precept of the love of God is not distinct from the precept of the love of our neighbor.

Obj. 4: Further, the Apostle says (Rom. 13:8): "He that loveth his neighbor hath fulfilled the Law." But a law is not fulfilled unless all its precepts be observed. Therefore all the precepts are included in the love of our neighbor: and consequently the one precept of the love of our neighbor suffices. Therefore there should not be two precepts of charity.

On the contrary, It is written (1 John 4:21): "This commandment we have from God, that he who loveth God, love also his brother."

I answer that, As stated above (I-II, Q. 91, A. 3; Q. 94, A. 2) when we were treating of the commandments, the precepts are to the Law what propositions are to speculative sciences, for in these latter, the conclusions are virtually contained in the first principles. Hence whoever knows the principles as to their entire virtual extent has no need to have the conclusions put separately before him. Since, however, some who know the principles are unable to consider all that is virtually contained therein, it is necessary, for their sake, that scientific conclusions should be traced to their principles. Now in practical matters wherein the precepts of the Law direct us, the end has the character of principle, as stated above (Q. 23, A. 7, ad 2; Q. 26, A. 1, ad 1): and the love of God is the end to which the love of our neighbor is directed. Therefore it behooved us to receive precepts not only of the love of God but also of the love of our neighbor, on account of those who are less intelligent, who do not easily understand that one of these precepts is included in the other.

Reply Obj. 1: Although charity is one virtue, yet it has two acts, one of which is directed to the other as to its end. Now precepts are given about acts of virtue, and so there had to be several precepts of charity.

Reply Obj. 2: God is loved in our neighbor, as the end is loved in that which is directed to the end; and yet there was need for an explicit precept about both, for the reason given above.

Reply Obj. 3: The means derive their goodness from their relation to the end, and accordingly aversion from the means derives its malice from the same source and from no other.

Reply Obj. 4: Love of our neighbor includes love of God, as the end is included in the means, and vice versa: and yet it behooved each precept to be given explicitly, for the reason given above.

* * * * *

THIRD ARTICLE [II-II, Q. 44, Art. 3]

Whether Two Precepts of Charity Suffice?

Objection 1: It would seem that two precepts of charity do not suffice. For precepts are given about acts of virtue. Now acts are distinguished by their objects. Since, then, man is bound to love four things out of charity, namely, God, himself, his neighbor and his own body, as shown above (Q. 25, A. 12; Q. 26), it seems that there ought to be four precepts of charity, so that two are not sufficient.

Obj. 2: Further, love is not the only act of charity, but also joy, peace and beneficence. But precepts should be given about the acts of the virtues. Therefore two precepts of charity do not suffice.

Obj. 3: Further, virtue consists not only in doing good but also in avoiding evil. Now we are led by the positive precepts to do good, and by the negative precepts to avoid evil. Therefore there ought to have been not only positive, but also negative precepts about charity; and so two precepts of charity are not sufficient.

On the contrary, Our Lord said (Matt. 22:40): "On these two commandments dependeth the whole Law and the prophets."

I answer that, Charity, as stated above (Q. 23, A. 1), is a kind of friendship. Now friendship is between one person and another, wherefore Gregory says (Hom. in Ev. xvii): "Charity is not possible between less than two": and it has been explained how one may love oneself out of charity (Q. 25, A. 4). Now since good is the object of dilection and love, and since good is either an end or a means, it is fitting that there should be two precepts of charity, one whereby we are induced to love God as our end, and another whereby we are led to love our neighbor for God's sake, as for the sake of our end.

Reply Obj. 1: As Augustine says (De Doctr. Christ. i, 23), "though four things are to be loved out of charity, there was no need of a precept as regards the second and fourth," i.e. love of oneself and of one's own body. "For however much a man may stray from the truth, the love of himself and of his own body always remains in him." And yet the mode of this love had to be prescribed to man, namely, that he should love himself and his own body in an ordinate manner, and this is done by his loving God and his neighbor.

Reply Obj. 2: As stated above (Q. 28, A. 4; Q. 29, A. 3), the other acts of charity result from the act of love as effects from their cause. Hence the precepts of love virtually include the precepts about the other acts. And yet we find that, for the sake of the laggards, special precepts were given about each act—about joy (Phil. 4:4): "Rejoice in the Lord always"—about peace (Heb. 12:14): "Follow peace with all men"—about beneficence (Gal. 6:10): "Whilst we have time, let us work good to all men"—and Holy Writ contains precepts about each of the parts of beneficence, as may be seen by anyone who considers the matter carefully.

Reply Obj. 3: To do good is more than to avoid evil, and therefore the positive precepts virtually include the negative precepts. Nevertheless we find explicit precepts against the vices contrary to charity: for, against hatred it is written (Lev. 12:17): "Thou shalt not hate thy brother in thy heart"; against sloth (Ecclus. 6:26): "Be not grieved with her bands"; against envy (Gal. 5:26): "Let us not be made desirous of vainglory, provoking one another, envying one another"; against discord (1 Cor. 1:10): "That you all speak the same thing, and that there be no schisms among you"; and against scandal (Rom. 14:13): "That you put not a stumbling-block or a scandal in your brother's way.".

* * * * *

FOURTH ARTICLE [II-II, Q. 44, Art. 4]

Whether It Is Fittingly Commanded That Man Should Love God with His Whole Heart?

Objection 1: It would seem that it is unfittingly commanded that man should love God with his whole heart. For the mode of a virtuous act is not a matter of precept, as shown above (A. 1, ad 1; I-II, Q. 100, A. 9). Now the words "with thy whole heart" signify the mode of the love of God. Therefore it is unfittingly commanded that man should love God with his whole heart.

Obj. 2: Further, "A thing is whole and perfect when it lacks nothing" (Phys. iii, 6). If therefore it is a matter of precept that God be loved with the whole heart, whoever does something not pertaining to the love of God, acts counter to the precept, and consequently sins mortally. Now a venial sin does not pertain to the love of God. Therefore a venial sin is a mortal sin, which is absurd.

Obj. 3: Further, to love God with one's whole heart belongs to perfection, since according to the Philosopher (Phys. iii, text. 64), "to be whole is to be perfect." But that which belongs to perfection is not a matter of precept, but a matter of counsel. Therefore we ought not to be commanded to love God with our whole heart.

On the contrary, It is written (Deut. 6:5): "Thou shalt love the Lord thy God with thy whole heart."

I answer that, Since precepts are given about acts of virtue, an act is a matter of precept according as it is an act of virtue. Now it is requisite for an act of virtue that not only should it fall on its own matter, but also that it should be endued with its due circumstances, whereby it is adapted to that matter. But God is to be loved as the last end, to which all things are to be referred. Therefore some kind of totality was to be indicated in connection with the precept of the love of God.

Reply Obj. 1: The commandment that prescribes an act of virtue does not prescribe the mode which that virtue derives from another and higher virtue, but it does prescribe the mode which belongs to its own proper virtue, and this mode is signified in the words "with thy whole heart."

Reply Obj. 2: To love God with one's whole heart has a twofold signification. First, actually, so that a man's whole heart be always actually directed to God: this is the perfection of heaven. Secondly, in the sense that a man's whole heart be habitually directed to God, so that it consent to nothing contrary to the love of God, and this is the perfection of the way. Venial sin is not contrary to this latter perfection, because it does not destroy the habit of charity, since it does not tend to a contrary object, but merely hinders the use of charity.

Reply Obj. 3: That perfection of charity to which the counsels are directed, is between the two perfections mentioned in the preceding reply: and it consists in man renouncing, as much as possible, temporal things, even such as are lawful, because they occupy the mind and hinder the actual movement of the heart towards God.

* * * * *

FIFTH ARTICLE [II-II, Q. 44, Art. 5]

Whether to the Words, "Thou Shalt Love the Lord Thy God with Thy Whole Heart," It Was Fitting to Add "and with Thy Whole Soul, and with Thy Whole Strength"?

Objection 1: It would seem that it was unfitting to the words, "Thou shalt love the Lord thy God, with thy whole heart," to add, "and with thy whole soul, and with thy whole strength" (Deut. 6:5). For heart does not mean here a part of the body, since to love God is not a bodily action: and therefore heart is to be taken here in a spiritual sense. Now the heart understood spiritually is either the soul itself or part of the soul. Therefore it is superfluous to mention both heart and soul.

Obj. 2: Further, a man's strength whether spiritual or corporal depends on the heart. Therefore after the words, "Thou shalt love the Lord thy God with thy whole heart," it was unnecessary to add, "with all thy strength."

Obj. 3: Further, in Matt. 22:37 we read: "With all thy mind," which words do not occur here. Therefore it seems that this precept is unfittingly worded in Deut. 6.

On the contrary stands the authority of Scripture.

I answer that, This precept is differently worded in various places: for, as we said in the first objection, in Deut. 6 three points are mentioned: "with thy whole heart," and "with thy whole soul," and "with thy whole strength." In Matt. 22 we find two of these mentioned, viz. "with thy whole heart" and "with thy whole soul," while "with thy whole strength" is omitted, but "with thy whole mind" is added. Yet in Mark 12 we find all four, viz. "with thy whole heart," and "with thy whole soul," and "with thy whole mind," and "with thy whole force" which is the same as "strength." Moreover, these four are indicated in Luke 10, where in place of "strength" or "force" we read "with all thy might."[1]

Accordingly these four have to be explained, since the fact that one of them is omitted here or there is due to one implying another. We must therefore observe that love is an act of the will which is here denoted by the "heart," because just as the bodily heart is the principle of all the movements of the body, so too the will, especially as regards the intention of the last end which is the object of charity, is the principle of all the movements of the soul. Now there are three principles of action that are moved by the will, namely, the intellect which is signified by "the mind," the lower appetitive power, signified by "the soul"; and the exterior executive power signified by "strength," "force" or "might." Accordingly we are commanded to direct our whole intention to God, and this is signified by the words "with thy whole heart"; to submit our

---

[1] St. Thomas is explaining the Latin text which reads "ex tota fortitudine tua" (Deut.), "ex tota virtue tua" (Mk.), and "ex omnibus viribus tuis" (Luke), although the Greek in all three cases has *ex holes tes ischyos*, which the Douay renders "with thy whole strength."

intellect to God, and this is expressed in the words "with thy whole mind"; to regulate our appetite according to God, in the words "with thy whole soul"; and to obey God in our external actions, and this is to love God with our whole "strength," "force" or "might."

Chrysostom[1], on the other hand, takes "heart" and "soul" in the contrary sense; and Augustine (De Doctr. Christ. i, 22) refers "heart" to the thought, "soul" to the manner of life, and "mind" to the intellect. Again some explain "with thy whole heart" as denoting the intellect, "with thy whole soul" as signifying the will, "with thy mind" as pointing to the memory. And again, according to Gregory of Nyssa (De Hom. Opif. viii), "heart" signifies the vegetative soul, "soul" the sensitive, and "mind" the intellective soul, because our nourishment, sensation, and understanding ought all to be referred by us to God.

This suffices for the Replies to the Objections.

* * * * *

SIXTH ARTICLE [II-II, Q. 44, Art. 6]

Whether It Is Possible in This Life to Fulfil This Precept of the Love of God?

Objection 1: It would seem that in this life it is possible to fulfil this precept of the love of God. For according to Jerome[2] "accursed is he who says that God has commanded anything impossible." But God gave this commandment, as is clear from Deut. 6:5. Therefore it is possible to fulfil this precept in this life.

Obj. 2: Further, whoever does not fulfil a precept sins mortally, since according to Ambrose (De Parad. viii) sin is nothing else than "a transgression of the Divine Law, and disobedience of the heavenly commandments." If therefore this precept cannot be fulfilled by wayfarers, it follows that in this life no man can be without mortal sin, and this is against the saying of the Apostle (1 Cor. 1:8): "(Who also) will confirm you unto the end without crime," and (1 Tim. 3:10): "Let them minister, having no crime."

---

1 The quotation is from an anonymous author's unfinished work (Opus imperf. Hom. xlii, in Matth.) which is included in Chrysostom's works
2 Pelagius, Exposit. Cath. Fid.

Obj. 3: Further, precepts are given in order to direct man in the way of salvation, according to Ps. 18:9: "The commandment of the Lord is lightsome, enlightening the eyes." Now it is useless to direct anyone to what is impossible. Therefore it is not impossible to fulfill this precept in this life.

On the contrary, Augustine says (De Perfect. Justit. viii): "In the fulness of heavenly charity this precept will be fulfilled: Thou shalt love the Lord thy God," etc. For as long as any carnal concupiscence remains, that can be restrained by continence, man cannot love God with all his heart.

I answer that, A precept can be fulfilled in two ways; perfectly, and imperfectly. A precept is fulfilled perfectly, when the end intended by the author of the precept is reached; yet it is fulfilled, imperfectly however, when although the end intended by its author is not reached, nevertheless the order to that end is not departed from. Thus if the commander of an army order his soldiers to fight, his command will be perfectly obeyed by those who fight and conquer the foe, which is the commander's intention; yet it is fulfilled, albeit imperfectly, by those who fight without gaining the victory, provided they do nothing contrary to military discipline. Now God intends by this precept that man should be entirely united to Him, and this will be realized in heaven, when God will be "all in all," according to 1 Cor. 15:28. Hence this precept will be observed fully and perfectly in heaven; yet it is fulfilled, though imperfectly, on the way. Nevertheless on the way one man will fulfil it more perfectly than another, and so much the more, as he approaches by some kind of likeness to the perfection of heaven.

Reply Obj. 1: This argument proves that the precept can be fulfilled after a fashion on the way, but not perfectly.

Reply Obj. 2: Even as the soldier who fights legitimately without conquering is not blamed nor deserves to be punished for this, so too he that does not fulfil this precept on the way, but does nothing against the love of God, does not sin mortally.

Reply Obj. 3: As Augustine says (De Perfect. Justit. viii), "why should not this perfection be prescribed to man, although no man attains it in this life? For one cannot run straight unless one knows whither to run. And how would one know this if no precept pointed it out.".

* * * * *

SEVENTH ARTICLE [II-II, Q. 44, Art. 7]

Whether the Precept of Love of Our Neighbor Is Fittingly Expressed?

Objection 1: It would seem that the precept of the love of our neighbor is unfittingly expressed. For the love of charity extends to all men, even to our enemies, as may be seen in Matt. 5:44. But the word "neighbor" denotes a kind of "nighness" which does not seem to exist towards all men. Therefore it seems that this precept is unfittingly expressed.

Obj. 2: Further, according to the Philosopher (Ethic. ix, 8) "the origin of our friendly relations with others lies in our relation to ourselves," whence it seems to follow that love of self is the origin of one's love for one's neighbor. Now the principle is greater than that which results from it. Therefore man ought not to love his neighbor as himself.

Obj. 3: Further, man loves himself, but not his neighbor, naturally. Therefore it is unfitting that he should be commanded to love his neighbor as himself.

On the contrary, It is written (Matt. 22:39): "The second" commandment "is like to this: Thou shalt love thy neighbor as thyself."

I answer that, This precept is fittingly expressed, for it indicates both the reason for loving and the mode of love. The reason for loving is indicated in the word "neighbor," because the reason why we ought to love others out of charity is because they are nigh to us, both as to the natural image of God, and as to the capacity for glory. Nor does it matter whether we say "neighbor," or "brother" according to 1 John 4:21, or "friend," according to Lev. 19:18, because all these words express the same affinity.

The mode of love is indicated in the words "as thyself." This does not mean that a man must love his neighbor equally as himself, but in like manner as himself, and this in three ways. First, as regards the end, namely, that he should love his neighbor for God's sake, even as he loves himself for God's sake, so that his love for his neighbor is a *holy* love. Secondly, as regards the rule of love, namely, that a man should not give way to his neighbor in evil, but only in good things, even as he ought to gratify his will in good things alone, so that his love for his neighbor may be a *righteous* love. Thirdly, as regards the reason for loving, namely, that a man should love his neighbor, not for his own profit, or pleasure, but in the sense of wishing his neighbor well, even as he wishes himself well, so that his love for his neighbor may be a *true* love: since when a man loves his neighbor for his own profit or pleasure, he does not love his neighbor truly, but loves himself.

This suffices for the Replies to the Objections.

* * * * *

EIGHTH ARTICLE [II-II, Q. 44, Art. 8]

Whether the Order of Charity Is Included in the Precept?

Objection 1: It would seem that the order of charity is not included in the precept. For whoever transgresses a precept does a wrong. But if man loves some one as much as he ought, and loves any other man more, he wrongs no man. Therefore he does not transgress the precept. Therefore the order of charity is not included in the precept.

Obj. 2: Further, whatever is a matter of precept is sufficiently delivered to us in Holy Writ. Now the order of charity which was given above (Q. 26) is nowhere indicated in Holy Writ. Therefore it is not included in the precept.

Obj. 3: Further, order implies some kind of distinction. But the love of our neighbor is prescribed without any distinction, in the words, "Thou shalt love thy neighbor as thyself." Therefore the order of charity is not included in the precept.

On the contrary, Whatever God works in us by His grace, He teaches us first of all by His Law, according to Jer. 31:33: "I will give My Law in their heart[1]." Now God causes in us the order of charity, according to Cant. 2:4: "He set in order charity in me." Therefore the order of charity comes under the precept of the Law.

I answer that, As stated above (A. 4, ad 1), the mode which is essential to an act of virtue comes under the precept which

---

[1] Vulg.: 'in their bowels, and I will write it in their heart'

prescribes that virtuous act. Now the order of charity is essential to the virtue, since it is based on the proportion of love to the thing beloved, as shown above (Q. 25, A. 12; Q. 26, AA. 1, 2). It is therefore evident that the order of charity must come under the precept.

Reply Obj. 1: A man gratifies more the person he loves more, so that if he loved less one whom he ought to love more, he would wish to gratify more one whom he ought to gratify less, and so he would do an injustice to the one he ought to love more.

Reply Obj. 2: The order of those four things we have to love out of charity is expressed in Holy Writ. For when we are commanded to love God with our "whole heart," we are given to understand that we must love Him above all things. When we are commanded to love our neighbor "as ourselves," the love of self is set before love of our neighbor. In like manner where we are commanded (1 John 3:16) "to lay down our souls," i.e. the life of our bodies, "for the brethren," we are given to understand that a man ought to love his neighbor more than his own body; and again when we are commanded (Gal. 6:10) to "work good ... especially to those who are of the household of the faith," and when a man is blamed (1 Tim. 5:8) if he "have not care of his own, and especially of those of his house," it means that we ought to love most those of our neighbors who are more virtuous or more closely united to us.

Reply Obj. 3: It follows from the very words, "Thou shalt love thy neighbor" that those who are nearer to us are to be loved more.

45. OF THE GIFT OF WISDOM (In Six Articles)

We must now consider the gift of wisdom which corresponds to charity; and firstly, wisdom itself, secondly, the opposite vice. Under the first head there are six points of inquiry:

(1) Whether wisdom should be reckoned among the gifts of the Holy Ghost?
(2) What is its subject?
(3) Whether wisdom is only speculative or also practical?
(4) Whether the wisdom that is a gift is compatible with mortal sin?

(5) Whether it is in all those who have sanctifying grace?
(6) Which beatitude corresponds to it?.

* * * * *

FIRST ARTICLE [II-II, Q. 45, Art. 1]

Whether Wisdom Should Be Reckoned Among the Gifts of the Holy Ghost?

Objection 1: It would seem that wisdom ought not to be reckoned among the gifts of the Holy Ghost. For the gifts are more perfect than the virtues, as stated above (I-II, Q. 68, A. 8). Now virtue is directed to the good alone, wherefore Augustine says (De Lib. Arb. ii, 19) that "no man makes bad use of the virtues." Much more therefore are the gifts of the Holy Ghost directed to the good alone. But wisdom is directed to evil also, for it is written (James 3:15) that a certain wisdom is "earthly, sensual, devilish." Therefore wisdom should not be reckoned among the gifts of the Holy Ghost.

Obj. 2: Further, according to Augustine (De Trin. xii, 14) "wisdom is the knowledge of Divine things." Now that knowledge of Divine things which man can acquire by his natural endowments, belongs to the wisdom which is an intellectual virtue, while the supernatural knowledge of Divine things belongs to faith which is a theological virtue, as explained above (Q. 4, A. 5; I-II, Q. 62, A. 3). Therefore wisdom should be called a virtue rather than a gift.

Obj. 3: Further, it is written (Job 28:28): "Behold the fear of the Lord, that is wisdom, and to depart from evil, that is understanding." And in this passage according to the rendering of the Septuagint which Augustine follows (De Trin. xii, 14; xiv, 1) we read: "Behold piety, that is wisdom." Now both fear and piety are gifts of the Holy Ghost. Therefore wisdom should not be reckoned among the gifts of the Holy Ghost, as though it were distinct from the others.

On the contrary, It is written (Isa. 11:2): "The Spirit of the Lord shall rest upon Him; the spirit of wisdom and of understanding."

I answer that, According to the Philosopher (Metaph. i: 2), it belongs to wisdom to consider the highest cause. By means of that cause we are able to form a most certain judgment about other causes, and according thereto all things should be set in order. Now the highest cause may be understood in two ways, either simply or in some particular genus. Accordingly he that knows the highest cause in any particular genus, and by its means is able to judge and set in order all the things that belong to that genus, is said to be wise in that genus, for instance in medicine or architecture, according to 1 Cor. 3:10: "As a wise architect, I have laid a foundation." On the other hand, he who knows the cause that is simply the highest, which is God, is said to be wise simply, because he is able to judge and set in order all things according to Divine rules.

Now man obtains this judgment through the Holy Ghost, according to 1 Cor. 2:15: "The spiritual man judgeth all things," because as stated in the same chapter (1 Cor. 2:10), "the Spirit searcheth all things, yea the deep things of God." Wherefore it is evident that wisdom is a gift of the Holy Ghost.

Reply Obj. 1: A thing is said to be good in two senses: first in the sense that it is truly good and simply perfect, secondly, by a kind of likeness, being perfect in wickedness; thus we speak of a good or a perfect thief, as the Philosopher observes (Metaph. v, text. 21). And just as with regard to those things which are truly good, we find a highest cause, namely the sovereign good which is the last end, by knowing which, man is said to be truly wise, so too in evil things something is to be found to which all others are to be referred as to a last end, by knowing which, man is said to be wise unto evil doing, according to Jer. 4:22: "They are wise to do evils, but to do good they have no knowledge." Now whoever turns away from his due end, must needs fix on some undue end, since every agent acts for an end. Wherefore, if he fixes his end in external earthly things, his "wisdom" is called "earthly;" if in the goods of the body, it is called "sensual wisdom," if in some excellence, it is called "devilish wisdom" because it imitates the devil's pride, of which it is written (Job 41:25): "He is king over all the children of pride."

Reply Obj. 2: The wisdom which is called a gift of the Holy Ghost, differs from that which is an acquired intellectual virtue, for the latter is attained by human effort, whereas the latter is "descending from above" (James 3:15). In like manner it differs from faith, since faith assents to the Divine truth in itself, whereas it belongs to the gift of wisdom to judge according to the Divine truth. Hence the gift of wisdom presupposes faith, because "a man judges well what he knows" (Ethic. i, 3).

Reply Obj. 3: Just as piety which pertains to the worship of God is a manifestation of faith, in so far as we make profession of faith by worshipping God, so too, piety manifests wisdom. For this reason piety is stated to be wisdom, and so is fear, for the same reason, because if a man fear and worship God, this shows that he has a right judgment about Divine things.

* * * * *

SECOND ARTICLE [II-II, Q. 45, Art. 2]

Whether Wisdom Is in the Intellect As Its Subject?

Objection 1: It would seem that wisdom is not in the intellect as its subject. For Augustine says (Ep. cxx) that "wisdom is the charity of God." Now charity is in the will as its subject, and not in the intellect, as stated above (Q. 24, A. 1). Therefore wisdom is not in the intellect as its subject.

Obj. 2: Further, it is written (Ecclus. 6:23): "The wisdom of doctrine is according to her name," for wisdom (sapientia) may be described as "sweet-tasting science (sapida scientia)," and this would seem to regard the appetite, to which it belongs to taste spiritual pleasure or sweetness. Therefore wisdom is in the appetite rather than in the intellect.

Obj. 3: Further, the intellective power is sufficiently perfected by the gift of understanding. Now it is superfluous to require two things where one suffices for the purpose. Therefore wisdom is not in the intellect.

On the contrary, Gregory says (Moral. ii, 49) that "wisdom is contrary to folly." But folly is in the intellect. Therefore wisdom is also.

I answer that, As stated above (A. 1), wisdom denotes a certain rectitude of judgment according to the Eternal Law. Now rectitude of judgment is twofold: first, on account of perfect use of reason, secondly, on account of a certain connaturality with the matter about which one has to judge. Thus, about matters of chastity, a man after inquiring with his reason forms a right judgment, if he has learnt the science of morals, while he who has the habit of chastity judges of such matters by a kind of connaturality.

Accordingly it belongs to the wisdom that is an intellectual virtue to pronounce right judgment about Divine things after reason has made its inquiry, but it belongs to wisdom as a gift of the Holy Ghost to judge aright about them on account of connaturality with them: thus Dionysius says (Div. Nom. ii) that "Hierotheus is perfect in Divine things, for he not only learns, but is patient of, Divine things."

Now this sympathy or connaturality for Divine things is the result of charity, which unites us to God, according to 1 Cor. 6:17: "He who is joined to the Lord, is one spirit." Consequently wisdom which is a gift, has its cause in the will, which cause is charity, but it has its essence in the intellect, whose act is to judge aright, as stated above (I-II, Q. 14, A. 1).

Reply Obj. 1: Augustine is speaking of wisdom as to its cause, whence also wisdom (sapientia) takes its name, in so far as it denotes a certain sweetness (saporem). Hence the Reply to the Second Objection is evident, that is if this be the true meaning of the text quoted. For, apparently this is not the case, because such an exposition of the text would only fit the Latin word for wisdom, whereas it does not apply to the Greek and perhaps not in other languages. Hence it would seem that in the text quoted wisdom stands for the renown of doctrine, for which it is praised by all.

Reply Obj. 3: The intellect exercises a twofold act, perception and judgment. The gift of understanding regards the former; the gift of wisdom regards the latter according to the Divine ideas, the gift of knowledge, according to human ideas.

* * * * *

THIRD ARTICLE [II-II, Q. 45, Art. 3]

Whether Wisdom Is Merely Speculative, or Practical Also?

Objection 1: It would seem that wisdom is not practical but merely speculative. For the gift of wisdom is more excellent than the wisdom which is an intellectual virtue. But wisdom, as an intellectual virtue, is merely speculative. Much more therefore is wisdom, as a gift, speculative and not practical.

Obj. 2: Further, the practical intellect is about matters of operation which are contingent. But wisdom is about Divine things which are eternal and necessary. Therefore wisdom cannot be practical.

Obj. 3: Further, Gregory says (Moral. vi, 37) that "in contemplation we seek the Beginning which is God, but in action we labor under a mighty bundle of wants." Now wisdom regards the vision of Divine things, in which there is no toiling under a load, since according to Wis. 8:16, "her conversation hath no bitterness, nor her company any tediousness." Therefore wisdom is merely contemplative, and not practical or active.

On the contrary, It is written (Col. 4:5): "Walk with wisdom towards them that are without." Now this pertains to action. Therefore wisdom is not merely speculative, but also practical.

I answer that, As Augustine says (De Trin. xii, 14), the higher part of the reason is the province of wisdom, while the lower part is the domain of knowledge. Now the higher reason according to the same authority (De Trin. xii, 7) "is intent on the consideration and consultation of the heavenly," i.e. Divine, "types"[1]; it considers them, in so far as it contemplates Divine things in themselves, and it consults them, in so far as it judges of human acts by Divine things, and directs human acts according to Divine rules.

Accordingly wisdom as a gift, is not merely speculative but also practical.

Reply Obj. 1: The higher a virtue is, the greater the number of things to which it extends, as stated in De Causis, prop. x, xvii. Wherefore from the very fact that wisdom as a gift is more excellent than wisdom as an intellectual virtue, since it attains to God more intimately by a kind of union of the soul with Him, it is able to direct us not only in contemplation but also in action.

Reply Obj. 2: Divine things are indeed necessary and eternal in themselves, yet they are the rules of the contingent things which are the subject-matter of human actions.

Reply Obj. 3: A thing is considered in itself before being compared with something else. Wherefore to wisdom belongs first of all contemplation which is the vision of the Beginning, and afterwards the direction of human acts according to the Divine rules. Nor from the direction of wisdom does there result any bitterness or toil in human acts; on the contrary the result of wisdom is to make the bitter sweet, and labor a rest.

* * * * *

---

1 Cf. I, Q. 79, A. 9; I-II, Q. 74, A. 7

FOURTH ARTICLE [II-II, Q. 45, Art. 4]

Whether Wisdom Can Be Without Grace, and with Mortal Sin?

Objection 1: It would seem that wisdom can be without grace and with mortal sin. For saints glory chiefly in such things as are incompatible with mortal sin, according to 2 Cor. 1:12: "Our glory is this, the testimony of our conscience." Now one ought not to glory in one's wisdom, according to Jer. 9:23: "Let not the wise man glory in his wisdom." Therefore wisdom can be without grace and with mortal sin.

Obj. 2: Further, wisdom denotes knowledge of Divine things, as stated above (A. 1). Now one in mortal sin may have knowledge of the Divine truth, according to Rom. 1:18: "(Those men that) detain the truth of God in injustice." Therefore wisdom is compatible with mortal sin.

Obj. 3: Further, Augustine says (De Trin. xv, 18) while speaking of charity: "Nothing surpasses this gift of God, it is this alone that divides the children of the eternal kingdom from the children of eternal perdition." But wisdom is distinct from charity. Therefore it does not divide the children of the kingdom from the children of perdition. Therefore it is compatible with mortal sin.

On the contrary, It is written (Wis. 1:4): "Wisdom will not enter into a malicious soul, nor dwell in a body subject to sins."

I answer that, The wisdom which is a gift of the Holy Ghost, as stated above (A. 1), enables us to judge aright of Divine things, or of other things according to Divine rules, by reason of a certain connaturalness or union with Divine things, which is the effect of charity, as stated above (A. 2; Q. 23, A. 5). Hence the wisdom of which we are speaking presupposes charity. Now charity is incompatible with mortal sin, as shown above (Q. 24, A. 12). Therefore it follows that the wisdom of which we are speaking cannot be together with mortal sin.

Reply Obj. 1: These words are to be understood as referring to worldly wisdom, or to wisdom in Divine things acquired through human reasons. In such wisdom the saints do not glory, according to Prov. 30:2: "The wisdom of men is not with Me": But they do glory in Divine wisdom according to 1 Cor. 1:30: "(Who) of God is made unto us wisdom."

Reply Obj. 2: This argument considers, not the wisdom of which we speak but that which is acquired by the study and research of reason, and is compatible with mortal sin.

Reply Obj. 3: Although wisdom is distinct from charity, it presupposes it, and for that very reason divides the children of perdition from the children of the kingdom.

* * * * *

FIFTH ARTICLE [II-II, Q. 45, Art. 5]

Whether Wisdom Is in All Who Have Grace?

Objection 1: It would seem that wisdom is not in all who have grace. For it is more to have wisdom than to hear wisdom. Now it is only for the perfect to hear wisdom, according to 1 Cor. 2:6: "We speak wisdom among the perfect." Since then not all who have grace are perfect, it seems that much less all who have grace have wisdom.

Obj. 2: Further, "The wise man sets things in order," as the Philosopher states (Metaph. i, 2): and it is written (James 3:17) that the wise man "judges without dissimulation[1]". Now it is not for all that have grace, to judge, or put others in order, but only for those in authority. Therefore wisdom is not in all that have grace.

Obj. 3: Further, "Wisdom is a remedy against folly," as Gregory says (Moral. ii, 49). Now many that have grace are naturally foolish, for instance madmen who are baptized or those who without being guilty of mortal sin have become insane. Therefore wisdom is not in all that have grace.

On the contrary, Whoever is without mortal sin, is beloved of God; since he has charity, whereby he loves God, and God loves them that love Him (Prov. 8:17). Now it is written (Wis. 7:28) that "God loveth none but him that dwelleth with wisdom." Therefore wisdom is in all those who have charity and are without mortal sin.

I answer that, The wisdom of which we are speaking, as stated above (A. 4), denotes a certain rectitude of judgment in the contemplation and consultation of Divine things, and as to both of these men obtain various degrees of wisdom through union

---

1 Vulg.: 'The wisdom that is from above ... is ... without judging, without dissimulation'

with Divine things. For the measure of right judgment attained by some, whether in the contemplation of Divine things or in directing human affairs according to Divine rules, is no more than suffices for their salvation. This measure is wanting to none who is without mortal sin through having sanctifying grace, since if nature does not fail in necessaries, much less does grace fail: wherefore it is written (1 John 2:27): "(His) unction teacheth you of all things."

Some, however, receive a higher degree of the gift of wisdom, both as to the contemplation of Divine things (by both knowing more exalted mysteries and being able to impart this knowledge to others) and as to the direction of human affairs according to Divine rules (by being able to direct not only themselves but also others according to those rules). This degree of wisdom is not common to all that have sanctifying grace, but belongs rather to the gratuitous graces, which the Holy Ghost dispenses as He will, according to 1 Cor. 12:8: "To one indeed by the Spirit is given the word of wisdom," etc.

Reply Obj. 1: The Apostle speaks there of wisdom, as extending to the hidden mysteries of Divine things, as indeed he says himself (2 Cor. 1:7): "We speak the wisdom of God in a mystery, a wisdom which is hidden."

Reply Obj. 2: Although it belongs to those alone who are in authority to direct and judge other men, yet every man is competent to direct and judge his own actions, as Dionysius declares (Ep. ad Demophil.).

Reply Obj. 3: Baptized idiots, like little children, have the habit of wisdom, which is a gift of the Holy Ghost, but they have not the act, on account of the bodily impediment which hinders the use of reason in them.

* * * * *

SIXTH ARTICLE [II-II, Q. 45, Art. 6]

Whether the Seventh Beatitude Corresponds to the Gift of Wisdom?

Objection 1: It seems that the seventh beatitude does not correspond to the gift of wisdom. For the seventh beatitude is: "Blessed are the peacemakers, for they shall be called the children of God." Now both these things belong to charity: since of peace it is written (Ps. 118:165): "Much peace have they that love Thy law," and, as the Apostle says (Rom. 5:5), "the charity of God is poured forth in our hearts by the Holy Ghost Who is given to us," and Who is "the Spirit of adoption of sons, whereby we cry: Abba [Father]" (Rom. 8:15). Therefore the seventh beatitude ought to be ascribed to charity rather than to wisdom.

Obj. 2: Further, a thing is declared by its proximate effect rather than by its remote effect. Now the proximate effect of wisdom seems to be charity, according to Wis. 7:27: "Through nations she conveyeth herself into holy souls; she maketh the friends of God and prophets": whereas peace and the adoption of sons seem to be remote effects, since they result from charity, as stated above (Q. 29, A. 3). Therefore the beatitude corresponding to wisdom should be determined in respect of the love of charity rather than in respect of peace.

Obj. 3: Further, it is written (James 3:17): "The wisdom, that is from above, first indeed is chaste, then peaceable, modest, easy to be persuaded, consenting to the good, full of mercy and good fruits, judging without dissimulation[1]." Therefore the beatitude corresponding to wisdom should not refer to peace rather than to the other effects of heavenly wisdom.

On the contrary, Augustine says (De Serm. Dom. in Monte i, 4) that "wisdom is becoming to peacemakers, in whom there is no movement of rebellion, but only obedience to reason."

I answer that, The seventh beatitude is fittingly ascribed to the gift of wisdom, both as to the merit and as to the reward. The merit is denoted in the words, "Blessed are the peacemakers." Now a peacemaker is one who makes peace, either in himself, or in others: and in both cases this is the result of setting in due order those things in which peace is established, for "peace is the tranquillity of order," according to Augustine (De Civ. Dei xix, 13). Now it belongs to wisdom to set things in order, as the Philosopher declares (Metaph. i, 2), wherefore peaceableness is fittingly ascribed to wisdom. The reward is expressed in the words, "they shall be called the children of God." Now men are called the children of God in so far as they participate in the likeness of the only-begotten and natural Son of God, according to Rom. 8:29, "Whom He foreknew ... to be made conformable to the image of His Son," Who is Wisdom Begotten. Hence by participating in the gift of wisdom, man attains to the sonship of God.

---

[1] Vulg.: 'without judging, without dissimulation'

Reply Obj. 1: It belongs to charity to be at peace, but it belongs to wisdom to make peace by setting things in order. Likewise the Holy Ghost is called the "Spirit of adoption" in so far as we receive from Him the likeness of the natural Son, Who is the Begotten Wisdom.

Reply Obj. 2: These words refer to the Uncreated Wisdom, which in the first place unites itself to us by the gift of charity, and consequently reveals to us the mysteries the knowledge of which is infused wisdom. Hence, the infused wisdom which is a gift, is not the cause but the effect of charity.

Reply Obj. 3: As stated above (A. 3) it belongs to wisdom, as a gift, not only to contemplate Divine things, but also to regulate human acts. Now the first thing to be effected in this direction of human acts is the removal of evils opposed to wisdom: wherefore fear is said to be "the beginning of wisdom," because it makes us shun evil, while the last thing is like an end, whereby all things are reduced to their right order; and it is this that constitutes peace. Hence James said with reason that "the wisdom that is from above" (and this is the gift of the Holy Ghost) "first indeed is chaste," because it avoids the corruption of sin, and "then peaceable," wherein lies the ultimate effect of wisdom, for which reason peace is numbered among the beatitudes. As to the things that follow, they declare in becoming order the means whereby wisdom leads to peace. For when a man, by chastity, avoids the corruption of sin, the first thing he has to do is, as far as he can, to be moderate in all things, and in this respect wisdom is said to be modest. Secondly, in those matters in which he is not sufficient by himself, he should be guided by the advice of others, and as to this we are told further that wisdom is "easy to be persuaded." These two are conditions required that man may be at peace with himself. But in order that man may be at peace with others it is furthermore required, first that he should not be opposed to their good; this is what is meant by "consenting to the good." Secondly, that he should bring to his neighbor's deficiencies, sympathy in his heart, and succor in his actions, and this is denoted by the words "full of mercy and good fruits." Thirdly, he should strive in all charity to correct the sins of others, and this is indicated by the words "judging without dissimulation[1]," lest he should purpose to sate his hatred under cover of correction.

---

[1] Vulg.: 'The wisdom that is from above... is... without judging, without dissimulation.

46. OF FOLLY WHICH IS OPPOSED TO WISDOM (In Three Articles)

We must now consider folly which is opposed to wisdom; and under this head there are three points of inquiry:

(1) Whether folly is contrary to wisdom?
(2) Whether folly is a sin?
(3) To which capital sin is it reducible?.

* * * * *

FIRST ARTICLE [II-II, Q. 46, Art. 1]

Whether Folly Is Contrary to Wisdom?

Objection 1: It would seem that folly is not contrary to wisdom. For seemingly unwisdom is directly opposed to wisdom. But folly does not seem to be the same as unwisdom, for the latter is apparently about Divine things alone, whereas folly is about both Divine and human things. Therefore folly is not contrary to wisdom.

Obj. 2: Further, one contrary is not the way to arrive at the other. But folly is the way to arrive at wisdom, for it is written (1 Cor. 3:18): "If any man among you seem to be wise in this world, let him become a fool, that he may be wise." Therefore folly is not opposed to wisdom.

Obj. 3: Further, one contrary is not the cause of the other. But wisdom is the cause of folly; for it is written (Jer. 10:14): "Every man is become a fool for knowledge," and wisdom is a kind of knowledge. Moreover, it is written (Isa. 47:10): "Thy wisdom and thy knowledge, this hath deceived thee." Now it belongs to folly to be deceived. Therefore folly is not contrary to wisdom.

Obj. 4: Further, Isidore says (Etym. x, under the letter S) that "a fool is one whom shame does not incite to sorrow, and who is unconcerned when he is injured." But this pertains to spiritual wisdom, according to Gregory (Moral. x, 49). Therefore folly is not opposed to wisdom.

On the contrary, Gregory says (Moral. ii, 26) that "the gift of wisdom is given as a remedy against folly."

I answer that, Stultitia (Folly) seems to take its name from *stupor;* wherefore Isidore says (loc. cit.): "A fool is one who through dullness *(stuporem)* remains unmoved." And folly differs from fatuity, according to the same authority (Etym. x), in that folly implies apathy in the heart and dullness in the senses, while fatuity denotes entire privation of the spiritual sense. Therefore folly is fittingly opposed to wisdom.

For "sapiens" *(wise)* as Isidore says (Etym. x) "is so named from *sapor* (savor), because just as the taste is quick to distinguish between savors of meats, so is a wise man in discerning things and causes." Wherefore it is manifest that *folly* is opposed to *wisdom* as its contrary, while *fatuity* is opposed to it as a pure negation: since the fatuous man lacks the sense of judgment, while the fool has the sense, though dulled, whereas the wise man has the sense acute and penetrating.

Reply Obj. 1: According to Isidore (Etym. x), "unwisdom is contrary to wisdom because it lacks the savor of discretion and sense"; so that unwisdom is seemingly the same as folly. Yet a man would appear to be a fool chiefly through some deficiency in the verdict of that judgment, which is according to the highest cause, for if a man fails in judgment about some trivial matter, he is not for that reason called a fool.

Reply Obj. 2: Just as there is an evil wisdom, as stated above (Q. 45, A. 1, ad 1), called "worldly wisdom," because it takes for the highest cause and last end some worldly good, so too there is a good folly opposed to this evil wisdom, whereby man despises worldly things: and it is of this folly that the Apostle speaks.

Reply Obj. 3: It is the wisdom of the world that deceives and makes us foolish in God's sight, as is evident from the Apostle's words (1 Cor. 3:19).

Reply Obj. 4: To be unconcerned when one is injured is sometimes due to the fact that one has no taste for worldly things, but only for heavenly things. Hence this belongs not to worldly but to Divine wisdom, as Gregory declares (Moral. x, 49). Sometimes however it is the result of a man's being simply stupid about everything, as may be seen in idiots, who do not discern what is injurious to them, and this belongs to folly simply.

* * * * *

SECOND ARTICLE [II-II, Q. 45, Art. 2]

Whether Folly Is a Sin?

Objection 1: It would seem that folly is not a sin. For no sin arises in us from nature. But some are fools naturally. Therefore folly is not a sin.

Obj. 2: Further, "Every sin is voluntary," according to Augustine (De Vera Relig. xiv). But folly is not voluntary. Therefore it is not a sin.

Obj. 3: Further, every sin is contrary to a Divine precept. But folly is not contrary to any precept. Therefore folly is not a sin.

On the contrary, It is written (Prov. 1:32): "The prosperity of fools shall destroy them." But no man is destroyed save for sin. Therefore folly is a sin.

I answer that, Folly, as stated above (A. 1), denotes dullness of sense in judging, and chiefly as regards the highest cause, which is the last end and the sovereign good. Now a man may in this respect contract dullness in judgment in two ways. First, from a natural indisposition, as in the case of idiots, and such like folly is no sin. Secondly, by plunging his sense into earthly things, whereby his sense is rendered incapable of perceiving Divine things, according to 1 Cor. 2:14, "The sensual man perceiveth not these things that are of the Spirit of God," even as sweet things have no savor for a man whose taste is infected with an evil humor: and such like folly is a sin.

This suffices for the Reply to the First Objection.

Reply Obj. 2: Though no man wishes to be a fool, yet he wishes those things of which folly is a consequence, viz. to withdraw his sense from spiritual things and to plunge it into earthly things. The same thing happens in regard to other sins; for the lustful man desires pleasure, without which there is no sin, although he does not desire sin simply, for he would wish to enjoy the pleasure without sin.

Reply Obj. 3: Folly is opposed to the precepts about the contemplation of truth, of which we have spoken above (Q. 16) when we were treating of knowledge and understanding.

* * * * *

THIRD ARTICLE [II-II, Q. 46, Art. 3]

Whether Folly Is a Daughter of Lust?

Objection 1: It would seem that folly is not a daughter of lust. For Gregory (Moral. xxxi, 45) enumerates the daughters of lust, among which however he makes no mention of folly. Therefore folly does not proceed from lust.

Obj. 2: Further, the Apostle says (1 Cor. 3:19): "The wisdom of this world is foolishness with God." Now, according to Gregory (Moral. x, 29) "the wisdom of this world consists in covering the heart with crafty devices;" and this savors of duplicity. Therefore folly is a daughter of duplicity rather than of lust.

Obj. 3: Further, anger especially is the cause of fury and madness in some persons; and this pertains to folly. Therefore folly arises from anger rather than from lust.

On the contrary, It is written (Prov. 7:22): "Immediately he followeth her," i.e. the harlot ... "not knowing that he is drawn like a fool to bonds."

I answer that, As already stated (A. 2), folly, in so far as it is a sin, is caused by the spiritual sense being dulled, so as to be incapable of judging spiritual things. Now man's sense is plunged into earthly things chiefly by lust, which is about the greatest of pleasures; and these absorb the mind more than any others. Therefore the folly which is a sin, arises chiefly from lust.

Reply Obj. 1: It is part of folly that a man should have a distaste for God and His gifts. Hence Gregory mentions two daughters of lust, pertaining to folly, namely, "hatred of God" and "despair of the life to come"; thus he divides folly into two parts as it were.

Reply Obj. 2: These words of the Apostle are to be understood, not causally but essentially, because, to wit, worldly wisdom itself is folly with God. Hence it does not follow that whatever belongs to worldly wisdom, is a cause of this folly.

Reply Obj. 3: Anger by reason of its keenness, as stated above (I-II, Q. 48, AA. 2, 3, 4), produces a great change in the nature of the body, wherefore it conduces very much to the folly which results from a bodily impediment. On the other hand the folly which is caused by a spiritual impediment, viz. by the mind being plunged into earthly things, arises chiefly from lust, as stated above.

TREATISE ON THE CARDINAL VIRTUES (QQ. 47-170).

47. OF PRUDENCE, CONSIDERED IN ITSELF (In Sixteen Articles)

After treating of the theological virtues, we must in due sequence consider the cardinal virtues. In the first place we shall consider prudence in itself; secondly, its parts; thirdly, the corresponding gift; fourthly, the contrary vices; fifthly, the precepts concerning prudence.

Under the first head there are sixteen points of inquiry:

(1) Whether prudence is in the will or in the reason?
(2) If in the reason, whether it is only in the practical, or also in the speculative reason?
(3) Whether it takes cognizance of singulars?
(4) Whether it is virtue?
(5) Whether it is a special virtue?
(6) Whether it appoints the end to the moral virtues?
(7) Whether it fixes the mean in the moral virtues?
(8) Whether its proper act is command?
(9) Whether solicitude or watchfulness belongs to prudence?
(10) Whether prudence extends to the governing of many?
(11) Whether the prudence which regards private good is the same in species as that which regards the common good?
(12) Whether prudence is in subjects, or only in their rulers?
(13) Whether prudence is in the wicked?
(14) Whether prudence is in all good men?
(15) Whether prudence is in us naturally?
(16) Whether prudence is lost by forgetfulness?.

* * * * *

FIRST ARTICLE [II-II, Q. 47, Art. 1]

Whether Prudence Is in the Cognitive or in the Appetitive Faculty?

Objection 1: It would seem that prudence is not in the cognitive but in the appetitive faculty. For Augustine says (De Morib. Eccl. xv): "Prudence is love choosing wisely between the things that help and those that hinder." Now love is not in the cognitive, but in the appetitive faculty. Therefore prudence is in the appetitive faculty.

Obj. 2: Further, as appears from the foregoing definition it belongs to prudence "to choose wisely." But choice is an act of the appetitive faculty, as stated above (I-II, Q. 13, A. 1). Therefore prudence is not in the cognitive but in the appetitive faculty.

Obj. 3: Further, the Philosopher says (Ethic. vi, 5) that "in art it is better to err voluntarily than involuntarily, whereas in the case of prudence, as of the virtues, it is worse." Now the moral virtues, of which he is treating there, are in the appetitive faculty, whereas art is in the reason. Therefore prudence is in the appetitive rather than in the rational faculty.

On the contrary, Augustine says (QQ. lxxxiii, qu. 61): "Prudence is the knowledge of what to seek and what to avoid."

I answer that, As Isidore says (Etym. x): "A prudent man is one who sees as it were from afar, for his sight is keen, and he foresees the event of uncertainties." Now sight belongs not to the appetitive but to the cognitive faculty. Wherefore it is manifest that prudence belongs directly to the cognitive, and not to the sensitive faculty, because by the latter we know nothing but what is within reach and offers itself to the senses: while to obtain knowledge of the future from knowledge of the present or past, which pertains to prudence, belongs properly to the reason, because this is done by a process of comparison. It follows therefore that prudence, properly speaking, is in the reason.

Reply Obj. 1: As stated above (I, Q. 82, A. 4) the will moves all the faculties to their acts. Now the first act of the appetitive faculty is love, as stated above (I-II, Q. 25, AA. 1, 2). Accordingly prudence is said to be love, not indeed essentially, but in so far as love moves to the act of prudence. Wherefore Augustine goes on to say that "prudence is love discerning aright that which helps from that which hinders us in tending to God." Now love is said to discern because it moves the reason to discern.

Reply Obj. 2: The prudent man considers things afar off, in so far as they tend to be a help or a hindrance to that which has to be done at the present time. Hence it is clear that those things which prudence considers stand in relation to this other, as in relation to the end. Now of those things that are directed to the end there is counsel in the reason, and choice in the appetite, of which two, counsel belongs more properly to prudence, since the Philosopher states (Ethic. vi, 5, 7, 9) that a prudent man "takes good counsel." But as choice presupposes counsel, since it is "the desire for what has been already counselled" (Ethic. iii, 2), it follows that choice can also be ascribed to prudence indirectly, in so far, to wit, as prudence directs the choice by means of counsel.

Reply Obj. 3: The worth of prudence consists not in thought merely, but in its application to action, which is the end of the practical reason. Wherefore if any defect occur in this, it is most contrary to prudence, since, the end being of most import in everything, it follows that a defect which touches the end is the worst of all. Hence the Philosopher goes on to say (Ethic. vi, 5) that prudence is "something more than a merely rational habit," such as art is, since, as stated above (I-II, Q. 57, A. 4) it includes application to action, which application is an act of the will.

* * * * *

SECOND ARTICLE [II-II, Q. 47, Art. 2]

Whether Prudence Belongs to the Practical Reason Alone or Also to the Speculative Reason?

Objection 1: It would seem that prudence belongs not only to the practical, but also to the speculative reason. For it is written (Prov. 10:23): "Wisdom is prudence to a man." Now wisdom consists chiefly in contemplation. Therefore prudence does also.

Obj. 2: Further, Ambrose says (De Offic. i, 24): "Prudence is concerned with the quest of truth, and fills us with the desire of fuller knowledge." Now this belongs to the speculative reason. Therefore prudence resides also in the speculative reason.

Obj. 3: Further, the Philosopher assigns art and prudence to the same part of the soul (Ethic. vi, 1). Now art may be not only practical but also speculative, as in the case of the liberal arts. Therefore prudence also is both practical and speculative.

On the contrary, The Philosopher says (Ethic. vi, 5) that prudence is right reason applied to action. Now this belongs to none but the practical reason. Therefore prudence is in the practical reason only.

I answer that, According to the Philosopher (Ethic. vi, 5) "a prudent man is one who is capable of taking good counsel." Now counsel is about things that we have to do in relation to some end: and the reason that deals with things to be done for an end is the practical reason. Hence it is evident that prudence resides only in the practical reason.

Reply Obj. 1: As stated above (Q. 45, AA. 1, 3), wisdom considers the absolutely highest cause: so that the consideration of the highest cause in any particular genus belongs to wisdom in that genus. Now in the genus of human acts the highest cause is the common end of all human life, and it is this end that prudence intends. For the Philosopher says (Ethic. vi, 5) that just as he who reasons well for the realization of a particular end, such as victory, is said to be prudent, not absolutely, but in a particular genus, namely warfare, so he that reasons well with regard to right conduct as a whole, is said to be prudent absolutely. Wherefore it is clear that prudence is wisdom about human affairs: but not wisdom absolutely, because it is not about the absolutely highest cause, for it is about human good, and this is not the best thing of all. And so it is stated significantly that "prudence is wisdom for man," but not wisdom absolutely.

Reply Obj. 2: Ambrose, and Tully also (De Invent. ii, 53) take the word prudence in a broad sense for any human knowledge, whether speculative or practical. And yet it may also be replied that the act itself of the speculative reason, in so far as it is voluntary, is a matter of choice and counsel as to its exercise; and consequently comes under the direction of prudence. On the other hand, as regards its specification in relation to its object which is the "necessary true," it comes under neither counsel nor prudence.

Reply Obj. 3: Every application of right reason in the work of production belongs to art: but to prudence belongs only the application of right reason in matters of counsel, which are those wherein there is no fixed way of obtaining the end, as stated in Ethic. iii, 3. Since then, the speculative reason makes things such as syllogisms, propositions and the like, wherein the process follows certain and fixed rules, consequently in respect of such things it is possible to have the essentials of art, but not of prudence; and so we find such a thing as a speculative art, but not a speculative prudence.

* * * * *

THIRD ARTICLE [II-II, Q. 47, Art. 3]

Whether Prudence Takes Cognizance of Singulars?

Objection 1: It would seem that prudence does not take cognizance of singulars. For prudence is in the reason, as stated above (AA. 1, 2). But "reason deals with universals," according to Phys. i, 5. Therefore prudence does not take cognizance except of universals.

Obj. 2: Further, singulars are infinite in number. But the reason cannot comprehend an infinite number of things. Therefore prudence which is right reason, is not about singulars.

Obj. 3: Further, particulars are known by the senses. But prudence is not in a sense, for many persons who have keen outward senses are devoid of prudence. Therefore prudence does not take cognizance of singulars.

On the contrary, The Philosopher says (Ethic. vi, 7) that "prudence does not deal with universals only, but needs to take cognizance of singulars also."

I answer that, As stated above (A. 1, ad 3), to prudence belongs not only the consideration of the reason, but also the application to action, which is the end of the practical reason. But no man can conveniently apply one thing to another, unless he knows both the thing to be applied, and the thing to which it has to be applied. Now actions are in singular matters: and so it is necessary for the prudent man to know both the universal principles of reason, and the singulars about which actions are concerned.

Reply Obj. 1: Reason first and chiefly is concerned with universals, and yet it is able to apply universal rules to particular cases: hence the conclusions of syllogisms are not only universal, but also particular, because the intellect by a kind of reflection extends to matter, as stated in De Anima iii.

Reply Obj. 2: It is because the infinite number of singulars cannot be comprehended by human reason, that "our counsels are uncertain" (Wis. 9:14). Nevertheless experience reduces the infinity of singulars to a certain finite number which occur as a general rule, and the knowledge of these suffices for human prudence.

Reply Obj. 3: As the Philosopher says (Ethic. vi, 8), prudence does not reside in the external senses whereby we know sensible objects, but in the interior sense, which is perfected by memory and experience so as to judge promptly of particular cases. This does not mean however that prudence is in the interior sense as in its princip[al] subject, for it is chiefly in the reason, yet by a kind of application it extends to this sense.

* * * * *

FOURTH ARTICLE [II-II, Q. 47, Art. 4]

Whether Prudence Is a Virtue?

Objection 1: It would seem that prudence is not a virtue. For Augustine says (De Lib. Arb. i, 13) that "prudence is the science of what to desire and what to avoid." Now science is condivided with virtue, as appears in the Predicaments (vi). Therefore prudence is not a virtue.

Obj. 2: Further, there is no virtue of a virtue: but "there is a virtue of art," as the Philosopher states (Ethic. vi, 5): wherefore art is not a virtue. Now there is prudence in art, for it is written (2 Paralip. ii, 14) concerning Hiram, that he knew "to grave all sort of graving, and to devise ingeniously (prudenter) all that there may be need of in the work." Therefore prudence is not a virtue.

Obj. 3: Further, no virtue can be immoderate. But prudence is immoderate, else it would be useless to say (Prov. 23:4): "Set bounds to thy prudence." Therefore prudence is not a virtue.

On the contrary, Gregory states (Moral. ii, 49) that prudence, temperance, fortitude and justice are four virtues.

I answer that, As stated above (I-II, Q. 55, A. 3; Q. 56, A. 1) when we were treating of virtues in general, "virtue is that which makes its possessor good, and his work good likewise." Now good may be understood in a twofold sense: first, materially, for the thing that is good, secondly, formally, under the aspect of good. Good, under the aspect of good, is the object of the appetitive power. Hence if any habits rectify the consideration of reason, without regarding the rectitude of the appetite, they have less of the nature of a virtue since they direct man to good materially, that is to say, to the thing which is good, but without considering it under the aspect of good. On the other hand those virtues which regard the rectitude of the appetite, have more of the nature of virtue, because they consider the good not only materially, but also formally, in other words, they consider that which is good under the aspect of good.

Now it belongs to prudence, as stated above (A. 1, ad 3; A. 3) to apply right reason to action, and this is not done without a right appetite. Hence prudence has the nature of virtue not only as the other intellectual virtues have it, but also as the moral virtues have it, among which virtues it is enumerated.

Reply Obj. 1: Augustine there takes science in the broad sense for any kind of right reason.

Reply Obj. 2: The Philosopher says that there is a virtue of art, because art does not require rectitude of the appetite; wherefore in order that a man may make right use of his art, he needs to have a virtue which will rectify his appetite. Prudence however has nothing to do with the matter of art, because art is both directed to a particular end, and has fixed means of obtaining that end. And yet, by a kind of comparison, a man may be said to act prudently in matters of art. Moreover in certain arts, on account of the uncertainty of the means for obtaining the end, there is need for counsel, as for instance in the arts of medicine and navigation, as stated in Ethic. iii, 3.

Reply Obj. 3: This saying of the wise man does not mean that prudence itself should be moderate, but that moderation must be imposed on other things according to prudence.

* * * * *

FIFTH ARTICLE [II-II, Q. 47, Art. 5]

Whether Prudence Is a Special Virtue?

Objection 1: It would seem that prudence is not a special virtue. For no special virtue is included in the definition of virtue in general, since virtue is defined (Ethic. ii, 6) "an elective habit that follows a mean appointed by reason in relation to ourselves, even as a wise man decides." Now right reason is reason in accordance with prudence, as stated in Ethic. vi, 13. Therefore prudence is not a special virtue.

Obj. 2: Further, the Philosopher says (Ethic. vi, 13) that "the effect of moral virtue is right action as regards the end, and that of prudence, right action as regards the means." Now in every virtue certain things have to be done as means to the end. Therefore prudence is in every virtue, and consequently is not a special virtue.

Obj. 3: Further, a special virtue has a special object. But prudence has not a special object, for it is right reason "applied to action" (Ethic. vi, 5); and all works of virtue are actions. Therefore prudence is not a special virtue.

On the contrary, It is distinct from and numbered among the other virtues, for it is written (Wis. 8:7): "She teacheth temperance and prudence, justice and fortitude."

I answer that, Since acts and habits take their species from their objects, as shown above (I-II, Q. 1, A. 3; Q. 18, A. 2; Q. 54, A. 2), any habit that has a corresponding special object, distinct from other objects, must needs be a special habit, and if it be a good habit, it must be a special virtue. Now an object is called special, not merely according to the consideration of its matter, but rather according to its formal aspect, as explained above (I-II, Q. 54, A. 2, ad 1). Because one and the same thing is the subject matter of the acts of different habits, and also of different powers, according to its different formal aspects. Now a yet greater difference of object is requisite for a difference of powers than for a difference of habits, since several habits are found in the same power, as stated above (I-II, Q. 54, A. 1). Consequently any difference in the aspect of an object, that requires a difference of powers, will *a fortiori* require a difference of habits.

Accordingly we must say that since prudence is in the reason, as stated above (A. 2), it is differentiated from the other intellectual virtues by a material difference of objects. *Wisdom, knowledge* and *understanding* are about necessary things, whereas *art* and *prudence* are about contingent things, art being concerned with *things made,* that is, with things produced in external matter, such as a house, a knife and so forth; and prudence, being concerned with *things done,* that is, with things that have their being in the doer himself, as stated above (I-II, Q. 57, A. 4). On the other hand prudence is differentiated from the moral virtues according to a formal aspect distinctive of powers, i.e. the intellective power, wherein is prudence, and the appetitive power, wherein is moral virtue. Hence it is evident that prudence is a special virtue, distinct from all other virtues.

Reply Obj. 1: This is not a definition of virtue in general, but of moral virtue, the definition of which fittingly includes an intellectual virtue, viz., prudence, which has the same matter in common with moral virtue; because, just as the subject of moral virtue is something that partakes of reason, so moral virtue has the aspect of virtue, in so far as it partakes of intellectual virtue.

Reply Obj. 2: This argument proves that prudence helps all the virtues, and works in all of them; but this does not suffice to prove that it is not a special virtue; for nothing prevents a certain genus from containing a species which is operative in every other species of that same genus, even as the sun has an influence over all bodies.

Reply Obj. 3: Things done are indeed the matter of prudence, in so far as they are the object of reason, that is, considered as true: but they are the matter of the moral virtues, in so far as they are the object of the appetitive power, that is, considered as good.

* * * * *

SIXTH ARTICLE [II-II, Q. 47, Art. 6]

Whether Prudence Appoints the End to Moral Virtues?

Objection 1: It would seem that prudence appoints the end to moral virtues. Since prudence is in the reason, while moral virtue is in the appetite, it seems that prudence stands in relation to moral virtue, as reason to the appetite. Now reason appoints the end to the appetitive power. Therefore prudence appoints the end to the moral virtues.

Obj. 2: Further, man surpasses irrational beings by his reason, but he has other things in common with them. Accordingly the other parts of man are in relation to his reason, what man is in relation to irrational creatures. Now man is the end of irrational creatures, according to Polit. i, 3. Therefore all the other parts of man are directed to reason as to their end. But prudence is "right reason applied to action," as stated above (A. 2). Therefore all actions are directed to prudence as their end. Therefore prudence appoints the end to all moral virtues.

Obj. 3: Further, it belongs to the virtue, art, or power that is concerned about the end, to command the virtues or arts that are concerned about the means. Now prudence disposes of the other moral virtues, and commands them. Therefore it appoints their end to them.

On the contrary, The Philosopher says (Ethic. vi, 12) that "moral virtue ensures the rectitude of the intention of the end, while prudence ensures the rectitude of the means." Therefore it does not belong to prudence to appoint the end to moral virtues, but only to regulate the means.

I answer that, The end of moral virtues is human good. Now the good of the human soul is to be in accord with reason, as Dionysius declares (Div. Nom. iv). Wherefore the ends of moral virtue must of necessity pre-exist in the reason.

Now, just as, in the speculative reason, there are certain things naturally known, about which is *understanding,* and certain things of which we obtain knowledge through them, viz. conclusions, about which is *science,* so in the practical reason, certain things pre-exist, as naturally known principles, and such are the ends of the moral virtues, since the end is in practical matters what principles are in speculative matters, as stated above (Q. 23, A. 7, ad 2; I-II, Q. 13, A. 3); while certain things are in the practical reason by way of conclusions, and such are the means which we gather from the ends themselves. About these is prudence, which applies universal principles to the particular conclusions of practical matters. Consequently it does not belong to prudence to appoint the end to moral virtues, but only to regulate the means.

Reply Obj. 1: Natural reason known by the name of synderesis appoints the end to moral virtues, as stated above (I, Q. 79, A. 12): but prudence does not do this for the reason given above.

This suffices for the Reply to the Second Objection.

Reply Obj. 3: The end concerns the moral virtues, not as though they appointed the end, but because they tend to the end which is appointed by natural reason. In this they are helped by prudence, which prepares the way for them, by disposing the means. Hence it follows that prudence is more excellent than the moral virtues, and moves them: yet synderesis moves prudence, just as the understanding of principles moves science.

* * * * *

SEVENTH ARTICLE [II-II, Q. 47, Art. 7]

Whether It Belongs to Prudence to Find the Mean in Moral Virtues?

Objection 1: It would seem that it does not belong to prudence to find the mean in moral virtues. For the achievement of the mean is the end of moral virtues. But prudence does not appoint the end to moral virtues, as shown above (A. 6). Therefore it does not find the mean in them.

Obj. 2: Further, that which of itself has being, would seem to have no cause, but its very being is its cause, since a thing is said to have being by reason of its cause. Now "to follow the mean" belongs to moral virtue by reason of itself, as part of its definition, as shown above (A. 5, Obj. 1). Therefore prudence does not cause the mean in moral virtues.

Obj. 3: Further, prudence works after the manner of reason. But moral virtue tends to the mean after the manner of nature, because, as Tully states (De Invent. Rhet. ii, 53), "virtue is a habit like a second nature in accord with reason." Therefore prudence does not appoint the mean to moral virtues.

On the contrary, In the foregoing definition of moral virtue (A. 5, Obj. 1) it is stated that it "follows a mean appointed by reason . . . even as a wise man decides."

I answer that, The proper end of each moral virtue consists precisely in conformity with right reason. For temperance intends that man should not stray from reason for the sake of his concupiscences; fortitude, that he should not stray from the right judgment of reason through fear or daring. Moreover this end is appointed to man according to natural reason, since natural reason dictates to each one that he should act according to reason.

But it belongs to the ruling of prudence to decide in what manner and by what means man shall obtain the mean of reason in his deeds. For though the attainment of the mean is the end of a moral virtue, yet this mean is found by the right disposition of these things that are directed to the end.

This suffices for the Reply to the First Objection.

Reply Obj. 2: Just as a natural agent makes form to be in matter, yet does not make that which is essential to the form to belong to it, so too, prudence appoints the mean in passions and operations, and yet does not make the searching of the mean to belong to virtue.

Reply Obj. 3: Moral virtue after the manner of nature intends to attain the mean. Since, however, the mean as such is not found in all matters after the same manner, it follows that the inclination of nature which ever works in the same manner, does not suffice for this purpose, and so the ruling of prudence is required.

* * * * *

EIGHTH ARTICLE [II-II, Q. 47, Art. 8]

Whether Command Is the Chief Act of Prudence?

Objection 1: It would seem that command is not the chief act of prudence. For command regards the good to be ensued. Now Augustine (De Trin. xiv, 9) states that it is an act of prudence "to avoid ambushes." Therefore command is not the chief act of prudence.

Obj. 2: Further, the Philosopher says (Ethic. vi, 5) that "the prudent man takes good counsel." Now "to take counsel" and "to command" seem to be different acts, as appears from what has been said above (I-II, Q. 57, A. 6). Therefore command is not the chief act of prudence.

Obj. 3: Further, it seems to belong to the will to command and to rule, since the will has the end for its object, and moves the other powers of the soul. Now prudence is not in the will, but in the reason. Therefore command is not an act of prudence.

On the contrary, The Philosopher says (Ethic. vi, 10) that "prudence commands."

I answer that, Prudence is "right reason applied to action," as stated above (A. 2). Hence that which is the chief act of reason in regard to action must needs be the chief act of prudence. Now there are three such acts. The first is *to take counsel,* which belongs to discovery, for counsel is an act of inquiry, as stated above (I-II, Q. 14, A. 1). The second act is *to judge of what one has discovered,* and this is an act of the speculative reason. But the practical reason, which is directed to action, goes further, and its third act is *to command,* which act consists in applying to action the things counselled and judged.

And since this act approaches nearer to the end of the practical reason, it follows that it is the chief act of the practical reason, and consequently of prudence.

In confirmation of this we find that the perfection of art consists in judging and not in commanding: wherefore he who sins voluntarily against his craft is reputed a better craftsman than he who does so involuntarily, because the former seems to do so from right judgment, and the latter from a defective judgment. On the other hand it is the reverse in prudence, as stated in *Ethic.* vi, 5, for it is more imprudent to sin voluntarily, since this is to be lacking in the chief act of prudence, viz. command, than to sin involuntarily.

Reply Obj. 1: The act of command extends both to the ensuing of good and to the avoidance of evil. Nevertheless Augustine ascribes "the avoidance of ambushes" to prudence, not as its chief act, but as an act of prudence that does not continue in heaven.

Reply Obj. 2: Good counsel is required in order that the good things discovered may be applied to action: wherefore command belongs to prudence which takes good counsel.

Reply Obj. 3: Simply to move belongs to the will: but command denotes motion together with a kind of ordering, wherefore it is an act of the reason, as stated above (I-II, Q. 17, A. 1).

* * * * *

NINTH ARTICLE [II-II, Q. 47, Art. 9]

Whether Solicitude Belongs to Prudence?

Objection 1: It would seem that solicitude does not belong to prudence. For solicitude implies disquiet, wherefore Isidore says (Etym. x) that "a solicitous man is a restless man." Now motion belongs chiefly to the appetitive power: wherefore solicitude does also. But prudence is not in the appetitive power, but in the reason, as stated above (A. 1). Therefore solicitude does not belong to prudence.

Obj. 2: Further, the certainty of truth seems opposed to solicitude, wherefore it is related (1 Kings 9:20) that Samuel said to Saul: "As for the asses which were lost three days ago, be not solicitous, because they are found." Now the certainty of truth belongs to prudence, since it is an intellectual virtue. Therefore solicitude is in opposition to prudence rather than belonging to it.

Obj. 3: Further, the Philosopher says (Ethic. iv, 3) the "magnanimous man is slow and leisurely." Now slowness is contrary to solicitude. Since then prudence is not opposed to magnanimity, for "good is not opposed to good," as stated in the Predicaments (viii) it would seem that solicitude does not belong to prudence.

On the contrary, It is written (1 Pet. 4:7): "Be prudent ... and watch in prayers." But watchfulness is the same as solicitude. Therefore solicitude belongs to prudence.

I answer that, According to Isidore (Etym. x), a man is said to be solicitous through being shrewd *(solers)* and alert *(citus)*, in so far as a man through a certain shrewdness of mind is on the alert to do whatever has to be done. Now this belongs to prudence, whose chief act is a command about what has been already counselled and judged in matters of action. Hence the Philosopher says (Ethic. vi, 9) that "one should be quick in carrying out the counsel taken, but slow in taking counsel." Hence it is that solicitude belongs properly to prudence, and for this reason Augustine says (De Morib. Eccl. xxiv) that "prudence keeps most careful watch and ward, lest by degrees we be deceived unawares by evil counsel."

Reply Obj. 1: Movement belongs to the appetitive power as to the principle of movement, in accordance however, with the direction and command of reason, wherein solicitude consists.

Reply Obj. 2: According to the Philosopher (Ethic. i, 3), "equal certainty should not be sought in all things, but in each matter according to its proper mode." And since the matter of prudence is the contingent singulars about which are human actions, the certainty of prudence cannot be so great as to be devoid of all solicitude.

Reply Obj. 3: The magnanimous man is said to be "slow and leisurely" not because he is solicitous about nothing, but because he is not over-solicitous about many things, and is trustful in matters where he ought to have trust, and is not over-solicitous about them: for over-much fear and distrust are the cause of over-solicitude, since fear makes us take counsel, as stated above (I-II, Q. 44, A. 2) when we were treating of the passion of fear.

* * * * *

TENTH ARTICLE [II-II, Q. 47, Art. 10]

Whether Solicitude Belongs to Prudence?

Objection 1: It would seem that prudence does not extend to the governing of many, but only to the government of oneself. For the Philosopher says (Ethic. v, 1) that virtue directed to the common good is justice. But prudence differs from justice. Therefore prudence is not directed to the common good.

Obj. 2: Further, he seems to be prudent, who seeks and does good for himself. Now those who seek the common good often neglect their own. Therefore they are not prudent.

Obj. 3: Further, prudence is specifically distinct from temperance and fortitude. But temperance and fortitude seem to be related only to a man's own good. Therefore the same applies to prudence.

On the contrary, Our Lord said (Matt. 24:45): "Who, thinkest thou, is a faithful and prudent [Douay: 'wise'] servant whom his lord hath appointed over his family?"

I answer that, According to the Philosopher (Ethic. vi, 8) some have held that prudence does not extend to the common good, but only to the good of the individual, and this because they thought that man is not bound to seek other than his own good. But this opinion is opposed to charity, which "seeketh not her own" (1 Cor. 13:5): wherefore the Apostle says of himself (1 Cor. 10:33): "Not seeking that which is profitable to myself, but to many, that they may be saved." Moreover it is contrary to right reason, which judges the common good to be better than the good of the individual.

Accordingly, since it belongs to prudence rightly to counsel, judge, and command concerning the means of obtaining a due end, it is evident that prudence regards not only the private good of the individual, but also the common good of the multitude.

Reply Obj. 1: The Philosopher is speaking there of moral virtue. Now just as every moral virtue that is directed to the common good is called "legal" justice, so the prudence that is directed to the common good is called "political" prudence, for the latter stands in the same relation to legal justice, as prudence simply so called to moral virtue.

Reply Obj. 2: He that seeks the good of the many, seeks in consequence his own good, for two reasons. First, because the individual good is impossible without the common good of the family, state, or kingdom. Hence Valerius Maximus says[1] of the ancient Romans that "they would rather be poor in a rich empire than rich in a poor empire." Secondly, because, since man is a part of the home and state, he must needs consider what is good for him by being prudent about the good of the many. For the good disposition of parts depends on their relation to the whole; thus Augustine says (Confess. iii, 8) that "any part which does not harmonize with its whole, is offensive."

Reply Obj. 3: Even temperance and fortitude can be directed to the common good, hence there are precepts of law concerning them as stated in Ethic. v, 1: more so, however, prudence and justice, since these belong to the rational faculty which directly regards the universal, just as the sensitive part regards singulars.

* * * * *

ELEVENTH ARTICLE [II-II, Q. 47, Art. 11]

Whether Prudence About One's Own Good Is Specifically the Same As That Which Extends to the Common Good?

Objection 1: It seems that prudence about one's own good is the same specifically as that which extends to the common good. For the Philosopher says (Ethic. vi, 8) that "political prudence, and prudence are the same habit, yet their essence is not the same."

Obj. 2: Further, the Philosopher says (Polit. iii, 2) that "virtue is the same in a good man and in a good ruler." Now political prudence is chiefly in the ruler, in whom it is architectonic, as it were. Since then prudence is a virtue of a good man, it seems that prudence and political prudence are the same habit.

Obj. 3: Further, a habit is not diversified in species or essence by things which are subordinate to one another. But the particular good, which belongs to prudence simply so called, is subordinate to the common good, which belongs to political prudence. Therefore prudence and political prudence differ neither specifically nor essentially.

On the contrary, "Political prudence," which is directed to the common good of the state, "domestic economy" which is of such

---

1 Fact. et Dict. Memor. iv, 6

things as relate to the common good of the household or family, and "monastic economy" which is concerned with things affecting the good of one person, are all distinct sciences. Therefore in like manner there are different kinds of prudence, corresponding to the above differences of matter.

I answer that, As stated above (A. 5; Q. 54, A. 2, ad 1), the species of habits differ according to the difference of object considered in its formal aspect. Now the formal aspect of all things directed to the end, is taken from the end itself, as shown above (I-II, Prolog.; Q. 102, A. 1), wherefore the species of habits differ by their relation to different ends. Again the individual good, the good of the family, and the good of the city and kingdom are different ends. Wherefore there must needs be different species of prudence corresponding to these different ends, so that one is "prudence" simply so called, which is directed to one's own good; another, "domestic prudence" which is directed to the common good of the home; and a third, "political prudence," which is directed to the common good of the state or kingdom.

Reply Obj. 1: The Philosopher means, not that political prudence is substantially the same habit as any kind of prudence, but that it is the same as the prudence which is directed to the common good. This is called "prudence" in respect of the common notion of prudence, i.e. as being right reason applied to action, while it is called "political," as being directed to the common good.

Reply Obj. 2: As the Philosopher declares (Polit. iii, 2), "it belongs to a good man to be able to rule well and to obey well," wherefore the virtue of a good man includes also that of a good ruler. Yet the virtue of the ruler and of the subject differs specifically, even as the virtue of a man and of a woman, as stated by the same authority (Polit. iii, 2).

Reply Obj. 3: Even different ends, one of which is subordinate to the other, diversify the species of a habit, thus for instance, habits directed to riding, soldiering, and civic life, differ specifically although their ends are subordinate to one another. In like manner, though the good of the individual is subordinate to the good of the many, that does not prevent this difference from making the habits differ specifically; but it follows that the habit which is directed to the last end is above the other habits and commands them.

* * * * *

TWELFTH ARTICLE [II-II, Q. 47, Art. 12]

Whether Prudence Is in Subjects, or Only in Their Rulers?

Objection 1: It would seem that prudence is not in subjects but only in their rulers. For the Philosopher says (Polit. iii, 2) that "prudence alone is the virtue proper to a ruler, while other virtues are common to subjects and rulers, and the prudence of the subject is not a virtue but a true opinion."

Obj. 2: Further, it is stated in Polit. i, 5 that "a slave is not competent to take counsel." But prudence makes a man take good counsel (Ethic. vi, 5). Therefore prudence is not befitting slaves or subjects.

Obj. 3: Further, prudence exercises command, as stated above (A. 8). But command is not in the competency of slaves or subjects but only of rulers. Therefore prudence is not in subjects but only in rulers.

On the contrary, The Philosopher says (Ethic. vi, 8) that there are two kinds of political prudence, one of which is "legislative" and belongs to rulers, while the other "retains the common name political," and is about "individual actions." Now it belongs also to subjects to perform these individual actions. Therefore prudence is not only in rulers but also in subjects.

I answer that, Prudence is in the reason. Now ruling and governing belong properly to the reason; and therefore it is proper to a man to reason and be prudent in so far as he has a share in ruling and governing. But it is evident that the subject as subject, and the slave as slave, are not competent to rule and govern, but rather to be ruled and governed. Therefore prudence is not the virtue of a slave as slave, nor of a subject as subject.

Since, however, every man, for as much as he is rational, has a share in ruling according to the judgment of reason, he is proportionately competent to have prudence. Wherefore it is manifest that prudence is in the ruler "after the manner of a mastercraft" (Ethic. vi, 8), but in the subjects, "after the manner of a handicraft."

Reply Obj. 1: The saying of the Philosopher is to be understood strictly, namely, that prudence is not the virtue of a subject as such.

Reply Obj. 2: A slave is not capable of taking counsel, in so far as he is a slave (for thus he is the instrument of his master), but he does take counsel in so far as he is a rational animal.

Reply Obj. 3: By prudence a man commands not only others, but also himself, in so far as the reason is said to command the lower powers.

* * * * *

THIRTEENTH ARTICLE [II-II, Q. 47, Art. 13]

Whether Prudence Can Be in Sinners?

Objection 1: It would seem that there can be prudence in sinners. For our Lord said (Luke 16:8): "The children of this world are more prudent [Douay: 'wiser'] in their generation than the children of light." Now the children of this world are sinners. Therefore there be prudence in sinners.

Obj. 2: Further, faith is a more excellent virtue than prudence. But there can be faith in sinners. Therefore there can be prudence also.

Obj. 3: Further, according to Ethic. vi, 7, "we say that to be of good counsel is the work of prudent man especially." Now many sinners can take good counsel. Therefore sinners can have prudence.

On the contrary, The Philosopher declares (Ethic. vi, 12) that "it is impossible for a man be prudent unless he be good." Now no sinner is a good man. Therefore no sinner is prudent.

I answer that, Prudence is threefold. There is a false prudence, which takes its name from its likeness to true prudence. For since a prudent man is one who disposes well of the things that have to be done for a good end, whoever disposes well of such things as are fitting for an evil end, has false prudence, in far as that which he takes for an end, is good, not in truth but in appearance. Thus man is called "a good robber," and in this way may speak of "a prudent robber," by way of similarity, because he devises fitting ways of committing robbery. This is the prudence of which the Apostle says (Rom. 8:6): "The prudence [Douay: 'wisdom'] of the flesh is death," because, to wit, it places its ultimate end in the pleasures of the flesh.

The second prudence is indeed true prudence, because it devises fitting ways of obtaining a good end; and yet it is imperfect, from a twofold source. First, because the good which it takes for an end, is not the common end of all human life, but of some particular affair; thus when a man devises fitting ways of conducting business or of sailing a ship, he is called a prudent businessman, or a prudent sailor; secondly, because he fails in the chief act of prudence, as when a man takes counsel aright, and forms a good judgment, even about things concerning life as a whole, but fails to make an effective command.

The third prudence is both true and perfect, for it takes counsel, judges and commands aright in respect of the good end of man's whole life: and this alone is prudence simply so-called, and cannot be in sinners, whereas the first prudence is in sinners alone, while imperfect prudence is common to good and wicked men, especially that which is imperfect through being directed to a particular end, since that which is imperfect on account of a failing in the chief act, is only in the wicked.

Reply Obj. 1: This saying of our Lord is to be understood of the first prudence, wherefore it is not said that they are prudent absolutely, but that they are prudent in "their generation."

Reply Obj. 2: The nature of faith consists not in conformity with the appetite for certain right actions, but in knowledge alone. On the other hand prudence implies a relation to a right appetite. First because its principles are the ends in matters of action; and of such ends one forms a right estimate through the habits of moral virtue, which rectify the appetite: wherefore without the moral virtues there is no prudence, as shown above (I-II, Q. 58, A. 5); secondly because prudence commands right actions, which does not happen unless the appetite be right. Wherefore though faith on account of its object is more excellent than prudence, yet prudence, by its very nature, is more opposed to sin, which arises from a disorder of the appetite.

Reply Obj. 3: Sinners can take good counsel for an evil end, or for some particular good, but they do not perfectly take good counsel for the end of their whole life, since they do not carry that counsel into effect. Hence they lack prudence which is directed to the good only; and yet in them, according to the Philosopher (Ethic. vi, 12) there is "cleverness,"[1] i.e. natural diligence which may be directed to both good and evil; or "cunning,"[2] which is directed

---

1   deinotike
2   panourgia

only to evil, and which we have stated above, to be "false prudence" or "prudence of the flesh.".

* * * * *

FOURTEENTH ARTICLE [II-II, Q. 47, Art. 14]

Whether Prudence Is in All Who Have Grace?

Objection 1: It would seem that prudence is not in all who have grace. Prudence requires diligence, that one may foresee aright what has to be done. But many who have grace have not this diligence. Therefore not all who have grace have prudence.

Obj. 2: Further, a prudent man is one who takes good counsel, as stated above (A. 8, Obj. 2; A. 13, Obj. 3). Yet many have grace who do not take good counsel, and need to be guided by the counsel of others. Therefore not all who have grace, have prudence.

Obj. 3: Further, the Philosopher says (Topic. iii, 2) that "young people are not obviously prudent." Yet many young people have grace. Therefore prudence is not to be found in all who have grace.

On the contrary, No man has grace unless he be virtuous. Now no man can be virtuous without prudence, for Gregory says (Moral. ii, 46) that "the other virtues cannot be virtues at all unless they effect prudently what they desire to accomplish." Therefore all who have grace have prudence.

I answer that, The virtues must needs be connected together, so that whoever has one has all, as stated above (I-II, Q. 65, A. 1). Now whoever has grace has charity, so that he must needs have all the other virtues, and hence, since prudence is a virtue, as shown above (A. 4), he must, of necessity, have prudence also.

Reply Obj. 1: Diligence is twofold: one is merely sufficient with regard to things necessary for salvation; and such diligence is given to all who have grace, whom "His unction teacheth of all things" (1 John 2:27). There is also another diligence which is more than sufficient, whereby a man is able to make provision both for himself and for others, not only in matters necessary for salvation, but also in all things relating to human life; and such diligence as this is not in all who have grace.

Reply Obj. 2: Those who require to be guided by the counsel of others, are able, if they have grace, to take counsel for themselves in this point at least, that they require the counsel of others and can discern good from evil counsel.

Reply Obj. 3: Acquired prudence is caused by the exercise of acts, wherefore "its acquisition demands experience and time" (Ethic. ii, 1), hence it cannot be in the young, neither in habit nor in act. On the other hand gratuitous prudence is caused by divine infusion. Wherefore, in children who have been baptized but have not come to the use of reason, there is prudence as to habit but not as to act, even as in idiots; whereas in those who have come to the use of reason, it is also as to act, with regard to things necessary for salvation. This by practice merits increase, until it becomes perfect, even as the other virtues. Hence the Apostle says (Heb. 5:14) that "strong meat is for the perfect, for them who by custom have their senses exercised to the discerning of good and evil.".

* * * * *

FIFTEENTH ARTICLE [II-II, Q. 47, Art. 15]

Whether Prudence Is in Us by Nature?

Objection 1: It would seem that prudence is in us by nature. The Philosopher says that things connected with prudence "seem to be natural," namely "synesis, gnome"[1] and the like, but not those which are connected with speculative wisdom. Now things belonging to the same genus have the same kind of origin. Therefore prudence also is in us from nature.

Obj. 2: Further, the changes of age are according to nature. Now prudence results from age, according to Job 12:12: "In the ancient is wisdom, and in length of days prudence." Therefore prudence is natural.

Obj. 3: Further, prudence is more consistent with human nature than with that of dumb animals. Now there are instances of a certain natural prudence in dumb animals, according to the Philosopher (De Hist. Anim. viii, 1). Therefore prudence is natural.

On the contrary, The Philosopher says (Ethic. ii, 1) that "intellectual virtue is both originated and fostered by teaching; it therefore demands experience and time." Now prudence is an

---

1   synesis and gnome, Cf. I-II, Q. 57, A. 6

intellectual virtue, as stated above (A. 4). Therefore prudence is in us, not by nature, but by teaching and experience.

I answer that, As shown above (A. 3), prudence includes knowledge both of universals, and of the singular matters of action to which prudence applies the universal principles. Accordingly, as regards the knowledge of universals, the same is to be said of prudence as of speculative science, because the primary universal principles of either are known naturally, as shown above (A. 6): except that the common principles of prudence are more connatural to man; for as the Philosopher remarks (Ethic. x, 7) "the life which is according to the speculative reason is better than that which is according to man": whereas the secondary universal principles, whether of the speculative or of the practical reason, are not inherited from nature, but are acquired by discovery through experience, or through teaching.

On the other hand, as regards the knowledge of particulars which are the matter of action, we must make a further distinction, because this matter of action is either an end or the means to an end. Now the right ends of human life are fixed; wherefore there can be a natural inclination in respect of these ends; thus it has been stated above (I-II, Q. 51, A. 1; Q. 63, A. 1) that some, from a natural inclination, have certain virtues whereby they are inclined to right ends; and consequently they also have naturally a right judgment about such like ends.

But the means to the end, in human concerns, far from being fixed, are of manifold variety according to the variety of persons and affairs. Wherefore since the inclination of nature is ever to something fixed, the knowledge of those means cannot be in man naturally, although, by reason of his natural disposition, one man has a greater aptitude than another in discerning them, just as it happens with regard to the conclusions of speculative sciences. Since then prudence is not about the ends, but about the means, as stated above (A. 6; I-II, Q. 57, A. 5), it follows that prudence is not from nature.

Reply Obj. 1: The Philosopher is speaking there of things relating to prudence, in so far as they are directed to ends. Wherefore he had said before (Ethic. vi, 5, 11) that "they are the principles of the ou heneka"[1], namely, the end; and so he does not mention euboulia among them, because it takes counsel about the means.

---

1 Literally, 'for the sake of which' (are the means)

Reply Obj. 2: Prudence is rather in the old, not only because their natural disposition calms the movement of the sensitive passions, but also because of their long experience.

Reply Obj. 3: Even in dumb animals there are fixed ways of obtaining an end, wherefore we observe that all the animals of a same species act in like manner. But this is impossible in man, on account of his reason, which takes cognizance of universals, and consequently extends to an infinity of singulars.

* * * * *

SIXTEENTH ARTICLE [II-II, Q. 47, Art. 16]

Whether Prudence Can Be Lost Through Forgetfulness?

Objection 1: It would seem that prudence can be lost through forgetfulness. For since science is about necessary things, it is more certain than prudence which is about contingent matters of action. But science is lost by forgetfulness. Much more therefore is prudence.

Obj. 2: Further, as the Philosopher says (Ethic. ii, 3) "the same things, but by a contrary process, engender and corrupt virtue." Now the engendering of prudence requires experience which is made up "of many memories," as he states at the beginning of his Metaphysics (i, 1). Therefore since forgetfulness is contrary to memory, it seems that prudence can be lost through forgetfulness.

Obj. 3: Further, there is no prudence without knowledge of universals. But knowledge of universals can be lost through forgetfulness. Therefore prudence can also.

On the contrary, The Philosopher says (Ethic. vi, 5) that "forgetfulness is possible to art but not to prudence."

I answer that, Forgetfulness regards knowledge only, wherefore one can forget art and science, so as to lose them altogether, because they belong to the reason. But prudence consists not in knowledge alone, but also in an act of the appetite, because as stated above (A. 8), its principal act is one of command, whereby a man applies the knowledge he has, to the purpose of appetition and operation. Hence prudence is not taken away directly by forgetfulness, but rather is corrupted by the passions. For the Philosopher says (Ethic. vi, 5) that "pleasure and sorrow pervert the estimate of prudence":

wherefore it is written (Dan. 13:56): "Beauty hath deceived thee, and lust hath subverted thy heart," and (Ex. 23:8): "Neither shalt thou take bribes which blind even the prudent [Douay: 'wise']."

Nevertheless forgetfulness may hinder prudence, in so far as the latter's command depends on knowledge which may be forgotten.

Reply Obj. 1: Science is in the reason only: hence the comparison fails, as stated above[1].

Reply Obj. 2: The experience required by prudence results not from memory alone, but also from the practice of commanding aright.

Reply Obj. 3: Prudence consists chiefly, not in the knowledge of universals, but in applying them to action, as stated above (A. 3). Wherefore forgetting the knowledge of universals does not destroy the principal part of prudence, but hinders it somewhat, as stated above.

48. OF THE PARTS OF PRUDENCE
(In One Article)

We must now consider the parts of prudence, under which head there are four points of inquiry:

(1) Which are the parts of prudence?
(2) Of its integral parts;
(3) Of its subjective parts;
(4) Of its potential parts.

* * * * *

ARTICLE [II-II, Q. 48, Art.]

Whether Three Parts of Prudence Are Fittingly Assigned?

Objection 1: It would seem that the parts of prudence are assigned unfittingly. Tully (De Invent. Rhet. ii, 53) assigns three parts of prudence, namely, "memory," "understanding" and "foresight."

---

[1] Cf. I-II, Q. 53, A. 1

Macrobius (In Somn. Scip. i) following the opinion of Plotinus ascribes to prudence six parts, namely, "reasoning," "understanding," "circumspection," "foresight," "docility" and "caution." Aristotle says (Ethic. vi, 9, 10, 11) that "good counsel," "synesis" and "gnome" belong to prudence. Again under the head of prudence he mentions "conjecture," "shrewdness," "sense" and "understanding." And another Greek philosopher[1] says that ten things are connected with prudence, namely, "good counsel," "shrewdness," "foresight," "regnative[2]," "military," "political" and "domestic prudence," "dialectics," "rhetoric" and "physics." Therefore it seems that one or the other enumeration is either excessive or deficient.

Obj. 2: Further, prudence is specifically distinct from science. But politics, economics, logic, rhetoric, physics are sciences. Therefore they are not parts of prudence.

Obj. 3: Further, the parts do not exceed the whole. Now the intellective memory or intelligence, reason, sense and docility, belong not only to prudence but also to all the cognitive habits. Therefore they should not be set down as parts of prudence.

Obj. 4: Further, just as counselling, judging and commanding are acts of the practical reason, so also is using, as stated above (I-II, Q. 16, A. 1). Therefore, just as "eubulia" which refers to counsel, is connected with prudence, and "synesis" and "gnome" which refer to judgment, so also ought something to have been assigned corresponding to use.

Obj. 5: Further, solicitude pertains to prudence, as stated above (Q. 47, A. 9). Therefore solicitude also should have been mentioned among the parts of prudence.

I answer that, Parts are of three kinds, namely, *integral,* as wall, roof, and foundations are parts of a house; *subjective,* as ox and lion are parts of animal; and *potential,* as the nutritive and sensitive powers are parts of the soul. Accordingly, parts can be assigned to a virtue in three ways. First, in likeness to integral parts, so that the things which need to concur for the perfect act of a virtue, are called the parts of that virtue. In this way, out of all the things mentioned above, eight may be taken as parts of prudence, namely, the six assigned by Macrobius; with the addition of a seventh, viz.

---

1   Andronicus; Cf. Q. 80, Obj. 4
2   Regnativa

memory mentioned by Tully; and *eustochia* or *shrewdness* mentioned by Aristotle. For the *sense* of prudence is also called *understanding*: wherefore the Philosopher says (Ethic. vi, 11): "Of such things one needs to have the sense, and this is understanding." Of these eight, five belong to prudence as a cognitive virtue, namely, *memory, reasoning, understanding, docility* and *shrewdness:* while the three others belong thereto, as commanding and applying knowledge to action, namely, *foresight, circumspection* and *caution.* The reason of their difference is seen from the fact that three things may be observed in reference to knowledge. In the first place, knowledge itself, which, if it be of the past, is called *memory,* if of the present, whether contingent or necessary, is called *understanding* or *intelligence.* Secondly, the acquiring of knowledge, which is caused either by teaching, to which pertains *docility,* or by *discovery,* and to this belongs to *eustochia,* i.e. "a happy conjecture," of which *shrewdness* is a part, which is a "quick conjecture of the middle term," as stated in Poster. i, 9. Thirdly, the use of knowledge, in as much as we proceed from things known to knowledge or judgment of other things, and this belongs to *reasoning.* And the reason, in order to command aright, requires to have three conditions. First, to order that which is befitting the end, and this belongs to *foresight;* secondly, to attend to the circumstances of the matter in hand, and this belongs to *circumspection;* thirdly, to avoid obstacles, and this belongs to *caution.*

The subjective parts of a virtue are its various species. In this way the parts of prudence, if we take them properly, are the prudence whereby a man rules himself, and the prudence whereby a man governs a multitude, which differ specifically as stated above (Q. 47, A. 11). Again, the prudence whereby a multitude is governed, is divided into various species according to the various kinds of multitude. There is the multitude which is united together for some particular purpose; thus an army is gathered together to fight, and the prudence that governs this is called *military*. There is also the multitude that is united together for the whole of life; such is the multitude of a home or family, and this is ruled by *domestic prudence*: and such again is the multitude of a city or kingdom, the ruling principle of which is *regnative prudence* in the ruler, and *political prudence,* simply so called, in the subjects.

If, however, prudence be taken in a wide sense, as including also speculative knowledge, as stated above (Q. 47, A. 2, ad 2) then its parts include *dialectics, rhetoric* and *physics,* according to three methods of prudence in the sciences. The first of these is the attaining of science by demonstration, which belongs to *physics* (if physics be understood to comprise all demonstrative sciences). The second method is to arrive at an opinion through probable premises, and this belongs to *dialectics.* The third method is to employ conjectures in order to induce a certain suspicion, or to persuade somewhat, and this belongs to *rhetoric.* It may be said, however, that these three belong also to prudence properly so called, since it argues sometimes from necessary premises, sometimes from probabilities, and sometimes from conjectures.

The potential parts of a virtue are the virtues connected with it, which are directed to certain secondary acts or matters, not having, as it were, the whole power of the principal virtue. In this way the parts of prudence are *good counsel,* which concerns counsel, *synesis,* which concerns judgment in matters of ordinary occurrence, and *gnome,* which concerns judgment in matters of exception to the law: while *prudence* is about the chief act, viz. that of commanding.

Reply Obj. 1: The various enumerations differ, either because different kinds of parts are assigned, or because that which is mentioned in one enumeration includes several mentioned in another enumeration. Thus Tully includes "caution" and "circumspection" under "foresight," and "reasoning," "docility" and "shrewdness" under "understanding."

Reply Obj. 2: Here domestic and civic prudence are not to be taken as sciences, but as kinds of prudence. As to the other three, the reply may be gathered from what has been said.

Reply Obj. 3: All these things are reckoned parts of prudence, not by taking them altogether, but in so far as they are connected with things pertaining to prudence.

Reply Obj. 4: Right command and right use always go together, because the reason's command is followed by obedience on the part of the lower powers, which pertain to use.

Reply Obj. 5: Solicitude is included under foresight.

49. OF EACH QUASI-INTEGRAL PART OF PRUDENCE (In Eight Articles)

We must now consider each quasi-integral part of prudence, and under this head there are eight points of inquiry:

(1) Memory;
(2) Understanding or Intelligence;
(3) Docility;
(4) Shrewdness;
(5) Reason;
(6) Foresight;
(7) Circumspection;
(8) Caution.

* * * * *

FIRST ARTICLE [II-II, Q. 49, Art. 1]

Whether Memory Is a Part of Prudence?

Objection 1: It would seem that memory is not a part of prudence. For memory, as the Philosopher proves (De Memor. et Remin. i), is in the sensitive part of the soul: whereas prudence is in the rational part (Ethic. vi, 5). Therefore memory is not a part of prudence.

Obj. 2: Further, prudence is acquired and perfected by experience, whereas memory is in us from nature. Therefore memory is not a part of prudence.

Obj. 3: Further, memory regards the past, whereas prudence regards future matters of action, about which counsel is concerned, as stated in Ethic. vi, 2, 7. Therefore memory is not a part of prudence.

On the contrary, Tully (De Invent. Rhet. ii, 53) places memory among the parts of prudence.

I answer that, Prudence regards contingent matters of action, as stated above (Q. 47, A. 5). Now in such like matters a man can be directed, not by those things that are simply and necessarily true, but by those which occur in the majority of cases: because principles must be proportionate to their conclusions, and "like must be concluded from like" (Ethic. vi[1]). But we need experience to discover what is true in the majority of cases: wherefore the Philosopher says (Ethic. ii, 1) that "intellectual virtue is engendered and fostered by experience and time." Now experience is the result of many memories as stated in *Metaph.* i, 1, and therefore prudence requires the memory of many things. Hence memory is fittingly accounted a part of prudence.

Reply Obj. 1: As stated above (Q. 47, AA. 3, 6), prudence applies universal knowledge to particulars which are objects of sense: hence many things belonging to the sensitive faculties are requisite for prudence, and memory is one of them.

Reply Obj. 2: Just as aptitude for prudence is in our nature, while its perfection comes through practice or grace, so too, as Tully says in his Rhetoric[2], memory not only arises from nature, but is also aided by art and diligence.

There are four things whereby a man perfects his memory. First, when a man wishes to remember a thing, he should take some suitable yet somewhat unwonted illustration of it, since the unwonted strikes us more, and so makes a greater and stronger impression on the mind; the mind; and this explains why we remember better what we saw when we were children. Now the reason for the necessity of finding these illustrations or images, is that simple and spiritual impressions easily slip from the mind, unless they be tied as it were to some corporeal image, because human knowledge has a greater hold on sensible objects. For this reason memory is assigned to the sensitive part of the soul. Secondly, whatever a man wishes to retain in his memory he must carefully consider and set in order, so that he may pass easily from one memory to another. Hence the Philosopher says (De Memor. et Remin. ii): "Sometimes a place brings memories back to us: the reason being that we pass quickly from the one to the other." Thirdly, we must be anxious and earnest about the things we wish to remember, because the more a thing is impressed on the mind, the less it is liable to slip out of it. Wherefore Tully says in his Rhetoric[3] that "anxiety preserves the figures of images entire." Fourthly, we should often reflect on the things we

---

1   Anal. Post. i. 32
2   Ad Herenn. de Arte Rhet. iii, 16, 24
3   Ad Herenn. de Arte Rhet. iii.

wish to remember. Hence the Philosopher says (De Memoria i) that "reflection preserves memories," because as he remarks (De Memoria ii) "custom is a second nature": wherefore when we reflect on a thing frequently, we quickly call it to mind, through passing from one thing to another by a kind of natural order.

Reply Obj. 3: It behooves us to argue, as it were, about the future from the past; wherefore memory of the past is necessary in order to take good counsel for the future.

* * * * *

SECOND ARTICLE [II-II, Q. 49, Art. 2]

Whether Understanding* Is a Part of Prudence?[1]

Objection 1: It would seem that understanding is not a part of prudence. When two things are members of a division, one is not part of the other. But intellectual virtue is divided into understanding and prudence, according to Ethic. vi, 3. Therefore understanding should not be reckoned a part of prudence.

Obj. 2: Further, understanding is numbered among the gifts of the Holy Ghost, and corresponds to faith, as stated above (Q. 8, AA. 1, 8). But prudence is a virtue other than faith, as is clear from what has been said above (Q. 4, A. 8; I-II, Q. 62, A. 2). Therefore understanding does not pertain to prudence.

Obj. 3: Further, prudence is about singular matters of action (Ethic. vi, 7): whereas understanding takes cognizance of universal and immaterial objects (De Anima iii, 4). Therefore understanding is not a part of prudence.

On the contrary, Tully[2] accounts "intelligence" a part of prudence, and Macrobius[3] mentions "understanding," which comes to the same.

I answer that, Understanding denotes here, not the intellectual power, but the right estimate about some final principle, which is taken as self-evident: thus we are said to understand the first principles of demonstrations. Now every deduction of reason proceeds from certain statements which are taken as primary: wherefore every process of reasoning must needs proceed from some understanding. Therefore

---

[1] Otherwise intuition; Aristotle's word is *nous*
[2] De Invent. Rhet. ii, 53
[3] In Somn. Scip. i, 8

since prudence is right reason applied to action, the whole process of prudence must needs have its source in understanding. Hence it is that understanding is reckoned a part of prudence.

Reply Obj. 1: The reasoning of prudence terminates, as in a conclusion, in the particular matter of action, to which, as stated above (Q. 47, AA. 3, 6), it applies the knowledge of some universal principle. Now a singular conclusion is argued from a universal and a singular proposition. Wherefore the reasoning of prudence must proceed from a twofold understanding. The one is cognizant of universals, and this belongs to the understanding which is an intellectual virtue, whereby we know naturally not only speculative principles, but also practical universal principles, such as "One should do evil to no man," as shown above (Q. 47, A. 6). The other understanding, as stated in Ethic. vi, 11, is cognizant of an extreme, i.e. of some primary singular and contingent practical matter, viz. the minor premiss, which must needs be singular in the syllogism of prudence, as stated above (Q. 47, AA. 3, 6). Now this primary singular is some singular end, as stated in the same place. Wherefore the understanding which is a part of prudence is a right estimate of some particular end.

Reply Obj. 2: The understanding which is a gift of the Holy Ghost, is a quick insight into divine things, as shown above (Q. 8, AA. 1, 2). It is in another sense that it is accounted a part of prudence, as stated above.

Reply Obj. 3: The right estimate about a particular end is called both "understanding," in so far as its object is a principle, and "sense," in so far as its object is a particular. This is what the Philosopher means when he says (Ethic. v, 11): "Of such things we need to have the sense, and this is understanding." But this is to be understood as referring, not to the particular sense whereby we know proper sensibles, but to the interior sense, whereby we judge of a particular.

* * * * *

THIRD ARTICLE [II-II, Q. 49, Art. 3]

Whether Docility Should Be Accounted a Part of Prudence?

Objection 1: It would seem that docility should not be accounted a part of prudence. For that which is a necessary condition of every intellectual virtue, should not be appropriated to one of them. But docility is requisite for every intellectual virtue. Therefore it should not be accounted a part of prudence.

Obj. 2: Further, that which pertains to a human virtue is in our power, since it is for things that are in our power that we are praised or blamed. Now it is not in our power to be docile, for this is befitting to some through their natural disposition. Therefore it is not a part of prudence.

Obj. 3: Further, docility is in the disciple: whereas prudence, since it makes precepts, seems rather to belong to teachers, who are also called "preceptors." Therefore docility is not a part of prudence.

On the contrary, Macrobius[1] following the opinion of Plotinus places docility among the parts of prudence.

I answer that, As stated above (A. 2, ad 1; Q. 47, A. 3) prudence is concerned with particular matters of action, and since such matters are of infinite variety, no one man can consider them all sufficiently; nor can this be done quickly, for it requires length of time. Hence in matters of prudence man stands in very great need of being taught by others, especially by old folk who have acquired a sane understanding of the ends in practical matters. Wherefore the Philosopher says (Ethic. vi, 11): "It is right to pay no less attention to the undemonstrated assertions and opinions of such persons as are experienced, older than we are, and prudent, than to their demonstrations, for their experience gives them an insight into principles." Thus it is written (Prov. 3:5): "Lean not on thy own prudence," and (Ecclus. 6:35): "Stand in the multitude of the ancients" (i.e. the old men), "that are wise, and join thyself from thy heart to their wisdom." Now it is a mark of docility to be ready to be taught: and consequently docility is fittingly reckoned a part of prudence.

Reply Obj. 1: Although docility is useful for every intellectual virtue, yet it belongs to prudence chiefly, for the reason given above.

Reply Obj. 2: Man has a natural aptitude for docility even as for other things connected with prudence. Yet his own efforts count for much towards the attainment of perfect docility: and he must carefully, frequently and reverently apply his mind to the teachings of the learned, neither neglecting them through laziness, nor despising them through pride.

---

1   In Somn. Scip. i, 8

Reply Obj. 3: By prudence man makes precepts not only for others, but also for himself, as stated above (Q. 47, A. 12, ad 3). Hence as stated (Ethic. vi, 11), even in subjects, there is place for prudence; to which docility pertains. And yet even the learned should be docile in some respects, since no man is altogether self-sufficient in matters of prudence, as stated above.

* * * * *

FOURTH ARTICLE [II-II, Q. 49, Art. 4]

Whether Shrewdness Is Part of Prudence?

Objection 1: It would seem that shrewdness is not a part of prudence. For shrewdness consists in easily finding the middle term for demonstrations, as stated in Poster. i, 34. Now the reasoning of prudence is not a demonstration since it deals with contingencies. Therefore shrewdness does not pertain to prudence.

Obj. 2: Further, good counsel pertains to prudence according to Ethic. vi, 5, 7, 9. Now there is no place in good counsel for shrewdness[1] which is a kind of eustochia, i.e. "a happy conjecture": for the latter is "unreasoning and rapid," whereas counsel needs to be slow, as stated in Ethic. vi, 9. Therefore shrewdness should not be accounted a part of prudence.

Obj. 3: Further, shrewdness as stated above (Q. 48) is a "happy conjecture." Now it belongs to rhetoricians to make use of conjectures. Therefore shrewdness belongs to rhetoric rather than to prudence.

On the contrary, Isidore says (Etym. x): "A solicitous man is one who is shrewd and alert (solers citus)." But solicitude belongs to prudence, as stated above (Q. 47, A. 9). Therefore shrewdness does also.

I answer that, Prudence consists in a right estimate about matters of action. Now a right estimate or opinion is acquired in two ways, both in practical and in speculative matters, first by discovering it oneself, secondly by learning it from others. Now just as docility consists in a man being well disposed to acquire a right opinion from another man, so shrewdness is an apt disposition to acquire a right estimate by oneself, yet so that shrewdness be taken for eustochia, of which it is a part. For eustochia is a happy

---

[1] Ethic. vi, 9; Poster. i, 34

conjecture about any matter, while shrewdness is "an easy and rapid conjecture in finding the middle term" (Poster. i, 34). Nevertheless the philosopher[1] who calls shrewdness a part of prudence, takes it for eustochia, in general, hence he says: "Shrewdness is a habit whereby congruities are discovered rapidly."

Reply Obj. 1: Shrewdness is concerned with the discovery of the middle term not only in demonstrative, but also in practical syllogisms, as, for instance, when two men are seen to be friends they are reckoned to be enemies of a third one, as the Philosopher says (Poster. i, 34). In this way shrewdness belongs to prudence.

Reply Obj. 2: The Philosopher adduces the true reason (Ethic. vi, 9) to prove that euboulia, i.e. good counsel, is not eustochia, which is commended for grasping quickly what should be done. Now a man may take good counsel, though he be long and slow in so doing, and yet this does not discount the utility of a happy conjecture in taking good counsel: indeed it is sometimes a necessity, when, for instance, something has to be done without warning. It is for this reason that shrewdness is fittingly reckoned a part of prudence.

Reply Obj. 3: Rhetoric also reasons about practical matters, wherefore nothing hinders the same thing belonging both to rhetoric and prudence. Nevertheless, conjecture is taken here not only in the sense in which it is employed by rhetoricians, but also as applicable to all matters whatsoever wherein man is said to conjecture the truth.

* * * * *

FIFTH ARTICLE [II-II, Q. 49, Art. 5]

Whether Reason Should Be Reckoned a Part of Prudence?

Objection 1: It would seem that reason should not be reckoned a part of prudence. For the subject of an accident is not a part thereof. But prudence is in the reason as its subject (Ethic. vi, 5). Therefore reason should not be reckoned a part of prudence.

Obj. 2: Further, that which is common to many, should not be reckoned a part of any one of them; or if it be so reckoned, it should be reckoned a part of that one to which it chiefly belongs.

---

[1] Andronicus; Cf. Q. 48, Obj. 1

Now reason is necessary in all the intellectual virtues, and chiefly in wisdom and science, which employ a demonstrative reason. Therefore reason should not be reckoned a part of prudence

Obj. 3: Further, reason as a power does not differ essentially from the intelligence, as stated above (I, Q. 79, A. 8). If therefore intelligence be reckoned a part of prudence, it is superfluous to add reason.

On the contrary, Macrobius[1], following the opinion of Plotinus, numbers reason among the parts of prudence.

I answer that, The work of prudence is to take good counsel, as stated in *Ethic.* vi, 7. Now counsel is a research proceeding from certain things to others. But this is the work of reason. Wherefore it is requisite for prudence that man should be an apt reasoner. And since the things required for the perfection of prudence are called requisite or quasi-integral parts of prudence, it follows that reason should be numbered among these parts.

Reply Obj. 1: Reason denotes here, not the power of reason, but its good use.

Reply Obj. 2: The certitude of reason comes from the intellect. Yet the need of reason is from a defect in the intellect, since those things in which the intellective power is in full vigor, have no need for reason, for they comprehend the truth by their simple insight, as do God and the angels. On the other hand particular matters of action, wherein prudence guides, are very far from the condition of things intelligible, and so much the farther, as they are less certain and fixed. Thus matters of art, though they are singular, are nevertheless more fixed and certain, wherefore in many of them there is no room for counsel on account of their certitude, as stated in Ethic. iii, 3. Hence, although in certain other intellectual virtues reason is more certain than in prudence, yet prudence above all requires that man be an apt reasoner, so that he may rightly apply universals to particulars, which latter are various and uncertain.

Reply Obj. 3: Although intelligence and reason are not different powers, yet they are named after different acts. For intelligence takes its name from being an intimate penetration of the truth[2], while reason is so called from being inquisitive and

---

1 In Somn. Scip. i
2 Cf. II-II, Q. 8, A. 1

discursive. Hence each is accounted a part of reason as explained above (A. 2; Q. 47, A. 2, 3).

* * * * *

SIXTH ARTICLE [II-II, Q. 49, Art. 6]

Whether Foresight[1] Should Be Accounted a Part of Prudence?

Objection 1: It would seem that foresight should not be accounted a part of prudence. For nothing is part of itself. Now foresight seems to be the same as prudence, because according to Isidore (Etym. x), "a prudent man is one who sees from afar (porro videns)": and this is also the derivation of providentia (foresight), according to Boethius (De Consol. v). Therefore foresight is not a part of prudence.

Obj. 2: Further, prudence is only practical, whereas foresight may be also speculative, because seeing, whence we have the word "to foresee," has more to do with speculation than operation. Therefore foresight is not a part of prudence.

Obj. 3: Further, the chief act of prudence is to command, while its secondary act is to judge and to take counsel. But none of these seems to be properly implied by foresight. Therefore foresight is not part of prudence.

On the contrary stands the authority of Tully and Macrobius, who number foresight among the parts of prudence, as stated above (Q. 48).

I answer that, As stated above (Q. 47, A. 1, ad 2, AA. 6, 13), prudence is properly about the means to an end, and its proper work is to set them in due order to the end. And although certain things are necessary for an end, which are subject to divine providence, yet nothing is subject to human providence except the contingent matters of actions which can be done by man for an end. Now the past has become a kind of necessity, since what has been done cannot be undone. In like manner, the present as such, has a kind of necessity, since it is necessary that Socrates sit, so long as he sits.

Consequently, future contingents, in so far as they can be directed by man to the end of human life, are the matter of prudence: and each of these things is implied in the word foresight,

---

[1] "Providentia," which may be translated either "providence" or "foresight."

for it implies the notion of something distant, to which that which occurs in the present has to be directed. Therefore foresight is part of prudence.

Reply Obj. 1: Whenever many things are requisite for a unity, one of them must needs be the principal to which all the others are subordinate. Hence in every whole one part must be formal and predominant, whence the whole has unity. Accordingly foresight is the principal of all the parts of prudence, since whatever else is required for prudence, is necessary precisely that some particular thing may be rightly directed to its end. Hence it is that the very name of prudence is taken from foresight (providentia) as from its principal part.

Reply Obj. 2: Speculation is about universal and necessary things, which, in themselves, are not distant, since they are everywhere and always, though they are distant from us, in so far as we fail to know them. Hence foresight does not apply properly to speculative, but only to practical matters.

Reply Obj. 3: Right order to an end which is included in the notion of foresight, contains rectitude of counsel, judgment and command, without which no right order to the end is possible.

* * * * *

SEVENTH ARTICLE [II-II, Q. 49, Art. 7]

Whether Circumspection Can Be a Part of Prudence?

Objection 1: It would seem that circumspection cannot be a part of prudence. For circumspection seems to signify looking at one's surroundings. But these are of infinite number, and cannot be considered by the reason wherein is prudence. Therefore circumspection should not be reckoned a part of prudence.

Obj. 2: Further, circumstances seem to be the concern of moral virtues rather than of prudence. But circumspection seems to denote nothing but attention to circumstances. Therefore circumspection apparently belongs to the moral virtues rather than to prudence.

Obj. 3: Further, whoever can see things afar off can much more see things that are near. Now foresight enables a man to look on distant things. Therefore there is no need to account circumspection a part of prudence in addition to foresight.

On the contrary stands the authority of Macrobius, quoted above (Q. 48).

I answer that, As stated above (A. 6), it belongs to prudence chiefly to direct something aright to an end; and this is not done aright unless both the end be good, and the means good and suitable.

Since, however, prudence, as stated above (Q. 47, A. 3) is about singular matters of action, which contain many combinations of circumstances, it happens that a thing is good in itself and suitable to the end, and nevertheless becomes evil or unsuitable to the end, by reason of some combination of circumstances. Thus to show signs of love to someone seems, considered in itself, to be a fitting way to arouse love in his heart, yet if pride or suspicion of flattery arise in his heart, it will no longer be a means suitable to the end. Hence the need of circumspection in prudence, viz. of comparing the means with the circumstances.

Reply Obj. 1: Though the number of possible circumstances be infinite, the number of actual circumstances is not; and the judgment of reason in matters of action is influenced by things which are few in number.

Reply Obj. 2: Circumstances are the concern of prudence, because prudence has to fix them; on the other hand they are the concern of moral virtues, in so far as moral virtues are perfected by the fixing of circumstances.

Reply Obj. 3: Just as it belongs to foresight to look on that which is by its nature suitable to an end, so it belongs to circumspection to consider whether it be suitable to the end in view of the circumstances. Now each of these presents a difficulty of its own, and therefore each is reckoned a distinct part of prudence.

* * * * *

EIGHTH ARTICLE [II-II, Q. 49, Art. 8]

Whether Caution Should Be Reckoned a Part of Prudence?

Objection 1: It would seem that caution should not be reckoned a part of prudence. For when no evil is possible, no caution is required. Now no man makes evil use of virtue, as Augustine declares (De Lib. Arb. ii, 19). Therefore caution does not belong to prudence which directs the virtues.

Obj. 2: Further, to foresee good and to avoid evil belong to the same faculty, just as the same art gives health and cures ill-health. Now it belongs to foresight to foresee good, and consequently, also to avoid evil. Therefore caution should not be accounted a part of prudence, distinct from foresight.

Obj. 3: Further, no prudent man strives for the impossible. But no man can take precautions against all possible evils. Therefore caution does not belong to prudence.

On the contrary, The Apostle says (Eph. 5:15): "See how you walk cautiously [Douay: 'circumspectly']."

I answer that, The things with which prudence is concerned, are contingent matters of action, wherein, even as false is found with true, so is evil mingled with good, on account of the great variety of these matters of action, wherein good is often hindered by evil, and evil has the appearance of good. Wherefore prudence needs caution, so that we may have such a grasp of good as to avoid evil.

Reply Obj. 1: Caution is required in moral acts, that we may be on our guard, not against acts of virtue, but against the hindrance of acts of virtue.

Reply Obj. 2: It is the same in idea, to ensue good and to avoid the opposite evil, but the avoidance of outward hindrances is different in idea. Hence caution differs from foresight, although they both belong to the one virtue of prudence.

Reply Obj. 3: Of the evils which man has to avoid, some are of frequent occurrence; the like can be grasped by reason, and against them caution is directed, either that they may be avoided altogether, or that they may do less harm. Others there are that occur rarely and by chance, and these, since they are infinite in number, cannot be grasped by reason, nor is man able to take precautions against them, although by exercising prudence he is able to prepare against all the surprises of chance, so as to suffer less harm thereby.

50. OF THE SUBJECTIVE PARTS OF PRUDENCE (In Four Articles)

We must, in due sequence, consider the subjective parts of prudence. And since we have already spoken of the prudence with which a man rules himself (Q. 47, seqq.), it remains for us to discuss the species of prudence whereby a multitude is governed. Under this head there are four points of inquiry:

(1) Whether a species of prudence is regnative?
(2) Whether political and (3) domestic economy are species of prudence?
(4) Whether military prudence is?.

* * * * *

FIRST ARTICLE [II-II, Q. 50, Art. 1]

Whether a Species of Prudence Is Regnative?

Objection 1: It would seem that regnative should not be reckoned a species of prudence. For regnative prudence is directed to the preservation of justice, since according to Ethic. v, 6 the prince is the guardian of justice. Therefore regnative prudence belongs to justice rather than to prudence.

Obj. 2: Further, according to the Philosopher (Polit. iii, 5) a kingdom (regnum) is one of six species of government. But no species of prudence is ascribed to the other five forms of government, which are "aristocracy," "polity," also called "timocracy"[1], "tyranny," "oligarchy" and "democracy." Therefore neither should a regnative species be ascribed to a kingdom.

Obj. 3: Further, lawgiving belongs not only to kings, but also to certain others placed in authority, and even to the people, according to Isidore (Etym. v). Now the Philosopher (Ethic. vi, 8) reckons a part of prudence to be "legislative." Therefore it is not becoming to substitute regnative prudence in its place.

On the contrary, The Philosopher says (Polit. iii, 11) that "prudence is a virtue which is proper to the prince." Therefore a special kind of prudence is regnative.

I answer that, As stated above (Q. 47, AA. 8, 10), it belongs to prudence to govern and command, so that wherever in human acts we find a special kind of governance and command, there must be a special kind of prudence. Now it is evident that there is a special and perfect kind of governance in one who has to govern not only himself but also the perfect community of a city or kingdom; because a government is the more perfect according as it is more universal, extends to more matters, and attains a higher end. Hence

---

[1] Cf. Ethic. viii, 10

prudence in its special and most perfect sense, belongs to a king who is charged with the government of a city or kingdom: for which reason a species of prudence is reckoned to be regnative.

Reply Obj. 1: All matters connected with moral virtue belong to prudence as their guide, wherefore "right reason in accord with prudence" is included in the definition of moral virtue, as stated above (Q. 47, A. 5, ad 1; I-II, Q. 58, A. 2, ad 4). For this reason also the execution of justice in so far as it is directed to the common good, which is part of the kingly office, needs the guidance of prudence. Hence these two virtues—prudence and justice—belong most properly to a king, according to Jer. 23:5: "A king shall reign and shall be wise, and shall execute justice and judgment in the earth." Since, however, direction belongs rather to the king, and execution to his subjects, regnative prudence is reckoned a species of prudence which is directive, rather than to justice which is executive.

Reply Obj. 2: A kingdom is the best of all governments, as stated in Ethic. viii, 10: wherefore the species of prudence should be denominated rather from a kingdom, yet so as to comprehend under regnative all other rightful forms of government, but not perverse forms which are opposed to virtue, and which, accordingly, do not pertain to prudence.

Reply Obj. 3: The Philosopher names regnative prudence after the principal act of a king which is to make laws, and although this applies to the other forms of government, this is only in so far as they have a share of kingly government.

* * * * *

SECOND ARTICLE [II-II, Q. 50, Art. 2]

Whether Political Prudence Is Fittingly Accounted a Part of Prudence?

Objection 1: It would seem that political prudence is not fittingly accounted a part of prudence. For regnative is a part of political prudence, as stated above (A. 1). But a part should not be reckoned a species with the whole. Therefore political prudence should not be reckoned a part of prudence.

Obj. 2: Further, the species of habits are distinguished by their various objects. Now what the ruler has to command is the same as what the subject has to execute. Therefore political prudence as regards the subjects, should not be reckoned a species of prudence distinct from regnative prudence.

Obj. 3: Further, each subject is an individual person. Now each individual person can direct himself sufficiently by prudence commonly so called. Therefore there is no need of a special kind of prudence called political.

On the contrary, The Philosopher says (Ethic. vi, 8) that "of the prudence which is concerned with the state one kind is a master-prudence and is called legislative; another kind bears the common name political, and deals with individuals."

I answer that, A slave is moved by his master, and a subject by his ruler, by command, but otherwise than as irrational and inanimate beings are set in motion by their movers. For irrational and inanimate beings are moved only by others and do not put themselves in motion, since they have no free-will whereby to be masters of their own actions, wherefore the rectitude of their government is not in their power but in the power of their movers. On the other hand, men who are slaves or subjects in any sense, are moved by the commands of others in such a way that they move themselves by their free-will; wherefore some kind of rectitude of government is required in them, so that they may direct themselves in obeying their superiors; and to this belongs that species of prudence which is called political.

Reply Obj. 1: As stated above, regnative is the most perfect species of prudence, wherefore the prudence of subjects, which falls short of regnative prudence, retains the common name of political prudence, even as in logic a convertible term which does not denote the essence of a thing retains the name of "proper."

Reply Obj. 2: A different aspect of the object diversifies the species of a habit, as stated above (Q. 47, A. 5). Now the same actions are considered by the king, but under a more general aspect, as by his subjects who obey: since many obey one king in various departments. Hence regnative prudence is compared to this political prudence of which we are speaking, as mastercraft to handicraft.

Reply Obj. 3: Man directs himself by prudence commonly so called, in relation to his own good, but by political prudence, of which we speak, he directs himself in relation to the common good.

* * * * *

THIRD ARTICLE [II-II, Q. 50, Art. 3]

Whether a Part of Prudence Should Be Reckoned to Be Domestic?

Objection 1: It would seem that domestic should not be reckoned a part of prudence. For, according to the Philosopher (Ethic. vi, 5) "prudence is directed to a good life in general": whereas domestic prudence is directed to a particular end, viz. wealth, according to Ethic. i, 1. Therefore a species of prudence is not domestic.

Obj. 2: Further, as stated above (Q. 47, A. 13) prudence is only in good people. But domestic prudence may be also in wicked people, since many sinners are provident in governing their household. Therefore domestic prudence should not be reckoned a species of prudence.

Obj. 3: Further, just as in a kingdom there is a ruler and subject, so also is there in a household. If therefore domestic like political is a species of prudence, there should be a paternal corresponding to regnative prudence. Now there is no such prudence. Therefore neither should domestic prudence be accounted a species of prudence.

On the contrary, The Philosopher states (Ethic. vi, 8) that there are various kinds of prudence in the government of a multitude, "one of which is domestic, another legislative, and another political."

I answer that, Different aspects of an object, in respect of universality and particularity, or of totality and partiality, diversify arts and virtues; and in respect of such diversity one act of virtue is principal as compared with another. Now it is evident that a household is a mean between the individual and the city or kingdom, since just as the individual is part of the household, so is the household part of the city or kingdom. And therefore, just as prudence commonly so called which governs the individual, is distinct from political prudence, so must domestic prudence be distinct from both.

Reply Obj. 1: Riches are compared to domestic prudence, not as its last end, but as its instrument, as stated in Polit. i, 3. On the other hand, the end of political prudence is "a good life in general" as regards the conduct of the household. In Ethic. i, 1 the

Philosopher speaks of riches as the end of political prudence, by way of example and in accordance with the opinion of many.

Reply Obj. 2: Some sinners may be provident in certain matters of detail concerning the disposition of their household, but not in regard to "a good life in general" as regards the conduct of the household, for which above all a virtuous life is required.

Reply Obj. 3: The father has in his household an authority like that of a king, as stated in Ethic. viii, 10, but he has not the full power of a king, wherefore paternal government is not reckoned a distinct species of prudence, like regnative prudence.

* * * * *

FOURTH ARTICLE [II-II, Q. 50, Art. 4]

Whether Military Prudence Should Be Reckoned a Part of Prudence?

Objection 1: It would seem that military prudence should not be reckoned a part of prudence. For prudence is distinct from art, according to Ethic. vi, 3. Now military prudence seems to be the art of warfare, according to the Philosopher (Ethic. iii, 8). Therefore military prudence should not be accounted a species of prudence.

Obj. 2: Further, just as military business is contained under political affairs, so too are many other matters, such as those of tradesmen, craftsmen, and so forth. But there are no species of prudence corresponding to other affairs in the state. Neither therefore should any be assigned to military business.

Obj. 3: Further, the soldiers' bravery counts for a great deal in warfare. Therefore military prudence pertains to fortitude rather than to prudence.

On the contrary, It is written (Prov. 24:6): "War is managed by due ordering, and there shall be safety where there are many counsels." Now it belongs to prudence to take counsel. Therefore there is great need in warfare for that species of prudence which is called "military."

I answer that, Whatever things are done according to art or reason, should be made to conform to those which are in accordance with nature, and are established by the Divine Reason. Now nature has a twofold tendency: first, to govern each thing in itself, secondly, to withstand outward assailants and corruptives: and for this reason she has provided animals not only with the concupiscible faculty, whereby they are moved to that which is conducive to their well-being, but also with the irascible power, whereby the animal withstands an assailant. Therefore in those things also which are in accordance with reason, there should be not only "political" prudence, which disposes in a suitable manner such things as belong to the common good, but also a "military" prudence, whereby hostile attacks are repelled.

Reply Obj. 1: Military prudence may be an art, in so far as it has certain rules for the right use of certain external things, such as arms and horses, but in so far as it is directed to the common good, it belongs rather to prudence.

Reply Obj. 2: Other matters in the state are directed to the profit of individuals, whereas the business of soldiering is directed to the service belongs to fortitude, but the direction, protection of the entire common good.

Reply Obj. 3: The execution of military service belongs to fortitude, but the direction, especially in so far as it concerns the commander-in-chief, belongs to prudence.

51. OF THE VIRTUES WHICH ARE CONNECTED WITH PRUDENCE
(In Four Articles)

In due sequence, we must consider the virtues that are connected with prudence, and which are its quasi-potential parts. Under this head there are four points of inquiry:

(1) Whether *euboulia* is a virtue?
(2) Whether it is a special virtue, distinct from prudence?
(3) Whether *synesis* is a special virtue?
(4) Whether *gnome* is a special virtue?[1]

* * * * *

---

1 These three Greek words may be rendered as the faculties of deliberating well *(euboulia)*, of judging well according to common law *(synesis)*, and of judging well according to general law *(gnome)*, respectively.

FIRST ARTICLE [II-II, Q. 51, Art. 1]

Whether *Euboulia* Is a Virtue?

Objection 1: It would seem that euboulia is not a virtue. For, according to Augustine (De Lib. Arb. ii, 18, 19) "no man makes evil use of virtue." Now some make evil use of euboulia or good counsel, either through devising crafty counsels in order to achieve evil ends, or through committing sin in order that they may achieve good ends, as those who rob that they may give alms. Therefore euboulia is not a virtue.

Obj. 2: Further, virtue is a perfection, according to Phys. vii. But euboulia is concerned with counsel, which implies doubt and research, and these are marks of imperfection. Therefore euboulia is not a virtue.

Obj. 3: Further, virtues are connected with one another, as stated above (I-II, Q. 65). Now euboulia is not connected with the other virtues, since many sinners take good-counsel, and many godly men are slow in taking counsel. Therefore euboulia is not a virtue.

On the contrary, According to the Philosopher (Ethic. vi, 9) euboulia "is a right counselling." Now the perfection of virtue consists in right reason. Therefore euboulia is a virtue.

I answer that, As stated above (Q. 47, A. 4) the nature of a human virtue consists in making a human act good. Now among the acts of man, it is proper to him to take counsel, since this denotes a research of the reason about the actions he has to perform and whereof human life consists, for the speculative life is above man, as stated in *Ethic.* x. But *euboulia* signifies goodness of counsel, for it is derived from the *eu*, good, and *boule*, counsel, being "a good counsel" or rather "a disposition to take good counsel." Hence it is evident that *euboulia* is a human virtue.

Reply Obj. 1: There is no good counsel either in deliberating for an evil end, or in discovering evil means for attaining a good end, even as in speculative matters, there is no good reasoning either in coming to a false conclusion, or in coming to a true conclusion from false premisses through employing an unsuitable middle term. Hence both the aforesaid processes are contrary to euboulia, as the Philosopher declares (Ethic. vi, 9).

Reply Obj. 2: Although virtue is essentially a perfection, it does not follow that whatever is the matter of a virtue implies perfection. For man needs to be perfected by virtues in all his parts, and this not only as regards the acts of reason, of which counsel is one, but also as regards the passions of the sensitive appetite, which are still more imperfect.

It may also be replied that human virtue is a perfection according to the mode of man, who is unable by simple insight to comprehend with certainty the truth of things, especially in matters of action which are contingent.

Reply Obj. 3: In no sinner as such is euboulia to be found: since all sin is contrary to taking good counsel. For good counsel requires not only the discovery or devising of fit means for the end, but also other circumstances. Such are suitable time, so that one be neither too slow nor too quick in taking counsel, and the mode of taking counsel, so that one be firm in the counsel taken, and other like due circumstances, which sinners fail to observe when they sin. On the other hand, every virtuous man takes good counsel in those things which are directed to the end of virtue, although perhaps he does not take good counsel in other particular matters, for instance in matters of trade, or warfare, or the like.

* * * * *

SECOND ARTICLE [II-II, Q. 51, Art. 2]

Whether *Euboulia* Is a Special Virtue, Distinct from Prudence?

Objection 1: It would seem that euboulia is not a distinct virtue from prudence. For, according to the Philosopher (Ethic. vi, 5), the "prudent man is, seemingly, one who takes good counsel." Now this belongs to euboulia as stated above. Therefore euboulia is not distinct from prudence.

Obj. 2: Further, human acts to which human virtues are directed, are specified chiefly by their end, as stated above (I-II, Q. 1, A. 3; Q. 18, AA. 4, 6). Now euboulia and prudence are directed to the same end, as stated in Ethic. vi, 9, not indeed to some particular end, but to the common end of all life. Therefore euboulia is not a distinct virtue from prudence.

Obj. 3: Further, in speculative sciences, research and decision belong to the same science. Therefore in like manner these belong to the same virtue in practical matters. Now research belongs to euboulia, while decision belongs to prudence. There euboulia is not a distinct virtue from prudence.

On the contrary, Prudence is preceptive, according to Ethic. vi, 10. But this does not apply to euboulia. Therefore euboulia is a distinct virtue from prudence.

I answer that, As stated above (A. 1), virtue is properly directed to an act which it renders good; and consequently virtues must differ according to different acts, especially when there is a different kind of goodness in the acts. For, if various acts contained the same kind of goodness, they would belong to the same virtue: thus the goodness of love, desire and joy depends on the same, wherefore all these belong to the same virtue of charity.

Now acts of the reason that are ordained to action are diverse, nor have they the same kind of goodness: since it is owing to different causes that a man acquires good counsel, good judgment, or good command, inasmuch as these are sometimes separated from one another. Consequently *euboulia* which makes man take good counsel must needs be a distinct virtue from prudence, which makes man command well. And since counsel is directed to command as to that which is principal, so *euboulia* is directed to prudence as to a principal virtue, without which it would be no virtue at all, even as neither are the moral virtues without prudence, nor the other virtues without charity.

Reply Obj. 1: It belongs to prudence to take good counsel by commanding it, to euboulia by eliciting it.

Reply Obj. 2: Different acts are directed in different degrees to the one end which is "a good life in general"[1]: for counsel comes first, judgment follows, and command comes last. The last named has an immediate relation to the last end: whereas the other two acts are related thereto remotely. Nevertheless these have certain proximate ends of their own, the end of counsel being the discovery of what has to be done, and the end of judgment, certainty. Hence this proves not that euboulia is not a distinct virtue from prudence, but that it is subordinate thereto, as a secondary to a principal virtue.

---

1 Ethic. vi, 5

Reply Obj. 3: Even in speculative matters the rational science of dialectics, which is directed to research and discovery, is distinct from demonstrative science, which decides the truth.

* * * * *

THIRD ARTICLE [II-II, Q. 51, Art. 3]

Whether *Synesis* Is a Virtue?

Objection 1: It would seem that synesis is not a virtue. Virtues are not in us by nature, according to Ethic. ii, 1. But synesis is natural to some, as the Philosopher states (Ethic. vi, 11). Therefore synesis is not a virtue.

Obj. 2: Further, as stated in the same book (10), synesis is nothing but "a faculty of judging." But judgment without command can be even in the wicked. Since then virtue is only in the good, it seems that synesis is not a virtue.

Obj. 3: Further, there is never a defective command, unless there be a defective judgment, at least in a particular matter of action; for it is in this that every wicked man errs. If therefore synesis be reckoned a virtue directed to good judgment, it seems that there is no need for any other virtue directed to good command: and consequently prudence would be superfluous, which is not reasonable. Therefore synesis is not a virtue.

On the contrary, Judgment is more perfect than counsel. But euboulia, or good counsel, is a virtue. Much more, therefore, is synesis a virtue, as being good judgment.

I answer that, synesis signifies a right judgment, not indeed about speculative matters, but about particular practical matters, about which also is prudence. Hence in Greek some, in respect of *synesis* are said to be *synetoi,* i.e. "persons of sense," or *eusynetoi,* i.e. "men of good sense," just as on the other hand, those who lack this virtue are called *asynetoi,* i.e. "senseless."

Now, different acts which cannot be ascribed to the same cause, must correspond to different virtues. And it is evident that goodness of counsel and goodness of judgment are not reducible to the same cause, for many can take good counsel, without having good sense so as to judge well. Even so, in speculative matters some are good at research, through their reason being quick at arguing from one thing to another (which seems to be due to a disposition of their power of imagination, which has a facility in forming phantasms), and yet such persons sometimes lack good judgment (and this is due to a defect in the intellect arising chiefly from a defective disposition of the common sense which fails to judge aright). Hence there is need, besides *euboulia*, for another virtue, which judges well, and this is called *synesis*.

Reply Obj. 1: Right judgment consists in the cognitive power apprehending a thing just as it is in reality, and this is due to the right disposition of the apprehensive power. Thus if a mirror be well disposed the forms of bodies are reflected in it just as they are, whereas if it be ill disposed, the images therein appear distorted and misshapen. Now that the cognitive power be well disposed to receive things just as they are in reality, is radically due to nature, but, as to its consummation, is due to practice or to a gift of grace, and this in two ways. First directly, on the part of the cognitive power itself, for instance, because it is imbued, not with distorted, but with true and correct ideas: this belongs to synesis which in this respect is a special virtue. Secondly indirectly, through the good disposition of the appetitive power, the result being that one judges well of the objects of appetite: and thus a good judgment of virtue results from the habits of moral virtue; but this judgment is about the ends, whereas synesis is rather about the means.

Reply Obj. 2: In wicked men there may be right judgment of a universal principle, but their judgment is always corrupt in the particular matter of action, as stated above (Q. 47, A. 13).

Reply Obj. 3: Sometimes after judging aright we delay to execute or execute negligently or inordinately. Hence after the virtue which judges aright there is a further need of a final and principal virtue, which commands aright, and this is prudence.

* * * * *

FOURTH ARTICLE [II-II, Q. 51, Art. 4]

Whether *Gnome* Is a Special Virtue?

Objection 1: It would seem that gnome is not a special virtue distinct from synesis. For a man is said, in respect of synesis, to have good judgment. Now no man can be said to have good judgment, unless he judge aright in all things. Therefore synesis extends to all matters of judgment, and consequently there is no other virtue of good judgment called gnome.

Obj. 2: Further, judgment is midway between counsel and precept. Now there is only one virtue of good counsel, viz. euboulia, and only one virtue of good command, viz. prudence. Therefore there is only one virtue of good judgment, viz. synesis.

Obj. 3: Further, rare occurrences wherein there is need to depart from the common law, seem for the most part to happen by chance, and with such things reason is not concerned, as stated in Phys. ii, 5. Now all the intellectual virtues depend on right reason. Therefore there is no intellectual virtue about such matters.

On the contrary, The Philosopher concludes (Ethic. vi, 11) that gnome is a special virtue.

I answer that cognitive habits differ according to higher and lower principles: thus in speculative matters wisdom considers higher principles than science does, and consequently is distinguished from it; and so must it be also in practical matters. Now it is evident that what is beside the order of a lower principle or cause, is sometimes reducible to the order of a higher principle; thus monstrous births of animals are beside the order of the active seminal force, and yet they come under the order of a higher principle, namely, of a heavenly body, or higher still, of Divine Providence. Hence by considering the active seminal force one could not pronounce a sure judgment on such monstrosities, and yet this is possible if we consider Divine Providence.

Now it happens sometimes that something has to be done which is not covered by the common rules of actions, for instance in the case of the enemy of one's country, when it would be wrong to give him back his deposit, or in other similar cases. Hence it is necessary to judge of such matters according to higher principles than the common laws, according to which *synesis* judges: and corresponding to such higher principles it is necessary to have a higher virtue of judgment, which is called *gnome,* and which denotes a certain discrimination in judgment.

Reply Obj. 1: Synesis judges rightly about all actions that are covered by the common rules: but certain things have to be judged beside these common rules, as stated above.

Reply Obj. 2: Judgment about a thing should be formed from the proper principles thereof, whereas research is made by employing also common principles. Wherefore also in speculative matters, dialectics which aims at research proceeds from common principles; while demonstration which tends to judgment, proceeds from proper principles. Hence euboulia to which the research of counsel belongs is one for all, but not so synesis whose act is judicial. Command considers in all matters the one aspect of good, wherefore prudence also is only one.

Reply Obj. 3: It belongs to Divine Providence alone to consider all things that may happen beside the common course. On the other hand, among men, he who is most discerning can judge a greater number of such things by his reason: this belongs to gnome, which denotes a certain discrimination in judgment.

52. OF THE GIFT OF COUNSEL
(In Four Articles)

We must now consider the gift of counsel which corresponds to prudence. Under this head there are four points of inquiry:

(1) Whether counsel should be reckoned among the seven gifts of the Holy Ghost?
(2) Whether the gift of counsel corresponds to prudence?
(3) Whether the gift of counsel remains in heaven?
(4) Whether the fifth beatitude, "Blessed are the merciful," etc. corresponds to the gift of counsel?.

* * * * *

FIRST ARTICLE [II-II, Q. 52, Art. 1]

Whether Counsel Should Be Reckoned Among the Gifts of the Holy Ghost?

Objection 1: It would seem that counsel should not be reckoned among the gifts of the Holy Ghost. The gifts of the Holy Ghost are given as a help to the virtues, according to Gregory (Moral. ii, 49). Now for the purpose of taking counsel, man is sufficiently perfected by the virtue of prudence, or even of euboulia, as is evident from what has been said (Q. 47, A. 1, ad 2; Q. 51, AA. 1,

2). Therefore counsel should not be reckoned among the gifts of the Holy Ghost.

Obj. 2: Further, the difference between the seven gifts of the Holy Ghost and the gratuitous graces seems to be that the latter are not given to all, but are divided among various people, whereas the gifts of the Holy Ghost are given to all who have the Holy Ghost. But counsel seems to be one of those things which are given by the Holy Ghost specially to certain persons, according to 1 Macc. 2:65: "Behold . . . your brother Simon is a man of counsel." Therefore counsel should be numbered among the gratuitous graces rather than among the seven gifts of the Holy Ghost.

Obj. 3: Further, it is written (Rom. 8:14): "Whosoever are led by the Spirit of God, they are the sons of God." But counselling is not consistent with being led by another. Since then the gifts of the Holy Ghost are most befitting the children of God, who "have received the spirit of adoption of sons," it would seem that counsel should not be numbered among the gifts of the Holy Ghost.

On the contrary, It is written (Isa. 11:2): "(The Spirit of the Lord) shall rest upon him . . . the spirit of counsel, and of fortitude."

I answer that, As stated above (I-II, Q. 68, A. 1), the gifts of the Holy Ghost are dispositions whereby the soul is rendered amenable to the motion of the Holy Ghost. Now God moves everything according to the mode of the thing moved: thus He moves the corporeal creature through time and place, and the spiritual creature through time, but not through place, as Augustine declares (Gen. ad lit. viii, 20, 22). Again, it is proper to the rational creature to be moved through the research of reason to perform any particular action, and this research is called counsel. Hence the Holy Ghost is said to move the rational creature by way of counsel, wherefore counsel is reckoned among the gifts of the Holy Ghost.

Reply Obj. 1: Prudence or euboulia, whether acquired or infused, directs man in the research of counsel according to principles that the reason can grasp; hence prudence or euboulia makes man take good counsel either for himself or for another. Since, however, human reason is unable to grasp the singular and contingent things which may occur, the result is that "the thoughts of mortal men are fearful, and our counsels uncertain" (Wis. 9:14). Hence in the research of counsel, man requires to be directed by God who comprehends all things: and this is done through the gift of counsel, whereby man is directed as though counseled by God, just as, in human affairs, those who are unable to take counsel for themselves, seek counsel from those who are wiser.

Reply Obj. 2: That a man be of such good counsel as to counsel others, may be due to a gratuitous grace; but that a man be counselled by God as to what he ought to do in matters necessary for salvation is common to all holy persons.

Reply Obj. 3: The children of God are moved by the Holy Ghost according to their mode, without prejudice to their free-will which is the "faculty of will and reason"[1]. Accordingly the gift of counsel is befitting the children of God in so far as the reason is instructed by the Holy Ghost about what we have to do.

* * * * *

SECOND ARTICLE [II-II, Q. 52, Art. 2]

Whether the Gift of Counsel Corresponds to the Virtue of Prudence?

Objection 1: It would seem that the gift of counsel does not fittingly correspond to the virtue of prudence. For "the highest point of that which is underneath touches that which is above," as Dionysius observes (Div. Nom. vii), even as a man comes into contact with the angel in respect of his intellect. Now cardinal virtues are inferior to the gifts, as stated above (I-II, Q. 68, A. 8). Since, then, counsel is the first and lowest act of prudence, while command is its highest act, and judgment comes between, it seems that the gift corresponding to prudence is not counsel, but rather a gift of judgment or command.

Obj. 2: Further, one gift suffices to help one virtue, since the higher a thing is the more one it is, as proved in De Causis. Now prudence is helped by the gift of knowledge, which is not only speculative but also practical, as shown above (Q. 9, A. 3). Therefore the gift of counsel does not correspond to the virtue of prudence.

Obj. 3: Further, it belongs properly to prudence to direct, as stated above (Q. 47, A. 8). But it belongs to the gift of counsel that

---

[1] Sent. iii, D, 24

man should be directed by God, as stated above (A. 1). Therefore the gift of counsel does not correspond to the virtue of prudence.

On the contrary, The gift of counsel is about what has to be done for the sake of the end. Now prudence is about the same matter. Therefore they correspond to one another.

I answer that, A lower principle of movement is helped chiefly, and is perfected through being moved by a higher principle of movement, as a body through being moved by a spirit. Now it is evident that the rectitude of human reason is compared to the Divine Reason, as a lower motive principle to a higher: for the Eternal Reason is the supreme rule of all human rectitude. Consequently prudence, which denotes rectitude of reason, is chiefly perfected and helped through being ruled and moved by the Holy Ghost, and this belongs to the gift of counsel, as stated above (A. 1). Therefore the gift of counsel corresponds to prudence, as helping and perfecting it.

Reply Obj. 1: To judge and command belongs not to the thing moved, but to the mover. Wherefore, since in the gifts of the Holy Ghost, the position of the human mind is of one moved rather than of a mover, as stated above (A. 1; I-II, Q. 68, A. 1), it follows that it would be unfitting to call the gift corresponding to prudence by the name of command or judgment rather than of counsel whereby it is possible to signify that the counselled mind is moved by another counselling it.

Reply Obj. 2: The gift of knowledge does not directly correspond to prudence, since it deals with speculative matters: yet by a kind of extension it helps it. On the other hand the gift of counsel corresponds to prudence directly, because it is concerned about the same things.

Reply Obj. 3: The mover that is moved, moves through being moved. Hence the human mind, from the very fact that it is directed by the Holy Ghost, is enabled to direct itself and others.

* * * * *

THIRD ARTICLE [II-II, Q. 52, Art. 3]

Whether the Gift of Counsel Remains in Heaven?

Objection 1: It would seem that the gift of counsel does not remain in heaven. For counsel is about what has to be done for the sake of an end. But in heaven nothing will have to be done for the sake of an end, since there man possesses the last end. Therefore the gift of counsel is not in heaven.

Obj. 2: Further, counsel implies doubt, for it is absurd to take counsel in matters that are evident, as the Philosopher observes (Ethic. iii, 3). Now all doubt will cease in heaven. Therefore there is no counsel in heaven.

Obj. 3: Further, the saints in heaven are most conformed to God, according to 1 John 3:2, "When He shall appear, we shall be like to Him." But counsel is not becoming to God, according to Rom. 11:34, "Who hath been His counsellor?" Therefore neither to the saints in heaven is the gift of counsel becoming.

On the contrary, Gregory says (Moral. xvii, 12): "When either the guilt or the righteousness of each nation is brought into the debate of the heavenly Court, the guardian of that nation is said to have won in the conflict, or not to have won."

I answer that, As stated above (A. 2; I-II, Q. 68, A. 1), the gifts of the Holy Ghost are connected with the motion of the rational creature by God. Now we must observe two points concerning the motion of the human mind by God. First, that the disposition of that which is moved, differs while it is being moved from its disposition when it is in the term of movement. Indeed if the mover is the principle of the movement alone, when the movement ceases, the action of the mover ceases as regards the thing moved, since it has already reached the term of movement, even as a house, after it is built, ceases being built by the builder. On the other hand, when the mover is cause not only of the movement, but also of the form to which the movement tends, then the action of the mover does not cease even after the form has been attained: thus the sun lightens the air even after it is lightened. In this way, then, God causes in us virtue and knowledge, not only when we first acquire them, but also as long as we persevere in them: and it is thus that God causes in the blessed a knowledge of what is to be done, not as though they were ignorant, but by continuing that knowledge in them.

Nevertheless there are things which the blessed, whether angels or men, do not know: such things are not essential to blessedness, but concern the government of things according to Divine Providence. As regards these, we must make a further observation, namely, that God moves the mind of the blessed in one way, and the mind of the wayfarer, in another. For

God moves the mind of the wayfarer in matters of action, by soothing the pre-existing anxiety of doubt; whereas there is simple nescience in the mind of the blessed as regards the things they do not know. From this nescience the angel's mind is cleansed, according to Dionysius (Coel. Hier. vii), nor does there precede in them any research of doubt, for they simply turn to God; and this is to take counsel of God, for as Augustine says (Gen. ad lit. v, 19) "the angels take counsel of God about things beneath them": wherefore the instruction which they receive from God in such matters is called "counsel."

Accordingly the gift of counsel is in the blessed, in so far as God preserves in them the knowledge that they have, and enlightens them in their nescience of what has to be done.

Reply Obj. 1: Even in the blessed there are acts directed to an end, or resulting, as it were, from their attainment of the end, such as the acts of praising God, or of helping on others to the end which they themselves have attained, for example the ministrations of the angels, and the prayers of the saints. In this respect the gift of counsel finds a place in them.

Reply Obj. 2: Doubt belongs to counsel according to the present state of life, but not to that counsel which takes place in heaven. Even so neither have the theological virtues quite the same acts in heaven as on the way thither.

Reply Obj. 3: Counsel is in God, not as receiving but as giving it: and the saints in heaven are conformed to God, as receivers to the source whence they receive.

* * * * *

FOURTH ARTICLE [II-II, Q. 52, Art. 4]

Whether the Fifth Beatitude, Which Is That of Mercy, Corresponds to the Gift of Counsel?

Objection 1: It would seem that the fifth beatitude, which is that of mercy, does not correspond to the gift of counsel. For all the beatitudes are acts of virtue, as stated above (I-II, Q. 69, A. 1). Now we are directed by counsel in all acts of virtue. Therefore the fifth beatitude does not correspond more than any other to counsel.

Obj. 2: Further, precepts are given about matters necessary for salvation, while counsel is given about matters which are not necessary for salvation. Now mercy is necessary for salvation, according to James 2:13, "Judgment without mercy to him that hath not done mercy." On the other hand poverty is not necessary for salvation, but belongs to the life of perfection, according to Matt. 19:21. Therefore the beatitude of poverty corresponds to the gift of counsel, rather than to the beatitude of mercy.

Obj. 3: Further, the fruits result from the beatitudes, for they denote a certain spiritual delight resulting from perfect acts of virtue. Now none of the fruits correspond to the gift of counsel, as appears from Gal. 5:22, 23. Therefore neither does the beatitude of mercy correspond to the gift of counsel.

On the contrary, Augustine says (De Serm. Dom. iv): "Counsel is befitting the merciful, because the one remedy is to be delivered from evils so great, to pardon, and to give."

I answer that, Counsel is properly about things useful for an end. Hence such things as are of most use for an end, should above all correspond to the gift of counsel. Now such is mercy, according to 1 Tim. 4:8, "Godliness[1] is profitable to all things." Therefore the beatitude of mercy specially corresponds to the gift of counsel, not as eliciting but as directing mercy.

Reply Obj. 1: Although counsel directs in all the acts of virtue, it does so in a special way in works of mercy, for the reason given above.

Reply Obj. 2: Counsel considered as a gift of the Holy Ghost guides us in all matters that are directed to the end of eternal life whether they be necessary for salvation or not, and yet not every work of mercy is necessary for salvation.

Reply Obj. 3: Fruit denotes something ultimate. Now the ultimate in practical matters consists not in knowledge but in an action which is the end. Hence nothing pertaining to practical knowledge is numbered among the fruits, but only such things as pertain to action, in which practical knowledge is the guide. Among these we find "goodness" and "benignity" which correspond to mercy.

---

1 *Pietas,* whence our English word *pity,* which is the same as mercy; see note on II-II, Q. 30, A. 1

53. OF IMPRUDENCE (In Six Articles)

We must now consider the vices opposed to prudence. For Augustine says (Contra Julian. iv, 3): "There are vices opposed to every virtue, not only vices that are in manifest opposition to virtue, as temerity is opposed to prudence, but also vices which have a kind of kinship and not a true but a spurious likeness to virtue; thus in opposition to prudence we have craftiness."

Accordingly we must consider first of all those vices which are in evident opposition to prudence, those namely which are due to a defect either of prudence or of those things which are requisite for prudence, and secondly those vices which have a false resemblance to prudence, those namely which are due to abuse of the things required for prudence. And since solicitude pertains to prudence, the first of these considerations will be twofold: (1) Of imprudence; (2) Of negligence which is opposed to solicitude.

Under the first head there are six points of inquiry:

(1) Concerning imprudence, whether it is a sin?
(2) Whether it is a special sin?
(3) Of precipitation or temerity;
(4) Of thoughtlessness;
(5) Of inconstancy;
(6) Concerning the origin of these vices.

* * * * *

FIRST ARTICLE [II-II, Q. 53, Art. 1]

Whether Imprudence Is a Sin?

Objection 1: It would seem that imprudence is not a sin. For every sin is voluntary, according to Augustine[1]; whereas imprudence is not voluntary, since no man wishes to be imprudent. Therefore imprudence is not a sin.

Obj. 2: Further, none but original sin comes to man with his birth. But imprudence comes to man with his birth, wherefore the

---

[1] De Vera Relig. xiv

young are imprudent; and yet it is not original sin which is opposed to original justice. Therefore imprudence is not a sin.

Obj. 3: Further, every sin is taken away by repentance. But imprudence is not taken away by repentance. Therefore imprudence is not a sin.

On the contrary, The spiritual treasure of grace is not taken away save by sin. But it is taken away by imprudence, according to Prov. 21:20, "There is a treasure to be desired, and oil in the dwelling of the just, and the imprudent [Douay: 'foolish'] man shall spend it." Therefore imprudence is a sin.

I answer that, Imprudence may be taken in two ways, first, as a privation, secondly, as a contrary. Properly speaking it is not taken as a negation, so as merely to signify the absence of prudence, for this can be without any sin. Taken as a privation, imprudence denotes lack of that prudence which a man can and ought to have, and in this sense imprudence is a sin by reason of a man's negligence in striving to have prudence.

Imprudence is taken as a contrary, in so far as the movement or act of reason is in opposition to prudence: for instance, whereas the right reason of prudence acts by taking counsel, the imprudent man despises counsel, and the same applies to the other conditions which require consideration in the act of prudence. In this way imprudence is a sin in respect of prudence considered under its proper aspect, since it is not possible for a man to act against prudence, except by infringing the rules on which the right reason of prudence depends. Wherefore, if this should happen through aversion from the Divine Law, it will be a mortal sin, as when a man acts precipitately through contempt and rejection of the Divine teaching: whereas if he act beside the Law and without contempt, and without detriment to things necessary for salvation, it will be a venial sin.

Reply Obj. 1: No man desires the deformity of imprudence, but the rash man wills the act of imprudence, because he wishes to act precipitately. Hence the Philosopher says (Ethic. vi, 5) that "he who sins willingly against prudence is less to be commended."

Reply Obj. 2: This argument takes imprudence in the negative sense. It must be observed however that lack of prudence or of any other virtue is included in the lack of original justice which perfected the entire soul. Accordingly all such lack of virtue may be ascribed to original sin.

Reply Obj. 3: Repentance restores infused prudence, and thus the lack of this prudence ceases; but acquired prudence is not restored as to the habit, although the contrary act is taken away, wherein properly speaking the sin of imprudence consists.

* * * * *

SECOND ARTICLE [II-II, Q. 53, Art. 2]

Whether Imprudence Is a Special Sin?

Objection 1: It would seem that imprudence is not a special sin. For whoever sins, acts against right reason, i.e. against prudence. But imprudence consists in acting against prudence, as stated above (A. 1). Therefore imprudence is not a special sin.

Obj. 2: Further, prudence is more akin to moral action than knowledge is. But ignorance which is opposed to knowledge, is reckoned one of the general causes of sin. Much more therefore should imprudence be reckoned among those causes.

Obj. 3: Further, sin consists in the corruption of the circumstances of virtue, wherefore Dionysius says (Div. Nom. iv) that "evil results from each single defect." Now many things are requisite for prudence; for instance, reason, intelligence, docility, and so on, as stated above (QQ. 48, 49). Therefore there are many species of imprudence, so that it is not a special sin.

On the contrary, Imprudence is opposed to prudence, as stated above (A. 1). Now prudence is a special virtue. Therefore imprudence too is one special vice.

I answer that, A vice or sin may be styled general in two ways; first, absolutely, because, to wit, it is general in respect of all sins; secondly, because it is general in respect of certain vices, which are its species. In the first way, a vice may be said to be general on two counts: first, essentially, because it is predicated of all sins: and in this way imprudence is not a general sin, as neither is prudence a general virtue: since it is concerned with special acts, namely the very acts of reason: secondly, by participation; and in this way imprudence is a general sin: for, just as all the virtues have a share of prudence, in so far as it directs them, so have all vices and sins a share of imprudence, because no sin can occur, without some defect in an act of the directing reason, which defect belongs to imprudence.

If, on the other hand, a sin be called general, not simply but in some particular genus, that is, as containing several species of sin, then imprudence is a general sin. For it contains various species in three ways. First, by opposition to the various subjective parts of prudence, for just as we distinguish the prudence that guides the individual, from other kinds that govern communities, as stated above (Q. 48; Q. 50, A. 7), so also we distinguish various kinds of imprudence. Secondly, in respect of the quasi-potential parts of prudence, which are virtues connected with it, and correspond to the several acts of reason. Thus, by defect of "counsel" to which *euboulia* corresponds, "precipitation" or "temerity" is a species of imprudence; by defect of "judgment," to which *synesis* (judging well according to common law) and *gnome* (judging well according to general law) refer, there is "thoughtlessness"; while "inconstancy" and "negligence" correspond to the "command" which is the proper act of prudence. Thirdly, this may be taken by opposition to those things which are requisite for prudence, which are the quasi-integral parts of prudence. Since however all these things are intended for the direction of the aforesaid three acts of reason, it follows that all the opposite defects are reducible to the four parts mentioned above. Thus incautiousness and incircumspection are included in "thoughtlessness"; lack of docility, memory, or reason is referable to "precipitation"; improvidence, lack of intelligence and of shrewdness, belong to "negligence" and "inconstancy."

Reply Obj. 1: This argument considers generality by participation.

Reply Obj. 2: Since knowledge is further removed from morality than prudence is, according to their respective proper natures, it follows that ignorance has the nature of mortal sin, not of itself, but on account either of a preceding negligence, or of the consequent result, and for this reason it is reckoned one of the general causes of sin. On the other hand imprudence, by its very nature, denotes a moral vice; and for this reason it can be called a special sin.

Reply Obj. 3: When various circumstances are corrupted for the same motive, the species of sin is not multiplied: thus it is the same species of sin to take what is not one's own, where one ought not, and when one ought not. If, however, there be various motives, there are various species: for instance, if one man were to take another's property from where he ought not, so as to wrong a sacred place, this would constitute the species called sacrilege, while if another were to take another's property when he ought not, merely through the lust of possession, this would be a case of simple avarice. Hence the lack of those things which are requisite for prudence, does not constitute a diversity of species, except in so far as they are directed to different acts of reason, as stated above.

* * * * *

THIRD ARTICLE [II-II, Q. 53, Art. 3]

Whether Precipitation Is a Sin Included in Imprudence?

Objection 1: It would seem that precipitation is not a sin included in imprudence. Imprudence is opposed to the virtue of prudence; whereas precipitation is opposed to the gift of counsel, according to Gregory, who says (Moral. ii, 49) that the gift of "counsel is given as a remedy to precipitation." Therefore precipitation is not a sin contained under imprudence.

Obj. 2: Further, precipitation seemingly pertains to rashness. Now rashness implies presumption, which pertains to pride. Therefore precipitation is not a vice contained under imprudence.

Obj. 3: Further, precipitation seems to denote inordinate haste. Now sin happens in counselling not only through being over hasty but also through being over slow, so that the opportunity for action passes by, and through corruption of other circumstances, as stated in Ethic. vi, 9. Therefore there is no reason for reckoning precipitation as a sin contained under imprudence, rather than slowness, or something else of the kind pertaining to inordinate counsel.

On the contrary, It is written (Prov. 4:19): "The way of the wicked is darksome, they know not where they fall." Now the darksome ways of ungodliness belong to imprudence. Therefore imprudence leads a man to fall or to be precipitate.

I answer that, Precipitation is ascribed metaphorically to acts of the soul, by way of similitude to bodily movement. Now a thing is said to be precipitated as regards bodily movement, when it is brought down from above by the impulse either of its own movement or of another's, and not in orderly fashion by degrees.

Now the summit of the soul is the reason, and the base is reached in the action performed by the body; while the steps that intervene by which one ought to descend in orderly fashion are *memory* of the past, *intelligence* of the present, *shrewdness* in considering the future outcome, *reasoning* which compares one thing with another, *docility* in accepting the opinions of others. He that takes counsel descends by these steps in due order, whereas if a man is rushed into action by the impulse of his will or of a passion, without taking these steps, it will be a case of precipitation. Since then inordinate counsel pertains to imprudence, it is evident that the vice of precipitation is contained under imprudence.

Reply Obj. 1: Rectitude of counsel belongs to the gift of counsel and to the virtue of prudence; albeit in different ways, as stated above (Q. 52, A. 2), and consequently precipitation is opposed to both.

Reply Obj. 2: Things are said to be done rashly when they are not directed by reason: and this may happen in two ways; first through the impulse of the will or of a passion, secondly through contempt of the directing rule; and this is what is meant by rashness properly speaking, wherefore it appears to proceed from that root of pride, which refuses to submit to another's ruling. But precipitation refers to both, so that rashness is contained under precipitation, although precipitation refers rather to the first.

Reply Obj. 3: Many things have to be considered in the research of reason; hence the Philosopher declares (Ethic. vi, 9) that "one should be slow in taking counsel." Hence precipitation is more directly opposed to rectitude of counsel than over slowness is, for the latter bears a certain likeness to right counsel.

* * * * *

FOURTH ARTICLE [II-II, Q. 53, Art. 4]

Whether Thoughtlessness Is a Special Sin Included in Imprudence?

Objection 1: It would seem that thoughtlessness is not a special sin included in imprudence. For the Divine law does not incite us to any sin, according to Ps. 18:8, "The law of the Lord is unspotted"; and yet it incites us to be thoughtless, according to Matt. 10:19, "Take no thought how or what to speak." Therefore thoughtlessness is not a sin.

Obj. 2: Further, whoever takes counsel must needs give thought to many things. Now precipitation is due to a defect of counsel and therefore to a defect of thought. Therefore precipitation is contained under thoughtlessness: and consequently thoughtlessness is not a special sin.

Obj. 3: Further, prudence consists in acts of the practical reason, viz. counsel, judgment about what has been counselled, and command[1]. Now thought precedes all these acts, since it belongs also to the speculative intellect. Therefore thoughtlessness is not a special sin contained under imprudence.

On the contrary, It is written (Prov. 4:25): "Let thy eyes look straight on, and let thine eye-lids go before thy steps." Now this pertains to prudence, while the contrary pertains to thoughtlessness. Therefore thoughtlessness is a special sin contained under imprudence.

I answer that, Thought signifies the act of the intellect in considering the truth about something. Now just as research belongs to the reason, so judgment belongs to the intellect. Wherefore in speculative matters a demonstrative science is said to exercise judgment, in so far as it judges the truth of the results of research by tracing those results back to the first indemonstrable principles. Hence thought pertains chiefly to judgment; and consequently the lack of right judgment belongs to the vice of thoughtlessness, in so far, to wit, as one fails to judge rightly through contempt or neglect of those things on which a right judgment depends. It is therefore evident that thoughtlessness is a sin.

Reply Obj. 1: Our Lord did not forbid us to take thought, when we have the opportunity, about what we ought to do or say, but, in the words quoted, He encourages His disciples, so that when they had no opportunity of taking thought, either through lack of knowledge or through a sudden call, they should trust in the guidance of God alone, because "as we know not what to do, we can only turn our eyes to God," according to 2 Paral. 20:12: else if man, instead of doing what he can, were to be content with awaiting God's assistance, he would seem to tempt God.

Reply Obj. 2: All thought about those things of which counsel takes cognizance, is directed to the formation of a right judgment,

---

[1] Cf. Q. 47, A. 8

wherefore this thought is perfected in judgment. Consequently thoughtlessness is above all opposed to the rectitude of judgment.

Reply Obj. 3: Thoughtlessness is to be taken here in relation to a determinate matter, namely, that of human action, wherein more things have to be thought about for the purpose of right judgment, than in speculative matters, because actions are about singulars.

* * * * *

FIFTH ARTICLE [II-II, Q. 53, Art. 5]

Whether Inconstancy Is a Vice Contained Under Imprudence?

Objection 1: It would seem that inconstancy is not a vice contained under imprudence. For inconstancy consists seemingly in a lack of perseverance in matters of difficulty. But perseverance in difficult matters belongs to fortitude. Therefore inconstancy is opposed to fortitude rather than to prudence.

Obj. 2: Further, it is written (James 3:16): "Where jealousy [Douay: 'envy'] and contention are, there are inconstancy and every evil work." But jealousy pertains to envy. Therefore inconstancy pertains not to imprudence but to envy.

Obj. 3: Further, a man would seem to be inconstant who fails to persevere in what he has proposed to do. Now this is a mark of "incontinency" in pleasurable matters, and of "effeminacy" or "squeamishness" in unpleasant matters, according to Ethic. vii, 1. Therefore inconstancy does not pertain to imprudence.

On the contrary, It belongs to prudence to prefer the greater good to the lesser. Therefore to forsake the greater good belongs to imprudence. Now this is inconstancy. Therefore inconstancy belongs to imprudence.

I answer that, Inconstancy denotes withdrawal from a definite good purpose. Now the origin of this withdrawal is in the appetite, for a man does not withdraw from a previous good purpose, except on account of something being inordinately pleasing to him: nor is this withdrawal completed except through a defect of reason, which is deceived in rejecting what before it had rightly accepted. And since it can resist the impulse of the passions, if it fail to do this, it is due to its own weakness in not standing to the good purpose it has conceived; hence inconstancy, as to its completion, is due to a defect in the reason. Now just as all rectitude of the practical reason belongs in some degree to prudence, so all lack of that rectitude belongs to imprudence. Consequently inconstancy, as to its completion, belongs to imprudence. And just as precipitation is due to a defect in the act of counsel, and thoughtlessness to a defect in the act of judgment, so inconstancy arises from a defect in the act of command. For a man is stated to be inconstant because his reason fails in commanding what has been counselled and judged.

Reply Obj. 1: The good of prudence is shared by all the moral virtues, and accordingly perseverance in good belongs to all moral virtues, chiefly, however, to fortitude, which suffers a greater impulse to the contrary.

Reply Obj. 2: Envy and anger, which are the source of contention, cause inconstancy on the part of the appetite, to which power the origin of inconstancy is due, as stated above.

Reply Obj. 3: Continency and perseverance seem to be not in the appetitive power, but in the reason. For the continent man suffers evil concupiscences, and the persevering man suffers grievous sorrows (which points to a defect in the appetitive power); but reason stands firm, in the continent man, against concupiscence, and in the persevering man, against sorrow. Hence continency and perseverance seem to be species of constancy which pertains to reason; and to this power inconstancy pertains also.

* * * * *

SIXTH ARTICLE [II-II, Q. 53, Art. 6]

Whether the Aforesaid Vices Arise from Lust?

Objection 1: It would seem that the aforesaid vices do not arise from lust. For inconstancy arises from envy, as stated above (A. 5, ad 2). But envy is a distinct vice from lust.

Obj. 2: Further, it is written (James 1:8): "A double-minded man is inconstant in all his ways." Now duplicity does not seem to pertain to lust, but rather to deceitfulness, which is a daughter of covetousness, according to Gregory (Moral. xxxi, 45). Therefore the aforesaid vices do not arise from lust.

Obj. 3: Further, the aforesaid vices are connected with some defect of reason. Now spiritual vices are more akin to the reason than carnal vices. Therefore the aforesaid vices arise from spiritual vices rather than from carnal vices.

On the contrary, Gregory declares (Moral. xxxi, 45) that the aforesaid vices arise from lust.

I answer that, As the Philosopher states (Ethic. vi, 5) "pleasure above all corrupts the estimate of prudence," and chiefly sexual pleasure which absorbs the mind, and draws it to sensible delight. Now the perfection of prudence and of every intellectual virtue consists in abstraction from sensible objects. Wherefore, since the aforesaid vices involve a defect of prudence and of the practical reason, as stated above (AA. 2, 5), it follows that they arise chiefly from lust.

Reply Obj. 1: Envy and anger cause inconstancy by drawing away the reason to something else; whereas lust causes inconstancy by destroying the judgment of reason entirely. Hence the Philosopher says (Ethic. vii, 6) that "the man who is incontinent through anger listens to reason, yet not perfectly, whereas he who is incontinent through lust does not listen to it at all."

Reply Obj. 2: Duplicity also is something resulting from lust, just as inconstancy is, if by duplicity we understand fluctuation of the mind from one thing to another. Hence Terence says (Eunuch. act 1, sc. 1) that "love leads to war, and likewise to peace and truce."

Reply Obj. 3: Carnal vices destroy the judgment of reason so much the more as they lead us away from reason.

54. OF NEGLIGENCE (In Three Articles)

We must now consider negligence, under which head there are three points of inquiry:

(1) Whether negligence is a special sin?
(2) To which virtue is it opposed?
(3) Whether negligence is a mortal sin?.

* * * * *

FIRST ARTICLE [II-II, Q. 54, Art. 1]

Whether Negligence Is a Special Sin?

Objection 1: It would seem that negligence is not a special sin. For negligence is opposed to diligence. But diligence is required in every virtue. Therefore negligence is not a special sin.

Obj. 2: Further, that which is common to every sin is not a special sin. Now negligence is common to every sin, because he who sins neglects that which withdraws him from sin, and he who perseveres in sin neglects to be contrite for his sin. Therefore negligence is not a special sin.

Obj. 3: Further, every special sin has a determinate matter. But negligence seems to have no determinate matter: since it is neither about evil or indifferent things (for no man is accused of negligence if he omit them), nor about good things, for if these be done negligently, they are no longer good. Therefore it seems that negligence is not a special vice.

On the contrary, Sins committed through negligence, are distinguished from those which are committed through contempt.

I answer that, Negligence denotes lack of due solicitude. Now every lack of a due act is sinful: wherefore it is evident that negligence is a sin, and that it must needs have the character of a special sin according as solicitude is the act of a special virtue. For certain sins are special through being about a special matter, as lust is about sexual matters, while some vices are special on account of their having a special kind of act which extends to all kinds of matter, and such are all vices affecting an act of reason, since every act of reason extends to any kind of moral matter. Since then solicitude is a special act of reason, as stated above (Q. 47, A. 9), it follows that negligence, which denotes lack of solicitude, is a special sin.

Reply Obj. 1: Diligence seems to be the same as solicitude, because the more we love (*diligimus*) a thing the more solicitous are we about it. Hence diligence, no less than solicitude, is required for every virtue, in so far as due acts of reason are requisite for every virtue.

Reply Obj. 2: In every sin there must needs be a defect affecting an act of reason, for instance a defect in counsel or the like. Hence just as precipitation is a special sin on account of a special act of reason which is omitted, namely counsel, although it may be found in any kind of sin; so negligence is a special sin on account of the lack of a special act of reason, namely solicitude, although it is found more or less in all sins.

Reply Obj. 3: Properly speaking the matter of negligence is a good that one ought to do, not that it is a good when it is done negligently, but because on account of negligence it incurs a lack of goodness, whether a due act be entirely omitted through lack of solicitude, or some due circumstance be omitted.

* * * * *

SECOND ARTICLE [II-II, Q. 54, Art. 2]

Whether Negligence Is Opposed to Prudence?

Objection 1: It would seem that negligence is not opposed to prudence. For negligence seems to be the same as idleness or laziness, which belongs to sloth, according to Gregory (Moral. xxxi, 45). Now sloth is not opposed to prudence, but to charity, as stated above (Q. 35, A. 3). Therefore negligence is not opposed to prudence.

Obj. 2: Further, every sin of omission seems to be due to negligence. But sins of omission are not opposed to prudence, but to the executive moral virtues. Therefore negligence is not opposed to prudence.

Obj. 3: Further, imprudence relates to some act of reason. But negligence does not imply a defect of counsel, for that is precipitation, nor a defect of judgment, since that is thoughtlessness, nor a defect of command, because that is inconstancy. Therefore negligence does not pertain to imprudence.

Obj. 4: Further, it is written (Eccles. 7:19): "He that feareth God, neglecteth nothing." But every sin is excluded by the opposite virtue. Therefore negligence is opposed to fear rather than to prudence.

On the contrary, It is written (Ecclus. 20:7): "A babbler and a fool (imprudens) will regard no time." Now this is due to negligence. Therefore negligence is opposed to prudence.

I answer that, Negligence is directly opposed to solicitude. Now solicitude pertains to the reason, and rectitude of solicitude to prudence. Hence, on the other hand, negligence pertains to imprudence. This appears from its very name, because, as Isidore observes (Etym. x) "a negligent man is one who fails to choose *(nec eligens)*": and the right choice of the means belongs to prudence. Therefore negligence pertains to imprudence.

Reply Obj. 1: Negligence is a defect in the internal act, to which choice also belongs: whereas idleness and laziness denote slowness of execution, yet so that idleness denotes slowness in setting about the execution, while laziness denotes remissness in the execution itself. Hence it is becoming that laziness should arise from sloth, which is "an oppressive sorrow," i.e. hindering, the mind from action[1].

Reply Obj. 2: Omission regards the external act, for it consists in failing to perform an act which is due. Hence it is opposed to justice, and is an effect of negligence, even as the execution of a just deed is the effect of right reason.

Reply Obj. 3: Negligence regards the act of command, which solicitude also regards. Yet the negligent man fails in regard to this act otherwise than the inconstant man: for the inconstant man fails in commanding, being hindered as it were, by something, whereas the negligent man fails through lack of a prompt will.

Reply Obj. 4: The fear of God helps us to avoid all sins, because according to Prov. 15:27, "by the fear of the Lord everyone declineth from evil." Hence fear makes us avoid negligence, yet not as though negligence were directly opposed to fear, but because fear incites man to acts of reason. Wherefore also it has been stated above (I-II, Q. 44, A. 2) when we were treating of the passions, that "fear makes us take counsel.".

* * * * *

THIRD ARTICLE [II-II, Q. 54, Art. 3]

Whether Negligence Can Be a Mortal Sin?

Objection 1: It would seem that negligence cannot be a mortal sin. For a gloss of Gregory[2] on Job 9:28, "I feared all my works," etc. says that "too little love of God aggravates the former," viz. negligence. But wherever there is mortal sin, the love of God is done away with altogether. Therefore negligence is not a mortal sin.

---

[1] Cf. Q. 35, A. 1; I-II, Q. 35, A. 8
[2] Moral. ix. 34

Obj. 2: Further, a gloss on Ecclus. 7:34, "For thy negligences purify thyself with a few," says: "Though the offering be small it cleanses the negligences of many sins." Now this would not be, if negligence were a mortal sin. Therefore negligence is not a mortal sin.

Obj. 3: Further, under the law certain sacrifices were prescribed for mortal sins, as appears from the book of Leviticus. Yet no sacrifice was prescribed for negligence. Therefore negligence is not a mortal sin.

On the contrary, It is written (Prov. 19:16): "He that neglecteth his own life [Vulg.: 'way'] shall die."

I answer that, As stated above (A. 2, ad 3), negligence arises out of a certain remissness of the will, the result being a lack of solicitude on the part of the reason in commanding what it should command, or as it should command. Accordingly negligence may happen to be a mortal sin in two ways. First on the part of that which is omitted through negligence. If this be either an act or a circumstance necessary for salvation, it will be a mortal sin. Secondly on the part of the cause: for if the will be so remiss about Divine things, as to fall away altogether from the charity of God, such negligence is a mortal sin, and this is the case chiefly when negligence is due to contempt.

But if negligence consists in the omission of an act or circumstance that is not necessary for salvation, it is not a mortal but a venial sin, provided the negligence arise, not from contempt, but from some lack of fervor, to which venial sin is an occasional obstacle.

Reply Obj. 1: Man may be said to love God less in two ways. First through lack of the fervor of charity, and this causes the negligence that is a venial sin: secondly through lack of charity itself, in which sense we say that a man loves God less when he loves Him with a merely natural love; and this causes the negligence that is a mortal sin.

Reply Obj. 2: According to the same authority (gloss), a small offering made with a humble mind and out of pure love, cleanses man not only from venial but also from mortal sin.

Reply Obj. 3: When negligence consists in the omission of that which is necessary for salvation, it is drawn to the other more manifest genus of sin. Because those sins that consist of inward actions, are more hidden, wherefore no special sacrifices were prescribed for them in the Law, since the offering of sacrifices was a kind of public confession of sin, whereas hidden sins should not be confessed in public.

55. OF VICES OPPOSED TO PRUDENCE BY WAY OF RESEMBLANCE (In Eight Articles)

We must now consider those vices opposed to prudence, which have a resemblance thereto. Under this head there are eight points of inquiry:

(1) Whether prudence of the flesh is a sin?
(2) Whether it is a mortal sin?
(3) Whether craftiness is a special sin?
(4) Of guile;
(5) Of fraud;
(6) Of solicitude about temporal things;
(7) Of solicitude about the future;
(8) Of the origin of these vices.

* * * * *

FIRST ARTICLE [II-II, Q. 55, Art. 1]

Whether Prudence of the Flesh Is a Sin?

Objection 1: It would seem that prudence of the flesh is not a sin. For prudence is more excellent than the other moral virtues, since it governs them all. But no justice or temperance is sinful. Neither therefore is any prudence a sin.

Obj. 2: Further, it is not a sin to act prudently for an end which it is lawful to love. But it is lawful to love the flesh, "for no man ever hated his own flesh" (Eph. 5:29). Therefore prudence of the flesh is not a sin.

Obj. 3: Further, just as man is tempted by the flesh, so too is he tempted by the world and the devil. But no prudence of the world, or of the devil is accounted a sin. Therefore neither should any prudence of the flesh be accounted among sins.

On the contrary, No man is an enemy to God save for wickedness according to Wis. 14:9, "To God the wicked and his wickedness are hateful alike." Now it is written (Rom. 8:7): "The prudence [Vulg.: 'wisdom'] of the flesh is an enemy to God." Therefore prudence of the flesh is a sin.

I answer that, As stated above (Q. 47, A. 13), prudence regards things which are directed to the end of life as a whole. Hence prudence of the flesh signifies properly the prudence of a man who looks upon carnal goods as the last end of his life. Now it is evident that this is a sin, because it involves a disorder in man with respect to his last end, which does not consist in the goods of the body, as stated above (I-II, Q. 2, A. 5). Therefore prudence of the flesh is a sin.

Reply Obj. 1: Justice and temperance include in their very nature that which ranks them among the virtues, viz. equality and the curbing of concupiscence; hence they are never taken in a bad sense. On the other hand prudence is so called from foreseeing (providendo), as stated above (Q. 47, A. 1; Q. 49, A. 6), which can extend to evil things also. Therefore, although prudence is taken simply in a good sense, yet, if something be added, it may be taken in a bad sense: and it is thus that prudence of the flesh is said to be a sin.

Reply Obj. 2: The flesh is on account of the soul, as matter is on account of the form, and the instrument on account of the principal agent. Hence the flesh is loved lawfully, if it be directed to the good of the soul as its end. If, however, a man place his last end in a good of the flesh, his love will be inordinate and unlawful, and it is thus that the prudence of the flesh is directed to the love of the flesh.

Reply Obj. 3: The devil tempts us, not through the good of the appetible object, but by way of suggestion. Wherefore, since prudence implies direction to some appetible end, we do not speak of "prudence of the devil," as of a prudence directed to some evil end, which is the aspect under which the world and the flesh tempt us, in so far as worldly or carnal goods are proposed to our appetite. Hence we speak of "carnal" and again of "worldly" prudence, according to Luke 16:8, "The children of this world are more prudent [Douay: 'wiser'] in their generation," etc. The Apostle includes all in the "prudence of the flesh," because we covet the external things of the world on account of the flesh.

We may also reply that since prudence is in a certain sense called "wisdom," as stated above (Q. 47, A. 2, ad 1), we may distinguish a threefold prudence corresponding to the three kinds of temptation. Hence it is written (James 3:15) that there is a wisdom which is "earthly, sensual and devilish," as explained above (Q. 45, A. 1, ad 1), when we were treating of wisdom.

* * * * *

SECOND ARTICLE [II-II, Q. 55, Art. 2]

Whether Prudence of the Flesh Is a Mortal Sin?

Objection 1: It would seem that prudence of the flesh is a mortal sin. For it is a mortal sin to rebel against the Divine law, since this implies contempt of God. Now "the prudence [Douay: 'wisdom'] of the flesh . . . is not subject to the law of God" (Rom. 8:7). Therefore prudence of the flesh is a mortal sin.

Obj. 2: Further, every sin against the Holy Ghost is a mortal sin. Now prudence of the flesh seems to be a sin against the Holy Ghost, for "it cannot be subject to the law of God" (Rom. 8:7), and so it seems to be an unpardonable sin, which is proper to the sin against the Holy Ghost. Therefore prudence of the flesh is a mortal sin.

Obj. 3: Further, the greatest evil is opposed to the greatest good, as stated in Ethic. viii, 10. Now prudence of the flesh is opposed to that prudence which is the chief of the moral virtues. Therefore prudence of the flesh is chief among mortal sins, so that it is itself a mortal sin.

On the contrary, That which diminishes a sin has not of itself the nature of a mortal sin. Now the thoughtful quest of things pertaining to the care of the flesh, which seems to pertain to carnal prudence, diminishes sin[1]. Therefore prudence of the flesh has not of itself the nature of a mortal sin.

I answer that, As stated above (Q. 47, A. 2, ad 1; A. 13), a man is said to be prudent in two ways. First, simply, i.e. in relation to the end of life as a whole. Secondly, relatively, i.e. in relation to some particular end; thus a man is said to be prudent in business or something else of the kind. Accordingly if prudence of the flesh be taken as corresponding to prudence in its absolute signification, so that a man place the last end of his whole life in the care of the flesh, it is a mortal sin, because he turns away from God by so doing, since he cannot have several last ends, as stated above (I-II, Q. 1, A. 5).

If, on the other hand, prudence of the flesh be taken as corresponding to particular prudence, it is a venial sin. For it happens sometimes that a man has an inordinate affection for

---

[1] Cf. Prov. 6:30

some pleasure of the flesh, without turning away from God by a mortal sin; in which case he does not place the end of his whole life in carnal pleasure. To apply oneself to obtain this pleasure is a venial sin and pertains to prudence of the flesh. But if a man actually refers the care of the flesh to a good end, as when one is careful about one's food in order to sustain one's body, this is no longer prudence of the flesh, because then one uses the care of the flesh as a means to an end.

Reply Obj. 1: The Apostle is speaking of that carnal prudence whereby a man places the end of his whole life in the goods of the flesh, and this is a mortal sin.

Reply Obj. 2: Prudence of the flesh does not imply a sin against the Holy Ghost. For when it is stated that "it cannot be subject to the law of God," this does not mean that he who has prudence of the flesh, cannot be converted and submit to the law of God, but that carnal prudence itself cannot be subject to God's law, even as neither can injustice be just, nor heat cold, although that which is hot may become cold.

Reply Obj. 3: Every sin is opposed to prudence, just as prudence is shared by every virtue. But it does not follow that every sin opposed to prudence is most grave, but only when it is opposed to prudence in some very grave matter.

* * * * *

THIRD ARTICLE [II-II, Q. 55, Art. 3]

Whether Craftiness Is a Special Sin?

Objection 1: It would seem that craftiness is not a special sin. For the words of Holy Writ do not induce anyone to sin; and yet they induce us to be crafty, according to Prov. 1:4, "To give craftiness [Douay: 'subtlety'] to little ones." Therefore craftiness is not a sin.

Obj. 2: Further, it is written (Prov. 13:16): "The crafty [Douay: 'prudent'] man doth all things with counsel." Therefore, he does so either for a good or for an evil end. If for a good end, there is no sin seemingly, and if for an evil end, it would seem to pertain to carnal or worldly prudence. Therefore craftiness is not a special sin distinct from prudence of the flesh.

Obj. 3: Further, Gregory expounding the words of Job 12, "The simplicity of the just man is laughed to scorn," says (Moral. x, 29): "The wisdom of this world is to hide one's thoughts by artifice, to conceal one's meaning by words, to represent error as truth, to make out the truth to be false," and further on he adds: "This prudence is acquired by the young, it is learnt at a price by children." Now the above things seem to belong to craftiness. Therefore craftiness is not distinct from carnal or worldly prudence, and consequently it seems not to be a special sin.

On the contrary, The Apostle says (2 Cor. 4:2): "We renounce the hidden things of dishonesty, not walking in craftiness, nor adulterating the word of God." Therefore craftiness is a sin.

I answer that, Prudence is *right reason applied to action,* just as science is *right reason applied to knowledge.* In speculative matters one may sin against rectitude of knowledge in two ways: in one way when the reason is led to a false conclusion that appears to be true; in another way when the reason proceeds from false premises, that appear to be true, either to a true or to a false conclusion. Even so a sin may be against prudence, through having some resemblance thereto, in two ways. First, when the purpose of the reason is directed to an end which is good not in truth but in appearance, and this pertains to prudence of the flesh; secondly, when, in order to obtain a certain end, whether good or evil, a man uses means that are not true but fictitious and counterfeit, and this belongs to the sin of craftiness. This is consequently a sin opposed to prudence, and distinct from prudence of the flesh.

Reply Obj. 1: As Augustine observes (Contra Julian. iv, 3) just as prudence is sometimes improperly taken in a bad sense, so is craftiness sometimes taken in a good sense, and this on account of their mutual resemblance. Properly speaking, however, craftiness is taken in a bad sense, as the Philosopher states in Ethic. vi, 12.

Reply Obj. 2: Craftiness can take counsel both for a good end and for an evil end: nor should a good end be pursued by means that are false and counterfeit but by such as are true. Hence craftiness is a sin if it be directed to a good end.

Reply Obj. 3: Under "worldly prudence" Gregory included everything that can pertain to false prudence, so that it comprises craftiness also.

* * * * *

FOURTH ARTICLE [II-II, Q. 55, Art. 4]

Whether Guile Is a Sin Pertaining to Craftiness?

Objection 1: It would seem that guile is not a sin pertaining to craftiness. For sin, especially mortal, has no place in perfect men. Yet a certain guile is to be found in them, according to 2 Cor. 12:16, "Being crafty I caught you by guile." Therefore guile is not always a sin.

Obj. 2: Further, guile seems to pertain chiefly to the tongue, according to Ps. 5:11, "They dealt deceitfully with their tongues." Now craftiness like prudence is in the very act of reason. Therefore guile does not pertain to craftiness.

Obj. 3: Further, it is written (Prov. 12:20): "Guile [Douay: 'Deceit'] is in the heart of them that think evil things." But the thought of evil things does not always pertain to craftiness. Therefore guile does not seem to belong to craftiness.

On the contrary, Craftiness aims at lying in wait, according to Eph. 4:14, "By cunning craftiness by which they lie in wait to deceive": and guile aims at this also. Therefore guile pertains to craftiness.

I answer that, As stated above (A. 3), it belongs to craftiness to adopt ways that are not true but counterfeit and apparently true, in order to attain some end either good or evil. Now the adopting of such ways may be subjected to a twofold consideration; first, as regards the process of thinking them out, and this belongs properly to craftiness, even as thinking out right ways to a due end belongs to prudence. Secondly the adopting of such like ways may be considered with regard to their actual execution, and in this way it belongs to guile. Hence guile denotes a certain execution of craftiness, and accordingly belongs thereto.

Reply Obj. 1: Just as craftiness is taken properly in a bad sense, and improperly in a good sense, so too is guile which is the execution of craftiness.

Reply Obj. 2: The execution of craftiness with the purpose of deceiving, is effected first and foremost by words, which hold the chief place among those signs whereby a man signifies something to another man, as Augustine states (De Doctr. Christ. ii, 3), hence guile is ascribed chiefly to speech. Yet guile may happen also in deeds, according to Ps. 104:25, "And to deal deceitfully with his servants." Guile is also in the heart, according to Ecclus. 19:23, "His interior is full of deceit," but this is to devise deceits, according to Ps. 37:13: "They studied deceits all the day long."

Reply Obj. 3: Whoever purposes to do some evil deed, must needs devise certain ways of attaining his purpose, and for the most part he devises deceitful ways, whereby the more easily to obtain his end. Nevertheless it happens sometimes that evil is done openly and by violence without craftiness and guile; but as this is more difficult, it is of less frequent occurrence.

* * * * *

FIFTH ARTICLE [II-II, Q. 55, Art. 5]

Whether Fraud Pertains to Craftiness?

Objection 1: It would seem that fraud does not pertain to craftiness. For a man does not deserve praise if he allows himself to be deceived, which is the object of craftiness; and yet a man deserves praise for allowing himself to be defrauded, according to 1 Cor. 6:1, "Why do you not rather suffer yourselves to be defrauded?" Therefore fraud does not belong to craftiness.

Obj. 2: Further, fraud seems to consist in unlawfully taking or receiving external things, for it is written (Acts 5:1) that "a certain man named Ananias with Saphira his wife, sold a piece of land, and by fraud kept back part of the price of the land." Now it pertains to injustice or illiberality to take possession of or retain external things unjustly. Therefore fraud does not belong to craftiness which is opposed to prudence.

Obj. 3: Further, no man employs craftiness against himself. But the frauds of some are against themselves, for it is written (Prov. 1:18) concerning some "that they practice frauds [Douay: 'deceits'] against their own souls." Therefore fraud does not belong to craftiness.

On the contrary, The object of fraud is to deceive, according to Job 13:9, "Shall he be deceived as a man, with your fraudulent [Douay: 'deceitful'] dealings?" Now craftiness is directed to the same object. Therefore fraud pertains to craftiness.

I answer that, Just as *guile* consists in the execution of craftiness, so also does *fraud*. But they seem to differ in the fact that *guile* belongs in general to the execution of craftiness, whether this be effected by words, or by deeds, whereas *fraud* belongs more properly to the execution of craftiness by deeds.

Reply Obj. 1: The Apostle does not counsel the faithful to be deceived in their knowledge, but to bear patiently the effect of being deceived, and to endure wrongs inflicted on them by fraud.

Reply Obj. 2: The execution of craftiness may be carried out by another vice, just as the execution of prudence by the virtues: and accordingly nothing hinders fraud from pertaining to covetousness or illiberality.

Reply Obj. 3: Those who commit frauds, do not design anything against themselves or their own souls; it is through God's just judgment that what they plot against others, recoils on themselves, according to Ps. 7:16, "He is fallen into the hole he made.".

* * * * *

SIXTH ARTICLE [II-II, Q. 55, Art. 6]

Whether It Is Lawful to Be Solicitous About Temporal Matters?

Objection 1: It would seem lawful to be solicitous about temporal matters. Because a superior should be solicitous for his subjects, according to Rom. 12:8, "He that ruleth, with solicitude." Now according to the Divine ordering, man is placed over temporal things, according to Ps. 8:8, "Thou hast subjected all things under his feet," etc. Therefore man should be solicitous about temporal things.

Obj. 2: Further, everyone is solicitous about the end for which he works. Now it is lawful for a man to work for the temporal things whereby he sustains life, wherefore the Apostle says (2 Thess. 3:10): "If any man will not work, neither let him eat." Therefore it is lawful to be solicitous about temporal things.

Obj. 3: Further, solicitude about works of mercy is praiseworthy, according to 2 Tim. 1:17, "When he was come to Rome, he carefully sought me." Now solicitude about temporal things is sometimes connected with works of mercy; for instance, when a man is solicitous to watch over the interests of orphans and poor persons. Therefore solicitude about temporal things is not unlawful.

On the contrary, Our Lord said (Matt. 6:31): "Be not solicitous . . . saying, What shall we eat, or what shall we drink, or wherewith shall we be clothed?" And yet such things are very necessary.

I answer that, Solicitude denotes an earnest endeavor to obtain something. Now it is evident that the endeavor is more earnest when there is fear of failure, so that there is less solicitude when success is assured. Accordingly solicitude about temporal things may be unlawful in three ways. First on the part of the object of solicitude; that is, if we seek temporal things as an end. Hence Augustine says (De Operibus Monach. xxvi): "When Our Lord said: 'Be not solicitous,' etc ... He intended to forbid them either to make such things their end, or for the sake of these things to do whatever they were commanded to do in preaching the Gospel." Secondly, solicitude about temporal things may be unlawful, through too much earnestness in endeavoring to obtain temporal things, the result being that a man is drawn away from spiritual things which ought to be the chief object of his search, wherefore it is written (Matt. 13:22) that "the care of this world ... chokes up the word." Thirdly, through over much fear, when, to wit, a man fears to lack necessary things if he do what he ought to do. Now our Lord gives three motives for laying aside this fear. First, on account of the yet greater favors bestowed by God on man, independently of his solicitude, viz. his body and soul (Matt. 6:26); secondly, on account of the care with which God watches over animals and plants without the assistance of man, according to the requirements of their nature; thirdly, because of Divine providence, through ignorance of which the gentiles are solicitous in seeking temporal goods before all others. Consequently He concludes that we should be solicitous most of all about spiritual goods, hoping that temporal goods also may be granted us according to our needs, if we do what we ought to do.

Reply Obj. 1: Temporal goods are subjected to man that he may use them according to his needs, not that he may place his end in them and be over solicitous about them.

Reply Obj. 2: The solicitude of a man who gains his bread by bodily labor is not superfluous but proportionate; hence Jerome says on Matt. 6:31, "Be not solicitous," that "labor is necessary, but solicitude must be banished," namely superfluous solicitude which unsettles the mind.

Reply Obj. 3: In the works of mercy solicitude about temporal things is directed to charity as its end, wherefore it is not unlawful, unless it be superfluous.

* * * * *

SEVENTH ARTICLE [II-II, Q. 55, Art. 7]

Whether We Should Be Solicitous About the Future?

Objection 1: It would seem that we should be solicitous about the future. For it is written (Prov. 6:6-8): "Go to the ant, O sluggard, and consider her ways and learn wisdom; which, although she hath no guide, nor master ... provideth her meat for herself in the summer, and gathereth her food in the harvest." Now this is to be solicitous about the future. Therefore solicitude about the future is praiseworthy.

Obj. 2: Further, solicitude pertains to prudence. But prudence is chiefly about the future, since its principal part is foresight of future things, as stated above (Q. 49, A. 6, ad 1). Therefore it is virtuous to be solicitous about the future.

Obj. 3: Further, whoever puts something by that he may keep it for the morrow, is solicitous about the future. Now we read (John 12:6) that Christ had a bag for keeping things in, which Judas carried, and (Acts 4:34-37) that the Apostles kept the price of the land, which had been laid at their feet. Therefore it is lawful to be solicitous about the future.

On the contrary, Our Lord said (Matt. 6:34): "Be not ... solicitous for tomorrow"; where "tomorrow" stands for the future, as Jerome says in his commentary on this passage.

I answer that, No work can be virtuous, unless it be vested with its due circumstances, and among these is the due time, according to Eccles. 8:6, "There is a time and opportunity for every business"; which applies not only to external deeds but also to internal solicitude. For every time has its own fitting proper solicitude; thus solicitude about the crops belongs to the summer time, and solicitude about the vintage to the time of autumn. Accordingly if a man were solicitous about the vintage during the summer, he would be needlessly forestalling the solicitude belonging to a future time. Hence Our Lord forbids such like excessive solicitude, saying: "Be ... not solicitous for tomorrow," wherefore He adds, "for the morrow will be solicitous for itself," that is to say, the morrow will have its own solicitude, which will be burden enough for the soul.

This is what He means by adding: "Sufficient for the day is the evil thereof," namely, the burden of solicitude.

Reply Obj. 1: The ant is solicitous at a befitting time, and it is this that is proposed for our example.

Reply Obj. 2: Due foresight of the future belongs to prudence. But it would be an inordinate foresight or solicitude about the future, if a man were to seek temporal things, to which the terms "past" and "future" apply, as ends, or if he were to seek them in excess of the needs of the present life, or if he were to forestall the time for solicitude.

Reply Obj. 3: As Augustine says (De Serm. Dom. in Monte ii, 17), "when we see a servant of God taking thought lest he lack these needful things, we must not judge him to be solicitous for the morrow, since even Our Lord deigned for our example to have a purse, and we read in the Acts of the Apostles that they procured the necessary means of livelihood in view of the future on account of a threatened famine. Hence Our Lord does not condemn those who according to human custom, provide themselves with such things, but those who oppose themselves to God for the sake of these things.".

* * * * *

EIGHTH ARTICLE [II-II, Q. 55, Art. 8]

Whether These Vices Arise from Covetousness?

Objection 1: It would seem that these vices do not arise from covetousness. As stated above (Q. 43, A. 6) lust is the chief cause of lack of rectitude in the reason. Now these vices are opposed to right reason, i.e. to prudence. Therefore they arise chiefly from lust; especially since the Philosopher says (Ethic. vii, 6) that "Venus is full of guile and her girdle is many colored" and that "he who is incontinent in desire acts with cunning."

Obj. 2: Further, these vices bear a certain resemblance to prudence, as stated above (Q. 47, A. 13). Now, since prudence is in the reason, the more spiritual vices seem to be more akin thereto, such as pride and vainglory. Therefore the aforesaid vices seem to arise from pride rather than from covetousness.

Obj. 3: Further, men make use of stratagems not only in laying hold of other people's goods, but also in plotting murders, the former of which pertains to covetousness, and the latter to anger. Now the use of stratagems pertains to craftiness, guile, and fraud. Therefore the aforesaid vices arise not only from covetousness, but also from anger.

On the contrary, Gregory (Moral. xxxi, 45) states that fraud is a daughter of covetousness.

I answer that, As stated above (A. 3; Q. 47, A. 13), carnal prudence and craftiness, as well as guile and fraud, bear a certain resemblance to prudence in some kind of use of the reason. Now among all the moral virtues it is justice wherein the use of right reason appears chiefly, for justice is in the rational appetite. Hence the undue use of reason appears chiefly in the vices opposed to justice, the chief of which is covetousness. Therefore the aforesaid vices arise chiefly from covetousness.

Reply Obj. 1: On account of the vehemence of pleasure and of concupiscence, lust entirely suppresses the reason from exercising its act: whereas in the aforesaid vices there is some use of reason, albeit inordinate. Hence these vices do not arise directly from lust. When the Philosopher says that "Venus is full of guile," he is referring to a certain resemblance, in so far as she carries man away suddenly, just as he is moved in deceitful actions, yet not by means of craftiness but rather by the vehemence of concupiscence and pleasure; wherefore he adds that "Venus doth cozen the wits of the wisest man"[1].

Reply Obj. 2: To do anything by stratagem seems to be due to pusillanimity: because a magnanimous man wishes to act openly, as the Philosopher says (Ethic. iv, 3). Wherefore, as pride resembles or apes magnanimity, it follows that the aforesaid vices which make use of fraud and guile, do not arise directly from pride, but rather from covetousness, which seeks its own profit and sets little by excellence.

Reply Obj. 3: Anger's movement is sudden, hence it acts with precipitation, and without counsel, contrary to the use of the aforesaid vices, though these use counsel inordinately. That men use stratagems in plotting murders, arises not from anger but rather from hatred, because the angry man desires to harm manifestly, as the Philosopher states (Rhet. ii, 2, 3)[2].

---

[1] Cf. Iliad xiv, 214-217
[2] Cf. Ethic. vii, 6

56. OF THE PRECEPTS RELATING TO PRUDENCE (In Two Articles)

We must now consider the precepts relating to prudence, under which head there are two points of inquiry:

(1) The precepts of prudence;
(2) The precepts relating to the opposite vices.

* * * * *

FIRST ARTICLE [II-II, Q. 56, Art. 1]

Whether the Precepts of the Decalogue Should Have Included a Precept of Prudence?

Objection 1: It would seem that the precepts of the decalogue should have included a precept of prudence. For the chief precepts should include a precept of the chief virtue. Now the chief precepts are those of the decalogue. Since then prudence is the chief of the moral virtues, it seems that the precepts of the decalogue should have included a precept of prudence.

Obj. 2: Further, the teaching of the Gospel contains the Law especially with regard to the precepts of the decalogue. Now the teaching of the Gospel contains a precept of prudence (Matt. 10:16): "Be ye ... prudent [Douay: 'wise'] as serpents." Therefore the precepts of the decalogue should have included a precept of prudence.

Obj. 3: Further, the other lessons of the Old Testament are directed to the precepts of the decalogue: wherefore it is written (Malach. 4:4): "Remember the law of Moses My servant, which I commanded him in Horeb." Now the other lessons of the Old Testament include precepts of prudence; for instance (Prov. 3:5): "Lean not upon thy own prudence"; and further on (Prov. 4:25): "Let thine eyelids go before thy steps." Therefore the Law also should have contained a precept of prudence, especially among the precepts of the decalogue.

The contrary however appears to anyone who goes through the precepts of the decalogue.

I answer that, As stated above (I-II, Q. 100, A. 3; A. 5, ad 1) when we were treating of precepts, the commandments of the decalogue being given to the whole people, are a matter of common knowledge to all, as coming under the purview of natural reason. Now foremost among the things dictated by natural reason are the ends of human life, which are to the practical order what naturally known principles are to the speculative order, as shown above (Q. 47, A. 6). Now prudence is not about the end, but about the means, as stated above (Q. 47, A. 6). Hence it was not fitting that the precepts of the decalogue should include a precept relating directly to prudence. And yet all the precepts of the decalogue are related to prudence, in so far as it directs all virtuous acts.

Reply Obj. 1: Although prudence is simply foremost among all the moral virtues, yet justice, more than any other virtue, regards its object under the aspect of something due, which is a necessary condition for a precept, as stated above (Q. 44, A. 1; I-II, Q. 99, AA. 1, 5). Hence it behooved the chief precepts of the Law, which are those of the decalogue, to refer to justice rather than to prudence.

Reply Obj. 2: The teaching of the Gospel is the doctrine of perfection. Therefore it needed to instruct man perfectly in all matters relating to right conduct, whether ends or means: wherefore it behooved the Gospel teaching to contain precepts also of prudence.

Reply Obj. 3: Just as the rest of the teaching of the Old Testament is directed to the precepts of the decalogue as its end, so it behooved man to be instructed by the subsequent lessons of the Old Testament about the act of prudence which is directed to the means.

* * * * *

SECOND ARTICLE [II-II, Q. 56, Art. 2]

Whether the Prohibitive Precepts Relating to the Vices Opposed to Prudence Are Fittingly Propounded in the Old Law?

Objection 1: It would seem that the prohibitive precepts relating to the vices opposed to prudence are unfittingly propounded in the Old Law. For such vices as imprudence and its parts which are directly opposed to prudence are not less opposed thereto, than those which bear a certain resemblance to prudence, such as craftiness and vices connected with it. Now the latter vices are forbidden in the Law: for it is written (Lev. 19:13): "Thou shalt not calumniate thy neighbor," and (Deut. 25:13): "Thou shalt not have divers weights in thy bag, a greater and a less." Therefore there should have also been prohibitive precepts about the vices directly opposed to prudence.

Obj. 2: Further, there is room for fraud in other things than in buying and selling. Therefore the Law unfittingly forbade fraud solely in buying and selling.

Obj. 3: Further, there is the same reason for prescribing an act of virtue as for prohibiting the act of a contrary vice. But acts of prudence are not prescribed in the Law. Therefore neither should any contrary vices have been forbidden in the Law.

The contrary, however, appears from the precepts of the Law which are quoted in the first objection.

I answer that, As stated above (A. 1), justice, above all, regards the aspect of something due, which is a necessary condition for a precept, because justice tends to render that which is due to another, as we shall state further on (Q. 58, A. 2). Now craftiness, as to its execution, is committed chiefly in matters of justice, as stated above (Q. 55, A. 8): and so it was fitting that the Law should contain precepts forbidding the execution of craftiness, in so far as this pertains to injustice, as when a man uses guile and fraud in calumniating another or in stealing his goods.

Reply Obj. 1: Those vices that are manifestly opposed to prudence, do not pertain to injustice in the same way as the execution of craftiness, and so they are not forbidden in the Law, as fraud and guile are, which latter pertain to injustice.

Reply Obj. 2: All guile and fraud committed in matters of injustice, can be understood to be forbidden in the prohibition of calumny (Lev. 19:13). Yet fraud and guile are wont to be practiced chiefly in buying and selling, according to Ecclus. 26:28, "A huckster shall not be justified from the sins of the lips": and it is for this reason that the Law contained a special precept forbidding fraudulent buying and selling.

Reply Obj. 3: All the precepts of the Law that relate to acts of justice pertain to the execution of prudence, even as the precepts prohibitive of stealing, calumny and fraudulent selling pertain to the execution of craftiness.

57. OF RIGHT (In Four Articles)

After considering prudence we must in due sequence consider justice, the consideration of which will be fourfold:

(1) Of justice;
(2) Of its parts;
(3) Of the corresponding gift;
(4) Of the precepts relating to justice.

Four points will have to be considered about justice: (1) Right; (2) Justice itself; (3) Injustice; (4) Judgment.

Under the first head there are four points of inquiry:

(1) Whether right is the object of justice?
(2) Whether right is fittingly divided into natural and positive right?
(3) Whether the right of nations is the same as natural right?
(4) Whether right of dominion and paternal right are distinct species?.

* * * * *

FIRST ARTICLE [II-II, Q. 57, Art. 1]

Whether Right Is the Object of Justice?

Objection 1: It would seem that right is not the object of justice. For the jurist Celsus says[1] that "right is the art of goodness and equality." Now art is not the object of justice, but is by itself an intellectual virtue. Therefore right is not the object of justice.

Obj. 2: Further, "Law," according to Isidore (Etym. v, 3), "is a kind of right." Now law is the object not of justice but of prudence, wherefore the Philosopher[2] reckons "legislative" as one of the parts of prudence. Therefore right is not the object of justice.

Obj. 3: Further, justice, before all, subjects man to God: for Augustine says (De Moribus Eccl. xv) that "justice is love serving

---

1 Digest. i, 1; De Just. et Jure 1
2 Ethic. vi, 8

God alone, and consequently governing aright all things subject to man." Now right (jus) does not pertain to Divine things, but only to human affairs, for Isidore says (Etym. v, 2) that "fas is the Divine law, and jus, the human law." Therefore right is not the object of justice.

On the contrary, Isidore says (Etym. v, 2) that "jus (right) is so called because it is just." Now the just is the object of justice, for the Philosopher declares (Ethic. v, 1) that "all are agreed in giving the name of justice to the habit which makes men capable of doing just actions."

I answer that, It is proper to justice, as compared with the other virtues, to direct man in his relations with others: because it denotes a kind of equality, as its very name implies; indeed we are wont to say that things are adjusted when they are made equal, for equality is in reference of one thing to some other. On the other hand the other virtues perfect man in those matters only which befit him in relation to himself. Accordingly that which is right in the works of the other virtues, and to which the intention of the virtue tends as to its proper object, depends on its relation to the agent only, whereas the right in a work of justice, besides its relation to the agent, is set up by its relation to others. Because a man's work is said to be just when it is related to some other by way of some kind of equality, for instance the payment of the wage due for a service rendered. And so a thing is said to be just, as having the rectitude of justice, when it is the term of an act of justice, without taking into account the way in which it is done by the agent: whereas in the other virtues nothing is declared to be right unless it is done in a certain way by the agent. For this reason justice has its own special proper object over and above the other virtues, and this object is called the just, which is the same as *right*. Hence it is evident that right is the object of justice.

Reply Obj. 1: It is usual for words to be distorted from their original signification so as to mean something else: thus the word "medicine" was first employed to signify a remedy used for curing a sick person, and then it was drawn to signify the art by which this is done. In like manner the word jus (right) was first of all used to denote the just thing itself, but afterwards it was transferred to designate the art whereby it is known what is just, and further to denote the place where justice is administered, thus a man is said to appear in jure[1], and yet further, we say even that a man, who has the office of exercising justice, administers the jus even if his sentence be unjust.

Reply Obj. 2: Just as there pre-exists in the mind of the craftsman an expression of the things to be made externally by his craft, which expression is called the rule of his craft, so too there pre-exists in the mind an expression of the particular just work which the reason determines, and which is a kind of rule of prudence. If this rule be expressed in writing it is called a "law," which according to Isidore (Etym. v, 1) is "a written decree": and so law is not the same as right, but an expression of right.

Reply Obj. 3: Since justice implies equality, and since we cannot offer God an equal return, it follows that we cannot make Him a perfectly just repayment. For this reason the Divine law is not properly called jus but fas, because, to wit, God is satisfied if we accomplish what we can. Nevertheless justice tends to make man repay God as much as he can, by subjecting his mind to Him entirely.

* * * * *

SECOND ARTICLE [II-II, Q. 57, Art. 2]

Whether Right Is Fittingly Divided into Natural Right and Positive Right?

Objection 1: It would seem that right is not fittingly divided into natural right and positive right. For that which is natural is unchangeable, and is the same for all. Now nothing of the kind is to be found in human affairs, since all the rules of human right fail in certain cases, nor do they obtain force everywhere. Therefore there is no such thing as natural right.

Obj. 2: Further, a thing is called "positive" when it proceeds from the human will. But a thing is not just, simply because it proceeds from the human will, else a man's will could not be unjust. Since then the "just" and the "right" are the same, it seems that there is no positive right.

Obj. 3: Further, Divine right is not natural right, since it transcends human nature. In like manner, neither is it positive right,

---

[1] In English we speak of a court of law, a barrister at law, etc.

since it is based not on human, but on Divine authority. Therefore right is unfittingly divided into natural and positive.

On the contrary, The Philosopher says (Ethic. v, 7) that "political justice is partly natural and partly legal," i.e. established by law.

I answer that, As stated above (A. 1) the "right" or the "just" is a work that is adjusted to another person according to some kind of equality. Now a thing can be adjusted to a man in two ways: first by its very nature, as when a man gives so much that he may receive equal value in return, and this is called "natural right." In another way a thing is adjusted or commensurated to another person, by agreement, or by common consent, when, to wit, a man deems himself satisfied, if he receive so much. This can be done in two ways: first by private agreement, as that which is confirmed by an agreement between private individuals; secondly, by public agreement, as when the whole community agrees that something should be deemed as though it were adjusted and commensurated to another person, or when this is decreed by the prince who is placed over the people, and acts in its stead, and this is called "positive right."

Reply Obj. 1: That which is natural to one whose nature is unchangeable, must needs be such always and everywhere. But man's nature is changeable, wherefore that which is natural to man may sometimes fail. Thus the restitution of a deposit to the depositor is in accordance with natural equality, and if human nature were always right, this would always have to be observed; but since it happens sometimes that man's will is unrighteous there are cases in which a deposit should not be restored, lest a man of unrighteous will make evil use of the thing deposited: as when a madman or an enemy of the common weal demands the return of his weapons.

Reply Obj. 2: The human will can, by common agreement, make a thing to be just provided it be not, of itself, contrary to natural justice, and it is in such matters that positive right has its place. Hence the Philosopher says (Ethic. v, 7) that "in the case of the legal just, it does not matter in the first instance whether it takes one form or another, it only matters when once it is laid down." If, however, a thing is, of itself, contrary to natural right, the human will cannot make it just, for instance by decreeing that it is lawful to steal or to commit adultery. Hence it is written (Isa. 10:1): "Woe to them that make wicked laws."

Reply Obj. 3: The Divine right is that which is promulgated by God. Such things are partly those that are naturally just, yet their justice is hidden to man, and partly are made just by God's decree. Hence also Divine right may be divided in respect of these two things, even as human right is. For the Divine law commands certain things because they are good, and forbids others, because they are evil, while others are good because they are prescribed, and others evil because they are forbidden.

* * * * *

THIRD ARTICLE [II-II, Q. 57, Art. 3]

Whether the Right of Nations Is the Same As the Natural Right?

Objection 1: It would seem that the right of nations is the same as the natural right. For all men do not agree save in that which is natural to them. Now all men agree in the right of nations; since the jurist[1] "the right of nations is that which is in use among all nations." Therefore the right of nations is the natural right.

Obj. 2: Further, slavery among men is natural, for some are naturally slaves according to the Philosopher (Polit. i, 2). Now "slavery belongs to the right of nations," as Isidore states (Etym. v, 4). Therefore the right of nations is a natural right.

Obj. 3: Further, right as stated above (A. 2) is divided into natural and positive. Now the right of nations is not a positive right, since all nations never agreed to decree anything by common agreement. Therefore the right of nations is a natural right.

On the contrary, Isidore says (Etym. v, 4) that "right is either natural, or civil, or right of nations," and consequently the right of nations is distinct from natural right.

I answer that, As stated above (A. 2), the natural right or just is that which by its very nature is adjusted to or commensurate with another person. Now this may happen in two ways; first, according as it is considered absolutely: thus a male by [his] very nature is commensurate with the female to beget offspring by her, and a parent is commensurate with the offspring to nourish it. Secondly a thing is naturally commensurate with another person, not according as it is considered absolutely, but according to something resultant from it, for instance the possession of property. For if a particular

---

1   Ulpian: Digest. i, 1; De Just. et Jure i

piece of land be considered absolutely, it contains no reason why it should belong to one man more than to another, but if it be considered in respect of its adaptability to cultivation, and the unmolested use of the land, it has a certain commensuration to be the property of one and not of another man, as the Philosopher shows (Polit. ii, 2).

Now it belongs not only to man but also to other animals to apprehend a thing absolutely: wherefore the right which we call natural, is common to us and other animals according to the first kind of commensuration. But the right of nations falls short of natural right in this sense, as the jurist[1] says because "the latter is common to all animals, while the former is common to men only." On the other hand to consider a thing by comparing it with what results from it, is proper to reason, wherefore this same is natural to man in respect of natural reason which dictates it. Hence the jurist Gaius says (Digest. i, 1; De Just. et Jure i, 9): "whatever natural reason decrees among all men, is observed by all equally, and is called the right of nations." This suffices for the Reply to the First Objection.

Reply Obj. 2: Considered absolutely, the fact that this particular man should be a slave rather than another man, is based, not on natural reason, but on some resultant utility, in that it is useful to this man to be ruled by a wiser man, and to the latter to be helped by the former, as the Philosopher states (Polit. i, 2). Wherefore slavery which belongs to the right of nations is natural in the second way, but not in the first.

Reply Obj. 3: Since natural reason dictates matters which are according to the right of nations, as implying a proximate equality, it follows that they need no special institution, for they are instituted by natural reason itself, as stated by the authority quoted above.

* * * * *

FOURTH ARTICLE [II-II, Q. 57, Art. 4]

Whether Paternal Right and Right of Dominion Should Be Distinguished As Special Species?

Objection 1: It would seem that "paternal right" and "right of dominion" should not be distinguished as special species. For it

---

[1] Digest. i, 1; De Just. et Jure i

belongs to justice to render to each one what is his, as Ambrose states (De Offic. i, 24). Now right is the object of justice, as stated above (A. 1). Therefore right belongs to each one equally; and we ought not to distinguish the rights of fathers and masters as distinct species.

Obj. 2: Further, the law is an expression of what is just, as stated above (A. 1, ad 2). Now a law looks to the common good of a city or kingdom, as stated above (I-II, Q. 90, A. 2), but not to the private good of an individual or even of one household. Therefore there is no need for a special right of dominion or paternal right, since the master and the father pertain to a household, as stated in Polit. i, 2.

Obj. 3: Further, there are many other differences of degrees among men, for instance some are soldiers, some are priests, some are princes. Therefore some special kind of right should be allotted to them.

On the contrary, The Philosopher (Ethic. v, 6) distinguishes right of dominion, paternal right and so on as species distinct from civil right.

I answer that, Right or just depends on commensuration with another person. Now "another" has a twofold signification. First, it may denote something that is other simply, as that which is altogether distinct; as, for example, two men neither of whom is subject to the other, and both of whom are subjects of the ruler of the state; and between these according to the Philosopher (Ethic. v, 6) there is the "just" simply. Secondly a thing is said to be other from something else, not simply, but as belonging in some way to that something else: and in this way, as regards human affairs, a son belongs to his father, since he is part of him somewhat, as stated in *Ethic.* viii, 12, and a slave belongs to his master, because he is his instrument, as stated in *Polit.* i, 2[1]. Hence a father is not compared to his son as to another simply, and so between them there is not the just simply, but a kind of just, called "paternal." In like manner neither is there the just simply, between master and servant, but that which is called "dominative." A wife, though she is something belonging to the husband, since she stands related to him as to her own body, as the Apostle declares (Eph. 5:28), is nevertheless more distinct from her husband, than a son from his father, or a slave from his master: for she is received into a kind of social life, that of matrimony, wherefore according to the Philosopher

---

1   Cf. *Ethic.* viii, 11

(Ethic. v, 6) there is more scope for justice between husband and wife than between father and son, or master and slave, because, as husband and wife have an immediate relation to the community of the household, as stated in *Polit.* i, 2, 5, it follows that between them there is "domestic justice" rather than "civic."

Reply Obj. 1: It belongs to justice to render to each one his right, the distinction between individuals being presupposed: for if a man gives himself his due, this is not strictly called "just." And since what belongs to the son is his father's, and what belongs to the slave is his master's, it follows that properly speaking there is not justice of father to son, or of master to slave.

Reply Obj. 2: A son, as such, belongs to his father, and a slave, as such, belongs to his master; yet each, considered as a man, is something having separate existence and distinct from others. Hence in so far as each of them is a man, there is justice towards them in a way: and for this reason too there are certain laws regulating the relations of father to his son, and of a master to his slave; but in so far as each is something belonging to another, the perfect idea of "right" or "just" is wanting to them.

Reply Obj. 3: All other differences between one person and another in a state, have an immediate relation to the community of the state and to its ruler, wherefore there is just towards them in the perfect sense of justice. This "just" however is distinguished according to various offices, hence when we speak of "military," or "magisterial," or "priestly" right, it is not as though such rights fell short of the simply right, as when we speak of "paternal" right, or right of "dominion," but for the reason that something proper is due to each class of person in respect of his particular office.

58. OF JUSTICE (In Twelve Articles)

We must now consider justice. Under this head there are twelve points of inquiry:

(1) What is justice?
(2) Whether justice is always towards another?
(3) Whether it is a virtue?

(4) Whether it is in the will as its subject?
(5) Whether it is a general virtue?
(6) Whether, as a general virtue, it is essentially the same as every virtue?
(7) Whether there is a particular justice?
(8) Whether particular justice has a matter of its own?
(9) Whether it is about passions, or about operations only?
(10) Whether the mean of justice is the real mean?
(11) Whether the act of justice is to render to everyone his own?
(12) Whether justice is the chief of the moral virtues?.

* * * * *

FIRST ARTICLE [II-II, Q. 58, Art. 1]

Whether Justice Is Fittingly Defined As Being the Perpetual and Constant Will to Render to Each One His Right?

Objection 1: It would seem that lawyers have unfittingly defined justice as being "the perpetual and constant will to render to each one his right"[1]. For, according to the Philosopher (Ethic. v, 1), justice is a habit which makes a man "capable of doing what is just, and of being just in action and in intention." Now "will" denotes a power, or also an act. Therefore justice is unfittingly defined as being a will.

Obj. 2: Further, rectitude of the will is not the will; else if the will were its own rectitude, it would follow that no will is unrighteous. Yet, according to Anselm (De Veritate xii), justice is rectitude. Therefore justice is not the will.

Obj. 3: Further, no will is perpetual save God's. If therefore justice is a perpetual will, in God alone will there be justice.

Obj. 4: Further, whatever is perpetual is constant, since it is unchangeable. Therefore it is needless in defining justice, to say that it is both "perpetual" and "constant."

Obj. 5: Further, it belongs to the sovereign to give each one his right. Therefore, if justice gives each one his right, it follows that it is in none but the sovereign: which is absurd.

---

[1] Digest. i, 1; De Just. et Jure 10

Obj. 6: Further, Augustine says (De Moribus Eccl. xv) that "justice is love serving God alone." Therefore it does not render to each one his right.

I answer that, The aforesaid definition of justice is fitting if understood aright. For since every virtue is a habit that is the principle of a good act, a virtue must needs be defined by means of the good act bearing on the matter proper to that virtue. Now the proper matter of justice consists of those things that belong to our intercourse with other men, as shall be shown further on (A. 2). Hence the act of justice in relation to its proper matter and object is indicated in the words, "Rendering to each one his right," since, as Isidore says (Etym. x), "a man is said to be just because he respects the rights *(jus)* of others."

Now in order that an act bearing upon any matter whatever be virtuous, it requires to be voluntary, stable, and firm, because the Philosopher says (Ethic. ii, 4) that in order for an act to be virtuous it needs first of all to be done "knowingly," secondly to be done "by choice," and "for a due end," thirdly to be done "immovably." Now the first of these is included in the second, since "what is done through ignorance is involuntary" (Ethic. iii, 1). Hence the definition of justice mentions first the "will," in order to show that the act of justice must be voluntary; and mention is made afterwards of its "constancy" and "perpetuity" in order to indicate the firmness of the act.

Accordingly, this is a complete definition of justice; save that the act is mentioned instead of the habit, which takes its species from that act, because habit implies relation to act. And if anyone would reduce it to the proper form of a definition, he might say that "justice is a habit whereby a man renders to each one his due by a constant and perpetual will": and this is about the same definition as that given by the Philosopher (Ethic. v, 5) who says that "justice is a habit whereby a man is said to be capable of doing just actions in accordance with his choice."

Reply Obj. 1: Will here denotes the act, not the power: and it is customary among writers to define habits by their acts: thus Augustine says (Tract. in Joan. xl) that "faith is to believe what one sees not."

Reply Obj. 2: Justice is the same as rectitude, not essentially but causally; for it is a habit which rectifies the deed and the will.

Reply Obj. 3: The will may be called perpetual in two ways. First on the part of the will's act which endures for ever, and thus

God's will alone is perpetual. Secondly on the part of the subject, because, to wit, a man wills to do a certain thing always, and this is a necessary condition of justice. For it does not satisfy the conditions of justice that one wish to observe justice in some particular matter for the time being, because one could scarcely find a man willing to act unjustly in every case; and it is requisite that one should have the will to observe justice at all times and in all cases.

Reply Obj. 4: Since "perpetual" does not imply perpetuity of the act of the will, it is not superfluous to add "constant": for while the "perpetual will" denotes the purpose of observing justice always, "constant" signifies a firm perseverance in this purpose.

Reply Obj. 5: A judge renders to each one what belongs to him, by way of command and direction, because a judge is the "personification of justice," and "the sovereign is its guardian" (Ethic. v, 4). On the other hand, the subjects render to each one what belongs to him, by way of execution.

Reply Obj. 6: Just as love of God includes love of our neighbor, as stated above (Q. 25, A. 1), so too the service of God includes rendering to each one his due.

* * * * *

SECOND ARTICLE [II-II, Q. 58, Art. 2]

Whether Justice Is Always Towards Another?

Objection 1: It would seem that justice is not always towards another. For the Apostle says (Rom. 3:22) that "the justice of God is by faith of Jesus Christ." Now faith does not concern the dealings of one man with another. Neither therefore does justice.

Obj. 2: Further, according to Augustine (De Moribus Eccl. xv), "it belongs to justice that man should direct to the service of God his authority over the things that are subject to him." Now the sensitive appetite is subject to man, according to Gen. 4:7, where it is written: "The lust thereof," viz. of sin, "shall be under thee, and thou shalt have dominion over it." Therefore it belongs to justice to have dominion over one's own appetite: so that justice is towards oneself.

Obj. 3: Further, the justice of God is eternal. But nothing else is co-eternal with God. Therefore justice is not essentially towards another.

Obj. 4: Further, man's dealings with himself need to be rectified no less than his dealings with another. Now man's dealings are rectified by justice, according to Prov. 11:5, "The justice of the upright shall make his way prosperous." Therefore justice is about our dealings not only with others, but also with ourselves.

On the contrary, Tully says (De Officiis i, 7) that "the object of justice is to keep men together in society and mutual intercourse." Now this implies relationship of one man to another. Therefore justice is concerned only about our dealings with others.

I answer that, As stated above (Q. 57, A. 1) since justice by its name implies equality, it denotes essentially relation to another, for a thing is equal, not to itself, but to another. And forasmuch as it belongs to justice to rectify human acts, as stated above (Q. 57, A. 1; I-II, Q. 113, A. 1) this otherness which justice demands must needs be between beings capable of action. Now actions belong to supposits[1] and wholes and, properly speaking, not to parts and forms or powers, for we do not say properly that the hand strikes, but a man with his hand, nor that heat makes a thing hot, but fire by heat, although such expressions may be employed metaphorically. Hence, justice properly speaking demands a distinction of supposits, and consequently is only in one man towards another. Nevertheless in one and the same man we may speak metaphorically of his various principles of action such as the reason, the irascible, and the concupiscible, as though they were so many agents: so that metaphorically in one and the same man there is said to be justice in so far as the reason commands the irascible and concupiscible, and these obey reason; and in general in so far as to each part of man is ascribed what is becoming to it. Hence the Philosopher (Ethic. v, 11) calls this "metaphorical justice."

Reply Obj. 1: The justice which faith works in us, is that whereby the ungodly is justified: it consists in the due coordination of the parts of the soul, as stated above (I-II, Q. 113, A. 1) where we were treating of the justification of the ungodly. Now this belongs to metaphorical justice, which may be found even in a man who lives all by himself.

This suffices for the Reply to the Second Objection.

Reply Obj. 3: God's justice is from eternity in respect of the eternal will and purpose (and it is chiefly in this that justice consists);

---

[1] Cf. I, Q. 29, A. 2

although it is not eternal as regards its effect, since nothing is co-eternal with God.

Reply Obj. 4: Man's dealings with himself are sufficiently rectified by the rectification of the passions by the other moral virtues. But his dealings with others need a special rectification, not only in relation to the agent, but also in relation to the person to whom they are directed. Hence about such dealings there is a special virtue, and this is justice.

* * * * *

THIRD ARTICLE [II-II, Q. 58, Art. 3]

Whether Justice Is a Virtue?

Objection 1: It would seem that justice is not a virtue. For it is written (Luke 17:10): "When you shall have done all these things that are commanded you, say: We are unprofitable servants; we have done that which we ought to do." Now it is not unprofitable to do a virtuous deed: for Ambrose says (De Officiis ii, 6): "We look to a profit that is estimated not by pecuniary gain but by the acquisition of godliness." Therefore to do what one ought to do, is not a virtuous deed. And yet it is an act of justice. Therefore justice is not a virtue.

Obj. 2: Further, that which is done of necessity, is not meritorious. But to render to a man what belongs to him, as justice requires, is of necessity. Therefore it is not meritorious. Yet it is by virtuous actions that we gain merit. Therefore justice is not a virtue.

Obj. 3: Further, every moral virtue is about matters of action. Now those things which are wrought externally are not things concerning behavior but concerning handicraft, according to the Philosopher (Metaph. ix)[1]. Therefore since it belongs to justice to produce externally a deed that is just in itself, it seems that justice is not a moral virtue.

On the contrary, Gregory says (Moral. ii, 49) that "the entire structure of good works is built on four virtues," viz. temperance, prudence, fortitude and justice.

---

1 Didot ed., viii, 8

I answer that, A human virtue is one "which renders a human act and man himself good"[1], and this can be applied to justice. For a man's act is made good through attaining the rule of reason, which is the rule whereby human acts are regulated. Hence, since justice regulates human operations, it is evident that it renders man's operations good, and, as Tully declares (De Officiis i, 7), good men are so called chiefly from their justice, wherefore, as he says again (De Officiis i, 7) "the luster of virtue appears above all in justice."

Reply Obj. 1: When a man does what he ought, he brings no gain to the person to whom he does what he ought, but only abstains from doing him a harm. He does however profit himself, in so far as he does what he ought, spontaneously and readily, and this is to act virtuously. Hence it is written (Wis. 8:7) that Divine wisdom "teacheth temperance, and prudence, and justice, and fortitude, which are such things as men (i.e. virtuous men) can have nothing more profitable in life."

Reply Obj. 2: Necessity is twofold. One arises from constraint, and this removes merit, since it runs counter to the will. The other arises from the obligation of a command, or from the necessity of obtaining an end, when, to wit, a man is unable to achieve the end of virtue without doing some particular thing. The latter necessity does not remove merit, when a man does voluntarily that which is necessary in this way. It does however exclude the credit of supererogation, according to 1 Cor. 9:16, "If I preach the Gospel, it is no glory to me, for a necessity lieth upon me."

Reply Obj. 3: Justice is concerned about external things, not by making them, which pertains to art, but by using them in our dealings with other men.

* * * * *

FOURTH ARTICLE [II-II, Q. 58, Art. 4]

Whether Justice Is in the Will As Its Subject?

Objection 1: It would seem that justice is not in the will as its subject. For justice is sometimes called truth. But truth is not in the will, but in the intellect. Therefore justice is not in the will as its subject.

---

[1] Ethic. ii, 6

Obj. 2: Further, justice is about our dealings with others. Now it belongs to the reason to direct one thing in relation to another. Therefore justice is not in the will as its subject but in the reason.

Obj. 3: Further, justice is not an intellectual virtue, since it is not directed to knowledge; wherefore it follows that it is a moral virtue. Now the subject of moral virtue is the faculty which is "rational by participation," viz. the irascible and the concupiscible, as the Philosopher declares (Ethic. i, 13). Therefore justice is not in the will as its subject, but in the irascible and concupiscible.

On the contrary, Anselm says (De Verit. xii) that "justice is rectitude of the will observed for its own sake."

I answer that, The subject of a virtue is the power whose act that virtue aims at rectifying. Now justice does not aim at directing an act of the cognitive power, for we are not said to be just through knowing something aright. Hence the subject of justice is not the intellect or reason which is a cognitive power. But since we are said to be just through doing something aright, and because the proximate principle of action is the appetitive power, justice must needs be in some appetitive power as its subject.

Now the appetite is twofold; namely, the will which is in the reason and the sensitive appetite which follows on sensitive apprehension, and is divided into the irascible and the concupiscible, as stated in the First Part (Q. 81, A. 2). Again the act of rendering his due to each man cannot proceed from the sensitive appetite, because sensitive apprehension does not go so far as to be able to consider the relation of one thing to another; but this is proper to the reason. Therefore justice cannot be in the irascible or concupiscible as its subject, but only in the will: hence the Philosopher (Ethic. v, 1) defines justice by an act of the will, as may be seen above (A. 1).

Reply Obj. 1: Since the will is the rational appetite, when the rectitude of the reason which is called truth is imprinted on the will on account of its nighness to the reason, this imprint retains the name of truth; and hence it is that justice sometimes goes by the name of truth.

Reply Obj. 2: The will is borne towards its object consequently on the apprehension of reason: wherefore, since the reason directs one thing in relation to another, the will can will one thing in relation to another, and this belongs to justice.

Reply Obj. 3: Not only the irascible and concupiscible parts are rational by participation, but the entire appetitive faculty, as stated in Ethic. i, 13, because all appetite is subject to reason. Now the will is contained in the appetitive faculty, wherefore it can be the subject of moral virtue.

* * * * *

FIFTH ARTICLE [II-II, Q. 58, Art. 5]

Whether Justice Is a General Virtue?

Objection 1: It would seem that justice is not a general virtue. For justice is specified with the other virtues, according to Wis. 8:7, "She teacheth temperance and prudence, and justice, and fortitude." Now the "general" is not specified or reckoned together with the species contained under the same "general." Therefore justice is not a general virtue.

Obj. 2: Further, as justice is accounted a cardinal virtue, so are temperance and fortitude. Now neither temperance nor fortitude is reckoned to be a general virtue. Therefore neither should justice in any way be reckoned a general virtue.

Obj. 3: Further, justice is always towards others, as stated above (A. 2). But a sin committed against one's neighbor cannot be a general sin, because it is condivided with sin committed against oneself. Therefore neither is justice a general virtue.

On the contrary, The Philosopher says (Ethic. v, 1) that "justice is every virtue."

I answer that, Justice, as stated above (A. 2) directs man in his relations with other men. Now this may happen in two ways: first as regards his relation with individuals, secondly as regards his relations with others in general, in so far as a man who serves a community, serves all those who are included in that community. Accordingly justice in its proper acceptation can be directed to another in both these senses. Now it is evident that all who are included in a community, stand in relation to that community as parts to a whole; while a part, as such, belongs to a whole, so that whatever is the good of a part can be directed to the good of the whole. It follows therefore that the good of any virtue, whether such virtue direct man in relation to himself, or in relation to certain other individual persons, is referable to the common good, to which justice directs: so that all acts of virtue can pertain to justice, in so far as it directs man to the common good. It is in this sense that justice is called a general virtue. And since it belongs to the law to direct to the common good, as stated above (I-II, Q. 90, A. 2), it follows that the justice which is in this way styled general, is called "legal justice," because thereby man is in harmony with the law which directs the acts of all the virtues to the common good.

Reply Obj. 1: Justice is specified or enumerated with the other virtues, not as a general but as a special virtue, as we shall state further on (AA. 7, 12).

Reply Obj. 2: Temperance and fortitude are in the sensitive appetite, viz. in the concupiscible and irascible. Now these powers are appetitive of certain particular goods, even as the senses are cognitive of particulars. On the other hand justice is in the intellective appetite as its subject, which can have the universal good as its object, knowledge whereof belongs to the intellect. Hence justice can be a general virtue rather than temperance or fortitude.

Reply Obj. 3: Things referable to oneself are referable to another, especially in regard to the common good. Wherefore legal justice, in so far as it directs to the common good, may be called a general virtue: and in like manner injustice may be called a general sin; hence it is written (1 John 3:4) that all "sin is iniquity.".

* * * * *

SIXTH ARTICLE [II-II, Q. 58, Art. 6]

Whether Justice, As a General Virtue, Is Essentially the Same As All Virtue?

Objection 1: It would seem that justice, as a general virtue, is essentially the same as all virtue. For the Philosopher says (Ethic. v, 1) that "virtue and legal justice are the same as all virtue, but differ in their mode of being." Now things that differ merely in their mode of being or logically do not differ essentially. Therefore justice is essentially the same as every virtue.

Obj. 2: Further, every virtue that is not essentially the same as all virtue is a part of virtue. Now the aforesaid justice, according to the Philosopher (Ethic. v. 1) "is not a part but the whole of virtue." Therefore the aforesaid justice is essentially the same as all virtue.

Obj. 3: Further, the essence of a virtue does not change through that virtue directing its act to some higher end even as the habit of temperance remains essentially the same even though its act be directed to a Divine good. Now it belongs to legal justice that the acts of all the virtues are directed to a higher end, namely the common good of the multitude, which transcends the good of one single individual. Therefore it seems that legal justice is essentially all virtue.

Obj. 4: Further, every good of a part can be directed to the good of the whole, so that if it be not thus directed it would seem without use or purpose. But that which is in accordance with virtue cannot be so. Therefore it seems that there can be no act of any virtue, that does not belong to general justice, which directs to the common good; and so it seems that general justice is essentially the same as all virtue.

On the contrary, The Philosopher says (Ethic. v, 1) that "many are able to be virtuous in matters affecting themselves, but are unable to be virtuous in matters relating to others," and (Polit. iii, 2) that "the virtue of the good man is not strictly the same as the virtue of the good citizen." Now the virtue of a good citizen is general justice, whereby a man is directed to the common good. Therefore general justice is not the same as virtue in general, and it is possible to have one without the other.

I answer that, A thing is said to be "general" in two ways. First, by *predication:* thus "animal" is general in relation to man and horse and the like: and in this sense that which is general must needs be essentially the same as the things in relation to which it is general, for the reason that the genus belongs to the essence of the species, and forms part of its definition. Secondly a thing is said to be general *virtually;* thus a universal cause is general in relation to all its effects, the sun, for instance, in relation to all bodies that are illumined, or transmuted by its power; and in this sense there is no need for that which is "general" to be essentially the same as those things in relation to which it is general, since cause and effect are not essentially the same. Now it is in the latter sense that, according to what has been said (A. 5), legal justice is said to be a general virtue, in as much, to wit, as it directs the acts of the other virtues to its own end, and this is to move all the other virtues by its command; for just as charity may be called a general virtue in so far as it directs the acts of all the virtues to the Divine good, so too is legal justice, in so far as it directs the acts of all the virtues to the common good. Accordingly, just as charity which regards the Divine good as its proper object, is a special virtue in respect of its essence, so too legal justice is a special virtue in respect of its essence, in so far as it regards the common good as its proper object. And thus it is in the sovereign principally and by way of a mastercraft, while it is secondarily and administratively in his subjects.

However the name of legal justice can be given to every virtue, in so far as every virtue is directed to the common good by the aforesaid legal justice, which though special essentially is nevertheless virtually general. Speaking in this way, legal justice is essentially the same as all virtue, but differs therefrom logically: and it is in this sense that the Philosopher speaks.

Wherefore the Replies to the First and Second Objections are manifest.

Reply Obj. 3: This argument again takes legal justice for the virtue commanded by legal justice.

Reply Obj. 4: Every virtue strictly speaking directs its act to that virtue's proper end: that it should happen to be directed to a further end either always or sometimes, does not belong to that virtue considered strictly, for it needs some higher virtue to direct it to that end. Consequently there must be one supreme virtue essentially distinct from every other virtue, which directs all the virtues to the common good; and this virtue is legal justice.

* * * * *

SEVENTH ARTICLE [II-II, Q. 58, Art. 7]

Whether There Is a Particular Besides a General Justice?

Objection 1: It would seem that there is not a particular besides a general justice. For there is nothing superfluous in the virtues, as neither is there in nature. Now general justice directs man sufficiently in all his relations with other men. Therefore there is no need for a particular justice.

Obj. 2: Further, the species of a virtue does not vary according to "one" and "many." But legal justice directs one man to another in matters relating to the multitude, as shown above (AA. 5, 6).

Therefore there is not another species of justice directing one man to another in matters relating to the individual.

Obj. 3: Further, between the individual and the general public stands the household community. Consequently, if in addition to general justice there is a particular justice corresponding to the individual, for the same reason there should be a domestic justice directing man to the common good of a household: and yet this is not the case. Therefore neither should there be a particular besides a legal justice.

On the contrary, Chrysostom in his commentary on Matt. 5:6, "Blessed are they that hunger and thirst after justice," says (Hom. xv in Matth.): "By justice He signifies either the general virtue, or the particular virtue which is opposed to covetousness."

I answer that, As stated above (A. 6), legal justice is not essentially the same as every virtue, and besides legal justice which directs man immediately to the common good, there is a need for other virtues to direct him immediately in matters relating to particular goods: and these virtues may be relative to himself or to another individual person. Accordingly, just as in addition to legal justice there is a need for particular virtues to direct man in relation to himself, such as temperance and fortitude, so too besides legal justice there is need for particular justice to direct man in his relations to other individuals.

Reply Obj. 1: Legal justice does indeed direct man sufficiently in his relations towards others. As regards the common good it does so immediately, but as to the good of the individual, it does so mediately. Wherefore there is need for particular justice to direct a man immediately to the good of another individual.

Reply Obj. 2: The common good of the realm and the particular good of the individual differ not only in respect of the many and the few, but also under a formal aspect. For the aspect of the common good differs from the aspect of the individual good, even as the aspect of whole differs from that of part. Wherefore the Philosopher says (Polit. i, 1) that "they are wrong who maintain that the State and the home and the like differ only as many and few and not specifically."

Reply Obj. 3: The household community, according to the Philosopher (Polit. i, 2), differs in respect of a threefold fellowship; namely "of husband and wife, father and son, master and slave," in each of which one person is, as it were, part of the other. Wherefore between such persons there is not justice simply, but a species of justice, viz. domestic justice, as stated in Ethic. v, 6.

* * * * *

EIGHTH ARTICLE [II-II, Q. 58, Art. 8]

Whether Particular Justice Has a Special Matter?

Objection 1: It would seem that particular justice has no special matter. Because a gloss on Gen. 2:14, "The fourth river is Euphrates," says: "Euphrates signifies 'fruitful'; nor is it stated through what country it flows, because justice pertains to all the parts of the soul." Now this would not be the case, if justice had a special matter, since every special matter belongs to a special power. Therefore particular justice has no special matter.

Obj. 2: Further, Augustine says (QQ. lxxxiii, qu. 61) that "the soul has four virtues whereby, in this life, it lives spiritually, viz. temperance, prudence, fortitude and justice;" and he says that "the fourth is justice, which pervades all the virtues." Therefore particular justice, which is one of the four cardinal virtues, has no special matter.

Obj. 3: Further, justice directs man sufficiently in matters relating to others. Now a man can be directed to others in all matters relating to this life. Therefore the matter of justice is general and not special.

On the contrary, The Philosopher reckons (Ethic. v, 2) particular justice to be specially about those things which belong to social life.

I answer that, Whatever can be rectified by reason is the matter of moral virtue, for this is defined in reference to right reason, according to the Philosopher (Ethic. ii, 6). Now the reason can rectify not only the internal passions of the soul, but also external actions, and also those external things of which man can make use. And yet it is in respect of external actions and external things by means of which men can communicate with one another, that the relation of one man to another is to be considered; whereas it is in respect of internal passions that we consider man's rectitude in himself. Consequently, since justice is directed to others, it is not about the entire matter of moral virtue, but only about external actions and things, under a certain special aspect of the object, in so far as one man is related to another through them.

Reply Obj. 1: It is true that justice belongs essentially to one part of the soul, where it resides as in its subject; and this is the will which moves by its command all the other parts of the soul; and accordingly justice belongs to all the parts of the soul, not directly but by a kind of diffusion.

Reply Obj. 2: As stated above (I-II, Q. 61, AA. 3, 4), the cardinal virtues may be taken in two ways: first as special virtues, each having a determinate matter; secondly, as certain general modes of virtue. In this latter sense Augustine speaks in the passage quoted: for he says that "prudence is knowledge of what we should seek and avoid, temperance is the curb on the lust for fleeting pleasures, fortitude is strength of mind in bearing with passing trials, justice is the love of God and our neighbor which pervades the other virtues, that is to say, is the common principle of the entire order between one man and another."

Reply Obj. 3: A man's internal passions which are a part of moral matter, are not in themselves directed to another man, which belongs to the specific nature of justice; yet their effects, i.e. external actions, are capable of being directed to another man. Consequently it does not follow that the matter of justice is general.

* * * * *

NINTH ARTICLE [II-II, Q. 58, Art. 9]

Whether Justice Is About the Passions?

Objection 1: It would seem that justice is about the passions. For the Philosopher says (Ethic. ii, 3) that "moral virtue is about pleasure and pain." Now pleasure or delight, and pain are passions, as stated above[1] when we were treating of the passions. Therefore justice, being a moral virtue, is about the passions.

Obj. 2: Further, justice is the means of rectifying a man's operations in relation to another man. Now such like operations cannot be rectified unless the passions be rectified, because it is owing to disorder of the passions that there is disorder in the aforesaid operations: thus sexual lust leads to adultery, and overmuch love of money leads to theft. Therefore justice must needs be about the passions.

Obj. 3: Further, even as particular justice is towards another person so is legal justice. Now legal justice is about the passions, else

---

[1] I-II, Q. 23, A. 4; Q. 31, A. 1; Q. 35, A. 1

it would not extend to all the virtues, some of which are evidently about the passions. Therefore justice is about the passions.

On the contrary, The Philosopher says (Ethic. v, 1) that justice is about operations.

I answer that, The true answer to this question may be gathered from a twofold source. First from the subject of justice, i.e. from the will, whose movements or acts are not passions, as stated above (I-II, Q. 22, A. 3; Q. 59, A. 4), for it is only the sensitive appetite whose movements are called passions. Hence justice is not about the passions, as are temperance and fortitude, which are in the irascible and concupiscible parts. Secondly, on he part of the matter, because justice is about man's relations with another, and we are not directed immediately to another by the internal passions. Therefore justice is not about the passions.

Reply Obj. 1: Not every moral virtue is about pleasure and pain as its proper matter, since fortitude is about fear and daring: but every moral virtue is directed to pleasure and pain, as to ends to be acquired, for, as the Philosopher says (Ethic. vii, 11), "pleasure and pain are the principal end in respect of which we say that this is an evil, and that a good": and in this way too they belong to justice, since "a man is not just unless he rejoice in just actions" (Ethic. i, 8).

Reply Obj. 2: External operations are as it were between external things, which are their matter, and internal passions, which are their origin. Now it happens sometimes that there is a defect in one of these, without there being a defect in the other. Thus a man may steal another's property, not through the desire to have the thing, but through the will to hurt the man; or vice versa, a man may covet another's property without wishing to steal it. Accordingly the directing of operations in so far as they tend towards external things, belongs to justice, but in so far as they arise from the passions, it belongs to the other moral virtues which are about the passions. Hence justice hinders theft of another's property, in so far as stealing is contrary to the equality that should be maintained in external things, while liberality hinders it as resulting from an immoderate desire for wealth. Since, however, external operations take their species, not from the internal passions but from external things as being their objects, it follows that, external operations are essentially the matter of justice rather than of the other moral virtues.

Reply Obj. 3: The common good is the end of each individual member of a community, just as the good of the whole is the end of each part. On the other hand the good of one individual is not the end of another individual: wherefore legal justice which is directed to the common good, is more capable of extending to the internal passions whereby man is disposed in some way or other in himself, than particular justice which is directed to the good of another individual: although legal justice extends chiefly to other virtues in the point of their external operations, in so far, to wit, as "the law commands us to perform the actions of a courageous person . . . the actions of a temperate person . . . and the actions of a gentle person" (Ethic. v, 5).

* * * * *

TENTH ARTICLE [II-II, Q. 58, Art. 10]

Whether the Mean of Justice Is the Real Mean?

Objection 1: It would seem that the mean of justice is not the real mean. For the generic nature remains entire in each species. Now moral virtue is defined (Ethic. ii, 6) to be "an elective habit which observes the mean fixed, in our regard, by reason." Therefore justice observes the rational and not the real mean.

Obj. 2: Further, in things that are good simply, there is neither excess nor defect, and consequently neither is there a mean; as is clearly the case with the virtues, according to Ethic. ii, 6. Now justice is about things that are good simply, as stated in Ethic. v. Therefore justice does not observe the real mean.

Obj. 3: Further, the reason why the other virtues are said to observe the rational and not the real mean, is because in their case the mean varies according to different persons, since what is too much for one is too little for another (Ethic. ii, 6). Now this is also the case in justice: for one who strikes a prince does not receive the same punishment as one who strikes a private individual. Therefore justice also observes, not the real, but the rational mean.

On the contrary, The Philosopher says (Ethic. ii, 6; v, 4) that the mean of justice is to be taken according to "arithmetical" proportion, so that it is the real mean.

I answer that, As stated above (A. 9; I-II, Q. 59, A. 4), the other moral virtues are chiefly concerned with the passions, the regulation of which is gauged entirely by a comparison with the very man who is the subject of those passions, in so far as his anger and desire are vested with their various due circumstances. Hence the mean in such like virtues is measured not by the proportion of one thing to another, but merely by comparison with the virtuous man himself, so that with them the mean is only that which is fixed by reason in our regard.

On the other hand, the matter of justice is external operation, in so far as an operation or the thing used in that operation is duly proportionate to another person, wherefore the mean of justice consists in a certain proportion of equality between the external thing and the external person. Now equality is the real mean between greater and less, as stated in *Metaph.* x[1]: wherefore justice observes the real mean.

Reply Obj. 1: This real mean is also the rational mean, wherefore justice satisfies the conditions of a moral virtue.

Reply Obj. 2: We may speak of a thing being good simply in two ways. First a thing may be good in every way: thus the virtues are good; and there is neither mean nor extremes in things that are good simply in this sense. Secondly a thing is said to be good simply through being good absolutely i.e. in its nature, although it may become evil through being abused. Such are riches and honors; and in the like it is possible to find excess, deficiency and mean, as regards men who can use them well or ill: and it is in this sense that justice is about things that are good simply.

Reply Obj. 3: The injury inflicted bears a different proportion to a prince from that which it bears to a private person: wherefore each injury requires to be equalized by vengeance in a different way: and this implies a real and not merely a rational diversity.

* * * * *

ELEVENTH ARTICLE [II-II, Q. 58, Art. 11]

Whether the Act of Justice Is to Render to Each One His Own?

Objection 1: It would seem that the act of justice is not to render to each one his own. For Augustine (De Trin. xiv, 9) ascribes to justice the act of succoring the needy. Now in succoring the

---

1   Didot ed., ix, 5; Cf. *Ethic.* v, 4

needy we give them what is not theirs but ours. Therefore the act of justice does not consist in rendering to each one his own.

Obj. 2: Further, Tully says (De Offic. i, 7) that "beneficence which we may call kindness or liberality, belongs to justice." Now it pertains to liberality to give to another of one's own, not of what is his. Therefore the act of justice does not consist in rendering to each one his own.

Obj. 3: Further, it belongs to justice not only to distribute things duly, but also to repress injurious actions, such as murder, adultery and so forth. But the rendering to each one of what is his seems to belong solely to the distribution of things. Therefore the act of justice is not sufficiently described by saying that it consists in rendering to each one his own.

On the contrary, Ambrose says (De Offic. i, 24): "It is justice that renders to each one what is his, and claims not another's property; it disregards its own profit in order to preserve the common equity."

I answer that, As stated above (AA. 8, 10), the matter of justice is an external operation in so far as either it or the thing we use by it is made proportionate to some other person to whom we are related by justice. Now each man's own is that which is due to him according to equality of proportion. Therefore the proper act of justice is nothing else than to render to each one his own.

Reply Obj. 1: Since justice is a cardinal virtue, other secondary virtues, such as mercy, liberality and the like are connected with it, as we shall state further on (Q. 80, A. 1). Wherefore to succor the needy, which belongs to mercy or pity, and to be liberally beneficent, which pertains to liberality, are by a kind of reduction ascribed to justice as to their principal virtue.

This suffices for the Reply to the Second Objection.

Reply Obj. 3: As the Philosopher states (Ethic. v, 4), in matters of justice, the name of "profit" is extended to whatever is excessive, and whatever is deficient is called "loss." The reason for this is that justice is first of all and more commonly exercised in voluntary interchanges of things, such as buying and selling, wherein those expressions are properly employed; and yet they are transferred to all other matters of justice. The same applies to the rendering to each one of what is his own.

* * * * *

TWELFTH ARTICLE [II-II, Q. 58, Art. 12]

Whether Justice Stands Foremost Among All Moral Virtues?

Objection 1: It would seem that justice does not stand foremost among all the moral virtues. Because it belongs to justice to render to each one what is his, whereas it belongs to liberality to give of one's own, and this is more virtuous. Therefore liberality is a greater virtue than justice.

Obj. 2: Further, nothing is adorned by a less excellent thing than itself. Now magnanimity is the ornament both of justice and of all the virtues, according to Ethic. iv, 3. Therefore magnanimity is more excellent than justice.

Obj. 3: Further, virtue is about that which is "difficult" and "good," as stated in Ethic. ii, 3. But fortitude is about more difficult things than justice is, since it is about dangers of death, according to Ethic. iii, 6. Therefore fortitude is more excellent than justice.

On the contrary, Tully says (De Offic. i, 7): "Justice is the most resplendent of the virtues, and gives its name to a good man."

I answer that, If we speak of legal justice, it is evident that it stands foremost among all the moral virtues, for as much as the common good transcends the individual good of one person. In this sense the Philosopher declares (Ethic. v, 1) that "the most excellent of the virtues would seem to be justice, and more glorious than either the evening or the morning star." But, even if we speak of particular justice, it excels the other moral virtues for two reasons. The first reason may be taken from the subject, because justice is in the more excellent part of the soul, viz. the rational appetite or will, whereas the other moral virtues are in the sensitive appetite, whereunto appertain the passions which are the matter of the other moral virtues. The second reason is taken from the object, because the other virtues are commendable in respect of the sole good of the virtuous person himself, whereas justice is praiseworthy in respect of the virtuous person being well disposed towards another, so that justice is somewhat the good of another person, as stated in *Ethic.* v, 1. Hence the Philosopher says (Rhet. i, 9): "The greatest virtues must needs be those which are most profitable to other persons, because virtue is a faculty of doing good to others. For this reason the greatest honors are accorded the brave and the just, since bravery is useful to others in warfare, and justice is useful to others both in warfare and in time of peace."

Reply Obj. 1: Although the liberal man gives of his own, yet he does so in so far as he takes into consideration the good of his own virtue, while the just man gives to another what is his, through consideration of the common good. Moreover justice is observed towards all, whereas liberality cannot extend to all. Again liberality which gives of a man's own is based on justice, whereby one renders to each man what is his.

Reply Obj. 2: When magnanimity is added to justice it increases the latter's goodness; and yet without justice it would not even be a virtue.

Reply Obj. 3: Although fortitude is about the most difficult things, it is not about the best, for it is only useful in warfare, whereas justice is useful both in war and in peace, as stated above.

59. OF INJUSTICE (In Four Articles)

We must now consider injustice, under which head there are four points of inquiry:

(1) Whether injustice is a special vice?
(2) Whether it is proper to the unjust man to do unjust deeds?
(3) Whether one can suffer injustice willingly?
(4) Whether injustice is a mortal sin according to its genus?.

* * * * *

FIRST ARTICLE [II-II, Q. 59, Art. 1]

Whether Injustice Is a Special Virtue?

Objection 1: It would seem that injustice is not a special vice. For it is written (1 John 3:4): "All sin is iniquity[1]." Now iniquity would seem to be the same as injustice, because justice is a kind

---

[1] Vulg.: 'Whosoever committeth sin, committeth also iniquity; and sin is iniquity'

of equality, so that injustice is apparently the same as inequality or iniquity. Therefore injustice is not a special sin.

Obj. 2: Further, no special sin is contrary to all the virtues. But injustice is contrary to all the virtues: for as regards adultery it is opposed to chastity, as regards murder it is opposed to meekness, and in like manner as regards the other sins. Therefore injustice is not a special sin.

Obj. 3: Further, injustice is opposed to justice which is in the will. But every sin is in the will, as Augustine declares (De Duabus Anim. x). Therefore injustice is not a special sin.

On the contrary, Injustice is contrary to justice. But justice is a special virtue. Therefore injustice is a special vice.

I answer that, Injustice is twofold. First there is illegal injustice which is opposed to legal justice: and this is essentially a special vice, in so far as it regards a special object, namely the common good which it contemns; and yet it is a general vice, as regards the intention, since contempt of the common good may lead to all kinds of sin. Thus too all vices, as being repugnant to the common good, have the character of injustice, as though they arose from injustice, in accord with what has been said above about justice (Q. 58, AA. 5, 6). Secondly we speak of injustice in reference to an inequality between one person and another, when one man wishes to have more goods, riches for example, or honors, and less evils, such as toil and losses, and thus injustice has a special matter and is a particular vice opposed to particular justice.

Reply Obj. 1: Even as legal justice is referred to human common good, so Divine justice is referred to the Divine good, to which all sin is repugnant, and in this sense all sin is said to be iniquity.

Reply Obj. 2: Even particular justice is indirectly opposed to all the virtues; in so far, to wit, as even external acts pertain both to justice and to the other moral virtues, although in different ways as stated above (Q. 58, A. 9, ad 2).

Reply Obj. 3: The will, like the reason, extends to all moral matters, i.e. passions and those external operations that relate to another person. On the other hand justice perfects the will solely in the point of its extending to operations that relate to another: and the same applies to injustice.

* * * * *

SECOND ARTICLE [II-II, Q. 59, Art. 2]

Whether a Man Is Called Unjust Through Doing an Unjust Thing?

Objection 1: It would seem that a man is called unjust through doing an unjust thing. For habits are specified by their objects, as stated above (I-II, Q. 54, A. 2). Now the proper object of justice is the just, and the proper object of injustice is the unjust. Therefore a man should be called just through doing a just thing, and unjust through doing an unjust thing.

Obj. 2: Further, the Philosopher declares (Ethic. v, 9) that they hold a false opinion who maintain that it is in a man's power to do suddenly an unjust thing, and that a just man is no less capable of doing what is unjust than an unjust man. But this opinion would not be false unless it were proper to the unjust man to do what is unjust. Therefore a man is to be deemed unjust from the fact that he does an unjust thing.

Obj. 3: Further, every virtue bears the same relation to its proper act, and the same applies to the contrary vices. But whoever does what is intemperate, is said to be intemperate. Therefore whoever does an unjust thing, is said to be unjust.

On the contrary, The Philosopher says (Ethic. v, 6) that "a man may do an unjust thing without being unjust."

I answer that, Even as the object of justice is something equal in external things, so too the object of injustice is something unequal, through more or less being assigned to some person than is due to him. To this object the habit of injustice is compared by means of its proper act which is called an injustice. Accordingly it may happen in two ways that a man who does an unjust thing, is not unjust: first, on account of a lack of correspondence between the operation and its proper object. For the operation takes its species and name from its direct and not from its indirect object: and in things directed to an end the direct is that which is intended, and the indirect is what is beside the intention. Hence if a man do that which is unjust, without intending to do an unjust thing, for instance if he do it through ignorance, being unaware that it is unjust, properly speaking he does an unjust thing, not directly, but only indirectly, and, as it were, doing materially that which is unjust: hence such an operation is not called an injustice. Secondly, this may happen on account of a lack of proportion between the operation and the habit. For an injustice may sometimes arise from a passion, for instance, anger or desire, and sometimes from choice, for instance when the injustice itself is the direct object of one's complacency. In the latter case properly speaking it arises from a habit, because whenever a man has a habit, whatever befits that habit is, of itself, pleasant to him. Accordingly, to do what is unjust intentionally and by choice is proper to the unjust man, in which sense the unjust man is one who has the habit of injustice: but a man may do what is unjust, unintentionally or through passion, without having the habit of injustice.

Reply Obj. 1: A habit is specified by its object in its direct and formal acceptation, not in its material and indirect acceptation.

Reply Obj. 2: It is not easy for any man to do an unjust thing from choice, as though it were pleasing for its own sake and not for the sake of something else: this is proper to one who has the habit, as the Philosopher declares (Ethic. v, 9).

Reply Obj. 3: The object of temperance is not something established externally, as is the object of justice: the object of temperance, i.e. the temperate thing, depends entirely on proportion to the man himself. Consequently what is accidental and unintentional cannot be said to be temperate either materially or formally. In like manner neither can it be called intemperate: and in this respect there is dissimilarity between justice and the other moral virtues; but as regards the proportion between operation and habit, there is similarity in all respects.

* * * * *

THIRD ARTICLE [II-II, Q. 59, Art. 3]

Whether We Can Suffer Injustice Willingly?

Objection 1: It would seem that one can suffer injustice willingly. For injustice is inequality, as stated above (A. 2). Now a man by injuring himself, departs from equality, even as by injuring another. Therefore a man can do an injustice to himself, even as to another. But whoever does himself an injustice, does so involuntarily. Therefore a man can voluntarily suffer injustice especially if it be inflicted by himself.

Obj. 2: Further, no man is punished by the civil law, except for having committed some injustice. Now suicides were formerly punished according to the law of the state by being deprived of an honorable burial, as the Philosopher declares (Ethic. v, 11). Therefore a man can do himself an injustice, and consequently it may happen that a man suffers injustice voluntarily.

Obj. 3: Further, no man does an injustice save to one who suffers that injustice. But it may happen that a man does an injustice to one who wishes it, for instance if he sell him a thing for more than it is worth. Therefore a man may happen to suffer an injustice voluntarily.

On the contrary, To suffer an injustice and to do an injustice are contraries. Now no man does an injustice against his will. Therefore on the other hand no man suffers an injustice except against his will.

I answer that, Action by its very nature proceeds from an agent, whereas passion as such is from another: wherefore the same thing in the same respect cannot be both agent and patient, as stated in *Phys.* iii, 1; viii, 5. Now the proper principle of action in man is the will, wherefore man does properly and essentially what he does voluntarily, and on the other hand a man suffers properly what he suffers against his will, since in so far as he is willing, he is a principle in himself, and so, considered thus, he is active rather than passive. Accordingly we must conclude that properly and strictly speaking no man can do an injustice except voluntarily, nor suffer an injustice save involuntarily; but that accidentally and materially so to speak, it is possible for that which is unjust in itself either to be done involuntarily (as when a man does anything unintentionally), or to be suffered voluntarily (as when a man voluntarily gives to another more than he owes him).

Reply Obj. 1: When one man gives voluntarily to another that which he does not owe him, he causes neither injustice nor inequality. For a man's ownership depends on his will, so there is no disproportion if he forfeit something of his own free-will, either by his own or by another's action.

Reply Obj. 2: An individual person may be considered in two ways. First, with regard to himself; and thus, if he inflict an injury on himself, it may come under the head of some other kind of sin, intemperance for instance or imprudence, but not injustice; because injustice no less than justice, is always referred to another person. Secondly, this or that man may be considered as belonging to the State as part thereof, or as belonging to God, as His creature and image; and thus a man who kills himself, does an injury not indeed to himself, but to the State and to God. Wherefore he is punished in accordance with both Divine and human law, even as the Apostle declares in respect of the fornicator (1 Cor. 3:17): "If any man violate the temple of God, him shall God destroy."

Reply Obj. 3: Suffering is the effect of external action. Now in the point of doing and suffering injustice, the material element is that which is done externally, considered in itself, as stated above (A. 2), and the formal and essential element is on the part of the will of agent and patient, as stated above (A. 2). Accordingly we must reply that injustice suffered by one man and injustice done by another man always accompany one another, in the material sense. But if we speak in the formal sense a man can do an injustice with the intention of doing an injustice, and yet the other man does not suffer an injustice, because he suffers voluntarily; and on the other hand a man can suffer an injustice if he suffer an injustice against his will, while the man who does the injury unknowingly, does an injustice, not formally but only materially.

* * * * *

FOURTH ARTICLE [II-II, Q. 59, Art. 4]

Whether Whoever Does an Injustice Sins Mortally?

Objection 1: It would seem that not everyone who does an injustice sins mortally. For venial sin is opposed to mortal sin. Now it is sometimes a venial sin to do an injury: for the Philosopher says (Ethic. v, 8) in reference to those who act unjustly: "Whatever they do not merely in ignorance but through ignorance is a venial matter." Therefore not everyone that does an injustice sins mortally.

Obj. 2: Further, he who does an injustice in a small matter, departs but slightly from the mean. Now this seems to be insignificant and should be accounted among the least of evils, as the Philosopher declares (Ethic. ii, 9). Therefore not everyone that does an injustice sins mortally.

Obj. 3: Further, charity is the "mother of all the virtues"[1], and it is through being contrary thereto that a sin is called mortal. But not all the sins contrary to the other virtues are mortal. Therefore neither is it always a mortal sin to do an injustice.

On the contrary, Whatever is contrary to the law of God is a mortal sin. Now whoever does an injustice does that which is contrary to the law of God, since it amounts either to theft, or to adultery, or to murder, or to something of the kind, as will be shown further on (Q. 64, seqq.). Therefore whoever does an injustice sins mortally.

I answer that, As stated above (I-II, Q. 12, A. 5), when we were treating of the distinction of sins, a mortal sin is one that is contrary to charity which gives life to the soul. Now every injury inflicted on another person is of itself contrary to charity, which moves us to will the good of another. And so since injustice always consists in an injury inflicted on another person, it is evident that to do an injustice is a mortal sin according to its genus.

Reply Obj. 1: This saying of the Philosopher is to be understood as referring to ignorance of fact, which he calls "ignorance of particular circumstances"[2], and which deserves pardon, and not to ignorance of the law which does not excuse: and he who does an injustice through ignorance, does no injustice except accidentally, as stated above (A. 2)

Reply Obj. 2: He who does an injustice in small matters falls short of the perfection of an unjust deed, in so far as what he does may be deemed not altogether contrary to the will of the person who suffers therefrom: for instance, if a man take an apple or some such thing from another man, in which case it is probable that the latter is not hurt or displeased.

Reply Obj. 3: The sins which are contrary to the other virtues are not always hurtful to another person, but imply a disorder affecting human passions; hence there is no comparison.

---

1 Peter Lombard, Sent. iii, D. 23
2 Ethic. iii, 1

BIBLIOBAZAAR

The essential book market!

Did you know that you can get any of our titles in large print?

Did you know that we have an ever-growing collection of books in many languages?

Order online:
www.bibliobazaar.com

Find all of your favorite classic books!

Stay up to date with the latest government reports!

At BiblioBazaar, we aim to make knowledge more accessible by making thousands of titles available to you- *quickly and affordably*.

Contact us:
BiblioBazaar
PO Box 21206
Charleston, SC 29413